THE HEIRS OF THE KINGDOM

THE HEIRS OF THE KINGDOM

ZOÉ OLDENBOURG

Translated from the French by Anne Carter

PANTHEON BOOKS

A DIVISION OF RANDOM HOUSE, NEW YORK

 Published in the United States by Pantheon Books, a division of Random House, Inc., New York, and simultaneously in Canada by Random House of Canada Limited, Toronto. Originally published in France as *La Joie des Pauvres* by Éditions Gallimard.

Manufactured in the United States of America

AUTHOR'S NOTE

This is not a historical novel. Neither is it history dressed up as fiction, or even a historical pageant. It is not a work of scholarship, nor has it involved the author in extensive academic research.

The author wishes to declare her firm and considered conviction that: (1) To praise an author for his or her scholarship, whether real or presumed, amounts to calling that author a plagiarist and a pedant. (2) Source material is freely available to anyone, and the writer is at liberty to make use of it if he so wishes. It is of no interest in itself and is valuable only in relation to the interpretation which is put upon it. All novels, however "objective" they may seem to be, are portraits of their authors and conform to the laws of the writer's inner world and no other. Consequently, in order to avoid any misunderstanding, let me warn all those who are seeking information about the history of the Middle Ages, a fictionalized view of history, or a conventional "historical novel" combining entertainment with a modicum of instruction, but who do not believe that a story about the past can have anything important to say to them personally, *that they had better not read this book.*

A novel is a portrayal of the human condition. Call this one hallucination, dream, epic, statement, or inquiry: only cease to think of it in the context of "history."

For the rest, students of history may take comfort: the events described in the book are true. In fact, I believe that the picture I have given of the "poor," about whom historians are always so niggardly of information, comes very near the truth.

Hath not God chosen the poor of this world rich in faith, and heirs of the kingdom which he hath promised to them that love him?

James 2:5

PART I

1

There was a letter in a box. The box was red and studded with five iron nails. It lay on a table covered with a white cloth. The table stood on a wooden dais in the middle of the field. Above the dais a canopy had been set up on four black-and-white painted poles.

It might have been a fairground: such a crowd of men and women, a good thousand of them, maybe as many as three thousand, so packed together that if it had rained the ground would not even have been wet. Four mounted men were around the dais, two with oriflammes and two with tall crosses made of painted wood, and at the foot of the steps was a man dressed in a frieze habit, a small, thin man with a long beard like rain-sodden hay.

Such a hubbub rose from the crowd that it sounded like the groaning of a hundred wagons going through a henhouse where thousands of fowls were all cackling at once. But when the little man with the grey beard raised his arms, the noise subsided. The boards could be heard creaking under the man's feet as he climbed onto the dais and again lifted his arms.

They all knew the letter was in the box. Those who had seen it said that it was written in letters of gold upon parchment that shone like snow in the sunshine. So great was the virtue of those golden letters that even men who were able to read could not make them out: aye, and but for the tears with which God moistened their eyelids, their eyes would have been burned.

For the parchment of that letter was not made by hands: the archangel Gabriel had taken the finest snow crystals from the sky and melted them in the cold fire of the stars to make a parchment, and brought it to the Lord Jesus Christ before His throne on the right hand of the Father. The Lord Jesus Christ took a feather from the archangel Gabriel's wing and dipped it in the sun and wrote words. That was how it had happened.

Then the Lord Jesus Christ, who is truly man and truly God, breathed on the letter to make it appear as an earthly thing, for otherwise no man could have touched the letter and not died.

And as Peter lay asleep in the Church of the Holy Sepulcher, the Lord Jesus Christ summoned his soul to heaven. You who are little, poor, and humble, know that I have chosen you to be the bearer of My letter. And Peter, it was said, being a simple man, did not understand. So great was his joy at seeing the Lord that he believed himself already dead and received into the paradise of the elect. Do not rejoice, Peter, for I would gladly keep you with Me but the time is not yet come. You shall go back to earth and take My letter. Alas, Lord Jesus, am I not old and frail in body, have I not prayed and fasted and preached Your word for more than thirty years? Is it thus that You reward me? And the Lord spoke to him in anger, chiding him for being slothful and unkind. Oh, you bad servant, would you remain here, tasting the joys of heaven while the Cup that I hold in My hand runs over with the tears of the poor? Know that this Cup is bitter and ever I drink it to the dregs and yet it is always full.

But to whom, Lord, should I take Your letter? To the Pope, to the kings or emperors? To the bishops or the knights? Surely if I take them Your letter their hearts will be touched and they will end the sufferings of the poor.

My letter is not for them, Peter, for truly the rich have eyes and do not see and ears and do not hear. Take My letter to those whom I love best, to the poor and humble: to those who make the corn grow and have not bread, who spin and weave the wool and are not clothed, who tend the vines and yet drink only water; to those who delve in the mines for silver and copper and never see a coin; to those who tan leather for shoes and go barefoot, and those who heat the furnaces to make the iron with which the rich kill them. To all these, Peter, you shall carry My letter to tell them their time is at hand. Let them repent of their sins and come to Me. I appoint them to meet Me in Jerusalem.

And Peter took the holy letter and returned to earth. He hurried to find a goldsmith and asked him to make a box of pure gold with five crystals set in the lid in memory of the five wounds of the Lord, but no sooner did he place the letter in the box than the gold melted and the crystals shattered. Then he had a box made of silver with five emeralds in the lid, but the silver melted and the emeralds shivered in pieces. Then Peter had a box made of wood and studded with iron nails and painted red, in remembrance of the wood of the Cross and the nails of the Passion and the blood of Our Lord. And the letter was put into the box and remained there.

This was the story of the letter.

Peter described to the poor how God's pardon must be gained.

My beloved, he said, your sins are so great that were God to let you feel the true weight of them not one of you would cross the bridge over the Scarpe: the bridge would collapse. But see God's mercy toward you: your wretchedness is such that were God to let you feel the true weight of it not one of you would get over that bridge across the Scarpe. You have only to think of your wretchedness in order to understand sin. But as for the rich, how can they repent? Their life is so good that they can never know the evils of sin, for to know evil one must suffer evil.

You hear that the rich, your lords and abbots, are preparing to do God's work. Do not despise them; follow their armies if your families and friends prevent you from joining mine. I summon you all to the way of the Cross, and I go before you. Leave today, or leave tomorrow, but do not delay too long. The time of grace will be short.

You will be cold and hungry. Your feet will be bruised, your backs aching, and your legs swollen. You will be mocked at, stoned, and abused by the ungodly and your footprints on the road will be marked in blood. Whoever would find the Lord must first give all he has, and it is easy for you to give all who have only to take up a staff and walk.

He gave out crosses made of coarse, unbleached cloth. The pious men who served him cut the crosses from old sacks and blankets and gave them to him to touch. He touched a thousand or more in a single day. The men formed up on one side of the dais to receive their crosses, the women on the other.

Before each man took the cross he had to repent of his sins; then he took the cross in his hands and kissed it and stowed it away beneath his shirt, next to his heart. But before he kissed the cross he had to bathe it with the tears of repentance, and so movingly did Peter speak that God brought tears to every eye. All were weeping, even the bakers who hid their flour when the harvest was bad. This was a miracle indeed, to see two bakers weeping hot tears and lying down in the mud: Tread on us, tread on us, good people, remember the black bread we sold you at two deniers the pound! And Alix of the Thirty Pieces, the fairest harlot in Arras, laid everything she had about her before the dais, her girdle, her gown, her necklace and earrings, and her gilded leather slippers. She would have given her shift of fine red linen also but for the shame of going home naked. She wept until there was not a dry thread left in the fabric of her cross. And the vintner from the Street of the Weavers wept and fell on his knees before all those who came near him. He had given everything but his breeches and was calling everyone to look at his obese hairy chest: See this fat pig, good people, may all the water I used to baptize your wine bloat my body . . .

The crosses were made of sackcloth, it was true, but they were worth more than all the rich men's crosses sewn onto episcopal robes. The Lord Jesus is taking us into His service, who never wore brocaded silks or cloth of Bruges.

O Lord Jesus Christ, for You we would have woven cloth so fine that a piece an ell wide would have passed through a ring, so closely woven that a child's hair would not have passed between the threads of it! We would have woven cloth of seven colors, we would have spun thread finer than gossamer, so that not even the Virgin Your Mother ever spun finer, and all for no reward. For You we would have worked through the night and worn out our eyes in the candle smoke. No one would have clothed You better than the weavers of Arras.

Poor people as you are, Peter said, my head burns with pity for you. For you live only to eat and drink, like the beasts, and would to God that you were as the beasts, for neither God nor men deny them food. But you, the brethren of Jesus Christ, wear yourselves out body and soul, from childhood to old age, for a foul stew of rotten beans, and are lucky to get even a bowl of such stew each day. The fool Esau sold his birthright for a mess of pottage, but you, you sell much more for much less, for in bad years you sell your souls, and not for lentils but for turnip parings.

I have no bread to give to you today. The more I get, the faster it goes. I have fed multitudes, thanks to the charity of the faithful, and have given money to those who had no work. I have been like the sieve that is constantly refilled and yet is always empty; more money has passed through my hands than would suffice to buy the palace of the Greek Emperor. You fill an empty belly and the next day it cries again for food. And this, my dear hearts, is all our life. I do not come to say to you, hunger no more. You would laugh in my face. I do not come to say to you, eat, for I have no more bread to give. I come to say to you, come, and if need be suffer cold and hunger and hard labor. Come, and let it be for God and not for the sake of your own bellies.

To make the lords and the cloth merchants rich, you wear yourselves out, body and soul. If you can do this to make bad men wealthy, then rather come with us and your sufferings will enrich God.

I call you to the looms of God, where you will never be idle. The whole world is God's workshop and the pilgrim is His workman, and each day's toil is richly paid in forgiveness, in God's grace, in charity and heartsease.

God will give you glory among the angels and the rich spoils of His love, and in that place you shall dwell in peace and charity, sharing all things, like the Holy Apostles. And Jesus Christ shall be your only Lord and your only Bishop and your only King.

How could anyone remember all the things he said? He held up his arms like Moses as he spoke, and his body trembled and his face glowed bright as a lamp, and his hair shone like threads of pure silver. His voice was as beautiful as the music of hautboys and so powerful for his frail body that all could see it was not he who spoke but the angel that dwelt in him. When he cried "*Jerusalem!*" all the fields and meadows and woods rang back: Jerusalem! The heavens cried out Jerusalem.

And so it went on until nightfall. Cressets flared around the dais and torches and lanterns sprang to light all over the field, with here and there a wood fire burning. They sang psalms, and their voices rose in great discordant waves because not all were singing the same tune, but the responses and the alleluias were all roared out in unison.

Marie sang with the other girls, lost in the crowd, and laughed and clapped her hands and wept when they all wept. She and her friends Marie-Brune, Isabelle, and Jeannette had worked their way close to the dais where Peter stood beside the red box, praying with clasped hands. His hair in the torchlight was like a saintly crown. It hung in unkempt waves about his brow and cheeks, and the idea came to Marie that it was not real hair but gold and silver threads that God had brought to life and it was through this hair that the power of the angels entered his head. Marie did not understand very clearly what he was saying, for she was not yet fourteen, but she wanted to have a cross of her own and go to Jerusalem, where in the midst of darkness a thousand fires were lighted on earth and in heaven.

She laughed and cried and was happy.

Then she saw Jacques watching her, so hard that the weight of his eyes was like two stones. Marie could feel them pressing heavily on her own. She thought him very handsome standing there in the torchlight, in spite of his long nose and his long face and his big mouth. He had pink, freckled cheeks, narrow grey eyes, and straw-colored hair that covered his forehead and his ears. He had stopped looking at her now; he had turned as red as a carrot and looked away. Then he was watching her again. Lord, surely no starving man would ever look like that at a crust of bread! There was even a little smile on his lips, and his eyes were all dreamy with happiness. He was as red as a fine cloth made for a festival and so burning hot that Marie seemed to feel the heat at ten paces.

Somehow he managed, in three strides, to be beside her. He was grinning, showing his big white teeth, but not as though he felt like laughing—more as if he were afraid.

"Hey girls, aren't you hungry?"

Marie and her three friends said they were, very hungry.

"Come over here, then, to this fire."

People were sitting on the ground around a wood fire and a woman stood by the pot where soup was heating, stirring it with a stick. Jacques said, "Christians, a bit of soup for the girls, in Jesus Christ's name."

"I don't know you, my lad," the woman said to him. "You are not of our neighborhood."

"Go on," said Jacques, "we are all neighbors tonight!" He had a deep voice even then and a quick gruff laugh. He laughed and they all laughed with him: Well spoken, lad, we are all neighbors in Jesus Christ. The woman filled a ladle full of soup and offered it to Jacques. He drank some and then passed it to Marie. Oh joy, a good bean soup, almost hot, that sent a glow coursing through your whole body. There was another ladleful for each of the girls. Jacques said, "Thanks, good Christians, may your soup have such a savor every day."

"Your health, boy, and may you have a beard soon." Everyone was laughing; it was a real holiday.

Marie thought Jacques a good, steady boy and well spoken; it was a pity he came from a different street. The girls were laughing and wiping their soupy faces with the backs of their hands. Big Jacques was no longer laughing. He was looking at Marie and trembling like a nervous horse. They stood there amid the noise and the crowd, and no one noticed them: they might have been alone. Marie did not know what it was that made this boy so beautiful. His face was like an angel's. He had stopped talking, and when she looked at him he turned away, grinning and scratching his head.

Marie was the daughter of Mathieu Longbras, who had been a weaver all his life in the faubourg of Arras. Mathieu's father had been a weaver before him, and his grandfather, in the days when folk worked in their own villages. Now the weavers owned nothing in the world except a loom, for which they were often in debt all their lives, and a broken-down cottage in some street in the faubourg, and yet from these cottages the masters had the right to evict the workmen when they grew old or ill, so that it would be true to say that even the weavers, who were the best paid of all the workers in the faubourg, existed to some extent on sufferance in their own houses. The value of work had fallen off a great deal in the past five years because of weavers coming in from the villages, where admittedly they were starving. The price of a length of cloth had dropped so low that people had to work night and day to earn a living. Mathieu had a wife and children: his wife, Armelle, was a weaver also and Marie was a winder. Of the remaining children, three were still living but too young to work.

Marie was beautiful. It was a fact that to poor folk a beautiful daughter was like a gold piece in a beggar's bowl: a cause of trouble more than anything else. Even when she was quite small they had to frighten her to keep her close to her mother's skirts because of the wicked folk that lurked around every corner in the town, and especially in the faubourg.

When Marie was ten, a woman of Arras came to the faubourg where the weavers lived. She was a widow dressed in good cloth of Bruges, and she gave the children raisins and pinched Marie's chin and said what a shame to see a girl like her in such a place. Then she went and found Armelle in the church square and talked to her about what a hard life it was and how she would give her two silver pennies to put by against the time when there was no work: "And for six weeks, my good woman, you will be able to have soup every day . . . you must think of your little ones." A good house, she said, in a street of tradesmen, and the girls have beds to sleep in and bread to eat every day and are taught embroidery. The Countess of Boulogne herself comes to the shop. Marie listened and thought that she would like to learn embroidery. But Armelle said, "Do you think I was born in a village? Why don't you ask for Perrine's daughter? She's a hunchback, but you don't do embroidery with your back."

"Very well then, my good woman, I'll make it three pennies."

"Do you think this is the first time? The first time I've heard such promises?" Marie's mother took her by the hand and told her, "Take a good look at her. This woman is the Devil, and if ever you listen to women of her kind you know what will happen to you? Snakes will come and eat up your eyes and your belly will be filled with worms and you will go to hell. And as for the embroidery, it wouldn't be countesses that you'd be working for. The real work in that trade is not what folks are led to think!"

The woman was not angry. She shook her head. "The Devil is not so black as he is painted," she said. "If the girl were not so beautiful, I should say nothing. She will blame you for it later."

Then one day the overseer who came around to collect the finished cloth stopped at Mathieu's house.

"Hey, with a girl like that you'll not be finding yourself laid off!"

"I'd not say no to honest wedlock," Mathieu answered, and the other man laughed.

The next was a neighbor's son. He was quite old, twenty, with a big mustache, and he told Marie, "I'll marry you, right enough." She asked her mother what marrying was.

"It's nasty, and if anyone says it to you, you run off as fast as you can."

There was another woman also, an old one this time. Marie was at the washing place with the other girls when the old woman said to her, "Help me carry my basket. I'm too tired."

Marie took the basket of washing, and as they went the old woman told her, "I have the sight. I see it written in your face that you were made for the bed of a count." Marie shrieked with laughter.

"No, child, do not laugh. Do not waste your youth. I too was pretty once. Two or three years from now some beggarman will take you by force behind the huts, or the soldiers will carry you off and shut you up in some lord's house and it will be the lord first and the soldiers after, and after the soldiers all the rabble of lackeys. Believe you me, it's not so funny." Marie, gasping and panting under the weight of the basket, could not say a word.

"A fine sweetheart, child, with a fair body all washed and scented and hair as soft as silk, and who'll give you such a good time that you'll be all plump and pink and white and wear shifts of fine linen. And nothing to do all day but laugh and sing, you'd like that, eh?" The things the old woman described sounded nice and pleasant, but her voice was like dirty water and Marie felt a bitter taste in her mouth as she listened to her.

By the time she was fourteen Marie was as tall as a woman and quick at her work. For if the work was hard, no one complained: they were too much afraid of being without. Lord Jesus Christ, Holy Mary patroness of weavers, make the rich ten times richer so they will buy lots of cloth, both coarse and fine, and linen for their shifts, and let them give two sets of clothes to all their servants at Christmas! And when Benoît is old enough to watch the bobbins we'll buy old Micheline's loom and I shall learn to weave! Only wait and see the fine cloth I'll weave, fine cloth with stripes of red and blue. This linen is smooth as silk, whose work is it? Why, Marie's, the daughter of Mathieu Longbras in the street of Master Richard. I shall never be short of work and then no one will say, You can always get a living!

At Eastertide, while everyone was still talking of nothing but Little Peter and the miraculous letter, a cousin of Mathieu Longbras came to borrow two wooden bowls from him. Now, no man puts himself out just for bowls, so there was something else. A boy going on eighteen, he said, who could ply a shuttle with the best, as well as being able to make shoes and prepare hides for tanning. "Such clever fingers, he'll mend the most worm-eaten looms for you so that you'd think he was in league with the fairies." Mathieu had heard it all many times before.

"For my part," he said, "I've never been to look at how they work in the Bishop's street. If I do get her a husband it will be from our own street."

"Bernier is willing," the cousin said (Bernier was Jacques's father), "to let the girl work for you until your Benoît is old enough to take her place. To be frank with you, the boy is pining.

He breaks his thread ten times a day and talks of going back to the country if the business isn't settled."

"Then let him go. If he breaks his thread over a girl, he's no loss."

"The boy is young, Mathieu, but he is a good worker. I'd carry a red-hot iron from here to the Church of St. Eustace on that."

"Well, we'll talk about it," said Mathieu, "we can always talk, but I make no promises." Bernier and his son were good workers right enough, but the mother did not weave any more since she had her right hand smashed in the machine because of the evil eye. It was a good year to marry a daughter. There was no lack of work, what with all the shirkers who had taken the cross and were going away, and the holy war in the offing, because when barons and bishops went on their travels they were known to take great quantities of cloth as gifts for the people who gave them shelter, and the price of cloth was bound to rise.

For ten days Marie thought constantly about Jacques, and worried about what he thought of her. She did not sleep at night and had to keep herself from laughing and singing aloud, while during the day she sang more than ever at her work. Her voice rose loud and clear above those of the other women. She would have liked, God knows, to make a song about Jacques, but would not have dared to sing it before the others.

They slept on straw beside the looms, woke—oh, when we get to heaven, Lord God, how we shall sleep!—and gulped down a ladleful of soup, thanking God that if there was no salt at least there was onion; the onion crop had been a good one. Then it was back to work and the clatter of the looms began again, the bars rose and fell, the reel turned, and the torch smoked. Before daybreak the men, father and uncle, arrived and sat down at their big looms, after first tightening their belts and making the sign of the cross.

Marie was sleepy and sang to keep awake. When one reel was finished she ran to fetch a fresh ball of yarn, glancing at the men's looms with their cloth of colored threads, blood-red with white stripes, so beautiful it made your heart ache. It was like an enormous lute with a thousand strings that danced and quivered with each movement of the bar. Marie thought that if Jacques were to wear a cloak made of that cloth he would look like the archangel Michael painted in the church. Or suppose he were a count or a bishop and rode through the streets of the faubourg on a great horse with trappings of fringed woolen cloth, and suppose he came into our house all dressed for a procession with a candle in his hand . . .

Then one Sunday night, they told her that Jacques's father had come to ask for her in marriage. The shock made her laugh at first, but it was fear more than gladness that was the cause of her laughter. Then, when she could not stop laughing, her mother slapped her face and she flew into a temper: "If that's how it is, I'd rather drown myself in the Scarpe!"

She ran and threw herself down on the straw and cried and cried until her father smacked her bottom for her. "Devil take the wench! She can stop bawling. I've promised nothing. Now let me go to sleep."

So that was what he wanted! He wanted to marry her, just like all the rest. Unkind! His mother has a withered arm and they need a servant. As true as God was born of a virgin, Marie thought, let my father give me to any other man but not to him! In the morning, her mother told her, "Don't cry. They shall not have you. I'll go and speak to his mother." But Marie was frightened and said, "No, oh no, never! Don't go and see them."

"Well then, you've seen this Jacques? Don't you like him?"

"I dislike him so much I'd give myself to the river Scarpe sooner than to him."

So Mathieu sent word to Bernier that there had better be no more said about the matter for the present. That night Bernier came himself to speak to Mathieu, and he was not best pleased. This was no way to behave. No promise had been made, but as good as.

"To tell you the truth," said Mathieu, "the girl screeched loud enough to rouse the whole neighborhood. Your Jacques is a good-looking lad, he'll find himself another that's not so stubborn."

Bernier scratched his chin. "The trouble is, he's stubborn too. His blood's on fire and likely to bring on a morbid fever. The girl is young, she takes fright at a word."

Mathieu said, "Aye, maybe." He would have been glad enough to settle the business. When a girl had the boys so hot for her it was better to marry her quickly: girls who were too pretty were more apt to attract bawds than husbands. He went home and gave Marie the flat of his hand for form's sake. "You'll have this boy or it's out in the street you go!"

"I'm not afraid," she said. "I'll go to Lille and join the pilgrims going to Jerusalem." She got a couple more blows for that which left her face swollen all next day.

Oh God, indeed I will go to Jerusalem. Where there are no rich or poor and where there is as much light by night as by day. And Bernier's Jacques can come and find me if he likes. People there have no husbands or wives but live like the angels in heaven.

But here men do such hateful things to girls that it is shameful even to think of it. And don't think I'm a fool, my friends, for married people do the same! Only perhaps Jacques does not know that?

He is older than I am, how could he help knowing? In Jerusalem there is no sun nor moon nor torchlight. God is their torch and it is always light. No one is ever tired in Jerusalem.

Then her friend Jeannette, who was sixteen, came to talk to her on Jacques's behalf, saying that he was a good, steady lad and a good worker and so much in love that he had run away to his uncle in the country and might die of grief.

"And what did Bernier's wife promise you for telling me that? It wasn't Jacques told you to say it."

"It's true she promised me three eggs," said Jeannette, "but I'm saying this for your own good. I'm sure you love him, only you're ashamed to say so."

"And I'd be ashamed if it were true! I don't want to go to hell."

"You don't go to hell for it when you are married, stupid. The priest sprinkles you with holy water and says words to take away the sin."

"Ha ha! I'd like to see that," said Marie. "The priest telling people to do such things! I'm not such a fool, and I won't listen to another word from you, you wicked girl!"

This made Jeannette angry too, and they flew at each other so fiercely that both emerged with scratched faces and arms covered with bruises. Marie was so angry that she was not even ashamed of fighting in the middle of the street, not even though people were watching them and calling out: Have at her, goldilocks! Don't let her beat you, Marie! Afterward, she ran and hid in the church.

The church was half empty, and it was the first time Marie had been there alone, without her parents. She got her breath back, wiped the blood from her cheeks, and looked around at the pictures painted on the walls. There was a tall angel dressed in red with stern eyes. He was as tall as at least four men standing one above the other, and Marie thought that were he ever to step off the wall he would crush people underfoot as an ox crushes the grass. She forgot why she was angry. Already, she seemed to see the great angel striding down the nave with his sword gleaming in the sun.

From that day, Marie began to sicken. She would start to cry for no reason and she could not sing any more. Her heart seemed to swell until it grew too big for her chest and she could not breathe. She tangled the threads on her reel and got a scolding. Oh, throw me out of the house. I don't care. I'm going away! Her mother thought she must be ill.

"I'm not ill. I am bewitched. I want to be exorcised!"

"Who has bewitched you, do you know?"

She wanted to say, Bernier's Jacques, but the name would not come out. The more her mother pressed her to tell, the more steadfastly Marie refused. She would pretend to mouth the words and then say, "No, you see, you see I can't!"

Armelle was frightened and spoke to her husband: "It is a wicked shame, someone means to do the girl a mischief."

"I think it is Bernier, myself," said Mathieu, "because that lad of theirs has run away. It seems he isn't in the village with his uncle."

This was true: Jacques had disappeared. His father had brought in his nephew Philippe to take his place at the loom. Bernier said, "The young bastard has gone north to join the crusaders." But his mother wept: "He has thrown himself into the Scarpe, I feel it in my heart. Even now he may be floating out beyond the harbor on the tide, out into the salt sea!"

"He can swim," said his father, "so why should he drown himself?"

But like all women unable to work, Jacques's mother was given to crying and moaning. She came and stood at the door of Mathieu's house, sobbing and shrieking: "Witches! You that eat men's hearts, give me back my boy or I will tell the priest about you!"

"May your tongue rot, it's you, you and your Bernier, have put a spell on Marie out of jealousy!" But Bernette stayed at the door, shouting, "Man-eaters! Fiends that eat men's hearts! What have you done with my boy?"

In the end it was all a great fuss about nothing: four days later Jacques came back. By this time Marie, believing he had gone to Jerusalem, was really ill, overcome with misery at the knowledge that he was no longer there.

Jacques came back, but he had not changed his mind. If this was how matters stood, he said, then he was going to Jerusalem and let anyone try and stop him. Only he could not help wanting to see the girl again before he went.

"Girl!" said Bernier. "I'll give you girls." And he belabored him so thoroughly with his fists and his belt that Jacques was sick for three days afterward and lay in his corner unable to open his eyes for the swellings and with his mouth too raw and bleeding even to nibble a crust of bread. "That should have beaten the girl out of his system," Bernier said, but his mother knew the boy was stubborn.

Marie had gone back to her task of watching the reels, but she worked badly. Her mother put it down to her not getting enough to eat for a growing girl, but Marie kept on insisting that she wanted to be taken to church and exorcised.

Armelle took her to Catherine, the midwife, who was wise in matters of sorcery. Catherine said, "This is no witchcraft. Hot blood, that is what ails her. It is not long to Whitsuntide but time enough to agree with the boy's family."

"But what boy?"

"That's not for me to say, but it seems she means to have him since she's making herself ill over him."

On the way home, Armelle stopped suddenly and looked at Marie and then slapped her hard. "You deceitful girl, I might have known it. Lovesick, that's what you are!"

"No, no, no! Who should I be lovesick for?"

"For Bernier's Jacques, you wicked little liar."

Both fathers refused to listen to another word about the matter, but the whole street knew that Marie was sick with love for Bernier's Jacques. Songs were sung about Marie and how she would and she would not, until she herself was half demented and swore twenty times a day that she loathed the boy because he had put a spell of love on her the day of the preaching when they had drunk soup from the same ladle. And the end of it was that when Jacques had recovered a little from the thrashing his father had given him, the betrothal was discussed and Bernier made a formal application to the Bishop's office, because he and his family were bondsmen to the Bishop, while Mathieu belonged to the Viscount of Arras.

Then, on the second Sunday before Whit, Marie went with her friends to the big well in the center of the faubourg, and Jacques was there with the other lads. The meeting was an arranged one, though they all pretended it was not. The betrothed pair were both so bashful that they hardly dared to look at each other.

"Well," Jacques said, "it's all right, is it?"

"Why shouldn't it be?"

"Why wouldn't you have me before?" Marie blushed so hard that she was almost in tears. "They say you screamed so loud the whole street knew."

"Because you put a spell on me," she said.

"Liar," he answered. "It was you put a spell on me."

"No, it was you!"

"No, it was you!" They went on arguing like this until they both started to laugh and hid their faces, but every time they looked at each other they burst out laughing again, harder than ever, and if the bell had not begun to ring for vespers they would have stayed there until dark.

When it comes to earning money no one is greedier than the artisan, because his pay is small and bread is dear in the towns, while his masters are not God-fearing men. They are always saying that if the piece is not finished by tomorrow and taken to the fullers', then there will be no more orders. They say prices are falling, so you will get three deniers less the piece. The man that works on Sundays is like a brute beast, but the man that has no work at all is worse. Hunger makes him lightheaded so that he goes to the overseer and says, You are paying Peter eight deniers. I will do the same work for five.

If it were not for the girls, then, what fun would the young men get out of life? The time for loving is not long and he is a fool that lets it pass him by. A girl is a flower at fifteen, a ripe apple at eighteen, a turnip at twenty-five, and at thirty a shriveled onion with one child in her belly, another at her breast, a third clinging to her skirts, and two or three more in heaven. Girls lose their bloom sooner than in the country because they work winter and summer. The men are worn out sooner because in the villages, although the work is hard, it is not always the same. The craftsman thinks of nothing all year round, from morning to night, but shuttle, warp, weft, and bar; even in his sleep he sees them: the loom never lets you go until the day you die, but if it should, then that is worst of all. There is no place in town or country for a man without work, and the man that would take to robbery on the highways must fear neither man nor God.

Thirty years before, or forty, the faubourg had been little more than a village of weavers where the women busied themselves with their chickens and their vegetable patches and spun the woolen and linen thread themselves. There were holidays for the gathering of the flax and for the harvest; the weaver kneaded his own dough on Saturdays and could clothe his children in woolen cloth of his own weaving. Life was good then. But men are never satisfied with what they have. Once the wool started coming from all over the country to the markets of Arras and Béthune and the merchants had even begun importing it from England, then the bishop of the city wanted to have his own workshops, and after the bishop, the viscount, and then the merchants were no longer content with selling but wanted to have their own weaving industry as well. All this might have been thought a great advantage to the weavers, and to the fullers and wool-combers also, but far from it. They did more and better work, but for less money.

Now the faubourg was as big as a fair and so crowded that the grass no longer grew and children old enough to be breeched had never seen a cow or an apple tree. That is what comes of it when sinful man forgets his nature and thinks only of earning a living. The workers had no time now to celebrate the feast of the Ascension or of Saint Catherine or Saint Barbara, or Martinmas, and even Saint John's Eve and All Saints were all but forgotten.

Indeed it was a fact that what with some coming from Lens and others from Avesnes or even Boulogne, people hardly knew which saint to turn to. They had lost the saints of their own villages, and Saint Eustace, the patron of the faubourg church, could not cope with so many, and that was why things went so ill with them and they fell into sin for love of gain. People from neighboring streets would abuse one another for the sake of a girl seduced or a bale of wool stolen, the young men fought among themselves with cudgels and even knives, and now and then the body of some poor wretch who, for lack of work, had sold his services too cheap would be found lying by the banks of the river Scarpe.

True, if they had not worked until matins, or even until prime, the work would never have been delivered on time. They preferred to keep all the work in their own hands rather than let their masters employ other craftsmen. It was wrong, of course, and unchristian, but neighbors would get together and bring down their prices so as to get a bigger lot of yarn than the next street—and then God knows what a cross and a martyrdom it was, working all night in the reek of resin torches to make good their boast and get it done on time.

But then, when the work was done, at night in the fine weather or after mass on Sundays, the young lads not yet twenty were worse than stallions put out to stud, chasing after anything in petticoats, whether it was their own promised brides or girls from another street, or any little whore: it was all the same to them. But even this was better than knife play. And so, God be thanked, at Whitsuntide came the time of weddings and no one in the faubourg did any work for two whole days. A great feast was held in the meadow with torchlight and dancing. If all the lads of an age to take a wife had not been married off, there would have been so many brawls over the girls that were seduced that life would not have been worth living, because in the faubourgs the old ways fell into disrespect and were forgotten—there were too many people come from different villages.

Bernier's Jacques had fallen in love with Marie so suddenly that not only his parents and friends but his whole street were taken by surprise; even Master Gerard, their employer, was very nearly dragged into it, for it was a fact that the girl was beautiful and it was an honor for the Bishop's people to get such a lovely bride: not for five or six years had any girl so fair been seen in the faubourg, not since Père Malebouche's Alix, she that was now Alix of the Thirty Pieces. Jacques was a fine lad and sharp for his seventeen years. He had grown up with the looms at Bernette's knee, a child of the shuttle, brought into the world alongside the loom and suckled to the noise of the machines. At three years old he knew all the weavers' oaths, and by the time he was six was getting so much under the looms that it was dangerous and he had to be sent to his uncle in the country, where he remained for five years. Then Bernier brought him back to the faubourg and his grandfather taught him how to set up the loom, because the boy was strong for his age. And it was a blessing from heaven, for not long after that Bernette had her accident and Jacques was able to take her place. At fifteen they put him on the men's loom.

He had learned in the village to handle an awl, and in the faubourg when there was no work he spent hours with the joiner who mended the looms, watching him at work. He knew what he wanted to do, and that was to build his own loom.

"You'll go far," the joiner told him, "if you don't get yourself murdered first."

Jacques still carried the awl stuck in his belt, but with the extra money he earned unloading bales with his father he had bought himself a knife. Every night he whetted and sharpened it, but as for using it, he hardly ever did. He did not want to damage it with carving wood, while as for fighting his fists were enough, for he was not vicious. When the time came to be thinking about girls, his mind was on other things: on Sundays he would hurry into the town with his friends to linger in the space before the half-built cathedral, listening to the pilgrims. There were a whole crowd of small artisans who amused themselves in this way on such days as they were not at work, listening to stories or idling about the town watching the fine folk go by, or gathering at the base of the scaffold when a man had been condemned to death. Jacques was turning into something of a dreamer; in fact, he was agog with curiosity. The faubourg, even Arras itself, was no longer good enough for him; he wanted to see Bruges and Ghent, and why not Rome or Compostela?

Bernier was therefore glad to see his son settle down, for at his age a working man was easily led astray. Everyone knew what pilgrims' tales led to. Pilgrimages were all very well for the rich and idle, but God knows, Little Peter, although a holy man, would have done better to hold his peace and not go turning the heads of folk that had no call to go adventuring.

How many had gone, none could say. It was a veritable Exodus, made up not merely of vagabonds and workless men, as was to be expected, but of the peasants living near rivers and highways, and when these went it was whole villages at a time. For no apparent reason some villages had succumbed, just like that, to a kind of madness, while others had not; but then they set out, these peasants, with their livestock and their wagons, leaving behind them fields sown with wheat and rye where the green was already beginning to show, and calling themselves Hebrews fleeing from the tyranny of Pharaoh. And like latter-day Pharaohs, some lords pursued them and drove them back to their villages at the stave's end rather than lose their crops, but others let them go.

Already, it was said, the great valley of the Rhine had been drained of half its peasantry, besides innumerable workless men. All through the Easter period these travelers with their crosses had been seen straggling along the roads past the dark fields and green meadows, camping at night by woods and copses and lighting huge fires. They came from Normandy and even Brittany, and the Bretons were the craziest of all, speaking no Christian language and praying to saints no one had ever heard of. Such was the power of Peter and his miraculous letter that people who did not know one word of French understood and followed him; he had only to appear for Flemings and Germans to repent their sins and take up the pilgrim's staff. Toward Whitsun, however, many peasants remembered the hay and the harvest and crept back, rather shamefacedly, to their villages, their provisions exhausted and their livestock slaughtered. They said they had discovered that Jerusalem lay more than six months', even more than nine months' journey away and that to reach it one had to cross the sea in ships.

And yet this business of the letter went to men's heads like a spring gale: people were gathering everywhere, like swallows on the point of flight, on commons, in marketplaces, and in churches, arguing whether this pilgrimage was a righteous undertaking or an act of folly, for there must be moderation in all things. Wait for a sign from heaven. Oh yes, my friends, if your she-asses begin to talk, or if letters of gold appear on church walls and comets in the sky, then you can be sure that this great pilgrimage was ordained by God. O ye of little faith, how do you expect God to accomplish such prodigious things in these degenerate days? He meant to try you by sending His apostle to you in the guise of a poor, humble man, as He Himself came into the world poor and naked, lying in a manger between the ox and the ass.

"Well, you've got your girl, now are you happy?"

Happy Jacques certainly was, though he had little enough cause to be, for Marie still worked for her parents during the day and Jacques with his and they never met until after nightfall. The orders would not wait. All day long, Jacques fretted and gnawed his lips and fidgeted like a man whose clothes are too tight for him. Marie, as soon as her work was done, ran off without a look for her father or mother and flung herself into Jacques's arms. They would go to the fountain and drink and share the hunk of bread that Jacques had in his pocket. Their spirits rose again until each was shouting with laughter at every word the other said. O God, send us a slump to put us out of work so that we need never be apart!

"Out of work?" Jacques said. "I'd set fire to the looms only to see you three hours sooner!"

Marie pictured the looms burning and the flames like huge golden butterflies racing up the threads so that they crackled and the lovely striped cloth was all glowing and hissing, eaten up by the fire . . . And then the straw catching fire, and the bobbins and the bales of wool and people's clothes. She was half mad with love, her throat was parched with longing to feel Jacques's arms about her, the marrow of her bones was melting away and her eyes felt heavy as lead, her body was burning, her whole life was burning, let the whole faubourg burn!

Not many days before the feast of Saint John half the weavers were out of work owing to a shortage of wool while fresh supplies were on the way. That was life all over, you never had everything at once; when you were free, you had no soup and prices rose. People made soup from grass, watched the strings of dried onions growing shorter, and talked all day long about bread and cake and cheese and apples. "My uncle in the country had a goat—oh, that was the life! Fat white cheeses, just like cream, he used to wrap them in sprigs of mint, a row of ten cheeses each as big as your fist." "What became of the goat?" "Killed. For my cousin's wedding. How we all cried!" "Jacques, shall we go into the town? At the Bishop's palace they are giving soup to people who have no work."

"We are not beggars," Jacques said. But there was nothing else for it and so they went to the Bishop's palace. The street around the door was full of people and no more than fifty or sixty were let in at a time.

Marie drew her white shawl over her face so that no one should say, "Here she comes begging for soup when she could earn white bread," or other things more foolish still—Jacques had not sold his knife. In the Bishop's courtyard a well-spoken clerk was explaining to the people in a loud voice that it was wrong to neglect the old customs, failing to keep feast days and living like pigs on a dungheap all for love of money. Love of money leads to unemployment, he said, because there are more weavers and fullers in the land than are needed and it is a great sin to leave the earth that feeds us to run after base metal. He might say what he pleased but as for feeding, the year before, the harvest had been so bad that the peasants ate acorns, and children and old people without number had died of starvation. That, said the clerk, was the vengeance of God. In these days men think of nothing but gain and God closes the sluices of heaven and sends no rain. Oh, let him say what he likes as long as he gives us soup and takes away the ache in our bellies. They all filed through, gazing at the big wooden ladle as though it were the Holy Sacrament.

Oh, God bless our lord Bishop, and reward him for these bowls of soup at the Last Judgment; may one of his sins be remitted for every ladle!

Jacques and Marie walked back across the city through the narrow streets strewn with straw, talking as happily as if they had never been hungry. "It is a sin," Jacques said, "to think too much about one's belly. What good will it do me to have a loom of my own if it is only to live in constant dread of being idle? I have been thinking about it for a long time now: I am going to take you to Jerusalem."

"What about the cross?" said Marie. "We did not take the cross. The curé would never let us."

"There is a holy man," said Jacques, "who is to preach at Lens on Saint John's Day. He gives out crosses. We are not working, why shouldn't we go?"

They went in a group of some twenty boys and girls from the faubourg along with a few older men that were out of work, for the rumor of a holy man was too great a temptation for those out of work. Five or six leagues on foot was quickly covered if you sang as you went; the singing made you forget your hunger.

On the common outside Lens the holy man, who was dressed in frieze, his face tanned almost black, was talking about the end of the world. He had a wooden cross in his left hand, and his right was pointing up to heaven. "I see angels in the clouds," he said, "and shining trumpets. You shall march like the Hebrews in the desert with a pillar of fire before you by night and a pillar of smoke by day. God summons you to the Day of Judgment.

"It is written that He shall reign for a thousand years over a new earth, and every ear of corn shall bear seventy grains and every vine seventy bunches of grapes, and the olive trees shall bow down under the weight of olives and the apple trees no sooner flower than they shall bear ripe fruit, and there will be five harvests a year.

"Peter came and preached to you. Let those who have not yet taken the cross take it now. Let them sell all they have and give to those who lead them, and let no one keep anything for himself. They shall live like the Holy Apostles! Their way will lead through great valleys and across high mountains, they shall know much suffering and many will die on the way, but those who die so need have no fear, for their souls shall go on before, bearing the Cross of the Lord, and lead their brethren to the Holy City.

"While they who come to the end of the journey shall bring about Christ's great victory on earth. The time is come for God to receive His rightful heritage again. This is the day on which He says to His poor: You that are My true friends, it is through you I will bear witness. For kings and emperors have not aided Me, and the popes and the bishops have not aided Me, and the barons and the knights have not aided Me: all these think of nothing but making war from vain ambition to command! But you, that do not wish to command anyone, come to Me and I will command you.

"You shall follow the army of the counts and barons, and thus alongside a sinful army there shall be an army of saints, alongside an army of proud, greedy, and violent men shall be an army of the poor, the humble, and the meek. And for the love of this army, God shall give the Christians victory and a thousand crosses shall be raised on all the towers of Jerusalem."

The holy man spoke, and they listened to him gladly because he promised such things that even the curé had not promised better when he spoke of paradise. And he explained that the "crusaders" would be washed clean of all their sins; even if they had killed father or mother they would be forgiven. For there, in the holiest land in all the world, he said, heathens ruled that did not worship God and stabled their horses in the Christian churches and spat upon the cross, and put to death Christian men and took Christian women and sold them in the market like animals, and forced children to be baptized into their pagan faith. These Turks were so wicked that one lawful wife was not enough for them; they wed with several at a time, and feared the wrath of God so little that they coupled also with one another like degenerate beasts. They were so cruel that when a town resisted them they crucified the men and roasted little children alive, and so impious that they ate meat on Fridays in contempt of our faith. So that at last the patience of the Lord had been exhausted, for these men crucified Him anew each day. In all the churches of that land the images of Jesus Christ wept tears of blood and the holy lamps on the altars went out by themselves, and at Nazareth, in the house of the Virgin, the monks heard weeping in the night and great sighs.

When the crowd heard of weeping in the house of the Virgin, then weeping was heard indeed—even the men were in tears, while as for the women, they were sobbing for pity and wishing they were at Nazareth already to weep with the Holy Virgin.

Marie could see Her: she saw a white stone house and the Virgin seated inside the house before Her loom. She was ten times taller than a real woman and wore a blue veil over Her head, and She was all bowed down with grief and tears streamed silently from Her great eyes. Oh Mistress, that these accursed Turks should make You weep thus! "For these men do not honor the Blessed Virgin, they call Her plain Mary and say that She is not the mother of God, and destroy all Her images. And such is their contempt for the Holy Sepulcher that know, good people—I hardly dare to tell you—they call it nothing but 'Dunghill.'" At this there was such an outcry that the preacher must have wished he had not spoken, for the men nearest to the dais all but mobbed him. "May God punish you if you lie, old bearded one! Enough, tell us no more such things!" And then they were all shouting at once: *"The Cross! The Cross! The Cross!"* so that it could have been heard for a league around, and the people of Lens ran to the walls wondering what was the cause of such thunder on a sunny day.

The man took off his habit and began tearing it in pieces, and those standing nearest to the dais did the same. Two monks came out of the crowd and climbed onto the dais, and then it was a case of who could tear his robe best and make most strips. Soon there were six men half naked, dressed only in their linen breeches, and throwing strips of cloth into the crowd. "For God's sake do not trample one another, good people, there will be enough for everyone." The preacher could not call each crusader by his name; there were too many of them. "Jesus Christ hears your vows, it is to Him you swear fealty. Get your parish priests to confirm it. And if the priests will not, if your parents and friends will not, Jesus Christ must be first served and it is to Him that you have sworn."

Jacques and Marie took their two scraps of cloth and kissed them and hid them inside their clothes; then they fell into each other's arms. "We have taken the cross. Now we are bound to Jesus Christ forever and where He leads we will go." They were happy. Everyone was shouting and screaming and singing, and they sang too and embraced their comrades. And whosoever goes back on his word, may a hump grow on his back and may he spend the rest of his life bent over a loom scratching for money.

Jacques met his uncle in the crowd. They stared as though

seeing each other for the first time, and kissed on both cheeks as if they would never stop.

"I'm damned if I knew you were here too, uncle! Have you taken the cross?"

"I am old, Jacques, my time is past. You will pray for me there."

That night, the great Saint John's fires blazed in the meadow, lighting up the walls of the town with a ruddy glow. Boys and girls moved in long chains around the fires, singing psalms in honor of Saint John the Baptist to drive away the fairies that cut off girls' hair on that night. Couples, some married and some not, tumbled joyously in the coppices of young oak trees, rolling in the grass and the moss, oblivious of their neighbors, making love to the tune of the psalms, bathed in the red glow of the flames. Marie watched Jacques's face become a red flame. These crosses next to our hearts are burning us, heart against heart, cross against cross. Jacques, surely I have conceived a child today, I can feel it within me. He will be our eldest son and we shall baptize him in Jerusalem, our eldest son baptized in the spring of living water that never stales.

The next day Jacques sold his knife in the market at Lens.

Some thirty from the faubourg took the cross that day, and there were a number that had taken the cross at Easter but had not set out with Little Peter. As the period of enforced idleness was to last for another two weeks at least, the crusaders got into the habit of meeting near the city walls to talk about the journey. Nearly all were people who had never been farther afield than Béthune. The chief organizer for the Arras contingent was a mason named Baudry, a man of thirty, informed, shrewd, and articulate. He was assisted by Brother Barnabé, a monk of Bayeux, who had left his cloister but was known for a holy man.

Baudry had been making preparations for departure for three months and was well informed on all subjects. He had made the journey between Arras and Boulogne four times and had even been as far as Anvers. What they must not do, he said, was to take the road like a company of beggars going from fair to fair: "To my knowledge we shall be at least four months on the way and it is madness to think that we can live by alms. Remember that worthy bands of pilgrims are sure to set out from every town in Artois and Picardy and the Boulonnais and Hainault, and then think of the alms that would be needed. We should earn ourselves curses rather than blessings."

Therefore, he said, before setting out they must sell everything they could and make collections, and ask families and friends, from one a chicken, from another a sack of beans or a cheese, from another a sheep or a goat if possible. And as much money as they could scrape together. "Do not be ashamed to go begging in the merchant quarters, for such men must be made to understand that they are giving to God.

"After the Assumption, or later at Septembrate, there will be great armies of knights mustering from the whole province under the banner of the Duke of Lower Lorraine, a wise and gallant leader who has already assembled more than a thousand trained battle horses for his own knights alone. He is only waiting for the harvest to buy up half the corn in his duchy, and be it known he is a God-fearing man and pays the proper price. His brother, the Count of Boulogne, goes with him, and the Bishop of Arras and the Count of Béthune, for you should know that more than a thousand knights have taken the cross with all their men. Thus the pilgrims will travel in safety, as though behind a wall of spears, for it is right that men of war should protect those who pray."

Nay, was the answer, it will be like the tale of the clay pot and the iron pot. Is it really certain he will take the road with so many soldiers?

"And what can the soldiers take from you, fools that you are? Do you think they are taking the cross to steal your sacks of beans? Why should they desire your wives, all lean and brown and smelling of sweat as they are? They have enough pretty whores of their own and once in Turkish lands they'll take the heathen women. Be it known that they also have taken the cross because they desire to serve Jesus Christ, and we shall see the wolf and the young lamb eat from the same manger."

The families of those who had taken the cross were not thanking the Lord for it. Fathers said, Have we raised a son only to have him turn vagabond just when he could be useful to us? Bernier, for one, was bitterly angry with his son.

"Go where you like, you young bastard, you'll not see your loom again. The day we start work again I'll put your cousin Philippe in your place. He'll be only too glad of it."

"Very well, father. Philippe needs a livelihood, he has been laid off for a year."

"You crusading dog, is that all you can say to me? Are you

laughing at me?" Jacques was sorry for his father then. He sniffed back his own tears.

"I'd strangle myself with my own belt sooner than laugh! Don't miss me. Philippe is a good worker, you'll not lose by the change."

"Not lose by it? You tell me I'll not lose by it?"

The curé spoke to the people of the faubourg in the church, after mass. "Be patient, good people. It is not for nothing that God sends you this trial. It is a good work, since our lord Bishop goes and takes clerks and canons with him. It is a work of profit for the soul. Do not seek to constrain souls that have heard the Lord calling." (He could barely keep back his tears because his own son was going and his priestess was tearing her hair like a madwoman.)

"It is a good work, for he that thinks to lose shall gain and he that gives shall receive, for so God has told us." This priest, Father Aimery, was also one of those who had heard Little Peter's sermon and he felt a great longing to repent of his sins, for the laws of the Church compelled priests to sin, and to preach respect for marriage while living in a state of concubinage, and to preach charity while taking money from the poor for the sacraments.

"Jesus Christ's letter, curé, did you see it with your own eyes?"

"When I saw the box opened, an angel dazzled my eyes and I saw only gold stars. For my sins, God did not permit me to read the letter. But a learned clerk told me that the Latin words it contained expressed the Lord's mercy to poor folk, that whatsoever sins they have committed He will forgive them, if they only take the cross with a pure heart."

Owing to the lack of work, the crusade was talked of more and more, and when work started again the talk went on in the workshops. Those who were to go sat by their looms and watched the others at work, and more than one regretted in his heart that he was pledged to it. If they could only have gone directly after taking the cross! But they were losing their work and had to wait another three months yet, dragging on and tightening their belts.

Marie was still working as a winder. Her family loved her too much to punish her for her folly. But as for earning money to put by, that was another matter. Her earnings were meager and the price of bread was rising, as it did every summer. Mathieu said that the children were wasting away from eating nothing but rotten beans; they needed bread. Marie gave him her pay, or rather she dared not ask him for it. "Take it, father, take it all, at least let me be useful to you while I am still here!"

"Don't you flatter yourself," said Armelle. "Benoît is going on twelve, he will take your place." She said it out of a sense of bitterness and slapped her daughter more often than was necessary because she was unhappy. "God knows what will become of you, my poor child. Girls cleverer than you have finished up as soldiers' whores."

"Mother, you did not hear the holy man. I promise you, you would have done the same. He said the Holy Virgin weeps for the insults Her Son is made to suffer in those lands." Armelle tightened her lips and nodded. She was still strong and handsome and not much past thirty.

"Well, why shouldn't I go? If I knew they were short of weavers in that country, I would go. We have never liked to be idle, Mathieu and I. But with this cross, my poor girl, you'll lose your taste for work, and you'll not be able to settle to it again."

Marie thought her mother argued like an old woman. Did God create us weavers, or masons or tanners? He made us men. In paradise they do not ask you what your trade is. On Sundays she went to meet Jacques in the meadow where Baudry was assembling those who were to go. He said that by mid-September they would all go to join the pilgrims from Béthune and Avesnes and march to Boulogne because the Count's army would set out from there. In October, Duke Godfrey of Lower Lorraine was setting out and he had said that he would gladly take pilgrims with his army, but not too many, and they were not to bring too many of the old or sick and they must provide carts for them . . . It was easy enough for Duke Godfrey to talk; were even pilgrimages to be only for the rich?

They were learning to sing the psalms and canticles about Jerusalem, and cleaning and mending their clothes for the journey. The women sewed crosses onto the cloaks. And the citizens of Arras came bringing gifts of shoes, blankets of wool and skins, wool for spinning, and cuts of cloth. (The fact that plenty of weavers had never woven an ell of cloth for themselves in their lives had become a byword in those parts.) "So that you will not be cold on the way, good pilgrims. Pray for us." They would be traveling all winter, long enough to wear out three pairs of shoes. The weather was warm and often the crusaders would spend all night out of doors in the fields, listening to pilgrims and preachers. Brother Barnabé, who had a fine voice, deep as the tenor bell in the church, sang psalms about the way to Jerusalem. He taught the people to sing these psalms and advised them to practice walking, because the workers in the faubourg were rarely great walkers. "Walking," he said, "will be your trade for many a long month and you have not yet got your bodies used to pilgrimage. After a couple of weeks you will have got the habit, but it will be hard at first and you must not lag behind."

He was a good man, was Brother Barnabé; he knew every man and woman by name and had a good word for each. You are strong enough to break the heads of ten Turks. You are not much of a size, but you know God likes the little ones best. You, Lucie, do not be ashamed of your big belly. There will be no more fatherless children in Jerusalem. You, Michel, were a thief in your own country; now you are going to steal your own soul from the Devil.

To Marie he said, "You sing so well that you shall lead the women in the psalms. God will give you the gift of making new words, for although you are married you are pure in heart." "Let none of you," he would say, "covet his neighbor's wife. For pilgrims that is one of the worst sins. Rather get your betrothed and your wives to go with you so that they also may benefit from the great pardon." For it was true that the older women, mothers of several children, were afraid of such a long journey in winter and because of this fathers of families who had taken the vow were falling into sin and regretting their decision. "Go on, mother, we'll put the children on the carts and wrap them up well. They'll enjoy seeing something of the world."

Jacques had made a great many new friends. Now that he was not working he was finding out about other men's trades, talking building with the masons and stonecutters and dreaming of tall scaffoldings and the sound of hammers, and of good pay, for of all Christian men the masons were the best paid. He had a friend who was an apprentice armorer, and his mind ran on beautiful great steel blades shining like pure water in the sun. He thought of rings of steel put together and soldered so as to make a cloth of iron; such pieces were made in the lands of the East and in Spain, kings wore them when they went into battle, and they made helmets brighter than the sun and as sound as bells —why, if you got a dint on them you'd as good as hear the bells ringing for mass!

"You would that. There are some go deaf from it."

"The Turks must wear three suits of iron one on top of the other to be so strong."

"That they do! And helmets wrapped in great balls of wool so that they never feel any blows. Weapons are useless against them, unless they are armed with some good relic; then the Turks' armor shatters of its own accord."

Marie scarcely left Jacques's side and listened to everything his friends said. She thought about the Turks, seeing them as giants, with balls of wool in place of heads. Crack! The blessed sword touched them and they fell, sliced in two like a split log, and a fountain of black blood spurted out. She laughed.

"Oh, but Jacques, aren't you afraid?"

"Afraid? Afraid of what?"

"Of taking such a lovely wife with you. Even pilgrims are not made of wood. Suppose someone were to take her from you?"

Jacques laughed. "If anyone tried to take her from me, I'd cut off his head."

"What if it were a knight?"

"What of it, haven't knights got heads?" His big, deep laugh rang out at his own joke and the others all roared with laughter too, because it was often said in the faubourg that the rich and powerful did not need much brain and that was why they were more stupid than the poor.

It seemed as if they would never set out, but the day of departure came at last, and then the crusaders were forgiven and there were no more reproaches. Parents wept and gave their children all they could spare for the journey, which was not much. A few copper coins, a hat or a piece of cloth . . . No, they did not set out very rich, for nearly all had been out of work for several months. Jacques had given Baudry the money he got from the sale of his knife, but it was little enough. Marie had nothing. She had said, "I could sell my hair." Jacques flushed red at that.

"Your hair? Why not the rest of you?"

"Jacques, people have asked my mother for it more than once but she never would. She used to say how would I get married without my hair? For a married woman it's different. I promise you, I know the prices; long fair hair is worth more than ten knives."

Jacques was horrified. "If you say another word about it, I'll beat you. People would work magic with it and you would die."

Marie looked at him with a smile that was at once sad and tender.

"I should not be the only one, you know. You stop believing in magic very much when you are hungry. Fine ladies plait it into their own hair with embroidered ribbons."

"I'll starve first," said Jacques. "It's bad enough to be poor without the rich taking your hair for their wives!" So Marie kept her lovely hair, modestly twisted up at the back of her head and covered with her coif.

That same day, Jacques's uncle came to the faubourg from his village and brought an ax.

"Take it, my lad. I can't give you anything more, but it's given with good will. It belonged to your grandfather. It is good and heavy and the wood is sound. You'll chop the Turks if ever they try and attack our women."

It was a good present. Nearly all the men were bringing either an ax or a pitchfork or a stout cudgel. Baudry and even Brother Barnabé said that two precautions were better than one. "God watches over His own, but even so He doesn't ask them to walk on water or fly through the air. If evil men attack you, you cannot answer them with psalms, and it may be that God Himself will have need of your weapons."

"Master Baudry, what should we do if our comrades should be driven by the Devil to turn their pitchforks against other pilgrims?"

"If any man does that without good cause," said Baudry, he shall be hanged on the spot without trial and lose the benefits of the pilgrimage. Swear to me that you will respect this rule, for whoever uses a weapon dedicated to God to kill his brother is no Christian but a counterfeit made by the Devil, and it is right to send him back where he came from!"

The men swore. All knew that there were some among them under suspicion of murder, but all were of good faith and the greatest sinners were the most eager to repent.

That night Jacques found himself sitting next to a big man dressed in a short tunic of brown wool, who yet did not look like a poor townsman. He was tall and broad with massive shoulders, a short, springy beard, and long chestnut hair. His grey eyes held a look of calm, grave assurance which, though it would have been hard to say exactly why, made his presence among the pilgrims a little unexpected. He was known as "the knight," and it occurred to Jacques to ask him why he was called this.

The man smiled broadly as he answered: "Because for many years I lived by that unhappy trade, and by God's will I shall be called upon to practice it again."

"Lord!" said Jacques. "Were you a real knight with a helmet and a shirt of mail and a great sword?"

"Aye, and a white belt and a shield with the arms of my house upon it, all the panoply of the Devil."

Jacques laughed. "If it is the panoply of the Devil, how can you say that by God's will you will take it up again?"

The man smiled slowly and shook his head. "Life is not simple, my boy. See here, dung is a foul thing of itself and yet we use it to enrich the soil to grow good bread."

Jacques thought for a moment. "I should not care to practice a trade," he said, "and then call it dung."

"Nor I. Yet truly," the man went on quietly, "the knight is worse than dung, for dung is not honored or respected." Jacques snorted with laughter.

"That would be a fine thing!"

"Yes," the man said, "but you see, take a count or a baron or any petty knight: they have the best place in church and everyone speaks to them with respect. Because these are corrupt times when men grow rich and powerful by force of arms. The more murders a man has committed, the more respected he is. That is why we are worse than dung."

"I see," said Jacques. "You are a sensible man. But if you followed this profitable trade I wonder how you got your sense."

"You want to know too much for one of your age," the man said. "It came to me of itself. A lark came down from heaven to tell it to me."

Jacques went and told his friends and Marie and Brother Barnabé, who said that Sir Evrard (he concealed his family name out of humility) had indeed been converted to God by listening to Peter's sermons and had left everything to lead a Christian life. But now he had joined the band of crusaders from Arras (he was too well known in his own country) because he said that the pilgrims had need of an armed escort.

"This is not a joke," Brother Barnabé said. "He has several companions, converted likewise, and he possesses a horse and armor."

The young men listened and scratched their heads.

"But then," Lambert, the curé's son, said at last, "why doesn't he go with those from his own parts? You say he is too well known. He may be a great cutthroat."

Baudry was there, listening thoughtfully. "My friends, there must be no doubts and suspicions among us before we set out. Let us not judge one another. I have spoken with this man. He has sworn not to draw his sword until the day we are attacked by infidels. I must tell you it is four years since he was converted. He fasts four days a week and what is more to the point, he is a widower and has lived in chastity for four years."

Lambert crossed himself. "God save us! Do you expect us to travel with a knight who has lived without a woman for four years? And here is Jacques with a beautiful wife!"

Brother Barnabé was angry at this. "Here you are, all of you, talking about Jacques's wife. Have a care to yourselves. It is the Devil sends you these thoughts. The knight is no longer a young man."

So saying, he dismissed the lads. On their way home Jacques said to Lambert, "So Brother Barnabé says you have an eye to my wife, does he? Tell me, is that right of you?"

Lambert was a quiet, sober lad and one of Jacques's best friends.

"Brother Barnabé didn't mean anything," he said. "I was speaking for your sake, because you are like a brother to me. To be frank with you, I have some hopes that Mère Perrine's Isabelle will be willing to come with me to Jerusalem, only she is waiting until the last moment for fear of her mother."

"What!" said Jacques. "Isabelle has a hump."

Lambert blushed. "So what? That's why I haven't told you. She is pretty, you know, and her back is not so bad. She has promised me that on the day we leave she will hide among the other women and her mother will never see. She already has her pilgrim's cloak and cross."

"I'm damned if I had any idea!" said Jacques. "Here, Lambert, your father is more learned than mine. What shall we find there, in Jerusalem?"

"If we knew all beforehand," said Lambert, "we would never set out. My father says that when you are a Christian you must give and ask nothing in return."

"Whoever touches the Holy Sepulcher," said Jacques, "fountains of living water spring up in his heart and he will never be sad again."

Jacques was a youth who was sometimes sad, for other causes than hunger. It came from the time when he lived in the country where people were not always working. Sometimes, as he watched the sheep, he would let fall the rope he was plaiting or the wooden bowl he was carving with his knife. On summer evenings he would gaze at the sun going down into the earth. The sun rose out of the sea, far away in the east, and drowned itself every day in another sea in the west, and the lands near to the sea where the sun rose were warm and rich, and there was never snow or rain or clouds.

Once he had seen sailors in the market square of Arras that were not Picards or Flemings or English. They came from Marseilles, but they talked like Christians. They had dark skins and brass rings on their wrists and in their ears and big knives in their belts. They talked of a land where there was no winter, where the apple trees blossomed all year round and golden apples grew on the trees and silk cost less than linen does here . . . There in the levantine seas, dragons made great storms in which a single wave could engulf a church tower. These dragons with golden scales guarded the place where the sun slept at night, and the nearer one got to that place the more the sea shone red and boiling, and no sailor ever returned from it alive. Those who were not eaten by the dragons were burned alive and melted in the sun like moths in the flame because the sun was really as big as a mountain. It rose from the water with a great rushing and the singing of thousands of angels, and every morning the sea burst into flames and burned so that the flames of its burning could be seen all over the world.

In the lands of the sunrise life was good; the people lived on boats with colored sails and caught as much fish as they wanted. The towns were rich, the houses were painted in gold and black and red, and the people walked abroad in silken robes. Their markets were so full of fruit and vegetables and fish of all colors that no one thought of stealing; there were heaps of things piled up on mats and the sellers offered them to you in courtesy. For those people did not worship the true God, but this was from ignorance and apart from that they were wise and courteous; they had always a smile on their lips and when they spoke it was like singing. In Arras, Jacques had once seen, in a procession, the new canopy for the shrine of Saint Vaast, made of silk woven in China: for such a fabric a man might risk damnation. Bernier had said, "What do you think? The work is fine but do you think it pays? What kind of a reed would you need for a loom like that?

You know how it is with a fine weft: you are paid three times as much for the piece and it takes ten times as long." But for some reason Jacques thought that in those lands there were no workers and no workshops, as if those fine silks were all woven by lords and ladies who made them only for their pleasure, in painted rooms where troubadours sang sweet songs to them.

Jacques was a cheerful lad, but when he was sad the mood persisted. He was always thinking life was better somewhere else, an idea common to many young men with too much joy in their hearts and too few reasons to be glad. In spite of all that Baudry and Brother Barnabé and the curé could say about the pilgrims being ready to face great hardships, even the mention of hardship was enough to make Jacques see joy ahead of him. He thought of hardship joyfully endured, of singing, of palms, great suns, the red lifeblood of martyrs. His mother wept: "What have I done to the Holy Virgin that the one child left to me should go and starve by the roadside? Oh, if it were not a sin, I should curse this cross!"

"Me, starve?" said Jacques. "The rich, perhaps, but we know all about that. We know what it is to eat nettles."

"Nettles! Who says you'll find any in those places?"

In the camp, all was in readiness for departure. They were only waiting for the distribution of grain. The lords and bishops who were going had bought up so much for the journey that there were fears in case not enough should be left to last until Christmas. Baudry was taking up collections: "For the pilgrims, good people, so that they may pray for you in Jerusalem." It had not been a good year and rye was expensive. The sacks were heaped on the carts and covered over with strawcloth, and Baudry counted and re-counted them every day. He also counted the pilgrims.

The pilgrims numbered two hundred by this time, which meant that the day of departure would be a day of great weeping.

When that day came, Alix of the Thirty Pieces made her appearance in the camp of those who were to go. She came leading by the bridle a mule laden with sacks and baskets, and with her came her old bawd, weeping bitterly. It was an unusual sight to see Alix dressed as she was, in a plain robe of coarse linen and a brown hooded cloak, with a staff in her hand and a red cross sewn on her right shoulder. Even so she attracted attention, because neither her manner nor her bearing was that of a poor woman. She would do better, the women said, to be off and go with the knights. But the pilgrims soon found that Alix knew how to defend herself.

She stood in the middle of the field at Baudry's side, and threw back her cloak and unfastened the neck of her dress, disclosing the shift she wore beneath it, made of rough dark sackcloth such as even a beggarwoman would have rejected.

"See, my friends," she said, "I am not a false pilgrim, and if I have not joined you before this, it was for shame because of my evil fame. Yet however bad that may be it is still too good, for truly I have been the Whore of Babylon with whom the kings of the earth have committed fornication and who is herself drunken with the blood of the righteous! Truly I have sucked the blood of the poor and drunk the widows' tears, and I a daughter of the faubourg of the weavers. I have denied my own people and loved only the rich. Brothers and sisters, forgive a miserable creature who, inflamed with devilish greed, has made her beauty into a trap for men's lust! Know all of you that I have had no God but Mammon and have made gold pieces my sacred Hosts!"

She wept as she spoke and the tears ran down her cheeks and into her mouth. The onlookers nudged one another and murmured, "At least she has not lost everything. She talks like a clerk so that it's a pleasure to listen to her."

"My dear brothers, my dear sisters," she said, "I am an abominable sinner. Despise me, for truly I have deserved it. In a single day I earned as much as a high-grade weaver gets in a month, and in three days as much as a winder gets in a year. In my frantic greed I have gorged myself, my dear friends, on your sweat and your tears, luring your masters and your merchants into my bed, along with knights and churchmen and sundry strangers. And so it is right that you should despise Alix and trample her under your feet, but do not take it as an outrage that I ask you to receive me as one of you, for the Lord Jesus Christ Himself has pity on the lost sheep when she finds her way back to the fold. See, I bring you here the goods I have amassed, all that I have left; they are ill-gotten gains, my friends, but I promise you they are not stolen goods! And if you will not forgive me, I will follow you, walking alone ten paces behind the last wagons, and even that I shall hold high honor. But if you forgive me, I swear to you that I will never in my life forget your charity!"

She was no longer weeping as she spoke, but the young women and even some of the men were in tears. Baudry told her, "God alone is the judge of your sins, but it is for our women to decide whether they are willing for you to march with them. For women of your trade repent easily, but their bodies are light."

"That is true," Alix answered, "but my repentance has not been easy. As for my body, it is like a field trampled by many flocks."

Baudry looked her in the eyes, and his own fell. Her gaze was so grave and clear that he was ashamed of having spoken to her as he had.

The older and wiser women in the company declared that if Alix Malebouche wished to follow the pilgrims, no one could prevent her from doing penance as she chose, but unless she found a man willing to marry her she must keep herself apart from the families and walk with the other repentant sinners. She was therefore given into the care of two elderly nuns who were going with special permission from their abbess. These two good sisters were to take care of the repentant prostitutes, since these unhappy girls were in great danger of falling back into their old sinful ways. The unmarried men hovered around them like flies around a honeypot.

And so Alix kissed her old procuress and begged her to return to Arras. "From this day," she said, "I am beginning my new life and I do not wish to see anything that may remind me of the old one. The shortest farewells are the least painful." And she sat down among the other girls, who eyed her resentfully, saying, "Here is this rich man's whore come to mortify us with her fine speeches."

The leaders of the party were in something of a quandary. It seemed to them that Alix of the Thirty Pieces would have done better to become a crusader at her own expense since she had the means. It was not that her contribution was unwelcome; far from it. At that price her presence must be endured.

"Charity is a fine thing," Baudry said, "but shall we be kind to the wolf at the expense of the sheep?"

"We do not know yet," said Brother Barnabé, "which of our pilgrims are wolves and which lambs. This woman talks too much, but she is sincere."

On the eve of their departure, when all over the field nothing was heard but sounds of singing, laughter, and weeping, the leaders of the company remained in their tent going over the accounts, more anxiously than the bride's father on the eve of the wedding. None of them, with the exception of Brother Barnabé, had ever traveled far afield. The knight was from Perche and familiar with Normandy, Picardy, and Beauce. Baudry had been as far as Bruges and Ghent.

"Three or four months on the road, and not one of our pilgrims in ten will have a whole pair of shoes."

"Leave it to God's grace," said Brother Barnabé. "Were the Hebrews in the desert any richer than we?"

"The Hebrews journeyed for forty years and they had holy Moses in person with them."

"And we," said Brother Barnabé, "have the Cross of Jesus Christ."

"Listen to them," said Mère Corneille, "howling like lunatics. Do they call those psalms? More like drunkards singing, for God forgive me they are drunk."

The curé nodded. "Go and speak to them, brother, that so holy an undertaking may not be taken for mere drunken bravado."

"Oh, let them drink and enjoy themselves, curé. It is a holy joy. They are drinking to the feast of Our Lord and here we are like the Pharisees blaming them for it!"

Brother Barnabé was prone to such moods of mingled gaiety and sadness which made him indulgent, while at other times he would see red if a man so much as sneezed in his presence.

"Here we are," he went on, "setting out to find God, and are we to be afraid of what the townsmen of Arras might think? For God's sake, let them think us drunkards and madmen! Today all loss is a gain."

There had been plenty of townsmen and clerics only too ready to censure the crusaders. "This enterprise of yours is pure madness," they said. "God has sent no miracles to prove that you are right. Your journey will only lead to endless debauchery, thieving, adultery, and even murder, so that instead of saving souls you are bound to damn them. Never since Jesus Christ came into the world have so many folk armed and unarmed been seen to set out together on a pilgrimage. Everywhere you go you will be greeted like an army of locusts, and that is just what you will be." A man that spent his life listening to good advice would never stir a step outside his own house. But Baudry was a sensible man and he tried to foresee and guard against all possible causes of trouble and disagreement. It left him feeling depressed. "We would flee from the world," he said, "and yet we have to begin by making all our arrangements in accordance with the wisdom of this world.

We have to rely on the support of armed men and count our pennies like misers."

They had to set out at dawn. Priests sang matins in the big meadow beside a fire of branches, and the faithful chanted the responses. The parents and friends of those who were to go spent the last night with the crusaders. People came out from the city, drawn by the fires and the singing. Some brought a gold coin, others a chicken or a sack of beans. Everything was piled onto the wagons, which by now were so loaded down that the axles were in danger of breaking. Pray for us, good pilgrims, do not forget us in Jerusalem!

A lady on a grey horse rode around the meadow, giving a copper denier to each man she met. Her eyes were red from crying and her cheeks scratched, and she was telling everyone, "Good pilgrims, remember the knight Rufin of Sacy, my brother, who is going on the crusade. Remember his name well and pray for him." Girard the Jay, a notorious rogue, said to her, "Madame, for a copper denier our memories will not be long, but for a silver mark we would remember till the Day of Judgment!" This made his comrades laugh, but the lady cried out, "What, churl, would you have me give a mark to each one of you? I give what I have."

Marie prayed, watching the curé's hands lifted to the dark sky and illumined by the firelight. If I forget thee, O Jerusalem, let my right hand wither and my tongue cleave to the roof of my mouth. O Jerusalem. Her father, mother, and brother were there and they thought as they looked at her: It would be a sin to keep her back, she hears the voice of God. Her face was grave and glad and her eyes, wide open and unblinking, shone as though the light of angels' wings had got into them. Her face was pale and smudged with tears, and with her swollen and quivering lips she looked more like a child than a married woman. Her mother thought: She has never been more beautiful.

Her brother said, "Marie, what are you looking at?"

She shivered as the child tugged at her arm, shivered and then turned and kissed first her brother and then her mother as passionately as if she were trying to hurt them.

"Oh, if you could only come too, if only I did not have to leave you! I love you so much and now I am going away!" She kissed her mother on both cheeks, again and again. "I did not know how much I loved you! And now I am going away!" And she burst into tears.

"Marie, what was it you were looking at just now?" The little boy kept pulling at her skirt and repeating his question. Marie stroked his hair.

"Benoît, my lad, you want to know too much. I saw a white crow riding on a blue horse no bigger than my finger." Then, seeing her brother pout, she stopped laughing and said, "Benoît, I saw crowns of stars. That is all I can tell you." Her parents looked at her and shook their heads. It was not often a girl had visions once she was married; either Marie was lying or she had received a gift from God.

They sat there on the ground, the four of them, among all the other pilgrims saying goodbye to their families. They had stopped talking and shared their crust of bread in silence. The two little ones slept, lying on the ground beside them. Twenty yards away, the flickering wood fire threw long shadows across them as men passed before it. A group of young men were singing an improvised song, clapping their hands in time to the refrain.

The words of the song said: Farewell our own land, farewell father and mother, do not weep. We go to find the land of Jesus Christ, who has never failed or been false to anyone. He has given us a pledge to lead us to paradise if we are willing to win it. Up and be bold, friends! And we will win it!

They were bawling the words at the tops of their voices and pounding as hard as they could with their hands. Jacques was one of them, sitting next to his cousin Philippe, who was not going and was beginning to wish now that he was.

Marie, her head resting on her mother's shoulder, blinked as she watched the firelight flickering on her small sister's sleeping face. How beautiful she is, how beautiful they all are, father, mother, Benoît, the curé, Mère Perrine, all of them. God has transfigured them tonight. This is how they will be on the Day of Judgment. The song pounded in her brain like the clatter of a thousand looms, and all at once she seemed to see a thread of gold finer than a hair unwinding on a shining bobbin and a voice was saying, This is fairy hair, and she thought: No, it is the Virgin's hair, it will never break, and from this hair we shall weave a banner to deck the throne of God . . . The reel was turning and turning, shooting out flames. Oh no, it cannot break, it is the Virgin's hair! Let it not break! Marie's head sank more and more heavily on her mother's shoulder. "She is asleep," said

Mathieu. "It is as well. They must be at Béthune by tomorrow night." Armelle dared not move for fear of waking her daughter, but the more she forced herself to keep still, the more her shoulders shook with sobs.

The procession made its way slowly out of the meadow and past the walls of Arras. People were waving and shouting from the top of the walls and the church bells were ringing. The poor had no fine banners, but they had made some from what they could find, from woolen cloaks and scraps of braid given in charity. They had tall crosses made of plain painted wood. The banners went in front, swaying in time to the movements of their bearers. The men were all singing. Men and women walked together, grouped by neighborhoods and families, and after them came the carts, some drawn by donkeys and others pulled by men, bearing the smallest children and pregnant women, the sick and the aged. The big wagons piled high with provisions and the flocks of sheep and cattle were escorted by Sir Evrard and his ten men mounted on somewhat seedy-looking horses, and bringing up the tail of the procession came the repentant sinners, the whores and those for whom the crusade was a penance laid on them by their priest. A sight which came as a surprise to many people was that among these sinners, walking barefoot in their shifts and beating their breasts, were the curé of the faubourg and his priestess, who, rather than part from their son, had made up their minds together at the last minute.

As long as the pilgrims were still in their own country where people spoke their language, before they joined up with the other companies and with the Count of Boulogne's army, they did not feel that they were really on their way; it seemed as if they were on an ordinary pilgrimage, although an unusually solemn one. The peasants in the villages they passed through watched them go by, calling out, "Pray for us, good people, remember us in Jerusalem." Some brought chickens or eggs or pots of honey and these gifts were piled onto the wagons. Already there was no more room for the chickens in the cages and the frightened fowls cackled and fluttered about while the people laughed and said, At least we won't starve to death. It was true they had succeeded in collecting more than two hundred sheep, but Baudry was relying more on the money stored in the communal chest, for what were two hundred sheep on such a journey? He knew little of foreign lands: it was said that in Germany the people were charitable, in Hungary very cruel, while as for the Greek lands, the peasants there were said to be poor so that they would have to find provisions in the towns.

Brother Barnabé was a man of eager, restless temper. In his monastery he had acquired the reputation of an uncomfortable bedfellow. He saw the Devil everywhere: in the refectory and in the chapel, in the vegetable garden, in the monks' habits, and even in his abbot's beard. Surely the abbot tended that beard too lovingly? Perhaps he wished to make it as fine as the prophet Elijah's? Surely beneath their black woolen habits the monks concealed a greedy appetite for wine and fresh fish, not to mention demons of pride and envy? A devil dwelt in all of them, even—oh sacrilege!—going so far as to sit on the cantor's psalter to make that monk show off his fine voice (all too often this was the case with Brother Barnabé himself) and jumping into the holy-water stoup to make the monks cross themselves ostentatiously. In short, there was not a flea on Brother Barnabé that he did not take for the Devil.

His abbot accused him of being possessed by a devil of censoriousness, and imposed penance after penance on him. I may be possessed by a devil of plain speaking, Brother Barnabé would say, but not of ill will, because my tongue denounces evil in order to amend it. This demon that dwells in me is not evil, for it hates, with a deadly hatred, corruption and sloth and cowardice and all the impure things of which this house is truly the chosen land. The abbot, unable to cope with this intractable nature and seeing that the monk, far from mending his ways, was growing increasingly outspoken, and having in other respects nothing against Brother Barnabé, who was conscientious in his prayers, chaste, sober, and a hard worker, therefore decided to send him on a penitential pilgrimage to St. James of Compostela. Brother Barnabé duly set out, performed his devotions at Compostela, and handed his abbot's letter to the superior of the Monastery of St. James, but he never returned to his own monastery.

He did not allow himself to fall a victim to the profane desire to see new lands, although this desire was very strong in him, but a strange adventure befell him. One evening as he was walking along the road between Carcassonne and Albi, he saw a man dressed in rags, bent double and apparently hardly able to walk. As a charitable duty, he went up to the man and offered to carry him on his back to the next village.

He was already preparing to take him on his back when he caught sight of his companion's face, swollen and misshapen with a nose bigger than a turnip. His heart failed him and without another word he fled, thinking: God be thanked I did not touch him, and telling himself that the man was wrong to walk the highways like that with his leprosy without shaking a rattle.

That night, Brother Barnabé had a dream. He saw the Lord Jesus Christ in such a blaze of white light that His face was hidden, and the Lord said, "Last night you denied Me and did not know Me."

"Lord, would You take such a loathsome form?"

"Can you read, yet do not know My Scriptures?"

Brother Barnabé awoke weeping and hurried away in search of his leper. He found him sitting at a crossroads at the foot of a stone cross. Filled with joy, Brother Barnabé went up to the man and kissed him on both cheeks and clasped his fingerless hands. "Forgive me, friend," he said, "for not knowing you last night."

"Do you know me?" the man said.

"Yes, I am sure I have seen you before. Get on my back and let me carry you."

He took the man for his companion, sharing his food and drink with him. He would have taken him to the leper hospital at Albi, but the leper stoutly refused. He was an evil, boorish fellow who talked of nothing but his desire to get himself a woman, one that was not a leper. Owing to his insistence on living in the open, after two weeks he caught cold and died. Brother Barnabé, convinced that he must have caught leprosy, would not go back to his monastery, but he could not bear to shut himself up at once in a leper hospital and so wandered the roads, begging his bread and waiting for the first signs of the disease to declare themselves.

He fell into a state of extreme melancholy and was filled with self-pity for his strong young body, for he was barely thirty, blaspheming against God for leading him to destroy himself in this way. He even believed that he had been the victim of temptation by the Devil. He committed a variety of sins, telling himself he would have plenty of time to repent them in the leper hospital. Every morning he inspected the palms of his hands and the soles of his feet for the white spots of leprosy. Months passed and at last he realized that the disease had spared him. He had never been in better health.

By that time he had reached the vicinity of the Spanish town of Seville, for the demon of curiosity had led him into that distant land where Moslems were almost as common as Christians. Saint Thomas appeared to him in a dream and said to him:

"Weak and foolish monk that doubted your Lord! Had you caught leprosy, should you not have rejoiced at it? With your own hand you have touched the wounds of Our Lord."

Brother Barnabé meditated on these words for a long time; then he went into the church of Seville and gave thanks to God. There, at last, he was visited by a revelation.

The Lord Jesus Christ called him, not to care for lepers only, but to be the brother of all God's poor. Were you not living in a monastery, safe from hunger and peril? To those who live thus I shall say on that Day: I was hungry and you gave Me no food. Instead of the suffering body of your Lord, you saw only monks eager to please their abbot and chant their prayers well. Brother Barnabé understood, and he began to haunt battlefields in order to care for the wounded and comfort the dying. He begged money or earned it by menial work and bought bread which he distributed to the sick. For five years he traveled the roads of Castile, Murcia, Catalonia, and Provence in this way, striving to put his hand in the Lord's wounds and touch evil so as to find the means of curing it.

But he saw so much poverty and suffering that the further he advanced on his quest, the further he felt from his goal.

You are too great for me, Lord, Your body bleeds and weeps in a thousand, in a hundred thousand of Your brethren and in a hundred times a hundred thousand! Here are beggars with rotting limbs, soldiers trampled beneath horses' hoofs, peasants in burned lands writhing in pain from eating earth; here are women with empty breasts and nurslings skinnier than little birds; here are the poor chained for stealing bread and hanged for stealing a pig. Here are workers toiling day and night with empty stomachs, and starving men that have no work driven off with whips. Here are aged whores stoned like stray dogs and old soldiers without hands or feet; here are lepers, their faces white and swollen with rottenness. So great is Your poverty, Lord, that soon our degenerate age must perish from its own hardness of heart, for God Your Father cannot endure it much longer! More than a thousand years have passed since men set You on the Cross; how can You bear to be thus mutilated and dishonored every day? Brother Barnabé talked in this way to all charitable men he met. His anger against the sins of men grew stronger, since for one trouble that came from God there were ten caused by the wickedness of men.

"Oh my brothers, shall we see our bishops riding through the streets dressed in silks and sables, shall we see our abbots sitting in well-heated rooms bursting with pride? Shall we see our kings and princes adorning their deadly weapons with gold and precious jewels and trampling the poor man's field and taking his bread to buy themselves horses and lances? Worse than Caiaphas, Pilate, and Herod, all these men daily spit in the face of Our Lord, and if God's law commands us to obey them, then let us obey but let us not make ourselves their accomplices. For all I am a wandering monk, I have not renounced my vows, and if all my brethren did as I am doing the wretchedness of the poor would be greatly relieved, for the monks are many and sound in body and mind."

By these fierce words he extorted alms from the rich and sometimes earned himself a beating. He would run after merchants or knights in the street, calling out, "You that have beaten and robbed Jesus Christ, give me a little of that money you have stolen from Him so that I may give it Him again!"

One day, after he had been cudgeled and left for dead, he was rescued by a man who took him to his cave and talked to him of the Revelation of Saint John. The end of this century, this man said, would see the fulfillment of these prophecies. Antichrist had appeared in the East and he was called the Sultan. He was coming at the head of his armies to conquer Christendom. He was on the point of capturing Constantinople and had stabled his horses in the churches of Jerusalem.

At first Brother Barnabé had not paid much attention to this news; then he saw that the signs were more or less in agreement. If the Sultan defiles Jerusalem in this way, he thought, it is because the sins of Christians have made the cup run over and soon the sufferings we complain of now will seem to us like the dew of morning. And so he made his way back to the North, meditating on the prophecies, and there joined the band of volunteers who followed Little Peter, gathering alms and tending the sick. For a time he lived happily as one of that traveling township of people converted to the life of Christ, where everything was shared according to each one's needs, where all—cripples, thieves, madmen, and prostitutes—were welcome, and where each man had a right to be called brother and friend.

These, he thought, are the signs of the times. Communities like this are helping the world to prepare for the great ordeal. But although Peter himself was a man both wise and just, some of his lieutenants were not easy men to deal with, or possibly Brother Barnabé was not very patient. He left the community, regretfully, just at the time when the great news of the crusade was beginning to spread. Pope Urban, inspired by the Holy Ghost, had seen the image of Jerusalem in a dream with every stone bleeding and groaning. The Sultan was persecuting the Christians of that land, the Saracens and the Jews were violating Christian virgins and roasting little children alive on spits. After he had had the same dream three times, Pope Urban left his city of Rome and summoned a great assembly of bishops, abbots, and secular princes in France, at Clermont in Auvergne, and told them what the Holy Ghost had revealed to him. Every man that valued his soul's salvation should leave lands, goods, and kin and make a great pilgrimage to Jerusalem.

Deeply stirred by this news, Brother Barnabé, who had heard that this Pope was a good and worthy man, hurried to his friends in the community to ask them what Peter thought of it. They told him that Peter had had visions and that great events were certainly coming to pass: the cup of Jerusalem's woes was very near to overflowing. Brother Barnabé pondered these words and discussed them with his friends. "We are the salt which has lost its savor," they said. "We must go to the spring of all virtue to get it back, for it is in that blessed land, close to the Sepulcher where the body of Our Lord lay, that God's grace manifests itself fully. Shall we venerate the relics of saints that were mere men and leave the place where God was willing to die for us at the mercy of the heathen?"

"But," said Brother Barnabé, "what can we do against the heathen?"

"Brother, the Kingdom of God must be won by force. We sit here and fold our arms and look on while Christendom falls deeper and deeper into sin and wretchedness. In their weakness men fall back into pagan superstition or become like beasts. The

Holy Land is like the sun hidden behind clouds, for too long now it has been hidden by the clouds of impious heathendom!"

"In God's name, will the Pope's prayers be strong enough to drive the infidel out of Jerusalem when he cannot drive the Germans out of his own city of Rome?"

"Brother, Jerusalem is the center of the world. It is from and with Jerusalem that God's true victory shall begin."

Then Brother Barnabé learned that Little Peter was to go all through Normandy and as far as the Ile-de-France, preaching the crusade. He went to Chartres and remained for twenty-four hours prostrate in the crypt before the miraculous statue of the Virgin, waiting for a sign. In a dream he saw the Lord Jesus Christ, His face shining like a thousand diamonds. He wore a pilgrim's cloak and carried a heavy cross on His right shoulder and seemed to go forward painfully. His feet were bare and bleeding and His knees buckled at every step.

"Lord, where are you going thus?"

The Lord made no answer but in his heart Brother Barnabé heard a voice say, "To Jerusalem to be crucified." Wakened from his sleep by the feet of the worshippers shuffling against him as they passed, Brother Barnabé got up and left the church in tears.

He turned back toward Normandy and on the way told everyone he met, Go to Jerusalem and help the Lord to carry His Cross. There was a fire in his heart. We shall all carry His Cross together, into His hands we shall commend ourselves, body and soul. He preached in this way in every village, saying, "I have come to rouse you. Leave your own lives, the Lord is calling you, make ready His road."

Reaching Rouen, he learned that his friends had gone northward preaching the crusade, led by a pious knight named Walter Sans-Avoir. He too began to preach in the marketplaces, and the townsfolk listened to him eagerly and would have followed him then and there had he not told them, "I am only a voice crying, go and find Peter or Walter." Then word came to him that the abbot of his monastery had discovered he was in the area and was seeking him out to apprehend him. He sent one of his friends, a cleric, to plead his cause with the abbot. The abbot was an easy-going man, and when he learned that Brother Barnabé was preparing to take the cross he agreed to look the other way.

"That monk has a devil in him," he said, "and even kept in confinement in the monastery he would cause trouble. Let him go and get himself hanged somewhere else, but he must leave the locality this very day."

This was how Brother Barnabé came to be in Arras, where he became friends with Baudry the mason, a man of great piety and a former follower of Peter's like himself. The two of them set about recruiting crusaders from the region of Arras.

Brother Barnabé was popular with the members of the company. He treated everyone with the same simple kindness, and did not repulse the women and treat them as unclean vessels and snares of Satan. He himself was not yet forty, but he was as cold to women as an old man. He had a ready smile for the children and young girls, and when the company stopped to rest he would stroll about the camp with his brown beard flowing down his chest and people would pause in their talk and turn to look at him, not in fear but because they were glad to see him.

"Look at him, isn't he beautiful, like an angel out of heaven." Not that he was at all beautiful, dressed in an old habit that had once been black but was now so filthy and discolored and worn out at the knees, seat, and shoulders that it was almost indecent. He had a tanned, bony face with a jutting nose and firm lips, and his faded brown, rather prominent eyes had a directness and intensity in their expression that reminded one of a hawk. When he smiled, strong yellow teeth showed through the bristly growth on his upper lip, making his face look curiously young. It gave him no pleasure to be admired. "What are you gaping at me for?" he would say. "Am I a fairground juggler?" But he could not endure to be disobeyed.

Everyone had to keep in step with him. If he caught a man begging a mouthful of soup from his neighbor he would lose his temper, and when he raised his voice it carried a long way: "Child of Cain, would you rob your brother? He has had no more than you!" And the sound of quarreling was enough to bring him running: "Here we are, hardly on our way, and already you return to your vomit! Shame on you, you defile the cross you wear!" Sometimes his anger would so get the better of him that he struck the guilty ones, and when he had sinned in that way he took it on himself.

Baudry, who was a man of more even temper, would take him

to task over it: "What right have you to strike a brother and a friend? Do you think these people have not had blows enough in their time?"

"There are blows and blows. Mine can do no harm, they are not unkindly meant. If we allow disputes before we have even reached the Scheldt, we shall have our men murdering each other in Germany and Hungary, and what will they be like in Constantinople? By the time we get to the Holy Land they will be worse than the heathens. Not all our pilgrims are lambs."

This was true. There were many repentant sinners in the company, and one false step was enough to make the rougher elements use their fists without a moment's thought. It was what they had done all their lives.

"Tame the beast that is in you, children of wolves that you are, tame it every day, for the Lord comes seeking the lost sheep, but if it strays again and again it may be that He will tire of it at last!"

"But Brother Barnabé, is it true that the Lord tires after seventy times?"

"No, nor even after seventy times seven. But take care lest the beast that is in you draw you far away to a place where the Lord can no longer find you!"

By the time they reached the Scheldt, the company of pilgrims had been joined by those from Béthune, Lens, Beauvais, and Lille and already numbered more than two thousand. They waited for the barons' army, and for a whole morning the pilgrims watched as it passed by along the road. Here were the knights belonging to the Count of Boulogne and the Count of Béthune, to the Duke of Brabant and the Bishop of Liège, as well as lords of lesser importance. At the sight of this army the pilgrims felt humbled, even afraid. They had known that these were powerful men but never had they envisaged such a sea of men and horses, of wagons, litters, sheep, and cattle. At first, as they waited at the crossroads and in the meadows by the road, they greeted with shouts of joy the banners of Duke Godfrey who, as the leader of this army, rode at its head. There were knights bearing oriflammes blazoned with the cross and after them the banners of Brabant, of Hainault and the Ardennes, and then the Duke on horseback in a green mantle with a coronet of silver on his brow and his fair hair and beard flowing over his shoulders and his breast.

He was a handsome figure, tall and slim with a truly royal bearing. His riding horse was a deep-chested bay, richly caparisoned, its reins, saddle, and bridle studded with plaques of silver and trimmed with fringes of red leather. On either side and behind him rode his knights, all dressed in cloaks of colored woolen cloth, wearing their long, smoothly flowing beards with pride, their gorgeous belts and embroidered gauntlets gleaming in the sun. They were followed by their squires, each leading alongside his own mount a destrier with glistening coat and plaited mane. The magnificent creatures had their heads muzzled and their legs hobbled and their huge bodies were all sweating and trembling. Next came the archers, carrying their long bows over their right shoulders and their quivers on the left, all marching in step like one man and singing as they came. For the first time in their lives the pilgrims, watching them, rejoiced at the sight of soldiers. All the fine men and splendid animals and fair banners! They acclaimed every lord that passed by. But after a while they grew tired of cheering. There were too many of them, too many knights, too many noble dames on horseback and in litters, too many gold-fringed banners, too many wagons as long and high as houses, wagons with huge wheels the size of millstones and drawn by six or eight oxen that gouged ruts a foot deep in the road already churned up by the horses' hoofs.

The air was filled with a dull, monotonous rumbling made up of the thud of hoofs, creaking wheels, men's voices, and the bellowing of cattle. The column advanced steadily, at a pace that was neither fast nor slow, without gaiety or sadness, for these people had been on the road for several days and the joy and sadness of the start had been, as it were, laid aside, put away for some later date. Only from time to time a young man would cry out "Praise God!" or "God wills!" or a young woman setting her hawk at a sparrow would laugh merrily.

Hour after hour the column moved along the road, flowing over into the fields and flattening the grass. When the Walloon pilgrims had gone by, the company that had set out from Arras joined line, stumbling forward over a road that was now no more than churned and beaten mud, crisscrossed with ruts and thick with the dung of cattle and horses. The women began to look forward longingly to a halt. It was as if the passage of the army had tired them more than five hours' walking. Everywhere in the crowd people were singing hymns and marching songs, but it was hard to keep in step because of the need to jump over the furrows and the heaps of ordure. Before long it was all beaten down again and fresh ruts carved out, while the sheep slipped and slithered in them and the packs on the donkeys' backs swayed dangerously and the children yelled and cried for their supper.

2

The marching host was spread out for a league along the road, and sometimes it split into two and traveled by two different routes to the same place, while other travelers on the same roads at that season had to draw their carts aside into a field and wait until the column had passed by, which took several hours.

They traveled along rivers, and the normal traffic of the waterways was brought to a standstill by the countless barges and transports laden with livestock, food, and military supplies. The journey led through increasingly mountainous country: high ranges of hills rose on either side of the valleys, their sides covered with woods and vineyards and their summits crowned with castles. The woods were brown, the bare fields black, and the greyish-yellow meadows were thick with crows. Flights of storks and wild duck were setting out for sunnier lands and the sky overhead was filled with crying and the beat of wings. Every now and then some of those with the army loosed their hawks, and then there would be battle in the heavens and a rain of blood.

"Have they no fear of God that they set their hawks to prey on these birds? The birds are pilgrims like ourselves, seeking the warm lands across the seas." But others said, "No, they are right, they want to save their provisions and eat fresh game while they can get it."

The long days' marches were all very much alike. Little by little they grew accustomed to the rivers, mountains, fortified towns, castles, and villages and ceased to stare at them. To begin with everything seemed new, but after three or four weeks they realized that apart from the changing height of the mountains all Christian lands were much the same. The trees were the same and lost their leaves in the same way, the sky was the same, covered with white or grey clouds from which the rain fell more often than anyone liked. On clear nights the moon rose and set, waxed and waned, the same as ever, just as though they had not traveled two hundred leagues to the east.

The tremendous fatigue of the early days had passed; they walked now without even being conscious that they were walking and were quite surprised to hear the call to halt. The knights were the first to stop, and the barons went to get lodgings in the nearest town; the soldiers set up camp, and the pilgrims settled in as best they could in the fields and copses. Fires were lighted, and when it rained, small tents had to be made up out of sacks and pitchforks. The old people complained of pains in their joints from the cold and the wet.

The pilgrims had looked forward with great dread to the journey through Hungary because they had heard much about the cruelty of the inhabitants of that land. In the event the crusaders scarcely set eyes on them, as they were told to keep away from the villages, but the Hungarians seemed to be neither tall nor broad, rather dark-skinned, and dressed in embroidered stuffs and sheepskin coats. If the Turks were like them, as they were said to be, then surely they could not be so very terrible.

"The Turks, my friends, are of no great stature, but each one has in his body the strength of three men, for their wizards have the power to draw the spirits of their ancestors into them and they dip their arrows in the blood of a he-goat that has been sacrificed to Satan, and these arrows are like living things and can find their marks of themselves."

"Is that true, sir knight?" Sir Evrard looked thoughtful.

"As to that, I do not know, but I have never seen such arrows nor have I heard of any spell which could produce such an effect. It may be that the Turks are more powerful than we are in witchcraft."

"And what shall we do if they fire such arrows at us?" Jacques asked. Lambert said that calling on the name of Jesus Christ would surely break the spell. The knight shook his head.

"In these days," he said, "even the sacred name of Jesus Christ no longer has the virtue it once had. Against the power of a wizard, great strength is needed such as only holy men or very venerable relics possess."

"Have you such relics in your sword?" Jacques asked.

"No, lad. Not in my sword or around my neck. It is a great sin to buy holy things for money, and a greater to buy them for use in deadly weapons. I dare to hope that God will aid me, such as I am, if ever I have to raise my sword in defense of His poor. For I shall not raise it ever again in my own."

The knight was a quiet man and this was one reason why he was so much beloved. His voice was slow and level and his broad smile came more from the goodness of his heart than from any great gaiety. The young men liked to talk to him. He could tell tales of chivalry, stories of the days of Charlemagne and his twelve peers. He would always put a few children up on his horse and tell them these tales as he walked beside them, leading the horse by the bridle. The young men would follow, eager to hear also, but he scarcely glanced at them, much preferring the company of the children, and it was for these he told his stories, describing Charles's big white beard, his wonderful gardens and the shining swords of Roland and Oliver, called Durandal and Hauteclaire.

"Have you lost your own children," Jacques asked him one day, "that you like to be with these so much?"

The knight thought for a moment. "Those I have lost," he said, "I hardly knew. They died in infancy while I was still away campaigning."

"Was that the reason you gave yourself up to Jesus Christ?" said Jacques.

"No, that was not the reason."

"Were you rich once, sir knight?"

"I do not know. Who is rich? Look at Duke Godfrey: he is very rich, but beside the King of the Greeks he is very poor. No one is rich, not even the King of the Greeks, for beside the King of Babylon he is very poor."

Jacques said, "Listen, sir knight, you believe yourself converted to Jesus Christ but the truth is you are proud. You do not like to talk of your own affairs."

"It may be so. Would you have the wolf turn into a lamb? I have been a wolf among wolves, let me tell you, and have shed Christian blood, burned villages, and robbed the poor, while thinking myself a good man. That is my history. It is nothing to boast of."

It was to Jacques, however, that the knight one day told the story of his life. The two of them were engaged in putting up a tent for the sick. The knight was very good at it. Using sticks and some old hides, he was very soon able to improvise a tent of sorts. Jacques was helping him, and the work had to be done quickly because the rain was turning to hail.

"No shoemaker could manage an awl better than you do," Jacques said.

"You take us for fools," the knight said, "but you are wrong. We are taught as children to turn our hands to anything, and if I cannot weave I promise you I'd learn in two days if I had to."

"Ah ha," said Jacques, "that is some boast!"

"No, truly. Tighten the pegs now and give me the end of the rope. An awl, you say! I can make rafts and drawbridges and ladders. Not like a proper carpenter, but well enough at a pinch."

"You," Jacques said respectfully, "must be a very good knight."

The tent was up, and all that remained to do was to pull the ropes tight around the pegs. Four men set to, their teeth chattering and the hail beating down on their backs.

"Ha! God help us, there is the tent up, bring the sick! Who ever saw a hailstorm last so long?"

The attendants waded through a thick layer of hailstones, carrying the sick all bundled up in sackcloth.

Seeing that Sir Evrard was bareheaded, Jacques offered him his cloak. "Take this. I am younger than you."

"Good. We will share it," the knight said. The hailstones were not large but they hurt, and under the cape you did not feel them so much. The two men laughed and shook themselves, mingling their streaming hair.

"Is it true," said Jacques, "that in the Holy Land there is no winter?"

"So they say. They say the trees are always green."

"Is it true," Jacques said again, after a moment's pause, "that you have killed men?"

"Why?"

"You don't look like it."

"I have killed," said Evrard, "in battle. But I have never known whether I wanted to kill."

"How could you not have known?"

"I did not know. You do not think about it, you simply strike out. You think that sounds hard? It is easier than driving in tent pegs."

"And you were sorry afterward, and that was how you were converted?"

"No. That was Peter. He came and preached at Nogent. I had gone there for a tournament. I had won five silver marks that day, for I had unhorsed two men. And afterward, like everyone else, I went to hear the preaching. And when Peter saw the knights there he began to urge us to renounce a trade which was leading us to perdition, body and soul, and made us glory in our shame. He said that no murderer should ever enter into the Kingdom of God, much less the man who, like a vulture, grew fat on murder and the sufferings of the poor. To put it briefly, he said so much and spoke so well that my heart was stirred, and when the preaching was over I went up to him and knelt before him and asked, 'Man of God, what must I do?'

"He looked at me and said, 'Have you money on you?' 'Yes,' I said, 'five marks.' 'Give them to me.' I gave them to him. Then he told me, 'If you mean what you say, sell all you have and give to the poor. How much do you think you are worth?' I thought and said, 'Taking into account what is due to my brothers, if I get the right price I might perhaps raise fifty silver marks.' 'Very well,' he told me, 'come and find me a month from now and bring me fifty silver marks.' Then he began to talk to other men, because as you can guess men were flocking to him like flies to honey. But for his bodyguard they would have torn the clothes from his body and the hair from his beard!

"And so I went home and told my brothers and my friends what had passed. What I could sell I sold, some to one man, some to another; my lands I leased to the abbey, and drove such a bargain that in the end I was not far off sixty marks. But the time was almost up and Peter had left those parts and was preaching in the neighborhood of Rouen. I took my money and the one horse I had left and scoured the roads looking for Peter. When I came to Rouen I was told that he had gone with all his community on the road to Coutances. I caught up with his camp and asked for him, and I was taken to his tent. 'I am three days late,' I told him, 'but I could not find you sooner.' He said to me, 'Who are you? What do you want with me?'

"'I am the knight you asked for fifty marks at Nogent,' I told him. At that he looked at me and his face brightened like the sun. 'You are on the right road,' he told me. 'Stay with us. You shall help us in our work.' For three years I followed him. It was my task to see to the transport of the sick and to the supplies. It was then I met Brother Barnabé and other men who had given themselves to Jesus Christ. Then one day Peter said to me, 'Wheelwrights do not weave cloth or potters shoe horses.' 'What,' said I, 'am I unfit for the work you have given me to do?' He gave me money and told me to buy a horse, and arms and accouterments.

" 'The time is coming,' he said, 'when the poor will have need of men to defend them and you shall serve the Lord in the estate to which, by His will, you were born.' This grieved me, for already talk in those days was of a crusade. He told me that such perils lay in wait for the pilgrims on the road to Jerusalem that without an armed escort they would surely perish. He said it was necessary to equip a company of peace-loving knights to go with the poor and help them in case of peril. 'Bear your weapons,' he told me, 'as Jesus Christ bore His Cross. Let what was once your shame become the means of safety for your brothers.' I did as he told me. But he would not let me go with him because there were several knights in his company who were jealous of me, not out of vanity but from zeal in his service. He told me to join the company of the weavers of Arras, where our friend Baudry was already. The rest of my story you already know."

"And before that?" Jacques said. "What happened before that? You had a wife when you were young?"

"I had a wife. You ask me that because you are thinking of your own."

"She must have been very beautiful," said Jacques.

"No, not so. Away with you, keep your mind on your own wife."

Everyone knew that Jacques was in love, but none envied him his happiness. It was of a kind that all too often brings a man misfortune in its train.

In order to avoid trouble, no one was allowed to leave the camp. Whenever they came in sight of a village, the leaders issued instructions to all the men: if they came up with pilgrims belonging to that land or any other travelers, they were to close up their ranks and pull in the carts to the side of the road and let them go by in silence, for there was no telling but what, if they had greeted them with a common "good day" even, these ignorant Hungarians might not take it for an insult, so strange was their language. Even the children were told not to laugh too loudly at the sight of strangers.

"Know, good people, that Duke Godfrey has pledged his honor and has sent his own brother as a hostage to the King of Hungary. You see that he keeps faith with you. Let there be no pillaging or marauding, so that we may not wrong other pilgrims who come this way after us!"

Even so, there was little enough provision left. The barons purchased cattle in the towns when the people were willing to sell them. The pilgrims had not so much as a sheep left, not even a chicken, and there was no question of buying from the local inhabitants. You had to apply to the quartermaster of the army, and he would tell you that everything had been sold already for six leagues around and you must be patient until Bosnia, which was in the domains of the King of the Greeks. Letters had been written to him and he was sending convoys of food from Belgrade. Not even Sir Evrard or Brother Barnabé had ever heard of Belgrade.

In November, the pilgrims of Arras had lost two old men who had caught cold and died of malignant coughs and fevers. Graves were dug hurriedly at night because there must be no dawdling on the march. Father Aimery, the curé from the faubourg, sang the mass for the dead, and all the pilgrims, even the children, gathered around, singing and weeping. Farewell, our first martyrs, we are leaving your bodies in a strange land but your souls go with us on the way and may God resurrect you soon! Your deaths were not caused by the heathen but by the rain and cold and winds of a harsh land. Farewell, martyrs to the cold and the bad roads, and God restore your bodies as fresh and fair as they were in your youth!

Marie had known one of the dead men well and she wept and mourned loudly at his grave. "Ah, Père Guillaumin, now your thread is broken and your warp is cut! Ah, Père Guillaumin, no man ever wove a finer cloth! Ah, Père Guillaumin, how beautiful is the stuff that you have woven to honor Jesus Christ, how fair the web of prayer and suffering you have spread before His feet!"

She tore her cheeks and beat her brow, while Mère Perrine's Isabelle and Jean-Michel, who were from the same street, echoed her lament. Brother Barnabé rebuked them:

"Is it fitting to mourn for martyrs as you would for men who have died in sin? You should rejoice, your Père Guillaumin has given all he had. His soul goes with us to Jerusalem."

Marie gazed at Brother Barnabé with shining eyes. "Oh, that

is well said, brother! We will set aside a share for Père Guillaumin at every meal and leave a place for him in our ranks so that his soul may march with us!"

The priests said that the souls of martyrs were the pilgrims' greatest wealth. It was a wealth that a few snowstorms or too many days of watery soup would very soon have given them, and in fairness neither the men nor their leaders had any wish for it; they did not long to sing, "O death, where is thy sting?"

"Brother, what will it be like in Jerusalem?"

"God will judge us according to our faith. He will make us see clearly with the eyes of the soul, and our souls will illumine our bodies."

"Will we never be hungry any more?" Marie asked. "Will we never be tired?"

"Child, do you think that God calls us to a life of pleasure such as the rich have who are never hungry and sleep as much as they like? These are great things, indeed, but only for him that has them not. But for ourselves, God calls us to Him in such a way that hunger shall become a joy and pain ineffable delight."

Marie understood this. She had often sung for hunger and weariness. She missed her parents, and sometimes at night she would dream of the reels and the hanks of thread. But this was an additional joy: she was discovering the pleasure of picturing her father and mother and Benoît and her friends, and it seemed to her that God sent her these pictures. Even when she was cold she enjoyed looking at the black and white and blue of the mountains and the dull, leaden light on the unfamiliar rivers and the flight of crows across the white sky. The broad, icy road with its reeking puddles was still the same under her feet—and whenever she chanced to catch sight of it winding away in front or behind her, lined with hills and fields and rocks and covered with a long moving ribbon of swaying banners, this endless road made her think of the great river of souls flowing to paradise.

She thought very often that the child she waited for was too long in making its presence known—and she who hoped to enter Jerusalem with a new babe in her arms! She and Jacques did all that was required to make a child come, but perhaps she was too young? She was fifteen, but girls who worked hard as children were slow to mature . . .

She loved Jacques so much that every night she promised him to conceive. Oh Jacques, Jacques, I have paradise within me, I shall die of it, I want to give you twenty children all as beautiful as the sun. She thought Jacques too good for her. It was lucky there were few young, unmarried girls about the camp or she would have been jealous.

He was the one who ought rather to have been jealous, because there were at least three times as many men as women among the pilgrims. The men of Arras generally left married women alone, but if a pilgrim from another region or a soldier happened to come along it was as well to beware. It was the same tale every time: "Lucifer! A man could go to paradise with that one!" or "She'll be a sultana if the Turks get their hands on her!" or "Cover your face, can't you, a man's not made of wood!" Marie's friends would say to her, "What is it they see in you? Are you sure you aren't a fairy?"

"Me? I never saw a fairy in my life! Did you ever hear of a fairy in the faubourg? With the looms banging away day and night?"

By some lucky chance for which she thanked God, Marie was not molested, but others were less fortunate. Even Isabelle, although she had been married to her Lambert two days after they set out, was forced to slap some man's face at least once a day.

"Be off with you, my lad! Think you're the only fish in the sea? Wait till I tell Lambert, and see what he'll do to you!" She did not tell him. They were too much afraid of trouble, and the women more than the men.

Trouble came, nevertheless, and brought with it some unexpected changes in the lives of the pilgrims of Arras. Élie le Grêlé, a weaver from the Bishop's workshops, so called because of his deeply pockmarked face, had a daughter, Marina. She was young and silly, a fair-haired, pink-cheeked child of twelve running about in a dress two winters old, so short and tight it showed her calves and was bursting across her chest. Old Mère Corneille had given her another, but Marina did not like it and went on wearing the old rag her mother had made for her. She was asking for trouble, and she got it. There was a fuller named Guillaume. He was thirty and a widower and was always watching Marina and brooding about her, until at last he could not help himself. One night he crept into the wagon where she slept, gagged her, then carried her off and lay with her on the still-warm ashes of the campfire. When it was over she broke free, tore off her gag, and like the idiot she was, ran screaming to her father.

When Élie le Grêlé saw the state she was in, all bloody and smeared with ash and crying her heart out, he went for his knife and hunted Guillaume all around the camp. It was late at night, and only a single fire had been left burning. They fought, but Guillaume had no knife. He was cut about the face and arm and would undoubtedly have lost his life if others had not separated them.

The pair of them were taken to Baudry's tent. Brother Barnabé, the knight, and Mère Corneille were there also, and all wanted the matter settled quickly because by now everyone in the camps of Arras and Béthune had been roused. Brother Barnabé dealt Élie le Grêlé several blows to calm him down. "Are you out of your minds, you sons of Satan?"

Élie gasped and spat and then recovered his breath and his rage together. "Let me go and I'll have the nose and ears off him! Give me back my knife!"

The matter was explained to Baudry. Guillaume was standing half naked and shivering, bound with the torn halves of his jerkin, while the men who held him had to fight to keep off the women, a number of whom were already prowling around the tent screaming, "Hang him! Put him to death!"

"Hell-cats, you may well howl for his death," Brother Barnabé cried furiously. "Was not Woman the cause of his sin?"

"You, Élie le Grêlé," Baudry said, "forgive him. You have already shed the man's blood, and both of you are pilgrims. He shall marry your daughter and God will wipe away the sin."

Élie swore he would drown his daughter in the Danube first.

"Can it be that he has already asked you for your daughter and you have refused him?"

"This robber has asked nothing of me. If she wants to have him now, I'll drown her in the Danube."

The men and women crowding around the tent were calling out for judgment. "Judgment, Baudry! Let us judge him for ourselves!" For no one wished to carry a complaint before the leaders of the army.

Baudry said, "I will not hang a brother crusader. Bind his arms and let him drag a cart until we reach Constantinople. But let none lay violent hands upon him."

Élie and his friends cried out that this was not a fair sentence; they said they had not taken the cross to have their leaders stand by while their daughters were dishonored. However, there were also a number of fullers in the company and these took Guillaume's part, in which they were joined by some fullers from Picardy. They said this was unjust, that here as elsewhere the weavers wanted things all their own way, and that Élie should have taken better care of his daughter. It was not right, they said, to put any man to death for so natural a sin.

"Then let us take your daughters and your wives," the weavers retorted. "Do you think we are all married men?"

Mère Corneille took Marina by the hand. The girl had been hastily cleaned up by some of the women, but she was shuddering and biting her wrists to stifle her sobs.

"Is she a bag of flour? It's time someone asked her what she wants."

"Well, my child?" Baudry said. "Will you wed with Guillaume?" She screamed in terror.

The leaders were in something of a dilemma because there was truth in what the fullers said. Even if husbands were found for all the widows and unmarried girls, there would still be too many single men.

"You have whores," one of the fullers burst out, "and you set nuns to guard them!"

"Shame on you!" Brother Barnabé cried. "Would you insult your sister crusaders? They have repented."

"So it's better to let them take our daughters, is it?" le Grêlé said, and at that they all started talking and shouting at once until neither Baudry nor Brother Barnabé could make himself heard.

It was at this point that Alix pushed her way through the crowd and came to stand at Baudry's side.

"Hear me, good pilgrims," she cried, "and I will reconcile you all. Let there be no more talk of our making a pretense of guarding the thing we have already lost, and standing by while those who have it still are spoiled! I and my companions, Arlette and Honorée, here make a vow that we will be wives to those that have no wives as long as this journey lasts. And for the future, keep your eyes off innocent virgins and honest wives, and let there be no more hatred and bloodshed among you for this cause which springs from the infirmity of your natures! Such as you are, you should all weep for pity and shame at the crime perpetrated against this child!

"But I give you my word that I am the fairest woman in all Arras and I am not yet three-and-twenty, and my friends also are young. At least you are in no danger of damning our souls. What we have done for money, we will do again freely, asking nothing more than God's forgiveness."

They heard her in silence, and when she had finished speaking there was a long pause, because there was no denying that even the most stupid of the men there were ashamed, even those whose first thought was: Here's good news.

"I will not stand for any such thing," Baudry said. "You have taken the cross."

"What of it?" said Alix. "I am a free woman. Did you not say we must forgive this poor fuller who has done this dreadful thing? In Jerusalem, God will forgive us all."

Brother Barnabé ordered everyone back to sleep. He said that Guillaume would not be put to death but that he would be punished, and the matter would be settled at the next day's halt. Baudry took Alix into his tent and rebuked her sternly.

"What do we gain," he said, "by exchanging leprosy for the plague? Is it right to incite pilgrims and crusaders to such debauchery?"

"It would be a greater evil," Alix said, "to have the pilgrims killing each other over their wives and daughters."

"You are no better than a bitch in season. You have taken the cross the better to wallow in the lusts of the flesh."

She did not take her long grey eyes from his face. "Go on, Baudry, insult me some more." Baudry flushed and shrugged his shoulders.

"I have no call to insult you. You are nothing to me. I speak for your own good."

She gave a short, bitter laugh. "Baudry, you know little of women. Do you think a worse penance could be invented for a woman such as I than to give myself freely to beggars? If penance there must be, then let me do it to the end and pay the full price for my sins!"

She was silent, and Baudry looked at her with a beating heart and could find nothing to say. She sighed.

"No, believe me, it is better so."

At the next day's halt, Alix and her two companions took about ten young widowers and other lads into the blacksmiths' tent, and if there was nothing to drink, there was much laughter and singing of bawdy songs. Alix could have made a desert father laugh.

"We'll keep open house on Mondays and on Thursdays, my friends," she said, "and get ourselves drunk on this good Danube water! And each one of you shall have a silver mark or a gold piece according to my fancy, because that was my price, let me tell you, and some I charged even more!

"But as for you, my lambkins, I like you all so much that you shall be the very first men to have me for nothing at all, and so you see how much money you'll have saved!" The lads laughed and squabbled over who should be first, and Alix laughed at them. "You foolish boys, there are no first and last with us! You shall all have your turn. I'll draw straws for you." Her voice had sunk to a low, caressing note, as if the Danube water had really made her drunk, and the men asked her what witch's brew she had in her cup.

"A good harlot, my lads, must be able to look drunk when she isn't and not show it when she is. I am drunk on laughter, my lambkins, because I am with you, my brothers, my own people. I have come back to you, to the faubourg where I belong, when for so long I have lain with those who have never known hunger! Let us drink and enjoy ourselves, my lovely little white stallions, my beautiful gold pieces that you are! Today I send no one away! Kiss one another, everyone, you are all brothers and friends!" She said so many foolish things that the men began to feel drunk as well, as if they had been drinking wine.

To amuse them, Alix imitated the cock crowing, and the song of the nightingale, and then she jumped up and crossed her arms and mimicked the voice of the Bishop's overseer (her own father having worked for the Bishop), who was a man universally hated because he always managed to say that the work was ill-done and to pay less than the price which had been fixed. Alix caught the likeness so well that suddenly she even seemed to look like him, and the things she made him say had the young men rolling on the ground with laughter.

"Oh boys," she said, "we have left all that behind us forever. God has set us free. No more working all night, and spoiled cloth and falling prices! Let us drink to that, my wolves, my lambkins, there are no masters in Jerusalem, save Jesus Christ and He shall be our master!"

Drunk she was, and very gay, and with every man she took with her to the old cart that had once held chickens she was as blithe as a woman entertaining her lover.

The next day she was very tired and nearly asleep on her feet. The other two girls who had volunteered walked beside her, crying from exhaustion and misery.

"Oh God, Alix, that was a bad day's work we did. We'll be

ruined body and soul, you wait and see." Alix yawned and stumbled.

"This morning I'd give body and soul for a glass of wine. God bless you, my doves, I haven't worked so hard for three years. Not since the great fair in Ghent. Eight silver marks in a single night. Knights coming away from the tournament."

"When you stop boasting," Honorée told her, "horses will sing!"

"Honorée, my sweet, my little quail, how can I help but boast now that I am back at my old trade? Eight silver pieces and an emerald ring into the bargain. *And* I paid for the wine out of my own pocket, but I promise you it was good."

Until this time the female penitents had kept to themselves. The two good sisters who were with them were old women, but they were hale and armed with stout sticks. The three backsliders now had to travel with the other women since the nuns, fearing their evil influence on the rest, treated them like plague-carriers. They begged to be allowed to join the respectable wives, who accepted them not unkindly. Alix was brave and not proud, and if it had not been for her flowery way of talking might have been taken for an honest woman.

Alix of the Thirty Pieces was so well known for her beauty throughout Arras that the poor excused her and the rich respected her. Such a woman, they said, was made for the pleasure of many men rather than just one. Let her make the most of it while she was young. She had been born in the faubourg and her father, Malebouche, a serf in the Bishop's domain, was a notoriously bad weaver, so bad that he spent three parts of his time out of work. His wife had died young, and Alix had learned to set up the loom by the time she was twelve. But she soon tired of being beaten and half starved and went off with the first procuress who came her way. She was no fool and she found herself a place in a good house where the girls were given a proper training. They were taught to cater for the pleasures of the rich, and quite a number finished honorably as the mistresses of canons or knights. More than one visiting lord and foreign merchant offered a high price for Alix, but she brought in a good profit and her employers would not let her go. But she doubled her price in secret and hid the money until one fine day she fled the house, hired the services of a clever and cunning old woman, purchased a lodging for herself in the goldsmiths' quarter, and set up in business on her own account. She had two stout serving-men, and a money box with a secret lock set in the wall. She had a great greed for money because love was something she had never known. Her passion for money and the pleasures it could buy was so all-consuming that the best-looking man in the world would not have earned a second glance from her. She dressed better than many noble dames and when she was present at a tournament, sitting in the stands reserved for the citizens' wives, it was necessary, rather than provoke a scandal, to warn contestants from other provinces for fear they should pay their respects to her, believing her to be the wife of some important citizen. Once warned, these stranger knights were not slow to dispatch a messenger to her go-between.

Alix insisted on payment in advance, but she never cheated, and acquired herself an excellent reputation. It was said that on one occasion in her early days, the provost's wife, whose husband was neglecting her for Alix, obtained a judgment against her and got her whipped at the church door as a common harlot. A month later, Alix sent her a present of a turquoise necklace with a message to the effect that she felt she owed her this return for all the new clients her chastisement had brought her. There was nothing that the provost's wife could do: Alix had the protection of the highest cleric in the diocese.

One day the Bishop himself issued a privy summons against her because ill-wishers had accused her of attracting men by witchcraft. Alix appeared before the Bishop carrying a huge bunch of flowers, lilac and periwinkles, mayblossom and gillyflowers, all so beautifully arranged that my lord Bishop and his clerks were delighted with it and complimented her on her nosegay. Alix asked the Bishop respectfully whether he considered that these flowers had been created by God or if those heretics were to be believed who held them to be the work of the Devil. "For," said she, "I swear by the Cross that I have no other commerce with the Devil than my face which seems fair to men. What my enemies call witchcraft is in truth the work of God."

It was useless for the Bishop to retort that she was putting God's work to very bad use. Alix promptly quoted to him the cases of Rahab, who harbored the Israelites from charity, and of Tamar, who disguised herself as a harlot in order to have a child by her father-in-law Judah and so became the ancestress of Jesus Christ, and of Saint Mary Magdalene and Saint Mary the Egyptian, and insisted that she was no unbeliever and that she wished to make a gift of thirty silver pieces to the poor of the see of

Arras. The end of it was that the Bishop let her go upon her making a promise to repent, and from that day on she was known everywhere as Alix of the Thirty Pieces, for she gave them right enough and made no secret of the rich gift. She was only nineteen years old at the time and proud of the fact that already she was a rich woman.

Avarice had hardened her heart. She had many friends among her wealthy lovers and she hardly ever came to the faubourg to visit her father, although she sent him money by her servants. Not that she despised her own people; she loved them still, but she had little time to spare for visiting. They did not blame her overmuch: if a girl from the faubourg was beautiful and clever enough to make her fortune, she had a right to be a little proud.

But on the day when she listened to Little Peter's sermon and was converted, she realized the error of her ways. She suffered a change of heart and swore faithfully that never again would she enrich herself at the expense of the poor. Her parish priest, fearing that this repentance was no more than a flash in the pan, dissuaded her from setting out with Peter and told her to wait for the departure of the barons' army. It was said that in the meantime she had prepared herself by giving up wine and going on foot, a habit she had forgotten. Right from the start of the pilgrimage, her companions could see that she was not delicate. She was not fat, but well built, and boasted that she was as strong as a man. There seemed nothing she did not boast of. She was skilled at hawking and could even draw a bow.

"Did they teach you that in your house as well?"

No, but there had been some young squires who had taken her to a feast at a castle near Lille. Later, she had challenged them all to stand up with a fox's mask fastened to their hats to be a target for her.

"By some miracle, I did not kill anyone. But it was a near thing!"

She had seen life, had Alix. She always had some tale to tell. It was impossible to be bored in her company.

Even the two nuns had grown to be fond of her, for her manner was quiet and unassuming; she wore her hood pulled well down over her face, fasted and prayed earnestly, and could altogether be held up as a model of what a female penitent should be. But the day when, on an impulse of mercy, she changed her ways, the nuns called her a snare of Satan and a wanton bitch.

Alix bowed humbly to the good sisters and thanked them for their kind words, then she cast herself on the charity of the married women.

By God's miracle, there was not too much dissension among these women, though they were not all of the same quarter or the same trade. The cross they bore on their shoulders saved them and they bore their trials patiently and helped one another gladly, saying that the rich women with the army must not be given the chance to scoff. Whenever a child became overexcited and got into a fight with the others, its mother would quiet it with a slap, saying, "Jesus Christ won't let you into His house. Just you wait and see!" The children were none too sure where Jesus Christ was; they had been told so often that He was marching on before them that some of them thought Brother Barnabé was Jesus Christ and others Duke Godfrey, while the brighter ones pictured an invisible man riding at the head of the army, but all of them believed that He was there and could see them.

As for the women, they thought about the evening's soup and the clothes that were beginning to wear out and the little hands chapped with cold. What a bleak, barren country! No one ever saw such winters at home, or so much snow or such hard frosts. Alix put herself out to be helpful, offering to carry children who cried too loudly to be left on the cart. "It's a shame you are so beautiful," the women said. They did not say it out of jealousy but because the girl's beauty was out of place, like a golden flower woven in the middle of a coarse linen cloth. It made no difference that Alix had renounced all her fine clothes; she still had all the softness of a woman who, for ten years, has bathed every day and never gone short of food. In the evenings, when the women sat around the fire searching for lice in one another's hair and doing the same office for their menfolk, Alix kept her blond hair hidden. She could not unbind the scarf from her head without someone accusing her of displaying herself for admiration.

She became friendly with Marie because Marie was beautiful; this helped them to understand each other. Marie was little more than a child and innocently self-assured in a way that appealed to Alix.

"If God had willed you to be born sooner, he would have chosen you for the Holy Virgin."

Marie, unaware that she was being teased, was angry.

"That is blasphemy. God will make your tongue shrivel up!" She thought that Alix was a wicked woman but even so could not help liking her. How could anyone dressed in a simple pilgrim's robe stay so lovely? Only to look into her eyes, the color of clear water and bright as crystal, was enough to make your heart turn over with mingled happiness and grief. "Alix, in Jerusalem, will you become a nun in a convent?"

"I do not know. Perhaps we shall all live like saints and there will be no need for convents."

"You will go and live in a hermitage in the desert and become like Saint Mary the Egyptian."

"Maybe," said Alix with a sigh. "If only that could be true, my heavenly dove! Not the bit about being a saint, I mean—not even my boasting goes as far as that. But to perform the same penance, alone in the desert with the Lord. You'd never think to look at me that I would want any such thing. How did you guess?"

"Saint Mary the Egyptian must have been like you."

Alix gazed dreamily into the fire. "You see, people in these days have no faith any more, that is why we have to go to Jerusalem. I used to say to myself, Here am I, Alix Malebouche of the diocese of Arras, the daughter of a weaver and a fallen woman. Why should God work a miracle for me? And here He has worked the miracle for a hundred thousand souls and more. He is calling us all to Him. And I play the strumpet twice a week to keep a few poor lads happy and they all tell me it is a sin. And yet to me it is like saying good morning or good evening. Not even that can stop me praying."

"You must be hardened in sin indeed! You would do better to repent again, you know, or I shall be ashamed to speak to you. I am married before God, and it may be that I carry a child in my womb."

Alix said no more but held her long fingers, chapped but still beautiful, up to the fire. She had had two children, both of whom had died while put out to nurse, and they had hardly even interrupted her in her work. Two girls, and she had grieved for them a little. My little girls, what a bad mother to let you be born the daughters of a whore. I have done such penance that it may be I shall meet you again in paradise, my little sacrificial lambs, my blessed little souls . . . Overcome by a sudden longing to weep for herself and for her daughters, Alix made a face and then started to laugh. She had no scruples about crying in public when she wanted to, but that night she did not want to in the least.

In the mountains of Bosnia, three children died of cold and fevers and one woman died in childbirth. This was only among the folk of Arras, as they were called, though not all of them came from Arras. By this time, the other companies of pilgrims had no lack of martyrs. Digging was hard, and Jacques had labored at the earth for hours with his ax. His two friends, Lambert and Gautier, set to with spades, and Gautier broke his. It was hard to comfort the mothers. Brown-haired Jeanne wanted to keep her baby and take it with her to Jerusalem. "It will keep," she said, "in this cold."

"But my daughter, it will be hot between here and Jerusalem, and indeed, in those lands it is always hot."

"In the Holy Land," she persisted, "in the Holy Land it is different. It may be he will come to life again."

Only the rich embalmed their children and carried them to Jerusalem. They took the little thin blue body away from the mother and laid it in the hole beside the woman dead in childbirth.

"She is not his mother," Jeanne was saying. "Why has she taken him from me? Curé, tell the good God that she is not his mother!"

They put big stones on the grave, arranged in the form of a cross. This was a Christian land. The graves would be respected.

The baby born to the woman who had died in childbirth was given into the care of a seamstress named Marguerite of Lens, who had a three-month-old child. They called him Guillaume the Firstborn because he was the first child to be born on the journey.

While the army was encamped outside Belgrade, where they were to remain for four days, there was news which sent a thrill of horror through the pilgrim camp. It started in the Flemish camp, which was nearest to the tents of the knights. Hearing the sounds of wailing and lamentation from this camp, people from the other pilgrim companies came running to find out what the matter was. Some were talking of plague while others were saying that the Count of Flanders must be dead. But it was not long before everyone knew the truth: disaster had struck the crusaders under Peter's leadership. The Turks had attacked them before they even reached the Holy Land, and it was said that never before in the history of Saracens or Normans had there been such a massacre of Christians.

Fifty thousand men, women, and children had died, even a hundred thousand, and it was said that Peter himself had been swept up into the air by God and carried to Constantinople.

"You fools, however saintly Peter may be, he is still a man! Can he fly through the air? If they are telling you such things it must mean that he too is dead." From end to end of the great pilgrim camp there was nothing but voices crying and mourning, while even in the knights' camp men were to be seen tearing their beards and crying aloud for grief. Everyone was running to their leaders and clergy, demanding that a deputation be sent to the barons, who were sure to have the most information.

The fact of the matter was that some men from Peter's host, sixty or so Frenchmen from the Ile-de-France and Champagne, had come from Constantinople, seeking refuge with Duke Godfrey. The Duke suggested that they should remain with his army, but the men were determined on getting back to France at all costs.

Of these men, three only had been present at the battle, and to tell the truth even they had no very clear idea of what had happened. Peter was certainly at Constantinople, having gone there to beg for reinforcements from the Emperor. He knew that his followers were ill-armed and that there were few able-bodied men among them, and still fewer with any experience of fighting. Unfortunately, nearly all the pilgrims had gone off in the wake of a few bold spirits to lay siege to the city of Nicaea. According to the accounts brought back by the men who escaped after the great battle, the Turks had descended on them with thousands of horsemen, so suddenly that no one had even seen them coming. They had begun by shooting arrows and had then overrun the camp, laying about them with sabers and battle-axes and trampling every living thing, young and old, beasts and men, beneath their horses' hoofs, while for the few knights who were able to defend themselves and who sold their lives dearly, there were hordes of poor people seeking only to escape. But it was little use fleeing on foot with the Turkish horses coming from all directions and the sabers rising and falling everywhere on heads and shoulders. So much noise and screaming, such quantities of blood and corpses had never been seen, while as for the Turks, no man could ever describe them. They were not men but devils and wild beasts, and those few men who had escaped the holocaust would shudder at the horror of it until Judgment Day.

This was the tale told by the Frenchmen who had survived the battle of Nicaea. The whole host had fallen, they said, all, all the men-at-arms with Walter Sans-Avoir at their head, all the monks, all the old men, the women and children, all! Those who had escaped could be counted on the fingers of both hands. Peter was a fool not to have foreseen more clearly what the Turks were like, for against men such as these resistance was impossible.

The pilgrims' camp was in an uproar, for many had relatives and friends in Peter's army. There was much weeping and in everyone's mind was the thought: If Peter himself has failed, will God protect the dukes' and the counts' armies any better? And who knows whether it is true Peter is still alive, or whether they are only saying that to reassure us?

Brother Barnabé called his flock together to remind them of their duty.

"Do you call yourselves Christians? Have you not taken the cross? Did God promise you an easy journey and green pastures? Has He not promised you a thousand sufferings, temptations, and agonies, by which you may be purified? Shame on you if you allow yourselves to be defeated by bad news! Turn back and run home again with your tails between your legs! Who is to say that this news is true, that it is not a temptation of the Devil, or that the disaster is as great as people say? Have they counted the dead? And how do you know that those who died did not act foolishly, for there are fools even among crusaders. And those who were made innocent victims, how do you know they are not shining in God's heaven this day? They are all marching before us on the road to Jerusalem, dressed in white and bearing palms."

By order of the commanders, all mourning for the martyrs of Nicaea was forbidden, for when people begin to mourn, especially for great numbers of dead, the cries and lamentations easily lead to excesses resulting in convulsions and people fainting and serious injuries. But, as Baudry and Brother Barnabé explained to the people of Arras, it was wrong to dissipate to no purpose the strength which should be employed in God's service. Keep your grief for the day when you have to fight the Turks and it will give you the strength to repel these evil men.

The curé of the faubourg comforted the more nervous of them. "It will not happen to us. We have with us all the chivalry of the Duke of Brabant and the Count of Flanders and the Count of

Boulogne and the Bishop of Liège, and we will have powerful support from Constantinople in the armies of the Count of Toulouse and the Count of Blois, and with them rides the noble Bishop of Le Puy, the Pope's legate, who is one of the wisest men in France. With such armies the pilgrims will be as safe as if they were behind strong walls."

There was no mourning, but great masses were celebrated for the souls of the martyrs. While the barons rested in Belgrade, the soldiers went the rounds of the camps, singing psalms and led by priests bearing aloft crosses. In this way the leaders kept them occupied and showed the inhabitants of Belgrade that theirs was a pious army, because it must be confessed that the people of these parts bore a grudge against Peter's crusaders, who had plundered towns and burned monasteries.

The civilian pilgrims took advantage of the halt to carry out repairs to their equipment, mending carts and altering harnesses, most of which had to be remade to fit men's shoulders since not many animals were left. They stitched shoes and jerkins, and the young men went in groups into the nearby forest and cut down young trees to make poles for stretchers and carts and collected dead wood for the fires. The people of the place would retreat to a safe distance when they saw them coming.

"They are Christians, surely? Do they take us for robbers?"

"The truth is," said a soldier from the Boulonnais, "they are alarmed because there are a great many tall fair men among you. They think you are Normans."

"In the old days," Lambert explained, "the Danes came as far as the region of Arras and even farther. They used to come just after the harvest, so they say, and take all the crops and rape all the women, and that is why there are so many people with fair hair in those parts."

"Are the women handsome hereabouts?" asked Girard the Jay.

"How should I know?" the archer said bitterly. "Our orders are that anyone who lays a finger on a local woman will be hanged on the spot. We'll make up for it with the Turks."

Lambert crossed himself. To him, it was as if the other man had said, We'll make up for it with she-wolves.

"Do you think it's true that men can lie with Turkish women?"

"Turks take Christian women, all right. And as for me, if ever I get my hands on the Sultan's wife—"

"The Sultan," Girard said, "we'll flay him inch by inch. Just like that. For days on end, we'll tear off all his skin in little pieces and put salt and pepper on the wounds. For all the poor that he has killed."

"Would you do that indeed?" Lambert said thoughtfully.

In the camps it was no longer possible to hear oneself speak for the din of hammering and banging and chopping and singing. The women were mending cloaks and cleaning the dirt from the men's coats by rubbing them with ashes. Dirt rots clothes worse than moths. Hot stones were carried into the tents and the sick wrapped in skins. Courage, in two or three weeks now we shall be outside Constantinople. They say the winters are mild there and the Emperor is getting ready supplies of grain and cattle for us.

The great army took the road again. The folk of Arras had a new member of their company, one of the Frenchmen who had come from Constantinople and who had chosen to resume his pilgrimage. He had never intended to return home, he said, he had simply come to greet Duke Godfrey because he had heard of his zeal and his courage. But the Duke had been ill-advised and declined to receive him and so he preferred to travel humbly with the poor. "March with us," Baudry told him. "We welcome all men of good will. But you are young and you will have to draw a cart one day in three."

The Frenchman expressed his willingness, since he was to share the lot of God's poor. He went on to say that he passed for a native of the Nivernais, the son, according to the general belief, of an armorer from La Charité-sur-Loire, but that he should more properly be called the son of the fisherman. His name was Jean.

"You are a bad Christian," Baudry told him, "to speak so of your mother. I asked no questions."

The man said, "Did I speak of my mother? Here are mysteries beyond your comprehension."

This Jean was a man of about twenty-three or twenty-four, tall and thin and with a pale face, brown hair, and a curling, youthful beard. He was a handsome lad, though his brown eyes were rather too big for his face and somewhat too heavily shadowed, soft and brooding like the eyes of a child. Brother Barnabé told Baudry, "Take care. He is simple."

"God loves a simple heart," said Baudry. "He does not look dangerous."

For the first few days, Jean was the center of attention. Everyone wanted to hear him talk about his travels. He had not been at the battle and had not seen the Turks, and for the rest, he had not a great deal to tell. All he said was that the Emperor had not given him an audience, which was a great pity, but that in Jerusalem the truth would be revealed at last.

That night, seeing Marie sitting by the fire with Jacques, mending a woolen cloak, he went up to her and asked her name.

"Marie."

"*Ave Maria gratia plena,*" he said.

"Whatever ails you?"

"I say that to all women called Mary. They are all images of the Virgin." Marie broke into laughter.

"You should see Marie the Whip, the overseer's wife!"

He squatted down beside her and stared into the fire.

"You are quite pretty," he said, and gave her a shy smile.

"And you had better be careful," Jacques said. "She is my wife."

"Your wife. Very well," the other said, "I like her. She has a good face."

"That's enough," Jacques said. "You may be older than me but I am stronger. Take yourself off." Jean rose and moved away from the fire.

"Can't you see the poor boy means no harm?" said Marie.

"The poor boy has wit enough to see that you are beautiful, hasn't he?"

Marie nodded. She felt sorry for the Frenchman and the next time she saw him, after the shared meal, she smiled at him.

"You will find out," she said, "that it does not do to tell a married woman she is pretty. Where are you from?" He gazed at her earnestly for a while.

"Why do you ask me that?"

"No reason. You have a beard and yet you behave like a child."

"Look at me well," he said.

"All right. I'm looking at you."

"Do you see nothing? On my face?"

"I see a nose."

He gave a melancholy smile. "I had thought you saw deeper. Can you not see the light? On my face?"

"No, I swear it."

"That's strange," he said. "I can see it. Even in the dark."

Marie laughed aloud. "Liar! How can you see your own face?"

"Shall I tell you the truth?" he asked her.

"Go on, then."

"I am Saint John."

"Well, well!" Marie said. "Well, well! Which Saint John, to start with?"

"You are no scholar. The Evangelist. You must know he never died? The others died."

Marie asked herself if she should laugh or pity the boy.

"So you have gone on living for a thousand years! But look at yourself, you are young!"

"This is to protect me from the hatred of the ungodly," Jean said gravely. "I take on the shape of other bodies that are born and die, and yet I never die. For as soon as a body is worn out, I discard it like an old garment and put on a new one. In that way I have changed my fleshly envelope eleven times, and this is the twelfth, and God has given me the appearance of an armorer's son from La Charité-sur-Loire. But in reality I am still John, the son of Zebedee."

"Very well," said Marie. "What was the name of Zebedee's mother?"

"That is not given in the Scriptures."

"But if she was your grandmother, you must know her name?"

"That is true," he said. "Well, then—she was called Marie. No. Salome."

"What I see," Marie said, "is that you are a liar and a braggart. You'd better change your tune, my poor boy. You may be mad but there's others won't be as patient as I am." She said it kindly and gently, and he did not take offense at her words.

"One day," he said, "I will tell you my story and then you will believe me."

Marie told Jacques and her friends that the newcomer believed he was Saint John the Evangelist, so that by that evening everyone was calling the lad Saint-John. He did not seem to mind, although he could see they called him so in mockery.

"All we needed was a madman," Brother Barnabé said. "He is one of those whose heads have been turned by the teachings of the heretics." The curé, Baudry, and Sir Evrard thought the simpleton would bring them luck. He was gentle and pious and his folly came from God, not from the Devil.

Fifteen days' march from Constantinople, before the end of Advent, Guillaume the fuller was found dead in his cart with his throat cut. Ever since the night of his crime he had walked with his arms tied behind his back and his legs shackled, hauling alone the two-wheeled cart that carried the blacksmith's tools and forge, and at night he slept in the cart, underneath the covers. He had suffered no beating or torture, but the load he had to pull was so heavy that even the weavers were sorry for him and said that he would never reach Constantinople alive. And then one fine morning the child who carried his food to him lifted the cover and screamed. The cart was covered with blood and Guillaume's head was lolling, half severed from his body.

There was no need to go far to find the murderer. Baudry sent for Élie le Grêlé to his tent, to protect him from the anger of the fullers.

"You child of the Devil," he said, "how dared you damn your soul like this? Now I suppose I shall have to hand you over to the army court."

Élie said, "I am willing to drag the cart with the anvil in the place of the dog on whom I have revenged myself. You did not hand him over."

"Haven't I wedded your daughter to the son of Mathieu the grinder? Surely she is consoled by now?"

"She, maybe, but not I. I got my consolation last night."

"And what of the cross on your shoulder? Do you think to accomplish your vow, stained with blood as you are?"

"In Jerusalem all will be forgiven. I shall do penance for all."

Once again the leaders were at a loss what to do, for they hated the thought of going to the army commanders. It was time to take down the tents and harness the carts, and this must be done hurriedly, as every morning. The barons had made it clear that there would be no tolerating any delay. Baudry soothed the fullers by promising them that justice would be done that evening, at the next halt. The body was wrapped in the sacking covers and Élie, his arms bound, took Guillaume's place, with a good hundred pounds of dead meat added to the load on the cart. He might be big and strong, but his eyes were starting from his head and he was as red as a beet while his breath rasped at every step. The mounted soldiers who rode up and down the convoy said, "It is a shame. Let someone share the man's load."

"Let be," was the answer. "It is a penance that he is doing."

It was already known among the Walloons that the folk of Arras were carrying a man with his throat cut among their baggage. Baudry sent the curé to tell the Walloons, "For God's sake do not bring the soldiers down on us. Your honor is at stake as well as our own. You too are workers and humble folk." And the curé told a white lie to the effect that the fuller had been possessed by the Devil and committed the crime of Judas. He had cut his own throat in despair.

That night they dug a grave in a wood near the camp. "It is permitted for us to pray for this man's soul," the curé said. "It was not his fault that he died without absolution. But let no one think of him as a martyr to Jesus Christ."

Guillaume's comrades said that he was a martyr all the same, since but for the crusade such a fate would never have befallen him. Moreover, le Grêlé had wrongfully prevented him from completing his penance.

"Friends," said Brother Barnabé, "you do not know what you are asking. It is not right that the rich should sit in judgment on the crimes of the poor. We have not taken the cross in order to submit ourselves to unjust laws. Be very sure the nobles avenge themselves for such an outrage, and if the offender is a poor man they do not pay the price for his blood. If Guillaume had dishonored the daughter of a knight, the knight would have killed him like a dog and not even paid a fine. Yet for the same vengeance, you would have a judge from among the rich hang one of your brothers. Neither Baudry nor our brother Evrard will take such a sin on himself. Because one man has been killed, would you have another put to death?

"Let le Grêlé do his penance. The day we come face to face with the Turks he will find a better use for his knife—and if God wishes his death it is the Turks who will punish him for his crime."

So there was no more talk of killing Élie le Grêlé. It was enough to harness him to the cart. Now that he no longer had to drag Guillaume's body as well, he would manage. He was one of the strongest men in the company.

The newcomer, Saint-John, took le Grêlé's place in the team drawing the big wagon on which, in addition to the material for the tents, were the pregnant women, the old, and the sick. Saint-John was not the equal of Élie, far from it. Not only was he not as strong, he was restless and could not walk at a steady pace, so that he only succeeded in making himself a nuisance to his companions, until in the end they told him he was good for nothing but tending the geese. They let him walk with the women and gave him some bundles to carry. The women did not trust their babies to him because they feared his folly might be contagious. He walked alongside Marie, who was sorry for him, but two of the female penitents and the wife of a weaver named Jean listened to him eagerly, saying that one could never tell and he might really be Saint John, or at least a little piece of the saint's spirit might have lodged in him.

"When I was a child, you know," he told Marie, "I did not know who I was."

"And how did you find out?"

"I was a boy like any other," he said. "My brother Bernard and I were apprenticed to become armorers like our father. Bernard was kind to me. He was the elder, I should tell you, my elder by five years, and he always protected and stood up for me. No one ever beat me. And then—I am telling you how it began—and then, one day we were crossing a field on our way home to the town, Bernard and I. There was a storm. Bernard was walking in front and I had stopped to tie my leggings. Then all at once the sky above me was rent apart with such a crash that I fell down. I saw a light brighter than ten suns which tore the sky asunder and consumed the woods, and I was blinded and deafened. I stayed there, lying on the ground, without moving. It shimmered all around me and seared my eyes so that everything looked red.

"And later when I got up, what did I see before me? Bernard, or rather someone about Bernard's size and wearing Bernard's clothes, but there was nothing left of his face but something black and twisted and hideous to look on. He was lying on the ground, struck by lightning. Some people found us and carried us to our parents' house. For days, I lay without speaking. My mother had me carried to the church porch to be exorcised but it did no good. Then my parents sent me to the monks in the Abbey of La Charité.

"There, I came to myself at last. But I would not go back home. You understand, the house without Bernard! I cried and cried. I yearned for the light from God that I had seen that day. I had seen the heavens open and the earth gape. The monks were kind to me. And then, suddenly, I began to understand. A voice spoke to me at night, and even during the day, in Latin, and although I knew little Latin, I understood. I understood that I was John, and that on John God would build His Church. My parents took me home, but still I heard that voice and still I did not understand. I answered, 'Lord or Demon, whichever you be, I know that my name is John'—for my parents had been divinely inspired to christen me with my true name—'but I do not understand your words.' And my curé, seeing my anguish, went so far as to give me some advice which was sensible in the eyes of the world but contrary to God's law—for I was nearing eighteen—and told me that my troubles might cease perhaps if I knew a woman.

"And so, with my father's permission, I went to a prostitute in the town and she offered me wine and made a lewd show of herself, but I took fright and fled. I ran out into the street and still the voice kept repeating to me *Tu es Johannus, tu es Johannus,* and lo, I saw in the air a man, all bright and beautiful, with his garments stained with blood and bearing a palm in his hand. He came down, and he drew near to me and held his arms open wide and smiled at me. 'Oh blessed martyr, who are you?' 'What?' he said. 'Do you not know your elder brother?' 'Bernard!' I cried. Oh, you can never know the joy I felt. 'I am James, the holy martyr. I am James and you are John, the son of Zebedee. Has not the Lord named us Boanerges, which means the sons of thunder? Did you not know that you should never die?' And then a great light shone within me and I understood all. He told me, 'I accepted martyrdom a thousand years ago for the glory of Jesus Christ, but you lived on, and have lived for a thousand years awaiting the second coming of Our Lord. The time of His coming is at hand and with your eyes you shall behold His glory.' I wept for joy, and for fear also, because you can imagine how hard it is to believe such a thing.

"I ran to tell my parents of my vision, but they would not believe me. They treated me as if I were mad. You cannot imagine the torments I suffered: the baths in ice-cold water, the burnings with hot irons, the leeches to my head, for my parents were rich, you see. And the exorcisms and the herbal potions and the witches' incantations. It nearly killed me. I was still so innocent, I thought that in the end they would come to understand. I told them, 'I am not who you think I am. I am Saint John. I have lived for a thousand years. Can any cure take this eternal life from me?' They even forced me to lie with a woman, but that remedy served them no better than the rest. Did they think to bring me to contrition by such means? 'My body is glorious,' I told them, 'sin cannot sully it. Let me go since you will not know me.'"

At this, his lips began to quiver as though he wept.

"Then they wanted to shut me up in a hospital for madmen. I knew this for one of the traps of the Devil, who wants the truth to remain hidden under a bushel. I feigned submission and escaped by night over the rooftops. And while I was climbing up a roof I found that I had no need of any light because my face was giving out rays of light. The next day I left the town and walked along the road, begging my bread and singing God's praises. I came to a village where the people received me joyfully at first, but when I did not perform miracles they called me a liar and drove me away with stones."

"There, you see," Marie said. "You see. The real Saint John, wherever he may be now, performs miracles."

"That cannot be. I tell you I am Saint John. Do you imagine that Saint John is constantly visited by the Holy Ghost? If he were, Marie, he would have performed so many miracles in a thousand years, and written so many holy books, that neither the age nor the Church could endure it. For men love the light, but they cannot bear too much light. And that is why Jesus Christ desired His servant John to live as it were in disguise in a humble form, so as not to trouble men before the return of the Lord. For the authority has been given into the hands of the Church and the vicar of Saint Peter . . . Look, think a little, Marie, who would be willing to listen to the popes and bishops if everyone knew that Saint John was still living and where he was, and if he was constantly making himself known by miracles?"

Marie frowned and tried to understand. "Listen, Saint-John. You are more learned than I am. But this is what I think: the real Saint John is hiding in the desert. He would perform miracles if he wished, but he is hiding and will not appear until the Last Day."

"Exactly," the young man said with calm obstinacy. "He is hidden under a humble exterior. I too said to myself, Lord, can this thing be? I am almost illiterate, I do not even know Latin. Then the Lord sent the holy archangel Gabriel to me and he spoke to me for a long time: John, you must submit to the laws of the flesh. For the time is near and it is among the poor and humble that you must be found on the day of Our Lord's coming. That is why He has made you forget your learning, so that you may be poor among the poor. You will remain with them, hidden like a pearl in an oyster, to escape the hatred of Antichrist, who has not forgiven you for having revealed the great secrets of the last days.

"And so for a long time I have lived on the road among the pilgrims, only revealing my true name to those who are worthy of it. And many have believed in me, and pious women have followed me and worshipped me. But the instruments of Satan set it about that I was mad, or even heretical, and drove me out and prevented these worthy women from following me. Then I learned that the man of God called Peter, who was famous for his great works, was summoning Christians to Jerusalem, and I understood that this was the sign for which I had been waiting. I went in search of Peter and he told me, 'I am willing to take you into my holy company provided only that you do not speak of these things. I have had no visions concerning you.'

"'But I,' I said, 'I have visions every day.' He said to me, 'If you wish to go to Jerusalem with us, do not speak of these things.' And James my brother appeared to me and told me, 'Obey Peter. It is Peter who today is the head of the Church of the poor and the true successor of Saint Peter. At Jerusalem all truth shall be revealed, and I shall be revived in the flesh and we shall be reunited again. Then your voice will be mighty again before the throne of Jesus Christ.'"

Marie sighed and continued to look thoughtful. "Oh," she said, "Peter was quite right to tell you not to speak of it. You muddle my mind. I do not know what to think of you, for you speak too well for a madman and too wildly for a wise man." And as she looked into the simpleton's face she felt more and more perplexed, because the face was beautiful and the eyes shone with a flame that was both candid and melancholy.

3

It was right that before the great trial began the pilgrim army should have the opportunity to gaze on the Wonder of Wonders and refresh themselves with the sight of it after the fatigues of so long a journey. Oh, fairest of all cities, oh, delight of the eyes and of the heart, most precious pearl, witness to the glory of men and to the glory of God!

They seemed to breathe more easily now that they were in this blessed land. Their bodies were no longer cramped with cold, the wind was soft and the roads no longer icy, and after the cold of the past months, even mud underfoot seemed pleasant. See, we have arrived, this is the great Haven, the harbor of rest where we can regain our strength. The poor and even to some extent the rich were amazed. Everything that earlier pilgrims to Constantinople had said now seemed empty words, for who could describe such a thing? What daring mind could invent such a city, not like a city but rather a forest of houses, a forest that stretched as far as the eye could see, covering the broad hills on either side of a winding arm of the sea that was like a great river. No, truly, this was no city but a hundred cities merged into one. Even at a league's distance the eye could not take it all in at a glance.

From a distance it was a shimmer of white and gold, green and rose, a gigantic, softly colored carpet flung across the plain and the hills; yes, as far as eye could see was nothing but houses, towers, and castles, with not a field or a wood but houses everywhere and here and there a garden. A double curtain wall ran around it like a white, fretted cincture, from which a thousand towers rose above wide moats filled with water that was now shining and now dull. The city was so large that its bounds were lost in a rosy mist, while to the right, across the wide river, lay a rich countryside of vines and trees that even in mid-January were green, and white villages, and beyond that again, on the horizon, could be seen the flat, violet-blue line of the sea.

Happy the people who lived all their lives in such a land. All their days were spent in a place that was like a foretaste of paradise. The company leaders and the sutlers of the army brought wagons loaded with sacks of grain and flocks of sheep into the camps, and all said, These are the gifts of the Emperor Alexius; it is his desire that the Christians shall lack for nothing in his realm. The men put up their tents in the fields and spreading orchards, feeling faintly astonished when they thought that they would not have to pack up again tomorrow or the next day. The army criers had proclaimed long since that at Constantinople there would be a long halt, of several weeks perhaps, since before crossing the Straits of St. George—this was the name of the sea dividing Constantinople from the coast of Asia—they must await the coming of the Count of Toulouse, who was still in Hungary with his army.

The military camp was large, three times as large as those of all the pilgrims put together. The poor were lodged in a very confined space and they had been made to dig ditches and build a palisade all around their quarters, for here as elsewhere the rich distrusted the poor and were afraid they would cause trouble. The Count of Boulogne and the Count of Flanders placed guards around the perimeters of the camps because, they said, the people who had come with Peter had not respected the Christians of the country and had even plundered churches.

Some of these people had come to beg a place among the pilgrims. They had been in camp there for four months and they said they knew the place and could make themselves useful, although how they were to be useful was not clear since it was forbidden to leave the camp. These people—French, Normans, Picards, and Germans—were unhappy and embittered. They said the Emperor had done wrong and that it was his fault their friends were dead, for he should surely have known what the Turks were like. And moreover, they said, when our people asked him for boats to take them to the country of Nicaea, he said no, and said that the country was not safe, but in the end he gave them the boats just the same and afterward he said, You brought it on yourselves. Did we know? How could we have known?

Baudry told them, "Make your camp further off, for we have too little room already and you are always telling sad stories. Our pilgrims set out joyfully and they are about to face great hardship. And you come and upset them with your tales of bad pilgrims and disorders in the camp."

"But it is true that it is partly Peter's fault. If he had stayed with us instead of going away to Constantinople to fetch help, the disaster would never have happened."

"Be quiet, ye of little faith," cried Baudry. "I know Peter. He knew what he was doing. If your people were fools enough to disobey him, they alone are to blame."

Peter was indeed in Constantinople, but he came out of the city into Duke Godfrey's camp, which was a great joy for everyone. The pilgrims were allowed to go in turn, in small groups, to the Duke's camp to greet the man of God. He spoke to them kindly and urged them to persevere in their faith so that all, dead and living alike, should be a single great body, one great flame of love. He told the men to obey their leaders and to respect the lords and bishops so that, when the hour of battle came, they would be only one great body, all for one and one for all. He commanded the women to be brave and chaste and not to panic in the hour of battle, but to stand firm like men.

And he added that salvation was to be won by the sword, for before they reached Jerusalem they would have to cross the seven abysses of hell and conquer the seven armies of the sons of evil, and to overcome infidelity, ungodliness, pride, lechery, covetousness, cowardice, sloth, and doubt. He that feared nothing would see God.

"But what of those who shed blood?" Brother Barnabé asked. "What of those who shed blood and are killed before they can do penance, will God absolve them?"

"This is a great mystery, brother. Indeed it seems to me that the time is coming when God Himself will make the great division: those who attack us will be sons of Belial with the faces of men. To shed their blood in defense of Jesus Christ will not be a mortal sin. In these days even monks and priests will be authorized to take up arms."

So Brother Barnabé told his pilgrims, "Have a care how you scorn knights and soldiers; in these days their work is pleasing to God. You, too, sharpen your knives and your axes, for if ever the

Turks attack us no man must hang back for fear of sin. What happened to the martyrs of Nicaea must not happen to us. God has need of His Christians to dethrone Antichrist."

He talked to them in this vein and ordered public prayer and fasting, because he feared the pilgrims would exhaust their provisions too quickly and get into the habit of eating more than was necessary. For the halt promised to be a long one. There were already rumors that when Duke Godfrey returned to his tent after his interview with the Emperor he was both worried and angry. Princes are men of uncertain temper; pride makes them suspicious of one another and they neglect the interests of the poor for the vanities of this world. If the Duke were to quarrel with the Emperor Alexius and the halt continue on indefinitely, then it seemed they would be in danger of running short of supplies.

Moderate rations were therefore distributed to the children, the sick, and women with child, but the rest fasted twice a week and satisfied themselves with soup and bread on other days. But all were pining to visit the city, however much the preachers might call it profane curiosity. They were restless, and the young people were forever finding excuses to rush off to the camps of the bowmen or the men of Boulogne because from there it was possible to get a better view of the city. Why will they not let us go and venerate the holy relics and pray in the churches? The barons and high-ranking knights and noble ladies can go.

In fact there was some disagreement between the barons of the army and the Emperor, and as the days passed there was some doubt as to how the matter would end. The criers of the army went the rounds of the camps giving out the news: Have no fear, good pilgrims. It takes time to make ready the boats and assemble the supplies on the other side of the strait, but do not believe those who tell you that our barons and the Emperor are not at one.

Meanwhile, the pilgrims and the humble folk with the army were making increasingly loud demands to be allowed to visit the city. For, they said, if the Emperor is our friend he should not be suspicious of us. Does he think we are going to plunder the shops? What difference can it make to the barons? What difference can it make to the Emperor? We are here for Jesus Christ's sake and their disputes are nothing to us.

Not long before Lent, the barons, seeing the unrest among the pilgrims and the soldiers, came to an agreement with the city authorities; the criers announced that the crusaders were to be allowed to go into the city in groups of a hundred persons at a time escorted by priests or monks, and that they would be guided by Frenchmen who lived in Constantinople and spoke Greek.

Then there was a fine stir in the camps, with people scrubbing and cleaning their clothes and hair and hands, and discovering all at once how very poor they were and wondering how they could go into the city without shocking the Greeks. The wives of noble lords came into the camps on horseback surrounded by their serving-women, and gave the pilgrims gowns—worn, no doubt, but still in one piece—as well as girdles and coifs and lengths of cloth and needles and thread, all gifts which were accepted with great gratitude though they caused a good many arguments, for they were all too few. When the time came for them to be shared out there were many tears and entreaties and much bargaining among the younger women. "There, now!" said Corneille. "If you aren't turning these good ladies' gifts into a snare of the Devil! You took the cross to face martyrdom and great hardship, and here you are upsetting yourselves over a few embroidered girdles!"

"Mère Corneille," said hunchbacked Isabelle, "it's not that we would give offense to Jesus Christ, but here are such pretty things that we might never have been given in all our lives, and there should at least be something for everyone."

"Get along with you," said the old woman. "There will be much more than that for everyone in Jerusalem."

The men walked together, led by Brother Barnabé, and the women followed, led by Mère Corneille. Marie would have preferred to make this pilgrimage at Jacques's side, but Brother Barnabé said that it was more fitting to separate the sexes. The pilgrims might be married but this was not written on their faces, and they must not let the Greeks think the crusader pilgrims were savages, abandoned to the lusts of the flesh—for, as he said, the married couples were bound to express their feelings at the marvels they beheld by happy laughter and kisses. So Marie walked between Isabelle and Bernarde, craning her neck now and then to catch a glimpse of Jacques, who was walking in front with the young men.

The entered through a great fortified gateway flanked by tall towers, grander than any church towers. The double gates were wide enough for wagons to pass with ease, and inside the archway was a mass of chains and iron bars and pulleys, while the doors themselves were covered with massive sheets of iron and held together by crossbars. The people of Arras had never seen a gateway like it and wondered what would happen if that gate once closed behind them.

The soldiers guarding it were huge fellows with blond hair and long whiskers drooping down on either side of their shaven chins. They were dressed in shirts of bright ring mail and carried tall halberds. Plumes of horsehair swung from their helms. The pilgrims had thought they were already inside the city, but now they saw a further set of ramparts ahead of them with a second gate and more towers. It took them by surprise at first because it seemed to them as if, by some magic, this city was continually closing up before them. On the walls, they could see a great many soldiers clad in handsome, gaily colored tunics with fur caps on their heads. These men were small and slight, like the Hungarians, and carried light spears and small round shields. They left their fires, on which sheep were roasting, and gathered in silent groups to watch the pilgrims, baring their white teeth in a fixed, mirthless grin.

Brother Barnabé asked the Norman priest who was their guide if these soldiers were the true Greeks, since these men were clearly not of the same race as the blond giants. He learned to his astonishment that the little dark men were Turks and Moslems. Neither were the fair men Greeks. They came from the far North and they at least were baptized, though according to the priest there were still men in some of their companies who continued to worship idols in defiance of the Emperor's ban.

"But why does the Emperor employ Moslems in his service?" Brother Barnabé asked. "Does he not fear God? Are these men to be trusted?" The Norman said that the men were well paid and would cut the throats of their own mothers and fathers for money. The word soon went around among the pilgrims that these were Turks, and the women clutched one another in terror and wondered if this visit to Constantinople were not a trap. What if they had been magically transported into pagan lands without their knowledge? They passed by the strange soldiers without daring to utter a word, hoping that no unforeseen danger lay in wait for them beyond the farther gate.

In the event it was quite otherwise. Once inside the second gate, the pilgrims found themselves confronting a fine tall house, at least five stories high. This was a barracks. In the open space before it, tables had been set up on trestles and on these tables was white bread and dried plums and bunches of raisins and fat earthenware jugs. Two priests with long hair hanging to their shoulders and a number of ladies dressed in silken gowns with embroidered trimmings came forward to greet the pilgrims.

The Norman priest explained that they were the parish priests and townswomen from this part of the city who had come to make the pilgrims welcome and beg them to take a little food. Brother Barnabé bowed to the priests, who seemed highly respectable though they spoke no Latin. The priests blessed the bread and the ladies poured beer and hydromel into painted wooden cups, which they offered to each of the crusader women in turn. The pilgrims bowed low, uncertain whether to return the ladies' smiles which, though gracious, seemed also slightly unnatural. The ladies, who were all advanced in years, had brown faces with delicate features and fine grey eyes and moved in such a measured, rhythmic way that they seemed to be dancing in time to a slow music.

Curé, are you sure that these are townsmen's wives? The gracious ladies were speaking in low voices in some incomprehensible tongue. "They say that God will reward you for the great sacrifices you are making for Him. They say you are good people."

The men fell on the white bread eagerly; for many of them this was the first they had ever eaten. Little by little, the square filled up with a crowd of citizens, both rich and poor, beggars and children. The crusaders felt embarrassed, eating their bread and dried fruits in the presence of this excited chatter punctuated now and then by laughter, but the kindly welcome was reassuring. See, these people who are so wise and rich treat us with honor. How surprised the citizens of Arras would be to see that!

After this, they walked in a long column through narrow streets and broad thoroughfares with carts passing along them, and across squares big enough for tournament grounds. Most wonderful of all, the streets were paved like churches and strewn with sawdust so clean that no one would have dared to spit or make water on it. The houses were tall and built of dressed stone, with grilles over the doors and windows of the finest workmanship and painted in different colors. Many of the walls were decorated with paintings of trees, flowers, and birds, so that the very streets were like gardens and churches all at once.

At first the pilgrims were nervous, but they soon forgot their shyness and could not stop nudging one another and exclaiming: "Oh, look! Look at that lovely fountain, just like a reliquary!

Look at those flowers in the garden behind those golden bars. Look! Are those precious stones? No! A whole wall built of precious stones? What is the picture on it? Surely it must be Saint George and Saint Hubert in the gardens of paradise. No, look at that hitching post, it is fairer than any church pillar! Oh, a house made all of rose-colored crystal! No, it is marble. How do they polish it to make it shine like that? It looks like glass."

Bells were ringing as they passed by a large church that shone with multicolored fires. The walls were faced with pink, white, and greenish-colored marble and all around the doors and windows were patterns of gems arranged to form holy pictures. The bells were ringing, and through the open doorway came the sound of music and a hundred angel voices singing.

The pilgrims fell on their knees, there in the square before the church, and crossed themselves reverently, not daring to sing a psalm.

Oh God, would they let us enter such a church, to hear the singing? Those who were able to look inside the door could make out, through a bluish haze, the glitter of a thousand candles and knew that it must be as bright as day within.

It was a mild morning. Shreds of blue sky moved slowly between greyish clouds above the roofs of the houses and the domed churches, and the sea wind brought great white gulls skimming low over the rooftops. The gilded cupolas shone with a soft, cold brilliance and sweet and solemn voices mingled in such harmony that the air in the square seemed vibrant with it, as if a single superhuman voice were singing in several moods at once, a music both triumphant and heartbreaking, both serene and sad, a single voice flowing like a great river of joy in God. The pilgrims crossed themselves with wonder at the heavenly singing and threw themselves down, and many wept, but in a little while the sacristans closed the doors.

"Why do they not let us in?" Brother Barnabé asked. The streets and the square were empty now except for a group of blond, mustached soldiers in pointed helmets, armed with light spears. The Norman priest said that it was not seemly to interrupt the sacred mystery of the mass, and that the pilgrims had already heard mass in their camp, but that very soon he would take them to a convent where the monks would give them food.

"Are we here to fill our bellies?" Brother Barnabé said. "Do they think we are starving? We have come here to visit the shrines and to pray in the churches." He had such a powerful voice that he did not have to raise it very much to make people turn around. The soldiers posted at the far end of the square came running up.

"It is nothing, friends," the priest told them. "This monk is a worthy man and comes from our own land. He is from Rouen."

"From Bayeux," Brother Barnabé corrected him. The priest shrugged and turned back to the soldiers: "You will not make trouble for a good Norman? We are leaving the square at once." The soldiers regarded the pilgrims with expressions of amused disdain. "Excellent," their leader said. "We shall go with you."

"Why the Devil did you say you were from Bayeux?" said the priest to Brother Barnabé under his breath. "These fellows happen to be Rouennais and they loathe the folk of Bayeux."

"Good God, do we have to come all the way to Constantinople to find Rouennais who loathe the folk of Bayeux! Why do these soldiers mean to go with us? Is there some danger?"

"No, no," the other man answered, smiling a little, "it is only that the city authorities have given orders to avoid any disturbance. They have the idea that those of the Latin rite are too excitable. At this hour, all the citizens are in church and so there must be no noise in the streets."

They went on along handsome, quiet streets lined with houses of painted stone and across squares with huge fountains of carved marble surmounted by statues of naked men. The fountains had as many as four to ten jets, columns of clear shining water falling into smooth pearly-pink basins. Pigeons, white and smoky grey, perched on the statues and walked sedately about the pink-and-grey pavements or fluttered idly up to roost in the barred windows of the houses. Curtains of red and yellow hung at the upstairs windows, rippling lightly in the breeze. Beggars with wooden bowls and crutches sat on the steps before a church whose doorway was bright with colors of blue and gold, and nearly all these beggars were better dressed than the crusader pilgrims.

The men crowded around the Norman priest, whose name was Father Albert, and asked him, "Are there no shops in this city? We were told that it was rich in merchandise of every kind."

"That is true," the priest said, "but I am taking you through the fine quarters. We shall not visit the commercial streets or the poorer parts. The city is too large, you could not see it all."

"We should like to see the shops of the cloth merchants," Jacques said. "There are many weavers among us."

"And the workshops," put in Girard the Jay. "We should like to see the workshops and see what their looms are like."

"That is not possible," said Father Albert. "It would take you three days. I have no instructions to take you to see the shops."

"Now here's foolishness," Brother Barnabé said. "They bring you to see holy churches and you ask for looms! Have you not seen enough of them? You are not weavers now, but soldiers of Jesus Christ."

Hearing this, the Norman soldiers roared with laughter and said that Jesus Christ must be needy indeed to be glad of such soldiers.

"Who do you think you are?" Jacques retorted. "We wear the cross on our shoulders. Jesus Christ was never rich. He is not the King of the Greeks."

The soldiers laughed. "Listen to the Picard oaf! The Turks know how to rate your crosses by now!" And the men of Arras, wrongly called Picards, wondered if they should retaliate. This was the first time they had come to words with a group of armed men.

They were still walking. The city was so big it seemed that two days would not be enough to walk around it. And they had seen only the grand parts as yet. The great basilica of the city was dedicated to Saint Sophia, a great Cypriot saint, as Father Albert explained; she was a widow who had lived in the time of the pagan emperors and she had three daughters named Faith, Hope, and Charity. This noble widow, the three maidens, and their maidservant, whose name was Agathoclea, were all five martyred on the same day, the eighth of September. The Greeks never invoked these martyred saints in vain, and this was why their basilica was the greatest and most beautiful in all Christendom.

"May we go inside?"

"Yes, certainly you may. The mass is over now but you may be present at the office of lauds. Take care you do not raise your voices, for the Greeks are a very religious people and such a silence reigns in their churches that when the choirs stop singing you can hear the candles sputtering."

The beauty of this Basilica of St. Sophia was beyond description; not even the angels in heaven could describe it. The pilgrim's eyes were already sated with the sight of a thousand beautiful things, but in this basilica, so vast that it could have contained three good-sized ordinary churches with their belfries; in this basilica with its twenty side chapels all ablaze with the light of white wax candles, its hundred golden candelabra hanging from the pillared arches, each one bearing twelve lamps that glimmered softly through thick guards made of colored stones; in this basilica where the domes, pillars, walls, and arches were all covered with mosaics of precious stones that sparkled like a thousand fires, even the most unfeeling men were breathless and could not help gasping for joy. All Father Albert's counsels were forgotten. Oh, who would not gladly travel three months, even three years, for such a sight! Surely God could have no better dwelling in the heavens.

The basilica was filled with worshippers, handsomely dressed people, very stiff and dignified, who stood devoutly looking toward the high altar, the men on the right, the women on the left. The officiating priests, dressed in long robes of purple silk woven with gold threads, swung heavy censers made of gold all set with crystals, from which came a thick blue smoke. The choir was singing a psalm. It was hard to tell where this choir was or how many voices were singing. The voices were like thunder, or the loud, muted rumble of a summer storm of pouring rain and hail and gusts of wind or gales. It was as if all nature had been fused into a song; heaven and earth were ringing with it; it was angel trumpets and no human voices.

That day, Marie's heart was pierced forever by the beauty of it.

She saw a vaulted sky of gold, as soft to the eye as a caress, against which holy bishops in white robes adorned with black crosses stood holding crosses and Gospels, staring with great eyes outlined in black. She saw garlands of green-black laurel and trees with dark foliage laden with golden fruit; she saw doves dazzling white against a background of dark-gold stones, and great soaring crosses, and in the center of each cross was a circle in which was a white lamb surmounted by a cross.

On the wall she saw Jesus Christ in a purple robe walking on green and blue waves and Saint Peter in the midst of the waves, stretching out his arms. She saw the face of Jesus Christ framed in bands of dark hair and a great circlet of gold and diamonds. This face was thin and all made of moonlit stones, with a small purplish mouth and lofty eyebrows and eyes of sparkling black stones. Those eyes saw and knew all things, for the real Jesus Christ looked through those stones, mild and terrible, merciful and stern, and seeming faintly surprised. Jesus Christ was there, His real gaze burning through the gemstones of His image. Saint Peter was there, looking up at the Lord, and the long white feet of Jesus Christ barely touched the waves where the fishes swam, all blue and rusty red.

The sky was dark gold and shimmering, and by the water stood a white chapel with a naked man coming out of it, his grey flesh covered with red circles. He was a leper, and another Jesus in a purple robe was stretching out His hand to him. This Jesus had the same eyes, but they were gentler and more grave. Here too! Marie wept. O Lord, do not look at me like that, or rather, look at me forever, look at us all and do not forget us! The choirs sang and stopped and sang again, and when they sang the holy images seemed to move. There were great angels with blue robes that seemed to be blown by the wind. Their vast wings were spread and they were blowing trumpets and their eyes were terrible, deep black and flashing with fire in the ruddy light of the great lusters.

The gold on the arches shimmered, now smooth now shining like a river in the sun, and all over the cupolas and the walls and the pillars Marie kept finding new faces, all pale and noble with sweet mouths and sad, shining eyes, and she longed to fall on her knees before each of them, as though she were not on her knees already; oh, not before each face only, but before each saint's garment made of subtly interwoven crosses, flowers, and strings of pearls, before each crown and palm branch, each fish with green and purple scales. She did not even know that she had crawled on her knees right around one huge pillar and then the length of a wall, brushing the gowns of the Greek ladies who were attending the service.

She backed away slowly, still on her knees, over the beautiful brown, black, and white stars that covered the floor of the great church. Oh wonderful! Oh happiness! Nothing the eyes rested on in this place but was a splendor, even this pavement with its tracery of precious marbles. The Greek ladies, whom she had disturbed without meaning to, looked at her kindly out of the corners of their eyes.

Then it was time to leave the basilica. Carried away by her fervor, Marie dared not stand up and leaned against the wall, her eyes wide open as though trying to absorb all the gold and brilliance of the sacred images and the majesty of the vast circular nave with its glittering golden dome and its great pillars. Jesus

Christ walking in the waters looked straight into her eyes. Poor Christian, have you never thought of Me before? Yes, yes, Lord, I swear it! That is how I knew You. O Lord, grant us the joy of seeing You again in Jerusalem!

Then they were outside the basilica in the great square, kneeling and praising God and gazing at the beautiful golden doors, the marble pillars and mosaics of the façade, as though they could never tire of such a holy sight. And the worshippers coming out of the church passed by them and paused for a moment to look, and nod and smile approvingly.

Marie was in the front row, and she saw a beautiful lady come out of the church, dressed in a gown of dark-red silk, and leading by the hand a little girl whose dress was all woven with gold flowers and whose fair hair, the color of pale gold, flowed over her shoulders; a little girl beautiful as the sun, with delicate cheeks and great eyes colored like wild honey and features that might have been carved from ivory. Oh heavens, she must be the daughter of the Emperor! The little girl—she could not have been much more than five years old—looked at the pilgrims with her bright eyes and tugged at the lady's sleeve. Then she took a small brown square from the lady's pocket, and running over to Marie, she put it into her hand. It was hard and dry—a sweetmeat, probably. When Marie saw the child so close to her, all gold and flowery and sweet-smelling, and saw her direct, solemn childish look, she was overcome by such tenderness that she clasped the child in her arms and kissed her on both cheeks. The child laughed happily and ran back to her mother, who dusted her dress and wiped her cheeks with the end of her veil.

Marie stayed where she was, in a daze, holding the sweet alms in her hand.

"What a lovely child," said Isabelle. "She must be the daughter of some great lord."

"Oh, she is the Holy Virgin as a child," said Marie. She raised her hand softly to her face to feel again the touch of those soft pink cheeks, oh, so soft and cool, sweeter than flower petals. She gazed at the cake reverently for a moment before hiding it away in the front of her dress, close to her heart. Oh no, I shall never eat it, of course. Her gift. Oh, the little angel, to think I was hungry, bless her!

It was true, in fact. She was hungry, because from excitement she had eaten nothing all day, but this was no ordinary hunger. She would have fasted for another whole day in spite of her aching head and burning eyes and stomach racked with cramps. Her heart was fainting with love, and she wanted nothing more than to contemplate the glory of God once more.

The pilgrims were sitting in a small square beside a convent wall. The wall was high and pink and crenellated, and behind it rose tall cypress trees, their tops swaying in the wind. By the gate was a fountain of white stone and opposite were houses with high smooth walls and windows framed in blue and green tiles. People passing by on foot and on horseback, coming and going, glanced curiously at the groups of pilgrims. Some came up and asked the Norman soldiers to explain the two banners with the cross that were propped against the wall. Others pulled their purses out of their pockets and seemed about to give them alms, but Brother Barnabé explained by signs that the pilgrims did not accept money, which seemed to surprise the charitable citizens.

"Why should you refuse?" Father Albert asked. "These people want to do a good deed."

"Then let them get up a collection and send the money to the camp. We have come here to worship God and not to beg."

Brother Barnabé had never refused alms before, but seeing his pilgrims so poorly clad while the servants of the citizens looked smarter than great lords, he was seized with a kind of inverted pride. "Tell these people that we will pray for them for their kind thoughts, but that we want for nothing."

All the same, these few dozen men and women with blackened feet seemed rather to want for everything. They were weary from walking all day long around a city where every house and every crossroads elicited cries of amazement. Their fatigue was a mixture of exhaustion and excitement, and they were beginning to feel stifled in this city that was larger than a forest. They felt like wild creatures trammeled in a house. League upon league, or so it seemed to them, with never a field or meadow. You could walk for hours on end without coming to the end of the city. It was like an enchantment.

The oldest among them had the glazed eyes of drunken men, but the young were consumed with the urge to get on and to see still more marvels. Evening was coming on. Must they go back to the camp? "It is too far, the roads will be all blocked by chains and the gates shut. We will go," said Father Albert, "to a terrace overlooking the port and ask permission to camp there in a pilgrim hospice. It is kept by Venetian merchants who will give credit to the Emperor. They care for all pilgrims to Jerusalem. You will have nothing to pay."

The Norman soldiers—there were ten of them not counting the captain—must have found means to obtain some wine, as they were growing boisterous, trying to walk alongside the women and accosting them with obscene gestures. The women dared not make a scene in the open street, but at last Mère Corneille reached the end of her patience and began shouting loudly for their captain.

"You great beanpole of a Norman, have your wits gone abegging? Keep your eye on your men. You are no conquering army! If it's trouble they're after, we've more than sixty men here!"

Startled by her shouts, the men realized what was happening to their women and swung around on their heels, intending to deal with the soldiers, who promptly held their lances at the ready.

"Now then!" said Father Albert. "Keep your men quiet, comrade Giraud, keep them quiet. If there is any trouble, you and I will have to answer for it."

The soldiers put up their lances but this did not silence them, and the women's ears were soon burning at the lewd things they said. The male pilgrims roared at them, "Drop your weapons, cowards, and we'll see how you can use your fists!"

"By Saint Eloi!" cried Brother Barnabé. "Make them be quiet, father! They had better have sent Turks to bear us company!"

"Have you never met soldiers before?" Father Albert said. "These women were not raised in ladies' chambers, that I know of!"

"No, nor in a barracks, either! They are honest Christian women, all married. I may have no spear, but my cross has a stout oaken staff!"

In the end the captain made his men march ten paces in front of the company of pilgrims, but both sides were angry and the women were alarmed. Who could say whether these Normans had not a whole company of their friends who were tired of Greek women and had made a plot to carry off the Christians who had come from France? What if all this were a trap? Their wonderment began to turn to fear.

In a little, they came to a wide terrace on which were two palaces of rose-colored stone and columns surmounted by winged beasts. From the terrace, a broad stepped street descended to a different quarter of the city. This must have been the port, because there was the sea beyond, a sea the color of lead and bronze with pale lights in it and by the shore a kind of moving city composed of hundreds upon hundreds of masts, big and small, masts that dipped gently in an immense white roadstead, and lines of black vessels tied up along the mole. In the distance, the sea vanished in a haze against which a long dark-blue line stood out. A pale light sprang up at the far end of the mole, and then they saw what looked like stars winking on the dark-blue band above the sea.

Stars? No, they were signals from the fortresses along the coast. Over there was the province of Nicaea. The pilgrims stared, only partly comprehending. It was like being shown yet another picture: this port that was so huge and yet so small, with its ships looking no bigger than sabots and that distant coast glimpsed through the evening haze beyond this sea of fast-changing colors, turning pale and silvered under a near-white sky filled with leaden, purple-rimmed clouds. It was on that shore that they would walk when they had crossed the Straits in ships. The wind was blowing from the sea, bringing the harbor smells and the sound of bells and distant voices. Was it near, or far off? In the city, the golden cupolas were gleaming bright among the dark roofs and towers and the black tufts of gardens and the heavily interlaced pattern of walls and streets.

Is that really Turkish country? No, it is a Christian land, but the Turks are ten leagues beyond, in Nicaea. It seemed strange that this coast, now black and scattered with winking beacons, should be so peaceful. They had expected to find it burning, a long line of dull-red fires. Is it far to Jerusalem? Nearly as far as from Arras to Constantinople.

Oh God, those who had crossed that sea six months ago, where were they now? Their souls are waiting for us over there, to go with us on the road to Jerusalem. Fifty thousand souls, or a hundred thousand. Oh Lord Jesus, if only we had wings and could fly straight across without waiting for the boats, crossing that black land with the souls of our martyred brethren to light us, bringing the great fire that shall consume all the Turks to a man!

The Venetian hospice was a kind of large brick-walled courtyard, with lean-to shelters made of wood along the walls. Some building work was in progress and piles of beams, bricks, and bags of mortar were stacked near the entrance. The lay brother who met the pilgrims spoke rather bad Norman, and he assured them that in a year's time the hospice of the Venetians would be the finest in the foreigners' quarter of the city and the cheapest.

"Very well," said Brother Barnabé, "we will hear vespers and compline in your chapel, but apart from that we shall not trouble you." He was told that the monastery chapel was too small, and Father Albert read the services in the open air by the light of torches and a wood fire.

"Oh Jacques, what a day! I feel ten years older."

"God forbid! That would make you twenty-five!" He was laughing and she laughed with him.

"No, Jacques, not twenty-five, or fifteen, but a thousand years old, like poor Saint-John." Her face grew serious. "The soul ages differently from the body. I have learned so many things that it seems as if yesterday I was still a child. What we have seen, Jacques, is truly an image of paradise."

Jacques pondered. "It is because the people here are so rich that they can have gold everywhere, and precious stones. It is very splendid. One single candlestick is worth as much as all the treasure in the church of Arras."

"No, you see—no, listen—an image, Jacques, an image is something real. The sun reflected in water is an image but it is real, do you understand?"

She took the little cake out of the front of her dress and showed it to her husband. "Do you see this? I shall keep it. It will keep quite well, and I shall give it to our child when he has teeth."

"You are not even pregnant!"

"I may be. I shall give this to our child, to bring him luck."

"Why not to me?"

She looked up into Jacques's face, red-brown and fined down by the distant glow from the wood fire.

"Oh Jacques, how beautiful you are! I am seeing everything with new eyes, even you. I can see the face that you will have in heaven. Here, we will share this thing. It is the bread of angels and it will be in you and in me."

The two of them bit into the little cake made of pressed figs and raisins. It was hard and rather musty, pungent and not very good, but to them it was as if they were sharing Communion, not with the body of the Lord, but in some holy rite that was yet at the same time somehow pagan. They thought of the Turkish lands before them, across the black gulf of the sea, beyond the twinkling watchfires of the last Christian outposts, and they thought of the possible joys of martyrdom and of the souls of the dead that were blazing over there on the other side, like a hundred thousand invisible torches.

It was a night of full moon and the great round face sailed out from time to time between the tattered, windblown clouds, its pale, brilliant light filling the sky around it with fringes of silver and milky rays, like long shores of white sand.

Brother Barnabé sat beside the red embers of the fire, occasionally throwing on a few dry sticks to keep it going until dawn. Father Albert, elbows on his knees and chin in his hands, watched the little yellow flames running up and down the wood.

"I should have gone home long since," he said, "if I had not been frightened of the journey. And you, who might have stayed there, come rushing like madmen in your thousands and your tens of thousands, and in such conditions! Is life so hard there nowadays?"

"Hard? I don't know. You heard about the famine two years ago?"

"Yes. But what of that, brother? Famines come every ten years or so, not more, and are soon forgotten. Do you think these people won't go hungry over there?"

"How can I tell? The barons are rich, they will not let us die."

"Your barons are false crusaders," the priest said. "They mean to take advantage of you and enrich themselves at your expense. That is what everyone here is saying."

"Do you think our poor are seeking to win lands and gold bezants? We leave that to men of little faith. We want something more."

"This is madness," Father Albert said. "I was a chaplain with the army in Paphlagonia. In the lands where you are going the roads are bad and the country poor. You will not cross it easily. Surely it is heresy to say a man cannot obtain God's pardon in the land where God gave him birth! Must God's poor go a thousand miles from their own lands to find forgiveness for their sins?"

"Pray God, father, pray God that at the end of a thousand miles they will be forgiven. Do you think I do not know them, God's poor? For ten years now I have lived with them, in every land, in sorrow and in gladness, because, father, Jesus Christ once showed Himself to me in the face of a poor sinner. I was a monk in an abbey and saw only other monks singing mass. It was easier than living with the poor, but it was a place of damnation. You too, father, are leading a life of damnation. In these days men must leave all for Jesus Christ."

"I have met more than one like you," the priest said, "and I have even seen the holy man, Peter. Was it not his fault so many poor folk were slain only twenty leagues from here, on the other shore?"

"Alas, father, what do we know of God's designs? If He wishes us to be martyrs, then we shall be so. Do you know the poor? The kings and the barons and the bishops give them bread and think themselves charitable. They give bread, and still the people are poor, for they take the grain which they grow and give them back only a tenth part and think themselves justified before God. Yet I do not blame them, for they might give nothing at all. They give bread and they say, Pray for us, and they believe that the prayers of the poor are powerful before God and that the souls of the poor have the better part, and so they are able to enrich themselves with a quiet mind at their expense."

"It is true, brother, that the poor have the better part. Jesus Christ said it is easier for a camel to go through the eye of a needle . . ."

A few of the older pilgrims, unable to sleep, had crept close to the fire to warm their feet. Brother Barnabé threw a handful of straw and some sticks on the embers and the flames crackled up, lighting the men's faces, bearded faces that were weatherbeaten and dulled with fatigue. Father Albert glanced inquiringly at his companion.

"No, father, what I am saying may be said before anyone. You say truly that it is easier for a camel—but what is it to me if the rich damn themselves? I am not their chaplain or their confessor! The rich take the earth and leave heaven for the poor. And it is a great lie, for the poor are damned also, a thousand times more, for there are a thousand times more poor than rich. The poor on earth are the image of Jesus Christ and that image is defiled in them, they sully and trample it, and they are wretched in this life only to be still more wretched in the next."

The priest listened, watching the old pilgrims with compassion. He himself was strongly built and well nourished, a blond, good-looking Norman with a hooked nose and a well-shaven chin with a cleft in it. He wore a brown woolen habit and good leather shoes.

"You speak harshly, brother," he said. "To those who are wretched on earth, God has promised forgiveness."

"Listen to me, father. God never promised any such thing, not to anyone. It may not be easy for a camel to pass through the eye of a needle, but it is not all that much easier for a mouse. You and your like are pleased to look on the poor as a flock of sheep. You think they are not given to all the same vices as the rich, that their blood is not as hot or their heads as hard, or their hearts as violent, and that they have only to let themselves be shorn and fleeced and let the lords take their daughters and the judges hang them for a stolen ewe. The wicked judge is damned, true, but the man who is hanged for stealing a sheep does not die a Christian death and he shall be damned as well.

"The truth is that the poor are as ravening wolves, as cunning as foxes and as lecherous as he-goats. I do not say this of all the poor but of a great many of them, for poverty never made any man better. It is easy not to tell lies when you are not afraid, not to steal when you are not hungry. But the person who acquires the habit of lying and stealing soon becomes like a beast.

"I have seen mothers sell their daughters. I have seen mothers abandon their newborn babes in the fields. I have seen men mutilate their children to make them better beggars. I have seen sons leave their aged fathers to starve because they themselves were hungry, and ten lepers band together to abduct and rape a girl, and great oafs steal alms from the blind, and cripples torture children and bind them with chains to stop their running off with the takings. I have seen people seek shelter with peasants and then make off in the night, taking with them the last sack of flour. The rich who rob the poor do not know what they do, but the poor man who robs the poor is an eater of human flesh.

"I have even known men lure children into the woods in order to eat them; they did it first from hunger, and as time went by they got a taste for it.

"I have seen men betray their friends for a promise of bread, and I have seen others eating the food of soldiers in the yard while the soldiers were with their wives inside the house, and others, too, father, cudgeling their brains to invent obscene songs and dances, playing the fool for the soldiers to get food . . . Wide is the gate, and broad is the way, that leadeth to destruction, and many there be which go in thereat. And for this the rich are surely to blame and they shall answer for it, but no man has more than one soul, and if the soul of a poor man is lost it matters little to him that the rich man's is lost also. For today it is too late. It is no longer bread which the poor lack.

"What Jesus Christ has revealed to us, father, is that it is time to rip off the bandages from running sores. Those who have taken the cross have accepted hardships for Jesus Christ. In the red fires of suffering the rottenness will be destroyed, and those who stand firm to the end shall be saved."

"Suffering, too," the priest said, "can lead to destruction. If you are hungry in the desert, will not your men be tempted to sell their womenfolk to the soldiers, even to the Turks?"

Brother Barnabé raised his head. "Have I not thought of that? If we weighed all the risks we would never stir from home. Men run with the pack, as they say, and even wolves would sing psalms when the men that sing them are truly devout. Alone, man is weak, but together we shall be strong. It is Jesus Christ who leads us.

"This is the revelation of our age, and this is what Jesus Christ told Peter, that by bowing to the wisdom of men, Christians have become like heathens. There is no salvation for mankind now except in madness. What we are doing is madness in the eyes of men."

The priest looked at the monk perplexedly, admiring the fine-drawn, bearded face and the big burning eyes that were like those of some beast of prey.

"You have the stuff of an abbot or a bishop in you, brother; you would have done credit to our province."

"The abbots and bishops of these times are the lackeys of the great ones of this world. You yourself are a lackey. Come with us, we have need of priests. You know the country, you speak Greek, your counsels will be useful to us."

Father Albert said that he was in the hands of his superiors and could not leave Constantinople without leave of his bishop.

"It is up to you. Jesus Christ is the greatest of all bishops."

At sunrise, the pilgrims retraced their steps along the terrace and beheld a dazzling pale-gold sea, with red and grey sails bobbing on the rose-pink waters of the harbor.

"Those are Venetian vessels bound for Smyrna," Father Albert said.

"What of our ships? When will they let us embark?"

The priest shrugged. "The sooner the better," he said. "This is a good season to travel. But it seems your barons are awaiting reinforcements. Between ourselves," he added to Brother Barnabé, lowering his voice, "the Emperor is much incensed against them because they will not follow his advice."

"And what kind of man is this Emperor? Have you spoken to him?" Father Albert crossed himself.

"I? Not even the leader of our company. Do you think it is easy to reach the Emperor? Even the noblest of the people here prostrate themselves in his presence. He is so proud that he makes even the Patriarch bow before him. For he is the most liberal and generous of men, but for pride he is like Lucifer."

Father Albert had arrived in Constantinople eight years before with a contingent of Norman mercenaries. At first he had liked the city for its wealth, but now he was used to it and saw only the faults of the Greeks, who, he said, were a proud, stiff, and suspicious people, devout, admittedly, but devout in their own fashion, for they held those of the Latin rite in contempt. "While their bishops," he said, "even go so far as to call us schismatics, which is truly heresy."

"Let it be, father! These are quarrels for princes and for the rich. We know they cannot help disagreeing: it is the law of the age."

Jacques stared suspiciously at the people passing in the street. The men were rather short, slender and dark, and all dressed with a mortifying elegance. With his weaver's eye he was assessing the quality of the thread and the fineness of the weave and thinking that no better could have been woven for the marriage of a count's daughter, yet these were ordinary citizens and today was not even a holiday. These people were mad. How much money did they spend only to house and clothe themselves?

Then they were back in the camp. It seemed to those who had seen the city that they had been away for a week, and it felt strange to find themselves back again among the wretched shelters made out of carts and the low tents of cracked hides. They were back again with the three emaciated mules and the mangy donkey, and the cooking pots hanging over brushwood fires, and the women paddling in the mud by the wooden tubs and the ill-washed garments hanging on strings between the carts.

How could we ever describe what it is like?

It is so beautiful that you could never imagine it, not even in dreams of paradise. It is like a city all made of shrines and reliquaries and the finest church ornaments, only all as big as great houses! And there are giant men there and giant horses all made out of gold encrusted with colored stones, and whole streets paved with stars and crucifixes, and marble fountains polished like crystal and whole walls glowing with jewels. And the basilica is so big that you could build three churches inside it, and all its vaults are covered with gold and gems set out like holy pictures, and there are so many precious stones on the candlesticks and the lamps and the crosses, red, blue, green, and purple, so many stones all shooting out glittering beams of light, that everything dances and shimmers before your eyes, so that only from looking you begin to see heavenly visions. And their singing is like the singing of angels. You would never believe that men could make such wonderful sounds. So each in his own way described the amazing miracle of the city that was so lovely and so big, so big that you could walk all day and never to the end of it.

"I am quite sure now," Marie told Saint-John, "that you are raving mad. You have been in this city and yet you never said a word about it. Are you blind into the bargain?"

"Yea, verily," the madman answered her. "Blind to all but the light of another world. I saw no divine light there."

"I did," said Marie. "I saw a thousand divine lights."

Saint-John shut his eyes in an effort to remember. "No. I saw nothing. They were all shouting aloud around me and swooning for joy. But for me, the light from my own face dazzled my sight and kept me from seeing. I walked as in a dream. In the Church of St. Sophia I saw a great burst of flames descending on me, and I saw only lights and more lights and I sang with the choirs. Then I felt my voice rising above the choirs and filling the whole basilica, and I was so tall that my head touched the top of the dome. And then the Holy Ghost ravished me and I lost consciousness."

Marie nodded. "There, you poor thing, you have a spirit in you, for sure. But it is not an evil spirit, even if it is not really the Holy Ghost."

"But Marie, how do you think I can help being a little out of my mind sometimes? Can one poor body contain such a great spirit within it? And to live for a thousand years and never die, with only this head which hurts me so? Some days it feels as if it will burst with all the thoughts that come to me and that I cannot utter!"

"Well, my friend," Baudry asked Brother Barnabé, "is it true, all that they say? Is it really so beautiful?"

"You will see for yourself when your turn comes. It is beautiful. But do not let yourself be taken in by appearances, for even in the churches there is much worldly pomp and all the gold and all the precious stones they have put there would have fed all the poor of the country for a hundred years. A single one of those stones is worth a hundred sacks of corn, and the bishop wears on his person enough to feed a whole great province. They are a proud people and wealth will not bring them happiness, for it is because of their pride that God has sent them the Turks."

On Ash Wednesday Peter came himself to preach the Lenten sermon. He had set up his camp not far from the Flemish barons and everyone, soldiers and civilians, came to hear him preach, to the neglect of the divine offices and the displeasure of the priests and bishops. "The man is not even a priest," they said, "maybe not even a monk. Is he possessed of sufficient authority? Let him preach, but let him not trespass on the hour of the offices!" "Can this holy man order the time when the Spirit speaks through him and tell it to be quiet when the time comes for vespers?" was the answer.

He spoke with such holy fervor that even the bishops were forced to weep, for at the beginning of Lent he had received the gift of tears and he wept aloud for the sins and the wretchedness of all the Christians and for the great desolation of the Holy Land. Our true home, the land where every pebble is more precious than all the stones of Constantinople, the roads where Our Lord's own pure feet once trod and which are trampled now by the horses of the infidel and are red with Christian blood. Let us this Lent, before we cross the sea, prepare ourselves worthily for this great honor which God has done us. It is His will that through us His land shall be purged and set free. Let us be strong, and not forget the martyrs who have blazed the way!

He wept, and even the most hardened soldiers wept with him. The very knights fell on their knees like penitents. And those who had set out to earn remission for some grave sin, or who had committed one such on the way, took off their shoes and their shirts and submitted to being flogged by their priests. By so doing, they hoped to obtain permission to take Communion either on Good Friday or on Easter Sunday.

On this occasion Élie le Grêlé was released from his bonds and allowed to join in the procession of the flagellants. He confessed his guilt and swore never again to fall into sin, but the curé of the faubourg did not promise him absolution until the day when he should give proof of his devotion to Jesus Christ. This was because he knew Élie for a man of uncertain temper: he had certainly taken the cross from motives of genuine piety, but he had been laid off work more than once for swearing and fighting.

"There's a penitent"—the captain in charge of the engines of war eyed le Grêlé's broad back—"there's a penitent we'd gladly employ as a stone-breaker. What was his trade in his own country?" And he added that it was a waste of good manpower for a fellow like that to work hunched over a loom.

"Give him to us, Master Baudry. We need men like that to carry loads and break stones for missiles."

"A pilgrim is not a horse to be traded. Besides, we need him also."

But when Élie heard of it, he went in search of the captain.

"If you can use me without my having to leave my own company, I will gladly work for you at breaking stones and I can help with the machines also, because I know about ropes and pulleys." The captain, looking at the man's thin face with the wolfish profile and the low brow overhung with thick, lank hair the color of dirty wool, the deep-set eyes and the dull, leaden gaze, thought that here indeed was good material gone to waste. Le Grêlé was past thirty and would never make a proper soldier.

"Can you handle an ax?"

"I can that. I have been a woodcutter when other work was scarce."

"When we have crossed over the sea, come and find Master Martin who commands the foot soldiers."

At the end of the third week in Lent, when the trees in the country round about, slender and dainty as small deer, were covered with pink blossom, there came a new sin into the Arras camp. The young wife of Bernard, a potter from Lens, went off with a Flemish soldier. There was nothing unusual in the sin itself, but in a camp of crusader pilgrims, in the middle of Lent, such behavior was shocking indeed. Bernard, a peaceable lad in general, flew into a rage and stormed off in search of Baudry and Brother Barnabé.

"It is all your fault for dragging us on this pilgrimage along with hordes of soldiers! If it had not been for these accursed soldiers coming and flaunting themselves in front of our womenfolk, Martine would never have left me. You fetch her back for me or I'll go and complain to the Count of Flanders."

"You shall have her back," Baudry said. "She shall be back tomorrow." But how he was to set about it, he did not know. The same thing had happened before among the Flemish pilgrims, and the army authorities had only said, So much the worse for you if your women are easy and our soldiers are fine, upstanding fellows.

"With the soldiers," Brother Barnabé said, "we shall always come off worst."

It was Alix who solved the problem. She went to Martine in the Flemish camp and frightened her so much by telling her that her Dirck would be punished, disgraced, and branded as an adulterer that the wretched woman agreed in tears to return to her husband.

"I would rather die," she said. "I shall die, but I wouldn't let anything bad happen to Dirck." Alix wept with her, and once back in the camp she told Baudry, "Above all, let no one scold her. She has done right and she really loves the fellow."

"It is well for you," Baudry said, "to be sentimental over a woman who plays the whore. She should be tied up and whipped for what she has done."

"I thought you were a good man," Alix said.

"It is your fault, you shameless woman, if I am unkind. If you had truly repented you would have scarred that face of yours before you set out on a pilgrimage."

Alix smiled rather wistfully. "Look," she said, "I like you well enough, Baudry, but not even for you would I destroy the face God has given me. And something else I'll tell you: if you had a wife, you would not grudge me my pretty face."

"A wife is the last thing I need! You judge all men by those you have known."

The more he thought of Alix, the more it grieved him to be obliged to despise her, for everything in her seemed good to him: her courage, her cheerfulness, her good sense, and her way of talking in that odd, rather learned and clerkly fashion which was so disturbing on a woman's lips. Baudry had taken no vow of chastity. His wife had died while he was still a young man and after that he had known several women, although he had never lived permanently with any one. Since his association with Peter, he had ceased to think of such things: there had been no time for it. Alix's beauty troubled him so deeply that he had many times been tempted to beg her to give him, also, a share in her favors. No one would have blamed him.

The two of them were standing outside Mère Corneille's hut. Martine was inside with the two nuns, and from the soft hiss of blows and muffled shrieks that could be heard it seemed the sinner was undergoing her punishment.

"Oh Baudry, let us go away from here. I do not want to hear."

Alix moved away in the direction of the ditch around the camp and Baudry followed her. It did not even occur to him that there was no reason why he should do as she said. Old pelts and babies' swaddling clothes were drying on the palisade along the ditch, and beyond it they could see the open country.

Over quite a wide area the trees had been cut down and burned, but on a hillside some way off was a large village of flat white houses surrounded by olive groves. Cypress trees were growing around the squat church, which was ornamented with big pink stones and topped by four cupolas. A long white wall ran around a grove of low, spreading trees with dark leaves and white flowers, and small black-and-pink bushes were scattered on a slope of bright-green grass and purple flowers. Peasants were leading carts drawn by small black donkeys.

"The villages in the Holy Land are said to be much like these," Baudry said.

"It is such a pleasant land!" said Alix. "How good it must be to live here. Just think, we are only in the third week of Lent, and at home not even the snowdrops would be out yet. If only they would let us walk in the country."

She sighed and looked at the camp with its bare, trampled earth, the same camp which, six months earlier, had been used by the martyrs of Nicaea.

"Baudry, this too is a part of our penance, to pass always before fair places, and to stand like starving men watching others eat. In the two months we have been here our camp has become more foul than the poorest street in the faubourg."

"We shall be leaving soon."

Alix stood with folded arms, gulping in the air as if trying to catch the scent of the white trees and the new grass across the stench of the ditch. And Baudry, looking at the woman, straight as a poplar tree and so slender and queenly in her bearing, could hardly believe she was Père Malebouche's daughter.

"Baudry," she said, "what are you thinking?"

"I am thinking, Alix, that this journey is too long. Patience is harder than martyrdom. I know that well, for Peter tried to teach us patience. But see for yourself, already seven of our company have sickened and died. We have borne with a murderer and an adulterer in our midst, and we have allowed unmarried men to wallow in debauchery."

"God leads us, and God will judge us. The Hebrews wandered for forty years to purge themselves of their sins, and that was better than remaining the slaves of Pharaoh."

"Was it? It is ten years since I left my trade and my family to live according to the laws of Jesus Christ. I was a mason, I worked on the churches of Arras and of Béthune, and on the town hall at Lens. I made a living. In these days masons do not want for work. But I had nothing to offer Peter but my head and my two hands. We went to villages ravaged by the wars and took care of the orphans and rebuilt the houses. We begged for seed corn from the lords of the land, and because there were no beasts for the plowing we harnessed ourselves to the plow. And the next year storms beat down the crops so that not a quarter was left.

"We took with us peasants who were afraid of famine and helped them to get work as journeymen in the cities of the North, but you know yourself that a laboring life leads to damnation and forgetfulness of God. And later, we went about the faubourgs and men with no work followed us, hoping that we would find them work in a wealthier city. And some of them got used to begging and doing nothing, and when we had no more bread for them they left us and became brigands.

"What was needed was not one man like Peter, or even two or three, but a thousand, and for all Christendom to rise and seek for justice. It was that made me realize, Alix, that there was no hope of salvation for Christians in our lands.

"And now that it is God's will that all should be changed, the rich have hastened to take the way of the poor, and here we follow them and depend on them and they shut us up in a stinking camp bounded by a ditch. Do you think that God will grant them victory, for the sake of the poor?"

"God would have spared Sodom if only ten righteous could have been found there. After all, even among the soldiers and the knights, there are some pious men." Alix sighed, and looked longingly at the blossoming countryside. A little troop of Walloon knights with their squires and two ladies were riding toward them up the yellow road which wound its way among the olive groves. They had hawks on their wrists, and Alix thought that if one of those knights had been her lover she too would have been able to ride in those meadows and run among the bushes with the pink flowers. Gaily, she laughed and shook her head. "Oh no,

Baudry, I still prefer this stinking camp! That is something you will never understand."

After Easter, people began talking seriously about the embarkation. The weather was fine and warm, and the sea as blue as cornflowers. The fields were beginning to turn grey and yellow. Heavy red-gold plums were ripening in clusters of three or four together on the trees of the village. Ships with big painted sails entered and left the port incessantly. The sea was dotted with them.

By the time they had been there four months, the pilgrims and the troops were on familiar terms. The Walloons mingled freely with the Picards and the Flemings with the folk of Arras, and if there were a few clashes and a few women seduced, people had ceased to notice it any more, so great was the fever of departure. During Holy Week, Duke Godfrey's men had marched into the city and plundered the outlying suburbs to avenge the insults put upon them by the Emperor, and many had returned with burns or other injuries, creating some surprise and a certain amount of anxiety in the camps.

But the criers went about proclaiming: Be not alarmed, good people, worthy soldiers of Christ, there is nothing to fear. Peace has already been made with the Emperor, and he has promised us ships for the week after Low Sunday. The Count of Toulouse is three days' march away, and very soon now the whole crusading army will be able to land on the farther shore and bear witness for God! The Emperor has offered us convoys and food for as long as the war shall last.

Good, people thought, matters are coming to a head at last. It is time to take the road again, for after all it is understandable that the Emperor and all his Greeks should begin to tire of having us encamped outside their city. It was time, high time even. Those who knew the country talked about the heat and foretold great hardships on the march.

The Flemish soldiers were the first to start going on board, with the cases of armaments, the equipment for the machines, and the pack animals. The Walloon camp was dismantled next and then the camps of the Picards and the Normans. The horses were led out, hobbled and blindfolded, in long files that passed through the camps, leaving a trail of yellow dung behind them. Getting the horses aboard would be difficult, it was said, because they were very high-strung. And what of us? the pilgrims thought. Are they going to forget about us? For the soldiers had been saying for a long time that they would not be much use in battle. But messengers came at last from the Count of Boulogne and the Count of Flanders to tell the different companies of pilgrims to strike camp and be ready to leave: they would be embarked in two days' time.

That day all sang the *Nunc Dimittis* together. Everyone felt a great shock, as if they had not really believed until that day that they were going to cross the sea. Beyond lay the fortresses and the mountains, and in the mountains the Turks. They had heard about them for so long that in the end they had come to listen to these stories rather as people listen to tales of remote lands. The fifty thousand martyrs of Nicaea and the thousands of Turkish horsemen and the hailstorms of arrows all took their place as part of those legends that every child knew.

And now, in two days' time, they would be going aboard. The sea was calm, but this did not prevent the spread of tales about vessels that were overloaded and sank. Have no fear: the Sultan is now in the mountains to the eastward making war on another Turk. He is so far away that he can never reach here before all the armies are disembarked.

How can this be? Will the Sultan wait, deliberately, until all the Christian armies have landed and are ready for battle? If he is as good a general as they say, he will not expose himself to such a risk. And at this moment all the cavalry is still in Constantinople, and all the leaders.

Are you soldiers of Christ? Those who died at Nicaea had hardly any soldiers with them, and they went forward into the lands of the Turks singing psalms.

Camp was struck. The shacks were torn down and the poles put back on the carts, and blankets, cooking pots, and all the clothes that were left heaped on top. The ladies with the army came on horseback and on foot and distributed lengths of cloth and needles and old shoes and wool for spinning, and salt and dried fruit. They were very gay and seemed glad to meet people from their own lands. They too were excited at the thought of crossing the sea. "May God help us! Pray for us, good Christians, pray for the good Duke and the counts and the Count of Toulouse, and that our knights will not be shamed before the Saracens!"

Marie was pregnant. She had found out from Mère Corneille, who was also a midwife, and at once she began to dance for joy and leap about like a goat among the puddles.

"There is nothing to dance about," Corneille told her. "Two or three months from now you'll feel it in your legs."

To Marie, two or three months seemed as long as three years.

"And when will he come out of me, Mère Corneille?"

"Not before Assumption, to be sure, and not later than All Saints. And well before we get to Jerusalem, at the rate we're going."

"Oh, if only I had the means to light a candle to Our Lady! If only my mother were here to teach me how to conjure away the evil eye!"

"Whatever next! Do you think I can't tell you just as well?"

Marie was dubious. She had always been told a mother's advice was best.

"Oh, I wish he was here already. I am dying of impatience." It was as if she had been told that she had unknowingly swallowed a magic pebble. She pictured the child in her body, like a huge and very precious ruby, all warm and soft. A good quarter of the pilgrims' wives were either pregnant or just out of childbed, yet it seemed to Marie that God was working a miracle for her alone.

"Jacques, Jacques! I am with child! You cannot see him yet, but he will grow. He will even move!"

"Oh God!" Jacques seemed thunderstruck. "This will be the first time!"

He was afraid because when his mother was pregnant he had always been sent away to neighbors—"Or the fairies will come and get you." It was a matter for the fairies, but as luck would have it, there had been none in the faubourg, still less in the pilgrim camp. He gazed hungrily at Marie, trying to see if she had changed, for to him all women with child were under an enchantment. She had become prettier, her breasts were like big round onions now, and she had grown two inches since they left home. It surprised him that after ten months of marriage he still wanted to make love to her, to kiss her and play with her beautiful golden hair like a lover. He was sure of her, he did not fear any rival, and yet she made his heart pound and when he laughed with her he felt a tickle in his nose as if he were about to cry. He had suffered a great deal before their marriage, when he had believed she would have none of him, and something of that suffering still remained with him.

"I wish," he said, "I wish you could have a litter drawn by horses, like great lords' wives when they are with child, and that I could give you a gown of gold thread and white wax candles and wine to drink for your lying-in."

"Ha! Rich women get their reward in this world. I do not envy them. They do not know what it is to share your bread with the man you love."

Jacques thought that what Marie said was true, only he himself did not possess such woman's wisdom. From listening to sermons and travelers' tales he had formed an idea of what it would be like when God's army reached Jerusalem. They would drive out the infidels and share out the houses and the lands, and there would be peace for a thousand years. There would be no more poor. But just by thinking about it, shivering under a thin coat on the march, mending shoes to buy a little more bread, the appetite grew, bringing more and more beautiful dreams. Jacques's brain reeled. He pictured Jesus Christ handing out gold candlesticks and brocaded silks to His poor, and chests covered with Damascus leather, and white horses. In his dreams he heard them neighing and snorting and saw great beams of light so bright they dazzled his eyes, and it seemed to him that these were fires of joy and grief blazing in the sky for the poor martyrs of Nicaea.

4

For the crossing of the Straits of St. George they had to embark first, by twenties and thirties, in small boats which moored up alongside a wooden ship as tall as a house, and then climb a swaying rope ladder above the water. The old and the sick were hauled up by ropes tied under their armpits, but the others had to get up on their own, and for the women that was no light matter because of the wind which blew up their skirts and bared their legs. There was much laughter and shouting and a good deal of shoving, and the great ship was soon so full that no one could move a foot. The sailors, half-naked, brown-skinned Venetians, shouted in their own tongue as they pushed past the people packed on the deck. When the anchor was raised, Brother Barnabé stood on a barrel with his back to the mast, holding his cross high in the air, and led the singing of the psalm of departure. Amid a roar of voices, the ship got under way. The sail was red like the setting sun, and the sea sparkled with myriad pale-golden fires until they no longer knew if it was the ship or the vast harbor, alive with shipping, that was moving up and down, or if the gilded and bejeweled city itself was moving, floating away into the distance like some gigantic ship.

The sea was a deep greenish blue with white caps on the waves and stains of green and purple along the shore. The ship dipped and swayed and with it the crosses and the white banners, the banners of the cross slapping in the wind and tangling in the rigging. The men and women sang to overcome their joy and terror and the vertigo which overwhelmed them on the rolling waves.

After half an hour or so, everyone was sick. Children were crying and old people fainting, and they were all so wedged together that no one could sit down. The ship moved forward slowly but it rolled alarmingly, and the sailors were cursing and saying that the vessel was overloaded and they would surely sink, but fortunately the pilgrims did not understand Italian. The sun was still high in the sky and yet they seemed to have been at sea for hours. Every roll seemed to last for a quarter of an hour and they were sure that time was standing still. Because they had lost all notion of time, they felt as if they had been on this ship forever and were doomed never to set foot on dry land. What little they had in their stomachs had been voided long ago, and it was more painful still to go on retching with nothing left to spew.

At length, fouled with their own vomit and drenched with sea water, they found themselves on ground that was no longer heaving. They were in a vast rocky harbor dominated by a castle built of yellow stone. The beach, the jetty, and the walls swarmed with a motley crowd of soldiers and sailors. The new arrivals collapsed exhaustedly on the stony beach and turned their backs on the gently swaying ships, the mere sight of which was enough to make them feel sick again.

They discovered the hitherto unsuspected bliss of standing on firm ground that did not shift under their feet. Could anything be more frightful than that immense blue landscape, a landscape of bottomless, moving waters? Beside it, the greatest rivers were mere ditches. If these waters ever rose in spate they would cover the whole earth in a second Flood! The still-bemused pilgrims were greeted with sardonic congratulations by the soldiers who had landed the day before and who had had their own share of terror and seasickness. We feared for you, truly we did. We thought you were going down. The water was almost up to the gunwales.

Brother Barnabé lay on the stones, slowly gathering his wits. He had not let go of his great cross and was still clutching it in his hands, his cheek pressed against the damp staff. Lord! he thought. No one dead? No one injured? All here? Sir Evrard sat beside him, calmly lacing up his sea-drenched leggings. He had been fortunate in feeling no ill effects, and was looking about him interestedly at the castle, the harbor, the sea, and the shore they had left that morning, now hidden in a rosy mist.

"No accidents?" Brother Barnabé asked, so hoarse that he could hardly speak.

"Not that I know of. The children are running off already to play in the water. They recover quickly at that age. Baudry has gone to find a place for the camp, and I am going along too. There are bound to be arguments with the Flemings over the baggage."

"Let there be no argument. Give them what they ask. We are not Picards or Flemings or French any more."

The knight made his way up to the castle to find out what was happening. The commander of the place was a Greek, but among his officers were two Norman knights from England who were at first inclined to scoff at Evrard.

"A man who turns himself into a beggar," they said, "must expect to be treated like a beggar, and kicked out like one!"

Evrard told them he was a Christian and would not take offense at insults, but that he was ready to treat them as brothers because they too were Christians, and he wanted to know more about the business in hand.

"This is what is happening," the knights told him, "we are preparing to mount a great attack on the city of Nicaea, which you can see from this tower, over there where the fires are being lighted. When the Emperor has concluded an agreement with your barons he will cross the sea with them and lay siege to that city. And if we succeed in taking the city, which is very strong, the Emperor will no doubt be very pleased and give your knights great gifts."

"Is it known when the siege is to start?"

The Norman whistled and snapped his fingers.

"From what we hear, your barons over there in Constantinople are a greedy lot and drive a hard bargain over the price of their services, but now that we have seen how many men you have we can understand that. If the cavalry is up to the foot, it is a fine army!" He went on to talk about the pilgrims of the previous year, and said it was a shame and that the Turks had laughed the Christians to scorn ever since. He said the Emperor must really have lost patience to send such a rabble across the sea, and that he would have done much better to have shipped them in leaky boats and drowned them all.

Evrard listened, controlling his temper with an effort.

"Even supposing there were some ruffians among them," he

said, "should innocent people, women and children and monks, be held to blame?"

"You have let yourself be carried away by this confounded Peter," said the Norman. "I'll not deny that he is a Norman and even, by what they say, of the nobility, but to my mind he is possessed of the Devil. The villeins will always be scum and it is nothing less than heresy to encourage them to leave the condition God put them in at birth. Give them a little freedom and you see how they behave."

It was said that Peter's pilgrims had committed great atrocities in the region of Nicaea.

Evrard went away much saddened, thinking about the knight's uncharitable words. The harsh things he had said were not wholly unjustified. Evrard looked with foreboding to the ordeals ahead, for he had heard enough about the Turks, and none had been able to withstand them yet. If our knights should fail, then what will become of the poor?

Another camp had to be set up, and this was complicated by the fact that some of the baggage had gone astray during the embarkation and the crossing. Hides, boards, and even cart wheels were missing. The two oxen belonging to the Flemings were too old and had to be left on the other side, as well as one she-ass that was about to foal. Father Berthold, the leader of the Flemish pilgrims, was a cheerful man and he said this was all to the good: the Christians would learn to help one another, and from now on all goods would be held in common, and, like the tower of Babel in reverse, the Christians would speak every language at once.

Sir Evrard called together all the grown men between the ages of sixteen and fifty and addressed them:

"My friends, now is the time to show that you are men. We are all soldiers of Christ, but you more than the rest because it is God alone who will pay your wages. You are fighting for Jesus Christ and in defense of your most precious possessions, your wives and children.

"While we are in camp or marching over the plain, the armies will protect us, but when we have to ride through valleys it will be impossible for you to be surrounded on all sides by armed men, and it will be against you, therefore, that the enemy will direct any attack at the flank. This is what we must do. You must swear not to give way whatever happens and to stand firm in case of attack as if you were rooted to the ground. You will send the young men into the woods with Greek guides to gather as many branches and young trees as you can, and you will have plenty of time before the army sets out to make screens and shields out of brushwood and cover the carts with them. Carry shields on your left arms and hold them over your heads in the event of an attack.

"You must know that we are going first toward Nicaea. We shall probably camp there for several weeks because the Emperor and the barons mean to take the city, which is one of the oldest in Christendom. The Turks hold it by treachery. But there we shall certainly be under attack, because the Sultan has his wife and children in that city and he will come to their rescue. You know the Turks are merciless and stick at nothing, and so you must be prepared to defend yourselves. It will be useless to run away, for you will not save yourselves by flight and will only hinder those able to fight."

It was unusual for the knight to speak at such length, and at the end of this speech all the men swore not to stir from their places in the event of a battle. Already they felt like soldiers in their hearts.

Between Easter and Whitsuntide the pilgrims watched the landings of the armies of Provence, and of the Normans of Prince Bohemond, and of the French led by the Count of Blois. Big ships sailed in three times a day and soldiers and yet more soldiers disembarked; other ships brought cargoes of horses and oxen and sheep by the hundred, and chests of arms and sacks of flour and beans and skins of wine and oil and coil upon coil of rope, and wheels and carts and litters, and after them, still more soldiers. There were soldiers of all sizes, dark and fair, talking in ten different languages, so many of them that it was a wonder any were left in France or in Provence, and the sight of so many soldiers all at once made people think that the Turks could surely never withstand such an army.

They came in companies of two or three hundred and set up their camps along the shore. All had crosses sewn on their banners, and they sang and shouted loud greetings to the Christians who had already landed. *God wills! Next year in Jerusalem!* Later vessels brought the Provençal pilgrims, three or four thousand of them, some rich but mostly poor, so that by the end all the camps had to close up together and people camped just as they were, in the open, without so much as a thought of getting properly settled in.

After the feast of Pentecost, the barons arrived at last.

It was a splendid sight: the gaily painted ships, their sails emblazoned with the cross and chivalric devices and their masts rippling with flags. Trumpets and clarions sounded from the decks where the barons stood with their wives, all dressed in brand-new tunics of silk shot with gold and of rare colors—light green, azure-blue, and blood-red; and as each one descended from the ship into the carpet-covered barge, dark-skinned Greek servants held red sunshades above the ladder. On the shore the drums were beating.

The great lords and their ladies were conducted up a pathway of carpets, scattered with sweet-smelling herbs, into the castle.

Out from the city to meet the noble crusaders came churchmen in full regalia and black-clad monks and leading citizens, bearing crosses and gold-fringed banners.

Walking at the head of the barons, dressed in purple robes, came the legate of Rome, the noble Bishop of Le Puy. This worthy man, although he had renounced this world, was the head of the great army. To mark the sacred nature of this cause, God had appointed a bishop to have command over the men of war.

The next to appear, after the Bishop's retinue, was that of Raymond, Count of Toulouse, who walked beside his wife, the Princess of Castile, a noble Spanish lady of great beauty, veiled in silver draperies. The Count was tall and broad-shouldered with a kingly beard, and his long brown curls swept the collar of his mantle. For all his age, the Count was a comely man, eagle-eyed, with a quick, springy walk, and from his massive belt there hung a sword so long that it almost dragged on the ground.

Next came Duke Godfrey and his suite. Beside him walked the Count of Boulogne, his elder brother, although now in his humility the elder was taking second place to the younger, for indeed the Duke was lord of wider lands. He was known as the fairest knight in all the Northern lands, lithe as a poplar, fair as ripened wheat, with a frank and smiling countenance. Behind these two came their younger brother Baldwin, with his wife and the nurse carrying their small children. Baldwin, though the youngest of the three, was also the tallest and fattest.

Stephen, Count of Blois, walked next to his kinsman the Duke of Normandy, and both these barons were so richly clad and proud and fair to look upon that there was little likelihood of either being thought inferior to the other. In fact, if the Count of

Blois passed for the wealthier and more powerful, Duke Robert was the better knight.

Next came Robert, Count of Flanders and the Count of Vermandois, brother to the King of France, both with their retinues. Then the renowned Norman prince of Italy, Bohemond, with his kinsmen. The crusaders had heard much of this man from the Normans in Constantinople. If he had possessed the wealth to equip a great army, it was said that he could have taken Cairo and Baghdad and Mosul. He was a Norman, tall and fair, dressed all in gold.

A great sigh of contentment and pride and even of some envy went up from the army to see so many great lords and bishops, abbots, and ladies and maidens passing by. There were lights on the castle walls that night, and singing around the fires in every camp. There was wine to drink the health of the barons and the Emperor and all Christendom. Peter had arrived also and his tent had been set up in Duke Godfrey's camp. Accompanied by those who were closest to him, he went the rounds from one camp to the next, still riding on his tiny donkey.

"I saw in the heavens," he said, "seven bloody swords. One fell on the army of Provence, another on the Normans, another on the French, another on the Walloons and the Picards, another on the Flemings, another on the Normans of Apulia, and the last upon the Greeks. But before they could strike, behold, seven swords of light sprang to meet them and so great was the shock that the whole sky was on fire with it. And the bloody swords were broken and shattered and fell to earth, wounding many Christians. But the swords of light blazed above the seven armies with a light fairer than the light of the seven candlesticks before the throne of God."

On the same day, Father Albert, the chaplain to the Normans in Constantinople, made his appearance in the camp of the pilgrims from the North, asking:

"Where is the tall, dark-haired monk who was with the pilgrims of Arras?"

And when he found Brother Barnabé, he went up to him and kissed him on both cheeks.

"I have come, brother. I did not forget your words. See, I have become a servant of Christ."

This made Brother Barnabé very happy. "Truly," he said, "the lion and the ox shall eat at the same manger! You have left a rich and peaceful life solely for love of God's poor. Do you stay with us, or are you leading some poor Normans who have come with the armies?"

"There are over a hundred Normans here," Father Albert said, "not from our own lands but from Sicily and Apulia, old soldiers and men of mixed race with their Italian wives. To be frank, they are a wild lot; they have hardly ever heard a sermon and their speech is very uncouth. Permit them to camp near you, so that these people may profit a little from the good sense of your pious pilgrims."

It was true that there was little fault to be found with the pilgrims of Arras. They had a good reputation in the camp.

Just as at home the people of Arras, and the weavers in particular, were looked at askance, so, in precisely the same degree, were they demonstrably brave and well behaved on pilgrimages. Even so, it was common knowledge that ever since they landed, Martine, the wife of Bernard the potter, had been meeting her Flemish soldier by the ditch, and Bernard had accepted it. All the same, it was a sin and a very bad example. Then there was Élie le Grêlé. He was no longer bound or harnessed to the cart. He had acquired himself an ax for his work in transporting the machines and seemed to have forgotten his crime all too easily.

It was three days' march to Nicaea, but before that the crusading army passed through the outer gates of hell.

It was hot and speed was called for, so there was no setting up of tents. They traveled chiefly at dusk and in the early morning, resting for three or four hours at night and for several more during the day. Those who were able to sleep in the middle of the day lay down in the shade of the wagons or underneath the folded tents. This mode of travel was no worse than any other. The country was beautiful, rich plains of olive trees, fields, and vineyards, though all suffering from neglect and overrun with grass that was scorched even at this season. The sky was a dense, flat blue and at sunset took on such garish colors that it seemed as if great fires were burning away on the seacoast.

It was one evening just as the last blaze of red light vanished, leaving the sky suddenly blanched, that the pilgrims of Arras saw the battlefield. They knew already, by the sounds of weeping and lamentation coming from the columns of the soldiers, that something unusual was happening, for the bulk of the troops were marching some way ahead and had already been crossing this accursed place for some time, but the mass of carts and animals stretching away in front of them and the companies of mounted men flanking the main column had cut off their view.

They had known, however, that the sides of the road, though not running into a defile precisely, had been drawing inward. For two hours or more, progress had been increasingly slow with long delays and a good deal of marking time, while up in front were shouts and horses neighing, and everyone was asking, Is it the Turks? Or some rough passage? What is all the shouting? People are crying and moaning up there. Little by little, as word was passed back down the line, they found out what it was: the martyrs, the martyrs, never was there such a thing seen in any land. Courage, good people. Be quiet and pray.

The western sky was still light, but in the east the blue was deepening and stars were coming out. The colors were fading from the earth but there was still plenty of light, and now, in that hard white light, they could see. What they could see lay on both sides of the road, a road which had narrowed suddenly because the army could no longer spread itself over the plain. In this place, a way had been made wide enough for three carts or ten horses to travel abreast. It was the field of battle.

Everything was white. For half a league to right and left, as far as the distant hills, the grey earth was covered with what looked like scattered patches of snow, while on both sides of the road rose white, uneven heaps, broken by black shadows. Some were big mounds with rounded tops, as high as a house; others were like great banks. Skulls, ribs, arms, remains of horses, whole skeletons, bits of broken bone, all entangled and heaped one on top of another, but nothing else, only bones. Even the dust underfoot was white with crushed and powdered bone. They had been stacked up here to make a passage, but the field on both sides was white and beyond the heaps of skeletons could be seen huddled and twisted forms that still lay on the ground, with limbs all twined together and many without heads, and numerous skulls like enormous white mushrooms.

Yet worst of all was still those ghastly heaps, those hills built out of white sticks, large and small, studded with death's-heads with great hollow eyes and gaping jaws, and here and there the skeleton of a baby hanging like some small animal with a large head and tiny, ravaged face.

They marched on, while the sky turned darker blue and the soldiers in the great column lighted torches and carried them aloft, and there was nothing visible on the plain except the flat grey-whiteness of that strange skeletal host. They marched on. The Bishop of Le Puy had passed word that the priests should pray for the dead, and that they were all to sing psalms for the dead, but without stopping. Let no one be afraid, for the bones that lie here are the remains of martyrs and this place is not haunted.

All the same, the older children were crying with fright and mothers hid their little ones under their cloaks. Even the men were wondering if these dismembered skeletons without arms or heads might not get up and start to dance. There was a sense of urgency, but no room to run. The column with its heavy wagons, its sheep and oxen, lumbered forward slowly. The ground echoed to the dull tramping and shuffling of many feet and the grinding of axles; the great stones of the road cracked as the wagons carrying the chests and engines of war rumbled over them, and the banks of skeletons shifted uneasily with little dry clicking noises horrible to hear—some of the soldiers cried out.

After they had passed the great heaps of bones the road was wider, but in the field beyond, the white carnage still continued. It was as if a storm had raged over a battlefield, as if some tempest of infernal power had in a moment made skeletons of all that lay there. They lay as they had fallen, cut down like corn, on their faces, on their knees, on their backs with their knees pointing at the sky. Here and there a horse knelt with its head drooping heavily on the ground at the end of a long neck made of a chaplet of white bones, and the skeleton of a headless mail-clad rider still hanging from its back. And there were other, quite small skulls, like big white apples.

Some heads still had a few shriveled hairs clinging to the scalp; some bodies wore the garments of soldiers, but most had nothing left on them: the clothes had rotted with the flesh in the course of those eight months. Winter had passed over them, and spring, and now a hot summer; the long process of putrefaction was over and the earth was dry. Thousands and thousands of pounds of rotted flesh had gone to fatten it and now it was dry. The grass had grown and was already browned by the sun. Underneath some battered trees, white, emaciated figures reared up on their knees, clutching the torn branches. Were they men or women? Who could tell? How many were there? The night was not dark. A waning moon was rising, yellow as a quince, and on the gently sloping field the same welter of dry bones could still be seen. They were more scattered now. These had run and been overtaken. They had run in all directions; there were patches of whiteness under the olive trees right at the far edge of the wide field. Farther on, underneath an upturned cart by the roadside, near the carcass of a donkey, was a skeleton clasping two tiny skeletons in its arms.

The strangest thing was that after an hour or two you grew accustomed to it and could look with pity, but without surprise, as if these were people like any others—poor, certainly, but already familiar. This must have been a woman, that an old man. Here's a hunchback, see his spine, and that one, he was a hefty fellow, those bones could have belonged to a horse! Let us pray, brothers. Brothers, let us pray, and if there were any sinners among them, may their sins be forgotten by God and men. They have paid their debt. The things their eyes saw that day count for all the torments of purgatory.

They were still marching, but now there were no more skeletons, or hardly any, just two or three here and there among the bushes.

When the signal came to halt, the moon was at its highest point in the sky, as small and clear-cut as a silver mirror and so white it hurt the eyes. The sides of the hills were like woolen blankets and against them the dark shapes of the trees stood out like huge nails.

The battlefield had been left behind, and yet it seemed to everyone that they could still see skeletons among the rocks. Whatever the priests might say, the fifty thousand dead behind them filled everyone with fear. It seemed incredible that after hearing so many prayers they should not rise up again and claim their share in the pilgrimage.

"How could they leave so many Christians unburied like that?"

"They had to wait. No one could have gone near such corruption. And even now, who could ever bury so many dead? The fields? They have not been cultivated for years on account of the Turks. Do the Turks come here? Yes, often enough, but they are quiet at present. They are afraid of the great army."

Tomorrow, we shall make camp before Nicaea. Nicaea stands on the shore of a great lake. The army lookouts on the top of the hill can see it.

No one slept that night. They sat or knelt on the ground, murmuring aloud the prayers for the dead. Among the poor pilgrims there were many with good reason to mourn, knowing that their own kinsfolk and friends were lying back there on the white field. They are in heaven, Marie, in heaven, surely, and happier than we. Isabelle had two cousins who had set out with their husbands on the day of Peter's preaching. Perhaps it was better so. Who could tell? Better to be dead than slaves . . .

They even killed the children. Marie crossed herself incessantly. She saw the sky turn a deeper and deeper black and the stars gleam more and more brightly. The moon had gone down and new stars were coming out all the time. There were so many of them at last that the sky was one vast carpet of stars, and as she watched them sparkling so brilliantly through her tears, Marie was afraid they would come unstuck from their holders and fall. So those are the martyrs, she thought, their souls are away up there, fixed in the sky! They all rushed upward, like a great shower of rain in reverse, a rain of glittering flames all shooting up to heaven. Such a noise! They must have heard them in Constantinople.

They are up there, following us on the way to Jerusalem. There are Isabelle's cousins, perhaps, and there is the old curé of Sarcelles, and there are lame Jean and his son Berthaut, and Marguerite, the whore from the ropewalk, and Marcellin that played the fiddle in the town on holy days, and André, the overseer's brother . . . and blind Giraud and Marie, the widow of Pierre le Brun, who was so rude to my mother, and how my mother slapped her face, poor woman! All turned into stars and light, oh please God, may none of their souls be wandering about back there on the field, trying to get back into their skeletons! Oh, the screams, how they must have screamed! Mercy on us, how brightly the stars shine!

Jacques was shaking her arm. "Marie, are you asleep? It is time to go."

She clung to him. "Oh Jacques, they are coming down. They are coming to us!"

"Who?"

"The martyrs. Their souls were waiting for us, they are coming with us."

Jacques crossed himself. "Do not say that. The Bishop promised us this place was not haunted."

"Oh no, not haunted, Jacques. They are blessed. They are coming down from heaven to go with us to Jerusalem."

Dawn came and the men began talking in overloud voices as they marched, denouncing the cruelty of the Turks as if no one had ever told them of it before. The cowardly devils, anyone could see there were hardly any soldiers among the dead lying on the field. They had not even stripped the bodies of the knights, and that meant they had not stripped anyone: those people were all unarmed. To massacre ten or a hundred or two hundred poor souls, well and good, it was not unheard of, but for an army to fall upon a defenseless host was worse than madness. If ever we come upon the Turks, by God, we'll make them pay for it. No quarter for their wives and children!

Toward evening they came in sight of Nicaea, which was quite the most magnificently fortified city the Christians had ever seen. No such towers and ramparts were to be found anywhere between Ghent and Barcelona. Prague and Belgrade were nothing to them. How was such a city to be taken? However brave our barons, they have no wings, and how may such walls be demolished?

Have faith, good people, God will help us. The Greeks have powerful machines and they know how to set about such walls as these, for they built them. The Turks took this city from the Greeks seven years ago and it is a venerable city, the home of many great saints. It is vital for us to take it. So said the criers of the army while the camps were being set up at a fair distance around the walls, well out of missile range.

The Turks were there all right, although they were still invisible because they were sheltering behind their walls. Sentinels could be seen marching up and down the ramparts, but they were so far away that they looked hardly bigger than mice. The Turkish banner with the golden crescent could be seen floating from the towers, and signal fires were lighted on the towers at night.

The army was large enough to invest the whole of the city except the side facing the lake, but this lake communicated with the sea and the Greeks had brought their warships into it. Then, when great public prayers had been offered up, the siege began. It was a grim business, and few had seen anything to compare with it in France. The Greek machines were so powerful that they could fling missiles bigger than horses' heads with such force that they could be heard nearly a mile away at the other end of the camp. Moreover, each machine could hurl between ten and fifteen missiles an hour. The stonecutters went to work quickly; hundreds of them were toiling in the nearby quarry. Altogether, from the start the siege made such a din by night and by day that in the camp only the children were able to sleep.

The nights were chill and the soldiers lighted fires every hundred yards, so that from a distance the city seemed to be surrounded by a ring of torches. All who were not soldiers worked by day on the trenches and the palisades that lined the trenches, while at night there was the watch to be kept, for what with the racket of the engines around the walls and all the other noises of the camp, a whole army of Turks could have come up without being heard. The sentinels in the part of the camp that faced east put their ears to the ground anxiously from time to time, always expecting to see the whole of the Sultan's army appear at the base of the ramparts.

One night Jacques was on watch by the ditch, in company with Lambert, Girard, and two Flemish soldiers: the men of the Flemish camp were in the habit of recruiting young pilgrims to relieve them. It was a Saturday night and fairly quiet for once. The infidels were shooting fire arrows down from the walls, but their range was not large and they were not falling inside the camp. They looked like firebirds. Jacques had been on watch the previous night and he was tired. He stood between two of the stakes in the palisade, gaping at the stars and yawning, and as he gazed upward, his eyelids drooped until he was almost asleep. He leaned both hands on his ax and had been standing like that, daydreaming, for a moment when he heard a sound like a rustle of cloth just beside him and looked around. A man had risen from the ditch as if by magic, and the sound that Jacques had heard was the swish of a sword being drawn from the sheath. The sword gleamed before his eyes. Jacques uttered a sharp yell of surprise, which made the man's hand pause for a second. The next instant, Jacques had brought his ax down on his head.

He heard a kind of muffled crack, and when he lifted the ax, intending to strike again, the man swayed and fell back beside the palisade. By now there were sounds of movement in the ditch, and Girard and the Flemish soldiers were sounding the alarm. Men came running up: The Turks! The Turks! It was simply an attack by marauding tribesmen.

Lambert held a torch and they all looked down at the man lying on the ground. He did not move. They took off his fur hat. His shaved head had been well and truly shattered, and the blood and brains had run out and mingled with the long fur of his hat.

"What," said Jacques, "is he dead already?"

"I'd like to see you still alive after such a knock!"

The man was quite young. He had a broad, harsh face with a small black beard on his chin and his narrow eyes were open, calm, and hardly even dulled. The blood had run from his hat down his forehead and over his nose.

Jacques did not understand. He stood leaning again on his ax, trembling and fighting off his dizziness. "Oh say, friends! Oh say, friends!" His teeth were chattering too much for him to say anything else, or even think anything else. They all thought that he was frightened. "Come on, Jacques, you're a brave lad. Don't look like that."

But he went on repeating, "Oh say, friends," and dropped the ax because his arms were shaking so much. "Oh say, what have I done?" At that moment he would have given anything for the man lying on the ground to be only wounded.

The captain of the Flemish foot was there, and Baudry too. The men were all talking at once, pointing at the body and at the ditch by which the raiders had got away.

"You," the Fleming said to Jacques, "tell me exactly what happened."

"Nothing," Jacques said, "nothing at all." His teeth were still chattering a little but he was recovering. "Nothing happened. I looked around and saw this fellow beside me and that thing shining, and I knocked him on the head with my ax, and he fell down."

"Well, my lad," the man said, slapping him on the back, "you may not have a beard but you've got pluck! You've got your first Turk already, and not many soldiers in my company can say as much. You're a lucky man. Would you like to enroll in my company?"

"No," Jacques said. "No."

He picked up his ax and walked away. He felt sick. Oh say, friends. His head felt empty and he could still feel the dull crack of breaking bone beneath the blade of his ax and the pull of the man's weight on his body as he swayed and fell, and he heard again the sound of smashing bone at the end of his ax, which had grown suddenly to a heavy weight on his arm. "Marie, I have killed a man."

Marie knew all about it already. No one had been talking of anything else for the past half-hour. "But you have done well, Jacques, you have done very well! It was you or him! Do you realize that? You had a lucky escape. It would have been the death of me!"

"You are a child, Marie. You cannot know."

Then the next day it was all finished. Everyone was congratulating him and saying that he was a credit to his father and his neighborhood, and that he had defended Jesus Christ indeed, by stopping the raiders from sneaking into the camp and murdering the Christians, and surely God had guided his ax. And indeed, he was glad he had been able to stop them. They would have murdered all his comrades, and his own head would have been the first to be struck off.

The raiders directed their attacks against the camps of the poor, because these were the least well defended. Knowing the lay of the land, it was child's play for them to slip through the palisades. The sentinels could do nothing to stop them: they made no more noise than rats. These were a kind of Turks known as Turkomans, who went about in roving bands, and by God, they were brave fellows, for they would attack without much hope of gain, merely to harass the Christians. Once they got into the camp of the Provençal pilgrims and killed ten of the guards in the way they had, creeping up quietly and lopping off a head before the man had time to know it, so well sharpened were their swords. Then they made a rush for the tents, and there they were trapped. The morning after the attack the martyrs were buried and the fifteen or so Turkish heads stuck on the stakes overhanging the ditch. Jacques's Turk adorned the palisade by the Flemish camp in the same way, and it was no pleasant sight because the head was soon black with flies. Even Jacques himself disliked passing it. During the day the children would go and stone it with their catapults.

The siege was a hard one. Burnt and injured men were brought in every day to the tents of the foot soldiers, and the Count of Toulouse's engineers went around all the civilian camps recruiting men for the mining operations. Hundreds of laborers were needed for digging and, still more important, for collecting and taking away the soil. The men formed long chains, passing buckets of earth from hand to hand, and the work went on so fast that after three days there were real mountains of earth and broken stones at the entrance to the gallery. Later on, other workmen carried this earth to a place opposite the tower, where they wetted it and packed it close to make a flat surface on which a wooden tower would be erected.

This was the only place where the work was dangerous; the defenders had machines with a long range, and although they sheltered behind large wooden boards, the workers were in considerable danger of being killed or maimed. The pilgrims of Arras lost two fullers in this way. Both were young men and one of them married. They told his widow, "Don't cry so hard. Your man is made a martyr." She stopped crying and, being a well-built woman, offered to take her husband's place as a laborer. She turned up wearing a man's breeches, with her braids wrapped around her head under a scarf.

If it had not been for the crashing of missiles and the dust around the walls and the Greek fire which now and then set fire to the palisades, the siege would not have been unpleasant. The Emperor was a good Christian, there was no denying that. He kept the army so well supplied that even the poorest had as much bread as they wanted, and wine on Sundays. A diet like that was enough to set you up for a year.

No one knew where they came from; they were simply there. Perhaps they managed to slip through the palisades, or made their way into the camp by following the supply columns, or even through some underground passage. Certain it was that from about this time, during the siege of Nicaea, they began to appear in greater and greater numbers. They preferred to mingle with the pilgrims because the soldiers drove them off unkindly. Many came after the battle which the Count of Toulouse and the French fought against a Turkish army right in the middle of the siege. This was not the Sultan's army, but only a small advance guard. The day the French and Provençal troops returned to camp proclaiming a victory, a whole company of these people came in the wake of the soldiers, bearing Turkish heads with them.

They were bone-thin, with blackened skin that had a strange sheen to it and large haggard eyes. They said little. At night they would sit close to the fires, giggling inhumanly and gazing hungrily at the bread and meat. They were given food and picked the bones clean voraciously, like animals, and did not ask for more. They were so strange that word began to spread that they were dead men brought to life again, and people began to be afraid of them and dared not drive them off.

One day, as Marie was sitting outside one of the tents stuffing padding into a man's hat, with Saint-John hanging around her as usual, one of these men came up and laid his dark hand on the madman's shoulder.

"Hey, Saint-John, a fine woman, eh?"

"Get thee behind me, Satan! She is a holy woman!" But the man only sniggered again.

"You," Saint-John said, "Richard. If you were raised from the dead it cannot have been for your good deeds, because you have grown fearfully ugly."

"I was never raised from the dead," the other answered. He sat down by Marie and folded his thin arms, like two sticks, on his sharp knees. He was all but naked: he had no shirt and the remains of his breeches did not cover his thighs.

"Black, eh?" he said, turning his wizened face with its beard the color of dead leaves toward Marie. When he talked, he bared his teeth in a kind of grin. "Black, eh, pretty girl? Black, am I?"

"Yes," said Marie. "Black as a devil."

"That is the sun and wind. Aren't you from Picardy?"

"No. I come from the faubourg of Arras."

"I am Richard, a weaver of Roubaix. I used to be a weaver in Roubaix. We were put out of work—the district was burned down."

"Mercy! With all the cloth?"

"And the workers. I managed to escape through the window. My brothers died."

"Oh, you poor lad!"

The black man stared straight in front of him with unseeing eyes.

"—and at Mainz, on the Rhine, we burned the Jews."

"Why the Jews?" Marie asked.

"Because they cast spells, of course. They mix their hosts with Christian blood, and it brings drought."

"It is not that, Richard," Saint-John said. "The Jews nailed Christ to the Cross."

"They still cast spells," the other said stubbornly. "They caused a slump, on the Rhine. The Bishop doesn't care if there is no work. He took the Jews' part." He nodded, lost in his own thoughts. "Everywhere they drove us out. Like stray dogs. Worse than stray dogs."

"What of your wife, Richard?" Saint-John asked. Richard laughed mirthlessly and made a gesture with his right hand across his throat.

"So. You understand? They are good at that game. One stroke of the sword and—bang! No head. I was lying on the ground, hurt. For three days I lay rotting under the carrion."

Marie crossed herself. "Oh God, are you sure you are not really dead?"

Richard laughed. "No, have no fear, my beauty, the real dead do not eat. No, they do not eat, the real dead. They cannot eat."

"Who knows?" Saint-John said dreamily. "How can we tell what they are like? You may be dead and not know it."

The other man emitted a dry chuckle. "Oh no! When I'm dead, I shall know it." He rose and moved away with his quick, loping tread, like a wolf, with his back bent and head thrust forward.

"He used to be a fine fellow," Saint-John told Marie. "But for the light which God has granted me, I should never have known him. He had a wife, Guillette. She was with child, but pretty. Eyes like little silver fishes."

Seeing these lost men made many people wonder if friends they had believed dead might not be among them, although it would have taken the supernatural insight of a Saint-John to recognize men so changed. Baudry and Sir Evrard and Father Berthold had agreed to approach Duke Godfrey's marshal with a request that these strange crusaders be rounded up and placed in one closed camp, because they were so filthy and they stank and frightened the children and walked about unclothed in a way that was hardly decent. Moreover, in spite of all the priests' assurances that the thing was highly unlikely, no one could be sure they had not risen from the dead.

One of them, a young man who was still quite well preserved, told Baudry that there was a considerable number of such people in the area. Up to two thousand of them were living hidden in the hills and had elected a king to lead them, and they prayed to God and obeyed the rules of their community so scrupulously that any man among them who transgressed was immediately put to death by his fellows.

The youth, whose name was André, said they would willingly offer their services to the barons of the army, provided they were allowed to live after their own fashion.

"And you, André," Baudry asked, "how have you lived and why have you not sought to make your way back to some seaport?"

"We hid. The people of the land would stone us when they saw us. You see, how could we tell if the people were Greeks or Turks? Some of those we killed may have been Christians. We get to a village and they come out at us with pitchforks. But we're hungry, see? We go for them with our knives. All dead.

After that, we eat what there is. It never lasts long. We used to envy the martyrs. Hunger is worst of all."

"You lost your family in the battle?"

"My father and two little sisters. Thank God my mother died in Hungary. I was from Rouen. We were craftsmen. Fullers. When Peter came and preached, God's curse on him, the merchants had been cutting down the prices so that you either worked yourself to death or starved. My father said we might as well go. So we did. We should have done better to have stayed. Hunger is the same everywhere. There have been worse things here."

"We will keep you with us," Baudry said. "If God wills, we shall reach the Holy Land."

"Holy or not, it's all the same to me. All I want is to be revenged on the Turks, see? I made a vow to kill three hundred with my own hands."

"That's some vow! How many have you killed so far?"

"Four. All the rest were Greeks."

"Well, my lad, we ought rightly to hand you over to the Emperor's officers. But after all you've been through, you may be sure we won't do that. You've a good head on you still, so stay with us."

"No. With us, it's live or die together. Even if they put us in a camp under guard."

The city of Nicaea surrendered to the Christians. There was no assault or sack, but for those in the camp who watched the thing from a distance it was still a splendid sight. The barons had built wooden towers as tall as the towers of the city, and their fire was so well directed that by the end of three weeks whole sections of the wall and parts of the towers were to be seen subsiding into the ditch with great crashes and clouds of dust and smoke. The great eastern tower had been undermined and whole cartloads of pitch and resin and the inflammable water of the Greeks placed in the mines and ignited by means of fuses soaked in resin. There was a rumbling sound as the ground was blown open on all sides, and at the same time pandemonium broke loose underneath the tower and clouds of smoke belched out, hiding the castle altogether. And the screams! It was no longer possible to tell who was screaming, Christians or infidels, for joy or for pain. Look, look there, she is going! And through the smoke a huge round tower, more massive than the strongest belfry, could be seen toppling over slowly, slowly, tearing apart great sections of the wall, as if it meant to dive into the moat. It was a terrifying sight, as if the tower had taken on a life of its own.

It did not fall, however. The men of the garrison were running about the walls amid the smoke, at the risk of their lives because the stones were still falling, carrying picks and buckets of mortar, while others fought to save the mangonels and set them upright again. All this took place opposite the Count of Toulouse's camp, and at the same time, on the other side by the gate, the Greeks were repulsing a sortie with their cavalry and their rams all ready to go into action. Turks and Greeks alike were falling into the water-filled moat off the plank bridge the Christians had thrown across it.

Even so, the city was not taken by storm. The next day the Greek standards were to be seen on all the towers, while inside the city the church bells pealed joyfully and the Greek trumpets sounded triumphantly on the walls. White banners with the cross. Thanks be to God, the Virgin, and Saint George! And to Saint Michael and Saint Nicephorus and Saint Mercury! The noble city of Nicaea is freed from the yoke of the heathen Hagarenes, whom others call the Saracens or Turks!

The only thing was that in the army there was a good deal of unrest and even mutiny. The priests and monks were forced to talk to the men at length, brandishing their crosses and protecting the barons' criers with their own bodies. "God and Jesus Christ and Holy Cross! Are you a Christian army or beasts without understanding? Before you start shouting, first hear how matters stand!"

"Oh, indeed! And who was it shed their blood? We or the knights? Who worked on the machines under the missile fire, who dug the mines and watched the walls? Let the barons have the honor and the Emperor's gifts, and give us the town! Give us the garrison, and the Sultana! They killed more than ten thousand of our women back there, on that white field of the slain! The Sultana and the garrison are ours by right! It was not the knights' wives who were killed back there, or the Emperor's daughters!"

The criers proclaimed that the Christian army had won a great victory. Fires were to be lighted in celebration, and that very day the Emperor was sending dozens of barrels of good wine into every camp and every soldier would receive his reward. All this they proclaimed, and back the answer came: He can keep his money! Let him open the gates to us! We did not fight for nothing. The town is ours!

"For shame, you bad Christians! Was it for the sake of plunder that you took the cross?" The priests and preachers climbed onto carts and rent the necks of their habits to make the people listen to them. "Shame on you! What plunder would you have? This is a Christian city. Only the citadel was held by the Turks! The Emperor does well to deny such savages entry into the city!" The priests were obliged to say this, but privately they themselves thought that a wrong was being done to the poor.

"Tell us, did we swear fealty to the Emperor? Give us the garrison, and the Turks' wives and their goods!"

"But what goods?" they were asked. "Those goods, the Turks stole from the Christians! Would you lay hands on that which is your brothers'? Do you dream of coupling with heathen women? Know that all union with unbaptized flesh is a mortal sin. Even tomorrow we strike camp to go and meet our enemies in the open field. It is in prayer and fasting that this day should be spent."

Brother Barnabé was depressed and irritable. "We have scarcely set foot on soil occupied by the infidel," he said, "we have hardly liberated one Christian city, and already the crusading soldiers have lost their heads and think of nothing but plunder." There were plenty of pilgrims also ready to shout with the soldiers, demanding the spoils and the Sultana, and fiercest of all was Élie le Grêlé.

Baudry had taken him aside and tried to make him ashamed. "That for the spoils," le Grêlé said. "Let them give us the Turks."

"It is not for you to say," Baudry told him. "God has not yet forgiven you."

Élie drew himself up and looked Baudry in the eyes unflinchingly.

"What do you know of that and what right have you to speak to me like this? A weaver is as good as a mason any day. I have sinned. But who is without sin?" He held himself so straight, looked so determined, and spoke so arrogantly that Baudry fell back a pace. Two months earlier he would have punched le Grêlé in the jaw.

"Wiser men than you," he said, "have chosen me willingly to lead them. If you will not obey me, then take your daughter and her husband and go to the soldiers or wherever you please."

Élie smiled grimly. "You are jealous, Baudry, because men know that I am braver than you."

Baudry shrugged and turned away.

Braver. It was true that during the siege works Élie had been singled out by one of the Norman knights, and all the pilgrims knew it. The scaffolding of one of the wooden towers had caught fire and a dozen Norman soldiers had been trapped, unable to get down, when Élie, who was sorting stones nearby, had run to find a long ladder and had held it until all the soldiers were down, and this under a heavy rain of missiles. The Norman knight had praised him for it. "You are a brave man, whoever you are. You saved my men. Here is money for you." Élie had refused.

"I did not do it for money. We are all Christians."

"Truly," the knight had exclaimed, "here is a man who should have been born noble!" Élie's head swelled with pride after that.

It was common knowledge that when the armies had struck camp and taken the road eastward the Sultan would come in person to fight the Christians. There was no time to waste in plundering or allowing the men to rest. It was necessary to get away quickly and be ready to meet the enemy on ground where the cavalry could be deployed. "Unless," said some of the more ignorant pilgrims, "he fears to attack such a mighty army?" We cannot count on that. His honor is at stake. His capital city has been taken from him with his wife and his best emirs! The reason he has not attacked yet is because he is gathering fresh troops, and according to the Greek spies he has been on the march for two weeks at the head of countless legions.

In any event, they all knew he could not be far off. At the end of the day's march, the eyes of the whole army were on the horsemen sent out to scout along the hilltops, watching for the alarm. On the third day after they left Nicaea, the signal came.

They were in a wide, almost empty stretch of slightly rolling country of fields crisscrossed by roads. There were signs that many flocks and herds or armies were accustomed to pass that way, and the villages were all abandoned or destroyed. May God defend us! In the quiet of evening they could hear the ground rumbling a long way off. *The baggage and the litters and the women and children are to go to the ruined village, by the well, and no one is to stir from his place. It is time to prepare for battle.*

The order was passed down the line: Stand firm at all costs. Stand firm even if all their horsemen fall on you at once. The knights were drawn up in battle order to one side and the bowmen on the flanks prepared their defense, sticking the points of their long shields into the ground and standing shoulder to shoulder so as to make a wall five feet high. *For God and Jesus Christ, friends! Stand firm.* There are thousands and thousands of horsemen coming. Flight will not save us now. All the noises of the camp were drowned in the thunder of tens of thousands of hoofbeats on the plain.

It was worse when they came in sight. They came fast: in less than an hour all the plain and the hills were thick with them. The swarming hills came suddenly alive. No one knew where the Sultan was; all they could see was the massed horsemen in white or grey cloaks mounted on their small dark-colored horses, advancing in orderly ranks at a smooth, easy gallop and all yelling as they came. They could not hear themselves speak for the din.

Then followed hour upon hour of hell. It was a clever man who could understand what was going on in that great tumult in the dark. In the middle of the camp, the terrified women were dressing themselves hurriedly and running in search of news. Children were bundled for safety underneath the carts and told, "No, it is nothing. Only a storm," or "It is only the machines firing," when that was the last thing it sounded like. All the men, soldiers and pilgrims, stood in close ranks, enclosing the camp and the wall in a series of human ramparts, each man gripping his weapon and protecting his head with shield, board, or bucket, whatever came to hand.

For it was like a cloudburst. It rained arrows. They whistled and flew, they fell and buried themselves in the wooden shields with a thud and a low, vibrating hum, they clattered against the rocks or stuck silently in an arm or leg—silent, but followed instantly by a scream or an oath. *Keep your heads down, lads, cover your eyes,* nothing else is fatal, *and above all, stand your ground, keep the ranks closed!* Protected by their shields, the bowmen stood firm, bending their bows and firing their arrows in quick succession, but for every one they fired, fifty came back. They were taking aim, but the Turks for their part scarcely needed to pause to find a mark; their arrows fell so thickly that there were enough for all. God! How long will it take them to empty their quivers? The men serving the archers were the most exposed and a great many of them fell.

The enemy came on, charging with such a thunder of hoofs and shouting and raising such a dust that in those hours before dawn the archers must surely have earned their place in paradise for not giving ground. They waited until the Turkish horses were no more than ten yards away and then they loosed their arrows all together. The Christians' bows were much stouter than the Turks' and the great *bang* made by their bowstrings drowned all other sounds. Nearly every arrow found its mark in one of the horses and the beasts reared up and fell. The enemy ranks were broken, and the riders swung away and galloped off. More came on instantly, bows bent, still yelling their shrill war cries that were like the howling of wild beasts.

How many of them are there? Or are they the same ones coming back again? Hour after hour, and already the sun was high in the sky, although few had marked its coming through the dust and the din. A whole row of the front rank of archers were ridden down and trampled so that not even their shields were left to show where they had stood, next to the Walloon and Flemish foot soldiers. *Lord Jesus have mercy on us!* At that moment they regretted the shields almost more than the men.

The archers in the second rank re-formed and went down on one knee to fire through the gaps between the shields. And their shields shuddered and split as one by one the arrows thudded into them. Thanks be to God these were light arrows, otherwise they would have overthrown the shield and the man with it. Those that passed over the heads of the archers were worse than angry wasps, like live things seeking out their prey. No more trenches were being dug, but the men stood ready with whatever they had in their hands, a weapon or a tool, and if these archers too were overrun they would go to it with their picks and axes. Meanwhile, the swiftest and most active ran to refill the bowmen's quivers, while others stood behind them as they fired and handed them their arrows.

Oh, those gallant archers! For hours on end—was it hours indeed? It may have been—they knelt there, like machines, bending their bows, loosing the string, taking fresh arrows, and bending the bow again until you would have thought their arms must be as insensible as mill wheels from repeating the same actions.

No one had the strength to speak any more; it was all they could do to breathe and now and then to spit. Over there, fifty yards away, or thirty yards, the Turks were making such a din that it seemed there never had been any other sound or ever would be but the thunderous gallop of the charge and then their shouting: *this was no continuous sound, but every ten seconds it broke out afresh, now shrill now hoarse, and every time it pierced your flesh like thorns,* until you could stand no more and not go mad. They would come tearing on at gallop, shoot their arrows, and then swerve away to one side while others came on, until at last you began to wish they would only come straight on and let you meet them face to face with spears and axes, them and their horses, so that it would all be finished.

The thundering hoofs were nothing, or even the dust, *if only they would stop screaming like that,* like owls, like vultures, is that their war cry? Oh, when Joshua, that holy man, made the sun stand still in the sky, that was truly a miracle because the Jews were winning and putting their enemies to flight, but for men in a tight place the sun stopped of its own accord without a miracle, and took twenty hours to reach its zenith. Another incident occurred among the Walloon bowmen. They had discharged their arrows truly, almost at point-blank range this time, when three horses with their riders leaped into the air and came down on top of them, crushing them beneath their weight.

The breach! The breach! The men in the second rank ran to finish off the fallen Turks and make a rampart of the injured horses, while the archers to left and right turned their bows against the fresh wave of riders coming on. In the ensuing uproar no one so much as thought of taking shelter behind the boards and rush matting. They simply waded in with pitchforks, spears, and axes, slashing at the horses' muzzles and the men's legs and howling like animals, howling loud enough to strike fear into the Turks themselves. Men got arrows in the arm or shoulder and did not even feel them. The place was heaped with the bodies of men and horses, still kicking and screaming and dying, heaped so thickly that the Devil's chariot could not have driven over them. And the horsemen turned away and attacked in another place, away to the left.

There the bowmen stood their ground, but they needed time to reload: they did not have ten arms. They were panting like injured hounds and firing blind because everything in front of them, field, earth, and rock, was obscured by dust, and each time the horsemen charged they raised such clouds of it that even the sky was hidden. Wounded horses reared and pawed the air and plunged back through the unbroken ranks behind them. Then there would be a few moments' peace. *What bliss! No more ar-*

rows. It was too good to be true: nothing was falling on your head and it was almost possible to see in front of you.

Sweat was streaming down your body until you were drenched with it, as if you had been out in the rain, sweat running out of your hair, down your forehead, into your eyes, and dripping into your mouth. You put out your tongue and licked it off. *Look out for arrows! They are coming back! The breach, men, the breach,* there beside Master Martin! Mercy on us! They charged like furies right over a row of ten bowmen, the arrows sticking in their horses' bellies. The horses were down and their riders on the ground, swords in hand, while yet more horsemen came leaping over the fallen mounts. If they get through the third line they will be right in the camp! Pray God the women keep their heads and grab hold of anything that comes to hand—cooking pots, anything will serve. *Let no man give an inch.* The horses plunged full tilt into the compact body of men, spitting themselves on spears and pitchforks. There was nothing to choose now between soldiers and civilians; all were striking out like madmen, like madmen with axes, mallets, picks, and shovels, no longer knowing what they did.

Horses with heads split open, men trailing severed limbs, an arm lopped off by an ax blow, the hand still clutching a sword, gashed heads and shoulders, all passed unnoticed. But before the pressure of that roaring throng, bloody, deaf, blind, and terrible in its frenzied lust to kill, a host of wounded beasts driving forward with every ounce of strength, horses and riders fell back as though in the grip of sudden panic, helpless in the face of these men on foot who clung to their ground and pushed forward slowly, step by step, baying so ferociously that far back in the lines of mounted Turks the horses paused in terror and the riders wheeled and fled. Not even the Turks themselves, not even the Turks, had ever heard any sound to equal that vast howl of rage. It was not a cry of fear or hatred. There was nothing human in it any more.

Tired out with killing, the men stood panting, staring around at the fallen horses, the few Turks, or their remains, chopped worse than butcher's meat, at the bodies of their comrades slain, and at the blood, the bright red blood fast sinking into the thirsty ground. How quiet it is! We have driven them off, lads. *In God's name, fill the breach!* The bodies of men and horses must be thrust back swiftly to form a rampart. Pile them up into a breastwork. The women had formed a chain and were passing buckets of water. They came running up, gasping, with their buckets and their pitchers, and sacks or even old tubs on their heads. The men bent down and plunged their faces into the water and drank straight from the buckets.

Marie was there, an old sheepskin tied around her head and a bucket in her hands that was so heavy she had to lean right over backward to lift it. Quick, give it here, here, here! They lapped like dogs, spluttering and shaking their heads. To the archers, take some to the archers! The bowmen, drunk with fatigue, were settling their knees firmly on the stony soil and digging the points of their broken shields deeper into the ground. They could not bend their heads to drink because of their rigid helms. Marie gave them water in her cupped hands and they had no sooner drunk than they were asking for more. They were beyond speech. Marie splashed water in their faces and poured it over their necks, and they closed their eyes and made little croaking sounds of thankfulness. Their hands still grasped their bows, with the arrows ready to fire.

They are coming back, lads! They are coming back! You women, take cover! But there was no cover. *And the baying of the men.* The archers bent their bows and fired. Oh God, will the arrows last? There was a gap of some fifty yards or so where there were no more archers, and this had been filled in with corpses and dead horses. Twenty paces back the men waited, down on one knee, their weapons, spear or pike or pitchfork, pointing forward. If they leap the barricade they'll charge right onto them. The women, Marie and Alix and Bernard's Martine and the nun, Sister Hildegonde, were caught in between the men and the breastwork of corpses. They stood there, feeling rather foolish, with their buckets, like peasant women coming from the well. Take cover, by all the devils in hell, they'll ride right over us! The arrows whistled overhead, dense as a flight of storks, only a hundred times swifter. One stuck in Marie's sheepskin, another hissed past Alix's nose, a third struck Sister Hildegonde in the shoulder and the old woman fell on her knees, dropping her bucket of water. Five or six men were hit, but they were leaning forward with their left knees on the ground and did not flinch except for one who took an arrow full in the face; he fell back and his neighbor grasped his spear and held one in each hand. Get to the barricade, you women, to the barricade! A moment later, five Turkish horses sprang across the breastwork of dead, right over the women's heads, and in the melee that followed, Marie understood nothing at all; all she heard was voices screaming and screaming and the din of hoofs, and men and horses rolling headlong in the dust ten yards away from her, while she knelt where she was beside her half-empty bucket of water, repeating endlessly, "Oh Jesus Christ, Holy Virgin, Jesus Christ, Holy Virgin."

Her heart was hammering so fast that she could feel it in her temples and in her legs, her whole body was hammering like a banner in the wind, and in the pit of her stomach the child was hammering also, with a faint, uneasy rhythm.

The barricade. She was leaning against the barricade. It was warm and smelled strong, and it was moving. She turned and nearly cried aloud: another head was close to hers, other eyes looking into her own. A horse's head was jammed in between the black back of another horse and a big leather saddle with a man's leg in it. The head moved slightly as though trying to free itself. It was a noble head, young and highly bred. The pink, almost transparent nostrils were palpitating, and the big brown eyes outlined in black had a gentle, rather bewildered expression. The eyes met hers. Oh God, the lovely creature, Marie thought, *the poor little thing.* The animal must have been mortally hurt, for it lacked even strength to free its neck. Marie gave it some water in her cupped hands and saw the quiver of soft lips over its big white teeth.

Then she became aware of men, bloody and pouring with sweat, running to her bucket and dropping on their knees beside her to drink. She looked up. Three steps away, a disemboweled horse lay, legs in the air, with the headless body of a soldier next to it, his neck in a great pool of blood.

She screamed: "Jacques, Jacques, oh where is Jacques?" She began to run, staggering and tripping over the bodies. An arrow struck her left arm as she went. Its force knocked her over but she got up, holding the arrow in her right hand, and went on screaming, "Jacques, where is Jacques?" Jacques was there, standing, puffing like a bull, his ax in his hand.

He dropped the ax for a second and took Marie in his arms, still puffing and wheezing with exhaustion. "Oh Marie, oh Marie, oh there, there!"

He was brick-red, bareheaded, his hair and his shirt soaking wet, his face spattered with mud and blood and his narrow eyes half shut with the look of a blind man, while his nostrils dilated slowly.

"Go on," he said hoarsely, "get back to the camp, I'm telling you."

"Yes, Jacques, yes, I'm going." She ran to take a bucket of water from the hands of one of the Picard women and came back with the arrow still dangling from her left arm and hurting badly.

"Here, someone take out this arrow for me." The soldier nearest to her gripped her arm and tugged at the arrow, gently at first, then with one swift pull: he knew what he was about. Marie bit her lip while the man tore a piece from her sleeve and made her a tourniquet.

"Don't keep it on too long."

He looked at her then and his eyes brightened suddenly. "Well, beautiful!" He took the bucket out of her hands and put it on the ground. "How about it, then?"

She thought he must be mad. They were standing in the middle of the throng, a few yards from the barricade, and all around them were injured men trying to bandage their wounds and men fastening their helmets. However, since the soldier seemed set on violating her on the spot, Marie pushed her fist into his face and fled with her bucket.

The archers were still shooting, but the Turks came no nearer and contented themselves with emptying their quivers from a distance so that their arrows fell well short of the bowmen's lines. They had a breathing space and the men drank and drank like madmen, fighting over the fresh buckets of water as they arrived. If they come back again . . . Oh God, if we have to go through that again we shall all go mad. Already they were up to their ankles in the mud and blood and dust, and it was only just past noon.

The clouds of dust had settled. In the distance the long lines of Turkish horsemen could still be seen, wheeling in tight formation, and they still surrounded the camp on all sides. They must be resting now but they'll come on again, let's take the chance to build a barricade. Then they heard the heavy, regular beat of galloping hoofs, and for once it was not the Turks. A company of Provençal knights and their squires—a good hundred of them—rode past at full tilt, and all the length of the camp people were calling out to know what was happening. *They rode straight for the end of the valley,* where the clouds of red dust glittered in the sunshine. "There is hot work over there. Courage, stand firm!"

Just then Sir Evrard, who had been fighting with his men on

the other slope of the hill, guarding the wagons of the Normans and Picards, came riding back to where the bowmen stood, his shield, his helmet, and his horse's headband all stuck with arrows and holding aloft his great spear which had once been white and was now red with blood. Five of his men followed him. They were walking their horses and did not appear to be in retreat, which was a good sign.

The knight came toward them, swaying to the movement of his lamed horse, his shield, heavy with the weight of arrows, hanging loosely from his left arm and his spear jogging in the crook of his elbow. His beard was dark with sweat, his lips compressed, and his eyes as heavy as lead weights. The men clutched his stirrups as he passed. What news?

"Not bad," he answered hoarsely. "Not bad. They are giving ground." Messengers arrived at a gallop from the Provençal camp, holding trumpets to their lips. "Forward, the brave! For God! Forward to victory!"

"What victory?"

"They're breaking, can't you see?"

All at once, the moving lines of Turks seemed to be melting away before their eyes like a cloud dispersing. "But we had orders not to budge!" "Then you'll stay here till Judgment Day! Clodpole, that order's out of date! My lord Bishop says, *Praise Jesus Christ!* And forward, to the kill!"

Not wholly understanding at first, the men who were unhurt began to move, almost regretfully leaving the bowmen's lines, the mound of dead bodies, and the women with their buckets of water. They seemed to have lived for so long in that place that they could not easily accustom themselves to being anywhere else. They walked forward in the wake of the mounted messenger, carrying their weapons and stumbling a little on the ground all churned up by the horses' hoofs and thick with arrows and horse dung, and the farther they went the more they understood: We've beaten them! They are running away! *We* are attacking.

And suddenly in every camp, all over the field, the same lightning thought shot through a thousand brains: WE'VE BEATEN THEM! JESUS CHRIST BE PRAISED! WE'VE BEATEN THEM! A roar of joy swept like a wave from end to end of the camp, reverberating like thunder till all the hills were shouting with one voice and men who half an hour before were hardly able to stand for weariness began to run.

They ran, leaping over rocks and stones, leaping over corpses, waving their spears and axes. Before them on the plain the knights were charging, spread out in the shape of a gigantic fan whose feathers were ten-foot spears. The knights were charging headlong at full gallop, crashing through the serried ranks of Turks like a huge foaming wave breaking on a heap of pebbles. Already they were on the Turks, *and their pace had hardly checked.* The Turkish horses were small and light-armed, something was known of them by now—yes, the great charge had hardly checked. As they came nearer they could hear the noise growing and swelling, and to the shouting and the trampling was added the hard clash of iron on iron, the din of a thousand smithies. Nothing could be seen for the dust except one thing: they were advancing, the cavalry were *advancing.* No more Turks on their flanks, no more Turks, they were in flight!

Then the foot soldiers were all running forward, except for the bowmen, who had earned their rest. All were thrown together that day, professional soldiers and amateurs alike, for the camps had all begun to move at once, and men were swarming over the whole breadth of the field crying death to the enemy.

Praise God! Praise God! No quarter, we have beaten them! For Jesus Christ! As the dust slowly settled, they found themselves stumbling over dead bodies and wounded horses. The cavalry had passed that way before them and done its work. Dismounted Turks in turbans and white burnooses fought with swords and javelins, but they could not defend themselves for long. The foot swept over them in such a ferocious onslaught that wounded men with faces slashed and hands hacked off still went on running as though they had felt nothing, while others came after them wielding clubs and axes for all they were worth.

On they ran until it seemed as if that race would never end and they were bound to pursue the Sultan throughout eternity, as the Devil's hounds pursued the impious knight. Joy gave them wings and took away all power of thought. For God. Until they could run no further. They were all drunk, even those that were half dead of thirst. *Night was falling.*

Now that the enemy was scattered beyond reach, the knights were tiring of pursuit and coming back slowly, looking solemn and somewhat bizarre because all the plumes and trappings from their helms and harness had been lost in the battle, their lances were broken and themselves all stuck with arrows. They were bloodstained and so dusty that even the colors of their shields were no longer visible. And seeing them return, the men on foot were obliged to stop their mad career and turn back also.

Orders: to finish off all wounded and round up the horses that are unhurt. God has granted us this day a great victory!

They will not come back. We have earned our night's rest.

The barons and the knights slept that night in the Sultan's tents. They had captured so much treasure and such quantities of livestock, sheep and cattle, that it seemed there would be enough to feed the army for the rest of the journey. The Bishop of Le Puy led a great service of thanksgiving, and the priests throughout the camp had orders to do the same. The division of the spoils could wait until the morrow; God must be served first. Hundreds of vultures were already wheeling in the red sky, spiraling down toward the field, and the Christian wounded must be brought in with haste, for indeed there were many of them.

Graves were dug near the camps. The army had lost more than three hundred archers that day, while as to the foot soldiers and the pilgrims, no one knew precisely. Each group was counting its own. They were laid ten to a trench, without tears or outward mourning. Theirs is the joy of martyrdom and the joy of victory, so great is the joy of the victors. Jesus Christ has triumphed over the Sultan!

In the camp, the children were crying and could not sleep for thinking that the Turks would come again. They heard the sound of trumpets and the crying of the vultures and began to scream, "The Turks! The Turks! The arrows!" The Sultan's sheep were roasting on spits over the fires, and the injured lanced their wounds and cauterized them with red-hot embers. No one complained. Thanks be to God, this field would not become a field covered with Christian bones. Friends and kinsmen met again as though after a long absence and kissed one another, weeping. All enmities were forgotten and everyone was laughing.

Bernard's Martine was sitting with her Flemish soldier on the slope near the fire belonging to the pilgrims of Arras. They were hugging and kissing openly and looking deep into each other's eyes as though they had been alone in the middle of a field. "Oh Dirck, oh Dirck, oh thank God, Dirck!" Martine was crying but they were tears of joy. She was laughing and crying and Dirck was crying too, and such was the grace of that strange night that no one, not even Bernard, dared to say a word.

Élie le Grêlé came in from the field with four of the young men. He held a torch and the young men carried big wicker baskets, bent double under the weight of them. "Hey, what have you got there?"

"Take a look." The baskets were set down on the ground and Élie lifted his torch. Inside were heads, human heads with shaven crowns and long whiskers and black beards.

"Thirty-six. Come here, children, no need to be frightened of the Turks any more. This is what we do to Turks."

When Brother Barnabé heard of it, he went straight up to le Grêlé and knocked him on the head with his staff.

"Get that lot out of here at once. Those heads will do better with the vultures than with you, you carrion bird."

Élie rubbed the bump on his head, impertinently.

"Saving your presence, Brother Barnabé, I am no carrion bird. Ask my boys here how many living men I killed with this same ax."

"You could hardly kill dead ones. The living we killed this day because God permitted it, but the dead will be left in peace. Do you understand that, excrement? Have you forgotten, by any chance, who it was saved your life?"

"By no means," said le Grêlé. "I have not forgotten, Brother Barnabé. If I had, I would not be listening to you now."

Jacques had slain three men with his ax that day, all of them probably more experienced fighters than himself, but smaller in stature and less enraged, and unused perhaps to being assailed by a man brandishing an ax. Where the good craftsman chisels the stone, the bad workman simply hacks away. It was not funny, it was dreadful even, yet at the time, amid the tumult and the dust, Jacques had not thought at all. He was out of his mind. It was during the pursuit, when they were all running and the Turks were running as well, so that it was hard to tell any more if a man was a Turk or not. You simply ran and shouted, and then this one had turned and raised his sword, and seeing the sword, Jacques had leaped back a pace and struck. The man fell, and he had gone on running. Now he was wondering how Jesus Christ had saved him. Only a scratch on his left thigh.

He had been so afraid that they would none of them live through it. Marie. Marie. The idiot, running about with a bucket of water and an arrow in her left arm, her pretty arm and that ugly wound that had to be cauterized with red-hot embers.

"Does it hurt?"

"Oh no." But her teeth were chattering.

Ever since Constantinople it had been common knowledge

that Alix nearly always managed to get hold of a little wine. She had some that night. They had not bothered to put up the tents, but the air was chill and a fire was burning, fed by the young men with an assortment of broken arrows, dry grass, and splintered shields. They were singing and Alix was sitting on a boulder, draped in a Turkish man's robe which someone must have plundered from the Sultan's baggage, for it was a robe of purple silk trimmed in gold, with wide sleeves. And Alix sat there on her boulder, clapping her hands in time to the singing.

"That's it, my children, for once you are entertaining me. I'm worn out, let's all sing! Let's have another one, for pity's sake!" The song was a merry one, one of those Jacques remembered hearing on his wedding night, and it made him want to dance, only they were all too tired to dance. Singing with them, Jacques was suddenly seized with a wild longing to be back again in the meadow beyond the faubourg, beneath the willow trees that grew along the Scarpe.

"Alix. Have you any wine, Alix? For Marie."

She bent down and gave him a small cask that stood at her feet. "It's lucky there's some left. Here, take it, take it and share it with Marie. Oh, my fine lad, God knows I love you, God knows I love you all! My heart is torn and bleeds with love for you!"

She spoke with a reckless tenderness, her voice breaking slightly, and in spite of all her efforts to be gay she suddenly let her lovely head with its long tumbled hair droop on her knees, and burst out crying.

"Alix," the young man said, "it is a sin on such a night!"

"Oh, I know, I know, if ever there was a day for joy it is today. Am I mad? I who have no one to mourn for? Ah, those brave archers! My friends, *never were there such brave lads as they!*" The young men cried with her, but they soon began to sing again. All of them were slightly drunk. Jacques went off with his few sips of wine in the cask, feeling almost sorry he was married, so pretty did Alix look in her Turkish gown.

Marie was asleep, still shivering with fever. He woke her and made her drink. "Jacques," she said, "the child."

"What is it?"

"He is still there. He is moving. He was scared today, but now he is jumping for joy."

"Marie, I got three Turks. Marie, they were real Turks. They were much older than I am. They had beards, too."

She was not listening. She was asleep with both her arms

twined fast around Jacques's neck. He was still thinking of the Turks, and as he sank into sleep the din of battle raged again inside his head: *the screams, the screams,* and the arrows, arrows falling all around him, and he felt again the weight of his ax heavy in his hands, hacking and hacking, hack away for love of Jesus Christ, hack for Jesus Christ. Oh God, God, is it true? That we have won?

Who could describe the Christians' joy and their just pride, and their gratitude to Jesus Christ? The next day was a trying one in itself. Everyone was feeling the pain of his wounds and the ache in all his limbs. They were dropping with sleep, but the heat and the flies and the screams of the vultures kept them awake. They dragged themselves about like drunken men from one place to the next, looking for a patch of shade. Yet all the time their hearts were filled with a joy that nothing could shatter. They had looked forward so long to this encounter, remembering the martyrs of Nicaea. And God had worked the miracle.

He will work others yet, believe it, brothers, if you persevere in faith and humility! *Beware of thinking you put the Turks to flight by your own merits. Stronger armies than yours have failed to withstand them!*

But God has delivered them into our hands because of the sign of the cross.

Let us not throw away the advantages of His great favor. Let us pray and purify ourselves and do penance for the blood that has been shed; let us praise our martyrs and do justice to those who fought so well.

Know that yesterday fiery angels came down from heaven and flew above the heads of our knights, spreading terror in the hearts of the Sultan and his emirs. Those angels were the souls of the martyrs of Nicaea, and on this day of grace have they been avenged. Let there be no weeping or mourning. Our friends go with us to Jerusalem, from the first of the sick buried in Hungary to our brothers who died of their wounds this morning!

But how long and painful the road would be, not even the wisest preachers could foretell. For the country they had to cross was like no other country. There were few villages, and all ruined or deserted; few fields, and most of those had long lain fallow: a parched land, without rivers, or with those there were nearly dried up. When the horses and oxen were led down to drink, they could hardly wet their noses and rasped their nostrils on the stones. It took a half-hour's scraping to fill a bucket, and water was so strictly rationed that the men had to be satisfied with three mouthfuls in the morning and three at midday, while even the children had very little more. The roads were stony and the wagons lurched and bumped so badly that the pregnant women actually preferred to walk, and the sick had to be carried on stretchers. The children could endure the jolting, but they cried with thirst all day long and nearly drove the people walking beside the carts insane.

It was impossible to travel through the middle of the day. The sun burned hotter the farther they went from the sea: every day two or three old people died of the heat, and the ground was so hard that they could not even be buried decently. The very earth cracked with the heat, and by noon no one could see at all; everything was white and there was a red mist before their eyes. Hardened soldiers, and even knights protected by their thick helmets lined with down, collapsed and fainted, lucky indeed if there was water to revive them. There was no shelter in the tents because the sun made them so hot that it was like being in an oven. The stones were burning hot to the touch.

It seemed a wonder that the flies did not drop down dead of the heat, but they followed the columns of the army in thick black clouds, settling on anything that still had a drop of moisture in it. The horses were soon spent and started trembling and pawing the ground, because they suffered more from thirst than the men, although three quarters of the water supply was kept for the horses and cows.

At every town they came to they drove out the Turks, and the free Christians came out in procession to greet the army, and the Greek and Syrian priests fell on their knees and gave thanks to God. Then quantities of jars containing water and wine and hydromel would be sent out to the army from the town, for these good people would themselves go without for the cause of Jesus Christ. These vessels were hoarded more carefully than holy relics, *and the order went out that any man who stole one would be put to death.*

But if the horses were not to die they had to have water, and the oxen also: there could be no cheating them. What a man may endure cannot be expected of an animal. The stores of water soon vanished. Is it right, to deprive children of water in order to give it to the animals? Which is more important, the child or the animal? Only fools said that. Without horses for battle or oxen for food and to draw the carts, how shall we cross this land? Without animals, we may as well lie down on the ground and die. Even the knights dismounted and went part of the day's march on foot to spare their horses, and they were all in full armor for fear of attacks by bands of Turkomans, so that walking was a great labor for them.

Fodder began to run short: the earth was too dry and nothing grew but hard, prickly scrub, all yellowed by the sun. Scouts were sent out in all directions, accompanied by men with scythes, to look for some hill or valley where the grass was sweeter, and sometimes they would return dragging sacks heaped with poor yellow fodder, drier than husks and all mixed with thistles. The beasts ate it because they were no more anxious than the men to die. But they died all the same. After each halt the army left behind a dozen horses, already covered with flies, like a fall of black snow, while clouds of vultures would appear from nowhere and start wheeling overhead. The farther they advanced into this country the bolder and more numerous these hordes of vultures became. Men shot arrows at them and they fell, which at least provided some blood to drink.

The flies stuck to everything, to the meat and biscuit, so that it was all anyone could do not to eat them. They got into your hair and your beard and even up your nostrils, until you wondered where they came from, there were so many. After all, there was not a great army every day for them to follow . . . They come from the sheep, the Turks have huge flocks, hundreds of thousands of them, and they take them up into the mountains in the summer.

It was true there were not many sheep to be seen, or many Turks either. They are wise to flee this land in summer. The Christians were all in fortified towns, but although these had fields and vineyards around them, the harvest and the vintage were over and everything, fields, meadows, and vineyards, had a scorched look as though nothing had ever grown there. By nightfall the stones were so hot that one could have cooked cakes on them, but the darkness fell swiftly and at once the air grew cold, and then a dry, suffocating heat rose from the earth and the rock. They walked with faces upturned to breathe the almost icy freshness that descended gradually from the starry sky.

And what a sky! It looked as hard and solid as one vast block of marble, cracked everywhere with stars all shivering at once with such a brilliance that it seemed as if any moment they might all come unstuck and fall to earth. There were so many shooting stars that people gave up counting them and merely cried out sharply to ward off the errant soul. Where do they fall? Far beyond the horizon, in the boundless seas where the sun rises. Ah, if it had not been for the thirst, the night marches would not have been too bad. For two months now they had been journeying like this, always wondering if the next day they would not leave some dead behind them. The endurance of the poor was almost unbelievable: at noon the old would lie, sick and shivering with fever, under awnings of scorching sacks, apparently at the point of death, while the priest administered the last rites. By the miracle of the sacrament, when evening came they had recovered their strength, and a few days later they would be insisting that they no longer needed to be carried on stretchers. The children were thin, their arms burned black by the sun and their bodies covered with insect bites, but they had grown so hardened to the life that they could run barefoot over the ground while it was still hot, and never cried when they cut themselves on sharp stones. The older ones made themselves useful by waving small thorny shrubs pulled up by the side of the road to drive away the flies, and those who were most popular in the camp, people like Brother Barnabé and Father Berthold, or Mère Corneille or even Alix, each had their own personal fly-swatters. Élie le Grêlé actually had two little fly-swatters vying as to who should serve him best.

Two of the women from Arras were brought to bed somewhat before their time as a result of the heat, both on the same day. They were put on stretchers as soon as they were delivered, because it was time to move on again. The newborn infants were strong and lusty and screamed at the top of their lungs, but within five days both were dead because their mothers had no milk. Marie was a little scared and her thoughts went to the fairies of her home who, poor things, were far away. Her belly was not very large and she was still quite slender, but Mère Corneille told her, "It will be your turn in a month or two, so take care. It is time you kept your eyes away from knives or anything that might frighten you."

That was easily said, and at home in Arras it would have been frightening to see two little dead babies laid in a stony hole in the ground, or the face of a blind person with the eyes crawling with flies and the nose eaten away by sores that were a mass of flies as well, or a maddened horse escaping from the knights' camp and plunging in among a flock of sheep, trampling and biting, or men writhing on the ground in convulsions; or vultures and rotting carcasses, and Turkish horsemen rising like phantoms on the hilltops and rolling huge boulders down the slopes. Here, nothing was frightening any more.

Not even the midday sun. You lay still under a sack, like one dead, waiting for the three mouthfuls of water. You held each mouthful in your mouth as long as possible and it was like coming to life again. The child kicked. He too was thirsty. God's little creature, if you are a boy I will call you Pierre and if you are a girl you shall be called Armelle.

When the sky began to glow red-hot in the west, gold and red about a huge fiery sun, then the men's thoughts began to turn to lovemaking. Then Jacques would come and lie beside her and make love to her, and whether it was in spite of his fatigue or because of it, he was growing more ardent than a flaming brand. He grew so fierce in his lovemaking that he would bite and gnash his teeth like a wolf, and even so Marie loved him, even with his face on fire and the sweat running out of his hair, even when his shirt was soaking and his whole body sticky with sweat and his arms and neck burnt by the sun (for the sun here raised sores on the arms and pierced through shirts and raised sores on backs and shoulders). So it was with many of the men: the heat and the flies and the glaring sunlight went to their heads and made them lie with their wives, like animals, in broad daylight and as it were in full view of anyone. In any case, it was hardly possible to put up a tent for every couple, and so even the most modest of women lost all sense of shame, not for their own pleasure but rather than disappoint their menfolk, and because of this no one thought to blame them.

Before they moved on, the jug would be passed around and everyone would receive his ration in an oxhorn and drink it slowly.

Truly, this land was the gateway to hell. Such water as there was was too brackish to drink and the plants, which in other places God made to grow for the refreshment of men, were misshapen and monstrous with thick, soft, snaky stems and leaves as big as flat cakes growing one out of another. These devilish plants were covered with spines that were thin but sharp as needles, so that when anyone tried to pluck them he pricked his hands and the prickles stung worse than mosquito bites. When these big leaves were broken open, the inside revealed a moist green flesh the mere sight of which was enough to make one's mouth water. People would suck and chew them as a cure for hunger and thirst, but the taste was bitter and this deceitful sap burned the stomach. Yet nevertheless people ate these plants, for even that was better than dying of thirst.

Then God took pity on His people and brought them into valleys where real trees grew and rivers ran. The Christians had endured the months of greatest heat as expiation for their sins, but alas for the animals and the little children who had not sinned, why must they be made to suffer such torment? The splendid horses purchased at such cost, cared for with such love, and trained with so much patience must now be watched sinking to their knees and scraping their muzzles on the ground and dying, all for want of a little hay and a little water which in Christian countries could be had for the asking.

By the time the nights grew as long as the days and the army entered a country of upland valleys, of wooded hillsides and blue distances, half the horses had perished and more than a third of the oxen and cows. Hundreds of soldiers had died of heat, for the sun here killed more swiftly than a spear thrust, while as for the poor, who had much less protection than the soldiers, they had died in even greater numbers. Yet God in His goodness did not send all hardships at once, and the Turks did not show themselves again. The moment the army came in sight of a fortified town, these devils were filled with terror at the sight of the cross and by the fame of the Christians, and they leaped into the saddle and left the town by night; or if they did not, the Christian inhabitants of these towns would drive them out or kill them and then come out to greet their brethren with tears of joy.

Praise be to Jesus Christ who has sent you to us from your distant lands in pity for our sufferings. People of Gaul, illustrious home of so many great martyrs and confessors, noble land of the setting sun, the glory of your arms makes the Hagarenes tremble as far as Babylon! May you soon restore the great city of Antioch, the home of Saint George, to Christendom! These people, who did not speak French, brought many Norman interpreters with them, and the Greek general Taticius, who was accompanying the army with three thousand of his men, went about everywhere with the barons to explain to them how matters stood in that country. But this general was not greatly loved in the land, and the nobles and prelates of the liberated cities sent their interpreters to the Count of Toulouse and Duke Godfrey. "We have great respect for your illustrious country and for the Pontiff of Rome," said the interpreters, "and we would have men of your race for our military governors, for their courage is without equal." Speeches of this kind traveled quickly through the camps until even humble soldiers of fortune and one-time craftsmen grew conceited at them and began to regard themselves as sons of Charlemagne.

Outside the city of Gocosa, Isabelle was brought to bed of her little girl. It was early in October and the weather was still hot and dry, but the place had a river and several springs. When they halted to make camp after a long march Isabelle was so thirsty that she drank three cups of water straight off. She was taken with her pains almost at once and delivered before the tents were up. This was a great joy to the pilgrims of Arras and of Flanders, because everyone loved Isabelle and the women had been afraid that, ill-made as she was, delivery might be impossible. But the child came into the world with no difficulty at all, underneath a big olive tree all covered with ripe olives. There was water, and Mère Corneille was able to wash the child in a full bucket of water, while the priestess and Alix and several women who were skilled in such matters stood around Isabelle in her labor, hiding her with their skirts and singing to keep away ill luck.

Because Isabelle had drunk water and because that day there was water for everyone, it was decided that the child should be baptized by a name associated with water. The curé, the child's grandfather, was consulted and chose the name Ondine. It was true that this was not a saint's name, but there is nothing holier than water to those who have known thirst.

May she be always like refreshing and life-giving water, may she be as good as clear water, and a joy to the hearts of her parents. Isabelle sat up proudly to catch a glimpse of her child as Corneille showed her off to the men. Ah, the darling baby, a real little bunch of wild roses! Already they had forgotten what it was like, that clear pink flesh, a little face untouched by the sun, and little new white hair that neither sun nor lice had ever touched!

While they were preparing the water for the baptism, a messenger came from the camp of the knights of Boulogne to find Lambert and the priestess. He told them that one of the Countess's ladies had just been brought to bed of a stillborn girl and that she begged Isabelle's family to accept a few presents for her sake: three wax candles for the baptism, some baby clothes and an embroidered bonnet, and a shift for the mother. Through these things which had been made ready for her child, the lady hoped to comfort herself a little in her own grief by joining in the joy of another mother. Lambert and his mother were both very nervous and wanted to refuse, but the curé told them they must not grieve a Christian woman for the sake of vulgar superstition. So they accepted the things, and when Isabelle saw the gifts she began to sing for joy and call all her friends. The clothes were of fine linen, the cap worked with the lady's arms in fine needlepoint, and the shift was red with a trimming of green embroidery. Oh Isabelle, it was no bad fairy who gave you your crooked back for a gift! You could have no better provision for your first lying-in. They do not make such fine stuff even in Ghent.

Little Ondine, in a cap rather too big for her and all embroidered in gold and blue and purple, looked like a fat flower bud in an enameled cup. Marie hung over her, crooning.

"Oh, she's so pretty, with her little white eyelashes and her little bright eyes! Oh, if only mine is a boy, we'll marry them to each other."

"Yes," said Isabelle, "and we'll lay them in the same cradle. And I'll lend you my shift for your lying-in."

"Oh, what a sweet girl you are!" Sweet Isabelle was, and pretty. Her face was round and soft, and her eyes very big, with dark-brown smudges under them. She was a funny girl, and when anyone mentioned her back she would open wide, astonished eyes as if she had never known she had a hump. Whether deliberately or from foolishness, she seemed never to remember her deformity. She was vain and lively and happy. "We pretty ones," she would say to Marie. The young men liked her too, and her husband was jealous. That day she was glowing with pride, as if her little Ondine would bring luck to the whole army.

Their stay in that place was a pleasant one, but the next day they had to go on. The vanguard of the army had set out long before, and they were loading skins full of water onto the carts when the criers came with a proclamation: To avoid Turkish ambushes in this region, we must go by a mountain road that is very hard and so narrow that two horses cannot go abreast. There will be no halts, by day or night, so be prepared. Get the sick and the children off the carts and harness the beasts in single file. Know that once we are over the mountains, we shall be in a land full of vines and orchards and you will have three days to rest.

What a march! First they had to wait all day long because drawn out in single file like this, the army did not move fast. The column of knights and foot soldiers and carts and cattle and pilgrims stretched out along that fiendish road, fit only for occasional mule-drivers, like a huge rope two leagues long. It was impossible to move fast because in places the stone-breakers had to go to work with picks and mallets in order to shift a portion of the rock and make a way for the largest wagons. This led to falls of rock which made the road more dangerous than ever, as it was not built for the passage of such vast numbers or for such heavy weights.

Unload the carts. Let the men share out all they can carry on their backs, and lay boards underneath the wheels. The boards slipped on the big rounded stones, and the wagons had to be held upright by main force and by ropes passed around the axles. The road had a wall of rock on the right and a precipice on the left so steep that no one who fell over could hope to climb up again. Moreover the cliff was three or four hundred feet high at the least, bare and stony, without a tree to cling to, only thorn-bushes. Even to look down was enough to make a man dizzy, and since the entire army had already passed along the road before the pilgrims, the surface was so worn that they could almost feel the earth giving way under their feet. Loud cries of men and animals could be heard all the time, as the horses and even the oxen and mules panicked in terror of falling over the cliff and had to be beaten to make them go on, while sometimes horses and riders lost their footing and hurtled down the slope, bouncing off the rocks, until the face of the cliff was stained all over with blood.

There were even some places where there was no slope at all, only a sheer and apparently bottomless precipice. The children screamed in terror. Be quiet, for God's sake, be quiet. You are frightening the animals. *Keep close to the wall.* For two days and two nights this march went on. The signal to halt was passed along the column to allow a chance to slow down and pause for breath. Pitchers of water and dry biscuits were passed from hand to hand. The old sat on the ground and the rest leaned back against the rocks and shut their eyes. At the bottom of the slope could be seen still figures lying in strange attitudes like stuffed dolls, with the vultures above, looking at that distance no bigger than blackbirds. They grew accustomed to marching like this. It began to seem as though they had been marching for a week and would go on marching for another month.

It was here that Marie's pains began. She could not have chosen a worse day. She was walking, leaning on Jacques's arm and carrying a big bundle of clothes. The pains came more and more frequently, but she took no notice. Then she screamed and Jacques said, "What is it? Did you twist your ankle?"

"No, no, it's nothing." But Mère Corneille, who was walking in front, turned around and looked straight at Marie with her little sharp black eyes and caught her lip between her teeth. Then she took Marie by the arm and pushed Jacques in front. "Let her be. This is not men's business. Catch up with Girard and don't look around."

Jacques was horrified. "What is happening?"

"Nothing for men's eyes. Pray to the Holy Virgin and stuff up your ears with your jacket."

"What?" Marie said. "Is it true?" She was frightened because although she was still walking, her legs were beginning to drag. Mère Corneille took hold of her left arm and a woman named Richaut grasped her right. "Walk. Walk. And if God wills, all will be well."

It was impossible to stop walking. Behind them were the Picards, with carts and mules and an ox.

"Mère Corneille, what will happen to me?"

"God willing, this will last until tomorrow and we may be in the valley by then."

Until tomorrow? Oh God, Holy Virgin, this pain until tomorrow! Keep walking, we're holding you. You won't fall. It was terrible, frightful, unbelievable, it was a red-hot iron searing and burning in her belly. She screamed with pain in a voice to split heaven and earth apart, and the two women on either side of her tightened their grip on her arms.

There was a sound of curses behind them and a clatter of hoofs and the noise of stones falling. "For God's sake, Marie, don't scream. Hold it back. You are frightening the mules."

"Yes, Mère Corneille, it's gone. It doesn't hurt now. Tell Jacques it is gone."

"You think so, my poor child! It's just beginning. Here, take my kerchief. Stuff it in your mouth and bite on it hard."

Jacques was trying to get back to her, but he was pitchforked on again. "Stay where you are, you fool! You'll bring the evil eye on her." Marie had stopped screaming, and when the pains came again she bit on the ball of cloth, all wet with spittle, that filled her mouth. Then the pains would go away again, and still she kept on walking. She would have given anything to go down on her knees. Walk, Marie. Walk, Marie. Don't stop. They'll give us a stretcher soon. Oh, the pain is unbelievable, it cannot be true, never was there such torture, such torture is impossible, impossible, any more and I shall jump over the edge. Why should it be such torture? It's not right! Don't excite yourself, don't worry, don't worry, you are not the first to go through it.

Marie felt her entrails tearing apart. Warm water was running down her legs. Some powerful animal was imprisoned inside her, thrusting outward, forcing her legs apart to free itself. She gave a triumphant sob, spat out her gag, and screamed, "Mère Corneille! Mère Corneille, he is here! He is coming! He has come!"

"Mercy!" the old woman cried. "Stop, you there, you behind, for pity's sake!" She knelt quickly at Marie's feet, holding out her skirt. The child slid into it. Marie felt it rush out of her and slip between her thighs. She had stopped walking, and the women with her. Mère Corneille cut the cord with her teeth and made a knot on the child's belly, and in her hands the baby shuddered and threw back its little head, all sticky with blood, and howled.

People behind were calling out: "Hey there! You from Arras, don't block the way! Keep moving! The Picard oxen are on top of us."

"Stop bellowing, back there. We can't help it. A woman's just given birth on her feet. You don't want to kill her?" Regardless of modesty, the men walking behind lifted Marie bodily and six of them made a litter for her with their crossed arms until a stretcher could be passed forward. And so they went on, with Marie lying on the men's arms with her head hanging back, clutching the child wrapped in Mère Corneille's kerchief to her breast.

All this took place in broad daylight under a glaring sun that drained sweat and strength from the body and caused blood vessels to burst, which was why many women were taken with their pains in the course of that forced march. The blood vessels burst in their bellies and brought on labor, even when they were a long way from their time. Bernard's Martine lost her child in this way, and God knows how many other women, rich and poor alike. In the course of that march the screams of women in labor echoed from end to end of the army, and for every child born alive there were at least ten more born prematurely, no bigger than rats or weasels.

By that night, under a moon so bright that sky and earth looked white, the whole army was already spread out along a flat road and the gentle slopes beside a little stream lined with willows and olive trees.

It did not seem possible that they could again see willows shining in the moonlight. They had forgotten that the earth could be rich and grassy. When the signal to halt was given, passed on from the front of the column to the rear, no one thought of putting up the tents. They lay down on the ground among the long dry grass and the stones, and under the thornbushes. They did not even think to unhitch the animals, they did not think at all. Everyone slept. The Turks could have come at that moment and slaughtered even the knights with no trouble at all. Even the sentries dropped like stunned men at their posts, and the sick no longer felt their aching teeth or the pains in their stomachs.

The next day they set up camp. It had been decided that they were to have a few days' rest. The town by which they were encamped was full of Christians, and the people of the villages were Christians also. All the Turks had gone, and those who would not go had been killed by the people of the place and their bodies hung on the walls. *Know, the barons proclaimed, know all of you, soldiers and pilgrims, that no wrong must be done to the people of this place, who all worship Jesus Christ!* You have come here to make them rich, not to despoil them. Pay the proper price for food and fodder, that you be not called robbers. The rich applauded these words, but not so the poor, for here was fruit and corn and beans but still there was not food for the whole army. The rich were able to pay, but the poor could not. God be thanked, there was water in the river, and for the length of a league the banks were turned into watering places and washing places and public baths, while the young men made rafts and fastened them with ropes to willow trunks and tried to catch fish in the center of the stream.

Marie lay on a sack slung between two olive trees and rested after the previous day's ordeal. The curé from the faubourg came to baptize the child and gave it the name of Pierre. Sir

Evrard and Alix, godfather and godmother, stood side by side, still pale and tired but smiling, for they were both courteous and mannerly. The curé himself could hardly stand upright. He muddled his Latin and his hands were shaking so that he could not hold up the child's head. When the baptism was over Alix said to him, "Father, I know where to get you some wine. Do not refuse it if I bring it to you."

"I thank you for your goodness, my daughter. My flock must forgive me, I have not much strength left to give them."

The good man kissed the baby Pierre and gave him back into Marie's arms. "Be happy, mother, and care for this child so that he may live and become a good Christian."

Then he went and lay down beside the cart that carried the tools and began quietly murmuring psalms. In a little while his voice gave out and he started sighing and moaning: "Lambert, Lambert, stay here, Lambert. Do not leave me. Do not leave me alone, Lambert—"

"Father, where is your pain?"

"In my whole body, son, and my whole soul. I shall not last beyond tomorrow."

He died the next day, in a gentle, Christian manner as he had lived, without great pain. He had no actual disease: he died simply of exhaustion. He confessed his sins to Father Berthold and received the sacrament. He wept and asked his life's companion to forgive him for causing her to live in sin for so many years.

"Have I ever complained, curé? *Have I ever complained?*"

She stayed there on her knees beside his bed, holding his hand and refusing to let it go. The curé asked forgiveness of all his parishioners who were in the camp, for what he called his idleness and lack of care for them. Then, as his death agony came on and he could find no rest, he begged Father Berthold, "Go and fetch the Bishop of Lille, since our own Bishop is far away. Perhaps a bishop will absolve me of my sin!"

"Father, you are absolved already by the sacrament of confession."

Seeing that the poor curé's soul could not bring itself to quit his body, Brother Barnabé took his great staff with the cross and set off, almost at a run, toward the barons' tents to find the Bishop of Lille, but they would not let him speak to the Bishop, and a message was conveyed to him on his behalf that the Bishop would not interrupt his devotions for a priest who had abandoned his ministry unlawfully and without leave.

"An act of charity," Brother Barnabé said, "is the best of all prayers."

"You yourself," said the Bishop's clerks, "are a wandering monk and a troublemaker. We know that your rightful place is in a prison cell in your own monastery. It is not for you to teach my lord Bishop what he should do."

"I am not teaching anyone," Brother Barnabé said humbly, "but a man is dying." But he could get nothing from them and went sadly back to the camp.

"Well," he was asked, "is the Bishop coming?"

The curé was still fighting death, his hands gripping the cross and his thin chest heaving with long, convulsive shudders.

"The Bishop over all bishops is here, curé," Brother Barnabé told him, "the King of kings, the Priest of priests. He is waiting for you to lift up your eyes to Him. Why do you need the Bishop of Lille?"

The dying man did not hear him. His breath came in gasps, like a dog panting for thirst; then it ceased altogether, and the priestess and Lambert and Isabelle began to wail and all the curé's old parishioners took up the cry.

There were some fifty there from the faubourg of Arras—fifty left of the eighty who had set out. Nine youths and unmarried men had enlisted in the Count of Boulogne's army and three women had disappeared, no one knew where, but the rest were dead, eighteen Christians in all. Now they were losing the curé, who had truly been a father to them though he was only a poor man, a father who had baptized all the young people and the children and had married even those aged forty or more, because he had been curé of the faubourg for twenty years. He had sung the mass for the dead for many, both old and young, and blessed the looms and the workshops, and led the processions in times of drought or scarcity of work. There had been times when people had been inclined to make fun of his priestess, who was pretty and liked to give herself airs, and at times they had held it against him when, at Christmas, he asked for payment of what was owing for the sacraments. Then he had come with them, leaving his parish, his church, and even his honor as a parish priest, to travel the roads like any workless man.

They all knew he had done it for Lambert's sake, yet all the crusaders from the faubourg had felt grateful to him and told themselves that he had chosen them of all his parishioners. He was not a very impressive man to look at, faded and stooping with a nose that almost met his chin, although not old: he was not quite fifty. For a year he had marched with his pack on his back and his pilgrim's staff, his eyes always searching the company of young men for his tall beanpole of a son, big bony Lambert with his bonnet forever askew. No doubt it was a sin for a priest to leave his curé for the sake of a carnal affection, but Jesus Christ, through the prayers of the Virgin, forgave a poor man for his loving folly! Now he lay on a litter of skins, lit by the last red glimmers of daylight, and his face, suddenly drained, seemed as if it were made of copper. His wife had combed his greying hair and folded his cold hands over the cross of oak. "Woman," Father Berthold said to her, "it is not for you to care for him any more."

The parishioners stood around the body, their arms hanging at their sides and their hearts too full to praise God. Why had the Bishop of Lille refused to come? It was Élie le Grêlé who spoke out that night, and he was known to be one who would rarely let his tongue run away with him.

"Brothers, friends, are we going to swallow this insult to our curé? There is a man who has traveled all this way on horseback, who has slept in a bed and never wanted bread, and yet he will not put himself out for the last wish of a pilgrim who has suffered hunger and weariness! Let us go, all of us, and tell this rich man's bishop that he is not a man and there will be no more bishops in Jerusalem! Jesus Christ wants no bishops who despise the poor!"

It was strange how they listened to le Grêlé, and before long he was standing up on a cart and waving his arms while all around him were crying out, "Shame on the Bishop!"

"They are made of the same flesh as we are," Élie was saying, "and they do not observe the vow of poverty! For a rich man he would have stirred himself, and he would have come with his cross and his ring!"

"You fools!" said Baudry. "What do you hope to gain? What is the good of making trouble?"

"You, Baudry," Lambert said, "you have never been one of us. He was never your curé."

"Look at them," someone said, "galloping over the fields with their hunting horns and their dogs and their prizes! Are they crusaders?" In fact, just at that moment, a number of knights and rich clerics who had been on a hunting party that morning were coming back from the forest. At once the rumor (actually quite untrue) began to circulate among the pilgrims of Arras that the Bishop of Lille had been one of the hunters. Loud, angry shouts arose in which the Walloons and Father Albert's Normans soon joined. Brother Barnabé appealed to Sir Evrard and his men: "There's to be no trouble in the camp. Keep your anger for the Turks."

"You blind fools!" said Father Berthold, getting up on the cart in his turn. "You call yourselves pilgrims and yet you insult Holy Church in the person of her pastors."

"We would be happy enough with pastors like you and Brother Barnabé," came the answer, "but we want nothing to do with rich people who go hunting and sleep on carpets!"

"Dolts! When a king rides through the streets, do you not lay carpets and flowers before his horse's hoofs? Is it the horse you honor? Do you complain if the horse drops dung on your woolen rugs? God's grace sits on the Bishop as the king on the horse. It is that grace you honor, because it comes to him direct from the Holy Apostles! Have a care lest in your dislike of the horse, you should spit on the king!"

These words of Father Berthold's provoked a good deal of laughter, and so, gradually, the anger of the people of Arras subsided.

Graves were dug, for the curé and for a number of other pilgrims who had died of exhaustion after the journey. The halt in this place of forests and streams should have been a time of rest, but the army was no longer in the mood for resting. The men were always on the move, strolling from one camp to the next gleaning news: where were the Turks, and what were they doing? Surely they must be gathering fresh armies. For three months now they had left the Christians in peace. Surely the winters must be mild in these parts and the infidels were waiting for the winter to renew the campaign? When they remembered the great battle, each one said to himself: God saved us then by a miracle but we shall never survive another such hard-fought battle!

After the ordeals of the previous week, Jacques could not get over the feeling that his body was young and strong again; even hunger made him feel like singing. To be in a land where there were real forests and vine-covered hillsides and where in the distance you could see a sparkling river deep enough to drown a man! It was neither hot nor cold and all the trees were still green. The far-off mountains were as blue as periwinkles and so cool that looking at them was like a drink of pure water. Is the Holy Land like this? So they say, only more beautiful because invisible angels hover over it continually and so the sky there is so pure and the air so full of light that every stone shines like gold, and the leaves are so green and the trunks of the trees so dark and the fruit so golden that it hurts the eyes.

We shall pass through great orchards where the apple trees are bowed down with fruit and vineyards where the grapes ripen three times a year. We shall go through fields of wheat where every ear bears seventy grains and meadows filled with black and white sheep. The wells there are deep and the springs are clear and cold.

Oh Lord, perhaps next summer we shall reach our journey's end!

Jacques thought about this land that was so holy and pictured it covered with white and gold crosses. The stars in the sky there arranged themselves in the form of a cross, the trees, the flowers, the birds were crosses, and the clouds stretched crosses of white and purple across the sky. Oh, what a light will shine that day when we touch the Sepulcher with our own hands! What shafts of invisible lightning are enclosed within it, so that each Christian who touches it shall be purged as though by fire and water!

How many of us will see that day?

He would never let himself die before that day. If he caught the plague, if he were mortally wounded, he would still cling to life, he would come alive through fire and water, but he would not be a martyr before he saw Jerusalem with his own eyes, with his, Bernier's Jacques's, own mortal eyes.

"Is it far yet?" He asked the question of Sir Evrard, who knew many people.

"Yes, over a hundred leagues, perhaps as much as two hundred. But the hardest part is still to come."

"What could be harder than last summer, with the battle and the heat?"

"There will be other battles. It is written in the Scriptures that the worst ordeals will come before the end."

The knight seemed out of spirits, and frowned when they talked to him about battles and the Turks.

"Surely," Jacques said, "God will help us."

"Listen to me, my lad, I made a vow once to love war no more. That vow I have kept, and I shall keep it, if God wills, as long as I live."

"You fought well when the Turks came!"

"Yes, lad, like a machine. If there had not been women and children to protect I should not have lifted a finger."

People were saying that Jacques of the Ax was a brave man and that he had already received his baptism of infidel blood. "God save him," they said, "you can see the weavers of Arras have good blood in their veins. The knights and the soldiers are not the only ones who can strike a good blow. We have our share of pluck."

"Father, I have killed." "A venial sin, my son. You were only defending yourself against the evil ones."

The other, they all knew, the other, the headsman, had plunged into the fray and brought down horses and riders with his ax. How had the Devil protected him? Surely God had forgiven him and accepted him into His service. Le Grêlé was well able to defend himself, and men respected him. It was during this halt that it became clear that in the eyes of the Normans from Italy, Élie was regarded as one of the leaders of the pilgrims of Arras.

Him! He's cracked or worse! But because he belonged to the faubourg, the weavers began to be proud of him.

At home Élie le Grêlé had not been regarded as a bad man. He was devout, he fasted when he ought, and never began a piece of work without first saying a prayer twice as long as that of any other weaver. Whenever he had no work, he would go off with all his family to the village from which his parents had come and live there as best he could by poaching in the lord's forests—a venial sin when a man has children crying for food—but in other respects he was honest, and he never borrowed a bowl of beans without returning it within the week. Moreover, at the time of taking the cross it was clear that he was no hypocrite: few men showed such sincere penitence on that occasion.

As he listened to Peter's sermon, he had had a terrible vision. When Peter described Our Lord's own land all bleeding from the cruel Turks, Élie had seen the body of Jesus Christ rise up before his eyes, so vast that it blotted out the mountains and the plains, lying at full length, white as wax and striped with bloody wounds which the Turks buzzed about like black flies, sticking lances and pikes into that most precious white flesh. In that moment

Élie was overwhelmed by such pity that he could not help himself and cried aloud for grief. He ran weeping to Peter's feet and made his vow and took the cross. But because his wife was very near her time he could not leave at once. (This was a thing that happened to many of those who took the cross in the beginning.)

But when the departure of the company from Arras under the leadership of Baudry and Brother Barnabé was settled on, Élie's wife was great with child again and she told her husband that far gone as she was, and with three children in arms, she would never take to the road, especially with winter coming on. So, seeing that neither blows nor prayers would overcome his wife's determination, le Grêlé set out alone, taking only his eldest daughter, Marina, who was old enough by then to look after a man. He was very fond of the little girl and hardly ever slapped her. When something had happened to Marina it had made him sick with anger, and that was the cause of his sin.

Immediately after the trouble, Baudry had arranged a marriage for the girl with a good stout lad, not much older than herself, who loved her. But for Élie, this was no consolation. A ruined girl was a ruined girl, and it seemed to him that all the weavers would have a right to spit in his face until he had his revenge. He lay awake night after night, brooding on his wrongs, until one day the temptation grew too strong for him. The fulfillment of his vengeance filled him with such joy that he accepted every punishment uncomplainingly. Dragging the heavy cart, enduring floggings, weeping and beating his breast, it all made him almost drunk with ecstasy and he would relive that winter's night near Belgrade, with the pale moon sailing behind small white clouds, the wagon where Guillaume lay asleep, then the slow, dreadful movement of his own arm, the grip of his hand on the knife, and the light, almost gentle action needed to slit a warm throat. The knife was well sharpened, and in one long, strong movement it had sliced through everything, until it met the resistance of the neckbone, scraping against the blade. And the way the warm lifeblood flowed out, pouring over knife and hand and trickling down his arm!

Élie le Grêlé was not a fine-looking man. His face had been so marked by the smallpox in childhood that it looked like a colander. He had a long, straight nose and colorless eyes set deep under pale, bushy brows. His head was rather small for his body, a big body, burly and powerful as a blacksmith's, and at thirty-three his back was hardly bent from his loom. He was not a bad weaver, but the loom was not in his blood. He was the kind of man that tends to imagine all sorts of things and is given to daydreaming, one of those who are forever thinking there is better work and better pay to be had elsewhere.

On the day of the great battle, he had been convinced that his forgiveness was complete. More than one man-at-arms had roared encouragement at the sight of him in his almost unpadded coat, swinging his ax and hurling himself furiously straight at the enemy horsemen. "What a pilgrim! There's a man who knows how to defend Jesus Christ! Have at them, villein! Stand firm, you're a credit to your village!" As if he came from some village! They took him for a peasant, him, a craftsman and the son of a craftsman! His dislike of Baudry sprang from the same cause, because Baudry treated him as an inferior, which he had no right to do. No, among pilgrims there were no masters and men.

PART II

5

At Antioch, the criers were sent around the whole army and to all the pilgrim camps with orders to prepare to go into winter quarters. A city such as this would never be taken by storm.

Because of the steeply undulating country, a good view of the city could be had from the hills across the river, and all knew that this was not going to be a matter of two weeks or a month or even, short of a miracle, of six months. The city was not so large as Constantinople, but it was still enormous. It spread over several hills along the river, and towering more than a thousand feet above at its eastern end was the citadel, perched on the side of a wooded, rocky height where there was no hope of establishing a camp. Double curtain walls a good two leagues in length ran around the city, broken every two hundred yards or so by strong defensive towers. These towers were tall and square with crenellated walls and were equipped to fire missiles from the roof, while in addition the river had been deflected by means of various channels to form a broad, water-filled moat around the whole west and southwest sides of the city.

At the sight of it, even those who were most ignorant of the arts of war breathed sighs of wonder and amazement, thinking: They were not mistaken when they foretold fresh ordeals in store for us. Jesus Christ is asking miracles of His followers! How did the Turks themselves ever take this city? For taken it they undoubtedly had, fifteen years earlier, profiting from dissension among the Christians.

Good God, is it so important that we take this city? Have we made any vows to liberate Antioch? Shall the home of Saint George take precedence over the home of God?

Unbelievers, will you incur the wrath of good Saint George in the very place of his earthly life? What saint could be a better protector to God's soldiers? *You ignorant fools, know that the end must be considered in all things. This stronghold is the real key to the Holy Land and as long as it is held by the infidel no Christian army can come to our relief,* and do you think the Sultan will sit by and watch with folded arms while we march into his domains?

Such is the ignorance and presumption of the poor and the common soldiery. When they set out from the West they were always talking about the Sultan and in Constantinople they were still talking about him, and after Nicaea, on the day of the battle, they had seen him at work with his terrible army. Now all those who knew anything about it were saying that there was more than one sultan and that the most formidable had his capital in Babylon, in other words Baghdad, five hundred leagues away. This great Sultan was so terrible that beside him the Sultan of Nicaea was no more than a petty princeling, and he ruled over all the countries of the East as far as India and all the Moslem kings were his vassals. In Babylon he was gathering unnumbered hosts to hurl against the Christians.

He had waited until they were close to his domains in order to make his attack more effective. And so, good pilgrims, if we fail to take this city we are lost, because we cannot withstand this army in the open field. Let us therefore pray to Jesus Christ and to Saint Paul and good Saint George.

Yet how is it possible to starve a city into submission when you cannot even surround it? It was so large and so widespread that the most that could be done was to dispose the various camps at a fair distance around the walls. For a good quarter of its length the outer wall could not be watched at all, either from close at hand or from a distance, while as for the rest . . . the Christian camps scattered on the plain and on the hillsides looked more like a tiny fair set up outside a great city. So, good crusaders, to work! Assemble all the men, except for the bowmen and the noble squires, and divide them into teams: some to fell trees and roll them down into the valley, others to dig trenches. If we are to stay here till spring, we must make permanent encampments before the winter rains begin.

The weather at this season was still mild and autumnal although the nights were cold: a beautiful autumn of golden skies and golden fruit, with the lovely dying leaves of autumn glowing in splashes of red and purple, gold and rusty brown, amid the dark green of those trees that did not lose their leaves. Great flights of birds passed crying overhead: black nets cast on the pale-yellow sky. At sunset, the white citadel poised high above the town turned pink and gold, like a lighthouse rising from the blue city that already was twinkling softly as the lights began to shine out on the rooftops.

As you climbed the hills to cut timber you could see the city, more wonderful than the city of the Queen of Sheba. It was full of gardens surrounded by cypress trees, tall spires of white and rose soared above azure-colored domes, and as the sun went down, the stained glass in the churches and the long windows of the dwelling houses blazed with incandescent red and gold as if a myriad pacific fires were burning. The slopes were terraced with sprawling, flat-roofed houses, and by screwing up your eyes you caught a glimpse of archways and stepped streets and open squares lined with big green trees.

Dusk plunged the city into a dark-blue haze through which small flickering lights moved slowly, signs that people were walking in the streets with torches. Cressets flared at night on the outer walls and the soldiers exchanged signals, calling with long, harsh cries like some strange kind of bird. What vast garrison was needed to defend such a city? Were there perhaps ten thousand of them?

Within a week the hills around Antioch had lost their thick dark verdure and were transformed into timber yards. The noise of picks and axes and heavy tree trunks crashing amid a welter of branches could be heard as far away as the camp and even in the city. Not all the pilgrims were very expert woodcutters—there was more than one broken arm and more than one tree fell the wrong way—but for zeal in their work it would have been hard to find any to compare with these joyous laborers. The days were cool and the work warming, and lines of women climbed up from the camp bringing baskets of bread and vegetables.

The men sat down for their midday break in the midst of a chaos of fallen tree trunks, stripped bark, wood chippings, and lopped-off branches. They made fires of dry wood and sang as they cooked their vegetables over the flames. This was the life! They had never dreamed of such freedom: these rich forests all to themselves, the trees of these ancient forests falling one by one beneath the ax, to be stripped of their great branches the way an animal is skinned. There were cedars and pines and oaks, so heavy that dozens of men were needed to line them up at the top of the slope.

Then with a great shout they would pull on the ropes that held the huge props and watch as the sea of barked wood rolled down to the bottom of the hill, flattening shrubs and bushes and bounding clumsily over sharp rocks. The trunks piled up into gigantic heaps at the foot of the slope. The knights brought dozens of pairs of oxen and the trunks were loaded onto wheel bases.

With all this wood they could have built a town. We must work quickly, friends, because in these parts, once the rains begin there can be no more work done. Jacques was happier than he had ever been in his life. The work was hard, but the ache in his back and arms only made his thoughts turn to food and sleep. With his ax he rooted up saplings and ripped out bushes, some to build huts, some to make brushwood screens. We are building our winter homes! Down there in the valley, only half a league from the river, we have our own camp, protected by a ditch and a palisade, and there are cows and goats and no shortage of milk. Oh, this beautiful land where there is food and drink for everyone! Oh, this beautiful land with the blue mountains pointed like church spires, and the blue plain stretching westward to the sea where the sun sinks red among purple clouds. *The golden rivers of paradise flowed through the skies at evening, encircling plum-and-amber-colored isles, long ships decked with red-gold streamers drifted slowly, and dazzling shafts like angels' wings shot through the clouds to light the lovely city of Saint George.*

Each evening the Turks within the city chanted their prayers; from every tower the same long, piercing, melancholy cry arose and all movement ceased upon the walls. Within the camp a thunder of solemn voices echoed, singing the vesper psalms. Picks and axes ceased their work while men crossed themselves and thought of the evening meal. The city lay before them, peaceful in spite of all the soldiers on the walls and the towering engines of war. How soon the body forgets, and the heart more quickly still! It seemed to Jacques that the miracle had already happened and the battles would be like joyous games, the blood like wine, the arrows like birds, and they would enter into this city with banners shining in the sun and the sound of the *Te Deum* covering all the screams.

He was, yes, he was surely past his eighteenth year, nineteen perhaps, and his whole body thrilled to the great joy of not going hungry, to the knowledge that there would be food that night and his lovely Marie, recovered from her labor, sitting by the campfire singing and weaving baskets. He no longer had any regrets for his loom. With this life they had led for more than a year now, his heart was growing light and carefree as a child's. Each halt had been the starting point for a new life, and in the two weeks the army had been encamped before Antioch he had begun to feel as if he had always lived there. This life held no tomorrows. The tomorrows were all so different that life held no future. There was no future but Jerusalem.

Baby Pierre had blue eyes and a grave, stern face like a small adult. Baby Pierre had a long tuft of fair hair on his head, a sign that he would live. "Marie, you do not love me as you used to do. You think too much of him." "What lies! I love you more than ever. You have a beard now." How they laughed together once again! When you can eat your fill you laugh at anything, a sneeze, a fly in the soup . . . The curé is dead. We really ought not to laugh. But even Lambert was beginning to laugh from time to time, hiding his face behind his hand.

Isabelle and Marie both had milk and sometimes for a jest they would swap babies. "They will be foster brother and sister. Will we be able to marry them all the same?"

"Of course, and they will get along even better."

The two babies hardly looked at each other yet: infants three or four weeks old are too young for friendship. Their mothers chattered like starlings, for the children had to learn to talk. From the first day she had seen her son, Marie had known he was intelligent, that all he lacked was the power of speech and in a year, or a year and a half, he would be talking like a true Christian.

"Isabelle, oh Isabelle, I think he loves Ondine already. See how he looks at her!"

"That wouldn't be hard!" Isabelle said, a little smugly. Ondine was pretty in a way that was rare for so young a child, just as pink and white and chubby as ever. Her embroidered bonnet just fitted her little head now, and she was truly the princess of the pilgrim camp. Even mothers who had lost their own babies looked at Ondine with pleasure.

They had huts now, with foundations sunk a good four feet into the ground, with walls made of tightly woven brushwood and roofed with a close covering of pine branches. Even the women had helped in the work, building their own homes as if they were to live in them for years. The siege was not making much progress; the Turks in the city sat still, knowing they were not to be shifted by an army such as this. Meanwhile in the army, gangs of workmen labored at consolidating the camp and building wooden towers. But if the Turks did not stir from the city, the Christians did—the Christians of Antioch, that is—and many of them came out in a sorry state, without horses or mules, carrying all they had in bundles or even bringing nothing at all, having been expelled from their city simply because they were Christians.

Consequently, by the middle of November, there were many of these poor Christians in the camp. The rich had somewhere to go: some had relatives in neighboring cities, while others made their way down to the sea and embarked on Greek ships. The poorer ones went to the barons and explained, through their Norman interpreters, that they lacked the means to leave the country and wished for lodging in the shelter of the army lines because bands of Turks were roaming the mountains and the land was full of brigands. Moreover, the valiant Gauls owed them hospitality, for it was on account of their army that the Turks were treating the Christians so harshly. What could the barons do? They sent criers out: Soldiers and pilgrims, show a Christian spirit to your brothers and share your food with them. When the city is taken the Emperor will repay you for all.

All of which was quite right and proper, only as ill luck would have it, in November when the weather was beginning to change for the worse in earnest, the army commanders realized that provisions were left in the stores and reserves for only another two weeks at most, while the flocks and herds acquired from nearby villages had melted away like snow in sunshine. The land was rich but such a great army, numbering more than sixty thousand people, had never been encamped there before. Soldiers are big eaters and all the men, long hungry and underfed, were having to work hard. In a month they had eaten up reserves which should have been enough for twice that time.

The result was that throughout this great city-without-a-city which was the camp, there began to be talk of shortages of bread, of meat, of beans. It was useless to go and forage for them in the surrounding countryside; the peasants had sold all they could and were themselves on the verge of starvation. As time went by, the talk grew more and more alarming. It will be a hard winter; if you have any animals left, slaughter them but do not eat them, dry the meat, mix husks and powdered chaff in with your flour, do not eat more than once a day.

In short, there would be famine very soon. Then, since troubles never come singly, the weather broke suddenly and the country which had been so beautiful became horrible. For in France or Flanders or Brittany the rains fell in their season, more in one place and less in another, but always in reasonable amounts, so that even in the North drought was a more serious threat than rain. But here, with all due respect to Saint George, when it began to rain it ceased to be rain at all and became a flood!

At first the crusaders were amazed and said, "This is a fine downpour! The land needed it."

It was a quite extraordinary downpour. In three hours it rained as much as in three days in Normandy. In three hours. It went on all day long and all night too, and all the next day. And after that? After the torrents that came down in those two days there could be no more water left in the sky! And still it went on raining.

The river rose visibly. The trenches filled with water. The moat around the city overflowed. The hills became rushing torrents. Ditches had to be dug around the huts, but soon, although everyone spent the day digging ditches and building dikes, the huts themselves filled with water, and the children could not be left inside. They were not houses any more but water tanks. The men dug holes in the ground while the women scooped up the water in buckets and tubs and threw it outside, and all this in a driving rain that filled the little drains in two minutes so that more ditches had to be dug quickly to keep the water out of the houses. To no avail: the water came in everywhere. You could not even tell where it was coming from, whether from the overflowing ditches or the buckets as they were emptied, or out of the sky. There was no time even to pray, and yet they needed prayers! Lord Jesus Christ, Holy Mary, Saint George, have mercy, shut the sluice gates of heaven. We can take no more. We'd rather have the Turks!

In such weather as this not even the Turks could do anything except pray to their god Mahomet to make the rain stop.

It was some relief when this diabolical rain, although it did not stop completely, began to turn to something more like an honest autumn downpour in Artois. The water was still falling but quietly, in soft, fine sheets. By then many of the men had not eaten for twenty-four hours: there had been no time. They had been driven so hard that they were almost asleep on their feet.

They dropped onto sodden tree trunks, spitting out the water which ran from their hair into their mouths and wiping off their soaked jerkins with the flat of their hands. This rain was cold. In the panic rush of work no one had noticed. You had to work quickly, sweating and shivering at the same time. It was not until you rested that you became suddenly aware that your body was clamped between sheets of ice. No garments could keep it out. Those with fewest clothes were the lucky ones.

Well, it is still raining. If this will only stop, then, God willing, we can dry out the houses. Oh, the poor houses! Panting, Marie lifted the little screen of boards and skins they had erected to shelter the cradle containing the two babies. They were still quite dry and sleeping as soundly as in a house of stone. "Ouf, my little ones, you're lucky! It's good to see something dry." All day long Marie had done nothing but empty buckets, standing in the hut with the water up to her knees, and feeding the baby standing up, with a wooden tub over her head to protect the child. The bed that she and Jacques had made, the good bed of grass and dry leaves, was swamped in mud. It had been all she could do to save Pierre's things and their Sunday shifts by stuffing them into the cradle.

She and Isabelle fed the babies, crouching underneath the floorboards of a big wagon with three other women. The children were not wet but the mothers, sitting on the ground, were up to their waists in the muddy water that poured under the cart. Isabelle, who because of her crooked back had a thin and sunken chest and easily caught cold, was coughing.

"Goodness, Isabelle, how red you are!" Even when she stopped coughing her cheeks were on fire. "Oh, but it suits you, you know. You look so pretty, and your eyes are so bright."

Isabelle smiled, but her smile was a little twisted grin of pain.

The men stood about, dull and stupefied with exhaustion, too stunned to try and remedy the disaster. Over there, where the soldiers are, perhaps. Their houses are stronger and they have reserves of dry wood. But to reach the camp of the Boulonnais meant walking a good half-league across rivers of mud. Well, friends, if the Orontes floods we shall have to shift camp up the hill. They stared gloomily at the animals, shivering and snorting as they waded about in a black sea of mud and filth, munching at sodden hay. There were two donkeys, half a dozen goats, and one old cow, a local cow bought at Mamistra, besides Sir Evrard's three horses.

Brother Barnabé, after working all night digging drains, was able to say his prayers at last. It was still raining but this gentler rain, falling on clothes and bodies that were already soaked through, went almost unnoticed. You could see it falling in grey streaks and plopping into the puddles, but when it ran down your face you felt it no more than contact with the air. Brother Barnabé prayed, on his knees by a fallen tree trunk. He wondered what trials God still had in store for His poor. Men are such fools: they never know what they want. If anyone had said to us this summer that in three months' time we should be shivering and half drowned by torrents of water from the skies, we should have cried out, Oh for that blessed day!

Man is a miserable creature. He is never satisfied, for everything in this life is bad for him. This world, so wide and beautiful, was not made for man. This world is delightful to our eyes and fatal to our flesh. O Lord, we set out to seek Your love and Your forgiveness, and for a year all we have done is struggle over mountains and plains, through cities and deserts, fighting to keep alive.

And the poor, Lord, who in their own lands have known famine and weariness from childhood, in this year have known more weariness and thirst and hunger than they would have met with in their former state, but at least they have no other master but You. Will You be a worse master than the owners of the workshops and the great lords of this world?

O Lord, do not desert those who have left everything for You! It is Your will that they should have nothing left to lose, nothing left to sell, that they should come to Your Jerusalem as naked as the first man. A rich man loses only perishable things, Lord, but a poor man . . . It is on the flesh destined for resurrection that evil fastens, and when the flesh suffers so, the soul cannot easily escape harm. There are so many made martyrs that it is no longer a martyrdom but only a miserable death. Is it right that You should become a cause of shame for so many Christians?

It was a fact that everywhere, in the tents of the clerks and abbots as well as in the camps of the poor and among the soldiers' chaplains, people were beginning to argue increasingly about the fate of the martyrs who had fallen on the journey. The loss of human life was a surprise to no one. The general feeling was that the army had come out of it rather well to lose only one man in eight or ten.

It was a lot and at the same time very few. On the day of the battle the whole army, except for the knights, might have been left for dead. During the crossing of the desert, the officers of the Greek general Taticius had said that but for the visible help of God three times as many men must have perished of thirst and sunstroke. Your men are tough fighters, they said, because to fight the sun like this is more praiseworthy than fighting the Turks! Such endurance has seldom been seen, especially among men who are not of this land.

Yet already thousands of men had won forgiveness and many women, even among the richest and most noble. There was no one in the army who had not a kinsman or a friend to mourn.

What, have you forgotten the promises? No one shall lose the benefits of the great journey: today their souls are as it were in waiting, irradiated even now by the light of God's countenance. All shall share in the glorification of Jesus Christ, all but those wicked souls who have made the holy pilgrimage the occasion for sin. If these have met a martyr's death, they shall find their time in purgatory shortened but they are not yet in a state of grace. Therefore all Christians must remain vigilant and not say to themselves, Our sins do not matter, we shall become martyrs. *Let them strive not to die; if they are sinners, let them cling to life for as long as possible.*

They had hoped for a mild winter, but the winter was colder than any in France. The rains began again, and for the poor and for the common soldiery and lackeys the fight against the torrents of water that poured down from the sky became a losing battle, making them forget that the real enemy was the Turk. What mattered most was to build stout shelters, but there was no wood left; all the trees that had been felled had been taken to build towers. There were two towers now in Duke Godfrey's camp, one in Bohemond's, and one in the Provençal camp. These towers were as tall as the towers of the city and broader: they had four stories with platforms big enough for several catapults, protected by close buttresses of heavy timber. The soldiers of the Turkish garrison hurled missiles from the walls to such effect that now and then some part of the work would collapse, but these towers were so ingeniously constructed that even if the missile struck a king beam the rest held firm, and the broken part was replaced by a tree trunk from a store held in reserve.

In this way many men with no experience of carpentry became

excellent assistant engineers, for in this war all willing men were welcomed.

The camp commanders sent teams of men-at-arms, some with axes, others with picks and cudgels, into the hills west of the Orontes, which had not yet been deforested. There were good trees there, but unfortunately there were also Turkish ambuscades. When these Turks saw the Christian army virtually immobilized, they grew increasingly bold. It was not safe to venture into the hills except in companies of fifty men, and not always then. The Turks concealed themselves with drawn bows in the woods and loosed their arrows as the pilgrims drew near. Once they had broken cover, the important thing was to rush them with fearful shouts, waving axes and making as much noise as possible, before they could fit a fresh arrow to their bows. It was a kind of trick: you had to make them think there were a great many of you or else give the impression of being devils incarnate.

The trees were rolled down the slopes and then dragged along with the aid of big hooks, and eventually tied together in the form of rafts or floating bridges. In this way large and small trees were brought into the camp to build more huts. As to its being easy to work in driving rain on an empty stomach—well, it was not easy, but it had to be done in order to provide shelter for the sick and the young children at least, and if there were many fewer young children, there were vast numbers of the sick.

It had been raining for two weeks and in these two weeks, among the people of Arras and Liège and the Normans of Italy alone, half the infants in arms had died as well as fifteen children old enough to walk, and ten old men and four old women. It was the cold that killed them. It fastened on their chests, and it was no use going to the other camps in search of fire and dry skins. Burning brands were soon extinguished and skins were soaked again in a couple of hours because the roofs, hastily put together out of tree trunks, let in the water. As a result, both the old and the young started to cough and coughed incessantly, until at last their chests were so painful that they could no longer breathe. The old coughed out their lungs and died, the infants choked to death. They stopped digging ditches and dug graves instead, and the bodies were laid in trenches full of water.

Meanwhile the men shouldered their weapons, using tools as weapons and weapons as tools according to the needs of the moment, and ranged the countryside in search of food. For food was certainly running short, for the soldiers and even for the knights, and there was little to be had by begging, while to purchase even a crust of bread cost more money than a laborer could have earned in a month if he were working, and no one here was working except for those employed on the wooden towers. They went out in the rain along roads that had turned into stony torrents, heading toward the sea and avoiding the main road, following local guides who promised a quiet village where the peasants still had some sheep or olives or corn to sell. And when they got there they would find the village empty, or else the peasants would swear they had nothing left. Then the men—the soldiers, because they were always the boldest—would break into the houses and lay hands on anything they could find, chickens or sacks of corn. Rather than let the soldiers have it all, the others would follow suit, but the truth was that there was little enough to take. The peasant women wept and the men bared their chests to show the crosses they wore. Good people, if you knew what we have suffered this last year, you that have your chickens and your goats and your houses and fields!

Close to one village was a big abandoned house enclosed by stone walls. There was a way in through a gap in the wall, and inside was an orchard and cedars and black cypress trees. That day Baudry was leading a band of pilgrims, and he told his people to hunt underneath the trees for nuts or pine cones, or even for some olives still hanging ungathered on a branch, but the ground was sodden and everything they found was rotten. The most they managed to find was a few cedar cones. The men were so cold and hungry that they wept, their tears mingling with the rain on their faces.

The house must have been beautiful. Paintings of flowers and trees could still be seen on the walls, and the floors were paved with smooth black and yellow stones. The roof was falling in, and the small inner courtyard with a covered gallery and a pool in the center was all one puddle in which the big raindrops were performing a mad dance. The pilgrims sheltered under the colonnade of the gallery, and gazed up at the little red-and-black painted capitals, which showed here and there the marks of arrows. The marble basin of the tiny circular fountain was cracked in two and choked with broken tiles and fragments of ironwork. The house had been dead for some time, and now it seemed as if it had never been alive. The little columns looked so useless and pathetic in the driving rain that even the dead branches were a more agreeable sight. What a fine house, how rich the people must have been who lived there, and what a good life, in another age, when there was peace and sunshine.

There were shouts as something moved in one corner of the gallery, something the men had taken at first for a heap of dead leaves or old rags. A man rose and walked unsteadily toward them. They took him for a ghost or a Turk and reached for their weapons, but Baudry stepped forward, saying:

"Do not touch him. He is unarmed."

The ghost put aside his garments and showed his cross. He was dressed in a dark-blue robe and his hood had fallen back, revealing black, closely curling hair. He was very pale, his almost hairless cheeks were sunken and his eyes red and puffy. His lips parted to speak, but no sound came.

Baudry, although himself scared, tried to communicate by signs. Roumi? Antioch? The man spoke hoarsely—he had caught cold in his throat: "You, Gauls, Latins, brothers."

"You speak our tongue?"

"A little. Go with you. I go with you."

"We—no food," Baudry said. "You understand?" The man shrugged.

"What is your name?"

"Philotheus. Roman. Christian. Turks killed my father. My mother—" He began to cry, sobbing on a strange, high-pitched note.

And so Baudry's party returned empty-handed but bringing another local Christian, of whom there were already too many in the camp. The man did indeed speak French after a fashion, and he could understand nearly everything that was said to him. He told Father Albert that he had studied to become a commercial interpreter and had met many pilgrims and merchants from the West in Antioch. They adopted him because everyone was glad to find at last a man of the country with whom it was possible to talk. He was small and slightly built and his body was as soft as a woman's, with delicate hands, and feet that were now covered with sores because he must have been used to wearing good shoes. Although he had hardly any beard to speak of, he was not a youth but a rather withered young man, a true Greek of Antioch, the son of wealthy parents.

He wept as he told Father Albert that his father, a distinguished lawyer, had owned a great house in the city where his family had always lived, he said, and when the Turks came he had retained his post in the chancellery and, as a brave Roman who loved his country, had written secret letters in code which he succeeded in conveying to the imperial envoys. When the news of the great victories won by the Christians from the West reached Antioch, Philotheus' father had been unable to contain his joy, and there was such rejoicing throughout the city that the Turks themselves were afraid. The Christians sang in the streets and ran to the churches to give thanks, and the Patriarch commanded public and private prayers to be said for the success of the great undertaking by their Latin brothers.

Then, when the Christian army was already outside Antioch, someone who had a grudge against him had denounced Philotheus' father to the governor of the city, and on account of his secret letters the worthy man was dragged before the governor, tortured, and then crucified. As for his mother, oh his mother, would to God that she had died a week before, for in their hatred of the Greeks the barbarians had subjected her to the most shameful outrages so that this noble woman, finding herself so abused in her old age, had cursed the hour of her birth, and clasping an icon of the Virgin in her arms, had flung herself headlong from a tower. Miraculously, the icon had been preserved. Philotheus' brothers had had time to escape, and after his parents' death he had decided to flee also but had been waylaid by robbers who took from him all that he possessed, including his mule. He had wandered about the countryside, no longer having the spirit to leave his native land.

"Very soon now," Father Albert told him, "you shall have your house again and your enemies will be punished as they deserve."

What the Greeks and the other Christians had to say about the cruelty of the Turks increased the anger of the pilgrims. Their own sufferings seemed to them of little account: after all, they had brought them on themselves. But these good folk, who were being maltreated on their own lands and in their own houses, reminded the crusaders of their own homes and their aged parents, so that they began to picture the Turks violating their own aged mothers, and wept over the misfortunes of strangers for love of their own homes.

Because of this, these Christians who spoke an unknown language were well treated in the camp in spite of their complexions, which were in many cases dark. On the days when there was anything to eat, everything was shared with them, fairly. Unhappily, these people seemed to find the life of the camp offensive and tried to find shelter near the tents of the rich folk, who drove them away because they could not take in so many, so that Syrian and Armenian families were continually going from one camp to the next, taking advantage of a lull in the rain to gather up their belongings and move away down river toward the port of St. Simeon, only to come back again for fear of Turkish brigands. The camp was becoming more and more like a fairground, and finally the barons gave orders for all the local Christians to be put in one camp by themselves where food would be doled out to them by the officers of the Greek contingents.

Philotheus developed a great reverence for Brother Barnabé; he followed him everywhere and asked permission to become his disciple. Brother Barnabé answered that he did not surround himself with disciples but was the brother of all men. He himself worked as hard at the ditches and the building of shelters as any of the young men, and poor Philotheus tried to do the same, but he tired easily. However, though there was little strength in his arms, he surprised them all by the ease with which he learned the French tongue, and by his facility in interpreting other languages and working out prices and weights, so that by the end of two or three weeks he was able to be of great service to Baudry and Brother Barnabé.

He told them he spoke Arabic and Armenian and even a little Turkish and was able to write in all these languages. His Latin was not good, but he understood that also. Baudry, who could not read, was amazed to find so much learning in a man who was not even a churchman, and he asked the Greek how he was able to hold all these languages in his head without confusing them. Philotheus said it was because his parents, when they saw that he had a gift for learning, had made him a eunuch so that he should not be distracted in later life by the daily cares of a family and breadwinning, but would be able to devote himself wholly to some honorable career. Although he seemed proud rather than bothered by the fact that he was a eunuch, Baudry and Brother Barnabé pitied him exceedingly and privately condemned this cruel and unchristian behavior of his parents. "In our country," Baudry said, "you would never have been subjected to such treatment." But Philotheus said that it was good to make some small sacrifice and lessen the power of the flesh in order to augment that of the mind. He had two elder brothers, both of whom were married, and five nephews and four nieces, and at the present time could only be thankful that he himself had neither wife nor children.

"Only yesterday a baby died of the cold in the camp, and its father wept as he dug its grave. Indeed, the courage of the Latins is far greater than I knew, for we had expected men inured to the profession of arms, and indeed there are many such among you, but we never thought that you would expose women and children to so many perils!"

"You must know, Greek," Brother Barnabé said, "that the pilgrims who took the cross did not count the cost they would have to pay. They have given themselves wholly to Jesus Christ."

Philotheus nodded gloomily because, in common with many other Greeks, he thought it hardly possible that they would reach Jerusalem and believed the pilgrims were deceiving themselves with false hopes.

"If the Emperor does not come to our aid, we shall never take Antioch, and the Emperor is detained by his wars in the west and has few thoughts to spare for us!"

"Our Emperor, Greek, is Jesus Christ Himself. He has never yet suffered defeat."

These are more good people who will never see Jerusalem with their earthly eyes: Marguerite, Martin's mother, André the smith, Bernard Cutnose, Girard the Jay's uncle Marcel, little Sybille who was just losing her front teeth, and her big brother Thierry . . .

It has become so easy to die: the shivering and the fever, the hectic flush all through the body, the pains in the back and the coughing. Some linger for eight or ten days, others not so long, and all because of the water. The water is so cold there is no getting them warm again. No fire will catch, even under cover there is nothing but acrid smoke which only aggravates the coughing. You can go and beg some burning embers from the rich, but even the rich have none too much to spare, and by the time you have carried them back to our camp they are nothing but cold wet cinders. Can all this have happened in a month? It does not seem possible, and yet the local people say we must expect it to rain for three months, until Ash Wednesday. "Wait for the north wind, good people, that comes down from the mountains and brings snow and sleet!" Oh God, let even the snow come, then at least the mud will dry and we shall not have to sleep under water.

Marie stayed close beside Isabelle and big Berthier's Catherine, who also had a baby at the breast. The three of them fed their babies crouching on big stones under a wooden shelter which, inevitably, let in the rain. They sat huddled together with their legs tucked up, nursing the babies under their cloaks. Poor babies, it was all they dared do to change their swaddling clothes once a day, and funny swaddlings they were too, ill-washed and yellowed and half dried over the embers. It was a real miracle the delicate little bodies were not covered with sores.

He pulled and pulled at the milk with his strong little mouth, sucking the life out of her body, so that at every feeding Marie felt her head swimming from the weakness caused by cold and hunger. Everything went black before her eyes, and how the cold gnawed at her hands and numbed her feet! Could they ever have been hot? There was just one tiny spot of warmth at her breast, the small hot mouth, Pierre, Pierre with his blue eyes and the little yellow crust at his nostrils and eyelids. He was strong, was Pierre, he could draw all the juice out of your body, making you colder than ever. The grey rods of rain changed before Marie's eyes into lances, and in place of the black huts she saw ships with purple oars and dark-gold sails, and then it turned into a huge picture made of colored stones like those in the churches of Constantinople, the dark-gold sails with their black halyards swinging against a sky of deep blue, and the lances and the silver arrows fell in their thousands and went on falling, the silver arrows, oh yes, they are the arrows that took the lives of the martyrs at Nicaea, the arrows and the bright swords, no, you blessed souls, do not carry my soul with you, do not summon me aboard your ships. *Jacques! Jacques!* O Saint George, do not come for me yet. He is there on his white horse, walking on the sea. Isabelle.

"What, that white horse?" Isabelle too was slightly delirious. "Yes, that white horse is real. Isn't he beautiful, floating in the air like a great bird."

"You silly things," Catherine said, "it is a shroud floating in the wind. They are burying le Grêlé's daughter's husband."

"Ah, is that it?" Neither of the two women had known that the poor young man was dead. It was true, he had been coughing terribly. Oh, poor Marina! What a shame. Married scarcely a year, and a widow at thirteen. Ah, poor Mathieu! Poor young Jean, what a grief for your mother! She need not wait for you now, her candle can go out of its own accord, her soup be spilled among the embers, pray no more for the living, mother, say a mass for the dead in the faubourg church!

Huddled over their babies, numb with cold, the two friends

could hardly summon up the energy to mourn, and all too often now they had little heart for mourning. All they could think was, Oh that this rain would stop, we cannot go on! Weariness hardens the heart, and they were asleep on their feet. They wept when they remembered the dead, but only from weakness. Everything made them cry. Even when they saw someone slip in a puddle they cried instead of laughing; the tears streamed from their eyes as soon as they started to laugh, and very often over something sad they would be laughing and crying at the same time.

"Is your Pierre still feeding?"

"Isn't he just! I've hardly any milk but he is getting what he can."

"Mine's asleep. Look, isn't she pretty?"

It was a pleasure to see them, with their little faces all pink and dry and safe from the wet. Of the two, Pierre was the merrier. "Why is he so contented, Isabelle? I never saw anyone so happy."

Isabelle was fighting back her cough, so as not to wake the baby; she was gnawing her lips and turning purple in the face. The cough burst out, hard and piercing, like a little dog yapping. *Oh God, it will get me too.* Marie! Marie was half asleep. She shuddered, thinking she could hear the Turks, but it was only Isabelle coughing. The Turks have come, stand firm, everyone! Don't give an inch, lads!

"You're dreaming, love," Catherine said.

A pale face loomed up in front of Marie, a thin, ghostly face, with rain streaming down it and great eyes like deep pits. It hovered above a circular dish from which a rosy steam was rising, and she could feel a pleasant warmth on her face. She shrieked: the head of John the Baptist on a silver charger! He was looking at her with eyes that were still strangely sad, a faint, sweet smile on his lips.

"I have brought you some charcoal. Here, warm yourself."

It was only Saint-John. The lad was good to her, he looked after her like a brother. The women laid their hands on the bowl full of warm, glowing embers, taking greedy breaths of the dry air and holding their soaking-wet kerchiefs over the hot charcoal. Perhaps you really are Saint John, after all, just a little bit of the real Saint John. He nodded, a knowing glint in his dark eyes. One day, you will see. You will see in Jerusalem.

He was very well able to endure cold, hunger, and fatigue and this made it clear to everyone that he was a true madman and no imposter.

"In Jerusalem you shall see me with my true face, standing next to my brother James, the holy martyr."

"Saint-John," Marie said, "you should not talk so much, it will get you into trouble." He told her that since he could not die, he had nothing to fear. "Oh, if you were Saint John, you would work a miracle and make it stop raining!"

Everything rotted. The thatch rotted and the timbers and beams made of green wood warped and cracked and the huts collapsed. They spent their time mending them, but the truth was that there was not a dry thread in the whole camp, between the soldiers' tents and the hills, and it was all the women could do to find shelter for their babies. The worst trouble threatening the poor at this time was the lack of dry clothes. From the time the rain had begun and it was impossible to build up big fires any more, nothing had dried out and garments made of wool, linen, and leather were beginning to rot, turning black and soggy and slimy and smelling of death. Instead of keeping you warm they stuck to your body in the cold wind like lumps of icy mud, and whenever you managed to get into shelter near a fire they gave out an evil-smelling steam, but at least they warmed up a little and you could make some attempt to dry them by putting hot ashes on them. All the same, it was clear that these clothes would not last much longer and were bound to fall to pieces before Christmas. Would they be compelled to go about naked in the middle of winter?

People took the clothes from the dead, but they were only mildewed rags. The skins of the few beasts left in the camp, eaten long ago, had been given to the worst cases among the sick, but there had been no way of tanning the hides properly so that they rotted and smelled so bad that those in a fever threw them off, preferring to be cold. Everyone's skin became rough and moist and insensitive, like a toad's. They got used to the cold, to such an extent that when the young men went out to hunt for food they preferred to go naked, with a cloth wrapped around their loins for decency's sake. They strode along naked, swinging their arms across their chests to warm themselves till in the end they hardly noticed the rain. Even their eyes grew accustomed to it, so long as they remembered to keep shutting them to squeeze the water out.

They got into the habit of going farther and farther afield, following the armed bands led by the knights. Nor were the knights tender. If you beggars lag behind, the worse for you. We wait for no one! The advantages of the soldier's trade were clear enough now. The soldiers had leather shoes and the better-off among them had strips of leather to protect their legs. They hid among the rocks and bushes at a place where four roads met to keep watch for a convoy of supplies which the Arab Christians out of Antioch had said was expected to enter the city on the side nearest the citadel where the Turks came and went as they pleased. In due course the convoy appeared, with soldiers in front, bringing mules laden with huge sacks, and black and grey sheep. It made your heart beat faster only to look at those sheep. You could almost smell the aroma of roasting meat already! Ah, praise God, shall we set on them now?

"No, let the soldiers go first, we'll take them in the rear. One good charge!"

Careful, lads, let there be no mistake, and spare the horses. God's curse on these Turkish soldiers, they fight as if each man had three lives in his body! You fall on them from behind and in a trice they all wheel around without so much as breaking ranks, while the two knights who led the attack are still astride their rearing horses with their feet in the stirrups but no heads on their shoulders. Forward, my boys, don't let the sheep get away, we'll take care of the men.

The Turks sold their lives dearly that day, for there were less than fifty of them against more than two hundred. Through the curtain of rain, a few riders in white cloaks could be seen making off down the slope, but several dozen Turkish and Christian dead were left on the field. No one stopped to count. They were all running to round up the sheep and the horses, and stripping the Turkish bodies of their fine cloaks, made of good solid wool and scarcely even wet.

The leader on this occasion was a knight from Picardy named Aubry of Mailleraie, who treated the pilgrims well. "We have all worked together, lads, so it's the swords and the mail shirts for us and the cloaks and boots for you. You," he said to Jacques, "where are you from?"

"From the faubourg of Arras."

"By my faith, it was a knight of Arras that sired you."

"Here, don't insult my mother! We are fair-haired because of the Danes." Jacques looked at the stains on his ax. Two of them, he and le Grêlé, had both struck their blows at the Turk, and now their axes were all dirty, with fresh blood on top of the rust.

Le Grêlé's ax had struck a horse also, on the neck close by the mane, and the beast was glaring around wildly and trembling.

"What is that man, a butcher?" the knight asked. "There's a good animal done for."

"Do not blame him for it, sir knight," said Baudry. "He has fought well today." This was true. Philotheus the Greek, who had made one of the company on this occasion, had been almost trampled by a horse and Élie le Grêlé had sprung forward and caught the creature's bridle at the risk of having his own head struck off by its rider. Le Grêlé was generally regarded as a slow-witted fellow, but when action was called for he was quicker than anyone.

It was a good day. Two hundred sheep and the mules and the sacks of beans and the spoils stripped from the Turks. It was getting dark and still raining, and they marched through torrents of water, driving the sodden sheep before them, while the rain washed the blood from their wounds. They brought back twenty dead, but they sang for joy as they marched. As was right, the greater part of the spoils went to the knights and the soldiers, but even so the pilgrims got forty sheep for their part in the raid.

The meat was cold and half raw, but a great deal better than rotten beets. It was not surprising there was some argument over its division. Brother Barnabé said, "Friends, do not blame the soldiers. They are hungry, more so than you because they are not used to it. Have you counted their dead? There is no weeping and mourning when a soldier dies. Those lads have no families, and death is their trade."

The engineers and those in charge of the mines sent men to the pilgrim camp: *Who will work on the machines for the honor of Jesus Christ? Hot soup morning and night and meat on Sundays.* They knew that the work was hard and dangerous, that the tunnels collapsed on account of the rain while on the towers there was a risk of being hit by a missile, but the men went even so, not so much for the sake of the soup as because they could not bear to stay where they were any longer, forever mending shacks which only let the water in again as soon as they were done, and listening to the moans of the dying. Marie, Marie.

Marie, you used to be so pretty. Now she looked like a mangy filly, so thin, with grey rings around her big eyes, her skirts black and rotten, her cloak black and rotten, and her skin abraded by the water to the consistency of pumice stone. She had no milk and was giving the child rags soaked in soup or warm water to suck.

"He will not die, Jacques. I can see it written in his face."

At Christmas our son will be nearly three months old, Jacques thought, and he is still alive! Surely God is watching over us.

Jacques loved the boy, in spite of cold and hunger, he loved him. God keep you, Pierre. I am not jealous when I see you in the dry and with something to eat. You need it, my lad, you are not strong enough yet and your head is no bigger than my fist. Go on, laugh, little fellow, and God grant that we may keep you.

"I love him, Marie. I swear to you, every time I come back to camp, I am so frightened that my heart is thumping. Marie, if I were a squire, you and he would be in a sound tent with a carpet on the ground."

"Jacques, it is better so. God has never loved the rich."

"Better? That it is not. Over there in the city, Marie, the Turks' wives live in fine, well-heated houses with ovens to cook in and beds to sleep on. They say they do not even have to go to the well. The water comes into their houses of itself, by a fountain, and runs out through the wall." Marie laughed, convinced the Greeks were great boasters and were making game of the pilgrims.

It is not surprising if things do not go well: this is the greatest test. If only it were not quite so cold, that was all, and if Isabelle did not cough so much, if only . . . Oh Holy Mary, it rains and rains, it pours down until we dream about it in our sleep, living up to our necks in mud, all filthy and caked with it. Just like toads, we are, like pigs. To cross the camp we have to wade through dung up to our knees, and however much we may be used to it, there are times when the stench of it chokes us. And the rain dances on and on in the black pools of water and on what is left of the sacks, and on men's backs until it makes us feel drunk to look at it and we start seeing things double. Lord Jesus, we shall be washed clean of our sins sure enough. Enough rain has fallen on us to water all the corn harvests from the Meuse to the Seine!

Some of the women were weak, and they would go and hang about bareheaded near the knights' tents, trying to smile winningly, yes, only for the pleasure of lying down on a dry mat and spreading their clothes on hot bricks. More than one girl would have sold herself for that. The camp-followers were dying also, for they were girls used to wine and ill-equipped to withstand the cold. Even women who meant to remain good Christians went to the tents of the rich in the hope of finding work so they would be allowed inside to dry themselves for a little while.

One day Marie and Isabelle and Catherine and le Grêlé's Marina took their courage in their hands and went, just as they were, the first three carrying their babies on their left hips, to the tents of the Countess of Boulogne and her ladies, hoping there might be some linen to wash or mend or some dishes to scour. "There is nothing for you, not in those clothes. You'll infect the whole tent. Wash your own clothes first." Isabelle had the idea of showing them her daughter's little bonnet, embroidered with the arms of the lady of Marilly. "See," she said, "the lady gave it to me for my lying-in."

This time the lady came herself and asked to see little Ondine. She let the four women come into her tent, which had a good ditch around it and was strewn with dry straw, and there were bearskins and woolen blankets and a brazier full of red-hot charcoal standing on a tripod. The women stood in the doorway breathing in the dry air, almost ready to weep for joy.

The lady was young, tall, and white-skinned, with fair braids and smooth cheeks, and she took little Ondine in her arms and started to cry. She said, "Good women, I have no work for you, but I will gladly keep this child and I will give you two woolen cloaks and a silver piece."

"I am feeding her," Isabelle said in terror. "I still have milk."

"One of my women has just lost her boy. She will nurse her."

"Oh no," said Isabelle. "Oh no." She began to cough desperately, owing to the dry air. Marie had to take Ondine from the lady. She was frightened also and she said, "I beg you, for pity's sake, her father and her grandmother would grieve."

"You foolish creatures! You can see the mother's lungs are affected. I like the child. I will bring her up in my household and she shall want for nothing." And Ondine, silly little thing, opened her pretty grey eyes very wide and did not even cry.

"Oh no, my lady. Oh no, for pity!"

Disappointed, the woman gave back the child and told the pilgrims to seek work elsewhere. However, she gave them a piece of fine linen to make new clothes for the baby.

They found themselves out in the rain again. Isabelle was still coughing and sobbing with fright. "To think of it! She almost took her from me!"

Marie hugged her Pierre to her as if he were the one who had nearly been taken away. It was raining harder and the mothers bent over, protecting the tiny living bundles with their own bodies and trying not to slip on the boards that served as causeways between the tents. At last they came to a big hut full of soldiers and sat down on the ground by the door to get their breath back and wring out what remained of their cloaks. The soldiers laughed, but they were not bad fellows and they gave them a mutton bone to gnaw and even a bowl of soup.

"Well, my lovelies, have you come to give a little pleasure to God's soldiers?"

Catherine said, "No, we are not what you think. We are looking for work, but not that kind."

Since the soldiers' clothes, like everyone else's, were in rags, it was agreed that the women should mend some of their jerkins. Fortunately, Catherine and Marie still had their needles with them, but it was not easy to work. Their fingers were numb, and they felt very sleepy. It was so good to be in the dry, to be almost warm, so good, like sitting with their mothers in the chimney corner. They thought themselves back home again, with the soldiers' voices transformed into the sounds of the looms, and the reels, and the songs of home . . . Then they became aware of Marina's crying.

"Now then, what are you doing to the child?"

Two big fellows were pinching her cheeks and arms, teasing her like some small animal. They meant no harm, but Marina was trembling like a leaf. She flung herself down and started to scream so loudly that the captain of the soldiers came and drove the four women away.

Outside again, with their babies in their arms and Marina crying, the three mothers too could have thrown themselves on the ground and howled like dogs. It was still raining, and the rain seemed harder than ever. It beat down on their heads until it felt like hailstones as the four of them walked on, bent double in the gathering darkness among the tents and the ditches and crying aloud, shamelessly, like madwomen, weeping and crying out for no reason, like whipped children. It was raining so hard that those they passed did not even turn around to look. The whole camp would have burst into tears just as easily, and there were people crying everywhere for no reason. It was all the fault of the rain; no one could live like this for weeks on end, with no proper shelter, without food, and all this water falling. Better the Turks, better the thirst, have mercy!

The next day there was sleet, and by Christmas, snow. The fires went out and there could be no torchlight processions. *You bad Christians: to honor Him who came to earth to suffer for you, you should not fear wind or snow!* Brother Barnabé bore aloft a huge resin torch so thick and so thoroughly lighted well ahead of time that the snow and the wind might lash it but they could not put it out. The pilgrims tramped singing through the snow and slush with their eyes fixed on the flame. The singing was hoarse, like bellowing more than singing, because their voices were cracked and their lips stiff and swollen with the cold. The sick were carried on stretchers and the children hopped about their mothers, unable to walk slowly because the snow burned their bare, chilblained feet.

On such a night, amid just such a storm, in the biting snow, in the frozen slush, in the darkness and the howling wind, with no lodging but a stable, King of Kings who had a hundred thousand houses resplendent with light, He was willing to come down and come to us on such a night, that lovely Child hotter than a thousand suns, to become like our own little babes in the straw of a stable in Bethlehem. *Peace on earth.* Over in the beleaguered city the bells were ringing, and in the camps, in spite of the storm, great fires of logs were built up, making distant splashes of red all over the dark valley and the side of the hill. Stern is the joy of God. Do not weep for cold, the cold that burns you is the angels' greeting today. For you God left His rich dwelling place, and for you He shivered with cold upon the straw, He who with His own hands created the sun.

Toward morning the storm died down, and after a night spent in marching and singing the pilgrims warmed themselves around smoky fires, content that nothing was falling on them any more. God had granted them that joy for His birthday. The joy was not to be long-lived. Two days afterward came a heavy snowfall, thick wet snow that melted and turned into slush, followed by further downpours of rain, and then hail and then frost.

So long as they could remain on their feet, everyone hoped to stay alive.

The danger was in lying down and being unable to get up again. The day you had not the strength to get up and stand on your legs, even with the help of a stick, was the time to send for a priest because there was a strong likelihood that you would never rise again. The dying did not even suffer; they were so weakened by lack of sleep that they could hardly feel their arms and legs and were only conscious of the pain in their chests. They lay under their wooden shelters wrapped in damp clothes and covered with warm ashes, whenever their friends were able to get them, and the skin on their backs and limbs festered and became purulent and stank like the material of their garments, but they no longer felt it and in the end their faces turned blue and they could not breathe. By now they had all lost count of how many men, even young men, had died like this. The survivors, unable to dig any more graves, simply rolled the bodies into the ditch and flung a few spadefuls of earth on top. The bodies sank into the muddy water, and when the vultures descended the men shot arrows at them. Vulture flesh was foul, as was the flesh of rats also, but flavored with onion peel it was edible. At least it was not rotten.

And even sick men burning with fever, when they had eaten a leg of vulture, felt their fever lessen and found the strength to sit up. Courage, children, courage, spring comes early here. You wait and see. By the second or third week of Lent there will be sunshine and gentle breezes, and you will think yourselves in April!

The thing seemed hardly possible, and yet at daybreak on the Saturday of the second week in Lent the pilgrims saw, behind the citadel and the high wooded peak that loomed above its towers, a sky the pink of ripe strawberries, a sky of brilliant pink with streaks of violet-purple cloud, and the pink softened and gave way to golden rays that fired the clouds with gold, and the sun came up, making all the roofs and towers of the city shine. Then they realized that the country round about was green, the wide expanses of deforested hillside were covered with new grass, and the sky was growing more and more blue. The trumpets began to sound and drums were beaten. Such joy as this was worth ten years of a man's life!

You have fought the bad weather, now you must meet the real enemies of God. Let every man able to fight enlist in the barons' armies. There will be work for all! The wooden towers and the engines have suffered from the bad weather, there are no longer enough men to work on them, and the Turks are expecting reinforcements.

After two days of wild rejoicing and some disbelief (*Suppose the rains came back. We could not go through that again!*), the songs of joy ceased and the talk was all of the siege. The Turks were not idle. They had spent the winter snugly in their houses but now they were hurling missiles down into the camp from the walls, making repair work on the wooden towers impossible. These missiles were so large that they could carry away both shield and man, crash through three thicknesses of wood, and smash to pieces wooden palisades, and there was no way of reaching their machines because they had a longer range than those of the Christians. Moreover, seeing that the Christians were scattered in twenty different camps, all poorly guarded and very much the worse for wear, they were not content to shoot from a distance but would break out of the city from time to time, in companies of a hundred or two hundred horsemen, and contemptuously ignoring the fanfares of alarm and the arrows of the archers of the guard, make a direct rush for some undefended part of the camp. Their charge would carry them over the palisades into the very midst of their enemy's camp, sacking and destroying, riding down the tents and trampling out the fires, cutting off heads, shouting, and trumpeting. All too often they succeeded in winning back to the moats and re-entering the city. They might lose a few men, but they always caused more damage than they suffered.

Each time they were driven off, and new fortifications of wood and even of stone were erected opposite the gates.

The Turks stationed their interpreters on the top of the towers to proclaim: "Dogs of Roumis, pack your baggage, our Sultan is sending us an army from Baghdad the like of which you have never seen! Fly fast, but you will never fly far enough! It will catch up with you and crush you like flies. Your women will be sold in the markets at one dinar the pair! Pig-eaters, idolaters, and heretics! Your shame shall be a laughingstock for years to come!"

The men answered these insults with volleys of arrows and crossbow bolts fired from the summits of the wooden towers. The Turks, who had no crossbows, or even any bows as powerful as those of the pilgrims, and who could not fire missiles uninterruptedly, showed their anger by bringing up to the ramparts crosses and holy images taken from the churches of the city, and breaking them and trampling them underfoot. "Here are your idols, Roumi dogs, the Devil will not protect them!" Then interpreters were taken up onto the wooden towers and told to cry out: "We shall fasten the image of your god Mahomet to the tail of an ass! In a month from now you will all be dead or baptized. Shame on Mahomet! Your Sultan and your Pope shall be flayed alive, and your women made whores for lepers!"

It was not water that fell from the skies now but blood. Nearly every day some wounded were brought in from the ramparts, and prisoners did not survive for long: those that were common soldiers were killed to avenge the outrages offered to Christ. When the Turks took prisoners they used their heads as missiles, and the Christians retaliated with the heads of their own prisoners. A man's head is not such a hard projectile as some others, but even so it can crush another man's head. After a sortie and a skirmish near the ditches the Turks carried off as many men as they could, the wounded, and then, when they got them on the wall, they seized them by the hair and cut off their heads.

Then the heads came back, in the midst of the clamor and the screams, the hiss of arrows and the creak of pulleys. They smashed against the timbers of the towers, splashing the brains over them. They were gathered up, as they had to be because they were Christian heads. They could be known by the hair and beard, sometimes even by the features. There were several hundred of them, at least, during those spring months, in all the camps nearest the walls. At first, seeing the head of a comrade come back in such a fashion, even seasoned men-at-arms turned grey as stone and turned aside to vomit, and if the man chanced to be married his wife would go mad, for indeed it was a dreadful thing to see. As time went on, people ceased to feel the same horror. When the grim missiles arrived lackeys went about the camps calling out, "Whose head? Whose head?" so that the man's friends would recognize it and could say prayers and bury it. As for the bodies, it was a bold or a clever man who could find them in the waters of the moat. They sank deep into the mud and rotted there. Stones and spadefuls of earth and rotten boards and the bodies of prisoners were thrown into the moat every day to fill it in, and the stinking water overflowed so that canals and still more canals had to be dug to carry it away from the camp and keep it from flooding the underminings.

This meant that there was work for all the men, and even for the women if they were strong enough. Work, but no pay. Work, but no bread. Flowers were growing on the hills, so many that in places you could not see the grass any more, purple and pink flowers, white flowers and yellow flowers in clumps, more than there ever were in France. The hills where there were no more forests were like many-colored carpets. There were flowers in plenty but no bread; for that they had to wait. There was nothing more to be got from the land, nothing at all, not even an onion, and every day the criers went around saying, Courage, take heart, they are sending us ships from Cyprus and from Constantinople full of wheat and oats and barley. Soon they will reach the harbor. But the harbor was ten leagues away, and between the harbor and the city of Antioch were Turkish armies on the march.

If only there had been no famine, what a beautiful spring it would have been! The dark trunks of the olive trees rose out of the young grass, crowned with silver leaves, and the orange and lemon trees, in their heavy dark-green foliage, had already shed their white blossom and promised to bear fine fruit, although as yet there were only hard, green, inedible berries. To a hungry man, nothing seems beautiful, nothing except bread, meat, or bean soup, yes, or even a leg of vulture, even a mess of bran. Nothing can draw the eye but what is good to eat. They went out of the camp and picked the flowers just to chew them, or roots, or juicy stems.

From the ramparts came crashes and voices shouting. God! The soldiers still have some beans, they have a ration of soup a day, and oh God, within the city the Turks and even the Christians eat bread, they eat mutton and chicken, they eat fish, they have oil, they have honey . . . Oh God, in our own faubourg of Arras our families have soup each night unless they have been put out of work. Last Sunday, only last Sunday, some kind ladies, may God bless them, distributed oatcakes to us!

Marie had no more milk. Carrying little Pierre on her hip, cradled in a cloth tied around her neck, she went the rounds of the camps with the other mothers, begging for a mouthful of soup or a morsel of cheese, for it was known that the barons still had cows and ewes. You could not blame them for it. The rich were not accustomed to go hungry and with the few cows they had left the army would not go far . . .

Seeing that there was nothing else to do, the women went begging with their babies in their arms. "I ask nothing for myself, only for the child. We will pray for you, we will pray for your husbands, that slingstones and arrows may never strike them." Sometimes a soldier would give the babies a spoonful of soup; sometimes a woman, the servant of some rich dame, would even take a child in her arms and give it suck: "There, my good woman, mine has milk every day. He shall have a little less tonight." Isabelle was no longer able to walk. The cold had gone and now she was in a continual fever, and the priestess carried her child.

Then a woman from the Provençal camp stopped Marie and told her that over where the black men were, the Tafurs, they had meat to eat.

"Ah God, perhaps they have indeed found some. Who told you so?"

"I don't know. There are rumors. But people are afraid to go and see." Marie crossed herself.

"I will go."

"I am frightened," Marina said. "They say they are all naked."

Marie herself had no cloak any more and her dress had fallen to pieces, so that she had made herself a kind of garment out of a piece of an old Turkish cloak, a short kirtle that left her calves and shoulders bare.

"We are almost naked ourselves. It is too bad if these people are naked. It will not kill us." And she hurried away with the Provençal woman to where the black men were camped.

She had believed that she was familiar with poverty and stench and mud. She had seen nothing yet. Here in this accursed camp, all was filth underfoot and the men had no shelters, no huts, no palisade, only a few crosses set up in the midst of the camp and fires burning. Naked they were, some had not even a cloth to cover their loins, naked and their skins covered with scabs and sores, their hair and beards caked with dried mud and the hair on their bodies crawling with lice like a turned-up ant heap. Not daring to hold her nose, Marie stood staring at a group of men seated around a fire, gazing bemusedly at the spit on which were some long dark joints of meat. The meat was smoking and smelled bad, like carrion. But they had eaten carrion before and this was not yet too high.

One of the men asked, "What are you doing here?" They were sniggering, but they did not look dangerous.

"Did you find that by the river?" Marie asked. She could not bring herself to call it "meat"; she was so hungry that the word stuck in her throat. The men laughed.

"We found it in the dogs' burial ground," the first man told her.

"Dogs?" said Marie. "Is there a burial ground for dogs here?"

"Circumcised dogs. Dogs that worship Mahomet."

Marie stiffened, as if in response to a blow in the stomach. The man took one of the joints and wafted it under her nose.

"That's meat, isn't it?"

Lord, yes, that was meat! Good roast meat. Marie felt the muscles in her stomach and her cheeks contract. She could not have been more terrified if they had shown her the flayed leg of her own father. Her whole body revolted, as it had done when she was a child and heard stories of men in times of famine eating human flesh. Tales of how the peasants used to bury people alive and drive a boar spear into the grave.

"It will kill you," she said.

The men were enjoying her terror. Marie clutched little Pierre to her, shielding his head with her hands.

"In God's name, friends," she said, "renounce this sin! For this sin there is no forgiveness!"

"Maybe," one of the men said—he was a young man, you could see by his teeth—"maybe you bring us lambs and pigs?"

The others were laughing. "We never felt better. This is good infidel flesh, properly bled and baptized by Christian arrows. May the same fate befall all Turks!"

Marie could feel her hair standing on end with anger.

"There!" she said, and she leaned toward the dark meat and spat on it, with all the saliva and the bile which her stomach had thrown up into her mouth. "There is Christian vomit, eat that also while you are about it!" The men showed no sign of anger. They had nothing against it, they had known worse sauces. Marie and the Provençal woman fled, hand in hand, while the two infants woke and wriggled like worms on their mothers' hips and screamed.

Coming toward them was a tall man without hair or teeth, brandishing a heavy cudgel covered with filth. He was naked but for a rusty iron cross two handspans wide that hung upon his chest. He looked so evil that the two women shrank back, hugging their babies in their arms.

"What's this?" the man cried. "Whores here?"

"No," said the Provençal woman, "no, lord, we are married women. We came to beg."

"Ha ha! Beg here? To beg lice, maybe? Away, you vipers, mangy bitches, servants of the Devil, bags of filth!"

"Now then!" Marie said. "What need have you to rail at us? You are frightening our children." Her one thought was to get away as fast as possible. As they left the camp, a man caught her arm and she screamed aloud.

"Don't be scared. Remember me? I know you, you are a winder, one of the weavers of Arras." Oh God, Marie thought with horror, can this be a man from our own street? "Richard," the man said. "You remember Richard, the weaver of Roubaix. I saw you at Nicaea with Saint-John."

"Goodness, that's right. And your brothers were burned in the faubourg."

This reassured her a little, as though finding a man from Roubaix in this condition was somehow better than meeting a man from Arras.

"We frightened you, eh?"

"You did!" said Marie. "It turned my stomach. Worse than beasts."

"For God," said Richard, "we have made ourselves worse than the beasts. We are the real poor. Your men plunder. You are wearing Turkish wool on your body."

"Must I go naked? It is permitted to strip corpses."

"With us, it is not permitted." He stood before her, tall and thin, stooping a little, and beneath the lice that crawled on his chest could be seen two long red scars in the form of a cross. He was ageless now: gap-toothed, sparsely bearded, and filthy as the wool on a sheep's tail. There were black rings under his eyes and over half his cheeks. Only his hands, which were still smooth, and the way he laughed showed that he was young.

"You are sick," said Marie. "Come with us, we are camping with the folk from Lille now, and with some others, Picards. So many have died in all the camps."

Richard walked beside the women, scratching his scars and his head.

"I'll go with you as far as the beginning of the Greek camp. Not to your camp, no. That is all past. You see this cross? I burned it there myself with a red-hot iron. Tell the others. We have stripped the old man."

"What? What old man?"

"It is written in the Scriptures. The old man."

"But, Holy Mother of God, what old man? Is it a Turk?"

"Stupid. It is in the Scriptures. All, you see, all is forgotten, save only Jesus Christ. See: no plunder, and if you find a Turkish horse, slaughter it, and if you find a Turkish cloak, tear it in pieces, or a house, burn it, let nothing remain. That is God's will. But you, you deck your body in rottenness."

"God, no! This is good wool."

"We must go naked," Richard said, in his hoarse, staccato voice, "naked as God made us. Strip the old man. God on His cross was naked. Everything shall be burned. Whoever takes aught for himself, even so much as a thread, shall be hanged. That is how it is with us. The rest of you are robbers and camp-followers."

"Well!" Marie exclaimed. "At least you haven't stripped yourself of your tongue! What is all this about burning everything? What about the mills? And the churches?"

"As yet there are no prophecies concerning them. First the infidel rottenness. There is the greatest stench. And the Greeks also. Devils have been seen dancing on their church at Mamistra. They worship Mammon, that is why they are so rich. And all this shall burn, I tell you. For in Jerusalem there will be no need of gold wrought by men's hands any more."

"Who has told you all this?"

"Jean Vernet, our priest. It was God Himself made him a priest, not the bishops. He has visions every Friday, God signed him with a bloody cross upon his breast. He has visions. As long as one single Turk or infidel or Jew lives on this earth the wounds of Jesus Christ shall bleed. And when all rottenness has been consumed by fire there shall be a great light from East to West."

"That's as may be," said Marie. "But you will be damned first because you eat human flesh."

"Corruption feeds on corruption. Our bodies are corruption. Man, beast, or the grass of the fields, it is all one. You eat the vultures that feed on men. The corn is nourished with corpses. All corruption shall be consumed with fire by God on the Last Day."

Marie went back to the camp, after telling the Provençal woman that she ought to curse the people who had mocked her so. She was weeping and dizzy with hunger, and the child was crying. She gave him rags to suck that had been dipped in the water in which some vulture bones had been cooked. There was talk of a convoy expected, an armed convoy coming from the port of St. Simeon.

"They have food over there, Isabelle, among the living dead. They are digging up the corpses of the slain from the Turkish burial places and eating them."

"And a fine state they must be in, those corpses!"

"No, it was still quite fresh. I saw it." And Marie cried and could not stop. "Oh God, to have set out to find Jesus Christ and see men eating Christian flesh."

"The Turks," said Isabelle, "are not Christians."

"Well, they might as well be. If they had been baptized they would be. Baptism was not made for pigs."

The dead were laid in batches of ten in the ditch around the camp, and the people walked along the ditch to identify the bodies before they were covered up with earth. This was how they found le Grêlé's Marina, lying half naked between two weavers from Béthune, for everyone was so tired that all considerations of modesty were forgotten. Nonetheless, le Grêlé had to be told so that he could see her before the earth was thrown on her. He was still working on the wooden towers, like many of the other men and he came, carrying his ax on his shoulder, with his mouth gaping and his eyes blank. He went down into the ditch and pushed aside the bodies of the weavers, then sat down by his daughter and stroked her hair with both hands.

"But I gave her some soup yesterday," he said. "Soup. She had food yesterday. She had some soup."

"Come, Grêlé, do not stay here. You must let the gravediggers do their work."

He got up meekly and climbed out of the ditch. Then he sat down again beside it, with his head bent. He seemed not to understand.

"Come, Élie, do not stay there. You shall pray for her. You shall avenge her."

"Sure," he said. "Surely I shall avenge her."

"She is a martyr now, Élie. Do not worry about her any more."

He said, "We are all martyrs now."

The next day some convoys of food arrived and people were shrieking with joy in all the camps. Flocks of sheep, mules, camels, carts loaded with sacks of corn: when it was shared out, even on short rations, the army had enough food for four or five days at the most.

Sir Evrard was killed in the fighting around the north bridge, during the great sortie which the Turks of Antioch made while the barons of the army were away at the port to fetch the provisions and more workmen. His body was not found because it had fallen in the river, along with a great many other bodies, both Turkish and Christian. So much blood was shed in this battle that the river ran red for hours. The bridge which had been so dearly bought remained in Christian hands, and the armies of Toulouse and Bohemond returned, bringing Turkish heads and supplies and convoys of war machines. *Courage, soldiers of God, ships are coming, bringing us reinforcements from all Christendom.* Those inside Antioch will not hold out much longer.

They held out for another two months, and but for treachery which God willed to help the Christians, the city of Antioch would never have been taken, for at the very moment when the city fell, the great army sent from Babylon by the Sultan was less than ten leagues away from Antioch.

6 ✠✠✠✠✠✠✠✠✠✠✠✠✠✠

Plundering is permitted to everyone, soldiers and pilgrims, until the morning star.

No one is to touch the houses of any Christians, whether Greeks, Syrians, or Armenians.

All the rest, Turks, Arabs, and Jews, may be slain without mercy unless they ask for baptism. But any man killing women and children will be committing a sin.

Guarding the entrance to the big white stone house were four Turks armed with spears. This was how le Grêlé dealt with them. He had a dozen lads with him, five men of Arras, four Picards, and some Normans, with axes and Turkish spears, besides some big stones which they carried in their scrips. The stones first, and that was two Turks hit on the head. The other two crossed their spears as the whole band rushed them at once, so quickly that one of the Picards was spitted on a spear which went right through his body and came out in the middle of his back. The Turk had his brains beaten out because his spear was no more use to him with the Picard on the end of it. The door was smashed in with axes and then: "Victory, friends! The house is ours."

Ours? Nay, screams like the slaughter of a dozen pigs were coming from within, and not all of them were women's voices. The men ran on and found themselves before another closed door, a handsome door with a grille of metal wrought like black lace and behind it a red curtain billowing. Standing in front of this door was a man of fearful aspect, two heads taller than any Christian, naked to the waist and with a skin as black as if he had been roasted over a slow fire, grasping in both hands a sword as big as a plowshare.

He grinned, showing big white teeth, and took one step forward, swinging up his arms, and there were two lads from Arras, Martin and Ferri the fuller, *headless on the ground.* The two heads went rolling away across the black-and-pink tiled floor while the bodies were still kicking and spewing out rivers of blood from their severed necks. Was this the Devil incarnate? "Out with your spears, boys," le Grêlé said. Four spears ringed the black man round. He shook his head, laughing, and beat down two of the spears with his sword, but the other two pierced his flesh, and his body was not impenetrable for the blood was flowing, red on black. He swung around then and beat down the other two spears, ripping them from his side, yet he did not cry out; only the grin of his white teeth became more fixed.

One against ten, boys. We've got him. Like dogs about a bear. He still stood before the door, scything the air with his great sword, and how it came about Élie never knew, it happened so fast, but there were the three Picards lying headless at the black man's feet and the glistening black skin, stretched tightly over muscles that were knotted and writhing like fat snakes, was all streaked with red. The man was not smiling now. He leaned against the door with a Norman spear between his ribs, and his arm was not moving with the same speed. He cleft the Norman's shoulder, and le Grêlé stepped forward, wielding his ax. With a swish like a windmill sail, the sword swept down and rose again. Le Grêlé ducked just in time to avoid the blow. God be thanked, the ax had struck the giant right between the eyes.

He swayed like a tree trunk and fell, face downward in the blood of the headless men. Élie had just time to wrench out his ax and leap backward. In front of him was the black man's body, so splendid and well-proportioned that it would have done credit to a Christian. Blood and brains were spilling from the halves of his shattered skull and the brains were white, like the brains of a man. Le Grêlé turned at last and found himself alone with six dead men and the black. The rest had gone.

He smashed open the delicate iron grille with one blow of his ax and ran inside. The house is mine.

He was in a small square courtyard roofed with a yellow canvas awning, with clear water flowing from a fountain in the center into a grey marble basin. The court was paved with grey and white marble tiles and the sun shone through the yellow awning onto screens wrought of gilded metal. Sitting by the fountain, her hands crossed on her breast, was a woman, *naked,* stark naked, without a stitch of clothing on her, not so much as a bangle on her ankle.

Le Grêlé stood stock-still, as if he had been turned to stone. A Turk could have come at him with a sword and he would not have stirred. She was the loveliest thing that he had ever seen, as white as cream, white as the moon, with hair and brows and eyes like black crows on the snow. No man in Christendom ever saw such beauty of face or form, she might have been carved from some substance finer than lily flowers, but most terrible of all was the intense black of her wide-open eyes. She was staring at him all eyes, eyes that looked unblinking into his, the ultimate defense of a soul in deadly fear, knowing that if it lets that gaze once relax it will become no more than so much flesh to rend and devour.

Her servants had left her while she was in her bath, and had cruelly taken her clothes with them. Rather than run naked in the face of their gibes, she had stayed where she was to confront the savage beast. Now she was half dead with fear. The man with his bloody ax, his bloody beard, his garments torn and stained with red, his ravaged face, stood helplessly gazing. He all but fell upon his knees to pray.

The sound of voices made him swing around quickly and lift his ax. Four Norman soldiers came running in with bloody swords, Turkish heads tucked under their left arms. Élie faced them, stepping back toward the woman by the fountain.

"God! The fair infidel! Out of the way, peasant, and let us take our pleasure of her!"

Élie backed a step nearer to the woman, shielding her with his body, and hefted his ax in both hands.

"Don't stand in our way. Your turn will come."

Élie advanced on them, swinging his ax above his head, with a look so terrible that the men, who had already begun to loosen their breeches, fled, leaving the Turks' heads behind them on the ground. Le Grêlé turned to the woman, all white and black. She was now trembling so that he could hear her teeth chattering and her lips were blue.

"There, there," he said. "Me good Roumi, not be afraid—" He knew not one word of their accursed language. The woman was staring in horror at the severed heads. She could not have been used to them.

Le Grêlé tore the red curtain from the doorway and wrapped it around the beautiful girl. Then he hoisted her onto his shoulder like a parcel and left the house as he had come, striding over the bodies of the black man and his own slain companions. This was all the booty he took. His mind was reeling and he ran through the streets where men were dragging out corpses and tossing silken cloths and silver vessels from the windows, thinking of nothing but finding a place to stow his prize in safety.

Jacques strode along with his companions, his bloodied ax on his shoulder because there were no more Turks left to kill. He was not the kind to hunt down old men. It was almost dark and violet smoke was rising into the red sky above the roofs, while the streets were filled with people, like a market day.

Crosses and holy images had been fastened to the doors of the houses. Just our bad luck to have come upon a Christian quarter. Where can we find some plunder? The knights knew what they were about when they sent us back here. The city was swarming with men, but not with citizens. The people of Antioch had shut themselves inside their houses. They knocked on the doors: "Ho there, are you truly Christians?" A Greek appeared, quaking all over, and unfastened his collar to show his baptismal cross. "What are you shaking for, old curly beard? We are brothers."

Jacques roared with laughter as he uttered the mangled Greek words, and the people looked at the men of Arras with terror, because of their axes and cudgels all covered with blood. What old women they are, to be still afraid of blood. They have been living safe and sound inside their houses while in the nine months we have been outside this city, we have seen more severed heads than loaves of bread.

They were climbing up toward the citadel, through fine paved streets with houses of pink and white stone. Already if you climbed upon the roofs you could see the walls and the river and the bridge, and the hordes of pilgrims straggling with their bundles toward the open gates. Christian banners on all the towers! Only the citadel still held out. Night was falling and the sky away over the sea was blood-red, gold, and purple, and the vault of heaven turned white and then almost at once to violet-blue and the first star was shining out like the diamond on Saint George's breastplate. The camp was emptying. Hardly any fires gleamed there now; the fires were running along the walls instead. The cathedral bell was tolling, and cressets flared on the parvis and torches blazed within.

Jacques, Bernier, Garin, Mathieu, and a few Flemings who had joined up with them ran along a straight street, elbowing one another. Groups of Provençal soldiers, carrying heads under their arms and on the ends of their spears, were coming down the street in the opposite direction.

"See," Mathieu said, "see, they are coming from a Turkish quarter."

"Where are you off to, you men of Provence?"

"To the church. Can't you hear the bell? God knows if it be this way or that, there's no finding your way in this uproar." It was best to go forward, because it was from there that the shouting and the screaming were coming.

The road led into a square where torches were burning, stuck in rings in the walls. In the center was a fountain with four jets of water flowing from a stone pillar set in a square basin, and a number of naked bodies lay in a heap near the fountain. Shrill cries were coming from the buildings. Too late, we'll get nothing in these houses. In one torchlit doorway three women were wailing in a monotonous, dirgelike manner, while a fourth was on her knees beside a man who lay on the ground, her long thin arms rising and falling as she tore at her blue veil.

The dead man was a handsome youth with curly hair, a long, powerful neck, and lips that were only faintly blue and seemed to smile.

"That's a good head," said Bernier. He drew his long knife from his belt as he spoke. Jacques grasped his shoulder.

"Hey, that's not fair! It isn't yours."

"What of it? You can do the same."

He had thrust back the wailing woman and was bending over the dead man when the woman, seeing what he would be at, shrieked and clutched at his hair. With one quick thrust Bernier drove his knife into her throat, and she collapsed like an empty sack. Bernier turned his attention to the neck of the corpse. "You're wasting time," Jacques said. He looked at the woman who lay like a bundle of blue and black cloth and said, "She was his mother."

Mathieu and one of the Flemings went up to the other three women. They were dressed in long silken coats with striped veils over their heads, good enough for plunder. The Fleming tugged the girdle of one and then at the hem of her coat to tell her what he meant, but the silly creature started to scream so loudly that a group of Brabançon soldiers just then coming into the square stopped dead. They stopped and then ran over to the doorway by the torch at the very moment when Bernier was severing his Turk's head and fixing it on the end of his staff.

The woman who had screamed was young. Her veil was ripped off and then her silken coat and everything that she had on, and the Brabançons began to rape her then and there, in the torchlight, one after another. Jacques said, "Come, Mathieu, come on, lads. We'll find some plunder somewhere else."

At the next crossroads they ran into a company of French pilgrims carrying torches. "Where are you going?"

"How should we know? This town is a real Constantinople. How can anyone find their way? All we can see is Christian houses."

"We should go up toward the citadel."

"We've just come from there," one Frenchman said. "They drove us away with the butt ends of spears. Knights' quarters. There is still fighting there."

"Besides," said Garin, "can we be sure that these are Christian houses? We should go and find out." They knocked for a long time on the doors of a big house with strongly barred windows. A tall, bearded man opened to them, holding a silver cross in his right hand. They pushed past him and found themselves in a colonnaded room opening onto a court. Two oil lamps were burning on tripods in the court, where bushy shrubs grew with strong-smelling white flowers. The bearded man hurried after the pilgrims, saying something in Armenian. "Well," Mathieu said, "it's clear they are not Turks."

"He might be a renegade," said one of the Frenchmen. "We'd better make sure he's not circumcised."

There was a general roar of laughter, but the man was old and they did not like to strip him. Jacques, grinning widely, took the Armenian by the arm, and began making signs: food, food.

They went into a huge, low-vaulted room, all yellowed with smoke. At the far end was a hearth and near the hearth three servants, armed with hatchets and a cook's knife. The bearded man said something to them, and one opened a big hutch and took out two loaves of white bread. Oh, to think that outside in the camp people were dying of hunger, *and here they had white bread!* Jacques and one of the Frenchmen took the loaves and began breaking them and passing pieces to the others. It was years since they had eaten anything so good. They were in such a hurry to eat that they did not even cross themselves first. The Armenian watched them, shaking his head.

He was sorry for them. He said something else to his servant, who brought a third loaf and a handful of salt. Probably they were not even aware as they stood there, covered with blood and dust, that all their bones were sticking out, that their eyes were like saucers and their lips and eyelids swollen from starvation. They ate in silence, taking small mouthfuls to make the bread last longer, grown suddenly grave as in church, in the presence of a holy relic. Bernier was still holding his staff with the Turk's head, which made him look as if he had two heads. The Armenian must have thought the head honestly come by, because he smiled at Bernier and slapped him on the back, saying, in his own language, "Well done, worthy Christian!"

Yet, God knows, the dead man's head was handsomer than Bernier's, even so; calm and sadly smiling, with its straight nose, smooth, prominent cheekbones, and black eyes half closed. Bernier had a red scar on his nose, his hollow cheeks were scabbed, and blond stubble grew patchily on his chin. The oldest of the Frenchmen said, "Lads, the good man is a Christian and the servants also. We must say our thanks and be off."

"What about all the time we've wasted?"

"What about it? You've eaten, haven't you?"

They went, with their torches and their weapons, a little regretfully because the house seemed rich and handsome.

"We are lost in an Armenian quarter. We should have followed the knights, they know at once where to go."

"See what you can find left after they've been by!"

By now there was a crowd in the street. The Brabançons had arrived with the remainder of the archers and the engineers. They were singing songs of their native lands, and had evidently found something other than Turkish houses, for they reeked of wine.

"Ho there, friends, what good Christians have been treating you so well?"

"You, from Artois, you wait for your beard to grow a bit longer. A captured city is a captured city."

They were carrying full sacks and rolled-up carpets on their backs. "Here, listen, lads. There are women screaming down that way, at the end of the street. There's sure to be something worth having."

They ran toward the noise, but when they got there it was like the tower of Babel, the houses full of soldiers and lackeys, a jostling mass of people in the street, and men with torches dashing over the rooftops in pursuit of women and children who were screaming like stuck pigs. The people here were Turks beyond a doubt, but you would have had to get there early to get anything from them. The men with the torches were setting fire to the women's hair and the poor creatures, clad in nothing but their shifts, were jumping from the roofs like so many frightened sheep, their hair and their shifts ablaze, like great golden torches. While down below the soldiers were catching them on their spears, trampling them, and dashing them against the stones.

The fools! They'll set fire to the whole neighborhood at that game. A rosy smoke was rising from the inner courts and a cloud of pigeons and ducks flew out suddenly with a great beating of wings, pink and gold against the dark sky, before the wings caught fire and the birds fell on the roofs and in the streets. Roast fowl, boys, roast fowl dropping into our mouths! Who'll have one? It was impossible to hear anything for the shrill screams of the dying and the raucous bellowing of the soldiers. Keep close, lads, we're better off together than alone. We'll force a way through.

Numbers of pilgrims and poor soldiers who had been forced out of the Turkish quarter were pouring down a long stepped street with gardens on either hand. White fountains rose between the cypresses and small round orange trees. It would have been good to rest in gardens like these, but there was no time, the crowd was like a river bearing you onward, and any man that stopped was knocked down and trampled underfoot. They were running now without knowing whither, heads on pikes and torches bobbing above the crowd.

Then they came to an open space full of people, soldiers and inhabitants of the country all mingled together, and there was a church with its façade lit up from beneath by a hundred torches. A huge mosaic above the porch showed Jesus Christ at the Last Judgment. *And the horrible thing was that the image of Jesus Christ was all pitted with the marks of stones, with iron staples driven into the eyes and the holy face defiled with stains of mud and blood.* The crowd in the square was looking at it and weeping. See what they have done to Our Savior. In the torchlight, the great mutilated face with its gouged eyes shone through the covering of filth. O Lord, it is for our sins they have done this to You!

O Lord, it would have been better had our own eyes been put out!

The great face looked down on them with its eyes shattered by the iron spikes. The splashes of blood were like wounds on the cheeks, and a stone had made a direct hit on the mouth. The blind face seemed to scream, and yet the line of the brows was stern and serene. The moving torches gleamed on chips of red and gold between the dried clods of dirt, making the great countenance seem to breathe. Priests in the crowd were singing the *Miserere* and it was taken up by a thousand voices, while the Greeks chanted a hymn in their own language.

The church was already so full of people that it was impossible to get inside, and sounds of weeping mingled with the singing from within. The Greeks in the crowd embraced one another and embraced the Latin soldiers, and soon there was not a man in the whole square who was not weeping hot tears until the singing was drowned in sobbing and the whole square was all one clamor of lamentation.

Companies coming from the walls heard the crying as they approached the square and asked, What, is the Duke dead? Or gallant Bohemond? No, Christians, it is Jesus Christ, He, the Duke of all dukes, the Bravest of the brave, see what they have done to Him. See, see, was there ever such grief?

See throughout the city the holy images broken and defiled, and God sees this! May our faces be covered with sores, only let there be no more wounds on the face of Our Lord! May our bones be broken, so the holy crosses that are broken may be made whole again! O Lord, for our sins they have trampled You beneath their horses' hoofs. Friends, let us run to the churches and see what we have still to do. Could we know that such things were happening in this city?

The pilgrims were borne on with the crowd, blinded by tears, alternately sighing and calling one another's names. In the Greek quarter around the church, the doors of the houses were shut and there were lights in the windows and the sound of singing and happy, excited voices. Ah, they are celebrating their deliverance, but they will not ask us into their homes. The night was cold, and the sky between the torchlit walls so black that they could hardly see the stars. A group of Norman soldiers came toward them singing a psalm of Jerusalem. A red-bearded monk walked in front carrying a cross, and behind him came a big fellow in a coat of mail bearing a severed head on his spear. It was the head of an old man with a white beard and a white turban. It is their priest, they have caught their priest. Other soldiers had the old man's arms and legs stuck on their pikes. The turbaned head had had its eyes gouged out and the mouth was wide open. "Ho lads, this head is worth more than yours. This is worth the head of an emir!"

"Cowards," said Jacques. "An old man with white hair is no great matter."

"You poor clod of a weaver, have you no fear of God? This is their *imam,* who puts charms on their weapons!"

Jacques recoiled and crossed himself. "I may be a weaver," he said angrily, "but weaver or not, I've as much of their blood on my ax as you have on your spear."

"Let be, Jacques," Mathieu said. "Let them alone, it is the Normans' day." He turned to the soldiers. "You brave fellows, we would burn a big candle for your Bohemond. Tell us, is there anything still to be had back there where you come from?"

"Nothing, not even any women. Not even a goat."

"And over toward the citadel?"

"Go there if you've not had your fill of arrows and stones. There's some hard fighting there."

Jacques said, "Shall we go?"

"Yes, a lot of good you'd do," said Bernier. "We've earned our booty. What's the good of asking to get knocked on the head?"

"Oh, Lord Jesus," Jacques said. "Lord Jesus."

In the morning the plain before Antioch looked like a field ravaged by a storm. The night before, it had seethed with people; now it was empty, crisscrossed by trenches, dotted with the blackened scars of dead fires, the space near the walls heaped with broken planks, charred beams, and bones of animals, which the vultures were still picking over leisurely. The last lines of stragglers were hurrying to the open gates, carrying their sick on stretchers.

The sky was blanching rapidly and the mountain mists melting away, swifter than snow in the fire, revealing the blue and black slopes behind the citadel. Trumpets rang out from the walls and the criers sent out a roll of drums from every tower. They were crying out in every tongue: *Thanks be to God, Jesus Christ, and the great Saint George, Ansiau the coward has fled, all is ours save the citadel!*

The saintly Patriarch John has been set at liberty and goes to celebrate mass in his cathedral! Let none remain outside the walls, for the Turks are less than a day's march away! Immediately after the first mass the engines will be fired. Let each man go to the quarters of his own people. Anyone caught plundering Christians will be hanged! By order of Bohemond, Duke Godfrey, the Count of Saint-Gilles, and the Count of Blois. Every man-at-arms will be paid six deniers in the local coin, every knight one silver mark! No more women or children are to be killed, by order of the lord Bishop Adhemar! Everyone is to go to mass. There are thirty-six unprofaned churches in the city. Do not all rush to the Cathedral of St. Peter. Do not grieve immoderately for your dead. God will not forget His martyrs!

The pilgrims roamed the outskirts of the city, all searching for their fellow countrymen. They no sooner set foot inside a courtyard than someone would tell them, This billet belongs to the Flemings, or the Bretons, or the Picards. Brother Barnabé and Baudry had painted the arms of Arras on a large house near the ramparts and set three armed men to guard the door. The house was a Christian one, but it had been abandoned. It had belonged to poor people and contained one large courtyard with a floor of beaten earth and three floors above with some ten dwellings on each. These were windowless for the most part but had doors giving onto the gallery. The masonry was none too sound and there were a number of holes made by missiles in the roof, but apart from this the house was a good one; the poor pilgrims deserved that much.

By the end of the day most of them had gathered there, except for the ones killed during the night and there had been a few, though no one knew where to begin looking for their bodies. The city was large and there were surely over a thousand streets. In the poorer quarters the day was a fairly quiet one. Everyone was tired. The men lighted fires in the courtyard and burned the beds and benches they found in the house. The night was cold and there would be soup for all, a soup of barley and mutton bones. The mutton was for the children and the sick.

Jacques had found no booty all night long and at daybreak had found himself with his friends in an open space outside a house where some Picard men-at-arms were engaged in fixing a shield painted with bars of sable on gules above the door. A pile of booty was heaped outside with an archer standing guard beside it.

"You're rich," Mathieu said to the soldiers.

"Not us, lads, but the knight Jean of Vireleu. These are his pickings."

The knight came out of the house, dressed in a robe of green silk embroidered in gold. A bandage stained with dark blood was around his head. Jacques knew him from having served on the machines, and greeted him:

"Thanks be to Saint George, sir knight! May you always have as much joy as on this day!"

"Ha, so it's you! The brave fellow that carried up the bolts! By my faith, the arrows feared you, not you them!"

Jacques laughed and could think of nothing to say. The knight said, "You deserve to make your fortune. I can see your ax has not been idle." The ax was black with blood, and Jacques had blood on his shirt and a big raw bruise on his cheek. He laughed again.

"This is all my fortune," he said, stroking the iron axhead. "We've found nothing, not so much as a button."

"Here," said the knight, "do you want a button off my robe? They are chased silver."

"Well," Jacques said, "that is, of your goodness, if I might only choose something from off this heap of yours, a trinket for my sweetheart."

"Aha! So you had a Greek or Armenian girl in the camp, eh?"

"No indeed! My wedded wife that I brought with me from Arras!"

"If it is for a woman brought from Arras, lad, choose what you will, except for the silver vessels."

Jacques gazed at the heap in a daze. There were rolls of cloth, carpets, vessels, gloves and embroidered slippers, ribbons and small coffers and candlesticks. He would have liked to take it all. But he was ashamed to take a big thing, and so he chose a ribbon of kingfisher blue with an embroidered pattern of green and gold fish.

"And what about us?" Garin said, but the knight had gone and the soldiers said, "If every beggar in the army came and dug into the heap, the knight would not be rich."

Marie had entered the city before nightfall on that great day when pillage was allowed and all the men had gone in first. Plunder was not a woman's business. They went in groups through those districts which had been cleared of Turks, bringing with them the boys who were too young to fight but were already carrying weapons taken from dead Turks. They ran about like mountain goats, glad to walk on ground that was not mud and to see proper houses. *Oh, but the city was beautiful!*

The outer ramparts and the towers of the great houses were all thick with spears and on each spear was a Turk's head. It was nearly evening but at every crossroads the stone houses, baked by the sun since morning, sent back waves of heat into your face while the streets felt like cool cellars, with fresh air flowing out of the doors through the ironwork gratings. The houses were tall and well built of a fine pale stone. In one square with pink granite fountains in the four corners, dogs were fighting over the entrails of a dead horse. Three headless Turks, stripped of their armor, lay near the horse in a great pool of congealed blood black with flies. The square was littered with dung and broken spear shafts. There had been fighting here.

Men and women with brown faces, dressed in long dark-colored robes, peered down into the square from the tops of the houses. Someone had painted big Greek crosses in blood upon the walls.

The boys were like mad things. They ran along beside the houses, banging on the doors with their sticks, then back again to the bodies of the Turks, breaking the arms and legs with cudgels for fun and teasing the dogs with their pikes. The women sat down by the fountains to wash the babies. The water was cold enough to chill your hands, and oh, how good it was! They let it run into their mouths and down their necks, and splashed it over their heads, and put their hands over the mouths of the jets so that they made great fans of water brighter than silver, reflecting the rosy fires of the sky. There were shrill screams and laughter and no end of splashing. The children were washed and clean, their baby hair all wet, and pretty as lambs. Hurry, friends, hurry, before it gets dark, so there will be time to dry a bit! Cloth that is stiff with dirt takes a long time to dry.

A group of men and women with bundles on their backs came into the square, people with blue eyes and long noses and thin red cheeks.

"Hey, is that booty you've got there?"

They glared back fiercely and their speech was like nuts being broken on stones, not a word of any Christian tongue. For two years now, they had gone about with the cross on their shoulders and they had not yet learned to talk! There was a priest with them.

"You women of France," he said, "where is the church here? We would honor Saint Peter." One-eyed Mahaut, a clothworker from Amiens, told him they had seen no church, of Saint Peter or any other saint.

"Jades," the priest said, "washing yourselves like harlots before you have set foot in a church and prayed." He said something to his flock in Breton, and they hitched their bundles onto their backs again and went on by the street down which the riders had gone.

"Oh dear, it's true, it is a sin, but where are we to find a church? Who will tell us? Those people on the roofs are sure not to speak French."

The Bretons went on their way, dragging their feet a little because they were heavy laden and dying of the heat. They had brought with them every single thing they had in their camp, even down to the feeding troughs and the straw mattresses and the firewood. It was not that they were mean, poor things, only mistrustful, because they were all peasants.

"Isabelle, suppose we go with them. They are bound to find a church. They see angels."

"Who told you that?"

"Saint-John. He said the Bretons are great ones for that." But while the mothers were watching the Bretons, those of the small children who had learned to run had scampered over to the pool of blood and—the naughty little imps—were playing in it, drawing big crosses on all the dead bodies. One of them was squatting down by one of the headless trunks and peering inside with big round eyes and his mouth open in a look of ecstasy. Oh, those dirty children! Those little devils! Just when we'd washed them! Madeleine, look at your Thierry! What does he look like! Madeleine hated anyone to criticize her son.

"Leave him alone, you're only jealous. He's been baptizing himself in Turkish blood." She took him in her arms, all dirty as he was, and hugged him to her breast.

"There's my brave boy, there's my little king. It's good Turkish blood, better than water. You aren't dirty, you're the prettiest of them all."

"Well," said Marie, "that's a funny way to talk to a child. He'll be thinking he's the Pope." She hugged her Pierre to her, wrapping him in her skirts (what if anyone does see my legs?). "Oh, thank God, you are clean, like a little new-laid egg! Stop wriggling. Suck your finger, and we'll find some soup for you tonight."

Oh God, we've finished with the camp and the fevers and the hunger. The city is rich and beautiful. They have fresh water and there will surely be bread.

The sky had turned from red to white and then to dark blue, so fast, as it always did in this land. Oh God, we are only women and children, three dozen of us at most, where have the others got to? You could lose yourself in this city as in a forest, and the houses were all shut up and the people afraid to venture into the streets. From here and there beyond the tall houses came a distant clamor of voices and the din of knights charging, and ruddy smoke showed in the sky to the east. After the camp, the city seemed a desert of walls and pavements. No sounds of shouting came from behind the closed doors of the houses, only a kind of murmur as of people moving about and hushed voices, a sense of slowly mounting excitement. The people shut inside were restless, roaming about and pressing their faces to the windows, and they were afraid, God, how afraid, and who would not be afraid in their place, with a great army pouring into the city? The street was dark now and the windows glowed red and yellow as the lights came and went inside. Voices approached, breaking into Latin chants, loud, raucous voices bawling out psalms. The singing came nearer and then died away with only a glimpse of smoking torches at the end of the street.

Walking like this on empty stomachs in the cold and the dark, while inside those houses were people who had bread. The boys were getting more and more out of control, banging on the doors with their sticks and shouting at the tops of their voices. All of them knew a little Greek or Arabic, and they were shouting abuse and making such a din that the little ones started to cry. Most of the boys were orphans, and this was why no one said anything to them. At last One-eyed Mahaut shouted at them: "Stop that, you wicked boys, or the people here will not give you any food!" Whereupon they all started laughing and yelling: "Then we'll take it, we'll take it!" And they went on like this, louder and louder, in a rhythmic chant: "*We will take it we will take it we will take it!*" delighted with their own cleverness. It was a good thing the people in these parts did not speak French.

"We will take it, we will take it, gouge out their eyes, cut off their noses, roast their feet, smash their teeth, eat their hearts, cut off their heads . . ."

"Oh," said Marie, "what a dreadful song. Suppose Saint George were to hear them!"

Marcel, one of the boys from Arras, called out, "Saint George is on our side!" and then the little fools started up again: *"Cut off their heads, smash their noses, drink their feet,"* making themselves hysterical with laughter. There was no denying that however empty-headed they might be, their bodies had grown in this past year, though God knows how. They were thin but very nearly as tall as grown men. Bad weeds grow fastest, and these had grown up like proper little savages with no looms to stunt their growth.

Kind lords and ladies, be not afraid of us, our children are crying for hunger. *Christos Yesous, Hagia Maria,* Christians, Roumis, *eleison despoios, Kyrios, Hagios Ghiorgios, mulieres, pueris, miserere nobis!* But for all their crying, no one opened to them. To have spent a year in taking this city and now to be reduced to begging at windows! *Eleison, eleison Kyrios!* A window was opened above and someone let down a basket on a rope. Their eyes followed it, like an angel from heaven. Now then! At once the boys were thrusting with their sticks, pushing the women aside and scrambling with yells to get at the basket. Worse than a pack of hounds, what must the Greeks be thinking of us? The women were in tears as the boys ran off with the loaves.

"May it choke them! You wicked, unnatural rascals! Sons of heretics! May the Turks cut off your heads—"

Hoofs clattered over the flagstones, making the whole street shake. There were at least ten horses, maybe fifteen. Make way, make way, Jesus Christ and Saint George! The Count of Boulogne's men! At their head was a man in a shattered broigne, bearing a torch. The women pressed themselves against the walls, unable to see the horses for the yellow smoke. The horses came on, flies on their blood-flecked nostrils, flies on their glaring eyes, their flanks heaving. There were black stains on the riders' leathers. Squeezing herself back against the wall, One-eyed Mahaut called out loudly, "My lords, knights, Christians! We are women of Arras and Amiens. In pity, give us some bread for our children!" Oaths were the only answer. The horses thundered past and the mothers were kept busy stopping their little ones from diving underneath the horses' hoofs. "You fool, Mahaut, do knights carry bread on their saddlebows? Would you have them give you a Turkish head to eat?"

In the big courtyard, friends were meeting again after the night's confusion. People were kissing and crying and the ladle of soup was being passed around. There, you see, children, everything is all right now. We have a good house and we will not be roasted by the sun or choked with dust or have to wade through mud any more. Everyone can choose a room, they are not large but big enough for four or five to sleep in.

Out of the company from Artois and Picardy and Father Albert's Normans, only about ten men brought any booty with them. Everything was handed over to Baudry, with the exception of clothes and weapons and, of course, the women. The pilgrims were decent-living folk and deplored the soldiers' custom of drawing lots for the women: each man kept what he had got. There were some valuable things among the spoils, including a purse containing three silver coins and a Jewish candlestick made of silver, besides two geese, a goat, and three jars of olives. Brother Barnabé said, "We had better sell anything that can be sold as soon as possible for what it will fetch. In a week's time a silver candlestick will not be worth a measure of flour."

"I thought the city was rich," Baudry said.

"Yes, but I have seen what stores the Turks had in their cellars. If the Turks had little, the Christians must have even less, and what they have will be taken from them. It will be a sin, but it will feed the army for a week."

"Do not tell the poor. Not tonight. Let them have some rest."

All the women were talking of the beautiful concubine that le Grêlé had found himself in a Turkish house. Three other young men had also brought women captured in the fighting, but this was a pardonable sin in young men without wives. Élie, however, was past thirty and had a wife in Arras. He had commandeered a good room on the first floor above, all to himself and his concubine. He was feared, and he did as he liked. He had brought his heathen woman in stark naked, wrapped in a curtain, but during the day he had managed by some unknown means to procure from the city an Armenian woman's dress and even some slippers, as though the woman could not go barefoot like everyone else.

Le Grêlé was glum and said little. Six of his comrades had

died in the fighting over the spoils. He still had two erstwhile workless men from the faubourg and two fatherless boys under his protection who served him as varlets.

When Jacques gave Marie her blue ribbon, she gazed at him, blinking speechlessly, as if he had been showing her a reliquary of Saint Ursula. Her eyes widened and her cheeks flushed. She could not believe that this lustrous fabric, soft as a bird's plumage, with delicate silk and gold embroideries, could be for her, and she rubbed her grimy hands against her skirt, not daring to touch it.

"Well," said Jacques, "don't you like it?" Then, with a cry, she flung her arms around his neck and hugged him hard and kissed him, laughing and crying at the same time.

"Oh Jacques, Jacques, oh my Jacques, how kind you are! It is so lovely I could die! It is so lovely I can't bear it, I could eat it, it is so lovely." She laid the ribbon against her cheek, then held it away from her so as to see it better. "The people here do such beautiful work. This is fit for a queen."

"For you. You shall wear it in your hair on Sundays."

"Jacques, what should I look like, with my face all burnt black from the sun!" She twisted the ribbon around her brow, laughing, and Jacques's eyes lighted up with desire as he watched her. With a hoarse cry, she threw herself on him and drew him over to the corner of the room. "Oh, make me happy, ten times, a hundred times, I do so want a child to come to me. I feel as if it were already inside me!"

Carried away with their love for each other, neither cared that Isabelle was there, dozing feverishly in her corner. They sighed and laughed and cried until at last Isabelle too began to cry quietly, pressing her cheek against her baby daughter's head. She was thinking that she would never know the pleasures of love again. There was no fighting sorcery. The lady whose baby had died was rich, she could afford to pay for people to cast spells.

"Marie, the next city we take, I shall stay close to the soldiers, I'll hang on to the knights, and we'll be rich, you wait and see."

"No, Jacques. The first shall be last. In paradise you will have a horse and Duke Godfrey shall hold the stirrup."

Jacques laughed. "I'd like to see his face! Do you think there are horses in paradise?"

"Yes, but not the same as the ones here. They do not eat and do not make dung. It is written: a new heaven and a new earth. The horses will be new also. Like Saint George's horse."

In Jerusalem, Marie was thinking, there are fountains at every street corner and the water that flows from them sparkles like diamonds. It is the living water that gives eternal life. A great fire of a thousand lightnings falls on the holy city, the angels' wings blaze like lightning, they will burn everything and not one infidel shall remain. Then the towers of Jerusalem will be turned to precious stones. In the midst of the city the Church of the Holy Sepulcher will blaze like twelve suns, each one of its stones a living star revolving on itself.

Oh, let my Pierre live until then! Let us live until then. Let Isabelle live until then. "Jacques, is it true that Jerusalem is a hundred leagues from here?"

There were five, or rather seven of them living in this room: Jacques and Marie, Lambert with his mother and Isabelle, and the two small babies. There was room to lie down and a place in the center of the room to put their bundles, the earthenware pot, and the cradle made from Turkish shields where the two children slept side by side, rubbing their pink heads against the grey wool. Their arms were left free so that they could brush away the flies for themselves. Isabelle hardly ever left her bed of straw. Whenever she tried to walk, it made her head swim. She was prey to hopeless misery. "Oh mother, oh for my bobbins and the good smell of wool! Even the flies on the meat were less troublesome at home!"

"Just hark at the silly girl," her mother-in-law would say. "Moaning for the flies in the faubourg."

Brother Barnabé called le Grêlé into the courtyard on the second day and told him, "It's not the rod you are asking for now, but the rope. You are quite clearly living in adultery."

Élie said it was not his fault that his wife had refused to take the cross. He was not the only married man to live in a state of concubinage.

"At least other men's concubines are baptized. You have not had yours baptized."

Le Grêlé said there was nothing he would like more.

"Bring her here and we shall see."

Élie le Grêlé stubbornly refused to fetch the woman out of his room, and so Father Albert went up with him, saying that maybe this infidel woman understood Greek.

Élie's room was quite light because the door was wide and there was even a small window giving onto the street. A jar of water stood by the door and a tripod with some charcoal under the window. When Father Albert saw the woman the color rose in his cheeks, and he understood why le Grêlé would not bring her down to the courtyard.

She was sitting in a corner on some straw covered with a mat, wearing an Armenian dress of pink and green stripes with the red curtain torn up and arranged as a veil over her head. Her face, which was uncovered, was as white as milk, her eyes like two immense black scarabs, and her mouth as soft and delicately formed as a flower embroidered in silk. She could not have been more than eighteen years old and her features were drawn in lines so pure that no Greek painting of the Holy Virgin could have been fairer.

Father Albert scratched the back of his neck. "Well," he said, "now I have seen the Devil! How did you manage to discover such a vessel of damnation?"

"When you have got the Devil out of her," said Élie, "shall I have no more sin?" The priest shrugged and began speaking in Greek.

Evidently the woman understood this tongue very well. After listening to a few words of it, she opened her mouth and began to speak so quickly and at such length that poor Father Albert missed half of what she was saying, while le Grêlé stood blinking in amazement because in two days he had not once heard his infidel woman's voice and had thought she was dumb.

"My daughter," Father Albert managed to get in a word at last, "I have come to bring you the baptism of Jesus Christ, for I am a priest of the Christian religion and I would save your soul."

The woman sprang up with a look of horror, clasping her arms across her breast. No, she said, that could not be, it would be sacrilege. In the Greek Church, the only true one, to which she belonged, it was not permitted to be baptized twice over, and according to the Chalcedonian Creed there was certainly only one baptism, which was that given at birth, and whoever suffered themselves to be baptized twice were heretics!

"Are you then a Greek?"

She said that she was not a Greek, but of the Greek faith. She had been born in Georgia, in the hills beyond Ararat, and had indeed been compelled to honor the Prophet also, but since coming to Antioch she had reverted to her true faith and did not believe in the wisdom of the Prophet as a means to salvation.

Élie was tugging at Father Albert's sleeve. "What is she saying? What is she saying?"

"She says that she is Georgian and a Christian." It took a lot of words to say that!

"Then she is baptized? Then she has not got a devil in her and I am not in mortal sin?" He was watching her with a mixture of relief and mistrust; after all, Christian or not, she had been in a Turkish house, that she could not deny, and according to the rules of war she was a Turk.

The woman was speaking again. She had risen and gone to Father Albert, and she bowed her knee before him: if he was indeed a priest of religion, then let him go, for pity's sake, and seek out the leaders of the war and have word sent to the son of the Emir Kutchuk, if he were among the prisoners, telling him where she was so that he might ransom her. He had property at Bassorah. He would give a good price for her. Father Albert told her:

"My daughter, the son of the Emir Kutchuk will pay no more ransoms, for himself or anyone else." He could not bring himself to tell her that the head of the Emir's son adorned a battlement on the Tower of the Two Sisters.

At his words, the girl turned back to the mat and sat there for a while in silence. Her shoulders drooped and her face looked suddenly lifeless.

"What is the matter with her?" Élie asked. "What did you say to her?"

Filled with pity, the priest asked, "Was he your husband according to Moslem law?" She shook her head slowly. "No, not according to the law. But it is cruel to lose a ground for hope. And he was good to me."

"What does she say? Good God! What does she say?"

"She is grieving for her Turk."

"Sir priest, if you are truly a priest, I am a slave and can neither give nor promise anything, but will you, for pity's sake, go and seek out the wives of your generals and tell these noble dames of my sad case and beg them to have pity on me and take me for a servant. Tell them I was born of wealthy parents and that it was through no fault of my own that I became a captive in a harem. Remind them that in time of war, no woman is safe from such perils."

Le Grêlé listened to her and the more he listened, the more he loved that cooing voice, so soft and beseeching, a voice that spoke straight to the heart although the words were strange. When she finished he sighed, wishing he could have gone on listening.

"Well? What does she want?"

"Listen, Grêlé," Father Albert said, "let me tell you something, man to man, and as a good Christian. This woman is not for you. You would not wish to take advantage of the misfortunes of a Christian woman?"

Élie blushed red. "Why not? I won her fairly, and lost six of my comrades in the doing of it. And now, just because I am poor and ugly, I have no right to my share of the plunder?"

"She would be better with the knights' ladies."

"Say you so, Father Albert. Say rather with the knights. They would make her their harlot. I saved her from four soldiers who would have violated her."

"And did you yourself not violate her?"

Élie bit his lip. He had not thought of that. "That was different," he said.

"Very well, then suppose we could place her in a Greek convent?"

"But why should anyone take away my booty?" said Élie. "She is mine by right of conquest."

"My daughter," said Father Albert, "the rules of war are the same everywhere. It distresses me, but you were the concubine of a Turk, and therefore it is as if you were a Turk."

The woman leaped up, like a mother bird in defense of her young, and began speaking again, very red in the face. Surely, she said, surely this man's captain could release her. According to the rules of war, captives were sorted out and allotted to the best men, and her master had paid twenty gold bezants for her in the coin of the time of the Emperor Nicephorus. Did the Franks hold their slaves so cheap? She had never believed that a man who spoke Greek would abandon her to such misery, but if he had no pity for her as a woman, he should at least consider that she was made to be some noble's prize.

"With us," Father Albert said, "there are no slaves nor masters. This man is free to keep you if he will." He was beginning to find the woman insolent. She was clinging to his habit, but he pushed her away and left the room with le Grêlé.

"What did she say?"

"She is a knights' harlot. She will bring you trouble. In any case, I have wasted enough time on her."

"Hey, Father Albert! What's her name?"

"Fool! Much good it will do you to know her name."

That day the drums were beaten on the towers and the criers of each company summoned the men to the ramparts. All, soldiers and pilgrims, who were not too tired thronged the walls, packed as close as a crowd come to watch a festival. The Sultan of Babylon's great Turkish army was virtually underneath the walls and making camp as if it meant to stay. The whole plain appeared to be stirring, and through the clouds of dust thousands of helms were gleaming in the sun. Out there, where only three days before the Christians had been watering their animals and burying their dead, long rows of circular tents were standing now, with the crescent banners waving above them.

They had all known the army was coming. They had not guessed it was so large. They could see it coming down the slopes of the northern mountains in swirls of yellow dust: more and yet more troops. It would be child's play for them to encircle the city; they had more men than the Christians had ever had, and ten times as many horses. There was little noise on the ramparts. No one had much to say, but under the hot red sky, beneath the rank sweat of their long-suffering bodies, their hearts were beating hard. *O Lord, what have we escaped, O Lord, what yet awaits us?*

We sat for nine months outside these walls, but they can stay a year if they please. They will not need so long, not if we eat all our horses down to the last one. In the city, the criers were proclaiming in the squares: No goats or sheep are to be slaughtered. Rations must be cut by half and extra guards placed on all food shops. We must hold out for two weeks. The Emperor Alexius is sending us his whole army, thirty thousand knights and his engines of war.

This was good news. Through the hot streets, the pavements clogged with every kind of ordure, the Greeks in robes edged with bands of braid were going to vespers, long lines of them, walking sedately, their servants going before to sprinkle sacks of ashes on the ground. They passed along, tall and grave, speaking seldom and then in low voices, and only the hawklike brilliance of their eyes betrayed that they were glad. The women moved slowly, their veiled heads held high, their shoulders motionless, as if each one were carrying a cup full to overflowing on her head. In the great Cathedral of St. Peter, the smell of incense and hot wax was stronger than the smells of men, and the candlesticks before the altar carried an army of yellow flames that wavered gently to the thunder of the singing. Their Latin might be no Latin, but there was no doubt either that no choirs in the world could match the Greeks. Frenchmen in the church wept as they listened to their singing, and disturbed the divine office with their sobs.

The Turkish army was spread out around the walls and along the river, and its thousand campfires made it seem larger even than by day. Their monotonous chants could be heard from the ramparts, tuneless and melancholy. They are encamped on our dead. What rest for you, our friends, beneath the horses' hoofs, trodden by these dogs, whose wailings are your prayers? May your souls be not troubled by them, friends. For there were many recent dead in the burial ground, the dead of a week ago, or four days, to say nothing of those earlier dead whose bodies had now rotted right away: one vast charnel house. God grant that all the suffering that has soaked into the earth down there may recoil on the heads of Kerbogha and his soldiers. May it chill their hearts and put lead in their veins. Happy the rich who had their dead embalmed and brought them into Antioch with the baggage.

By morning heads were flying on the southern ramparts, smashing against the parapets or rolling into the outermost ward of the city. The garrison from the castle of La Mahomerie, across the river, came hurrying back into Antioch, and the castle itself was burning. Fighting broke out again before the citadel, for there were still Turks inside and they were letting in as many soldiers of the relieving army as they wished. Even the children were no longer frightened by the heads flying through the air. But the barons sent criers through the city to proclaim that workmen were needed for the building of a new wall within the city to contain the citadel. Bowmen maintained a running fire from the rooftops while the masons hurriedly built the wall, using stones from demolished houses and such quantities of mortar as would have served to bury whole houses in.

In the camp, the soldiers and knights of each company or region had been together in one place, but here they had dispersed rather than lose the houses they had taken. This meant that when it came to mounting guards and ordering the defense of the towers and of the new wall, they were forever having to run after one another or be summoned by criers. Moreover, the city was so large that it took several hours to cross it. For three days they ate well, but on the fourth even the knights had to be content with dried figs and a soup made from bones. By the fifth day, rich and poor were alike in the city, except among the local Christians, who, if they had any stores, knew where to hide them. Tradesmen dealing in corn and dried fruit barricaded themselves inside their houses and lowered the sacks out of the windows, insisting on payment in advance, while what had cost one denier on the first day had risen to a hundred by the sixth.

The fear of starvation preceded actual hunger. To hold out even for a week they needed something besides fresh water. The city was emptied of food overnight, as if the Devil had turned all the grain to gravel.

For three days Alix had wandered about Antioch, praying and weeping in all the churches, admiring the fine buildings, gardens, and public squares. In the evenings she came back to the big house and sat by the fire in the courtyard with her own people. "Oh my friends, my friends, what a beautiful city! If it were not for the war it could be paradise. If a rich Armenian would take me to wife I would stay here, and there would be an end to poverty. I should have a house with a courtyard full of fountains, and orange trees and white peacocks."

"Rich man's whore," said Madeleine, and Alix laughed.

"Do you think so? Not even if they offered me the Patriarch's own palace! I was daydreaming. I think about a thing, and then it is as if it had already happened and I do not want it any more. This is Saint Paul's city, my little ones, and Saint George's, a holy city, the pearl of Christendom. After Rome and Jerusalem, there is no holier city, do you realize that?

"When I think of that, it is as if I had been raised from the dead, like Saint-John. Let me tell you, friends, I am pledging myself to lead a goodly life and give myself to no more men. You have Armenians and Syrians now—take them to wife! It is time to prepare ourselves for Jerusalem: there we shall see such things that our hearts may burst, and stars will rain down on our heads!"

On the evening of the third day, Philotheus returned to the people of Arras. When nothing was seen of him, everyone had thought that he had found some of his family in the city. However, he came back to them in good earnest, rather neatly dressed as became a townsman and—much to everyone's surprise—very round and fat, at least in body. His gown, above the belt of studded leather fastened tightly around his waist, was so well filled out as to make the folk of Arras think: These Greeks are not made like us if they can fatten up like this in four days. Telling Brother Barnabé and Baudry that he wished to speak to them privately, Philotheus went with them to their room, where he unclasped his belt and let four long canvas bags like outsize sausages slip to the ground. In a moment he had become as thin as before.

Brother Barnabé and Baudry looked at one another in silence, and then at the Greek. All three were very red in the face and almost in tears.

Philotheus was the first to speak. They had better hide these things, he said. There was barley and flour and beans enough for four days, or perhaps longer on short rations. Of course, they were free to do as they liked with it, but he thought it best the others should not know how much food there was.

"We will repay you for this," Baudry said.

"What?" said the Greek. "When you have fed me for more than six months."

"Then you will stay with us?" said Brother Barnabé. "What about your family?"

He told them he no longer had anyone in Antioch apart from a married sister and a few friends, and would prefer to live as a pilgrim. He would go with them to Jerusalem, and after that would probably go and join his brothers in Melitene.

The three men sat on the ground, chin on hand. No one spoke but all their thoughts were the same: how many pots of soup could be got from one bag, how many ladles in a pot, how many days . . . In the camp on the other side of the ramparts, the Turks were hard at work digging trenches and rebuilding the partly burnt-out siege towers.

"What do your people say?" Brother Barnabé asked. "Is it true that your Emperor is bringing his army?"

"So true that we have already had letters from our cousins in Nicaea telling us our troops will be in Antioch before the Nativity of the Virgin."

"God bless the Emperor and let him make haste. We have done already more than mortal men can do."

A much thinner Philotheus returned to the courtyard, and seeing him as slender as a wraith once more, the men sitting under the gallery lifted their eyebrows and tensed like hounds on the scent.

"So that was it, eh, Philotheus? Flour?" Philotheus shrugged.

"A few beans. Keep it quiet, friends. The soldiers are already out searching the cellars."

Within minutes the whole courtyard knew there would be bean soup that night. The men were excited and sang cheerfully as they set about lighting the fires. The naked children ran around the fires, jumping for joy. It would be three hours yet before the beans were cooked, but they had learned to wait. Their lives had revolved around this for so long: food, and whether there would be soup that night or only a moistened rag to suck. They were in a dream. Big beans, big as goats' turds, big as dogs' turds, and then barley cakes, cakes as big as my hand, big as your face, big as the cooking pot! Cooked in sunflower oil, so greasy that your fingers were all sticky with it, and salty, oh so salty, nothing but salt! They dreamed of a city paved with barley cakes, where every leaf on the trees was a cooked bean and the wood fires had fagots of toasted bread you could crunch between your teeth. That is how it will be in Jerusalem; you can eat everything, you only have to lick the walls because they are all fat and covered with salt, and the streets are made of bread, real bread, we will all eat so much bread we'll be as fat as bladders, oh, everyone will eat two loaves apiece and still go on eating.

Isabelle was dying and Lambert stayed beside her, holding her hands. "No, sweetheart, no. Look, we have food. Don't cry. See, I'll give you my share. Soon the Emperor will come and there will be bread and wine."

"Oh Lambert, I am not hungry, that is what makes me so afraid. Eat my share, Lambert, eat it gladly. If they gave me bread I should not want it."

Her mother-in-law went off with little Ondine to the houses of the Syrians, for the poor are more generous than the rich. She went up to young women with infants in their arms (necessity breeds intelligence and she had picked up a few words of Arabic) and explained: "Her mother is dying. Only a little milk for the child. God will reward your child." The women were dark of face but they were good Christians, and Ondine was a pretty child. They gave her their breasts, and the baby was not slow to suck. The priestess would take the woman's child and nurse it and pet it to keep it quiet. "Ah, what a beauty. How strong he is, like a little Saint George! Happy is your mother, happy your father!" In this way she made friends, and she helped the women make their fires and scour their pots. They were good, simple women and they did not mind her blue eyes and her pale face, or her bad Arabic. When she came back to her own people's house, she would say one word in Arabic for every three in French. This made Marie laugh, and Isabelle would be cross.

"They will do my daughter harm with their infidel milk."

"Oh, you ungrateful girl, they are poor women and they have none too much milk even for their own children!"

There were already four infidel women in the house, now baptized by Father Albert and Father Berthold, and married in proper Christian fashion. Only le Grêlé's paramour was not married, but le Grêlé was feared and nothing more was said to him. Besides, how could you marry a man who was married already? The boys who waited on le Grêlé said the girl was lovely as a Greek princess, so beautiful indeed that they had never seen her like. The women peeped in at the door, exclaiming, "Oh how wonderful! How white she is, how delicately shaped! She is like an ermine! Such eyebrows, and that little mouth, *it might have been painted with a brush like a holy image!*" The woman listened to their chattering and looked at them as if they had been so many magpies—which indeed they were, the silly things, but it was a pleasure to see such a pretty creature when they themselves had long been dirty and burnt black by the sun.

Élie took Philotheus aside and explained to him that his paramour spoke Greek. He said he wanted to talk to her, and for her to speak to him. He did not even know what her name was. Philotheus owed him that, surely.

"Certainly," the Greek said, "I am willing." He did not like to be obliged to act as interpreter to a concubine, but he felt that he had no right to be proud with le Grêlé and so he went with him. And eunuch though he was, she took his breath away. Oh God, a goddess of antiquity, a houri, a peri! He stood for a moment unable to say a word, for love enters through the eyes and goes straight to the heart even when a man no longer has the right to call himself a man.

"Very well," he said to le Grêlé at last. "What would you have me say to her?"

"What is her name?"

Courteously, Philotheus asked the woman to reveal her name. She turned her violet-lidded eyes on him and the eyes lighted up with a spark of anxious joy that quickly died.

"You are their interpreter?"

"No, but I know a little of their tongue. I am a free man."

"Then, Greek, if you have the heart of a man, go and find our Patriarch, the most venerable John, and bid him intercede with the Frankish emirs to release me. I swear to you I am no renegade! I have never prayed to the Prophet unless I was compelled." She spoke Greek in a soft, cooing voice, and from the graceful carriage of her head and her slow, studied gestures, must have been trained for some princely harem. How came she to be found in the house of a Turkoman?

"She will not tell me her name, eh?" le Grêlé growled. "Tell her I am called Grêlé, Élie I mean, of the weavers of Arras, a pilgrim and a crusader, and that I want to know her name." Philotheus translated this speech and the woman's brows rose a little.

"Let it suffice you, Greek, to know that I am a native of Georgia, a land where the men are brave and the women beautiful. I shall not demean my father's race by speaking of it. My baptismal name is Euphemia."

"Euphemia," said Philotheus, and Élie repeated the name several times, as though afraid of forgetting it.

She did not look at him; her eyes were searching the Greek's as if she were trying to decide whether she could trust him. She asked:

"You are from Antioch?"

"Yes."

"What are you doing here, with these people?"

"I am their friend."

"Have you spoken with their emirs?"

"Oh no, they are too proud." She turned away forlornly and stared at the sky through the barred window. Élie gazed at her raptly. Her every movement left him wondering how any creature could be so beautiful. She had a hundred faces, all different. Even now, when he could see only her right cheek and the long line of her neck.

"Speak to her. Tell her more about me. Tell her I am kind, tell her some good of me." Philotheus began to speak, and gladly, for it is pleasant to repay a debt. He said that the man was not as brutal as he looked, he was worthy and devout and it was wrong to despise his poverty, he had the heart of a lion, although he was not a soldier, and had left his own land out of zeal for the cause of the Christians of Antioch. The young woman listened absently, frowning a little, as if she were thinking of something else. However, when Philotheus told her how le Grêlé had saved his life at the risk of his own, stopping a charging horse by the power of his arm, she glanced at Élie with a faintly wondering, almost kindly expression, rather as she might have looked at some large, powerful dog. Élie felt his heart thud: it was the first time she had looked at him as if she were conscious of his existence. It made him nervous and he grinned broadly at her, but he was not a man who often smiled and the effort of baring his big, broken yellow teeth gave him the air of a village idiot. The young woman looked away.

"Tell her. Tell her to speak to me." ("He wants you to speak to him.") The woman seemed to wonder what there was to say, but finally she said, "Ask him if he does not wish to go back to his own land." Philotheus repeated the words in French. Élie glowed with happiness. Why, he did not know, just because of those few words she had spoken to him, to him and no one else. He could have found a thousand words to answer her. Well, yes, he admitted, in his country, around Arras, the summers were not so hot and there was no drought and no khamsin, while as for work, no one need starve, even in a bad year, and it was a fact also that in his country even in a slack year you could find comrades to give you a hand, while at other times you could help them. The only thing was the taxes. There were too many taxes, nor was it fair to be a weaver and at the same time liable for feudal service. When you were a crusader, you went hungry but you had no taxes, nothing to worry about—didn't she see? Did she know what taxes were?

For some time past, the young woman had been counting the flies on the ceiling, and even Philotheus had not managed to catch all of what his Frankish friend was saying. However, he repeated the question, and Euphemia said gravely that she did indeed know what a tax was. Her lips twitched. Suddenly both of them wanted to laugh.

There were the taxes, Élie went on, and then children, and a wife always with one child in her belly and another at the breast, so that in the end you were as good as toiling all by yourself from dawn to midnight. Here the children that died were not your own and that did not hurt so much—except for Marina. Marina was the one I brought with me and that a son of a whore dishonored her for me. But she was dead now and it was like getting a bang on the head, it was all forgotten. There was only the cross he had taken, blood, and fire. Did she know what it was like, to take the cross?

"Yes, indeed," Philotheus said. "She knows." Élie blinked. He had been talking on and on, forgetting that the woman could not understand him.

"Well, what are you waiting for? Say it to her in Greek. Everything I have said."

From then on, Philotheus was always having to go to le Grêlé's room to act as interpreter. Euphemia never left the room, but Élie had developed a great longing to know all about her, and to talk to her himself. He had never been much of a talker, yet now he talked on and on, finding innumerable things to tell, and all to someone ignorant of French.

Even so, as a concubine Euphemia was not a great success. The Turks had an odd way of rearing their women, for what the Devil was the good of such a creature? She could not set eyes on a flea or a bedbug or a glob of spittle on the floor without making a face as if she were about to vomit. She refused to scratch your back or wash your feet or hunt for lice. She could not even mend a pair of shoes or patch a shirt, and she was so cold in bed that each time Élie had to pinch her to make sure she had not died on him. All this troubled him a little because he had known no women other than his wife, and this one was so different from his wife that she could have been an animal or bird of some unknown species.

The Turks outside the walls and famine within the city. Eight days they held out, ten days, and by the eleventh they were scraping the earth in the cellars, even in the houses where the knights were quartered. Stables and kitchen yards were bare. On the orders of the Bishop of Le Puy and of the Patriarch, all livestock had been requisitioned for the army, starting with that of the Syrians and then later of the Armenians and the Greeks, but it had all melted away in two days, for after one nine months' siege the citizens had few stores left. Their flour was taken, leaving only half a sack for every family; their oil, their dried figs, their wine, their honey, their dried meat, their preserves and pots of lard, their salted fruits, their jars of pimentos, their amphorae of milk of almonds. When the soldiers went around with their carts gathering up all these provisions there seemed to be a great deal, but once it was shared out among all sections of the army, the whole lot was swallowed up in one day, and even then on short rations.

So much delicious food all gone, turned into urine and the excrement that piled up in the corners of courtyards and in the street gutters, and the man that could eat that must have a stronger stomach even than the Tafurs. So much delicious food all lost in order that the army might eat for one more day, and what then? It was rumored in the town that some of the Italian and Provençal troops had managed to secrete some of the carts when the goods were being shared out and were selling a bowl of flour for a silver mark to anyone who knew the password. Bad Christians, worse than the Turks, and yet men hoped—hoped that they might meet these bad Christians, who were surely clever, prudent men, and pray God they had managed to steal a lot of food!

On the ramparts, things were getting hotter because the Turks, on their side, were by no means starving. They had brought flocks of sheep and cattle and caravans of grain with them from Mosul and had plundered all the crops along the way. They could hold out for a month or two. During the hours of truce the dogs would come and sit down underneath the walls to eat their half-roasted sheep, bringing baskets full of golden barley cakes. The word went around the city, spread by the Syrians, who spoke Arabic and could understand Turkish, that all those who left the city unarmed and promised to become Moslems would be given food and would suffer no harm, but only be put to work in the trenches.

Ten days after the capture of the city, the Christian forces were again engaged in fierce fighting, some on the walls and others around the citadel, fighting a full-scale battle in a vast city where the men were scattered in small companies through fifty different districts, and if any refused to go to the walls it was a clever man who could dig them out of their houses. *Christians, do not stand idle, for love of Saint George! Better to fight on an empty stomach than stay in bed to have your head cut off.* If we let them undermine the walls, none of us will want food or drink again.

Soldiers of Christ, be it known that any man leaving the camp to give himself up is first given food within sight of the ramparts, but then they take him farther off and flay him alive, and use his skin to cover their machines.

And be it known that those who desert for the sake of bread will think they were well off being flayed alive by the Turks when they are in the prisons of hell. Soldiers of Christ, remember that those who abandon Jesus Christ shall be flayed eternally, and their flesh pierced with red-hot needles for evermore. Rather than risk that, who would not go hungry for three days?

Three days, they said. The men drank their watery soup and climbed the steps up to the ramparts. The archers had barely strength to draw their bows and their aim was bad, while it took six men to work a mangonel instead of four. Three days. Moreover, it was not true that the Turks flayed them alive, because you could see our men with their fair beards and torn shirts working in the trenches along with the Turkish slaves. A curse on them, renegades and deserters, they have betrayed Jesus Christ for a crust of bread.

One night, the gateway of the Tower of the Two Sisters was opened and the people living nearby heard the sound of horses' hoofs and the jingle of arms. The Turks, or a relief force coming in? No, the horses were coming from inside the city, a great company passing in the dead of night, without torches, lighted only by a corpse-white moon. Pilgrims and local inhabitants watched from the rooftops as the knights rode by, fully armed, with lances at rest, the crests on their helms blanched by the moon like dead birds borne on a swift-flowing stream. Is there a sortie planned? Oh, the gallant knights, the men of noble race, they mean to take the Turks unawares by night! Those men who had the strength ran to the walls and went up the steep stone steps four at a time. A sortie? Who is going out? Those are French arms, it must be the Count of Blois, Count Stephen himself, who leads them. Have they gone mad? They are too few to tackle the whole Turkish army. They will need not only Saint George but ten legions of angels!

In the morning, the truth was known. Count Stephen and his followers had ridden at full tilt straight across the plain and were gone before the enemy had time to get to horse, gone to find food elsewhere. Cowards, may the rain never fall on them, may the bread for which they betrayed us turn to lead in their mouths and their wives and children spit in their faces! If the noblest men in France act thus, what will God think of the French and how should He defend them? In the poorer quarters a great shout went up that almost turned into a riot: *Christians, good pilgrims, they will all do as Count Stephen has done.* They will steal away like cowards in the night and leave us to the mercy of the Turks.

Bohemond's criers gathered together in the public squares all those able to understand French and told them: Soldiers, pilgrims, crusaders, do not waste your strength in shouting and fighting among yourselves. The good Emperor is coming to relieve us. The Turks will not dare to stay and meet him. Be patient for three more days. Of all those that are in this city, barons, knights, priests, clerks, soldiers, and pilgrims, not one more man shall leave it except to cut the Turks to pieces or for paradise.

Any man caught trying to leave the city will be hung from the walls as a target for the Turks, be he knight or priest even.

That same night, fifty pilgrims from the Ardennes stole a coil of rope from the machines and escaped out of the city by sliding down the wall near the citadel, next to a rocky ravine where the dead bodies were lowered. The next day it was being said in the quarters of the soldiers and the pilgrims that Peter himself had been caught by one of the postern gates with two companions, trying to get out of the city.

There was no means of telling if this was true or not and some squabbles arose as a result. Brother Barnabé called his people together in the courtyard and told them: "My friends, if you accuse Little Peter, the man of God, you might as well accuse God Himself. Peter has never betrayed you. If he was trying to leave the city, it was because in his charity he meant to go to the Turks and ask them to take pity on the poor, the women and children, and sell him some flour. For even the Turks listen to men of God. If, impossible as it seems, he can have acted foolishly, the reason was pure charity."

"And if that were true," said Alix, "why should the knights have stopped him from going?"

"Because Bohemond has sworn on the Holy Gospels that he will allow no man to leave the city. He must keep his oath. But if the Bishop of Le Puy should relieve him of that oath, he would himself send Peter to Kerbogha so that Peter might bring us back bread for the women and children."

"Yes," said the men, "and they would give that bread to the soldiers. They have already eaten horses that were neither dead nor dying. That is what they are saying."

"They are saying a great many things," Baudry replied. "Those are the emanations of hunger. People will say anything."

Queues of men, crusaders, Syrians, even Armenians, crowded outside every stable. If a horse died, the meat was for the baron's company, but still the poor people hoped. There was the head or the fetlock or the entrails: they could always make something of those with a little wood ash and some cypress leaves. There were plenty of rich men in the city, among the Franks and among the Greeks, yet even they would have given all their riches for some bread, but they could not. There might have been some who ate in secret in their palaces, but if there were no one knew of it.

Courage, Christians, a few more days and the Turkish camp will be ours with all their flocks and their grain. When the Emperor's army comes in sight our knights will sally forth from the city: the enemy will be caught between two fires and those that flee will take no thought for baggage.

The days of starvation were so long that two weeks after taking the city they already felt as if they had been there for months. The dead were let down the rocks near the citadel while priests stood on the wall chanting the prayers, some in Latin, others in Greek or Syrian. It was a great grief to be deprived of burial places in this way, but it was no longer possible to bury people within the city; the churchyards were so full of fresh graves that they resembled newly plowed fields. Oh, Christian friends, this is a sad deliverance we have brought you, if we must all die together. The natives of the place were amazed to see how soon the pilgrims, and even the rich, the knights and clerks, succumbed to hunger. They did not know what it meant to go hungry for a year. For it was only fair to say that ever since Constantinople, even when there was no shortage of meat, the noblest barons had seldom eaten their fill, but curbed their appetites for shame rather than incur the censure of their men.

The knights suffered more than the humble folk, for they spent themselves more and had more flesh on them to feed. There were some who ate the thistly straw provided for their horses. But what frightened them most of all was that the fodder was becoming poorer and poorer, and even of this there was only enough for ten days at the most. A horse is not like a man, and cannot live on promises. They knew, as the whole city knew, that if the Emperor did not come to their relief in ten or fifteen days there would be nothing for it but to eat the dead horses and wait for the end, for without horses there could be no battle. There would be the greatest slaughter in Antioch that had ever been seen since the time of the Romans, for whether they sold their lives dearly or not, the end would be the same for all.

The priests prayed day and night in all the churches, and the Patriarch proclaimed fasts—as if anyone could help fasting—and public prayers and processions. But God had little mercy on

His people: on the fifteenth day a courier sent by Bohemond's brother from Cilicia got into the city by way of mountain paths, bringing the worst possible news. The Emperor was not coming. Believing false rumors that Antioch had already fallen, he was leading his army back toward the sea, making for Nicaea.

This news would have been better kept from the soldiers and the people in the city, but when the whole city was on edge waiting for news, with people crowding around the palaces and dogging the leaders' footsteps trying to guess what was in their minds, bad news traveled like a river in spate. Very soon a wave of lamentation swept in some mysterious way through every court and square, over the ramparts and the rooftops. All was known, the Emperor was not coming, the Emperor was going home, he was not sending reinforcements. It was known from spies coming from the Turkish camp, though none had wanted to believe it; it was known from the cries of the Turkish interpreters; in the Turkish camp they were beating drums and lighting fires for joy. Die, infidel dogs, your king has flung you to the jackals, to him you are as dung, he will not tire his horse three days for you.

Tomorrow your women shall be delivered up to our men-at-arms, your children roasted on spits, your priests tied at our horses' tails.

We will fill wagons with your heads and make sheep pens of your swords and lances, for they are cowards' weapons.

Camels shall stall on your banners, and the images of your Messiah and your false prophets shall be trodden into dung-heaps.

All this they cried in Arabic, Greek, and French from the tops of their siege towers. Yield, slaves, they cried, and of our mercy we will give you bones to gnaw! If you deliver us your women, we will spare your lives and only cut off your ears and noses.

"Laugh, servile dogs, servants of the false prophet, soon your heads shall grin on the points of our spears.

"Draw up in your battle array and meet us if you dare. When we come out of the city you will not dare to stand and face us! Our spears are for your backs, not for your breasts!

"We have never seen such poor soldiers in our own lands. It hurts us sorely to draw sword against you."

The criers on the towers laughed. "Come on!" they cried, in Turkish and in Arabic, and God knows no one believed a word of it, because whether Mahomet was good or evil, the Turks were the bravest soldiers in the world. That was well known. When they rushed in to the attack, they would not flinch for arrows or missiles, and yet they fell and died, they were no more immortal than the Christians.

Isabelle died on the day they learned that the Emperor was not coming. She heard the wailing in the courtyard and dragged herself to the edge of the balcony, where she understood at last what was the matter. Then she went back and lay down on her mattress and closed her eyes.

When her mother-in-law came to bring her something to drink she said:

"It is finished. I shall not drink again except in paradise."

"Don't be so foolish, girl. Paradise is not for foolish girls who give up hope."

"Mother, you will not tell Ondine about my crooked back." This was the last thing she said.

The priestess summoned Father Albert and Lambert and Marie, but Isabelle had no time even for confession. She died just like that, tired and sad, her pretty face all shrunken like a little old woman's.

It is always sad to see a young mother die, and the folk of Arras and their companions were not yet so hardened that they could not mourn for Isabelle. They laid her on a bier and set it in the center of the courtyard, lighting torches for lack of candles. Marie bound her blue silk ribbon around her friend's brow and Alix covered her with the Turkish robe won at the great battle of Dorylaeum. It was half rotted now but the gold threads still held, covering Isabelle with a web of golden flowers interspersed with dark holes. Honorée put a silver chain around her neck.

That night was so heavy with grief that they all bade farewell to Isabelle as if this burial would be their last. God knows if there will be any lights or prayers or tears for us that are left. It may be the Turks who will attend our obsequies.

Father Albert and Brother Barnabé prayed aloud, raising their voices to be heard above the sobbing of the women. The men stood a little apart, leaning on their staffs, and the children sat on the ground, crying because they heard the women crying, and wondered if the dawn would ever come, and if they would be given something to eat that morning.

The dead cart came around at dawn, the man in charge asking at every house what was to be taken. Seven men and two women had already left the house this way since the capture of the city, as well as four infants, one already learning to talk. The torches had burned out; the cold came down from the pale sky like a great transparent shroud, and the grimy walls and flagstones of the court, the ragged garments, all congealed in a pure, cruel light. Farewell, cool night, the guardian of the dead, by noon the sun's heat will bring corruption and the flies. God guard all bodies that do not lie in earth.

Ah, Isabelle! Faithless friend, you are gone from us. Isabelle, whom we so loved.

Isabelle, your little Ondine was well named, *the bitter waters of salt tears shall be this child's drink.* Isabelle, whom God made so fair that the Devil grew envious and made her fall from a ladder. Her back was crooked but her soul was straight as the poplars, straight as a wax candle, *straight as Roland's sword, fair Durandal!*

In paradise you shall behold her straight and slender as an empress, O Lord Jesus! O Lord Jesus, how ill have You repaid her, O Holy Virgin Mary, did she not pray enough to You? Why have You let my poor Isabelle die? Even with her crooked back she was fair to us.

O Lord Jesus, You did not guard her well!

Oh Mère Perrine, your warp is broken, your shuttle has slipped from your hands! Oh Mère Perrine, your wool has perished and your cloth is wasted! Let him that should bear the news die before he reaches the faubourg. *Oh Mère Perrine!*

You let her follow the Lord Jesus with her cross on her shoulder, and the Lord Jesus has taken her to Him on His cross. *Oh Mère Perrine!*

He has taken her, your daughter, on His cross, He has made her His martyr. Oh Isabelle, now you are straight as a candle, your eyes shall weep no more tears.

Oh Isabelle, my star, oh my friend, my flower, my darling! Oh my sister, how could you leave me, poor as I am, without even bidding me farewell? Oh my Isabelle . . .

As she spoke, Marie's voice gained in strength and resonance, gliding imperceptibly into song, and the song turned to sobbing and the sobbing swelled to a fresh threnody of grief. Her body swayed to left and right in time to her words, and all those present, the folk of Arras and the men whose task it was to load the bodies onto the carts, listened to her. They were familiar with grief, but Marie sang her dirge in a voice so heartbreaking that it gladdened them to hear her and they said there was no finer mourner.

The cart was moving on, drawn by six men with ropes attached to long shafts, and already there were many other Christian bodies on the cart, laid out tidily and wrapped, some in a length of cloth, some in a garment, and the friends of the dead followed, weeping and rending their cheeks. The names and provenance and virtues of the dead were mingled in the general chorus of mourning until each mourner half forgot for whom he grieved.

Oh my friend, oh my brother, oh Bernard, oh Marcel my comrade, oh cursed Turks, may this rock smash the skull of him that sent it. Oh my fellow, oh Gerard, what a grief is this for your mother . . . You who were so strong, so true, who feared no arrows. Oh friend, you feel no hunger now, you have no fever, the gangrene cannot harm you, you go to meet your son. Oh Isabelle, oh Isabelle!

They followed the cart as far as the street corner, to the limits of their ward of the city. Beyond, the principal streets were controlled by the knights and the way had to be kept clear for the movement of troops. In any case, the families had neither the will nor the strength to go on to the end and see their dead cast over the walls. Once the Turks were gone, they would all be put in the earth, in one huge common grave. When the Last Day came, God would not fail to find them.

Later the same day, a Norman soldier came to the house of the pilgrims from Arras and approached Marie.

"Come with me," he said, "and mourn for my brother who got an arrow in the chest, for as sure as God lives I am in such pain that if I do not weep I shall go mad."

"How can I?" Marie said. "I have never seen your brother."

"Come," the man said, "and you shall see him." Marie took pity on him and went, taking Saint-John with her because a simpleton was better protection than a man who was too ready with his fists.

She was taken to the courtyard of a soldiers' billet where there were several dead and wounded, as well as a number of soldiers engaged in mending their equipment. The man's brother lay on his long shield, his hands folded on his breast. He was a tall, fair youth whose beard had not yet grown, and his face was a greyish brown except for the forehead and the lower part of the cheeks, which were quite white where his helmet had shielded them from the sun. He had not been dead long; his cheeks were smooth, his nose seemed chiseled out of marble, and his pale lips smiled with such sweetness and tranquillity that Marie cried out, "God, but he is happy!"

"He was my only brother," the soldier said. "Gilbert. I taught him his trade."

Fascinated, Marie stared at the dead man. She had never seen a more beautiful smile. The heavy eyelids, large and slightly bulbous, were firmly closed. It was hard to imagine that the eyes had ever looked upon this earth, they seemed to have seen only God. *He is a saint,* Marie thought.

To the man, she said, "Your brother's is the better part. All is well with him. Look at him, see how beautiful he is even now. Speak to him. He is going to Jesus Christ, but he can hear you still."

"No, already he is too far away."

"Oh no, he hears, but speak to him softly, we must not weep or moan for the happy dead. He is climbing the angels' ladder now and we must not cry out and make him fall."

The soldier knelt by the body, gazing intently at the still face and moving his hand to brush away the flies that settled persistently on the nostrils and at the corners of the mouth. "Only this morning, Gilbert, only this morning, at the dawn watch, you were bending your bow. Gilbert, tell Jesus Christ I had no other brother but you. Ask Him to let me die soon and follow where you have gone."

The captain of the archers was shouting to arms. "For God and Saint George, Normans, enough of weeping! Men are needed on the tower. We have priests for the dead."

The men were tightening their belts and settling their quivers on their left shoulders. From under their helms, the sweat ran in fat rivulets down faces that were grey with dust and flushed with weeping. Their eyes were the eyes of hunted wolves, but they held themselves upright and bared their teeth in a parody of a grin. Of all the men in the army, the archers were the toughest. In good times they were bad men, but when things were going badly they displayed a pride that put the knights to shame. They might be starving but they never mentioned food.

Marie and Saint-John watched them leave the courtyard. God keep them, you would find no such men even among the Turks. To see them march you would have thought that they came straight from eating.

A Norman knight came out of the house that gave onto the court, two squires still lacing his cuirass. He was swearing by all the saints and seemed in haste, but when he saw Marie he stopped and said, "Whose whore is this?"

"She is a married woman," Saint-John said. "A woman of Arras. She came here merely to help one of your men in his grief."

"Come hither, fair one, and I'll give you my ration of beans tonight."

Marie and Saint-John lost no time in argument but fled the courtyard. However, the knight on horseback caught up with them at the end of the street and leaned down from his saddle.

"You shall have anything you want, once the Turks are gone. White bread and oranges, and a room opening on the garden."

Marie made a face at him that would have frightened a Turk, but the man said, "I shall know where to find you."

Marie and Saint-John ran for safety to the courtyard of a house full of Syrians. "It is the fighting," Marie said, "it rouses their blood. Their heads are all upside down on account of the assault."

Saint-John had forgotten the knight already and was looking at the Syrian women seated on the ground in a corner of the court, wailing in unison, striking their breasts and their cheeks. They were poor women, blacker than Turks, with thin, aquiline faces, and wore robes of coarse blue-and-grey woolen.

"See, Marie," said Saint-John, "here are the holy women weeping over Christ at the descent from the Cross."

"You're dreaming, my lad. It is not Eastertide."

"It is Easter every day, Marie, for truly Jesus Christ is nailed to the Cross every day. These women look like Syrians but in reality they are Mary the mother of James and Salome and Joanna and Magdalene. They believe they are mourning for a Syrian of Antioch, but I say to you that all tears are truly for Jesus Christ. You thought last night you wept for Isabelle, but Isabelle is also Jesus Christ."

"Stop raving," said Marie, "and let us go home."

"I rave, Marie, because for me there is no difference between one year and a thousand years. Jesus Christ is the oak and men are the leaves which sprout and fall year by year. They are the same because the oak is always the same. Each man that dies is a leaf of Jesus Christ. They return to the mold and He draws them back again into Himself." Marie sighed, because she was fond of Saint-John, but all she said was, "You will be cured in Jerusalem."

• • •

They went back to the business of living. They had known for two days now that there was nothing more to hope for, least of all the Emperor.

If only we had Charlemagne instead of this degenerate Greek Emperor, then we would be in Jerusalem in no time!

But the days of the great men are past, and there is no going back. *Hear me, good Christians, God means to try us, but He does not purpose our deaths, for He cannot purpose His own shame.* We do not yet know how, but it is certain that He will deliver us before two weeks are out. There are still rats and mice in the cellars, we can even eat flies by pounding them with ashes, but anyone caught eating Christian flesh shall hang, be it even the flesh of a Syrian Christian, for they are our brothers. Hunger is better than thirst. Remember the crossing of the desert. Here you have water in plenty.

The men were growing so listless that they did nothing from morning to night but lie in their rooms, where at least the heat was more bearable. The strongest roamed about the city, scraping with their staffs in the gutters, where from time to time it was possible to find a dead rat that was still edible.

Jacques lay alongside Lambert in the room where there was no Isabelle any more. Where the door should have been, he saw a white horse, a big white horse with a broad, deep chest and lips drawn back in an enormous grin. Its black eyes with their blood-red lids expanded and contracted, seeming at the same time near and very far off; at times they were so near that Jacques felt as if they were merging into his own.

"The horse, Lambert."

"What horse? Saint George's horse?"

"In the doorway—or am I dreaming?"

"That's not a horse, it's a white rat."

"So big?"

Lambert shook himself and went over to the door.

"I was asleep, that's all. I was dreaming of—you know what? Of our church in the faubourg. It was white and newly painted and my father was wearing a chasuble all sewn with silver, and the stones above the chancel arch were singing. Think of that, singing stones!"

The priestess was nursing Ondine, but Ondine was crying and would not go to sleep.

"My son, I know what we must do. The spell was stronger than our prayers, and your Isabelle was willed to die. If that woman who wants your daughter has brought this trouble on us, she will surely lift the spell if she gets what she wants. She is rich. Ondine will be better off with her."

"Talk it over with Baudry," Lambert said. "I don't know what I'm doing any more."

Baudry, Brother Barnabé, Alix, and all those who had the heart to listen to the news from the city were sitting on the shady side of the courtyard, dipping their hands into a bucket of water from time to time to drink and cool their faces. The priestess went down to them, carrying Ondine in her arms, and told them of her belief that it would be best to let the child go to the woman who wanted her, or otherwise it would soon be Lambert's turn.

"Have you any proof," asked Brother Barnabé, "that there is any spell, and that it is indeed this woman who has cast it?"

The priestess said she had always felt it. She said that the woman had asked for the child on the day Isabelle went there to beg, and from that day on, Isabelle's malady had grown worse. She added that the woman was rich and would surely be able to find a nurse.

Marie was there, with baby Pierre on her knees, squirming like a little captive bear because he was hungry, and cramming both his fists into his mouth. She got up at once, dumping the child in Mahaut's lap, and began to speak her mind. She said that she would never let them do it, that they meant to take away her little Pierre's affianced bride and that Isabelle had promised her faithfully to him. She added that Isabelle was still quite close to them and could see everything: "And what shall I say to Mère Perrine, who is my mother's friend, if I let Isabelle's child go to strangers? Besides, Ondine and my Pierre already love each other, and if the priestess is too weak to beg, then I will beg for both. I will take the girl on one arm and the boy on the other."

"You!" the priestess said. "Your man should beat you, but he is too soft! You can hardly stand up yourself and yet you want to carry two children. If you manage to keep your own alive it will be a marvel!"

Brother Barnabé looked from the two women to little Ondine lying half asleep in her grandmother's arms, her head on its long slender neck lolling back and her big eyes half open behind wet lashes. She was pale, like a faded flower, but prettier than ever. Her thinness made her look less like a baby than a young girl in miniature.

"As the patriarchess Hagar in the desert went and laid her child afar off," Brother Barnabé said, "so as not to see it die, whereupon God made a spring of fresh water flow for her, so you, woman, would send this child away from you so that God may save her. It may be that the woman you speak of is richer than we are. The child seems fair and likely to live. Do as you think best."

"Oh no," Marie said, "Ondine is not for any wicked woman who puts spells on people. No, she shall never leave her own folk. Who then will tell her of her mother? Here she is loved by all, but who will love her there? Oh Isabelle, Isabelle my linnet, now that you have left this world they mean to take your daughter from you!"

"Peace, Marie," Baudry said, parting the two women. "The priestess is older than you are, let her do what is best for the child. You must not draw the spell upon yourself, you have a son to rear."

The priestess took Ondine away. She walked through the city, keeping close to the walls. The child was heavy, and she was tired to death. She tried to run, hugging her granddaughter in both arms, hobbling, bent double, through streets that were thick with ordure, hobbling with little zigzag skips like a wounded bird, bumping into soldiers and beggars. She showed the men-at-arms the little embroidered bonnet with the lady's blazon on it and asked them where the knight lived who bore this device on his shield.

Someone showed her the way at last, and she came to a large house with arched windows flanked by slender columns and the device of the Boulonnaise lady hanging with a number of other shields above the door. A soldier at the gate told her, "On your way, woman, the knights here have nothing for you."

"But I have something for them." She showed her embroidered bonnet. "I have come to find the wife of this knight."

She was allowed inside. Ondine was whimpering and tugging with her little hands at the tendrils of fair hair that curled about her face.

There were a number of women in the ladies' chamber, sitting some on coffers, others in the window embrasures. Two half-grown girls were lying on rugs. At least three of these women were noble; they wore long braids and ribbons studded with silver bound around their brows, but their gowns of Greek silk hung on them like rags, unfastened at the neck on account of the heat, and their faces were like everyone else's—gaunt, except for a puffiness around the lips and eyes, with the dulled expression of those whose thoughts are centered on food. But the priestess had sharp eyes and she recognized the lady, thinner and aged though she was. She went straight up to her and laid Ondine in her lap.

"There," she said. "Take her."

"What do you want of me?" the lady said, and then she recognized the bonnet.

"Her mother is dead. Take her."

"My poor woman, what can I do with her? None of our women have any milk. We have lost three infants for want of nurses."

"You will find one for her," the priestess said. "She is yours. It was for that her mother died."

The woman closed her arms around Ondine to prevent her from falling and the child, who was no fool, finding herself in a young woman's lap, set to at once with both hands to undo the bosom of her gown and find the breast, and clamping her little mouth to it, began to suck earnestly. The woman's whole face quivered with shock, her hands trembled, and she held the little girl close. "Ah, poor fool, what are you trying to get? I have nothing in my breasts for you." There were tears in her eyes. Ondine was sucking as hard as she could, biting angrily at the empty breast. Choking back her sobs, the woman asked, "What is her name?"

"Call her what you would have called your own dead daughter. Her true name God will not forget, but it has not brought her luck."

"Very well," the woman said at last. "She shall not die, or I shall. Not God nor the Devil shall take her from me."

The priestess went away. Her body felt lighter without Ondine dragging on her arms and breaking her back, but her heart was heavy: the little strumpet, the bad girl, to forget her granny who has kept her alive for three months at God knows what cost, to forget her for a woman who has not even any milk. She knew her because of the spells she put on us.

Ondine is dead. Stillborn. It is the soul of the other child that will live in her. She will never know her mother had a crooked back. No one will tell her now about the curé, and the faubourg of Arras, and about Mère Perrine.

A priest was addressing the crowd in the open space before a church porch where the beggars lay, so still that it was hard to distinguish the living from the dead. He had eyes like red-hot coals, grey, sunken cheeks, and a dirty grey beard like a goat's. He was trembling all over and speaking in a clipped, breathless voice like a man with hiccups.

"Fellow Christians! The envious Greeks are hiding the truth from us. Salvation is at hand. It lies not far away, in the Cathedral of St. Peter. This is why we are in Antioch, so that God may reveal the truth to us. If the barons will not search for it, we shall do it for them.

"It is here! Before three days are out you shall see it, if you do penance first. Even now it is talked of throughout the Provençal quarter, and the truth shall not long remain hidden! Because he that knows the truth is poor and mean and humble, they will not listen to him.

"God, to confound the rich and the mighty, has revealed His truth to a poor man, despised by all, but he shall not be despised for long. They shall turn to him as to their savior."

"What truth?" the people were asking.

"Not that which is in Constantinople. That is a falsehood, set up by the Greeks in their pride. But the one, the true, which shines so brightly underneath the earth that the righteous see it, like the sun in the bottom of a well. God has waited for us here to reveal this great secret to us."

"Surely," the people said, "it must be the crown of thorns, surely it is the Holy Grail. It is the head of John the Baptist."

". . . What have we been doing since God delivered this city into our hands? Shame on us! The Turks are at our gates and we howl like wolves because of our empty bellies! And no sooner do we find some gobbet of unclean meat to gorge ourselves with than we hasten to satisfy our fleshly lusts on women yet more unclean! Throughout this city are holy images defiled, crosses broken, the paintings in the churches defaced, and such is our slothfulness that neither the Bishop nor the Patriarch has succeeded in finding workmen enough to clean the churches. We should have washed them with our tears and worn our hands down to the bone to wipe away those stains. Repent and pray that God may yet reveal this great secret to you!"

"This is Provençal boasting," a Norman soldier said. "They need something to boast about because our men have the better billets. But who was first inside the city?"

"With miracle after miracle," the priest went on, "with miracle after miracle, the Lord Jesus Christ drives out Mahomet. At the hands of the poor, the humble, and the starving. Do not boast, Normans, you did not take the city. God gave it to us. One day later and we should all have been dead, for the Turkish army was at hand. God performed this miracle as He will perform a hundred more, until Jerusalem. The truth shall burst like lightning from East to West. I see the plain ablaze like a sea of torches: it is the Turks swept living into the fires of hell. The water under the bridge runs redder than the dyers' vats and the field is covered with a rich carpet of their slain! The banners of the cross wave over them, led by Saint George mounted on his white horse!" The priest sank to his knees, and men ran to lift him up. He was gasping for breath and there was foam on his lips. Ah God, how can a man half dead with hunger speak for so long? Give him some water, at least.

Slowly, trembling with exhaustion, the priestess made her way back to the house. There also, everyone was talking of the good news. A holy man from Provence had prophesied an end to the siege. Priests and clerks believed in him and he had been taken to the legate, the Bishop of Le Puy, who would very soon pronounce publicly on the truth of the prophecy. The priestess said there was talk of a miraculous relic, a relic of such power that the Turks would never stand against it but would be stampeded like a herd of cattle.

"In that case," Baudry said, "it would need to be the Holy Cross itself, and everyone knows that is not in Antioch."

"Well, whatever is in Antioch is buried underground, no one knows where, and no one will know until the sinners have repented."

"Well," said Alix, "there are plenty of sinners to be converted. We might wait until Christmas."

"Be silent, woman," Brother Barnabé said, "and do not mock. In our present plight, no sinner would fail to return to God: we are every one of us as good as dead."

The news of the hidden treasure spread through the city like a rising tide undermining the land from below, appearing now in one place, now in another, seeping into the subsoil and saturating it. It fermented like wine in the minds of men made light-headed by starvation until they no longer knew what to believe or even whether they should speak of it aloud.

It was treasure buried long before by the Roman emperors, sarcophagi filled with gold coins, enough to ransom every man within the walls.

It was the reliquary encrusted with diamonds and emeralds containing the head of John the Baptist.

It was the reserves of grain hidden by the Turks before the siege, a hundred bushels of corn in a cave a hundred feet underground, guarded by the ghosts of ten Turks slaughtered at the entrance to the cavern.

It was a subterranean kingdom where the grass grew and springs of fresh water flowed and white sheep grazed beneath orange trees, where it was always light, by night and day, because the walls of the underground cavern were made of luminous stones. The streams were alive with singing fishes and the birds in the trees had women's heads. Whoever entered there would not have far to walk, for it emerged in the grotto of the Holy Sepulcher, right in the middle of Jerusalem . . .

Beneath the floor of the Cathedral of St. Peter reposed the bodies of ten holy martyrs, crucified in the time of the Emperor Hadrian. They had been placed there to guard the sacred relic, but the Romans had killed all the Christians and profaned the tomb, setting up a statue of Jupiter in its place, in punishment for which crime God had decreed that the relic should remain hidden from all mortal eyes for seven hundred years, and the seven hundred years had now elapsed.

This relic was the Holy Lance that pierced the right side of Our Lord. For the lance Saint Helena had found was not the true one, though very like it; it was the lance of one of the other soldiers who had stood near the Cross and because of this it had some virtue also. But who could doubt that the virtue of the true Lance was such that if the Greeks had possessed it they would never have suffered defeat. *Because of their sins, God had not permitted them to find it. Instead, He had revealed the secret to the lowliest of all the poor pilgrims of Provence.*

All those who were not on the walls gathered their strength and went in procession to the churches, and when all the churches were full the hosts of worshippers crowded around the doors and in the streets and squares round about. Those unable to stand or kneel for very long sat or even lay down on the ground, and some of these did not get up again.

It was very hot and the flies born of the filth and the corpses hung like a thick black net above the half-naked bodies. The sky was bluer than the deepest sea and the sun so close to the earth that it seemed three times its size and all colors were consumed by it. Everything was white, walls, pavements, people's bodies; even the darkest clothes looked grey and the mosaics on the wall over the doorway burned like fire.

The voices singing the responses were so cracked that it seemed as if the whole city was at its last gasp.

Lord Jesus Christ, now is the time to keep Your promises. Behold us, nailed to Your Cross, pierced by the Lance. Reveal to us the Lance that pierced Your most pure side and is stained with the promised blood. *Kyrie eleison miserere Domine.*

The sky turned black and above the church the Lance was shining, a mighty, tapering barb of white-hot iron. In broad day the sky was black, the Lance drew all light into itself, it soared above the church, white-hot, and the blood upon it shone like the sun.

Jacques watched the dead walking in procession through the air, their feet brushing the roof of the church. At their head walked Sir Evrard, a fiery cross on his bloodstained broigne, blood on his beard, with eyes closed and lips moving in a psalm. Where are your psalms and your white robes, brothers? We are going with you to Jerusalem where all shall be fulfilled. Washed in the blood of the Lamb, washed in the blood, rivers of blood shall flow, drowning the whole city.

Sir Evrard passed on with closed eyes, his lance in his hand and the blood streaming in a red mantle over his shoulders, and the other dead followed him, arrows in their breasts or in their eyes, shattered heads and severed arms gleaming like rubies in the light of the Lance. Singing, they circled in the air above the church.

There will be blood up to the horses' nostrils. None shall see the new heavens and the new earth that are not washed in blood. Why does he keep his eyes shut? Oh, sir knight, oh, my friend, this is a cruel parting!

The square was full of voices. Many of those who saw the

Lance were sinners and they screamed because the Devil was leaving them.

Élie le Grêlé stood up and sang with all his might, he who had never sung. *Miserere nobis Domine.*

Lamb of God who takest away the sins of the world,
Blood of the Lamb,
Our sins are washed away, the Lance is found,
our bodies saved,
Our souls baptized with fire!

Once again he saw the body of Our Lord, huge as the sky and pierced all over with arrows of fire, and the crown of thorns set above the sun, dropping a rain of blood. As he sang his fingers clenched on the handle of his long knife, his throat tightened, and a great hunger and thirst rose from his whole body toward his heart; his other hunger was swallowed up in it like a brook in the sea. This hunger was for his ax; he longed to feel it grasped between his hands. Before his eyes was the black man, the giant with the white teeth, reeling under the ax, his skull split. His ax. He hungered for his ax. The sky had become a beast full of eyes and le Grêlé's heart beat faster as he saw those eyes gouged out—baskets, fountains, full of living eyes.

Big black, melancholy eyes, those big vacant eyes that could look right through a man. When will You look at me, what must I do to make You see me?—*Miserere Domine.* Oh, body of Our Lord pierced by the Lance, the strong Lance that pierced the earth and sky, the blood of the whole world has flowed from its point—the blood of the Turks shall flow, Orontes shall be red with it like a dyer's vat, with Turkish blood. Euphemia, I shall bathe you in Turkish blood, oh whitest of all, in blood I shall baptize you. Oh Lord, my ax.

Brother Barnabé was praying. They will go away, Lord. They shall flee before Your might, You will save the poor, the little children shall not die of hunger any more. You brought them here, now it is time for You to reveal Your miracles, O Lord, and more than time. A half and more are dead—who can perceive Your will? Our dead companions, from the first who died in Hungary right down to young Isabelle, *all with us, let none be forgotten.* In the mountains and the deserts, in the rivers and ravines, in the great burial ground down there beneath the Turkish tents, and in the gully beyond the wall, crusaders raised from the dead, all for one and one for all. At the touch of Your Holy

Lance may our sins be burned away like gangrene cauterized by red-hot iron. Lord, the sins of hunger are greater than all others but the first to be forgiven.

Bread of Life, because You suffered on the Cross, Bread of Life, by the Lance that wounded Your body, pierce us through, Lord, that the leprosy of hunger be burned out of us, give us bread, Lord, for the children who are dying.

Let our soldiers put the Turks to flight so swiftly that they leave us all the spoils—their flocks and their sacks of corn, their jars of olives and their baskets of fruit. Let them have no time to carry anything away, but all be left for us.

In the stables the horses snorted and neighed with human voices and beat down the walls with their flailing hoofs. They were horses trained for battle and their grooms said, "They can smell Turkish blood." They were the only creatures in the whole city that were well fed, and men gulped involuntarily at the sight of their chests and haunches. The horses were half mad and tried to bite all who came near them.

The flies were mad and settled in great black masses on the lips of the dying. Men gathered them up like handfuls of grain and there were some who pounded them with ashes to make a paste, and by a miracle God made of it a food, good to eat.

The Tafurs, the living dead who had been housed in the empty pens where once the people of the city had kept the animals destined for slaughter, were beginning to emerge in small groups, black and naked and so thin that their bones protruded through their flesh. No one knew whether they ate one another but it was certain they had little else to eat. Brothers, brothers, the day is come! Already the crows and vultures are leaving the city, they can see the blood upon the plain. Tomorrow they will be drunk with Turkish blood.

They screamed like men possessed and had to be driven away from doorways with spears to stop them forcing their way inside. They had no weapons other than broken Turkish swords or staves, but their teeth were known to be as sharp as those of dogs. Often as they crossed a square, shouting and singing, one of them would fall to the ground and be taken up dead, with the whites of his eyes showing and foam on his lips. The soldiers laid them down by the wall until the dead cart should come around.

The streets leading to the citadel were barricaded and guarded by soldiers. So many men wanted to worship the Holy

Lance that they had to be beaten off with cudgels, for already some people had been crushed to death or suffocated in the crowd around the cathedral. And there was such a clamor there that the Turks could have entered the city and no one would have heard them, so great a noise that not even horns or drums or church bells could be heard above it.

The uproar spread through the whole city until the carpenters and miners in the Turkish camp beyond the walls stopped their work and the men on the wooden towers forgot to shoot as if in terror, for no such din, no such roaring of voices was ever heard even on the day of a great battle. The whole vast city was shouting for joy, soldiers and knights, pilgrims and priests, men and women, Syrians, Greeks, Armenians, French, Provençals, Normans—the Lance is found, Jesus Christ is with us!

THE LANCE IS FOUND, THE BISHOPS HAVE RECOGNIZED IT, IT HAS REVIVED THREE MEN ALREADY!

In the streets leading up to the cathedral, the sick fell to the ground from their broken stretchers and were trodden underfoot by the crowd. No one could help it; those behind pressed forward as if the Turks were at their heels. The Holy Lance is not for the rich and the priests! Let us see it, we too have our dead and dying! It did not seem possible that the army was still so great, that there were so many pilgrims in the city, and so many Greeks and Syrians in the houses.

The Bishop of Le Puy will go out of the city first, bearing the Holy Lance, and let no man be so bold as to hinder him from doing what God has ordained. Once the Turks have been driven off, all may come and worship the Holy Lance, but until then it must remain on the altar in the cathedral and none may approach it.

That night the dead that had been thrown into the gully below the ramparts were seen to rise and walk upon the walls and descend in procession into the city. Just as they were, half eaten by the flies, their flesh torn off by vultures, the moisture oozing from their eyes and down their blackened faces, hair falling out, ragged shrouds spotted with brown. They sang as they walked, and it seemed that a mighty wind swayed them, though the air was still and heavy as solid rock, and this swaying was terrible to see. Their singing was a hoarse moan which came not from their mouths but from their chests. They were hungry for consecrated ground as the living for food, and they sang the psalms of Jerusalem, for the cross which they had taken would not let them rest. On the day of the battle we shall be with you, brothers, as you will be with us.

> We are going to show the Turks our ravaged faces
> black with flies, white with worms, see what they have done
> to us
> they will not dare to look us in the face
> brothers, when you come to bury us have no fear
> we are all the same flesh signed with the cross
> lay us in the earth with the cross over us
> our souls will go to Jerusalem
> with the Holy Lance we shall go and beat on the
> gates of Jerusalem
> and they will open and the light stream out like ten suns

The Lance was there in the cathedral, lying on the altar amid the candles.

Amid the golden candlesticks, on the cloth sewn with seed pearls. Three bishops and a hundred priests knelt in prayer, all night long in prayer; they were not to stir from the place. In the churches the barons were at prayer, on their knees, hearts beating, burning like an altar lamp, preparing for the hour of battle.

The Turks out there on the plain, eating their fill, do not know that we are done with hunger. We shall pursue them to the sea if need be. None shall lay a finger on the spoils, for so God wills it.

God wills it. No one shall lay a finger on the spoils till nightfall. Any man that picks up so much as a crust of bread dropped on the ground will bring misfortune on the whole army.

The sick and wounded had been carried into the churches, and those who were not sick were little better. They lay on the ground with closed eyes and listened to the cantors' monotonous chanting. The cantors were relieved at frequent intervals: their voices gave out and their eyes smarted from the hot fumes of wax and incense until they could not breathe and sang the psalms like drowning men calling for help.

> O Lord, deliver Israel
> Out of all its calamities.

Men clothed in white, of a miraculous beauty, their hair and beards shining like gold, passed through the crowd of worshippers without touching them with their luminous robes, and went and stood behind the altar. They were Saint Andrew and Saint Jude, Saint Matthew and Saint James, and they were seen that night in more than twelve churches at the same time. Their feet were bare and white as marble and their faces like lamps of alabaster. They stood behind the altar, their hands raised in prayer, and light descended from the dome to their white hands as if they drew it to them, and that night a great power descended from the skies on the city of Antioch. It rushed into men's empty hearts, and into their bodies that were emptied to the marrow by hunger. *Lord, those still alive tomorrow shall see Jerusalem with their mortal eyes!*

Not bread or wine, we shall be filled with prayer, and he who has not strength to hold out one more day is a coward.

The Provençals shall surround the citadel and guard the walls; all the rest shall go out, and let God decide between the Christians and the Turks.

The Holy Lance shall go forth to fight for you, and you shall fight for it! The Bishop of Le Puy shall carry it forth, raised high in both hands; he will go through the city and all shall have a sight of it.

Peter stood on a wooden dais surrounded by torches on the parvis of the Church of St. James and prophesied. The joy of God is on us, heaven is so close to earth that the angels brush us with their wings and stir our hair.

Their hunger was so great that it had mounted from their bellies to their heads and even the riffraff of the army, men who the day before would have killed to rob another of a dead rat, now cried aloud and saw visions. They saw angels walking on the rooftops carrying the heads of Turks in huge bread baskets. God has forgiven these His children. They are innocents and God makes them see what we shall all see tomorrow.

We shall have the heads first and the bread afterward.

Before dawn, in the hour when the sky whitened behind the citadel, the main streets were empty and the roofs of the houses thick with Christians.

The knights rode down toward the gates in full armor, with silken surcoats over their chain mail and the cross sewn on their shoulders. The sky was red above the mountains and white toward the sea, and in the cold light the faces of the knights, under their helms with visors up, looked grey as stone. Their eyes were fixed and vacant like the eyes of hawks, their mouths were set, and their hands lay lightly on the reins. They were preparing for the great work, and carried their strength within them like a full cup from which not a drop must be spilled before the time.

The gates of the tower giving onto the bridge opened with a groaning of iron bars, the portcullises rose, and the chains slid over the pulleys and fell with a clatter. The gate was open on the Turks.

They are all going out and not one will turn back while there is a single Turk left on the plain. They have sworn an oath to it. They are brave men. God has forgiven them their sins.

As the Holy Lance was carried by, a cry went up from the rooftops: See, it comes, it was true, it comes, Christians, who can harm us now? It comes, who shall overcome us? The Bishop moved on, fully armed on his white horse, the Lance held aloft in both purple-gloved hands. Two clerks rode on either side of him, supporting the Bishop's arms with their hands. Two arch-priests mounted on black stallions went before him, bearing oriflammes embroidered with the image of the Lord Jesus Christ; three priests followed with tall crosses encrusted with crystal and enamel, and monks walked beside them, brushing the walls, holding tall lighted candles. After them came the knights with drums beating. The drums sounded slow and muffled, like heart-beats, in time to the singing of the psalms.

The Holy Lance has come, it appoints us to meet it on the plain. Who will follow? Dead and living with it!

Knights and sergeants with it! Archers and pilgrims with it!

Today those on the plain shall see that Jesus Christ is truly Man and truly God.

He is our flesh and we are His, truly man, made like us. He knew hunger and death.

The Lance pierced His side that was made of real flesh, and real blood flowed from a real wound. *And there came out a little water and a little blood.* Truly Man He is, flesh of our flesh, and knew hunger and thirst.

They shall all know that He is truly God. They shall see the One who was pierced.

The knights rode out and formed up in battle order on the plain. They could be seen from the walls as they crossed the bridge, cohort upon cohort of them; Normans, Ardennais, Boulonnais, and French, they rode out and drew up in straight lines like furrows, facing the Turkish camp. The Turks were in no hurry to offer battle. They re-formed their cavalry on both sides of the bridge, believing themselves so strong that they had no need of haste. They had four times as many horses and ten times as many archers and must have thought: We can easily outflank these dogs of Christians and hurl them into the river.

They had eaten well the night before and eaten well that morning also. They thought: These Christians are coming out in desperation, because they are dying of hunger.

The trumpets rang out on the walls, and in all the ranks of the army the trumpets rang in answer. This was the miracle: the whole army was outside the walls, drawn up in battle array, and the Turks had come no nearer. They were waiting, because they had many more horses.

The Bishop raised the Holy Lance as a woodman raises his ax in both hands to split the stump of a tree. He lifted it and brandished it and waved it aloft with all the strength of his arms, and hurled it at the enemy in a movement that was suddenly arrested, a movement transformed suddenly into the immobility of stone. He held the Lance in both hands and gripped it fast as though it had been a piece of the sky. The sky came down to earth and the Lance plunged right into it and drew the power of God from it. This was the signal. The trumpets rang for the charge and the knights began to shout.

Their lances pointed forward and with a fearful yell, they began to move. The watchers saw them sweep across the plain toward the camp and then fan out into two solid wedges that lengthened into a single line made up of two close ranks, moving heavily at a steady gallop. There was a sudden check, a clash of shields and lances, and almost at once the charge swept on again.

They had ridden down horses and riders like a flock of sheep and were in among the mass of the Turkish horses, and still their advance was barely checked. Horses fell and rolled on the ground before the sheer force of their lances. From a distance the watchers could hardly make out the arrows that fell around the knights like a storm of black sleet.

Then the mass of the foot and archers was swarming over the plain toward the reeling Turks. And still the knights rode on, more slowly now, a great wave wearing itself out painfully on the shifting, trampled earth. They had reached the site of the old Christian camp and the great burial ground where the earth was soft and bare, and such a dust was rising that nothing could be seen in the glaring light but white and yellow clouds and the bright flash of sun on metal.

It was as if the sky had really come down to earth. The foot soldiers were still running, knives and cudgels at the ready. By now every gate was open and all able-bodied men pouring out of the city.

The Turkish ranks were broken and scattered, and still the knights pushed on. The watchers on the walls could see that beside every knight was a ghostly white companion, glinting like steel in the sun.

They saw them on the plain, flattened by the white sunlight, through the white dust; they saw them, white knights, flying in the air above the Turks' heads and striking out with their horses' hoofs.

The Turks were routed.

They fled both ways, some toward the sea, others northward, but the ranks of knights had never broken. In the distance the two lines rolled away like a mist; nothing more could be seen for the dust, and all the watchers knew was that the space between the abandoned camp and the battle was growing ever wider.

God save them, they are saints.

The field was strewn with the bodies of men and horses and with trampled tents as the foot soldiers advanced at a run. They finished off the wounded ridden down by the knights and hurried on.

No halt until nightfall, by order of God and Saint Andrew.

Gathering momentum, like rolling stones. Joy gave them strength. They had rushed out of the gates with a mighty roar, like stallions that see the mares, leaping forward brandishing their cudgels, their axes, and their knives. The Turkish foot, left far behind by the cavalry, now lost in clouds of dust, were reforming, digging in behind a barricade of dead horses. The heat was so fierce that the straw strewn about the camp caught fire of itself and stacks of hay were blazing. The Turks caught up wisps of burning straw on the ends of their pikes. Riderless horses galloped about aimlessly, trampling and biting all they met.

Those Turkish foot soldiers were brave. They sold their lives dearly, but such a host of men bore down on them that they were forced to give ground and were driven, packed close together, right into the river, and those that swam had stones thrown at them. Even so, many were able to save themselves by swimming.

Jacques's ax worked hard that day. He had recovered from his sickness, and it was true indeed that the mere thought of food that night was enough to give a man strength. After the first star they would be free to plunder the camp.

The ax had grown so heavy that Jacques could no longer carry it on his shoulder and was forced to drag it. The Turks, even the wounded, still had some power in their javelins. The first one Jacques saw he battered clumsily in the face with his ax, smashing nose and teeth to pulp, and the ax, drinking fresh blood, became a living thing once more. It was terrifying how men could surpass the limits of human strength.

A moment before a man had been thinking: I shall lie down and die, and the next thing he was swinging his ax in both hands. At anything that moved. If he had been alone in a host of Turks all armed with swords, he would not have noticed. All he saw before him was the heads of horses, grinning and baring bloody teeth. A javelin grazed his shoulder, three arrows whistled through his hair. He felt them and his courage soared: They dare not harm me, the Holy Lance protects us.

Strong red wine ran in his veins instead of blood, making his arms and legs work like engines moved by ropes. It was not his own blood, it was the blood of Jesus Christ.

"Jacques, oh Jacques!" "What do you want?" Mathieu was there, yes, surely it was Mathieu. Mathieu was down on his knees with an arrow in his right arm. Jacques bent over him and Garin with him.

"Come on, up with you, an arrow is no great matter, it won't be hard to get it out." Mathieu's lips were grey and his face the color of dirty wax. Had he fainted? Well, lads? No time to waste. They shook him and Jacques pulled out the arrow, but Mathieu's blue, parched lips did not quiver.

Just for an arrow! Alas, that is what hunger does to you. He could not take an arrow in his arm. Ten yards away a group of Turks were sheltering behind three horses, still shooting. "The dogs, why do they go on? The day is ours, they know well enough that they are lost."

They do not know, those who have food do not know, that mad dogs bite more fiercely than the rest.

Élie walked along the riverbank, keeping a grim look out for anything still living in the heaps of wounded. Long black ribbons of blood striped his bare legs; an arrow hung from his shoulder and another from his left hip. The ax twirled of its own volition in his two hands, crashing down to left and right on fallen bodies. He strode over chests and faces but it gave him no joy—they were only dead men. He was chopping at dead flesh. If by any chance something moved, he stopped and took aim so as to split the skull neatly down the middle. He had killed some that day who were still on their feet, how many he did not know, ten, twenty, a hundred; the lust to kill burned in him so that the same Turk was killed ten times over and ten Turks were as one. He saw himself surrounded by vast stalls of butcher's meat, his head was full of slaughterhouses where the blood ran in long rivulets across the floor, he was a poacher again, jointing deer in the lord's forest with his ax.

His companions followed after him like hounds after a huntsman. The day is hot but we will last out until the first star. So commanded Saint Andrew: no plunder, and whoever stops or draws back shall go to hell.

They marched through the devastated camp, leaving behind the tents and stores and the pens where, alongside the quietly browsing sheep, camels with great sad, bewildered eyes raised their haughty heads.

The knights were long out of sight but the hosts of foot marched on, marched as if they had forgotten they would ever have to return to the city.

At sunset, clouds of purple dust rose against the red sky. The knights were coming back, their exhausted horses treading heavily, heads stuck on their lances, their pennons stained with blood and their tunics black with dirt, so tired they could scarcely sit in the saddle.

Too tired to shout their triumph. The knights were coming back, unable to pursue the Turks any farther. No need to fear they would return.

They knew what an army scattered and fleeing was like, and they had pursued them without stopping until nightfall. The sky was sapphire-blue, with great streaks of milky white on the horizon, as the knights got down from their horses and camped out in the fields beside the river to drink and water their horses.

The Holy Lance returned, hedged in with banners and then by another hedge made of spears on each of which was a head. The heads of emirs, carefully selected, a finer sight than oriflammes. The clarions found their breath again to sound for victory.

They will not come back again.

THEY WILL NOT COME BACK, THEY WILL NOT COME BACK.

The plain is clear, all the way to the sea, the banners of the Count of Toulouse wave from the citadel.

The children have stopped crying; in three days they have got into the habit of eating again.

Long caravans are moving on the roads, vessels coming up the river. Antioch shall no longer want for bread, meat, fruit, and wine.

Those who cannot buy food may go and ask for it from the rich, from the monasteries and the barons' palaces. No one now will demand a gold piece for a sack of flour.

7 ✠✠✠✠✠✠✠✠✠✠✠✠✠✠

Shall we be in Jerusalem before All Saints? Or even before Saint Peter Advincula, for we must strike while the iron is hot. Today the Turks fear us so that they will let us pass without a blow struck.

Antioch, alas, was now a city given up to sin, full of harlots of all kinds, those men had taken before they entered the city and those they had found there. Even the priests were reluctant to put a stop to the fornication because, they said, once these women were married they would be obliged to follow their husbands and these vast numbers of women and small children with the army would impede the march.

All these young men who had taken the cross might as well wait until they had taken Jerusalem and get married then. On the other hand, God abominated sinful lust, and having once forgiven and absolved the Christians and delivered them from their enemies, He might easily repent of His forgiveness when He saw their bestial concupiscence.

In the house of the pilgrims of Arras, where since the night of the victory the number of men had been reduced by five who met their deaths on the battlefield, there were already six Syrian women living. All were legally married, though unable to speak French. Also, a young Picard named Jean the Fuller, one of the clothworkers from Lille, had brought back a girl called Selima who was black but comely. She was tall and shapely as a princess, only black, blacker than the skins of roasted chestnuts, with nothing of human coloring about her except the palms of her hands and the inner surface of her lips. She was not above fifteen years old, and she wished to be baptized. She knew a little Arabic, and one of the Syrians who understood Greek spoke for her to Father Albert, and Father Albert translated into French for Jean; they were a married couple who could only speak to each other through two interpreters. But Selima wished very much to become a Christian and believed in the Holy Lance, and since she was honest and a virgin it was right to marry her. Accordingly, she was baptized in the Church of St. James, but unfortunately the baptism did nothing for her and she remained as black as before. It was not long before she learned a little French, for Jean was very much in love with her.

Élie le Grêlé did not give up his paramour, and since his little band of followers now included, besides a number of young boys, three men from among those who were left of the pilgrims from Amiens, it was not easy to make him listen to reason.

By now this paramour was no longer a mystery; everyone had seen her. On the day of the victory she had come out into the courtyard with the other women and gone up to the roof to acclaim the knights with the rest. Even now, thin and starved, she was a pearl among common pebbles. Alix had gazed at her for a long time and it had made her very sad. What remained of the great beauty of Alix of the Thirty Pieces was still enough to make knights turn around as she passed, but beside the fair Euphemia no man on earth would have looked at her. The two women had eyed each other for a while, like two adversaries circling, and Euphemia's eyes had said, You must have been worth a good price in your day. Alix said, "They would have paid well at home for one night with her, but not for a second. I'll wager she can't laugh and tell stories."

There were plenty of people ready to tell le Grêlé that he could sell his concubine for a good price because the Greeks of these parts purchased slaves and there were even Frankish knights who would not despise her.

"Go sell your mother," was le Grêlé's answer.

It was advisable to wait for the end of the hot weather before setting out again.

There were fresh horses and weapons to be bought, armor to

be mended, and shields to be repainted. New carts and tents had to be made and sheep and cattle purchased, and for the latter it was necessary to search far afield because by now there were none to be had within twenty leagues of the city.

The dead had to be reburied and the burial ground desecrated by the Turks reconsecrated. The work was not proceeding very fast owing to the fearful stench that arose from the charnel in the gully, which made it necessary for the men working there to be relieved at hourly intervals, so that no more than a hundred or a hundred and fifty bodies could be moved each day. Oh God, should we have burned them and let them go without Christian burial?

The friends and relatives of the dead went out along the road to pray beside the huge trenches where the bodies, unrecognizable by now, were laid in rows.

Brothers, God in His mercy has allowed us to pass living into the shadow of death! Be not troubled, arm yourselves with patience, for to God the smell of corruption is no more unclean than the smell of lilac. Decaying flesh is fearful to us but does not offend God's sight.

Here, that which men hide away in the bowels of the earth is revealed to us in its truth. What we are and what we shall become, the truth of our flesh. Fear not, for the dead and the living are one.

God shows us our suffering brethren, humbled and crucified. Do not despise this flesh. It is our own. On the Last Day it will rise again, will rise up firm and fresh and living from this very earth. The bones shall be clothed in sinews and the sinews in muscle and the muscle in skin of dazzling whiteness, as the prophet Ezekiel has said.

For we shall not reach Jerusalem before all the terrors of hell have gone over us. Whoever stands firm to the end shall be saved.

So said Brother Barnabé, and with unrivaled courage he followed the pestilential biers and peered into the worm-eaten faces, a wooden cross clutched at his breast. His skin was dry and yellowed, his beard grew in dusty, reddish tufts on his hollow cheeks, and his deep, grey-shadowed eyes were scalded with tears.

Oh dear brothers, as we see you today the faces of lepers would seem fair by comparison, yet know, you that are still close at hand, that our love for you is not altered. Companions of our travels, now your bodies shall lie at peace in earth at last, while you go on with us to Jerusalem.

The men took up their spades and filled in the trenches, and rarely was the gravediggers' task carried out with such quiet content. Little by little the rottenness was swallowed up by the earth and the trenches filled in with good, wholesome yellow clay soil and broken stones. The priests moved along them followed by cantors, sprinkling the ground with holy water.

Isabelle. There was no telling now which body had been Isabelle's, with her crooked back and the blue ribbon around her head. Who could say? The bones were broken, the ribbon was no longer blue. Marie had the fever and had not gone down to the trenches. Marie had the fever, and in her delirium she talked about Isabelle and her ribbon and about Ondine. She believed that Isabelle was still alive. Oh, give me back my ribbon, it is Jacques's share of the spoils, give it back to me, let me look at it a little more, it belongs to both of us and we will give it to Ondine on the day of her marriage to Pierre. Oh, do not cry. Eat my biscuit, I don't want it, I promise you I am not hungry any more. Don't cry, my poor linnet, keep your ribbon. And she wept like a child, saying that she did not want any bread, that they must keep it for tomorrow, and pray to the Holy Lance to bring bread into the city. Many of those who had been bravest during the siege succumbed in this way when there was no more famine or danger. No one could blame them: in the time of trial they had wrenched more strength from their spirits than God gave them.

Baudry roamed from the house to the church and from the church back to the courtyard of the house as if he could not believe that now they had food for more than fifteen days, with two live sheep in the courtyard, the boys nibbling corn all day long, and the women squabbling over their washtubs, and that there was no longer any need for him to spend all his time hunting for food for his flock. After the joy of the first days he began to worry again, wondering why there was as yet no mention of setting out for Jerusalem.

The end of the hot weather—that was all very well, but surely it was better to set out while it was still hot than to risk another winter's siege. By now even the simplest and most ignorant knew what to expect of the country, and men said that the winters in Jerusalem were no milder than in Antioch—worse even, because the city lay among hills and the Syrians talked of snowstorms, of ice and frost and torrential rains. If it were not taken before winter, the knights might survive but not the poor people. Comrade, we are in God's hands; unless we hope for miracles we have no hope at all. Brother Barnabé believed in miracles, although he too was very weary, and he was sure it was much better to reach Jerusalem while they still had their mortal eyes and bodies of flesh and blood. Whoever stands firm to the end shall be saved.

Philotheus spent much time talking to the two leaders in the room they shared. He was well informed through his friends and his brother-in-law and always had some fresh news. He said that the Sultan would never be able to levy troops before the new year, and that the kings of Aleppo and Tripoli were quite ready to make peace with the Christians. He said that the Greeks who had come from Jerusalem were certain that the city would be liberated before the winter, and that the Christians of the West should not delay too long because the Church in Jerusalem was suffering a cruel martyrdom at the hands of the Egyptians, who were insolent masters and worse than the Turks.

"Is it to us that you should be saying all this, Philotheus? You must tell it to Prince Bohemond and Duke Godfrey."

"Have no fear. They have been told all this, and much besides."

The beautiful Euphemia's story was a sad but not uncommon one. The daughter of a wealthy armorer, she had been captured by pirates on the Hellespont while traveling with her family from Tiflis to Trebizond. She had been only eleven years old at the time, but her face was already so beautiful that she was not violated but sold in Ankara to the agent of a great slave merchant of Baghdad. In Baghdad, the biggest slave market in the world, she was given a good education: she learned to speak and to read Arabic and Greek, to play on three different musical instruments, to sing and recite poems, and to talk of love, since her master was negotiating with the chief eunuch of Prince Sanjar, King of Khorassan and brother to the Sultan, and was grooming her for the harem of this prince. The matter was settled finally and the young slave girl dispatched under a good escort to Khorassan, but the caravan was attacked by Bedouins. The girl was sold in the market at Aleppo and bought by Kutchuk, one of the emirs of Yaghi-Siyan, lord of Antioch, who intended her for his eldest son, Marduk ibn Kutchuk. This young man was suspected of adherence to the Party (the name given to those who recognized the descendants of Ali, the son-in-law of Mahomet, as caliph) and his father hoped, by promoting his union with a beautiful slave, to distract him from a preoccupation dangerous to his soul's salvation. The young man saw the Georgian girl and was struck by Cupid's darts, and since his nature was passionate used violent means to force her into his bed.

Compelled by these misfortunes, Euphemia began to reflect upon her life and remember the faith of her fathers. Her master, who had a kind heart, allowed her to keep an image of the Virgin in her chamber and had her conveyed to the Greek church on feast days. Euphemia had been Marduk's favorite for nearly a year when the city fell to the Christians. She was not quite eighteen years old; her breasts were still firm and shapely, her hips smooth and well covered. She considered herself worth a high price. There was no longer a proper slave market in Antioch, but agents were buying for the merchants of Aleppo and Homs. "Would you be willing to return to the infidels?" Philotheus asked her. "It would be a sin."

"The Holy Virgin is my witness, if I could live honestly among Christians I would not consider it!"

Philotheus visited her frequently, sometimes when le Grêlé was not there. He was the only man she was allowed to see because Élie was not suspicious of him. Father Albert asked Philotheus one day why he, an educated man, was so patient with such a boorish fellow.

"Was he any less boorish on the day he saved me from being trampled by the horse?" was Philotheus' answer.

Le Grêlé was working on the rebuilding of the walls. He returned at night tired out from breaking and heaving stones all day, breathless and filthy dirty, but happy because he brought back money, which he would hand over to Philotheus: "You know the city and the prices, you buy what is needed." The task was beneath the dignity of a free man, but Philotheus forgave the barbarian his ignorance. He had grown fond of Élie. What he hardly dared admit even to himself was that he was still fonder of the Georgian girl, and he would gladly have gone the rounds of all the shops in Antioch if it would make life easier for her. Often, when Élie's money was not enough, he would go and ask his friends for more.

After vespers, the Georgian girl would light a lamp in Élie's room and then warm up the soup on the brazier by the door. Élie ate noisily, growling and snuffling like a dog, his eyes on his food. When he had done, he would wipe his mouth on the palm of his hand, cross himself hastily, and look expectantly at his paramour.

This was when she had to talk. He persisted obstinately in his desire to hear her talk and listened, his pale, lusterless eyes fixed on the young woman's mouth. He followed her lips with his eyes, like a hunter peering through the undergrowth for a sight of his quarry. His own lips moved as if he were repeating the words after her, although he was too dull-witted to have picked up so much as a word or two of Greek. Philotheus translated while Élie said, Ask her some more—ask her, tell her . . .

He wanted to know if she was homesick for her own land, if life was good in that country, whether the corn was often frosted in the field. To his amazement she had no idea. Her family? How could she know? She had no means of knowing where they had been sold. Her father had been a brave man and was almost certain to have been killed by the pirates when they boarded the vessel, but she did not know. She had been carried off like a parcel, wrapped in a sheet.

"Ask her if she loved her Turk." No, she had not loved him. What woman could love a man who had taken her by force? "Ask her if she hated him." No, he was kind. He gave her everything she wanted.

"Ask her if she has ever loved a man."

"How can I ask her that?" Philotheus said.

"Ask her, I say."

"I can tell you, Philotheus, but he will not understand. For with all my heart I loved the Prince Sanjar to whom they were sending me, and now that I have been made unworthy of him, I shall never love another man."

"What does she say? Good God, what does she say?"

"Go on, tell him, I do not mind."

"But," said Élie, "I thought she had never seen this prince, God's curse on him for an infidel!" Euphemia said with a proud, gentle smile that women of sensibility had no need to see in order to love, and that the prince was renowned for his virtues and all the poets praised his courage.

"The little fool!" said Élie. "The silly girl, they have turned her head with songs! Tell her that her prince can never have lacked concubines and cares nothing for her." But this Philotheus would not translate.

"Ask her if she likes me."

"What is the use? She will say no."

"Ask her, all the same." Philotheus asked, with some embarrassment. The girl wrinkled her brows, briefly, as if to get rid of a fly that was bothering her.

"Very well, tell him I do like him."

"She says she does not know." Élie could not have been expecting this, for he looked very pleased, and Philotheus felt some compunction.

"Ask her—tell her I like her. That I love her very much." He watched the woman's face while the Greek was translating. It was sweet and cold, with eyes like the Holy Virgin's. A little glimmer of weary mockery shone in them for an instant and quickly died. A man may be a fool but, fool or no, he can learn from looking at a face to read its meaning.

"Tell her, Philotheus, tell her that the day I found her, she knows what the soldiers would have done to her. There were only four of them, but if it had not been for me the whole company of Rouennais would have had her.

"Tell her that after Brother Barnabé and Baudry, I am pretty well first in this house, that even Baudry dare not say a word out of place to me. And at Nicaea a knight told me I should have been born noble."

For once he was speaking so fast that Philotheus had difficulty in remembering it all to translate it. But Euphemia was not listening; she was polishing her nails idly on the end of her silken girdle.

"Tell her I am living in sin for her sake and getting little enough out of it because she cannot do anything, not even hunt for lice, I have to get my lads to do it. I almost have to get her food. Tell her that but for my pitted face, I'd be no worse-looking than the next man."

At daybreak the men left the courtyard to go and look for work. The masons were the luckiest, and then the stonecutters and the painters. For the rest there was nothing but day labor, and they had to be up early to get themselves hired for the day. The shops were open again in the streets of the corn merchants and the vegetable-sellers, but prices were high and pillaging forbidden. Only the children stole from the goods on display, but they had lithe bodies and long legs and were not often caught.

It is not easy to find work in a strange city, especially when there is no call for your particular trade.

There was plenty of weaving done in Antioch, but wool and flax were scarce this year, the looms had been badly damaged by fire, and the masters, installed once more in their houses, were harder than Turks and would not pay, pleading that they were ruined already and that "Celtic" workers, as they called them, were used to looms of a different type and the cloth they made too loosely woven. The few weavers who had found employment left after a fortnight, determined never again to work for Armenians. Workers in this country were treated worse than prisoners of war. If the Syrians wanted the work they were welcome to it. The laborers unloading the sacks of sand and assembling the timber for the scaffolding got three deniers a day and their midday meal.

The criers of my lord Bishop Adhemar delivered this proclamation. They said it was not right to leave the city like a pigsty, because it was a noble, a holy, and a Christian city and it was the duty of the Christians to repair the damage caused by the siege, to restore the churches desecrated by the Turks, and to strengthen the walls, lest the people of the land should say the remedy was worse than the disease and the Catholic Christians worse than the infidel.

They added that the army must be re-equipped to undertake the journey to Jerusalem and reinforcements of arms and horses brought from the port of St. Simeon. The pious pilgrims should be patient because, as they well knew, without the protection of the knights the same thing would befall them as had befallen those who perished at Nicaea.

They did know it, only too well. A week passed, and another, and at last a whole month. In the merchant quarters there were chains fastened across the streets and armed guards, the Greeks and the Armenians barricaded themselves inside their houses, and in the city the soldier was king.

Peter Bartholomew, the man who had found the Holy Lance, lived in the Provençal quarter, surrounded by priests and clerks who questioned him continually because he saw many visions. He was a holy man, to be sure, but the Spirit did not visit him every day.

Saint-John spent his whole time wandering from one church to another, and from the Bishop's palace to the Patriarch's. It was often after curfew when he came back to the courtyard, telling endless stories about meeting the Apostles or Mary Magdalene, Herod Antipas or Pontius Pilate. To him, every prostitute was Mary Magdalene and every knight cooling his face in a city fountain Pontius Pilate, and they had all ceased to pay any attention to him.

Marie had recovered from her fever and went out daily with the other women looking for work, carrying little Pierre, who was almost a year old now and getting heavy, on her hip. The rich Greeks had lost many of their servants during the siege and there was work to be had in the wealthy houses, scrubbing floors or carrying water. The Greeks did not pay but they fed well.

Philotheus came constantly to see Brother Barnabé and talk of the sufferings of Jerusalem. He said that priests and monks could hardly show themselves in the streets outside the Christian quarters, and every day some Greeks were arrested as enemy spies.

"I like you, Philotheus," said Brother Barnabé, "and I like to hear news of Jerusalem, however gloomy, because it is news of our brethren, but it would be better for you to spend more time with your friends in the city."

"Why?"

"They are saying here that you are hanging around le Grêlé's concubine."

Philotheus gave a faint, bitter smile. "What harm can I do anyone's concubine?"

"I do not know, Greek. You are not old or ugly." Philotheus shrugged, thinking Brother Barnabé sinned through excess of charity.

He went up to the gallery and paused outside the door of Élie's room. The watchdogs let him pass. These were two boys of thirteen or so who spent their days lazing about, scratching themselves and playing knucklebones, but they were stout lads, armed with spiked cudgels, and it was not safe to tease them.

Euphemia was kneeling on the floor, rolling out dough on a white cloth. Irritated by her inability to do anything useful, Élie had finally discovered that she could make cakes. Philotheus had procured her some flour, honey, and almonds and it emerged that she was an excellent pastry cook. She spent hours kneading, stretching the fine white paste with her long, slender fingers, folding and stretching it again to make transparent rounds which she covered with ground almonds. She let them stand for a while before cooking them on the brazier and rolling them in honey. This was how she spent her time. She did not eat much as a rule, but she was pleased when Philotheus brought her an orange or a fig. When she saw him come in, her face would light up and her eyes brighten with eagerness. There was no good news to give her, yet she still hoped. An obstinate, tenacious girl, not very intelligent.

She was always asking him to inquire in the city for news of merchants of Aleppo, who must surely have agents in Antioch.

"Am I a go-between?" Philotheus would say. "Is it my business to sell you?"

"I see no other way of getting out of here. He sets a guard over me and I can see no one. A merchant might give him a good price for me."

"He would never sell you."

She went and sat on a bale of straw by the window. The window was covered with a piece of yellow cloth suspended from the bars by means of leaden hooks. Élie was no more stupid than the next man and he was not going to have anyone looking in and seeing Euphemia. She sat there with her face pressed against the fabric, and in the yellow light her features had the warm pallor of a water lily in the setting sun. She sighed and began to talk about Baghdad, and how she used to read love poems in a room where the floor was paved with blue mosaic. She sighed over her lost love, feeling no shame at speaking of it to a man such as Philotheus.

"Who knows? You might have grown old in the harem of the King of Khorassan, you might have lost your beauty without ever catching a glimpse of the prince."

"Mine is not a mercenary heart," she said. "I would have given him my life and not asked for a glance from him in return."

"You know nothing of love. What you call love is no more than a childish dream."

"I know enough," Euphemia said, "to know what love is not. The beastliness of men is not love."

"The man with whom you live feels true love for you."

She looked up in faint surprise, as if he had suddenly said something in a language that was strange to her, and indeed it was cruel to plead Élie's cause.

"But, Euphemia, you might have fallen into the hands of some rich, depraved old man, a monster who was repugnant to you, and then you would regret the Celt."

She did not understand. She wanted to sleep in a bed, to have clean linen, baths, slaves to wait on her—in short, to live like a human being.

She could not stand it any more: the stench all around her, the lice that she could not get out of her hair, the disgusting food, the raucous voices of the savages in the courtyard, the filthy man who scratched his feet and then put his fingers in his soup, the scabby children sitting by the door. ". . . not even a woman to wait on me, and their women are as dirty as the men." Élie was too suspicious to allow any of the local women near her.

"Tell me," Philotheus said, "tell me if there is anything I can do to help you without wronging this man. He saved my life." Euphemia threw back her head and laughed contemptuously.

"A horse or a dog can save a man's life!"

"If my horse saved my life, I should not kill it."

Euphemia shook her head and reverted to her original idea of finding someone ready to pay a good price for her. Even among the Christian Celts, there must be men susceptible to female beauty.

"How great a price? He would never agree."

"But why not?" she asked. "*Why not?*"

"He is in love." Again that stubborn, uninterested look.

"I shall die," she said, "unless you get me out of here. I shall hang myself with my girdle and my soul will be damned and you will have to answer for me before God."

"Euphemia, I may no longer call myself a man, but I am a man nonetheless and my heart is on fire when I look at you. Do not play with me, the game is too easy. I will do anything you like, but I will not help you sell yourself to the Turks."

Euphemia began to cry. A tender heart, a vulnerable heart, a heart that she could take and knead between her hands as she kneaded her paste of sifted flour. She cried and said, "Save me, help me to escape and I will go with you. We will go away together and I will never leave you. Have you not wit enough to find a trick that will deceive this man?"

The next day was Sunday, and le Grêlé was surprised to hear his concubine singing as she set out her cakes on the window ledge. She had a pretty, clear voice like a bird's, a high clear trilling, unlike any human voice. She stopped and he said, "Sing, go on singing," and she resumed her song. He was surprised to find that she had obeyed. She was not a bad concubine after all. And her cakes were good. If she made some more he might send one of his boys to sell them in the knights' quarters. He did not set much store by money but he thought it right for a woman to earn her living. Every creature should be some use.

"Sing," he said to her. "Speak—*speak*." This was a word he had learned at last to say in Greek. She gave him a long look, an odd, almost mocking look, mocking but not unkind, and began to speak. It was not Greek, but Arabic, he knew that although he did not understand a word of it, but she was speaking, all to herself, like a dove cooing, and the fact that he did not understand what it was she said filled le Grêlé with a strange joy, touched with sadness.

Surely it was a fine thing to be so much in love with a woman who said a thousand lovely things you could not understand, words you would never understand. God bless her, she spoke better than the fairy Morgan. "Speak again, no woman has ever spoken so many words to me.

"I am a married man, but after all why should I remember that, even on Sunday? I have five children, Euphemia, as well as four already underground and Marina who died outside Antioch, and I was not a bad weaver but my master laid me off work more often than I deserved because I would not stand for injustice. Oh no, you don't know what injustice is like, when they dock you two deniers the piece off your pay because the men of Valenciennes will work for less." He was talking now, but the woman was not listening to him, he could see that, she was thinking of something else. "Euphemia, oh Euphemia, your breasts, your breasts are so soft, as soft as flour, and your eyes make me dizzy when I look into them." How strange it felt to say such things aloud, to dare to utter what was in your heart because no one could understand. She did not understand, she was not even listening; to her it was like the barking of a dog. "Am I a dog, Euphemia?"

Philotheus came in, dressed in his Sunday robe of dark blue trimmed with green, and that day le Grêlé knew that castrated or not, the Greek was a man. How did he know it? Philotheus avoided looking at the woman, and she turned her eyes the other way, but you could see that she was burning to look at him. As God lives, he is betraying me, he may even have found someone to buy her, he means to help her escape.

"Philotheus," he asked, "am I a dog?"

Euphemia looked up, hearing the hardness in his voice. Oh, those hostile eyes! It was the way one looked at a tiresome animal.

"Ask her, do you hear? Am I a dog, yes or no?"

Philotheus asked and she answered, "What have I done to make you angry?"

"Am I a dog?"

No, of course he was not, why was he so cross?

"Then what am I?"

"A man."

The two of them had retreated to the window, looking frightened. It did him good to frighten them. "A man, am I? You know I am a man. Tell her that, Philotheus, that she has cause to know I am a man." Philotheus repeated the words, but his cheeks were slowly turning the color of brick. "And now, Philotheus, tell her you are not a man, and if she does not know that, you have only to take off your clothes and let her see you naked. Just take off your fine clothes and she will see that you are not a man."

Philotheus said, "I will not repeat that to her."

"Yes, you will repeat it, you son of a whore. Or I will tear your clothes off you in front of her. You want to take her from me. That is why you cover yourself with scent."

Slowly, Philotheus turned to the woman and said something to her. He was very calm, almost smiling, but there was a small tic at the corner of his mouth and eyelids.

Euphemia listened, her face on fire. She looked so beautiful that Élie forgot his fear of her, because God knows, in spite of his own anger, he feared hers. Beautiful, Lord, so beautiful a man could die of it. She began to speak. Tell him, Philotheus, tell him everything. Word for word. She was speaking in Arabic, very fast, in a strong, resonant voice. Philotheus translated, his eyes very bright and his face suddenly hard.

"She says she worships you, she yearns for you. Your embraces are paradise to her. The mere thought of your face sends a thrill of pleasure through her. The wine of your caresses has made her your devoted slave." Even in French, Élie understood only half of what she was saying, but enough to know that she was mocking him. He understood that so well that he could not even bring himself to silence her. He just stared stupidly at the pair of them.

Euphemia was still talking, but after a while she started to laugh. It was such a pretty laugh, like the trilling of mad nightingales. Terrible, glad, cruel laughter—he could have listened to it all his life.

Élie stared at her, fascinated, until his pride came uppermost again. He would not stand there to be humiliated in front of a eunuch.

"You," he said to Philotheus, "think yourself lucky I spare your life, but what a man has once given he does not take away. I shall not ask you to translate again, and never let me see you in this room." He would have liked to kick him out bodily, but because of Euphemia he dared not.

Surely God was protecting the boys. God did not wish these innocents to perish for nothing, and He made them strong so that they at least might reach Jerusalem.

Somehow, they had all grown very fast. To those who did not die on the journey or during the winter of the siege, God had given a resistance to coughs and chilblains and the ability to eat the worst kinds of food without becoming ill. There were nearly a thousand children in the pilgrim quarters of Antioch old enough to run about on their own, and more than half of these were adolescents between ten and fifteen. God had cut down the little ones during the crossing of the desert, and the poor infant martyrs lay under heaps of sand and stones beside the scorched roads over which the great flocks of sheep passed in the spring.

During the siege, the survivors had scoured the fields, grubbing for roots, and gone down into the trenches in the heat of battle to tear chunks of meat from the dead horses. They even managed to kill jackals, whose meat sickened adults at the time of the siege, for the Christians thought they were hungry in those days but it was not until after the taking of the city that they knew real famine. These children went about in gangs, even those who still had father or mother preferring to be with comrades of their own age.

Le Grêlé had half a dozen boys whom he fed when he could. He had men also, two Picards and a Walloon, whom he took with him to the building sites, and he had become to some extent the leader of a band. He supervised their work, collected the pay for all, and shared it out. His judgment was fair and there were no arguments. He did not make the children work. He had come to a kind of understanding about them with the leaders of the pilgrim companies, and even half-grown lads of fourteen or fifteen who at home would have been more or less earning their own living were not expected to do anything beyond fetching wood or water now and then.

The most amazing thing was how big they had grown. As a result of staying for a year in the same place, without marching or working, and because the sun made everything grow more quickly in these lands, the children had grown, in spite of the shortage of food, five or even ten inches, and those who only yesterday had to be carried on men's backs were now man-sized themselves. However, they had not grown more intelligent for all that.

Nearly all of them, even the Breton children, were able to speak Arabic and beg for alms in Greek, but they spoke their own tongues worse than seven-year-old babes. It was as much as they could do to recite a *Pater.* They believed that Jesus Christ appeared to the knights mounted on a fiery steed and armed with a seven-bladed sword, and that the Holy Virgin was buried in the Church of St. Mary in Antioch, and that in Jerusalem milk and honey flowed from the public fountains and the sun never set.

They were strong and agile, though very thin, with sunburn blisters on their backs and shoulders and sores and scabby patches all over their bodies, but their flesh, beneath this wretched garment, was hard and firm, glowing with health. People who had lost their own children watched them go by in gangs, shouting, leaping over boundary stones, and banging on the house doors, and thought: At least these will see Jerusalem. Let them do as they like. At least they are alive.

Many of the girls dressed like boys, in coarse linen shirts that hung on their thin, flat-chested forms. The women had cut off their plaits, saying, They will grow again when we reach Jerusalem. They had done this on account of the famine during the siege, when it was impossible to keep the children from running wild about the camps or hanging around the soldiers' messes. The little girls hardly knew that they were girls; they had gruff voices and light fingers, and the boys treated them like other boys.

There were about fifteen of these half-wild children in the house of the pilgrims of Arras, and the smaller ones looked up to them and longed to go with them on their forays through the city. At night, when everyone gathered around the fires in the courtyard and the priests said prayers before meat, the children prayed hardest of all and went on prostrating themselves and making the sign of the cross, for this too was a game to them.

Euphemia would come out of her room and stand at the edge of the gallery, because this was the time of day when her small jailers went down to eat. She was so bored that it was almost an entertainment for her to look down on the courtyard full of ragged people milling around the two fires lighted as the last of daylight died. The people sat, lay, or squatted around the fires, passing a ladle of soup from hand to hand, while the children raced up and down the courtyard and the women nursed little naked infants on their laps.

They sang wild, rhythmic songs of their own lands, in voices that although rough were not unmusical, and listening to this barbarian singing Euphemia grew almost to pity these poor people; they reminded her of wild creatures, trapped and penned. They were a primitive, superstitious, and unstable race, yet one that could provide good mercenaries, and their women were known in the harems as excellent nurses.

Le Grêlé would come back from the ramparts, reeking of sweat and breathing hard, too tired to speak. Euphemia was afraid of him. She would put his bowl of soup down in front of him, and he would hurl himself on it like a famished dog. Afterward, he would talk. It amazed her that a man could talk like that when he knew he was not understood. He would say in Greek, "*Speak*, you, speak." She would say nothing, but remain silent, her head and heart quite empty, longing only for night and sleep. She had not seen Philotheus for two days and was dying of boredom and loneliness.

The Greek no longer went up to Élie's room, but he still came to talk to Brother Barnabé and Father Albert. When le Grêlé met him he said, "Go on, let's forget what happened. I can't talk to her without you."

"Find another interpreter."

"I don't know any."

"That's your bad luck."

"Listen, Greek, we have had words, but I like you. I said what I did because I was jealous, I know there was nothing in it. A woman needs to chatter." Philotheus shrugged and followed Élie to his room: such are the humiliations to which love reduces a man. He felt as if he were walking on hot coals. When Euphemia saw him come in, she gave a little gasp and her lips parted slightly, as if she were short of breath.

Jacques was working with his ax on the rebuilding of the fortifications. It was here that the knight of Vireleu spotted him as he was returning, hawk on wrist, from a hunting expedition with his squires. He stopped and spoke:

"A brave fellow like you, digging ditches! Leave that and come with me. Duke Godfrey is going to Edessa to help his brother drive the Turks out of that country." Jacques said he was no soldier. "All our countrymen are soldiers, my lad. You can help with the machines, and you'll find work for your ax among the men-at-arms as well." The knights of Picardy and the Ardennes had lost so many of their foot soldiers that they would gladly have recruited even monks.

Jacques was tempted. In the first place, he loved all knights because of Sir Evrard, and said so: "I had a friend that was a knight. He was a saint."

"Then you should wish to avenge him."

"As to that, I did somewhat to avenge him on the day of the victory."

"We need men, my lad, and your ax is worth as much as a mace. You'll be given a padded jerkin and a good leather cap."

Jacques thought this a good offer. Arrows rarely penetrated such jerkins. Besides, he wanted to see more of the world. "I have a wife in Antioch," he said.

"All the more reason to go. You'll have someone to brag to."

Jacques mentioned the matter that night around the fire and said he wanted to accept the offer. His earnings as a laborer were meager and the work was doing little good to Jesus Christ.

"You have a wife and son," Baudry reminded him.

"True enough. All the more reason. They will be proud of me."

"You are not a soldier," Brother Barnabé said. "You did not take the cross to follow that trade."

"We are all soldiers against the Turks. In the country of Edessa they are carrying off the wives of Christian men in revenge for their defeat."

"You should ask your own wife what she thinks," Baudry said.

Marie was sitting by the fire with Pierre asleep on her lap. She was tugging with both hands at the folds of her skirt, the better to wrap it around the child. Her eyes were wide open, and glowing, yet at the same time miles away.

"Marie, are you listening?"

She shivered and shook her head.

"Of course I was listening. You made me jump. I was asking Saint George for counsel."

"Well?"

"I saw him. Saint George. Over there on the other side of the fire, by the water jars."

"Well?"

"He looked into my eyes and he nodded his head. That means you will come back safely if you go."

"Do you think," said Brother Barnabé, "that Saint George comes at your beck and call? Think, suppose your man gets killed. It will be too late then to say your vision was wrong."

"Oh yes," said Marie. "I know it is true. I recognized Saint George by his face."

Jean the Fuller and his black girl were now living in Jacques's room along with the priestess and Lambert. Lambert was working in a church. He had got work as one of a gang scraping the walls to clean the pictures that the Turks had daubed with whitewash. He came home plastered white all over and his hair grey with it, and his mother set up a wail because it seemed to her an ill omen. Lambert said:

"Brother Jacques, do not think of your body, think of your soul. Turks or no, it is not a good trade."

"Oh yes, it is a good trade in these lands where we are now. And I am not pledging myself to it for life. A month from now I shall be free again."

Lying on the straw beside Jacques, Marie wept and clung to him, devouring his face with kisses. You are the bravest and handsomest of them all, Jacques. You are as good as a knight. You will show them what you are worth. I saw it in your face today: you will enter Jerusalem, striking out left and right with your ax, and at each blow a Turk will fall.

Jacques, in Jerusalem all the poor will be dressed as knights. You will have a horse of your own, and Pierre shall marry Ondine.

Élie le Grêlé was on his way back from the ramparts. Already the days were getting shorter, and the light in the streets was red and violet, turning almost immediately from violet to white. Élie walked slowly, breathing in the evening air. God be thanked, the coolness came quickly. He stumbled against some bales of straw lying in the street in front of the house and thought to himself, Fools, dumping straw in the middle of the street, supposing it caught fire? Just above the bales of straw was the window of his own room. He looked up. There were voices inside the room and he climbed onto the straw to hear better.

He knew the two voices well. He did not understand Greek, but there was no need to understand Greek to know what they were saying. The voices sang and wept, the voices were more deeply imbued with love than a caress, and he, a boorish man, had learned in these two months to know the voice of a woman in love, had learned it without ever hearing it. The love, the sweet tenderness in that voice, he learned it in a moment, in that very instant, as if he had known it all his life and had been waiting only for the joy of hearing that voice. Oh, the vicious, stupid woman—a gelded man! And she loved him.

He listened, his head almost touching the window ledge. The street was very quiet. Oh no, no need to know Greek. The two voices dovetailed and entwined, one warm and resonant, the other low, like the sound of a cracked reed. No need to know Greek. This was what they were saying: I love you, I love you, I love you! Do not say that, what is the use? I am a withered tree. I love you as you are, I will follow you anywhere! My love, do not ruin your life for me. I cannot live without you, do not leave me. Wretched creatures that we are, what are we to do? How can we escape? Oh my love, oh my beloved, oh sun of my life! Oh, you are so beautiful, what have I done to deserve such happiness?

That night le Grêlé received the gift of tongues. The voice of love cannot lie. If the words were not saying that, the voices were. So this was what she was, a shameless woman, throwing herself at the first man who spoke her language. And I, thought le Grêlé, God knows I wished the man no harm!

He was reluctant to go home. The Greek was not a fool: he would suspect. Better to hide behind the bales of straw and wait. Night had fallen, it was dark in the street, and on the roofs Syrian women were chattering together as they strung their vegetables on strings to dry for the winter.

Philotheus walked quickly. His step was light and slightly uneven. God knows why—there was nothing wrong with his legs.

He walked faster than usual because it was late, but le Grêlé knew why the Greek's feet had wings that night. His own legs, his whole body, were moving with the same unconscious, animal suppleness. He slid through the dark, keeping close to the houses, his bare feet making no sound. The curfew had sounded but there were still people moving about in the streets, Syrians talking in doorways, women calling across from roof to roof. Two priests passed, preceded by a sacristan bearing a lantern with blue and red glass. They came to a square, and Élie nearly lost the Greek. The doors of a church stood open, and in the space before them were some soldiers and Greeks, both men and women, interspersed with knots of beggars. Inside the church, a coffin covered with a silver cloth stood between two rows of lighted candles and cantors were singing dirges in Greek. Philotheus had paused to say a prayer. All the better, le Grêlé thought as the two men resumed their progress across the city.

In the light of the torches burning at street corners, le Grêlé could see the man walking twenty paces ahead of him, careless and preoccupied, thinking himself quite alone. He had a cheerful look, as if he were slightly drunk, and walked with his head in the air, so lost in his own thoughts that he had not once looked around. Sounds of voices and singing could be heard in the distance, but the street was deserted.

A group of drunken Norman soldiers came down the stepped street, and Philotheus stood back against the wall to let them pass. One spoke thickly: "Hey, little girl, come with us." The Greek shrugged off the hand that groped toward him and went on his way. Oddly, Élie was almost sorry.

"Bah, let the bugger alone," another of the Normans said. "We'll find some real girls somewhere." They did not see Élie hidden in the angle of a doorway and moved away, laughing, hiccuping, and singing in cracked, tuneless voices. Élie slipped through the darkness close to the wall, and as the drunken voices moved away a great sadness took hold of him, his heart contracted, and he would have been glad to see the men return. God, even their stupid songs were good to hear! There, just ahead, an unlighted turning gaped, black as the pit.

This was it. The Greek was still walking but, curiously, more slowly now; he had slowed down as if he too were conscious of a sudden sadness and regretted the Normans' passing. In a few silent bounds, Élie caught up with him.

Philotheus did not recognize him. It was too dark. He did not cry out, but he tensed and flattened himself against the wall. In one practiced movement, Élie pulled him forward onto his chest, and holding him by the hair like a sheep, drew the knife across his throat.

Never in all his life had Élie felt so deep a joy. A cry welled up from the bottom of his heart, and he choked it back for fear of rousing the neighborhood. It changed to a gurgle in his throat, echoing the swift, gurgling flow of blood, blood, waves of blood pumping from the gaping throat under his hand. A single flexing of the muscles in his arm, one quick movement of his hand coupled with the edge of a well-sharpened blade, so vertiginously easy, the blood gushed over his hand and down his arm, pulsed slower and slower until the body supported by his left hand ceased to twitch. He let go and the Greek sagged at the knees, slid slowly to the ground, and fell back at his feet.

On the roof of the house opposite, someone was moving about with a lantern and a voice said something nervously in Greek, something that must mean, "Who is there?" A third-floor window in another house sprang into yellow light. Élie froze against the wall. On the other side of the wall lay some rich man's garden; the tops of cypress trees stood out black against the blue-black of the sky, all wreathed in stars. The lantern went out and the stars shone as if they would fall to earth like hail. The air was vibrant with the concerted jar of crickets from the garden.

It seemed to Élie that all life had fled away from human bodies into the stars and the sky and the trees and the crickets, the crickets that were singing for joy over the dead stones and the dead souls; soon, today or tomorrow, we shall all be dead, may the Lord have mercy on the risen dead.

Soft and delicate as a woman, hardly more than a woman, his sins less than childish sorrows, God would not even recall them. He was quite dead, the flow of blood had stopped. Élie ran his hand over the still-warm face and open mouth and thought that he should finish by removing the head and taking it with him to give to Euphemia. That was how a man should take his revenge. He was so carried away by the joy of vengeance that he never thought of danger, but a stronger fear gripped him. How could he do such a thing to so delicate a woman? How would she look when she saw the severed head? Oh God, the shock of it would drive her mad!

No, he would not be strong enough for that. Much better that she should know nothing, that she should think her lover had left the city. He wiped his hands and arms on the dead man's clothing and walked away at random. His heart was beating very fast and he had no idea where he was going. He was half dead for want of food. At daybreak he went to the soldiers' billets and begged some bread, and then he went to work.

Next day, just before vespers, a number of black-bearded men dressed in Greek robes with embroidered trimmings appeared in the courtyard of the pilgrims of Arras. Father Albert went to meet them. One of them was a person of some importance, one of the secretaries to the Patriarch who had dealt with the administration of justice under the Turks. When Father Albert realized what he was saying, he sent in some alarm for Baudry and Brother Barnabé to come into the court.

The strangers waited, pale, erect and dignified, their hands hidden under their long cloaks. The matter was this: Philotheus Petrides, the brother-in-law of one of the men present, had been found murdered a hundred yards from his sister's house. He had been found at the hour of prime with his throat cut, stark naked and already stiff. His friends knew that he was a frequent visitor in the house of the people of Arras and that he had particular cause to fear the temper of a man named Élie. Father Albert said that in a city under military occupation, full of soldiers and suspicious persons of all kinds, there was no need to go to the faubourg quarters to look for murderers. "Our pilgrims," he said, "are not in the habit of roaming about the wealthy quarters of the city at night, and this Élie is not the man to murder a Christian in order to steal his clothes."

The Greeks held to their idea. Philotheus had told them several times that the man in question had a grudge against him. Brother Barnabé and Baudry, when this was explained to them, admitted that le Grêlé was a violent man and that there had apparently been some disagreement with Philotheus concerning his concubine, but that even so, no one had ever killed a eunuch out of jealousy. Both were extremely shocked because they were fond of Philotheus. The fact of his death came as no great surprise to them, for they had seen death often enough, but they thought: If it is le Grêlé who has done this, then we are all responsible.

"Élie will be home soon," Brother Barnabé said. "Question him."

As soon as he came into the courtyard after his day's work, Élie was taken to Baudry's room where the Greeks were waiting for him with Brother Barnabé and Father Albert. They all stood facing the door, looking at him, and he knew at once what they wanted. They asked him if he knew that Philotheus the Greek had been murdered the previous night.

I'm not such a fool, he thought. Aloud, he said, "No, how should I have known it? Where was this, that he was murdered?"

"Not far from his sister's house." Élie crossed himself.

The Greeks were speaking. They had faces like tax-collectors, stern and arrogant. Élie stood a head taller than they, but this irked him.

"Well," he said, "I didn't kill him."

"That is what they think," Father Albert said.

"How could I have done it? I don't even know where his sister lives."

"He was here last night. You could have followed him and killed him."

"I did not see him last night."

"Where were you all night?"

"In my room."

"Can you swear that you are innocent?"

He was frightened but he said, "Yes, I can. Tell me how I must swear."

Brother Barnabé and Baudry looked at one another in silence, a swift glance that said, We are not mistaken, it was him all right. Baudry said to Father Albert that this was a serious matter and that it was best to run no risk of perjury. They had better send for the two boys who slept outside le Grêlé's door and question them in turn.

The two boys were brought down. Everybody in the house was in the courtyard by now, crowding around the door of the room. They were anxious and inclined to be angry, saying that the Greeks meant to cause trouble and would lodge a complaint with the leaders of the army.

The first boy, Gillet, was made to stand by the door, and Father Albert held up an oil lamp to light the witness's face. Gillet was a lad of about thirteen, tall, thin and bony, with a certain puffiness around the eyes. He seemed to be half asleep. Had le

Grêlé come back to his room last night? Yes, he had. He had not left it? Yes, this morning at dawn to go to the wall.

"Tell us more about when he came home."

"At sunset."

"You are quite sure he came home last night?"

"Sure. He hit me."

"And after that?"

"He shouted at Feemy because the soup was cold."

"What did he say?"

"He bashed her. And then he said like, I piss on your mother. And your brother . . ."

"You are lying," said Brother Barnabé. "He did not say that."

The child crossed himself absently, as though brushing away flies. "He did so say it! And then he said like, Trollop, the whole faubourg knows why your mother was taken on to card wool . . ."

"Did he truly say that?"

"Sure," the child said. "He was drunk."

The other boy, Mardoche, had a long face and big sheep's eyes half hidden under a thatch of dry, tow-colored curls. He stood scratching his behind and eyeing the men who questioned him like a trapped animal. Had le Grêlé come home last night?

"Yes."

"He did not go out during the night?"

"No, he didn't."

"But you were asleep."

"No, I was too cold. I sleep during the day."

"What did he do?"

"He yelled at Feemy."

"Ah, and what did he say?"

The child bit his lip and gave a crow of laughter. "He said, You aren't a woman."

"And then?"

"Then he lay with her."

"He did not beat her?"

"He may have. I didn't see. She never screeches."

Father Albert translated the boys' words for the Greeks. He told them that if he had not been home that night, le Grêlé had certainly had no chance to warn them, and that if he had really spent the night in his room he must be innocent. The Greeks departed, more or less convinced, but still not entirely reassured.

The men in the courtyard began talking loudly, saying that if one of their people was to be tried it would not be by Greeks, but because they were poor everyone was trying to blame them for a murder committed in a rich neighborhood on the other side of the city. Le Grêlé had killed enough Turks and had no need to steal the clothes of any Greek.

"Well," Brother Barnabé said to Élie, "I think that clears you. I am glad."

"You thought I did it?"

"No, because you would certainly not have stolen his clothes . . . But God knows, my heart grieves for him. We shall miss him."

Almost ready to drop from hunger and exhaustion, le Grêlé could not bring himself to go up to his room. Instead, he lay down by the fire in the courtyard. His joy of the previous night was quite dead. We shall miss him. That was true. We shall miss him. He saw again the pale, gentle face, the weary twinkle in the narrow eyes, and wished that the unshriven dead could come to life again, come to life again every night so that every night he, le Grêlé, could slit that frail bare throat, come to life again and walk with his light step through the empty streets.

He let le Grêlé catch up with him, and in the light of the mortuary candles that streamed out through the open doorway of the church, he smiled. The mark of the knife on his throat had vanished and he smiled his pale smile—Philotheus, until the Last Judgment, until Jerusalem—until Jerusalem—you will walk before me like this and I shall seek your blood. What good was this woman to you?

Who was the son of a whore who took his clothes?

He said nothing to Euphemia, for the very good reason that he could not talk to her. She had not learned one word of French beyond bare yes and no. He said nothing, but in some mysterious way she knew it all. Perhaps some of the Syrian women had found the means to tell her. Brother Barnabé and the others might have been taken in, but Euphemia knew everything.

She knew that he was not a dog. That he was madly in love with her, she knew that too. That he had murdered a Christian for her sake, she knew. She eyed him warily as an animal mad with terror eyes the butcher's knife. She was so afraid of him that when he came into the room she cringed back into the corner and did not stir. It cost her an effort to get up when he spoke to her, and her legs gave way as if they had been made of wool.

A few days after Philotheus' death, Baudry and Brother Barnabé were sent for by the Bishop. There was such a crowd milling in the courtyard and in the galleries and guardroom and anterooms that they had to wait their turn until the evening. There were suppliants of every nation, even Moslems, because a great many infidels had filtered back into the city for reasons of trade, both rich and poor, knights and clerks. My lord Bishop was said to be sick, and in the city it was rumored that God was punishing him because he had told his friends that the true Lance was indeed in Constantinople.

One of the Bishop's clerks took Baudry and Brother Barnabé into a small vaulted room in which were several interpreters and a scribe. He told them that their people were causing trouble in the city and that in any event, pilgrims led by men who had been companions of Peter were not true crusaders. To this Brother Barnabé replied that God was the same for all, but that in His eyes the poor were worth more than the rich.

"Yes, indeed, but only if they are pure in heart. But his Holiness the Patriarch has informed our chancellery that among your men is one suspected of the murder of a Greek of good family." Baudry said that the man had been exonerated by two witnesses who had been questioned separately.

"I know that also," said the clerk, "and we have been informed that the witnesses seemed unworthy of credence and that they contradicted one another on various points. However, I am aware that the Greeks do not love us overmuch and I am willing to believe that your man is innocent. However, to prevent any trouble, I have to tell you that from now on the men of your house must not venture into the city or be employed anywhere except in the faubourgs or on the walls."

"What is this?" Baudry said. "Must they carry a rattle, like lepers?"

"No, because henceforth all pilgrims who are not soldiers and have no property of their own will be confined to the faubourgs."

"That is to say, all those who are poorly dressed without shoes?"

"You are sensible men," the clerk said. "You know yourselves that this is best for everyone."

Brother Barnabé and Baudry went away, feeling saddened and insulted, but reflecting that Antioch was not Jerusalem and that this would never happen in Jerusalem.

Marie and the other women fit to work were no longer able to earn their living from the Greeks and Armenians, and there was little work to be found elsewhere. Nor had they any desire to beg, because there were already far too many blind or crippled beggars, and they were afraid of being called lazy and told that their place was in a brothel. It was mortifying to beg unless people were dying of starvation in the city.

The priestess and Mahaut, who were no longer young, put themselves in the way of the knights as they came home from hunting, and clung to the squires' girths, offering to wash linen and mend clothes, but the knights evidently had washerwomen and seamstresses at home.

Then one day Marie was accosted by the same Norman knight who had importuned her once before, on the day after Isabelle's burial. He was walking near the ramparts and when he saw her he came running up to her, saying, "I have found you again at last!"

"You are mistaking me for someone else. I never set eyes on you before!" But he stood there, right in the middle of the street in front of the other women, telling her how beautiful she was, that there was no lovelier girl in all Antioch, and how after three months he had not forgotten her.

Marie wished that Pierre had not grown so heavy that she was forced to leave him at home.

"Go and tell that to some ugly girl. I've heard it all before. Besides, I'm not a girl, I am a married woman."

"You deserve better than a villein," he said. "A knightly sweetheart would become you more." He was young, tall, and fair with a face that was by no means ugly in spite of the tan which made it darker than his beard.

"There must be plenty of unmarried girls in the city who wouldn't say no to you," Marie said.

"They are not like you. You are fair and like the girls of my own land!"

"Then you should have stayed in your own land. There's no point in coming all the way to Antioch to find fair girls."

"Surely you are no villein's daughter," the man said. "Your mother got you of some knight."

"Well, that's the limit!" said Marie. "How dare you say such things about my mother, the most respectable woman in the whole faubourg! Do you think that is the way to please me? I wouldn't have a father such as yours, knight though he may be. He brought you up too badly."

She tried to walk on, but the man blocked her way. The street was a narrow one and the other women were saying, "Ah, Marie, this is dreadful. This man seems really set on you."

"Let us pass now," Marie said. "We shall be late for vespers."

"I'll let the others go, but not you. I have my men with me and they can easily carry you anywhere I wish."

"What!" Marie was really alarmed. "You wouldn't carry off a married woman in broad daylight? Oh, my friends, whatever you do, don't leave me!"

They were all walking on in this way, the knight with his two squires and the women huddled close together, when they came out into a small open square with a pink fountain in the middle. Here they saw some Syrian women, some poor Normans, and a handful of soldiers about to enter the church.

"You are not to go into that church," the knight said. "If you try to resist I shall tell them all you are my concubine who ran off with a Syrian."

"Oh, what lies! Who would believe you?"

"I care not who may believe me," he said.

It was impossible to run across the square full of people and so the five women linked arms more tightly, calling the importunate knight a dog and an infidel. "Oh, your mother back home would be ashamed of you!" It was then the knight attempted a trick. He pretended to be leaving the square but hid behind the fountain, and as soon as the women separated to go into the church he ran up to Marie and grabbed her by the shoulders, saying, "Now you shall come with me." Meanwhile his squires had got between Marie and her companions.

Screaming at the top of her voice, Marie wrenched herself out of the man's arms and sprang up onto the rim of the fountain. This raised her above the crowd in the square, and everyone looked at her. Some even came out of the church to see what was going on. Marie went on screaming. She was tired and hungry and beside herself with fury.

"Never!" she cried. "These are evil men and they shall not enter into the Kingdom of Heaven! Liars and traitors. They stop us going to the wealthy districts but they come into the poor quarters to steal honest pilgrims' wives! Oh, brothers, friends, see! Thanks to us they drove out the Turks and now they preen themselves on the miracle that God worked for His poor! And they take all the spoils that they won thanks to us and now they want to take our lives as well! This man would dishonor me because I am a poor man's wife, when my Jacques has killed more Turks with his ax than this ironbound coward with his lance!"

She balanced on the rim of the fountain, shouting, while the ice-cold water flowed out of a lion's head and soaked her dress. The knight and his two men had drawn their daggers from their sheaths and were retreating before the oncoming crowd, and all the time the knight's eyes never left Marie. She might have been the Holy Virgin and her words so many blessings.

When the three men had succeeded in forcing their way through the crowd, using their elbows and daggers, and had left the square, Marie came down chilled and trembling with excitement and threw herself into the priestess's arms. They went into the church. "Oh God," the priestess said, "These men will bring trouble on us."

As a result Marie returned to the house that night escorted by a crowd of Norman pilgrims and Syrian workmen, and as it turned out these kindly men were quite right to insist on going with her, because the mad knight was watching for her as she came out of the church and had even summoned another knight and five men-at-arms to his aid. However, when they saw the women of Arras protected by about fifty men armed with staffs and sheath knives, they dared not start a fight.

When the Normans and Syrians had gone away, Baudry barred the door into the courtyard and told the women to stop crying. "Marie," he said, "this is your fault. You would have done better to have stayed in the courtyard to look after the little children."

"Am I a prophetess? How was I to know we were going to meet that madman?"

"No," Baudry said, "but beautiful girls should not go wandering about in places full of soldiers."

"Maybe, Baudry, but this whole city is full of soldiers! And I am not so beautiful as I was."

"Apparently you are beautiful enough."

It was true that Marie's skin had turned the color of burnt toast from the sun, but this only made her eyes look bluer and her teeth whiter, while even starvation does not sit so ill on young faces. Marie was slim and lithe as a young filly and her fair hair, plaited into long braids, was not even dirty, for there was plenty of water in Antioch. But God, the way the poor women were dressed! It was a shame to speak of it, skirts that barely reached their calves and shifts tied with string at the neck; in Arras even the beggars would not have dared show themselves like that in the streets. If it were possible to be thought too beautiful like that!

"Listen, Baudry," said Brother Barnabé, "Marie has managed to look after herself well enough until today. Clearly she was up against a madman. We'll find out more about this man and make a complaint to his superiors."

The men sat around the fire, arguing.

"Marie, Marie," Alix said, "drink your soup. It will help cool your anger."

"Oh, what a good thing," Marie said, "what a good thing I advised Jacques to go away! It would have been the death of him. He would have gone rushing off to find that ruffian!"

"The man must have been the worse for drink, and when he sobers up he will forget all about it."

"Oh no, he was not drunk! It was sheer wickedness. They all saw him, the priestess and Mahaut . . . Oh Lord, these men have not taken the cross with a pure heart! They batten on the poor, here as elsewhere, they have taken the cross only to rob the poor of the heritage of Jerusalem. Has anyone counted up how many of our people have died and how many of theirs? They seek to win the paradise of Jerusalem through our martyrs and the best hire they can offer us is to abuse us! They deny us work, we are not good enough to wash their linen, and they would make us their whores."

The men had stopped talking to listen to her. Alix pulled her arm and said, "Sit down and get on with your food, you silly girl. No one has raped you."

Several of the men thought that what Marie said was true and the most outspoken of these was Élie le Grêlé. "If our women are violated," he said, "it is up to us to avenge them. If not, we shall have knights and their men coming to dishonor us in our own courtyard."

"You," said Brother Barnabé, "had better hold your tongue."

"For what I did at Belgrade, God has forgiven me," Élie said. "This time I shall take my ax, since Jacques is not here. And I shall not be the only one, because these people must be taught to fear us."

"We are not going to entrust the settlement of our affairs to you," Baudry said. "Father Albert and Brother Barnabé shall go and complain to the barons."

It was therefore agreed that Marie should stay in the house and look after the younger children, and that Father Albert should go and seek out the villain and complain to his leaders.

It took Father Albert some time to discover the name of Marie's attacker. The young knight was a nephew of the Viscount of Evreux. The Viscount was richly lodged in the mansion that served as a barracks for his company. The room that he and his knights occupied had a tiled floor covered with a Persian carpet, and silken cushions and serving dishes of enameled copper. They were not short of concubines, either: Father Albert caught a glimpse of four handsome girls, dressed only in diaphanous muslin, whisking themselves out of the room as he entered it. They were local girls, to judge by their long black hair which they had not even modesty enough to braid up. The Viscount was reclining on a heap of cushions while a small black-skinned boy waved away the flies with a peacock-feather fan. His knights sat around him, watching two of their number engaged in a game of chess.

When Father Albert explained his business to the Viscount, the knights roared with laughter and told him that he, a Norman, should not degrade himself by associating with a gang of weavers from the North. However, the Viscount, who was thin and pale and looked ill, raised himself on his elbow and said he had heard something of the story the night before and that there could be no doubt that the woman in question had cast a spell on his nephew, since there were known to be many witches and heretics among the weavers of Arras. It was awkward, he said, to speak about such things to a priest, but the young man was sick of love and if there was any way of tempting this woman with money, he thought that the sin was better than the risk of seeing a brave and handsome knight die.

Father Albert had lived long enough to be able to control his temper. "Lord Viscount," he said, "the people of those parts are a proud folk and accustomed to bloodshed. Advise your nephew not to show himself where he may meet with any men of Arras." The Viscount replied that it was not the first time the riffraff had tried to make trouble in the city. Only the Thursday before, three pilgrims from Provence had been hanged for the murder of a noble squire, and some French knights had been attacked quite openly outside the walls by a band of Flemish laborers, simply for making fun of their language. He said the pilgrims were becoming a real nuisance because they were not men born to the sight of blood.

Father Albert said that all the trouble was due to the indecision of the barons, because if the army were to pack up tomorrow and leave the city to march on Jerusalem, all quarrels between Christians would be forgotten. The knights listened thoughtfully and nodded, for even if they did not agree they would not have dared to say so.

Father Albert withdrew, therefore, with nothing gained or even asked, for he could see clearly that his endeavors were foolish and doomed to failure. What seemed a crying shame to the poor was so small a thing to the rich that they could not even understand what the fuss was about, and talking to them, even Father Albert himself was no longer quite sure what the matter was.

In the course of that same month of September, the order went out from the leaders of the army that all the lesser folk, civilians, foot soldiers, and lackeys, were to leave their houses. They were to gather up their belongings and go and camp in and around the city of Maarat an-Numan, which lay twenty leagues distant from Antioch. This was because Antioch was overcrowded since the return of its former inhabitants and the arrival of reinforcements by sea, and also of Christian refugees from Aleppo.

The army promised to keep the foot soldiers and the pilgrims supplied regularly with food at reasonable prices, on condition that the men neither returned to seek work in the city nor caused any trouble. Now that the walls had been repaired, the ditches cleared, and most of the houses put in order, the presence of such a vast number of poor people was turning the outer wards of the city into total slums which were becoming a real danger.

The end of it was that they had to go. At first the people all thought this departure was the real thing. Later, even when they found out they were merely moving camp, the pilgrims were inclined to welcome the change because they were growing bored in their houses. The only trouble was that winter was coming on and the leaders chose this of all moments to turn the people out of sound, easily warmed houses.

On the day before they were to leave, Father Albert went to visit le Grêlé's concubine. Ever since the Greek's death she had remained by herself in her room, and Father Albert was feeling a little guilty about her. He could have gone to see her now and then, but after all he was still in the prime of life and she was a very lovely woman. But now, when he saw her, he had a shock. She was thinner, there were purple shadows under her eyes, her hair hung lank and dull about her face, and her gown was all stained and dirty at the neck.

God knows, she was still beautiful, with a beauty that would bring tears to the eyes of the most hardened man. Nothing could take away her beauty, and the signs of despair and unhappiness on her were like the splendid ornaments of mourning.

"My daughter," the priest said, "tomorrow we leave the city. There may be some way of getting you carried off by the men of the Patriarch's guard and taken to some Greek house. I could find a white lie to tell le Grêlé."

Euphemia barely glanced at him; she seemed hardly to understand what he was saying. At last she said, "No, what is the use?"

"You do not wish to remain with this man?"

"It is all the same to me," she said.

"You do not mean to tell me that you care for him."

She answered with quiet indifference, "*I no longer care for anything.*"

"Do you fear him so much?"

She shook her head quickly and a little glimmer of suspicion flickered in her eyes. "No. I do not fear him."

Father Albert folded his arms and looked at her unhappily. He could not resist the temptation to ask her the question which had long been tormenting him: "Tell me, do you know something? Was it le Grêlé who killed Philotheus the Greek?" He saw the young woman's eyes go blank of all expression; her face became hard as marble. She answered almost angrily:

"How should I know? No, it cannot have been him."

Who could ever understand women? Father Albert, at all events, knew very little of them. Most of the confessions he had heard since becoming a priest had been from soldiers. It occurred to him that perhaps this lovely girl found satisfaction in the arms of a tough, brutal man.

And so Euphemia left the house and the city with the other women of the company from Arras, carrying on her back a bundle in which she had wrapped the few things le Grêlé had procured for her: a few pots and pans, a small rug, and a shift. The Syrians tried to talk to her in Arabic, but she would not answer them. The women of Arras looked at her and sighed: "Ah, what a shame! Holy Virgin, has he made her mad? Her eyes have no expression left in them."

Euphemia had no longer any wish to live. Nor had she any wish to die. She did not know what she hoped for. She prayed for this man to die, yet lacked the courage to kill him herself. When he lay beside her snoring, she was amazed that she should hate him so little; he was not dangerous, a poor animal. But during the day, even when he was not there, she was so frightened that she lived in constant expectation of seeing him appear in the doorway with his knife. The knife filled her vision. The whole world had shrunk to the dimensions of one big knife.

8 ✠✠✠✠✠✠✠✠✠✠✠✠✠✠

The camp settled down again at Maarat an-Numan, a small and not unpleasant fortified town from which all the Turks had gone. The professional soldiers occupied the buildings of the citadel, the former mosque, and the best houses, while the rest fought among themselves for the houses that were nearest to the wells or had the biggest courtyards, and by the end of a week the share-out was complete and some measure of peace restored. In the end there was room enough, because there were hardly more than a thousand Armenians left in the place and the richest of these had left when they saw the hordes of crusaders arriving. It was a fact that the people of these parts had no great opinion of the Christians from France; they said they were dirty and coarse and quarrelsome, which was hardly surprising. Poverty improves no one.

Outside the city, in the ruins of one of the outlying villages and what had once been wheatfields, the Tafurs had made their camp. They were not wanted in the city, and in any case they refused to take advantage of stolen houses: even if a house was used by right of conquest and with permission from the Bishop, the Tafurs called it stealing. In addition, the lepers from the leper hospital in Antioch, where they were certainly overcrowded, were transferred to a field which they fenced in with a palisade and were given canvas and skins to make themselves tents. The Bretons also settled outside the walls. Most of them were peasants, and they preferred it to being cooped up in houses perched one on top of the other.

These Bretons were a hardheaded and suspicious race. They dug deep trenches around their camp and lined them with pointed stakes, and some even began to dig the ground and plant vegetables. Between now and the barons' decision to set out for Jerusalem they would be able to grow not only beans but perhaps vines also and even apple trees, especially as in these lands everything grew more quickly than in Brittany.

The armies of Duke Godfrey of Lower Lorraine came back. They brought plunder and large flocks of sheep and goats, and some good news as well: there were no more Turks from Edessa to Melitene, and it was known throughout the country that the Sultan would send no fresh army, he was so discouraged to see how God favored the Christians. But in Baghdad the Moslems had their pope, who was called Calixtus, and he was preparing to preach a crusade against the Christians, so that when spring came it was to be feared that he would lead his armies in person to the defense of Jerusalem.

Jacques and some other men who had gone with the Duke's army came back very pleased with themselves after the good time they had had in the north. A country of clear air and rich soil, with vines, corn, olives, and oranges, where sheep and cattle were plentiful, the mountains higher than those around Antioch and well wooded—the timber in the pinewoods alone was worth a fortune—with streams lined with willows and elm trees and valleys where the grass was green, and white cities filled with churches and gardens: they had so much to tell that the others began to suspect them of bragging. But whether they were making it up or not, they certainly looked well and had put on a good five pounds of flesh and muscle fighting for Jesus Christ. There had been no great battles, only ambuscades and strongholds captured without much trouble, since the people of that country were Armenians and themselves concerned with driving out the Turks.

In the way of booty, they did not bring back a great deal: a few sheep, a little money, bows and arrows, a silver ewer, and two Turkish women's robes. One of these robes was for Marie; the other, which had been won by Bernier who had no wife, was bought by Élie le Grêlé.

Élie had taken possession of a small house not far from the Bishop's palace. Two small rooms gave onto a street too narrow for a cart to pass, making it permanently dark inside. The boys and the three Picards slept downstairs, Élie and the woman above, and Euphemia made cakes which one of the Syrians would then sell outside the Bishop's palace. This enabled Élie to say that his concubine was not a charge on anyone but, on the contrary, earned her living better than any other woman in the company. It was good for Euphemia, also. All day long she stretched and dried and rolled and garnished her pastry, and in the work she forgot time, her days flowed by, long, long weeks and months of endless day, while she sifted and sifted the same flour and spread out the leaves of pastry with slow concentration, seeing nothing, her head a hollow void, a bell without a clapper.

The days grew cool as they waited for the rains.

Élie gave Euphemia the green silk robe. Even when he meant to be kind, he looked like a man throwing a bone to a dog. Only his eyes were strange: uncertain, timid, with a little tawny glimmer in their depths.

"Well? Don't you like it?" Euphemia did not understand but she guessed and nodded her head.

"Smile, at least!" She guessed that too and the corners of her mouth turned up. He looked at her wonderingly, lost in blissful admiration. To him she was no less lovely than before. Far from it. Now, dirtier and thinner, he felt her closer to him, his wife for four months, four months which felt like a year to him. She had given him more anxiety than a woman brought to bed and nursing a child. His heart was heavy, so heavy because of her, he pitied her, did she think him a brute? He pitied her. If he could have brought her Greek to life again for her, he would have done it!

On Sunday he took her to mass in her green dress.

Here at Maarat there was no more work. He lived on what the cakes brought in and on the corn distributed on Saturdays. Often he stayed in the house, watching her make her pastry. Such deft, slender fingers she had, like a fairy! That was why the pastry was so good; it was said my lord Bishop himself ate it with relish.

After the feast of Saint Peter, two Turkish prisoners were brought into Maarat, marauders who had deserted from the great army. There had been twelve of them. Three had made their escape and the rest were killed, except these two who had been captured. There seemed no point in killing them: they could be put to work in the mill.

What happened, in the event, was this. The two prisoners had been left lying, bound, in a barn near the walls, when a gang of boys came along. The boys were at a loose end with no work to do, and it occurred to them that they ought to learn how to cut off a real Turk's head, but their small knives were blunt and broken and they did not know how to go about it. They set to, all together, each one hacking and sawing away in turn as best he could, while the Turk choked and struggled and his companion roared for help. The boys were discovered, all spattered with blood, gathered around the Turk whose head was hanging half off, and squabbling over whose turn it was to sever the next vein or sinew, while the blood gushed from the body all over their legs.

The men who had captured the Turks gave the boys a hiding and haled them off, all bloody as they were, to Baudry's house. What kind of behavior was that, to help themselves without so much as a by-your-leave, besides inflicting such a dreadful death on a fellow that had done them no harm? Baudry and Brother Barnabé were very angry, for the oldest of the boys was not yet fourteen.

Brother Barnabé had the five boys lined up along the wall, and then he took a leather strap and set about beating them with all the strength of his arm, on their faces and their backs and their legs, while the children howled and threw themselves on their knees, and still Brother Barnabé went on flogging them.

"Gently," Baudry said, "they are only children."

"Children of the Devil. And I mean to drive the Devil out of them."

The boys tried to run, but there was no way of escape. Brother Barnabé stood between them and the door, and the lash flew so fast that the holy monk might have handled a whip all his life. They squealed and sobbed and shrieked: "Mother! Mother! Mercy, we won't do it again!" They made such a racket that a crowd collected in the square in front of the house.

By the end the boys were huddled on the floor close to the wall, hiding their heads in their arms, covered all over with bloody weals. Brother Barnabé, exhausted, his face on fire, coughing his heart out, threw down his lash and said, "Get out, you devils! On your knees, like beasts, and never let me see your filthy faces again!" Then, when the boys were outside, he went and sat down on the floor in a corner and hid his face in his hands.

Under his frieze cloak, his broad, thin shoulders were shuddering convulsively. Baudry crossed to the door to make sure the boys could still walk, but they had disappeared into the crowd. Some of the men there were Provençals who did not know the cause of the trouble, and they were saying in their own dialect, "Lucky for you two you do not belong to us!" Baudry shrugged and went back to Brother Barnabé.

"Well," he said wearily, "do you think you have driven out the Devil?" Brother Barnabé sat very still, his bent head resting on his folded arms; only his shoulders were still jerking. "What is the use of crying?" Baudry said. "Are you weeping for your sin or theirs?" Brother Barnabé raised his head slowly.

"God knows, I have committed no sin. Even if I had killed them I should not have sinned."

"Brother, God is great."

"Yes. But why did He permit a thing like that?"

One of the boys who had been beaten was le Grêlé's protégé Mardoche, and on his account Élie went that same evening to see the two leaders of the company from Arras and told them it was not right to deal so harshly with an orphan. He, Élie, had known the boy's father well and had fed him since his father's death. It was for him to punish him if punishment was needed.

"Not so," said Brother Barnabé. "Here it is I who punish. And I would have whipped you likewise if I thought it would do you any good."

Élie said Mardoche's right eye was so swollen that he was likely to lose it.

"Let that be a lesson to him."

"These boys learn to fight as best they can," said le Grêlé.

"Get out," said Brother Barnabé. "I have seen enough of you."

Mardoche did not lose his right eye, but the story got about, and not only among the folk of Arras.

Élie le Grêlé now had the entry into the citadel and talked to the captains of the soldiers without taking off his cap. All the boys of Artois and Picardy were known to look up to him as to the Pope, and a round dozen of the men were ready to follow his lead. Among them was Jacques of the Ax, because Jacques had not forgotten that while he was away Élie had been ready to rush off with his friends to the mansion occupied by the Viscount of Evreux to make short work of the wicked knight, and between fellow countrymen such a service merited an oath of friendship.

"The boys have no business in guardrooms," Baudry said. "Their parents did not take the cross to make soldiers of them."

"We are all soldiers of Christ," Élie said.

"Of Christ, yes, but not of Master Jacques of Saint-Flour" (this was the name of the captain of the foot soldiers) "and we took the cross for prayer and penitence."

"Well, after all," One-eyed Mahaut put in, "what those boys did to the Turks, haven't the Turks done as much and worse to God knows how many of our own people?"

"And if we mean to do everything the Turks have done," said Brother Barnabé, "why don't we go and desecrate the churches and spit on the images of Jesus Christ? Truly, that is all we need, so do it and show everyone once and for all that you are children of the Devil!"

But neither his anger nor his prayers had any power to move the young men now, for they had all aged ten years in these past two and what Peter's companions had preached at Arras had become like old men's maunderings. Those are old men's tales, they said, things are different now. Brother Barnabé was not old, but his brown beard was grizzled and his large eyes had purple shadows around them and were bright with fever. His thunderous voice was cracked and gasping, and he was beginning to spit blood from his lungs.

Even faithful friends like Baudry and Alix were saying, In Jerusalem our sins shall be forgiven, but until we reach Jerusalem who can live without sin? If it is God's will that we should drive out the Turks, He will take our sins on Himself.

"The millstone around our necks, Baudry. The millstone around our necks, dragging us down, down to the bottom of the lake of boiling pitch."

"How now, brother, have you begun to feel the temptation of Judas?"

"Who would not be tempted? God promised us great hardships but I did not foresee this. And yet it was not hard to foresee!"

The rains began, and it was clear that the Bretons had not been mistaken in building houses for themselves. They were almost snug inside their huts dug deep into the ground, walled in by stones and roofed with straw and branches, and they said it was much better than the last winter, with no siege works to worry about and far fewer deaths. God was very good.

Caravans came from Antioch twice a week bringing supplies, and news as well. There would be no setting out tomorrow or even by All Saints. There was some kind of plague in the city; people turned as red as boiled crayfish, with a high fever and pains all through their bodies. The death rate was not unduly high, hardly one man in five, but many of the knights were sick and because of this the army could not set out.

What said the Holy Lance? For although it was true that the Lance itself uttered no words, it was through it that Peter Bartholomew, the man who had discovered it, saw visions. It said that God would surely deliver up Jerusalem to the Christians if they remained pure in heart, forgot their quarrels, and abstained from all commerce with women that had not been baptized. That these quarrels existed was known by now even to the men assigned to the supply convoys. The barons argued all day long over the division of Antioch and the province of the Orontes, each wishing to have pride of place there. They were all such great lords that none might yield to another without shaming all his kin.

And since the good Bishop of Le Puy, God keep his soul, was dead, and Jesus Christ was not revealing Himself clearly, and the Pope not answering the barons' letters, nor the Emperor either, how were such proud men to reach agreement?

It was well known they were men who would starve to death in front of a table laden with food if anyone suggested that one of lesser nobility should be served first.

Here were men who had taken on them the cross of Jesus Christ, who had pledged themselves to lead all their friends and their armies and the pilgrims to Jerusalem, and yet after the great miracles that God had performed for the Christians they could not bring themselves to waive their pride of race. The true Christian is willing to be the servant of all, yet there they sat, staring one another in the face, all with the one fear that they might be suspected of being willing to serve under one of their number.

The Christian's duty is to give away all he possesses, and if he has two shirts to keep only one of them, yet these men had weapons and horses and clothes in plenty and wealth of all kinds, and still they spent their time squabbling over who should keep the wealthiest districts and who should fly his banners from which towers. If this was how they behaved, it was not surprising God had sent this plague on them.

For no man may serve two masters and they chose Mammon. They said, In return for our zeal it is right that God should bestow on us the wealth of Mammon. God knows, they said, we have already done so much for Jesus Christ that He owes us our reward. We are not mercenaries, no, but we are His saviors.

If they had taken Jerusalem and Bethlehem and Nazareth and all the holy places, then perhaps they might have something to be proud of. But for Antioch, where Christ never set foot, they thought themselves already so thoroughly absolved by God that they forgot their oaths!

In Maarat, there was much talk of the bad faith of the barons and their knights. After All Saints, the weather seemed to be settling, but there was still no mention of departure. A week after All Saints, the Count of Toulouse sent a flock of five hundred head of sheep and ten wagonloads of corn as a present to the foot soldiers, and was much praised for his goodness, yet even the Provençal soldiers at Maarat were beginning to say, *Are we here to eat and drink?* Does he throw food to us as one might throw a bone to a growling dog? Don't they know the winters are mild down there in the south, by the sea, and that before Christmas we could be encamped outside Jerusalem?

Are they waiting until the Pope Calixtus has had time to raise a new Turkish army to come and slaughter us all in Maarat?

Is the Holy Lance a false lance, that they are afraid to march with it on Jerusalem?

Has the Holy Ghost sent word to them that Jesus Christ was born in Antioch and purchased the remission of our sins in Antioch?

They have sent us away and turned us out of the city for shame, so that the poor of the army shall not see the easy life they lead in their palaces and gardens, surrounded by Oriental carpets and silver vessels and beautiful Greek girls they have carried off by force from their families.

There was no work, and no famine. Tired of continual preparations for the great departure, the men went off in groups of two or three hundred at a time into the mountains or along the valley in search of God knows what: goods to plunder or bands of Turks to drive off? There were no more real Turks in the region, only brigands. These had horses, so that sometimes the soldiers came back with dead or wounded, but with two or three horses also.

Can it be, Élie thought, can it be that she is still thinking of her Greek? He had no way of finding out; he could not talk to her and dared not utter Philotheus' name in her presence. He had wanted to do it a hundred times, and his mouth had refused to open. Sometimes he would say, "Are you thinking of him? Did you love him as much as that?" but as he said it in French she did not understand. He told her, "You are as cold as a corpse, what pleasure can a man get from you?" And she would look at him with her huge, empty eyes. She was afraid of him, yes, there was nothing odd in that, but surely one got used to anything, even fear.

His desire for her was so strong that even in his first youth, in the early days of his marriage, he had known nothing to compare with it, but every night saw him disappointed, helpless with rage. She was cold enough to freeze the flames of hell.

If she had put her arms around his neck only once, he would have gone mad with joy. The mere thought of it was enough to set his face on fire. There were those who said that even a girl who was raped, who fought and screamed, could suddenly turn loving. No one could see if a man was ugly in the dark. This girl had a devil of ice in her body.

And even for the ice in her body he loved her.

Never once had that name been uttered. Perhaps she used to twine her arms about his neck. Perhaps she used to kiss his eyes—it was enough to drive a man mad. Jealousy does not die with the death of a man. "Well then? Smile at me. Smile." She must have understood because she turned her head slowly and her lip curled in a deathlike smile. The little coward—if she would only lose her temper, at least. Not even that, not even temper, not even hatred, only a little fear.

On Christmas Eve, Brother Barnabé spoke to le Grêlé: "When will you have done with the scandal? Somehow, I do not know how, you have acquired a band of friends who follow you everywhere, you are known for a brave man, the least you can do is refrain from setting a bad example."

"Am I the only one in the army? The knights and sergeants have their concubines as much and more."

"Did you take the cross to copy the knights' evil ways? At least, you need not be a public sinner. There are always whores."

Élie said he had never touched a whore in his life and was not going to begin now that he was thirty-three. Besides, he was attached to the woman, "not so much for what is in your mind, but—how can I put it—out of pity."

"Then you mean to take her with you to Jerusalem?"

"At the rate the barons are managing the business it will be a long time before we see Jerusalem."

"What if we were to leave tomorrow?"

Le Grêlé shrugged. He had no answer.

It was cold and gusts of wind blew down from the mountains, bringing mingled sleet and snow, but no one cared about the bad weather. On the contrary, the wind seemed to put heart into them. The louder it blew, tearing down the narrow streets, the louder rose the shouting, on every roof and at every crossroad, as though the whole town had gone mad. Every quarter had its fanatic, suddenly possessed by zeal for Jesus Christ, and when his voice wore out there was another to replace him instantly.

Brothers, what are we waiting for? Brothers, shall we desert Jesus Christ?

Brothers, Christmas is over that was our time of grace! If Jerusalem is not liberated by Easter, what will God think of us?

Brothers, friends, soldiers, shall we lie to our dead?

All of us here in Maarat and below the walls and out on the plain! All, the lepers and the Tafurs as well! With our axes and our hatchets, our cudgels and our pitchforks, our knives and our hammers!

They are maybe five thousand and we, with the women and children, more than twenty thousand, surely! More than thirty thousand! If we all march together on Antioch they will do as we want.

They are disputing over the spoils of Antioch, and for this stolen heritage they neglect the heritage of Jesus Christ, yet God knows, brothers, they did not take the cross to enrich themselves, and if they set out with that idea we will knock it out of their heads, for we have never sought to enrich ourselves, except with the only true wealth which is Jerusalem.

A consignment of oil and corn arrived that day. In actual fact it had been expected in time for Christmas, but for some unknown reason it was late and they had managed without it.

They had waited for the corn and oil, and when the barons had not stirred themselves to send this Christmas gift in time, the troops said to themselves, They will have feasted like kings and entertained ambassadors, Egyptian, Greek, and others, and much good may it do them. Then the convoy arrived and the mule-drawn carts came to a halt by the city gate, just inside the outworks, and the captains of the men-at-arms and the two knights who were in command of the town came out to ask those in charge of the convoy the reason for the delay.

One of these men, the Provençal quartermaster from Antioch, replied by telling them not to look a gift horse in the mouth. Jacques of Saint-Flour, himself a Provençal, retorted promptly that it was no gift horse, that neither the soldiers nor the pilgrims lived on charity but were paid a great deal less than their services had deserved, and if the barons chose to take it that way they could keep their oil and their corn.

In his anger, he raised his mace and struck such a blow at one of the jars of oil in the first cart that the jar broke and two more were cracked under the force of the blow, and oil began to pour out all over the sacks and the wheels. Seeing this, two friends of Jacques of Saint-Flour drew their swords and rushed up to a wagon of corn and began ripping open the sacks one by one.

There was already a crowd on the walls and the steps around the carts, and more people came running from the town. Small children began picking up the corn that was scattered in heaps around the wagons, and the soldiers drove them off with kicks. Let no one touch it. Let all this grain be swept into the ditches. By Saint George, we'd rather go and plunder every village for ten leagues around than submit to be called beggars!

A great shout went up. At that moment every one of all those looking on agreed with the soldiers. They were hungry enough to be quickly stirred to anger but not enough to be feeling the pains of dizziness and cramps, and even those who felt sick at the sight of all that wasted grain only rejoiced the more, and shouted all the louder: "Take it back! Throw it away! Give it to your dogs! Stuff yourselves, get as fat as pigs! If they have too much, let them send it to the Emperor in Constantinople!"

There were some priests on the walls who cried out, "Brothers, sons, this is a mortal sin. God's gifts are not to be thrown away!"

"The gifts of cowards! The gifts of robbers! Jesus Christ forbids us to take them!" The men sent to escort the convoy galloped off full tilt for Antioch.

There were certain men in the town who, while not entirely sane, were undoubtedly inspired, and these went up to the roof-tops and spoke to the people. It was a cold, clear day of sun and wind, like a foretaste of spring in midwinter. Gusts of wind buffeted the men's faces and the clean, dry air from the mountains went to their heads. All those who had eaten nothing since dawn were in such a state of excitement that they were laughing and crying at once, because to people who have known famine, to watch corn trampled underfoot is like tearing out their own entrails.

Lord Jesus, we will not eat this bread
We shall eat better in Jerusalem.

Let them stay and eat and drink in Antioch: we shall go on without them!

The town was in such a fever of excitement that men began packing up their belongings and the women sang as they wrapped pots and provisions in blankets. Tomorrow at dawn, we shall go on without them! They shall be lords of Antioch and we of Jerusalem!

"Soldiers! You have been deceived! Be sure they never meant to make this pilgrimage. They came here only to enrich themselves by your sweat and your blood!

"They said, these men will fight better if we make them believe they are fighting for Jesus Christ.

"They were wronging Jesus Christ Himself with their false promises! But Jesus Christ, who sees all men's hearts, has rejected their service. But for the love He bears His poor all these proud men would be dead today and their heads scattered from Baghdad to Aleppo and Damascus!

"You need not fear them. It is they who should fear you. If you desert them, God will desert them also."

The man who said all this was a priest, the chaplain to the Walloon troops. He had a strong voice, and a stage had been erected for him in the square outside the gate of the citadel. He climbed onto it, brandishing a cross of bronze. All men listened to him, including many who were neither soldiers nor Walloons. He had seen visions during the famine and ever since had worn a twenty-pound chain around his waist and slept on cinders.

"Men in this town are given up to sin and idleness, but their sin is less than that of the barons! For the barons are the head and you the body, and when the head is full of vanity, then let the arms and legs set to and lead the head!

"When God deprives the head of understanding, He permits reason to dwell in the heart, and you are the heart of the army!"

Many other priests and laymen were saying much the same thing. Agreement was general, and the Bishop of Maarat in his lofty palace promised to pick a delegation to go to Antioch. But everyone knew how delegations were received: with a great many promises and a lot of waiting about in anterooms. We have waited long enough.

No one would listen any more to either the Bishop or the commanders of the garrison. The captains of the men-at-arms and the leaders of the pilgrim bands assembled in the church, and this was what they decided:

Whereas, the leaders of the army are putting off the performance of their vow from wicked covetousness

and for six months have been disputing among themselves for possession of towers, castles, and mansions and have forgotten Jesus Christ

and neither prayers nor entreaties can move them, and God may grow tired of their idleness and abandon the Christians,

it is necessary to deprive these covetous men of the objects of their greed, and that these gorged dogs shall become famished dogs once more.

Since we hold the town of Maarat, we shall begin with this town, and after that go on to Antioch.

There are sappers and blasters among us, and miners and quarrymen, artillerymen and masons. Tomorrow there will be public prayers, and then all shall set to work! Soldiers and civilians, monks and laymen, men, women, and children!

By next week, let no stone of this fortress remain upon another.

And let them know that this is only a trial, and that in Antioch we shall do much more, however great the city.

Once this good news was proclaimed and cried from the rooftops, the people did not even wait for the public prayers. They had done enough work on the walls of Antioch, and it is easier to demolish than to build. Those of less account were the first to set to work—women and children. With mallets, cudgels, and even heavy stones they smashed down doors, windows, and timbers. They knocked down the walls of the less substantial buildings, using iron bars as levers. It was like a holiday.

Stop: someone must oversee the work. Call in the quarrymen at least, these houses are old, they may collapse on top of you! But the women only laughed. They were not afraid. God will protect us, we are doing His work.

They lived in such a din, and such a dust, that if God had descended out of heaven in all His glory they would not have seen or heard Him.

No one noticed the cold any more. The men of Arras were working on the walls. The stones there were strong, four feet across. A team of six men was assigned to each section of wall. They hammered the iron bar into the interstices between the stones with heavy mallets, then beat down the other end of the bar until the great squared stones shifted. The workmanship was Greek and very strong. Strength and skill were needed to unseat the stones and prize them out. As each stone came loose and tumbled down into the moat, the men in the team gave a great shout of triumph and then stood panting and mopping their brows.

The men had forgotten what it was like to be cold; they were streaming with sweat. Their hair and beards were dripping with it, and they were bright yellow from the dust that clung to their bodies. They laughed when they looked at each other, all red and yellow, their eyes clogged with dust and such a ringing in their ears as left no room for a single thought in their heads, nothing but hammer blows. They could not even speak; all they could manage was cries of "Heave ho! Easy! Easy, now! There she comes!"

Never was such backbreaking work done with such glee. A moment to get their breath, to look at one another and at the empty place where the stone had been: "We're doing fine, men! We're way ahead of the next gang." The walls cracked and shivered, but nothing could be seen for dust. Dust and splinters of granite stuck to their lips, their eyes were blinded with it, but from the direction of the town they could hear the roar of houses falling.

There were voices shouting, shrill, happy voices, and singing half drowned by the sound of hammering. The dust was worse in the town than on the walls, and columns of smoke were going up: the teams of blasters had lighted huge fires inside the most substantial houses and there was a sound of stones splitting and shattering and timbers crackling, and flames billowed out into the streets. Tomorrow half the town would have nowhere to sleep, but there was no one who was not working, except the old women who were looking after the small children, and these had taken refuge in the church at the foot of the citadel.

Baudry and Élie le Grêlé were on the same team. Both were tall, strong men, but Baudry had more experience with stone and he was in charge. For once there was no ill-feeling between them: strong proof that this was good work and according to God's will. Baudry had remembered his old skills and knew just where and how to strike, and in the manner of masons he gave each stone a name, and would say to himself, This was good work, there are no better workmen than the Greeks! By the end of the day the wall was so low that a child could have climbed it, and the space between the two enceintes was like a torrent of huge brown and yellow stones, their neatly dressed corners sticking up everywhere like the crests of waves. Faint with hunger, their clothes thick with dust and clinging to their bodies, the men ran out of the town toward the fires that had been lighted there.

There the priests were already chanting prayers. Whole sheep on spits were crackling golden-brown over the fires, and the women, drunk with fatigue, staggering and laughing, carried around jugs of water colored with wine.

The night was cold and piles of broken beams had been brought from the town. Fires were burning all the way to the lepers' camp. The lepers looked on, lining the inside of their palisade. "Good work, brothers? God bless you, brothers!" People answered them and almost invited them to come to the fires. They too are going to Jerusalem. "Courage, brothers. It may be at the Holy Sepulcher you will be cured." The lepers were used to the kindly wish, and the least affected even had some hopes. "Thanks, brothers, we are praying for you. Our prayers are strong with Jesus Christ."

They chanted the prayers and the lepers chanted with them.

There were young, handsome men among them and women whose faces were still whole, and these put themselves forward and made signs and called out greetings to remind the rest that they were not to be scorned. "Will they let us in also?" "Sure as God lives. You shall touch the Holy Sepulcher." No one knew, but they said this to comfort them.

Inside the town the houses were still burning, and the citadel shone red through the ruddy smoke. Piercing screams, screams as of beasts being flayed alive, rose from somewhere near the ramparts where the Flemish archers were burning the thirty prisoners they had been keeping in their billet, men from Aleppo who had promised ransom. The archers wanted no ransom; they wanted nothing. They had shut the men in a barn with some straw and fagots. The Flemings stood warming themselves twenty yards from the burning building, and any that got out they finished off with stones rather than waste arrows. Whoever spares a Turk out of lust for money is a traitor to Jesus Christ.

Jacques and Lambert were lying on some straw a few yards away from the lepers' enclosure. Marie had gone to fetch Pierre from the church. She came back to the big meadow and asked the men sitting around the fires where the folk of Arras were camped. No one knew. There were no more folk of Arras, or Lille, or Rouen, or Mantes: it was the tower of Babel. The men were gathered haphazardly around the fires, sharing whatever they had to eat without asking their neighbor where he came from. Marie hugged the sleeping child to her, wrapped in a sheepskin.

"Are you a widow, beautiful?" She crossed herself. "Good God, no! I am looking for my husband. I saw him this morning with some soldiers from Picardy."

"Then go toward the lepers, he should be over there. A pity, all the same."

The camp whores were kept busy that night, Syrian and Turkish girls, for there were few French ones left now.

Jacques was asleep, so broken with fatigue that a blow in the face would not have wakened him. Lambert was awake. "My mother?" he asked.

"In the church with the sick. Aubry, from Valognes, will not last much longer, God rest him."

"Marie, how many of us will enter Jerusalem alive?"

"As many as God wills. On that day all our dead shall find rest."

"Some of the priests say that they are already in glory."

Marie lay on her back and looked up at the stars. On this cold night, how they shone! Like rivers of diamonds. "Lambert, Jesus Christ would gladly bring them to glory and wipe all the tears from their eyes, but they will not be comforted while their brothers have not yet reached the end of their journey. I hear them singing a hymn of lamentation, a choir of a hundred thousand voices!"

"You hear them?" Lambert said.

"When I lie still and look at the stars. Yes, I hear them."

"As for me," said Lambert, "when I go to sleep I dream of home. I go back to the faubourg with my father and no one knows us."

Jacques was talking in his sleep. They could not catch what he was saying, it was nonsense or some unknown language, but he seemed happy and was laughing. It was a silly, almost childish giggle. Then he cried out, "His guts! His guts are full of pearls!" He started up suddenly and cried out again, "My ax!" Then he fell back. Lambert shook him to wake him from his ungodly dream, but without success. His sleep was as deep as an enchantment.

"Do you think," Marie said, "that we will destroy Antioch as well? That will be a job."

"If we have to," said Lambert, "we shall do it."

The Bishop had shut himself up in the citadel, along with the commanders of the garrison, the few Armenians who were left in Maarat, and a few dozen Turkish prisoners. In the morning he came out, surrounded by his clerks and his guard, riding a dapple-grey horse with a herald going before him.

He came to the billets of the Provençal troops, which were still intact. A great many of the sick and wounded had been taken there and women were drying dirty linen and babies' clothes around the huge fires that burned in the kitchen and the guardrooms. The men's captains were in the town, overseeing the demolition work. The Bishop asked that they be sent for.

The captains came, red-faced, out of breath and temper, and with them three or four of the leading pilgrims who did not want the soldiers to be the only ones to have a say in the matter.

The Bishop spoke to them severely at first, but afterward he softened a little. What did they want? Did they think they could do without the knights? The army was like a ram, with the knights as the pointed, iron-shod head that could do nothing on its own, but the ram was useless without it.

Jacques of Saint-Flour, being a Provençal like the Bishop, spoke in his own dialect in the name of all. They knew that, he said; that was why they were waiting for the barons. But their patience was at an end. The soldiers were not fools any more than the barons, or less well informed about what was happening in these lands. Had the defeated Turks not asked their pope to preach a crusade? Were they to wait until the new Turkish army was ready for war?

The Bishop replied that captains of bowmen were not invited to take part in the barons' councils, and that the barons had their reasons. He added that the siege of Jerusalem would be much stiffer than the siege of Antioch. The country was more barren, and they would have the Egyptian armies at their backs.

Jacques of Saint-Flour answered that he had not been present at the councils of the barons, or of the Turks or the Egyptians, but that the poor obeyed the counsels of Jesus Christ and His saints. He said that if God willed, He would perform more miracles, as He had done already, and that the present conduct of the troops and the pilgrims was dictated by the inspiration of the Holy Ghost. It seemed to the Bishop that to hear a captain of archers speak like this was a miracle of the Holy Ghost in itself.

The captains said that since Antioch was such an important stronghold and the Turks must on no account be allowed to recapture it, the best thing to do would be to raze it completely, and in that way all the army, from Prince Bohemond down to the meanest foot soldier, would be free to leave the city and resume their march to Jerusalem.

"I daresay," the Bishop said, "but there are a good fifty thousand and more Christians still living in that city. Where should they go to?"

"Where we are going, if God grant them grace. If not, they are in their own land, they will always find somewhere to go." Argument, in fact, was impossible. For once everyone was in agreement and hardened soldiers made common cause with monks: the same thing would happen to every town and every stronghold that the knights meant to take possession of for their own greed.

• • •

"With men like you, lads, we'll have the Tower of the Two Sisters and the citadel of Antioch down just as easily! Bring up the rams, sound the call to arms! With God's help, the work is moving fast."

Inside the town, men and women, young and old had seized on any scrap of iron they could find—pokers, door latches, pothooks—and were tearing up the paving in the streets, the doorsteps and window ledges, breaking the basins of the fountains so that the cold water swamped every crossroads and trickled away among the debris and the broken stones. And some were hurt at the work and did not even notice.

The sky was a clean, bright blue with white balls of cloud heading straight for the sea. The wind was strong and cold. The air was full of particles of ash and fragments of charred wood, blown from God knows where, and above the sharp, confused clamor of picks striking on stone, distant shouts could be heard: the hoarse, rhythmic shouts of the stonemasons.

The singing of the laborers attacking the stones of the larger towers with picks and mattocks.

By Jesus Christ and Holy Sepulcher and Saint George! This is one labor we undertake for no reward!

The next day was Sunday, and through the debris, past the gutted and demolished houses, the pilgrims went to mass in the three churches of Maarat. There was not room for a tenth of the army inside the churches, and so the priests held services on platforms erected outside the walls. Everyone needed a day of rest, and their heads were so full of the din of the day before that the silence rang in their ears like the tolling of a huge bell.

They sang—by the rivers of Babylon, they sang:

> If I forget thee, O Jerusalem
> Let my right hand forget her cunning.
> . . . If I forget thee, O Jerusalem.

And such a general sobbing echoed through the trampled field that the priests themselves were in tears and could not continue.

Lord, may our sins be forgiven us, and our forgetfulness.

For hunger and thirst, heat and cold, wounds and sickness

have long made us forget Your holy face and the sufferings of Jerusalem!

The men did penance and tore their hair and smeared their

faces with earth mixed with ashes and rubble. An end to fear and waiting: we shall force God and the barons to keep faith. This land has become more bitter to us than the antechamber of hell, and we will not remain here one more week.

If I forget thee, Jerusalem, let my tongue cleave to the roof of my mouth

He that will remain by the rivers of Babylon, let him be called a traitor to Jesus Christ.

O Babylon, the evil you have done to us! O Babylon of the Turks and the proud! *O Antioch!*

Antioch of blood and tears, Antioch of hunger, of freezing rain and burning sun and the smell of death!

Antioch of the Holy Lance and victory, graveyard of mud and blood, O camp, your trenches packed with our dead!

The evil you have done to us, O Babylon, let it remain with you, we are leaving it behind forever.

"Brothers," said Brother Barnabé, "brothers, friends, every one! Half our number we leave here, in the earth below the walls of Antioch; let the half that remain not force them to be false to their promise!

"Remember the words of Peter, that good and holy man whom the barons are holding as a hostage for God: through blood and fire and tempest

"through the raging waves and through deserts like furnaces, by yawning precipices and valleys swarming with reptiles

"through the hail of Turkish arrows and the charge of thousands of horsemen, through the torments of hunger, and plague and fire

"and through the waters changed into blood and the rains of fire

"we must go on without looking back, our eyes fixed on the light of Jerusalem,

"as moths and midges fly in the dark toward a torch, seeing nothing else, and are consumed in it, so may your souls be consumed in the love of Jerusalem.

"For if our love is great enough we cannot fail to reach it and to enter in and find our hearts' delight."

He wept as he spoke, they all wept. Brothers, repent of your sins, let us all repent, let us destroy the old Adam as we have destroyed this city.

We shall set out poorer and more naked, we shall lose everything, so that when we come to Jerusalem we shall have nothing but our thirst for Jesus Christ.

That Sunday was a great and blessed day. Everyone was talking of departure; they knew the time was near. The fifteen months they had spent in this land of Antioch had been so long that the remembrance of their journeyings, the days when they had marched by five-league stages and camped out in the open, those days seemed as sweet as memories of a happy youth gone by and the horrors of thirst in the desert, of precipices and perilous tracks, and of the great battle were all like an old tale that men are proud to recall with others who remember.

Even the dead were like long-buried ancestors to be thought of with mingled sorrow and pride, from Père Guillaumin who had died in Hungary down to young Mathieu, slain on the battlefield by an arrow in his arm. Do you remember Sir Evrard, do you remember Mère Corneille and Martine with her Fleming? And Philotheus the Greek—and young Marina, and Martin and Giscard, do you remember Isabelle? Lambert, even Lambert hardly thought of Isabelle, or of his father the curé whom he still saw in dreams.

These scars healed faster than bodily wounds. Oh Isabelle, my dear, six months already! Only six months ago. Last winter we were trudging with our babies through the rain to beg food from the soldiers' tents. Little fools, we were like two children ourselves. Isabelle, now you are wiser than the Pope.

"Jacques, will the lady give little Ondine back to us in Jerusalem?"

"Ondine will be a lady, she will not want us any more."

"Jacques, perhaps there will be no more ladies in Jerusalem?"

Too old, Jacques was thinking, too old, I am twenty now, too old to learn that trade, they all say so. A man-at-arms, yes, Jacques of the Ax, and when I have taken the spoils of Kerbogha's tent all for myself, with nothing but my ax, then they will see—so ran his thoughts—then they will see. He closed his eyes and saw himself on a big white horse, clothed in silk and riding with the knights, his ax carried high.

Élie le Grêlé had gone in search of Brother Barnabé. "Well, that's that," he said, "I have made up my mind."

"To what?"

"You know. I understood what you meant just now."

"Good," said Brother Barnabé.

"That we must look ahead and see the light. I saw a great flame coming toward me to consume me."

"Take care," said Brother Barnabé, "that it be not the flame of hell."

"No, it was white and not red. I shall go."

"I hope so."

"Then I swear it to you on my baptismal cross and on the name of the Holy Sepulcher. What else must I swear by?"

"That will do, I think."

"But I have sinned greatly."

"Very well," the monk said. "I ask no questions. God is your judge. Forgive me if I have misjudged you."

"Oh, as to that, gladly," Élie declared, with such cheerful confidence that Brother Barnabé's eyebrows lifted in some surprise. He had asked forgiveness only out of habit, without thinking, but now it crossed his mind to wonder: Blessed are the poor in spirit, and who knows whether this man is not better than I?

His eyes were seared by the sight of poverty, yet his heart was not hardened to it, and when he remembered Philotheus a worm began to gnaw at the pit of his stomach and he thought: I ought to have cleared up that business, I ought . . . No one wants to get a man hanged. God forgives all things. God forgives much besides.

If God did not forgive, then you might as well tie a stone around your neck and jump in the river. God forgives, and yet—a nice lad, intelligent and educated and so sweet-tempered, with an honest heart although he was a Greek. The dead are soon departed. No sooner dead than forgotten; they had to be. But he was one that you did not forget.

The evening was cold. The mist swept slowly down the mountains like the wing of some gigantic bird, and spread out over the plain until the campfires were like balls of yellow wool in the gloom. By the fires the men were shaking themselves like animals, clapping their hands to keep warm, and passing around the jug of water colored with wine.

From the direction of the soldiers' camp some way off came gusts of loud, raucous laughter broken by shrill, piteous screams. The girls. Those poor Turkish girls, God knows what they were doing to them. The soldiers wore them out in a month or two, they were Turks and they did not even baptize them so that they need feel no scruples, slim, black-braided girls with little narrow eyes. The men forced them to go naked in the midst of winter, or smothered them with fat and then rolled them in feathers, or thrust smoking torches into their faces, and worse things besides. More shameless even than wild beasts, forty or fifty of them would satisfy their lusts on a single girl in one night and leave her dead in the morning: that way they did not have to feed them.

Death, God knows, was the best that one could wish these girls, for what life was left in them was good for nothing but to howl and moan with pain, like a wounded animal. Jesus Christ, even this can You forgive? The soldier's sin. Lord, for his simple heart, and his inhuman trade? They also took the cross and seek forgiveness.

You could hear them hawking and hiccuping, neighing and bellowing, and singing, God forgive them, psalm tunes mingled with obscenities, for they too could sing psalms.

The men drew closer around the fires, toasting their toes, and the women held their babies to the warmth, those babies that were left—not many in our company, only eight. Since last winter, not one woman but was either brought to bed before her time or lost her newborn baby in the first three days, and these were strong, healthy women. Cold is no more merciful than great heat.

It was high time to set out again. Winter is milder by the sea.

It is easy for the barons, with their furs and their well-heated houses, to talk of waiting.

On Monday everyone was at work again. This was a new work, unpaid and unsolicited, a useless work—nay, the most useful work of all. *Let no stone be left standing upon another. Of this town where they have put us to keep us quiet, let no place be left to give shelter for a mule.*

The Turkish prisoners were dragged out of the citadel by main force. The commanders barricaded themselves in their room, powerless to prevent it. There were more than fifty prisoners, bound hand and foot. The pilgrims bombarded them with great stones, and fiercest of all were the children, even quite small girls. Then the soldiers came with their maces and battle-axes, and began cutting down the men penned in the castle courtyard as woodcutters chop down trees, shouting louder even than the wounded men, and God knows the inhuman cries the poor devils raised to their Prophet in heaven. The soldiers waded in among the dead to cut down those at the back—so many dead, lopped branches, black and blue and bleeding.

The soldiers of the garrison had joined the regular troops, and the knight who commanded them could do nothing but stand at the top of the tower with folded arms and watch. There was no way of telling which were wealthy prisoners. Only two or three had fine clothes; the rest had already lost all that they had, and their faces, what could be seen of them, were broad and dark with short beards, faces of terror, screaming faces, waxen faces striped with bright scarlet blood.

Mardoche returned to his companions bearing a severed hand, thin, yellow, and long-fingered. There were rings on the fingers, but these were so tightly clenched they had to be cut off to get at the rings. The boys hung the silver and enameled rings on threads from their ears. Le Grêlé, when he saw it, let them keep their booty, thinking that however precious the jewels, to the children they were only toys.

Euphemia was with the other women in one corner of the guardroom, and now that she was no longer alone and was able to talk to the three Syrians and Selima, she seemed less sad. She was even seen eating with a good appetite, and humming, and running with the others to the wall to see how the demolition was progressing. "We are going away," Élie told her. "You stay here." Selima, who understood French, translated. Euphemia looked at him incredulously, as though she could not believe the black girl had understood properly.

Élie said again, "I am going away, but not you." She looked at him, frowning, like a wary animal, then nodded to show that she had understood. She won't be sorry, Élie thought. She gave no sign of sorrow or of joy, yet he could sense—in that very moment he sensed it—that she felt suddenly a hundred pounds lighter, all at once her heart was light. She breathed differently, she walked with the grace of a tame fawn, and it came to him how young she was, a girl of seventeen; at that age you could survive anything. No, not everything. Poor girl. Ah yes indeed, poor girl.

The men were still at work, but with less enthusiasm now because they were tired and the idea of going on to demolish Antioch was beginning to look a little foolish. They all knew how big the city was, how broad and strong the double ring of fortifications, and how tall the houses built of fine dressed stone. To say nothing of the knights, who had their horses and their lances.

They still talked about it, but even the boldest and the most simple-minded did not really believe in it. Work on such a scale, without pay or provender? Besides, the first flush of their anger had cooled as they worked.

The Bishop returned with a delegation of barons and priests from Antioch. Do not despair, good Christians, do not be angry any more, restrain your pious indignation—you will need it against the Turks.

Know that the barons and princes, our leaders, are insulted by your accusations but they applaud your zeal. They have never considered abandoning the cause of Jesus Christ, and in three days from now the Count of Toulouse is to leave Antioch with his whole army and he will lead all men who are willing to follow him to Jerusalem.

On condition that you all do penance and take with you no whores, or thieves or murderers, but only those who have taken a vow to die for Jesus Christ.

Meanwhile, since you have this assurance, the barons ask you to stop your work of destruction, and spare what remains of this town.

The news the Bishop proclaimed was cried throughout the town and in the camp outside the town, and was received with some measure of distrust. Three days could easily turn into three weeks and even three months, who knows? The barons have so much baggage that they take a long time to get moving.

And so the soldiers' leaders made answer to the emissaries that the road to the coast passed by Maarat and they would see if the Count of Toulouse kept his promises. Our men and our pilgrims, they said, are all ready to strike camp and they will follow the knights as soon as they have seen them pass by on the road. Meanwhile, we are giving orders to suspend the work, but in three days we shall begin again.

The walls of Antioch were ringed with lights. Fires shone from the tops of all the towers. They were like a long serpent made of flickering flames winding up and down around the city to vanish in a greenish mist on the mountainside. Long yellow flames seemed to pour off the lighted bridge into the black water, and the river was crammed with barges full of horses.

The banners were big white butterflies flapping their wings in the torchlight. This was the last night, and the troops had gone down to the plain to say farewell to their dead. All along the length of that vast burial ground, fires were burning and the living sat in circles around the fires, not close together, but each man leaving room for his dead. All had one, and some had two or three.

Here they were singing hymns; elsewhere the voices joined in songs of home. The dead sat beside the living, nudging those who did not leave them room enough. You could not see them, but you felt their weight and their warmth.

All that lay under that earth, under the crackling fires, under the thousands of stones marked with a bare cross, all that lay there in that grievous earth transmuted into rich soil to nourish vines and olive trees.

Why have you come to trouble the rest of body and soul, singing songs we have forgotten, why do you warm our poor bodies that no longer feel the cold, why this salt and grain and these pitchers of water? We shall not hunger again.

Oh, companions of our journey, we are going away. Come with us, for we shall not easily return here. Comrades, you shall be with us on the way, you shall enter with us into Jerusalem the golden, we shall keep a share of food for you. Do not forget the songs of our own lands. For Jesus Christ does not forget, living and dead we are all one with Him, as raindrops that fall in the sea.

The voices of the dead joined in the singing and their breath was in the wind that made the flames dance. In the dark sky, among the clouds blanched by the moon, Saint George was passing on his white horse, a white cross in his right hand. The horse glided on, its legs hardly moving, its long tail sweeping the stars.

He was leaving Antioch and going away toward Jerusalem.

Slowly, a long way off, it was rising, away beyond the hills toward the sea it was climbing into the night sky with its twelve shining gates, as yet no bigger than a cluster of stars, *the true Jerusalem.* At the sound of Christian voices raised in prayer, it was floating free of its terrestrial form and showing itself in the night sky to remind them of their promise.

Even among the soldiers, there were some who saw it.

You must not believe, friends, you must not believe that those who see it are about to die.

• • •

At first light, the great gate across the bridge swung open to the sound of trumpets.

To the sound of drums and clarions, a man on foot came through the open gate onto the bridge, followed by two bishops and knights in full array. The man was tall and strong, straight and broad-shouldered; his long, curling beard fell in grizzled waves down his chest, greying fair hair lay on his shoulders. He advanced, bareheaded and barefoot, wearing a frieze shirt. With his left hand he leaned upon a pilgrim's staff, in his right he held aloft a silver cross.

The host of pilgrims shouted for joy and men fell on their knees and held out their hands and praised Jesus Christ aloud for the great miracle. The Count of Toulouse himself had become a simple pilgrim for the love of God, poor among the poor, a crusader clothed in frieze, he the richest and the wisest of all the barons.

He advanced, and his beautiful white feet that had been shod from his childhood did not disdain to tread upon the dirt and stones. Oh best and most faithful of men, will he go thus all the way to Jerusalem?

Is it right for a man of his age, who all his life has walked only upon carpets, voluntarily to endure such an ordeal? Here is enough to shame those who complain if they have so much as a corn on their feet: here is a man, strong in battle and in council, the equal of kings, yet in the middle of winter he puts off his robes of marten's fur and puts on frieze!

Men and women cheered him until their throats were hoarse. Oh long life, oh eternal salvation to the Provençal Count. He shall be king in Jerusalem.

He walked on, grave and resolute, at the head of the procession and after him came the priests and bishops and the knights, walking beside their horses out of humility and in imitation of the Count. They cheered them all, but what the Count had done was so fine a thing that all thoughts were for him. He walked stiffly and heavily, saying psalms, his eyes fixed on his cross, and if he was cold or if he felt the pain of his feet which had turned purple, there was no way of knowing it because he had all that famed endurance of the nobility who would die rather than lose face. He was so carried away with his own zeal and so moved by the acclamations of the crowd that he could have had little thought to spare for himself. Beautiful as a holy prophet, handsome as Charlemagne, oh my friends, God has spoken to him, he sees visions. Already he sees the walls of Jerusalem.

All day long, the army marched by in a long column and encamped toward evening south of Maarat. Thus the Lance was proved true and the Bishop of Le Puy, God rest his soul and pardon him, was wrong: it was the Holy Lance which had wrought this miracle in the Count's soul.

They were there. They were encamped, ready to march at dawn. Up, you Christians that believed this day would never come! God and men have heard you.

The whores were turned out of the camp. The soldiers were by now so filled with pilgrim zeal that they were swearing to live chaste and never touch another woman until Jerusalem was taken, although if truth were told, this was a vow they had made many times before. The girls, those of them who were natives of the place, the Syrians, Turks, and Arabs, were put all together in a field by the river and then told to go. When they hesitated, the soldiers began to drive them away with whips and stones, so that in the end they fled and scattered over the countryside. Those that came from the West, however, they kept. There were not many of them, and the men said they were comrades and after all that they had been through they deserved to do penance.

Alix stood on the roof of the barracks and wept as she watched the girls running.

"They are sinful vessels," Baudry told her. "You should forget that you were once like them."

"No," Alix said, "I was never like them. I was the whore of Babylon but truly these are the poorest of the poor, and those that are baptized shall be placed higher than we in paradise."

Baudry and Alix had become fast friends now, not as a man and a woman but as two friends. They were both in good health and felt themselves equal to enduring many further hardships, and already they were making plans to keep all their friends together in Jerusalem and live as true Christians, like the first apostles.

That night, Élie le Grêlé lay for the last time beside Euphemia. He did not regret the vow that he had made.

She felt the cold and he had made her a blanket of sheepskin and sheepskin slippers for her feet, because she could not sew the skins for herself. What fingers! More like candle wax than fingers! Well, it was lucky after all that there had not been much work in Maarat, but was it for a man to look after a woman? He knew that he would not stay behind; he thought of the white light, brighter than lightning, greater than the sun, that he had seen on the day when Brother Barnabé had talked of Jerusalem and which he saw still in his dreams. He would go straight toward it, straight as a great stone rolling downhill, and as he rolled the light grew stronger and stronger, blinding him, and came to meet him at great speed.

By this he knew that he must go, whether he would or not.

His knife was whetted, sharp enough to cut a piece of leather in two at a touch. It was a good blade, bought in Arras when he had sold his loom to his brother Mathieu. A good blade. He had spent an hour sharpening it.

If she could only speak French, or he could speak Greek. Sometimes at night he would tell himself these stories. If she could speak French and would say to him, Let us go away and desert to the Turks. If she would only say it in that voice she had once used, one evening as he listened underneath the window. *Oh that voice, he could have listened to it all his life!* Only to think of it, to think that she could ever speak to him in that voice, only to think of it made his heart leap and beat hard enough to burst.

Such was the strength and madness of this love.

She was asleep. She had pretended to be asleep when he had taken her, with sighs and tears, God knows, for the parting would be hard; with a man sobbing madly on her breast, she could pretend to be asleep. But that was how she was. She was really asleep now and it made him sad not to see her lovely face. He was trembling with a joy that was greater than the terrible sadness of not seeing her again. The hand might tremble but the knife was sharp enough to do its work unaided, or very nearly.

She scarcely even sighed, her throat cut in one stroke. Beneath the sheepskin coverlet that muffled its quick, gurgling rush, the blood flowed quietly, a sound of warm springs rippling, and once more a tremor shook the slender body. Élie was seized by such a frenzy of love that he could have plunged his face into the gaping wound and drunk that blood. A life was slipping away under his hand. He touched her. She was alive at last, she lived through him; he had taken her life in his hands with one stroke of the knife.

You know it now, Euphemia, you have always known it, I did you no harm and you martyred me. She was not moving now. She was warm, and limp, and soft. Her coldness gone, her ill will quenched. He was almost surprised to feel that she was no longer breathing. He wiped his knife and his hands on the rug. It was dark. Groping, he pulled the rug up over the still head. He would not uncover it at dawn. He would never see her face again.

At dawn he got up and took his bundle and his ax. The guardroom was emptying. Out in the square the women crossed themselves hurriedly before they ate, while the soldiers' trumpets were sounding for departure.

What are they hurrying for? Do they think we are likely to die of heat at noon? Ah well, friends, time to form up and take the road, the knights will be a league ahead of us. The knights were watering their horses, their tents already folded.

No one in France would ever have believed it, the Norman knights themselves did not believe it, that such a host of pilgrims and common men-at-arms could take their places in the column so quickly and with so little fuss. Already they were better disciplined than an army, quicker to grasp orders and to understand what was expected of them.

Everyone to his wagons! The children acted as scouts, running up the road and then coming back to their own groups to tell them where they were to go.

Hurry up and stop saying goodbye to your sick if you want to march with your own people, otherwise you will have a hard time finding them again before nightfall.

Saint-John was running along the demolished walls, waving his arms. There shall not be left here one stone upon another!

O Jerusalem, how many times I have longed to gather all your sons together as a hen gathers her chicks, *and you would not let me!* "Saint-John," his friends called, "come on, this town is not Jerusalem." Oh you fools, Jerusalem is everywhere. We have thrown down its walls, and elsewhere we shall find them still the same, and of its buildings there shall not be left one stone upon another.

He that works in the fields, let him flee into the hills.

"Saint-John, we are not going toward the hills now, but to the sea." He walked with the others, carrying a Picard child on his back. "Oh, if you knew, my friends, if you knew, these fallen walls are lower than heaps of broken stones, these hills less than molehills, each step we take is a league and yet we do not stir." The boys laughed at him because, with his dusty clothes, his beard and hair full of ashes, and his witless smile, all he needed was a hat with bells. "Hey, Zebedee, who are we?"

"The poor children of the Canaanite woman, possessed by the Devil." They pulled his hair and made water over his legs, and the women threw stones at them. "You wicked boys, he is one of God's innocents!" Marie, with Pierre fast asleep in a sling fastened on her back, ran to catch up with Saint-John. "Oh, you imps, sprung from the belly of Beelzebub, how you must grieve your fathers in paradise!"

"Where are we going, Marie?" said Saint-John.

"You know where. To Jerusalem."

"Yes," he said. "To be crucified."

"Think again, poor boy. We are not Jesus Christ."

"Yes, Marie. We are the flesh and blood of Jesus Christ and if we are going to Jerusalem it must be to be crucified."

Le Grêlé stood in the doorway of his billet and drank his soup standing, his bundle at his feet.

"Well, Élie, where's your concubine? Isn't she coming to say goodbye to you?"

"She is asleep," he answered. "Best not disturb her." The words did not come from his mouth but from the mouth of some invisible person standing beside him. He picked up his bundle and settled his ax on his shoulder, and his comrades looked at him in amazement. He seemed to have aged ten years in one night. Those in the camp were not much in the habit of worrying about their neighbors' health—it would have kept them too busy—but his friends said, "Listen, Grêlé, you are sick. Stay here and catch up with the column at the next halt."

He was so covered with grease and sweat that no one saw the bloodstains on him. His eyes, paler than faded cornflowers, were troubled and his jaw hung slack, like a dead man's. No one could doubt that he had seen a ghost. He went out of the courtyard without a glance at anyone and went to take his place in the team drawing the big wagon, settling the strap over his shoulder and running his hand along the pole. They would be six men pulling the wagon, six men where what was needed was two oxen.

Bernier, Giscard, Guillaume of Valognes, Marcel the Picard, Jacques le Roux, all tall, broad men over thirty, and stout walkers. Giscard was a woodcutter by trade. Marcel was almost blind and could see nothing in front of him but red and white shapes. Getting started was the hardest part, especially when the road was choked with stones and churned up by the horsemen, but even so, six good men were better than ten that included youngsters who fidgeted and pulled unevenly.

If I forget thee, O Jerusalem
If I forget thee
Jerusalem
if I forget thee . . .

It was hard to get started, but after that, by husbanding their breath, they would pull well; taking the weight on their backs and shoulders, they would pull all the way to Jerusalem without stopping. What, all the way to Jerusalem? A hundred leagues.

To have been for two years within a hundred leagues of Jerusalem and never stirred!

They will find her, in her corner behind the bale of straw, all sticky beneath her covers, congealed in her own blood like a newborn child. The billet is empty now, perhaps they will put some homeless Syrians in it, but they will not get around to looking underneath a pile of sheepskins all at once. But suppose they discover her today, le Grêlé thought, I shall not see Jerusalem. Strung up from a cedar tree at the first halt. Because she was a Christian.

Ah no, Brother Barnabé, what do you know of such things? Yet you have eyes, you know what becomes of soldiers' whores. They all say, To a convent, or to the Greeks, well then, why not to the King of Khorassan? In the barracks of Antioch, that is where she belongs.

So white and black, like crows in the snow, and oh her eyes, lively as birds, those two shining black orbs that could speak a language of their own, a language more alive than words. After all, who but an idiot would expect a girl like her to make sheep's eyes at you, a dog, a wolf, a wolf but no fool, and if I were a widower I should have married her and brought her with me. Never again. Not in the morning or the evening. It is easy to kill a body, but how do you kill a soul? Her soul clinging to your heels, gnawing at your heart, her poor, mute, foolish soul, as much alive as any heart that beats.

"Hey, Grêlé, what's wrong?" Guillaume of Valognes had glanced at his companion in harness, startled to hear him sniffing noisily. Élie was weeping so hard that the tears ran down his cheeks and soaked into his mustache. Big drops flowed from his wide-open eyes like water from a spring.

"Hey there, Grêlé!"

"What?" Crisscrossed rays, sharp as knives, moved through a watery veil before le Grêlé's eyes.

"Did she mean so much to you?" said Guillaume. "Your concubine?"

Through clenched teeth, because his nose and eyes were full of water, le Grêlé said, "That's my affair."

"Maybe you will see her again." Élie said nothing, but so much water was streaming from his eyes that he nearly drowned in his own tears, because his nose was blocked and he could not breathe. He would have given his knife and his ax to "see her again," as the other man had said, when he saw her and only her in every eye, in every stone along the road. Yet there was one of all these hundreds and thousands that he would never see again, the only real one, with real blood in her veins. And she would not speak French. Oh, those Greek words, Lord Jesus, those Greek words! The only real words!

Speak to me, speak to me again, speak Greek, Arabic, Turkish, what you like, only speak to me. Shall I ever recall one word of yours? He trudged on and even the hard, patient toil of a beast of burden could not kill the longing, like an aching wound, to roll on the ground and bang his head against a wall and scream aloud, but all these cures for grief were for a holiday, grief itself was a holiday, and we are a team of six men drawing a wagon heavy enough for a pair of oxen.

Tell them all: I am mourning. I have killed my concubine! Hang me, but let me have the right to scream. Yet it was not fear of hanging but pride that made le Grêlé keep silent that day and the days that followed.

At that night's halt, Father Albert rejoined the company from Arras. A chaplain belonging to the Norman engineers had died the week before and for three days and three nights he had been administering confession to the soldiers. The priests, few of whom were young, died more quickly than the soldiers, but Father Albert seemed cut out to live a hundred years. He had gone to the aid of his fellow countrymen. All the soldiers to a man wanted absolution, and it felt as if he had confessed the same man a thousand times over, their sins were so alike, and yet they were not venial ones.

After listening to the same things over again for hours on end Father Albert, for all his familiarity with fighting men, began to put himself in the place of Jesus Christ and wonder: Is it surprising that God should be slow in leading us to Jerusalem? The Hebrews journeyed for forty years, and they were better than we are.

"We must not compare ourselves to the Hebrews," Brother Barnabé told him. "Salvation and damnation happen more quickly in these days. God will not wait longer. This year of our lives is the last of our century. It is a sign: before the year's end, we shall be in Jerusalem."

"Then we must be there before Easter," Father Albert said. "Because if the barons invest the city in the summer, we shall not hold out. Judaea is known to be a dry country, and it will be far worse than Antioch. Before Antioch we were never short of water."

So the great army marched on, in good order and full of good intentions. The weather was mild; it was hard to believe that it was January. As they drew nearer to the sea they came to broad, cultivated valleys and hillsides thick with flocks of sheep, to immense groves of orange trees in blossom, to vineyards and dark plowed fields. White villages of square houses piled one upon another clung to the hillsides, with here and there a fortified castle painted blue and white, set among cypresses and groves of olive and orange.

If Judaea is as beautiful, the people said, no wonder Our Lord chose this land. For the weather was more like spring than winter, with cold winds and heavy showers followed the same day or the next by sunshine and blue skies in which the thick white clouds loomed up and spread and disintegrated astonishingly fast, moving over to drown themselves in a violet sea that turned at night to light grey streaked with pink below a horizon of red and purple, and the air was so clear that the island of Cyprus could be seen, a long, leaden streak on the horizon.

During the halts they camped in the wagons and underneath them, sheltered by sacks when it rained. The soldiers still had their tents in good condition, while as for the knights, let no one say they had ruined themselves in Antioch! Their tents were like real houses, with so many guy ropes around them that they resembled the masts of ships. And it was said that the Count of Toulouse had Kerbogha's own tent, made of brocaded tissue with silver poles. In the best room of this tent the Holy Lance was kept, with two priests watching over it by night and day.

It was not surprising that, owning such wealth and seeing that in these lands the meanest holder of a fief lived better than kings at home, the barons should be tempted by greed. For when, after a very few days' march, they came to Tripoli, they learned that a permanent camp was to be set up, and for all the Count might say that it was in the interests of Christendom to take this city, or any other along the coast, the men of the army wondered if it were not simply that he wanted the place for himself, especially since he had failed to gain possession of the citadel of Antioch.

Not so, Christians. *It is a prophecy of the Holy Lance that makes him encamp here.* Our army is not strong enough and we must wait for the good Duke Godfrey and Count Robert of Flanders to join us, for they are coming by a different route and are engaging the Turks somewhere in the region of Jebail. So there they were, in camp outside Tripoli, a large and splendid city with a seaport, and the king of this city, though a Moslem, was no enemy to the Christians, for he sent them quantities of provisions and even horses.

There was much talk at this time about the Pope Calixtus. He was said to be mustering an army of a hundred thousand Turks at Baghdad, while our own Pope had not even sent a new legate after all the letters the barons had written to him. The Turkish pope was not like other popes. He had wives and sons, and he chose the best of his sons to be pope after him. He could bear sword and lance, and he was so fond of killing Christians that the Turkish princes could not make him any finer gift than a Christian head. Whenever they killed a lord of great renown they had his head embalmed and sent it to their pope, so that Calixtus' oratory was filled not with holy relics but with the heads of Christian knights.

Well, people laughed as they told these stories, but there were some who, even while they laughed, said, "That is the kind of pope we should have had." "Listen, friends, is the Turks' faith better than ours, by any chance? It is because their religion is bad that their pope acts so. And on their Sunday, which is Friday, they like nothing so much as shedding blood!" To which there were plenty of men, and not only soldiers, ready to answer that since the time had come, they must not blow hot and cold at once. Such was the quality of Turkish blood that whoever shed it was like a man watering the fields to make the rain come: it was a blessed dew preparing the ground for the coming of Jesus Christ.

They were still arguing, even after two years of war they were still arguing about what was right to do and what was not. For the halt at Tripoli was a long one, the weather mild, and food plentiful.

All that we have done so far has been only a preparation and a trial. The real war will begin after Jaffa, when we come to the places where Jesus Christ lived.

The bishops who were with the army had sent men to preach in all the camps, and Peter himself had had a dais set up for him in the midst of a field on the side of a hill and spoke to the crowds, and his companions went around to those who were not able to hear and told them what he had said.

It may be that you will see valleys and hills and villages and towns in appearance like to what may be seen in other lands, but in truth, just as the relics of a blessed saint may look like the bones of any other man, these holy lands resemble others but they are very different. We must look at them with the eyes of the spirit.

You will set your feet on stones that may have been trodden by the feet of Our Lord. Like you, He went on foot and traveled the roads in plain sandals, and did not scorn to let the dust of the roads cover His feet.

With His hand, He touched the olive trees and the fig trees and the ears of corn; and the trees and the corn that you will see have sprung from the very fruits and seeds that Our Lord touched.

By the miracle of His mercy the ground was not burned that His feet trod, nor changed into stars the leaves of the trees that He touched with His hands! Truly, He left no more sign of His passing than the humblest pilgrim, for it is written: A bruised reed shall He not break.

He so humbled Himself in pity for our weakness, that He has permitted His earth to be defiled by impious men and has not swallowed them up in a lake of fire like Sodom and Gomorrah! This mystery is great, and this is the explanation of it: His love for His earthly home is so great that He would not destroy it in destroying the infidel. He has desired Christian hands to come and avenge the desecration.

There were many monks, and Peter chief among them, who taught that murder was a sin and that those who killed infidels in battle should do penance, nor should the pilgrims shed blood in these holy places except of dire necessity. They said it would not be right or decent to act as they had done in Antioch, ripping out men's entrails and hurling women from the housetops, and adorning the sacred walls with severed heads that soon decayed into objects of horror.

But even among the priests there were those who quoted the Scriptures and the words of the prophet Ezekiel, saying that the enemies of God should be wiped from the face of the earth and that it was not possible both to exterminate the infidels and to spare them. If a man can be forgiven for killing to avenge a member of his family, they said, how much less sinful is it when God is to be avenged? Indeed, it is not a sin at all, but a good work. For men burn the tares and kill wolves, which is proof that living creatures exist which are fashioned for evil and that God Himself commands us to destroy them.

My friends, you sit here arguing over what to do if God gives us the victory, and we have not yet reached the Holy Places, and the Count of Toulouse is making war on the King of Tripoli and laying siege to a city where Jesus Christ never set foot. It is nowhere written that He ever came anywhere near the land of Tripoli.

This is the real truth of the matter: the Count has lost faith once more and fears to march on Judaea; he fears lest, as a punishment for his sins, God may send a great army out of Egypt to bar our way. He is afraid that Pope Calixtus may come with his army from Baghdad and fall on us from behind. Oh, man of little faith! Is it for him that God has performed His miracles?

And if it is the Holy Lance that counsels him to waste his time in this way, waiting until summer when the sun of Judaea is much less fierce in spring, then the Holy Lance is not the true one.

And yet—in Antioch it worked a miracle.

It was Saint George who worked the miracle, and those who discovered the Holy Lance were deceived. It happens sometimes that two archers shoot together and when the center is hit, one man's arrow is mistaken for the other's.

On windy days the sea of rich blue, going from dark sapphire to turquoise, was flecked with lines of white foam. At midday it glittered like a golden shield and as evening came on it paled, merging toward the horizon into streaks of blood-red, tawny orange, and violet. The Turkish ships heading for Tripoli left golden trails behind them on the whitening water. At nightfall, the long, plaintive Moslem prayers rose from the tops of the minarets in the town of Arqa, which was invested by the Christian camp. This was the hour after vespers, the quiet hour when the red sky swiftly took all the colors from the earth and chilled them, before they were obliterated altogether by the coming darkness.

Flights of gulls soared above the castle, glided around the ships, and swooped down upon the shore.

On the other side, the mountains stretched away in long blue chains eastward and the nearer hills, covered with thick black forests, were like huge slumbering animals. The morning sky there was brilliant with a pure light that washed everything clean, from the weariest faces to the very mud in the ruts.

The distant mountains were drowned in a light of mingled blue and gold, and the grey olive trees shone like a woven carpet of dull silver. The orange groves toward Tripoli were so laden with ripe fruit that from afar they looked more red than black. The fruit was ready now for picking, and long lines of the grey-clad men and women of the region were going up into the city bearing baskets full of golden fruit on their heads.

All this could be seen, but from a distance. Within the ditch and palisade that marked the outer limits of the camp, the grass was so trampled after three weeks that not a living blade remained, only mud and dung and dry earth. It was a piece of luck to find an anemone or a jonquil still growing by the side of the ditch. Yet the country was not short of flowers; the meadows were mauve and white, and in the distance the almond trees spread their fragile arms full of pink blossom against a background of bright grass, like graceful girls decked out for Eastertide.

The blue air where the gulls and the swallows and the vultures wheeled was so pure that even those who were most inured to it began to suffer from the reek of the camp. The fleas and lice seemed to bite harder than in winter and the smell of urine permeated everything, along with the smells of moldy straw and bad soup and garments impregnated with stale sweat. By midday the sun was beginning to be really hot.

Arguments began to break out among those men who were young and strong as to who should be included in the teams that went off to cut wood. The woodcutters, with master carpenters in charge, set out at dawn and stayed in the forests for two or three days at a time. The work was hard. The Count was in a hurry and he needed wood for building siege towers. There was nothing he liked better than building wooden towers, and he knew as much about it as any professional. Within a fortnight whole hillsides were laid bare and turned into a sea of broken branches scattered among what remained of the felled trunks. The stripped trunks of hundred-year-old pines rolled down the cleared slope, flattening the meadows and the black mold of the fields with their weight.

There were not enough oxen or enough ropes to drag all this timber back to the camp, and men were needed. The carpenters saw to the building of a broad causeway made of logs along which the tree trunks could be made to slide. Each tree required a team of twenty stout lads, and by the time they reached the building site they were ready to throw themselves on the ground, panting like bellows.

In the forest you could look up between the strokes of the ax and see, through the sweat dripping from your eyebrows, a sky of turquoise-blue in which the frantic birds wheeled with flapping wings. But there was no time for stargazing. The work went on apace. The trees fell close together. If a man must meet martyrdom, let him not find it crushed beneath a pine.

With a great crack and a tearing and groaning of broken branches, the great tree swayed and fell slowly, to hoarse shouts from the workmen, a cry so loud it might have been that which struck the tree its final blow. Élie le Grêlé had been made leader of one team because he had a good ax and some knowledge of trees. God knows how it is, his comrades thought, God knows how this man always manages to come out on top.

Le Grêlé had some knowledge of leadership as well; he knew which man to put in which position, and on which side to make the cut. Jacques and Lambert, who were working with him, liked him well enough for that.

About an hour after noon, a halt was called for food, but they had to eat fast and drink little to remain active. They would say a prayer and talk a little. What a number of trades we shall have learned in God's service—soldiers, woodcutters, masons, quarrymen. Perhaps in Jerusalem Jesus Christ will have need of weavers also?

"Maybe someone will have to weave cloth for the churches and convents," Lambert said. "The Turks will have pillaged everything, worse than in Antioch."

"What about you, Grêlé?" Jacques said. "Will you go back to your loom?" Élie considered, as if the question were too difficult to answer. At last he said:

"We shall be new men. And not so as to become weavers again."

"To become what, then? Potters or dyers?"

His comrades felt sorry for him because ever since leaving Maarat he had been like a man suffering from a raging toothache. After all, they said, there are so many sins committed in the army, and his was not the worst. There are some men who were never meant to live like monks.

Toward the end of Lent a company of soldiers from Antioch caught up with the army, and with them some pilgrims who had been unable to leave with the rest. Brother Barnabé asked one of them what had become of the fair Euphemia. He learned that she was dead, found murdered in the barracks not long after the army had left. No one was surprised. Such a beautiful woman. In time of war it was better to be one-eyed or hunchbacked. "All the same," said Brother Barnabé, "we should not tell le Grêlé, for he loved her truly."

Baudry thought le Grêlé might well know more about the woman's death than anyone, but he kept his thoughts to himself because it was common knowledge that he had no love for Élie. When two men dislike each other and only one of them is moved by good will, it is bound to lead to trouble. According to Élie,

Baudry was unfair in dealing out the rations, did not know how to manage the camp, looked down on the weavers, and made it his boast that he had never killed a Turk in order to disguise his fear of fighting battles. "Thank God," Baudry said, "there are plenty of cutthroats in the army even among our own people, and if I have never killed I make no boast but thank God for it. It is not written that any of the Holy Apostles ever cut off a Turk's head."

"Maybe, but they all became martyrs."

"If ever I become one, Grêlé, it won't be thanks to anything you may say."

In spite of his lack of Baudry's wisdom and his unprepossessing countenance, Élie had plenty of friends who were given to saying openly that the mason had outlived his usefulness and they needed a man to lead the company who was not afraid of splitting a head with an ax, and that since there were many weavers among them it would have been better to choose a weaver. Besides, the Holy Virgin Herself was the patron saint of weavers and with her own hands had woven the veil preserved in the cathedral at Chartres.

Not that le Grêlé had any wish for the leadership; all he wanted was to annoy Baudry. Ever since parting from his concubine he had been like a mad dog wanting to bite but not knowing whom.

He tried asking those who came from Maarat if they knew what had become of Euphemia, but they told him they knew nothing of her. This was odd, because in a room occupied by several dozen people a corpse cannot go long undiscovered. She had gone, and gone for good; even in his dreams he could not see her. Night after night he would dream of a room, a door, a blanket, and she was behind it or beneath it, still alive, but when he put aside the blanket there was nothing there. Gone for good. An obdurate soul. In Jerusalem a light was burning, ruddier and ruddier.

Lord Jesus Christ, for the sake of my vow I sacrificed her. If You do not hold me absolved, then who shall absolve me? We set out on the road to Jerusalem and now once again we are wasting our time to no purpose. Have they not promised a rich harvest of Turks?

Are the knights to be allowed to make war as they please and make the rest of us serve them? Jerusalem. Shall we ever get there?

In the great camp, among the tents and wagons, people were coming together in groups that grew larger as time went by until no one stayed away minding their own business any more. And everywhere the theme was the same: *They are deceiving us, there is treachery at work, they are trying to make us stay here all summer and winter too, and maybe we shall set out again next spring only to stop again after another ten leagues to lay siege to another town where Jesus Christ never set foot.*

Surely the knights must be afraid to enter the Holy Places on account of their sins, or what is more likely, they do not care about Jerusalem because they know that there they will not dare display their pride.

They mean to rob the poor of the wages that Jesus Christ has promised them.

Let them keep Antioch and Tripoli for themselves, and Arqa and Beirut and Edessa and Maarat and all the cities that they please, if they are strong enough to take them, but let them leave us Jerusalem and let them begin by going on to Jerusalem, for we cannot get there without them. But neither can they remain here without us.

And if the troops down to the last engineer and archer desert them, they will not go far with their horses and their armor and their fine tents.

If the Holy Lance tells them to betray Jesus Christ, it is not holy, it is only a piece of iron and no more precious than a poker.

The test will show if it is real, or if what we have been told about it is all one great lie.

If they have decided to betray us and to rob us of our share in Jerusalem, we will set fire to their engines of war and their siege towers and force them to keep their promises.

Where they have lost two men in ten, we have lost fifty out of a hundred.

From camp to camp, songs were being sung to an old tune from the Ile-de-France which everyone had known for months. So many disputes are begun with songs.

For the Count had enough wood already and had no further need of woodcutters, or of men to cart timber, and those men who could not get work as carpenters were idle and confined to their camps.

It was not like this at Antioch. They have grown proud now. They employed hundreds of men in digging this ditch, on the pretext of giving them work, and now these same men are driven back by soldiers if they try to cross the ditch. And why? Because if there is disorder in the camp the siege works will not get done quickly, and the Count has made a vow to take the city.

And who forced him to make that vow? What holy relics lie hidden in Arqa?

And if he has taken this vow, the men who have sworn fealty to him may perhaps be bound by it, but such a vow does not bind the whole army. The only vow that holds good for everyone is the vow to take Jerusalem.

Consequently, the songs that were being sung were far from complimentary to the Count.

The Brabançons lighted their fires next door to the Provençal camp and sang at the tops of their voices, and the men of Provence sang back.

The Lance was with us
On that miraculous day
When the Turks fled
Ten men before one
A thousand before a hundred!
The Lance was with us
And we shall keep it still
A Provençal found it
Men of Provence shall keep it
And the envious shall be chastised!
We shall enter into Arqa
With the Count and Jesus Christ!

You can stay where you please
With the Count and his barons
And the Lance can stay with you
For Jesus Christ is with us!
He loves no laggards!
He was not born in Arqa
Nor did He preach in Arqa

He was betrayed and nailed on Cross
But never in Arqa!
He rose again from the dead
But not in Arqa
He ascended into heaven
But not from Arqa!
And your Count has made a vow
Never to quit Arqa
White hairs shall you have each one
Before you are lords in Arqa!
We shall conquer Jerusalem
And shame the Provence men
We will have no other Lance
But Godfrey's own!

Not only the Brabançons, and not only the Walloons and Lorrainers, but men of every country, the French pilgrims and the Normans, were beginning to sing:

We will have no other Lance
But Godfrey's own!
The good Duke has never lied
Or deceived Christian men
Godfrey himself shall be the first
First in Jerusalem
Where he has sworn to enter
Before Saint-Gilles's Count
Before the Duke of Normandy
Before the Count of Flanders
Before the Viscount of Evreux
And before the Count of Dreux!
He snaps his fingers at your Lance
He needs none but his own!

There was no finer man among all the barons than the Duke, and none mightier or stronger of arm, and his voice was so powerful that five thousand men could hear it at once.

It was known that he was anxious to strike camp and that there was no love lost between him and the Count for this reason. For all their brave words, therefore, the Provençals had little reason to feel proud, when even soldiers who would have fired their own fathers' fields if they had only been paid enough for it were growing impatient and murmuring that they were soldiers of Jesus Christ and wanted the wages of Jesus Christ.

As a result of the heat, the whole camp was crawling with flies and maggots. They were everywhere, in the dirt beneath the carts and in the cattle pens and in the beds of the sick, even in the bread they ate, and in the tents that served as chapels. Such a stench rose from the ordure in the ditches that the tents had to be moved farther away. Water was beginning to run short; the wells dried up, and teams of men had to be sent to the neighboring villages to water the beasts. The villages were almost deserted: the peasants of this region were Moslems who had fled into the hills. The cisterns were emptied. Then they started to slaughter the sheep.

This is nothing, my friends, everyone knows there is much less water in Judaea than there is here.

That is why the Count is afraid to march on Jerusalem. He himself will never go short of water, but he wishes to spare the men of the army.

Oh, there are no good reasons. We have not so much as set foot in Judaea and already the barons are calculating how many jars of water will be needed each day! Among the folk of Arras, Marie was now the one who talked loudest. "What does the Count know about it? In the desert we had to drink our own urine and we writhed in agony, but not he!

"These men have no hearts, they think we are animals needing nothing but to be fed and watered.

"Yet they know that Jesus Christ has performed miracles for us and not for them! But for their pride, He would do so again, and water would spout from the stones as it did for the Hebrews. That is what frightens them! In Jerusalem the living waters flow so plentifully that no one will be willing to serve them any more. They betray Jesus Christ because they wish to be served and not to serve."

This was the kind of thing Marie said. She sat on a cart with Pierre on her knees, and men came from all the camps, even soldiers and clerks, to listen to her. People liked to hear her because she had a fine voice. Therefore they said, She is a simple soul and her words are inspired by God. Brother Barnabé let her talk because he thought the same as she did.

One day, however, a chaplain came from the camp of the knights of Brabant and called Marie a shameless woman in front of everybody. There was a scuffle, and Brother Barnabé and Baudry succeeded in extricating the discourteous chaplain from the hands of the men who had fallen upon him and taking him to their tent.

"With all due respect, father, why speak like that in front of the crowd? You have more courage than sense." The chaplain had acquired a number of bruises and he was extremely angry.

"That woman," he said, "is a weaver and what she says is tainted with heresy."

Brother Barnabé vouched for Marie's faith, but that same evening he sent for Jacques.

"Your wife talks too much. She may get into trouble."

"How so?" said Jacques. "God gave her a tongue. He meant her to use it. Would God everyone could speak as well."

"It seems she does not speak so very well after all, since a priest has accused her of saying things that are heretical." Jacques flushed.

"They say that because we are from Arras. The wool merchants have invented that slander so as to pay the weavers less."

"Listen, Jacques, there are no wool merchants here. You will tell Marie to keep quiet. That is an order."

Jacques went back to his friends. "They are glad enough of a weaver's son when it comes to knocking Turks on the head, but to speak your mind you have to belong to a noble house."

Élie said, "Brother Barnabé is too friendly with Baudry. Baudry is a sheep, only asking to be shorn. A fine fool you'll look, telling your wife you've had orders to make her keep her mouth shut. We are strong enough to protect her."

Jacques said, "A promise is a promise. I promised Brother Barnabé." All the same, it was hard to lose face in front of his friends.

Marie readily agreed to say no more, but the next morning after mass she was off again. "Oh, they are envious, they want to silence us because we would make them keep their promises.

"Hunger and thirst are familiar to us. We did not come here to eat. Oh my friends, if we are hungry in Judaea, at least we shall know why. At least it will be worth it.

"In their jealousy they would take the reward from us because our share will be better than their own. And what do they fear? They too shall have their reward, the joy of the Holy Sepulcher is for all Christians, the rich shall have their share of joy also. But if they keep us here any longer, shame will be our heritage and theirs."

This time it was Brother Barnabé who took Marie's hand and said to her, "Listen, my daughter, I am very fond of you, but if you go on I shall have you bound and put away in a tent."

Such was the monk's authority that not one murmur of resentment was heard from the crowd. Starvation, sickness, and grief had combined at last to give him the beauty of a prophet, and he wore his rags like a kingly mantle.

"Then you speak, Brother Barnabé," Marie said. *"You speak better than I do."*

"It is useless," Brother Barnabé said, *"the very stones speak."*

By stones he meant the hearts of the soldiers. For several days past, in all the camps, outside the tents and the food stores, even on the sites of the siege towers, the soldiers had been making their voices heard, declaring that their patience was running out and that the troops were quite capable of doing the same here as they had done at Maarat; one fine day they would abandon work on the engines and set fire to them. It would not be so very difficult. At Maarat, they had done much more.

If the Count does not give the order to burn the engines, they will burn in spite of him. Even the Provençals were saying that although the Lance was holy, it was being kept a prisoner through the ambition of certain traitors. The knights themselves were growing anxious and beginning to wonder if the prophecies of Peter Bartholomew had been properly interpreted.

Among the Normans from Normandy, a number of learned priests were organizing large assemblies, and even going into the neighboring camps, claiming that the chaplains to the Duke of Normandy had uncovered the imposture at last. The man was a liar and a traitor and a scoundrel and had himself buried a piece of iron under the flagstones of the Cathedral of St. Peter in Antioch while he was working on the repairs to that church.

He had made up his visions and dreams for his own glorification. The army had believed in them because they were lightheaded with hunger, and Saint George had taken pity on the Christians and accomplished the great miracle.

Was it proven, they were asked, that Peter Bartholomew had really been one of the laborers working in the Cathedral of St. Peter?

"There were many Provençals there. He is believed to have remained behind, after they had finished work, to carry out his despicable task." There was no way of telling. Moreover, some of the building laborers said the thing was impossible: if the ground had been disturbed less than two weeks previously, anyone would have known it, and to bury a lance five feet underground beneath the paving of a church was such an undertaking that the next day everyone would have noticed that the floor had been lifted; therefore Peter Bartholomew must have acted in good faith.

All right: to begin with, were you there? Did you examine the flagstones? Was it really five feet underground? Have you forgotten how all the men, even the barons, were lightheaded and how their eyes were playing tricks on them? Men suffering from starvation will see the moon at midday.

In the hollow place through which the convoys were accustomed to enter the camp and which was used as a parade ground on ceremonial occasions, the Count's chaplains and their men had erected a double row of dry fagots. In order that the entire camp might witness the ceremony of the ordeal, the priests and clerks took up positions in a circle some twenty yards away from the fagots, the knights were ranged in close rows behind the clerics, and the soldiers massed together at some distance, while thousands more onlookers crowded the slopes. This time even the sick and wounded had been laid on carts so as to see the thing with their own eyes, because at last the truth was going to be made known.

The criers had proclaimed it throughout the camp, but ever since the departure from Maarat criers had been unnecessary: within two hours even the lepers knew all there was to know. Ditches and palisades there might be, but there were no barriers between men's hearts, and by now, soldiers or civilians, from North or South, they had developed a jargon of their own.

The heralds sent out by the council of barons and clergy said,

"Peter Bartholomew has accepted the challenge and submits himself to the Judgment of God. He will carry the Lance through the fire. Pray for him! Pray to God to make known the truth at last!"

If he was lying, would he be brave enough? The Lance is clearly genuine, for who should know better than he?

"Nay, but there are those that out of vainglory will eat hot coals. Let us see if he can come through the fire."

"Even if he is burned, brothers, even if he is burned, is it not clear that he has a pure heart and has not lied? It takes more than vainglory to make a man cast himself into the fire. It needs great faith. The Lance is genuine. God does not betray honest men."

From early morning everyone—soldiers, pilgrims, men and women—had been sitting in groups on the hillside or perched on the engines and the piles of sawn logs, waiting, oblivious of food or drink. People were promising children and men and women who were not tall enough that they would lift them up in their arms at the moment of the ordeal.

It was a day of blazing sun and wind; the clergy around the tribune called on the crowd to make room, as they were being forced to move back because of the danger of the wind spreading the flames.

The wind was blowing from the sea, cooling the sun's heat. Count Raymond and Duke Robert of Normandy and Duke Godfrey and the noble ladies on their stands fanned themselves with palm leaves. Their clothes were hot, and they were as excited as everyone else because, like it or not, they were going to know the truth at last. The Count of Toulouse sat in the best place with his wife at his side and their young son standing in front of them. He held up his head with pride because since the whole camp had heard of the courage of Peter Bartholomew, the enemies of Provence had talked less loudly.

Suppose that all the ill that had been spoken of the Lance was sacrilege, that it was truly real, had truly pierced the side of God and been stained with His blood.

Oh, the folly of men who mock today at what they worshipped yesterday, and are forever passing judgment on that which they cannot understand!

The excitement was so great that it could be felt flowing back and forth between the groups, surging to and fro in an ever-mounting wave as the drums began to roll.

The choir intoned the prayers for the man about to undergo the ordeal of God. If he is innocent, may God surround him with a cloud of coolness as He did the three young Hebrews in the midst of the flames; if he has lied, let him acknowledge his fault before he undergoes the ordeal.

Waves of blue smoke rose from the censers around the rows of fagots, and when the fire was lighted and the flames began to climb, crackling among the sticks until, caught suddenly by the wind, they burst into a thousand yellow tongues, enveloping the walls of fagots from top to bottom, a sudden gasp went up from the whole of that crowded arena. O Lord, O Lord, You accept the sacrifice. Right or wrong, this man will truly be a martyr.

He walked forward slowly, dressed in a white shift with sleeves tight to the wrist, very straight and stiff and well starched to prevent the flames from gaining a hold on it too swiftly. His hands were folded tightly on his breast, clasping the Lance like a great black bird against his heart.

The fire crackled and the yellow flames turned white and the air all about rippled and shimmered with a thousand invisible threads. The voices of the choir rose above the hiss of the flames and a priest held out a cross for the man to kiss before he went forward, alone, to meet the fire.

A lane had been left between the rows of fagots for him to walk along, but now this path was filled with flames.

The crowd roared. Louder and louder as the man knelt and prayed, his head thrown back, the Lance clasped in his arms. Go on! Liar, go on! Go on before we throw you in! Don't be afraid! Take no notice! Long live Peter! Peter, go on. Long live the Lance. The Lance! Go on, don't be afraid. Oh God! Oh God! The shouting grew louder still as the packed ranks of the crowd, like a slow landslide, surged forward on all sides toward the flames, sucked in, drawn forward in spite of themselves. Oh, go on! Liar, deceiver! Go on, Peter! Show them their mistake!

There he is, he is in! The Lance is in the fire. It is beating back the flames!

He had vanished into the fire. The double wall of flame shot up suddenly, trembling and hissing, in a shower of red sparks. The heat could be felt almost three hundred feet away. Lord, he is burning, he is dead, God has judged him! Is it possible? Can it be? A living man!

O Jesus Christ, Lord, for the love of the most Holy Lance!

A miracle. The shouting ceased, the noise of the flames could be heard as far as the lepers' camp. Time had stood still. Where is he, Lord, what have You done with him, what have You allowed to happen? He went living into that hell!

He did not draw back, he went straight ahead.

They saw him come out through the gateway of leaping flames, himself aflame from head to foot, the yellow tongues licking at his shift until it flickered and crawled with fire, and the Lance held aloft in both hands, pointing toward heaven. Even the flames seemed to waver at the piercing cry that was torn from the crowd. The man staggered, priests were around him wrapping him in blankets, while soldiers thrust back the crowd that surged forward irresistibly until the priests, the soldiers, even Peter himself, were almost pushed back into the fire. Those who were trying to kiss the martyr's hands and feet had to be beaten back with spears.

The Holy Lance, set high on its golden reliquary studded with crystal, gleamed in the sunshine. He has carried it, at peril of his life, right through the flames. God has saved him. He is alive!

People who had lost brothers, children, and friends wept for joy because a man who was nothing to them had emerged living from the fire. He has walked through the fire praying to Jesus Christ, he did not lose faith, he held the most pure Lance to his pure heart.

Be all such liars and you will conquer Jerusalem without a blow struck.

There was no thought of a return to camp. The cooks forgot to light the fires, there were no arguments around the wells. Men reeled like drunkards from one group to another, telling what they had learned from the criers or from the Provençals. He was injured, yes, a man must be pure and spotless from his birth for the fire to spare him wholly, and Peter Bartholomew was a man like any other. What sin was left in him had burned away in the fire.

His hair and beard had caught fire, and his shift also, but his body was unscathed, except for a slight reddening of the skin.

He was lying in the tent of the Bishop of Maarat, and his face was so beautiful that from his expression you would say that angels stood around his bed.

His enemies would have destroyed him because he is a poor and simple man. The rich abused his simplicity and interpreted his prophecies to suit their own designs. Now he will rise up and prophesy the deliverance of Jerusalem.

As soon as he is better, we shall set out.

See: Duke Godfrey is already beginning to strike camp, rounding up his cattle and mending his wagons.

There is no better Christian among all the barons than the Duke. He spends half his nights in prayer, and keeps no concubine but lives as chastely as a monk. He has precious relics in the hilt of his sword, and never wields his sword without first kissing it with reverence and commending his soul to Jesus Christ.

Moreover, he is descended through his mother from the line of the great and holy Emperor Charles, who made the pilgrimage to Jerusalem and obtained the keys of the Holy City from Pope Aaron of Baghdad. If any man deserves to conquer and govern Jerusalem, it is he.

So now they sang songs about the Duke and said that it was he who should have the keeping of the Holy Lance.

The Count, however, was recruiting more men to work the engines, promising them double rations and wine. Will you work against Jesus Christ? Surely you should rather set to work to destroy these wooden towers? It made no difference. The men went to work, especially those with wives or friends that were sick.

The Count, dressed in a simple brown tunic with a light helm on his head, walked about among the engines, climbed the ladders, and personally checked the strength of the bolts and levers. He was an old man, known to be over sixty, but good living is an excellent preservative, and he was alert and vigorous and showed more heart for the work than a master carpenter.

His advice was always good. He set such store by taking this accursed city that he could think of little else, and the workmen were amazed to see a man of such wealth and nobility, the leader of so great an army, expose himself to the arrows without bothering even to put on a shirt of mail.

He was melancholy and preoccupied, for it was known throughout the camp, in spite of what the Provençal clergy said, that Peter Bartholomew was dying. The crowds that gathered around the Bishop's tent were told that he was better, that already he was able to eat, but his groans and cries of anguish could not be stifled. It was a pity, oh a mortal pity to hear them, those animal howls. Few men recovered after such suffering.

He was nearly burned to death. His body was said to be all over burns, and the best doctors in the camp could do nothing to relieve his pain.

Arnoul, the well-known chaplain to the Duke of Normandy and the man possessing the finest voice in all the camp, rode about surrounded by his clerks, proclaiming everywhere that God had made known His judgment. The imposter was unmasked and was receiving the wages of his imposture. He passed through the fire under compulsion, shaking with fear. Not all the unguents of the Provençal doctors could prevail against the Judgment of God.

"Like Herod and the impious King Jehoram, this man is rotting alive, devoured by his sins. Now, from head to foot he is all one suppurating wound, because he dared to make a mockery of God's glory and the faith of Christian men.

"God has justified me and I no longer fear the judgment of men. I flung God's gauntlet in the face of the imposter. Now you see that you have been abused by a false prophet, and that it is time to strike camp and set out on the road to Judaea."

It was known that but for Arnoul, the Judgment of God would never have taken place: he had been the first to suggest it. And there were plenty to blame him for it, saying that even if the Lance were the true one, it was wrong to tempt God.

He will recover, God's poor man, the martyr of the Holy Lance. Jesus Christ will bind his wounds and make his skin whole again as a little child's. Feeling ran so high that it came to a pitched battle between the Provençals and the Normans, soldiers against soldiers, threatening one another with knives and javelins, and although no one was killed, a round dozen were injured.

The death of Peter Bartholomew was announced to the sound of muffled drums and trumpets. Whether he was a sinner or a righteous man, it was fitting to pray for his soul. If he had lied, he had paid dearly for it. The Count had withdrawn into the oratory in his tent in token of mourning, and was praying and weeping on his knees before the Holy Lance.

The next day the order to strike camp was given.

The Picards' mare had foaled.

The Picards were camped side by side with the pilgrims of Artois. Their leaders were a Benedictine monk named Brother Imbert and Jean-Marc, a weaver from Lille. The Picards had a mare, a fine Arab beast they had had with them ever since the great battle of Dorylaeum and had managed to keep alive during the famine by hiding her in the cellar of their house and swearing that she had been sold.

Now, ever since All Saints, the Picards had known that she was in foal, although this was something of a surprise because no one knew when she could have met a stallion. They endured a good deal of raillery on the subject of their mare being got with young by the Holy Ghost. A good many Picards really believed it.

Then one day, the Picard children came running and shouting for joy: "She has foaled! He has come, he is here!" And not before time either, because they were on the eve of departure. According to the children, God had waited for this month of May on purpose, since otherwise how would the poor creature have endured the journey? The colt was born and lay beside his mother on a litter of fresh hay while the children crowded around, silent and marveling. It was wonderful. There he stood, a little uncertain still, on legs that were too long for him and faintly swollen at the joints, the hair of his mane standing erect and his delicate arched neck carrying a head that seemed a bit too heavy for him, with big eyes not yet fully awake. His mother was golden, but he was white with pink ears.

The children sighed. "Did you ever see the like? All white . . . all white, not one yellow hair! Look at him breathing, see his muzzle quivering. Oh, isn't he sweet! Isn't he lovely! Don't talk so loud, you'll frighten him."

"There, he's come straight from paradise."

"Hey, Mardoche, we'll give him our sheepskin to sleep on."

"Do you think he needs it? We've got one too."

"All right, then, he can have several."

"Bertin, is it true he was sired by Saint George's horse?"

Bertin folded his arms proudly: "It's a mystery. We know what we've seen, but we mustn't tell."

"Tell me," Mardoche begged. "I'll give you my Turkish ring."

"I'll get thrush on my tongue if I tell."

Bertin was fair and slightly built with tawny eyes beneath pale lashes. His cheeks were brick-red and almost unmarked. He was the most agile of all the boys; there hardly seemed to be a bone in his body. He had the reputation of being either a liar or a visionary, and after three years only a very few, even among the Picards, remembered seeing him run about in plaits and a skirt. He had once been called Berthe. To keep this a secret, he had begun to wear a broad belt strapped tightly around his chest. Berthe was the daughter of a peasant family, and her mother and father had died of thirst in the desert.

"And do you think," said Gillet, "that Saint George's horse spends his time going around serving mares?" The children stared at the colt, fairly dribbling with tenderness.

"What are you going to call him?"

"Brother Imbert will tell us. Perhaps we'll call him Sun."

"Is it true," Mardoche asked, "that he will bring us luck?"

"What do you think? Why did God make him be born today of all days?"

"He's so pretty," Gillet said. "It would be a shame to pull out any of his hairs. But will you keep some for us if you find any in his litter?"

That night the children drove everyone mad with their chattering.

"All right! Have you never seen a mare foal?" To tell the truth, they had not seen it very often. Moreover, in their minds this colt was like Jerusalem. They were going to Jerusalem and it was white and there were no flies there, there was as much milk as you wanted and wheaten bread, and white horses and white doves everywhere. What else?

Bertin told how he had dreamed that Saint George took him up on his white horse and carried him off through the sky to Jerusalem.

"And what did you see in Jerusalem?"

"Rivers of fire. All the streets turned into rivers of fire!"

There was no doing anything with them. Instead of helping the men to pack up the tents, they ran about like young wild goats, dancing farandoles in their delight at the knowledge that they were going to move on at last. The tents might have been taken down on purpose to give them room to dance. They pulled handfuls of straw from the bales and made themselves belts and crowns, and ran to light dead branches at the cooking fires to make torches, at the imminent risk of setting themselves alight.

As they danced they sang a mixture of popular songs and the psalms of Jerusalem, and made up songs about the Holy Lance and Duke Godfrey and Pope Calixtus as they had heard their elders do. They rejoiced when they saw the Count's wooden tower over toward Arqa catch on fire and the black smoke and the flames licking it slowly, and when they saw the barons' convoys on the level ground at the bottom of the slope begin to move off and the knights forming up in long columns with their bright shields gleaming and their lances raised. They could feel the camp beginning to stir and work like rising dough.

Everywhere was the noise of men cursing impatiently, wheels creaking, sheep bleating as they were driven down into the valley, the crack of whips and the groaning of timbers. Every now and then would come a shrill cry as someone began to see visions: "*Jerusalem!* Oh Holy Mount! Oh Zion!"

"Long live the Duke! His head is crowned with fire! The chariots of Pharaoh have fallen into the sea!"

The children danced in the gathering dusk and waved their torches until the flames, yellow against the red sky, lit up their faces with a strange light that was not of day or night, nor of earth or sky: they had the light of Jerusalem in their eyes.

Now sings the lark and blooms the may
Jerusalem, we come to thee
  Before Midsummer's Day.
We'll light the fires of Saint John's Night
And every one in heaven shall see
  And Christ on earth alight.

Oh the innocents, all thin and brown from the sun, with their bare legs and their bare heads and their skins roughened to the texture of snakeskin from sores and infections. God watches over them. There were not many children under fourteen left now, only three or four hundred in the whole army. When they set out there had been at least two thousand in all the camps together. The desert had killed them: they had given up counting the dead then. These, the indestructible, the bad seed, with bodies made of wood and iron, God protected them. They tumbled twenty feet and fell on their feet like cats, they ate the most unwholesome food and were never ill. Watching them rush about like mad things, the women said, "Oh, the Devil's brood, can't anyone keep them quiet?" The men answered, "Let them be, they will sleep all the better tonight."

They threw their bunches of straw on the ground and set fire to them with their little torches, and then played at leaping over the flames. I am Peter Bartholomew. I am the Holy Lance. I am the martyrs, I am the burning brand.

I am Saint George—and I'm Saint Michael. I am the prophet Elijah, I am the Star and you are the Three Kings. I'm the ox and I'm the ass.

I'm the baby Jesus. I'm the Holy Innocents I'm the Yule log I'm the burning bush.

One, two, three, four, five
Great Saint Denis was alive
Six, seven, eight, nine, ten
At Montmartre he was slain
Took his head off, chop, chop, chop
Lost it in a butcher's shop
Make it into sausage meat
Black pudding and salt pig's cheek
    And if you eat it now you know
    Straight to heaven you will go.

"Why will they let them shout such rubbish?" Baudry said.

Brother Barnabé was mending the straps of his sandals, praying quietly as he worked. "All right. You stop them."

"They are not afraid of anyone but you."

"I don't mind their nonsense. It's no worse than the things we say ourselves."

"What did Peter say to you, Brother Barnabé?"

"Nothing. He says only what Jesus Christ commands. At Jerusalem he will be visited by an angel."

"What do you think the angel will look like?"

"He will look like Peter when Peter speaks the words of God."

That night, Count Raymond's tower burned down, lighting up the empty camp of the knights and the black walls of the fortress behind it. The men who had labored to cut down the trees folded their arms and smiled, some mocking, some resigned. Ah well, there goes another load of timber that won't do the King of Tripoli any good!

The Turkish prisoners were sent back to the King of Tripoli with honor, under a strong escort. The Count had made them gifts of fresh clothes and horses. This was only fair because the same king, whose name was Ammar, had given the Count a thousand horses and a great deal of money. So there was the Count, whose left hand never knew what his right hand was doing, laying siege to Ammar's castles and at the same time sending him tokens of friendship. No, do not laugh, for you must know that not all infidels are alike in their unbelief, and these of the coastal regions are not Turks but good and gentle knights.

At the time of the morning star, Brother Imbert spoke to his camp of Picards. The monk's beard was so long that he was obliged to tuck it into his belt and his hair hung to his waist, for he had made a vow not to cut either until Jerusalem. He was bent and thin with the look of a bird of prey, yet his heart was full of charity.

He spoke with tears and sighs. "*Nunc dimittis,* the Lord has granted us release at last. Be patient, be brave, this is the last march. You have suffered long but the Kingdom of God is yours.

"Behold, you are more naked than on the day of your birth, you have wasted your inheritance with harlots. Now you are walking toward your Father's house, your birthplace is in sight, already you see the smoke of its chimneys and hear the bleating of its sheep! Your Father is preparing to kill the fatted calf and you shall rest on the bench beside the door at sunset!

"He has said, Go out into the streets and hedgerows and seek out the poor, the beggars, the homeless, and bring them in that I may invite them to My feast. See, the tables are laid, spread with white cloths, and the torches are lighted! You shall go forward and these blessed days shall be to you as the time to recite a *Pater Noster*. Truly the days shall be few, for there will be no more delays!

"Let these be days of prayer and penitence and charity, for you shall see Jerusalem with your own eyes before the corn is gathered."

The carts moved off, hauled by the strength of men's arms.

The pilgrims crossed themselves and took their places in the column, singing as they went. From the top of one of the carts, surrounded by bales of hay, the little white colt gazed with innocent wonder at the stream of faces moving past, and all, as they passed by, greeted him with a smile.

PART III

9

Lord God! Where are Your promises?

For three days we have marched along waterless valleys, over treeless hills. Is this Your country?

Everything is turned to stone: trees, houses, cattle, corn. On these hills is nothing but stone and a sparse dry scrub. Only a few cypresses, a few stunted pines, and watercourses so dry that the sand burns your feet. The sky is a still, dense kingfisher blue, like no sky at all. In the noon light, everything is white. The rocks, the road, troops of men and horses, carts and banners, even men's faces are bleached white and quivering in the burning air. We shall die before we get there.

Jerusalem. When? These hills are all the same, the same ridges rising on every hand, with dried-up stream beds marked by clumps of dusty willows. We are lost. Ever since Bethlehem the Enemy of Man has been leading us around in circles. We shall miss Jerusalem altogether and stray off the road to lose ourselves in a further wilderness of hills.

Yet even here the villages are abandoned, the wells filled with carrion, and nothing left but stray dogs, crows, and jackals. The abomination of desolation. Courage, friends, if they have filled in the wells it is because they fear our coming, and if that is so then we are not far from our goal. These Moslem villages of small square white houses clustered on the hillside are almost invisible from any distance, the ground is so broken. Grey patches of olives are spread out below the villages and here and there an aged cypress tree stands up like a black candle. Walking is not hard before the sun has risen above the mountain. Courage, there will be water soon, but God, the sun travels fast in these parts! Almost before you know it, the white rays are over the hill, etching in white rocks and blue shadows.

They stopped to pray, and to drink. The little children, the few that were left, cried for more. Water, more water. The older ones did not even cry. They knew by now.

That day, the victorious clarions rang out loud and clear.

So loud was the song that echoed from end to end of the mile-long convoy, passing from mouth to mouth, from camp to camp, all along the road that wound about the broad shoulder of the hill, so loud was the song and so deafening the beating of drums and the fanfares that, miraculously, no one was thirsty any more. The music and the singing were water from heaven.

Jerusalem is in sight! The vanguard and the Norman army have reached the outskirts of the city. The word went around—within half an hour the news was known even to the tail end of the column. They were less than a league from Jerusalem.

Normans from Normandy, Flemings from Flanders, with their own sinful eyes, their mortal eyes, behold it. It cannot be true. It is a vision, one of those visions that come to men in the desert.

The cry that went up, swelling in volume until it rolled back from the rocky slopes, that cry was no mistake. It is there! It is there and they can see it. Oh, the holy miracle! Come, come all of you. Come, Christians, all, let none hang back. This is no time to rest!

From where they are, they can see it, spread out, as though on the palm of your hand. Come on, set spurs to your horses, pull, just one more effort and we shall drink on the plateau.

The sun was getting higher. You shall drink, my children, you shall drink, my friends, when we are in sight of Jerusalem. You shall drink to Jerusalem. There she lies. The promises have been fulfilled.

The road was not wide but the hillside was level. Suddenly as if by magic, the columns broke up and the slopes on both sides of the road swarmed with men, running and scrambling over the rocks; even mounted men risked their horses' knees and plunged forward among the stones. The carts and those men who carried children or heavy loads stuck to the road, but there was more room now and they were able to make better speed. The great column suddenly fanned out and shortened visibly as the soldiers clambered in groups and in files over the sloping ground, each one feeling he would get on faster if he left the beaten track.

The horsemen on the road pushed forward, almost riding down those on foot, who were compelled to scramble for safety up the slopes. *Salvation is there, who will seize hold on it?* The shouting had died down now: people needed all their breath for walking. They were all panting and gasping and pausing for breath.

Not long now, just around the bend. Not long now, over there where they are singing alleluias. The singing is closer now. It is not far. Can it be real?

The men hauling the carts were straining like the damned, scarlet and streaming with sweat, blue veins standing out on their necks and temples. To go any faster in such heat they had to forget both God and the Devil; they no longer knew where they were going or why, and still they pressed forward until they were almost running. The reason quite forgotten, their one desire was to go faster yet.

The farther they went, the louder and more sustained the shouts that came from around the shoulder of the hill. There was no room for thought, they went on mindlessly toward the shouting that was like a whirlwind, drawing all moving bodies into itself. They were drawn, physically, as if by suction.

Then they were there, they were on the plateau, running and staggering like drunken men and falling, and in between the ranks of men sitting and kneeling on the slope, they saw.

Not one Christian remained on horseback. All were prostrate on the ground, striking their brows against the stones.

The sun was high in the sky. It lay there, beneath the huge hot platter of bright blue sky. White. White and terrible with its domes and minarets painted in blue and gold, like fragments of the sun. Spread out on the hills, white walls outlined in dark-green foliage diving into sudden valleys. White amid the rocky slopes strewn with black scrub and the silvery patches of olive groves.

Drink, Christians, drink. This water is holy that is drunk in sight of Jerusalem. Drink and may this water be to you truly the water of life, so that all with one heart may sing alleluia. The women went around with pitchers and ladles, silently holding the water to swollen lips. The women with the army were thin and worn, so weary that they were no longer even conscious of their bodies.

Brother Barnabé was singing, both arms raised above his head, singing in a cracked voice that seemed to tear his chest apart. Oh, let me see, oh, let me see the walls of Zion.

We shall all go up to the Holy Mount, we will worship the Lord in Jerusalem!

Arms raised, palms stretched wide toward the city. His big eyes were blank, all fixed and burning fire, he saw without seeing, Jerusalem filled his sight like an ocean of suns. His song became a cry, he held his arms higher still until they stiffened so that he could no longer bend them, his legs became so stiff he could not kneel.

They had arrived. His poor, what were left of them. Their hearts consumed by the holy vision. God have mercy on their burnt-out hearts.

Their sins burn like straw in a brazier.

Baudry, his head on his knees, was weeping like a child. It was the first time anyone had seen him cry. They were all crying, kneeling or lying face down on the ground, scraping up the dust from between the stones to eat it, kissing the stones and rubbing their cheeks and temples against them.

Jacques had his son in his arms. He came up with Marie and the rest, a little ahead of those hauling the carts, stepping with care on the stony ground because a child is not a bundle of clothes. He walked tight-lipped, his eyes fixed eagerly on the plain unfolding before him. "This is Jerusalem, Pierre, look, soon we shall enter it." He could see it now, with those sharp eyes that could tell a blackbird from a magpie at two hundred paces, he could see it and already he was counting the towers and domes and gardens, oh the beautiful, the holy city, we shall take her, she is ours. God gives her to us! "Marie, oh Marie, say, which of these churches is the Holy Sepulcher?"

"How do I know? There are so many of them! How they shine! God has decked them with gold and diamonds to make Christians glad. It takes your breath away. It is not possible, not possible that such joy should be given to men."

Alix came toward them with a pitcher half full of water. They gave Pierre a drink first, then Marie. Jacques asked, "How much must we leave?"

"Drink it all, Jacques, I will find some more. Never mind if we are short tonight! Drink, it is the promise of the living water that we shall never lack in Jerusalem." Alix was very straight and proud, standing gravely with her pitcher, like one of the holy women at the tomb on the morning of the Resurrection. The mistress of the feast. She bent and dipped up water from the jar and offered it with her queenly smile, as though in this holy spot she found herself the lady of the house, for she was so framed for joy that even at such a time she did not lose her head.

"Where is Lambert?" said Jacques. "We have left him behind. I'll go and find him."

Then Lambert came up with his mother clinging to his arm.

"Lambert! What is it, Lambert? Oh, my God!"

"It will be all right, mother, you are dazzled, that is all."

The priestess was clinging to her son in terror, her feet stumbling on the stones and her legs giving way beneath her. "Lambert, I cannot see. It is dark. There was fire, and then nothing!"

"You shall drink. It will pass." The poor woman lifted a frightened face to her son, her eyes sought desperately for Lambert without finding him. "Lambert, my son, I am afraid!"

Lambert too was afraid, but he did not say so. Others before this had gone blind from too much sun and had not recovered their sight, but that was not at the first glimpse of Jerusalem. He was not looking at Jerusalem; he was blinking at his mother, as though his own eyes could bring the light back into hers. She clung to him and on her small, worn face with its faded eyes there was a look of piteous terror, like a scared child's. "It is not true, Lambert? God cannot do this to me? Not now! Oh, my God, not now! Not now!"

They had stopped moving, and all around her the priestess could hear people running and weeping for joy and calling out, pushing past her and Lambert because they were standing right in the way. Jacques came up and drew them both across to where the rest of their party stood. "What is it?"

"Tell him, Lambert, tell him, I cannot."

"It is her eyes."

"Turn me toward Jerusalem."

"It is there, facing us."

"You can see it?"

"Yes, mother. I will not look if you do not wish me to. We shall see it together."

"Oh, get along with you," she said sharply. "Go and sing with the rest, and I will sing too. I'll pretend to see it. Don't worry, I shall get better."

The men hauling the wagons came up, each team jostling the next in their eagerness to get by. The carts drew abreast, two or three together because the valley broadened out around the bend. They came up, gasping and staggering, their faces black with flies because their arms were fast in the traces and there was no one there to brush them off. People called out to them to leave their carts and come. No one will rob us today! They had no strength left to free their arms, and friends came to unfasten the traces and splash water on their faces.

Guillaume of Valognes and Élie le Grêlé were the first to be released from their cart and they plunged forward, holding out their arms like blind men. Guillaume gave a great cry and dropped to his knees, then fell face downward on the ground. Le Grêlé had fallen beside him and was kissing the earth before he could bring himself to look at what lay ahead. It was then he saw the pool of blood spreading beneath his comrade's head. "Hey, Guillaume, are you hurt?" He raised the other man's shoulders and saw that his beard was matted with blood, his eyes blank, and his face grey. The heavy breathing had stopped. His eyes were fixed forever on the image of Jerusalem.

Le Grêlé rolled the body over onto its back and closed the still-warm eyelids and crossed the two hands on the breast.

"Hey, Grêlé, what are you doing?"

"Guillaume is dead."

The others looked, too exhausted for grief. How great is the goodness of Jesus Christ to have allowed him to hold out until now. It was very close. He might so easily have fallen out before we got here.

He saw Jerusalem, and that was as good as dying shriven. It was a good death. He died of joy. Fresh arrivals pushed past the body, stepping in the pool of blood. Le Grêlé followed in their wake, thrusting a way with difficulty through the crowd.

It was unfortunate that they should have arrived just at noon, when the sun was at its height. Drained of all strength, men knelt or lay flat on the ground, dragging caps and hoods over their faces, while before their eyes, all they could see through the thornbushes was the terrible white glare of that white city with its burning cupolas and the blue mountains beyond.

It is there. The Lord is my shepherd, I will fear no evil . . .

He maketh me to lie down in green pastures, He leadeth me beside the still waters.

Green pastures—le Grêlé was sobbing. He lay with his body stretched out on the hot stones, while his sweat-soaked garments dried on the stones and burned his skin, and sobbed, his chin resting on his hands, without even bothering to wipe away the tears. After the agony of dragging the cart, all his strength had deserted him; even the pain came to him through a shimmering curtain of flame, as if another body were suffering that seemed to have no connection with himself. He did not see the white city before him as a city; he only saw something that moved and shimmered, bursting into flame, a thousand tongues of white flame shooting up to heaven.

A rain of shining swords, white birds rising and falling, wings outspread, and then—an immense cross of white light, cutting earth and sky into four parts, Jesus Christ on the Cross, dressed in raiment whiter than the sun. The Cross was hurtling toward him at such a dizzy speed that Élie leaped to his feet and sprang backward. The oncoming Cross filled the whole sky, the blue fell apart and crumbled into shreds all around. The whole sky was about to crash and burn.

He stood with his arms held out, but whether this was to ward it off or to rush to meet it he could not have said. Hands gripped him. He did not know that he was screaming aloud. The hands on his arms were lighter than the feet of flies.

Someone splashed water in his face. He filled his mouth, his teeth banging against the rim of the jug. He could see burning all around him. "Hey, Grêlé, have you had a vision?"

"No," he said.

"Drink some more, you're all in." The others had lost interest. He was not the only one crying out and seeing visions in that moment; all around was nothing but sobbing and crying.

He sat down on the ground. All he could see now was the prone figures, scarred, emaciated limbs, and dusty garments stained with blood. Wooden crosses held aloft. It seemed impossible to him that the sun would move across and sink again into the sea on this day as on any other, that this day would ever have an end.

The sun was sinking. Marie saw the angels. They were clothed in red and gold. Emerging in long streams from the skies, they moved through the air above the city. Their garments were made of rippling, liquid gold, their wings were red and purple, and their heads glowed like gold-rimmed lamps. They spiraled upward, and below them the city with its walls and houses glowed in tones of red and ochre in the sun. The angels wheeled about the city in a slow and solemn dance, their red wings sweeping the ramparts. Each one was as tall as a tower. A song came not from their lips but from their wings, a wordless song so powerful that it caused the trees to tremble and the rocks to shake. The song of the great beauty of God.

As the Christians sang the psalms in their poor cracked voices, the angels sang with their wings in a peace so royal that the voices of men, their sighing and crying, were lost in it as rivers in the sea. Marie stood still as a statue and watched, while rivers of sweat ran down her face like the dew from Gideon's fleece. For a long time she stood thus, so still that if she had not been on her feet she must have seemed dead or unconscious. Pierre tugged at her skirt and called to her, "Marie! Marie!" but she did not hear him and others hushed the child: "Leave her alone, she's having a vision." They were all praying.

Those who were nearest to Marie looked at her from time to time and wondered if, exhausted by her excess of joy, she would not fall into a fit. Yea, though I walk through the valley of the shadow of death, O Lord, behold Your promise, death is no more. Everlasting joy to our martyrs who pray with us! If I forget thee, O Jerusalem. O Jerusalem!

That night they camped within sight of Jerusalem.

Jerusalem was the promised Bride, prepared in her bridal chamber, lighted with torches.

The bread that was broken that night was the bread of the Sacrament. Higher up, among the barons' tents, torches were lighted and priests carrying banners gathered to walk in procession around the camp. Horses and sheep roamed over the hillside, browsing on the scanty bushes and the remnants of dry grass. Late-comers were still arriving, looking for a place to camp: the lepers and the living dead, who always marched at some distance from the rest, guarded by a detachment of charitable knights. They came up in time to see Jerusalem all rose and red and mauve with red-gold lights reflected from its domes and pale fires illuminating the tops of its towers.

The sun was flooding the city with blood, the towers rose from the deep blue shade of the valley, bathed in a red light that faded almost at once. Ever-brightening lights flickered up into the clear air among the pale, blue-shadowed masses of the houses and the clumps of black, rocket-slim cypress trees. Oh, do not sleep, most fair, awaiting your deliverance. We shall light you with so many torches that night shall be as bright as day.

Rejoice, O daughter of the King, thou whom the Lord has chosen before all others. Watch, Christians, this night your prayers are mighty with God.

It was time to rest, put up the tents, and dig graves. That last, forced march had been a grueling one and some even of the young soldiers had died. This ground is holy, friends, even if the grave is poor you will rest in sight of Jerusalem. All night long the sound of picks was heard, accompanied by singing, and when one voice was hoarse another took it up, while the soldiers held their hands in the flames to keep from falling asleep.

That first vigil was like a Christmas Night—happy the servant who shall be found by the Master awake and at his prayers! No one waited for their priests to tell them; all had decided for themselves that they could sleep tomorrow, but tonight was for watching. A white wall of angels' wings stood all around. There must be no sleeping on the bridal night, the night of the great arming.

There before us, in the silence of the night broken only by the cries of jackals. Henceforth let this silence be filled with psalms. Oh, such singing as you have long time lacked! We are pilgrims twenty thousand strong, come all together from the far ends of the earth.

May our singing bring down the infidels' walls like those of a second Jericho.

Inside the city enclosed within its gold-studded belt, small glimmering lights came and went among the blocks of houses. There seemed to be more of them than was usual in a sleeping town. They must have seen us. They know that we are here. We must not delay too long. They are preparing.

The Sultan of Egypt has sent two thousand of his best troops and the city is not difficult to defend.

A yellow moon climbed slowly over the crest of the hills, a waning moon, half devoured by shadows, edged like the blade of an enormous ax. It paled as it rose, throwing an icy brilliance on the earth that chilled bodies and rocks alike. The air of these uplands was so pure that the rays of the moon passed through it like fine steel blades and what was fire by day became ice. These regions were so close to the sky that men were no longer protected by the earth's warmth.

Brushwood fagots crackled on the fires, throwing up glancing flames that as quickly died away. More fuel had to be thrown on continually. We must not let the fires die. This night they are burning for our dead, all our dead are here to warm us, our dead have followed us from Antioch, bound by their crosses and their vows.

Suppose that they were here around the fires and God were suddenly to restore their earthly forms: there would be no room left on the plateau or the hillside. Before such a multitude the King of Egypt himself would throw down his arms! The invisible army was there, flowing down the hillside to Jerusalem and marching in procession around the walls. You that have stolen the heritage of Jesus Christ shall know that a hundred thousand living souls, sundered from their bodies, wait at the gates of Jerusalem for their hour.

The sky grew lighter, bathing everybody in a wash of cold, clean air that, far from doing harm, gave back new life. After the sleepless night, the dawn turned mortal weariness into a longing for joy and their bodies felt as light as if they were risen from the dead.

The knights were singing, kneeling with raised arms before the altars that had been set up in the open air. They flung themselves prostrate on the ground, bareheaded and bare-breasted, weeping and asking forgiveness for their sins. Then, one by one, they carried their swords up to be blessed.

Saint-John walked among the rocks, skirting the bushes, seeking a path that led down to the valley. He felt no weariness. The pains in his head that stretched a flaming curtain before his eyes did not defeat him. He had never been ill, even the flies scarcely touched him. He walked without thinking, amazed to find himself recognizing every bush and stone, the sides of the valley, and the massive earthworks, topped by strong white walls: Greek walls because the real ones had been destroyed long since. But—this was the miracle—even destroyed and rebuilt, Jerusalem was still itself, and he had returned to see Jesus Christ judged and crucified.

He saw through the rippling flames vultures wheeling in the blue sky, for wheresoever the carrion is, there will the eagles be gathered together. They are eagles. There will be thousands upon thousands of them. I was a fisherman on Lake Tiberias. Why, why was it necessary for all to begin again, why after a thousand years must I come back again to this place, which in truth I have never left? He found himself on a road and men were walking to meet him, priests with long black beards wearing tall, circular black hats, with monks and some other men in blue and brown robes. He thought to himself that these were the servants of Caiaphas, seeking to arrest Jesus Christ. One of the monks spoke to him in Latin and then in French, but he would not tell them who he was. A poor wandering pilgrim, he told them. And you? The monks came from the Hospital of St. John at Jerusalem, and those accompanying them were Greek priests. They came on behalf of the persecuted Christians to greet the gallant liberators come from Gaul. They came to place themselves under their protection and to assure them of the support of all the Christians of Jerusalem.

They went up toward the camp and Saint-John went with them. The strangers spoke in Greek among themselves and from time to time cast pitying looks at the thin, barefoot pilgrim with his garment hanging in rags and his beard white with dust, like a beggar. He kept close beside the two monks from the hospital, and fastening his great, unblinking eyes on them, he asked, "Why do these Greeks carry daggers?"

"They are obliged to arm themselves because such are the present misfortunes of our people that no Christian may be sure of his life. Inside the city, the religious houses are only spared because they have stout walls and pay a heavy tribute."

"You come from Jerusalem?"

"No, from Siloam, for the governor has expelled us from the

city. Those who were not driven out are fleeing of their own accord because the new masters are worse than the Turks."

"They are the Romans," Saint-John said, "and their governor is Pontius Pilate."

"That is so indeed," said one of the monks, "and he shall be justly rewarded for his cruelty."

The Greeks passed through the camps of the poor people on their way to the barons' tents, and it must be said that if they had pitied Saint-John they were now forced to realize that he was one of the more presentable of the pilgrims. The pilgrims themselves, when they saw the Greek priests with their scrubbed faces and their neat, clean robes, looked at one another with a sudden sense of shame. This was what men were really like, like the priests and townsmen at home. They had forgotten, after all these weeks of traveling with their reddened and blistered skins, their scabs and their sores, their fevered and swollen eyes, cracked lips, raw throats, and clothes so tattered and filthy that even the pus and bloodstains on them no longer showed. Feet hard as leather, hands raw, hair crawling with lice: they had been accustomed to it all for so long. Even the soldiers were no very splendid sight.

The Greeks observed them with a kind of horror and discreetly held their noses because the stench within the camp was worse than an untended stable. The stony ground was thick with blood and filth and the flies flew heavily, settling on anything—faces, arms, the refuse on the ground, wherever there was a trace of moisture. Children gripping dry sticks stared at the visitors with the half-scared, half-aggressive expressions of animals likely to bite.

Everyone looked uncertainly at the visitors, wondering how they should be received. Many were under the impression that these priests and citizens had come out especially on their account, and were thinking: Alas, what can we offer them?

Baudry ordered the pitcher of water, already three-parts empty, to be brought from his camp. Brother Barnabé, having first wiped it with the hem of his habit, dipped into it the one cup his people possessed and offered this first to the eldest of the Greek priests, who blessed it and drank it in one gulp.

Father Albert had been sent for hastily and he came, brushing the dust from his clothes with the palm of his hand. Since he was normally clean-shaven but had not shaved for several days, his brick-red countenance was adorned by a light stubble, while an infected sore on his right ankle added a pathetic touch to his walk, ill-suited to his imposing frame.

Unconscious himself, perhaps, that he scarcely resembled a priest any more, he talked while Brother Barnabé refilled the cup and passed it around to the other visitors in turn. The pilgrims looked on with dry throats, thinking: That is our water gone. Are these people not accustomed to short rations?

Father Albert spoke almost as well as a real Greek. He asked the visitors for news of his Holiness the Patriarch Simeon and told them what he knew of the reverend John, Patriarch of Antioch, and of the good understanding between the Greeks of Antioch and the Latin bishops and abbots: in short, he did his utmost to show them he was a person of some consequence. After five or ten minutes, when they realized that he had once been chaplain to the Emperor's Norman garrisons, the Greeks almost forgot his shabby appearance.

Before long they found themselves surrounded by a dozen priests and monks, the leaders of the poor pilgrims, all of whom insisted on escorting them to the barons' camp. Father Albert translated their greetings and blessings: this was indeed a joyful day and they had come in the name of the Christians of their country to greet the children of Christ who were suffering such cruel persecution in Jerusalem. The day was hot and the sweat ran from under the Greeks' black hats and down their faces as they listened, patient but unsmiling, to the Norman speaking on behalf now of one side, now of the other, and apparently translating the same speech over and over again, while the stench around them became more and more suffocating.

At last Father Albert said to the pilgrims, "My friends, these Greeks wish to see the abbots and barons. Let us lead them to the grand tents." They all went in procession, past the camps of the soldiers where the men lying exhausted on sacks hardly lifted their heads to see them pass. A few chaplains joined them, without much idea of what was happening, but thinking it must be some delegation.

"Who are these people you are with?" one of the Greek priests asked. "And why are there so many of them?"

"So many?" said Father Albert. "When I met them in Constantinople they were four times as many." The Greeks gasped in amazement. "What then do they seek?"

"Salvation, like all Christians. And I can promise you that each of these men is now worth a soldier. You must know that but for the prayers of these simple souls God would never have delivered Antioch to us and all Cilicia. It is through them that Jerusalem will be delivered."

The eldest of the Greeks, a tall, swarthy man with a flowing, grizzled beard, crossed himself devoutly. "Great indeed must be the faith of our Celtic brothers, since they place their trust in weapons other than those of this world! The army must endure heavy sacrifices in order to feed such hosts of beggars, and by so much are the rations of the soldiers diminished."

"There are no beggars among us," Father Albert said sharply. "Every man and woman here works according to his or her ability. Moreover, the poor are not beggars, but rich, and it is the chiefs of the army who should beg for their prayers and seek to deserve them!"

Other visitors were already waiting, drawn up in long lines around the barons' camp, and more could be seen climbing the stony track from the east in long processions, led by priests on horseback and on foot. Among them were people of all kinds, from Armenians in pointed hats to Syrians in white hooded burnooses, Greek merchants dressed in silk, and hairy, sun-tanned peasants with sandals and bare legs. Some had brought donkeys laden with panniers. They stood waiting, regarding with approval the tall tents decked with banners and shields.

The knights' servants and men-at-arms had no idea what to do with so many people. Those who seemed to be of most consequence had been led inside the barons' tents. The rest remained where they were, not daring to venture too far among the rows of tents, and after embracing the first sentinels they met, the Eastern Christians stared with dull bewilderment at the great force come from oversea. From afar, these famous men of iron had seemed to them much more formidable.

They were soldiers, tall and impressive though most were thin, with fair or nut-brown beards, light eyes, and noses rather short and broad; the skin of their eyelids and necks was oddly white: a race from the cold lands, not made to bear the sun's heat. Even when they smiled they seemed to be in pain. The visitors could not know that all these men were thinking of one thing only: how to supply themselves with water. That morning each man had taken the contents of one oxhorn from their reserves of water, and the horses must be watered first.

The Greeks and Syrians said they had come to ask for help and protection and permission to remain in the camp. The Latins said that they were preparing to storm the city on the next day but one, but that they must know where to find water: they had lost many sheep and cattle from thirst although they still had some reserves of corn and dried vegetables and a little wine.

Except for the pool of Siloam, which was in Greek hands, there was no other well in the vicinity of Jerusalem: on the orders of the governor Iftikhar, the Egyptian garrison had poisoned all the wells, and the springs were dried up until the autumn. The Egyptians had also rounded up all the flocks and herds and the reserves of corn. The Syrian peasants could show the water convoys the best way to reach the Jordan, or such Christian villages as had not yet been devastated.

"And inside the city, brothers?"

"Inside the city they have water in plenty, stored in clean, well-guarded cisterns, while for the public fountains they draw on the water of Siloam."

The Latins were expecting reinforcements from Jaffa. Did they know whether there were any enemy forces between Jerusalem and the coast? No armies, but bands of Bedouin. Where could they get hold of camels? They would be unlikely to find any nearer than Nablus or Ramleh; the garrison had taken them all. Those they could not take they had killed.

And so, by no wish of the knights, the news filtered little by little through the camps: there was no water nearer than ten leagues away and if they wanted to save the horses and cattle they would have to strike camp and graze the flocks around the pool of Siloam: tomorrow water convoys would be organized.

There were still some reserves for the men, and they could drink wine. Tomorrow there would be half a cup of wine for each soldier taking part in the assault.

We attack tomorrow. Sleep by day, and spend the night in prayer.

Oh, Baudry, what a night! God has granted us the miracle of a day of rest. The lion lies down with the ox and the sheep browse among the wolves as the prophet Isaiah foretold, and the desert blooms again, not with earthly flowers but with Christian hearts-ease and hope. Already we are one race sharing the water and the bread and the cares of the day! It may be that before tomorrow's sunset we shall be in Jerusalem.

"Has God revealed it to you in a vision, brother?" Brother Barnabé stood with folded arms, gazing about at the campfires and the men seated around them. They all seemed a little drunk, but there was no violence in their drunkenness, only a great gaiety and also a certain easy and infectious sentimentality. Yet no wine had been drunk. As at the marriage of Cana, Jesus Christ had changed their meager ration of water into the wine of mirth. A vision? I do not know. I see for tomorrow a great light which dazzles my sight. I know that it will be a great day. As far as my reason can understand it, the assault should be successful.

Le Grêlé came up to them with his catlike tread which always startled those he came upon suddenly: it seemed strange for so big a man to move like that, with long, soundless strides, like a ghost. He asked if anything was known about the next day's assault.

"The criers will go around before dawn," Baudry said. "I gather we shall be behind the Brabançons, who are to move forward up the slope on this side during the night."

Little could be seen of Jerusalem now beyond a vast shadowy expanse, blue and misty white, in which yellow fires were flickering. Small lights came and went on the sides of the steel-blue hills. Le Grêlé watched them, lost in thought, his lips murmuring a prayer. At last he asked, "Brother Barnabé? Is it true what they say? That they have put a heap of dung in the place of the Holy Sepulcher and call it—God forgive me—the midden."

"You know it is true. Everyone knows."

Élie bit back a growl of anguish. "We know, yes, but it is hard to believe it." His eyes were fixed on the city, in a dull, slack-jawed stare, as if he were seeing something fearful and terribly sad. "Yet surely they cannot have done that."

He crossed himself. It was on the tip of his tongue to confess all his sins to Brother Barnabé, but because Baudry was there he did not do it. For Jerusalem, God promised forgiveness for all sins, confessed or unconfessed. Two big black eyes opened wide in the blue night, opened wider still, bottomless pools, who would believe it was possible to feel such sorrow for a woman, that after six months there would still be a wound in the heart. God grant that all may feel the anger that I feel. Who would not weep for pity at the things those accursed devils have done in Jerusalem, those devils who have tortured and murdered Jerusalem? Who should know better what it is to feel pity?

No one had ever felt such tearing pity.

"We shall enter," he said, "at the same time as the knights. They will not dare to leave us outside."

"Wait until you get there," Baudry said.

"I am not asking you, you will not be in the front line."

"I shall be there before you, at the head of our men."

"He who would lead finds himself at the rear in the fight."

"Listen, Élie, I have never sought a quarrel with you, and tonight less than ever. If I have offended you, forgive me freely."

"And you," Élie said gruffly, "freely." As they embraced, Baudry seemed to feel a long cold blade pass right through him, and he was relieved when the other man moved away and was lost among the dark shadows moving around the fire. *That man is Judas.* He did not know why the thought came to him, and dared not utter it aloud.

Before dawn, a knight of the Duke's retinue, accompanied by an interpreter, reined in his horse before the Sion Gate, raised the herald's white flag, and announced on behalf of the leaders of the army that Jesus Christ had delivered Jerusalem into the hands of the Christians, and that the Christian barons made known to Iftikhar ad-Dawla, the governor, and his emirs that they were about to launch a general attack and were certain of victory. They granted the said Iftikhar one hour to surrender: his men were to lay down their arms and open the gates and swear to be converted to the faith of Jesus Christ, they and all the Moslems in the city, and all the Jews if they would listen to reason. If not, let them all prepare themselves to be slaughtered to a man.

The knight and the interpreter had to raise their shields to ward off a dozen arrows that sped toward them from the top of the tower. The answer came back that the governor of Jerusalem likewise placed his trust in God's help and was confident of repelling the assault with ease. His advice to all the Franks was to go back over the sea unless they desired to become food for vultures. However, they could if they chose be converted to the religion of the Prophet and abjure their idolatry, and their lives would be spared. He did not advise them to remain in Judaea longer than ten days, as the Vizier of Cairo was sending an army of two hundred thousand men to the relief of Jerusalem.

When these challenges had been exchanged, the signal was given to attack, which had to be done quickly if they were to avoid escalading the walls in the full heat of noon. The reserves of wine were distributed to the soldiers and to all men able to fight. It seemed to the barons that if they did not attack at once the men would be weakened by thirst and would fight badly, but it was well known that the garrison of Jerusalem had been preparing its defenses for two weeks and that the infidels in Jerusalem were rejoicing. We were expecting a lion, they said, and behold, a famished jackal. We were expecting an army whose numbers should be like a cloud of locusts, and this army will not even be able to encircle the city.

The Christian refugees confirmed that there were more than two thousand picked troops inside the city and that there was talk of arming the citizens and the slaves. It was therefore necessary to make haste, while there was still something left to drink and before the initial exaltation died down.

After mass, the signal was given. The troops who had been drawn up in long columns on the hillside facing the fortifications of the northern wall hurled themselves forward with a cry that alone seemed loud enough to bring the walls crashing down.

A roar that must be heard on the other side of Jerusalem.

The foot soldiers, dragging ladders and sows, ran as fast as the rest so that from a distance each ladder looked like a huge centipede, carried by two lines of men whose movements were as ordered as those of rowers in a galley. In between the ladders, the knights and every other man who could muster a helmet and broigne advanced in a solid body, shields raised. The archers followed, bows bent and directed at the ramparts. After the archers came the rest of the foot.

Nothing could be heard above the storm of roaring voices. Trumpet calls, drumbeats, screams of agony as the missiles fired from the walls straight into the advancing host smashed their way through men's ribs and carried off their heads, sending the fountains of scarlet blood gushing out: all were drowned in that storm of frenzied rage. And still the advance continued. The wounded man's neighbors got shakily to their feet after the impact and ran on, at the same pace as before, and those coming behind passed over the fallen body. As if they had not seen it—when their heads and shoulders were spattered with blood—they pressed on shouting "Jerusalem!" and "Holy Sepulcher!" and "God with us!" or simply shouting, with their mouths wide open, while the missiles whistled around them and beside them and above their heads and they themselves were like a solid hail of missiles surging forward irresistibly until they reached the foot of the walls.

The huge ladders, upended suddenly by means of ropes and pulleys, towered above the crowd and crashed against the walls with the full weight of their iron grapnels, and almost before they touched the walls they were swarming with men, all rank and precedence gone by the board, knights and common soldiers climbing faster than squirrels up a tree; the more men on a ladder, the harder it was to overturn. But the ladders were few, too few, there should have been ten times as many, and up above on the walls were cauldrons with great fires blazing beneath them.

The archers were shooting, but the walls were high and the spaces in between the battlements were narrow, so that most of the arrows ricocheted against the stones and fell back. As each ladder was set up such a roar rose from the host that those farther off took fresh heart, thinking the Christians were already on the walls. Then a dreadful scream rose even above the storm of voices as the men above wheeled one of the cauldrons to the head of a ladder and tipped it. Like apples beaten off a tree, the men burned by the boiling pitch dropped off the ladder, dragging their comrades with them, while those below thrust them off as best they could and climbed up in their turn. At all costs the ladder must not be dislodged.

Up, up, before they can bring another cauldron! We shall have them. The day will be ours.

The sun was high but thirst was forgotten in the fever of battle. Throats emitted only a hoarse croaking instead of a roar, like the growling of a thousand-headed lion mauling its prey. The ladders were falling back, crushing the wounded who had no time to crawl away, but they were got upright again and slammed back against the wall. At the gates, relays of men were swinging the only two rams in the camp, and the wounded were replaced so fast that they were trampled underfoot. The teams drew back, gathering themselves to hurl the massive wooden ram with all its force against the gate, which groaned through all its weighty ironclad timbering yet did not yield. All down the walls near the ladders the stones were streaked with blood and pitch.

Baudry, with his comrades, was assigned to the Brabançons' ladder. With thirty men-at-arms they had carried it and helped to set it up and held the foot of the ladder. After the first rush, they went up it with the soldiers, taking helmets from the wounded to put on their heads. They went up because they had to make weight, keep the foothold while on top of the walls black men armed with black hooks strove to dislodge the ladder and thrust it outward. There had to be a sufficient weight of men, and they all flung themselves at the wooden rungs, already hot and slippery with blood. The knight assigned to the ladder had just been killed. Men were struggling on the ladder, soldiers and pilgrims, some well armed, some not, hurrying to meet the men with the black hooks as if they had been angels in paradise!

Baudry was brandishing a nail-studded club, and he went up faster than he would ever have thought it possible to climb. With bare feet it was easier not to slip, and he was already grabbing for the top of the wall when he found himself suddenly face to face with a black man: there between two blocks of yellow stone was a coal-black face, the round black head swathed in a white cloth. Even as he raised his club he felt something sharp driven in below his left shoulder. He tried to snatch at it but was thrust backward and lost his footing. The man behind him, a Brabançon soldier, caught him around the waist and flung him into space.

He came to himself at the foot of the wall, lying on other bodies that were bloody and apparently dead. He tried to get up, but his right leg was as heavy as lead and he knew from the pain that he could not stand on it. Close by his own face was a head in a soldier's helm, and beneath the helm something that had once been a face but was now no more than dirty and bloody flesh. The eyes were a gruesome slime, and the beard red and sticky as though torn out in handfuls. Oh Lord, one of those first up the ladders, he got the pitch full in his face! He was burned all over, neck and shoulders and chest, with what remained of his clothing still clinging to the torn flesh. What a death! I was lucky, Baudry thought, damned lucky. I won't get out of this alive but at least I shall have escaped that.

He was in pain from his broken leg and from the wound in his shoulder. He raised his head to see what had become of his comrades. The ladder had gone. There was nothing but men lying all around him. Heaps of them. There were many there who had fallen like himself and lay one upon another. It was very hot. The dust had not yet settled on the glacis below the walls, and bodies lay scattered like dead leaves after a squall. On the far side of the great ditch beyond the curtain of dust there was still movement and shouting. There were voices shouting on top of the walls, shrill cries in some foreign tongue, and a sound of trumpets.

More trumpets are sounding from the other side, the other side, our side! *They are sounding the retreat.*

Baudry did not understand at once. Then he thought: Of course, there were not enough ladders, how can they storm the walls when there is nothing to climb? He began to crawl up the slope, using his hands and his sound knee. A soldier was walking toward him, leaning on his mace and clutching with his left hand at his stomach, which was bleeding badly.

"Greetings, comrade, where are you from?"

"The men of Arras."

"I'm from Namur. If you get out of this, tell them, our fellows, that Gerbert—that Gerbert—tell André, and Bermond of Namur, that Gerbert hated to leave them."

"Perhaps we'll both get out," said Baudry.

"No. I'm done for, man. I've got it in the guts." He stumbled to his knees and then rolled over on his side. "Go on, crawl if you can."

Baudry looked at the slope. All around him other men were crawling or struggling to their feet. He heard the hiss as an arrow buried itself in the ground three paces from him. Whew, he thought, that was close. A great weariness was creeping over him; every now and then everything went black before his eyes and he fell into a black hole, and came out again to find only the stones and dust and pools of congealing blood.

Then he saw two black men, naked to the waist with white cloths on their heads, coming toward him grinning. They had fine, strong white teeth and they grinned without amusement, like animals baring their teeth. Baudry remembered the black man on the wall between the battlements. He thought: It is true. I have never killed.

The Christians had withdrawn out of missile range. From the Count of Toulouse down to the meanest foot soldier, all knew, if the truth were told, that the day was lost. Beneath the walls, the army could do nothing but endure the missiles and the arrows and the boiling pitch, unable to retaliate in any way whatever.

Theirs was a seasoned army, full of fight and perfectly capable of taking the city if once it succeeded in getting a foothold, but with only forty ladders in all they were a sitting target. The barons, knowing they had none too many men to lose, had decided to call off the useless slaughter. The troops had retired in good order, taking the ladders, with the exception of those that had been set on fire, and the men were given the order to rest.

The local Christians formed a chain from the pool of Siloam as though for a fire, passing buckets and pitchers from hand to hand, because the sun was little past the meridian and just then water was a greater need than prayer.

The women had come from the camp and moved along the rows of men lying on the ground, holding the pitchers of water to parched and bloodied lips. All over the scorched hillside, white with dust, a long, gasping groan went up from many thousand throats. Injured and uninjured alike were in almost the same state, half dead from heat and thirst, limbs numb with fatigue, heads aching from the din, and nearly deafened by the terrible shouting which still rang in their ears.

The barons and the knights remounted and rode back to the summit of the plateau the better to observe the movements of the army and of the enemy. A glance at the number of bodies lying on the glacis below the walls was enough to tell the most obstinately determined that the attack had been madness.

If the enemy were to attempt a sortie at that moment, the army would have no chance even to defend itself. The criers and the trumpets sounded the retreat: each man to his own camp, keep together there! Bring up the carts for the wounded.

The soldiers picked themselves up, rubbing their legs, and shouldered their weapons once again. Among the wounded were many suffering from burns who begged their comrades to finish them off. For those with gaping wounds where the flesh had been torn away by the pitch there was little hope of survival. They were given water and loaded onto the carts, and the agony they endured, being jolted against each other in this way, made them gnaw their own flesh or that of their comrades in misfortune.

From their position on the far side of the ditch, some of the pilgrims stared across at the bodies lying at the foot of the wall. Some were still moving; possibly they were only stunned and could get on their feet again and back to camp. Some were walking; others, when they came to a place where the slope was steep, simply rolled down to the bottom, bouncing over the stones. With cries of "Courage!" the pilgrims ran down to meet them.

Then, through a postern at the side of the Sion Gate, soldiers started coming out of the city, spears in hand and swords at their belts.

An excited stir ran through the troops still in the open, facing the ramparts. They were not much more than a bowshot from the walls and the sight of the enemy so close roused them to sudden anger, not unmixed with fear.

"Halt! Back up the slope! Stand by your arms!"

Élie le Grêlé sprang forward, swinging his ax over his head. "Forward, lads! Can't you see what they're doing? They've come to finish off our wounded!" He succeeded in getting about thirty men to follow him, and they were already running down the slope when they were joined by a number of archers who advanced with bows drawn on their living targets. The temptation was too strong. The enemy soldiers were tall, black-skinned men, naked to the waist, those very Sudanese guards of whom they had all heard so much.

The Sudanese had indeed come to deal with the wounded. The pilgrims could see the glitter and the searing lightning-flashes of their swords as they strolled about the battlefield as calmly as in a cornfield, only they were reaping heads.

The little group climbing back up the slope halted abruptly as a missile brought down two of the pilgrims. Others were calling out to them from the camp: "Come back, you fools! Come back, for Christ's sake! A truce had been proclaimed."

"A truce! They are killing our wounded."

"That is their right."

They came back, dragging the two pilgrims whose legs had been broken. To see the Sudanese so close and not be able to kill one of them! Le Grêlé, walking alongside Lambert, was snorting like a bull. "Oh, the dogs! Oh, the brigands! The Devil flay them alive!" He was sick with rage, almost ready to turn his ax on his own comrades. "You have shown your courage, friend," Lambert told him. "What is the use of getting killed for nothing?"

"A truce? When they can fire at us? A truce?" The men paused to get their breath and wipe away the sweat that was running down their faces. "Baudry?"

"Him!" le Grêlé said. "He's probably back in camp long before this."

He was sorry for the words later, when the machines on the walls began firing again and they went to collect the missiles falling twenty paces away from where the men were standing, even at the risk of getting another on the head. They picked them up and carried them away, two or three at a time, in a fold of their cloaks. There were enough for a battalion.

Back in the camp, in the red hour of sunset, they counted the wounded: except for those who had been burned, nearly all would recover. The ones that were seriously hurt had all been left on the field. No one knew how many men had been lost. Some said eight hundred, others more than a thousand. Too many for an attack that failed.

Some of the severed heads were unrecognizable, the faces smashed against the rocks, for the Egyptian catapults were powerful and the ground hard. But there were others which had fallen more lightly and could still be known. Baudry's was among them.

This was a hard blow for the pilgrims of Arras. They had loved the mason better than they knew. They laid the head, along with another which might have been Bernier's, on the cleanest cloth they could find and all the dead men's friends came to pay their last respects. Baudry's bruised and battered head, now that the blood had been washed away, was seen to have the eyes still open and, in spite of the long purple weals disfiguring nose and cheeks, the expression was peaceful and the parted lips, surrounded by the blood-caked beard, seemed caught in the act of uttering some words of peace. Yet it was cruel to see the traces of a former beauty emerging from the ruined face as from a broken mirror. It was like a mist before your own eyes.

Jacques recalled having seen Baudry, from the foot of the ladder where he was occupied, climbing high up and struck by a spear and falling, and they all said that Baudry had died well, being almost at the top and on the point of entering Jerusalem.

Alix came and stood by the cloth on which the heads were laid and gazed for a long time with eyes that were fixed like those of a dead woman, and for once she did not speak. For once she had nothing to say. Then she asked Élie for his knife, which was known to be the sharpest in the whole camp of Arras. He gave it to her in silence. Brother Barnabé stepped forward.

"What are you going to do?" he asked. He was afraid that, seized by a sudden madness, she meant to kill herself for grief, but she answered him dully, "Nothing wrong."

She took her left plait in her hand and cut it off, just below the ear, and then did the same with the right. They were beautiful plaits, thick and fair, the color only a little faded from too much sun. She laid them around the severed head, so that they looked like a halo. Then she gave Élie back his knife. After that, she stayed for a long time on her knees beside the heads, praying quietly, her face as solemn as a child's.

Brother Barnabé did not weep, nor would he let his eyes dwell on the cruel object that was for him the last earthly reminder of his friend. In his mind he saw Baudry's tall, noble body, robed in a long white shift, laid on a black bier with three candles burning at its head and a crucifix between the clasped hands. He saw the face calm, clean, and smooth; he saw the eyes, their rounded lids closed on some great dream of happiness, and heard the solemn chanting of monastic voices: *Libera me, Domine, de morte aeterna.* He saw a body befitting that great, tranquil soul: such was Baudry as he slept in Abraham's bosom awaiting the Last Judgment.

His body will not rise up in the night, seeking its head. God Himself watches over the bodies of martyrs. Oh, my brother. All the severed heads are laid at the foot of the Holy Mount, at the foot of the Cross.

Night came, like a grievous vigil for the dead. The next day would be waterless, rationed down to a quarter of a pint. The pool of Siloam would never yield enough water to quench the thirst of more than twenty thousand souls in one day, in addition to horses and cattle. In this country it never rained in summer.

They have fountains in Jerusalem, and cisterns.

All the wine has been drunk.

There are more than a thousand who will not drink again, but are we the richer for it? Say a prayer as you drink the ration of the comrade who died.

Such a day of blood! Tonight hardly anyone gives it a thought, but tomorrow they will remember.

There were not enough ladders and the infidels laughed at us. They poured boiling pitch on us and we could not even retaliate with arrows.

O Jerusalem, if I forget thee! Bitter and cruel Jerusalem.

At Antioch it was easy to make as many ladders as were needed in two days, but in this country there are not even any woods.

These people defend themselves so well that a fresh assault will need long preparation.

The local Christians were already coming to say that there was great fear in the city and that the fury of the emirs was equally great: the infidel dogs were saying that they had never seen so reckless an army, the Frankish Christians were possessed by the Devil and had less regard for death than the Sudanese, and if the Vizier delayed in sending aid the city would not hold out. "Maybe, but do they know what it means to be thirsty?"

Many Greek and Syrian Christians, fearing the Moslems' anger, let themselves down into the ditch on ropes that night and made their way into the Frankish camp. By morning the army had a hundred more mouths to feed. "Go farther off," they told them. "Go to the Christian villages, go to Bethlehem, which has already been liberated. You know the Egyptians have poisoned all the wells." But they insisted on staying, because they were afraid to venture far along the roads infested with wandering bands of Bedouin.

Courage, Christians, if the city is not liberated by Saint John's Day it will surely be so before Assumption. You have waited three years. What are a few weeks to you? This defeat was God's will. He means to give you time to purify yourselves and prepare properly for the day of the great encounter.

The priests explained these things to the soldiers, who listened fearfully because no men were greater sinners. But the poor pilgrims murmured and said that there were not so many impure hearts among them, that even the criminals had sincerely repented, and they did not see how they could purify themselves any more. Sin as well as repentance came of suffering.

Beware, presumptuous men, lest God send plague to punish you for your pride! We are nearing our goal. Remember that the earth you tread may have been touched by the feet of Our Lord. Nothing can happen to you here that is not a blessing, except your own sins.

The barons sent out criers with orders that the camps were to separate. The city had to be surrounded, and this was no easy matter because there were two leagues of walls, or rather of moats. The city was built on hills, with more hills all around. The first thing to be done was to block all the valleys with bodies of troops, after which the camps could be extended up the hill-sides and suitable sites selected for the construction of siege engines. In pursuance of this plan, the Provençals marched around the city and took up a position opposite the Tower of David, while the French and the Normans remained where they were and extended their camps to the east. Here, what was needed was not so much to dig trenches as to erect barricades and watch-towers on the tops of the hills. All the workmen, crusaders and local Christians alike, were promised a double ration of water. The barons had taken charge of the water supplies in order to prevent any unfairness: if water had to be paid for, the poor would be in danger of dying of thirst. In two days the camps were completed and fortified on all sides, and all roads cut off except those leading to Jaffa and to Bethlehem.

Each camp had to provide its own water convoy, and the water it had brought was shared out by the leaders, but all the men employed on siege work were given their water on the spot. The army was short of laborers, and Frenchmen, Bretons, Provençals, Syrians, even women, were recruited and finally even the archers were compelled to carry stones, but what of that? It was not what the archers were paid to do, but they submitted. If the camp was undefended when an Egyptian army arrived, there would be no more archers or laborers or knights, no more rich or poor.

When the watchmen reported dust on the Jaffa road, the first thought was that the Egyptians were coming. The alarm was raised and a good deal of panic ensued. Then it was seen that the advancing company was only a small one. A mounted messenger arrived, bearing a banner with the cross. Greetings, friends! Soldiers of Christ, your brothers of Genoa have sent you victuals and reinforcements: three hundred sailors, skilled in woodwork, ready to work with a will at the siege of Jerusalem.

They passed through the camps going toward the Tower of David, led by their knights dressed in red tunics with plumes on their heads. They brought six-wheeled carts loaded with siege catapults and boxes of tools, pulleys as big as mill wheels, and a huge quantity of casks and earthenware jars the sight of which roused shouts of joy. Oh, worthy Christians, God has sent you. Truly this is a miracle of charity! The sailors walked alongside the convoy, dressed in bright clothes with turbans and caps of all nations on their heads.

It was a miracle of charity that a small company should have succeeded in crossing all the country between here and the sea and bringing such a convoy intact! The women came running from the camps of the poor and almost flung themselves into the sailors' arms. The blessing of Jesus Christ be on you, Italians. Gallant Italians, is it wine or water you bring in those casks?

For the love of God, brothers, a cask for our camp, we have children and wounded! The driver of the cart said he would gladly sell the cask, the water was for everyone, at three Genoese sous the cask. The women set up a howl, for who could pay so much? Ever since Arqa work had been paid for in food, and the people had sold all they had, even to their belts and amulets. They swarmed around the wagon, preventing it from moving on, demanding their cask of water. Oh, these unchristian men! We have done more than fetch water without seeking payment! Only a cask, one cask for our little ones who are biting their fingers and dying of thirst.

Oh, cursed Italians, worse than the Jews, Romans, sons of Pontius Pilate! We'll take it from them by force. We'll take two. Call up your men, call the soldiers; sisters, friends, these men are selling the lives of our children for three sous! Some fighting developed when the women began throwing stones. The soldiers drove them off with their spears and then the men came up with picks and shovels, saying that their women were being attacked.

One knight commanding the guard at the entrance to the Norman camp thrust his way into the crowd with his lance lowered, and the women scattered like sparrows. The Italians said they would rather die than yield before stones and abuse. They had orders not to waste their water. Oh, you evil men, may you go thirsty all your lives! Go and get yourselves covered with boiling pitch and see if you deserve a drink! It is God who sends this water for His poor.

In the end the knight ordered one cask of water to be set on the ground and the wagon released. The Italians were by no means pleased and said they had never encountered such disorderly behavior or such abusive women in any country, and not for want of seeing people who were hungry and thirsty.

In the Arras camp, the choice of a man to succeed Baudry was under discussion. Brother Barnabé could not cope singlehanded with the division of food, work, and other duties, or take command in the event of battle, and in any case he was known to be a sick man. In his own view there was no one capable of replacing Baudry and the best thing they could do would be to join forces with the Picard camp. Brother Imbert was a holy man and his chief lieutenant, Jean-Marc, had plenty of authority. To this, the men of Arras answered that by God's grace they had got as far as Jerusalem without being obliged to take orders from any men of Lille or Roubaix, Brother Imbert's company included men who were condemned and branded thieves, and there could be no real harmony except among tried friends.

The long and short of it was that a good many of them wanted le Grêlé for their leader because he was the strongest and bravest of all the men over thirty.

Brother Barnabé drew himself up to his full height, his teeth chattering so much with anger that he could hardly speak. At last he said that he would never countenance such a heresy. Let anyone dare talk of setting up a murderer and a public sinner in the place of a just man like Baudry. They might as well choose Mardoche!

Le Grêlé's friends all got up in turn, and finally Élie himself came forward to the fire. "For once," he said, "I am going to have my say."

"Who is to stop you?" Brother Barnabé said. "Your own words are your judge."

"Well then, Brother Barnabé," le Grêlé said, "why did you stop them hanging me at Belgrade, if it was only to cast my sins in my face at every turn?" At this all his friends began roaring agreement.

Élie held up his hand to quiet them. "And let me tell you also,

Brother Barnabé, that in all fairness my sins are not my own but God's, because if I had not taken the cross I should never have become a murderer or an adulterer. God alone is to blame for the sins of crusaders, for opportunity makes the thief, as they say. God has already promised forgiveness for all these sins to those who liberate Jerusalem!"

"I never heard such nonsense," said Brother Barnabé.

"Not so. I may be stupid, but today it is Jesus Christ who speaks through me, for I tell you truly that there is more joy in heaven over one man such as I than over ten like you and Baudry, God rest his soul, for I am a sinner that repents! I have more sorrow for my sins than you can ever know, because you have committed no sins."

"As for your repentance," Brother Barnabé said, "you have had your reward for that in this moment and God will not reckon it among your deserts in this world or the next. And now let me make it clear to all of you that while I live this Barabbas shall never take Baudry's place."

Then Alix rose also and said that Brother Barnabé was wrong. The man that could shout loudest and hit hardest was the best leader, and le Grêlé was a good leader in work and in battle.

"You too? Do you ask for Baudry's enemy to take his place?"

"Baudry no longer cares either for friends or enemies," Alix said. "Yet if anyone did anything to save the wounded left by the walls, it was le Grêlé. If more people had followed him, it may be that Baudry would not be dead, or many others of our comrades."

"Oh, you harlot!" Brother Barnabé said sadly. "Your true leaders are Mahomet and the Pope Calixtus, for many are called but few are chosen.

"Which of you," Brother Barnabé went on, "would see le Grêlé take Baudry's place? Let all who wish it stand up." It emerged that against le Grêlé there were only ten men, three of whom were old and sick. Élie himself was surprised. "Very well," said Brother Barnabé, "this very night we go over to the camp of the Picards. If there is no better man than le Grêlé among us, then you deserve to be governed by a weaver of Lille. Even Jean-Marc is too good a leader for you."

He turned away, followed by Saint-John, who had no love for Élie. He sighed dejectedly and his clasped hands, as he stared down at them, were trembling. Brother Barnabé looked around. "What are you doing here?" he said.

"I am your friend."

"Thank you. You would not be a bad fellow if you did not think you were Saint John, God forgive you."

"Perhaps you yourself are a holy apostle."

"Ha! Which one?"

"I do not know. I cannot see clearly. But once inside Jerusalem, we shall all know one another."

"Listen, my lad. We are going to live with Brother Imbert's Picards and I advise you not to talk so much there. Brother Imbert is as meek as a lamb, but Jean-Marc will accuse you of heresy."

Brother Imbert and Jean-Marc agreed that all things considered it would be wiser to live, eat, and work together and forget all past rivalries. It is no longer a case of Artesians or Picards, peasants or weavers. We must have the means to furnish our own water convoy.

Jean-Marc was a sensible man and he was thinking fast. "Putting both our companies together will make rather more than two hundred of us, including the children. If we provide a cart and six men to draw it and two men-at-arms, we shall be able to carry up to five casks every three days. Half that water will be ours, as the price of our labors. You have a good cart: it must be cleared and ready by tomorrow, and the men ready to go with the convoy at dawn."

"Very well," said Brother Barnabé, "but who will take charge of the distribution?"

"I will," said Jean-Marc, "but you shall stay by me to watch so that your men have no complaints."

That night the pilgrims of Arras took their carts and their sacks over to join the Picards. The children were highly delighted. They made a fire of their own and all made up their minds to sleep together. But first they went and hovered around the pen where the white colt was. The nervous, rawboned mare quivered through all the length of her hobbled legs whenever anyone attempted to touch her foal. The colt was beautiful: a month old, well fed, glossy, and white as milk with a touch of pink in his nose and tail. He was lively and full of fun, and in the absence of any other playmate he loved the children and would come prancing up to them, nuzzling them gently, and the ones he touched were as proud as if they had been patted by a bishop. Impudent and quarrelsome as they were, with the colt they were good as gold. The boys promised themselves that one day, in Jerusalem, he should be shod with silver. He had beautiful black eyes, such beautiful eyes, friends, beautiful, not even the fair Euphemia's were more beautiful!

The criers of the army were going around all the camps collecting volunteers to go to Cedron and Nablus, woodcutters preferably, but any able-bodied man could go. They would have water on the journey and a double ration on their return, because there were wheels and axles but few mules and they would have to drag the wood for four leagues over bad roads and do it quickly. For even with the best joiners in the world, how could battle towers be built when there were no trees to fell? And that was a fact: there were none. The few cypresses in the abandoned villages had already been taken. The olives were low and twisted and useless for any except the smallest crossbeams, and moreover, it was a pity to fell too many of them because of the distress this caused to the local Christians.

The city was more or less surrounded. The men rested in the fiercest noonday heat and set to work again at the first breath of cooler air, preparing the ground for the towers and digging mines, while the Egyptian garrison watched the camp from the ramparts but were unable to do very much because the camp was out of missile range. The things they were able to shout from the tops of the towers were largely inaudible, but messages flew back and forth fastened to arrow shafts and these were translated and cried throughout the camps. If the Egyptians thought to put fear into their enemies they were much mistaken. Their letters were read and then stuck on pikes and burned, and the soldiers made songs about them.

Let your Vizier come with his hundred thousand men or with two hundred thousand. We have beaten off the Turks, and one Turk is worth ten of you! We shall not die of hunger or of thirst. Hunger and Thirst are our sisters, we have long been familiar with them!

The crows will not eat us because we shall eat them!

If we are cowards, then come outside and show yourselves instead of skulking within your walls and never coming out except to finish off our wounded! We have too few pikes to hold your heads, but we shall stick them on our pitchforks and fire irons. We'll give them to our children to play with.

They have water in Jerusalem. They have fresh water fountains at the street corners, they have deep, dark cisterns and wells of icy water, they are stealing our water that God made for His Christians.

After two days the water convoys returned. The men were hailed as saviors and miracle-workers, and the water was shared out among the camps and put under guard: water for not less than three days, or even four if possible. Be wise, Christians, the laborer is worthy of his hire and today those who are working on the siege towers are the first to be served, for without these towers how shall we take the city?

Jean-Marc supervised the distribution twice a day and there was no appeal from his decision. He gave the men twice as much as the women, but the young children had as much as the men. Jean-Marc had a wife and two sons, and there were those who whispered unkindly that there was nothing wonderful in this since Jean-Marc had always had charge of the distribution of rations. His sons were strapping Picards with fair hair and red faces. They were good workers, and even if they did eat more than the rest they earned their bread. They had married in Antioch two Armenian girls, the daughters of an ironsmith, and the ironsmith and his wife had followed the army, drawn by the piety of the crusaders. The Armenian went to work in the camps of the rich and brought back a little money or some wine.

Until the day when the folk of Arras joined up with the Picards the two companies had been friendly enough, but once they were forced to share everything and at the same time there was less and less to share, they began to look askance at one another. The people of Arras were dissatisfied and missing Baudry: dead for four days now, and already he had become like the dead of Maarat and the dead of Antioch, truly dead and gone over to join the ranks of the martyrs for whom the dirges were sung around the campfire.

Alas for Baudry, best of men
To enemies and friends alike.

Arras to Rhine, Cologne to Hungary
From Hungary to Belgrade and
From Belgrade to the Straits
The fair city of Saint Sophia
  Valiant, just, and good
  You led our company.
The old men's brother, children's father
May God love you as you loved us.
First in the camp before Nicaea
First in the battle at Dorylaeum
That great battle which God won for us.
  You killed no man
  No man saw you draw back.
Baudry, our friend, our brother, father!
How great the heat was in the desert
One in ten the sun slew then
And one in ten would die of thirst.
Baudry, you never spared yourself
  God spared you for us.
Bitter the cold at Antioch
Our hands and feet were numbed like ice
The sky at noon was dark as evening
In torrents the rain from heaven fell
Cold water a bed for live and dead
As through the mire you led the march
  To bring us food to eat.
Let any speak who saw you eat
Before the last grain was shared out.

Alix has cut her golden hair
But not to sell to a baron's lady
Alix has made a costly shroud
For him who will never have a bier.
High on the walls of Jerusalem
Thirty feet from the Gate of Sion
High on the walls an angel drew him
The Devil in envy cast him down.
Forward darts Élie le Grêlé
Jacques and Lambert are with him

Pierre and Gilbert, Marc and Bernier
Baudry is hurt, we must save him!

The Nubian sabers shine like suns
At every stroke a soul flies up
At every stroke a body sundered
A Christian soul departs in blood.
No fireballs are the slingstones flying
But heads of saints Christ died to save
No further harm can now befall them
Their tears forever done.
They will rise up on the Judgment
Heads and bodies joined again
Dead and living reunited.

On Judgment Day the gates shall open
Weak and strong shall enter in
Rich and beggars, clerks and barons
For our tormentors then shall weep
Theirs the heads that fill our wagons
For Jesus Christ died not in vain.
Baudry, be with us on that day
None stay away from that High Feast
None shall be jealous of your goodness
Here, where Christ deigned to die for us.
Ah Baudry, who unwilling left us
Angels nor saints shall love you more.

So they sang during the night watches, and the pilgrims of Arras echoed the refrain. The men wept until they had no voices left. Marie had a voice and she stood up and sang; she had the skill to make up the right words. Marie of Arras, the sweetest mourner of all, whose voice called forth rivers of tears. Even in the Norman camp they were singing the lament for Baudry, with tears, for all had lost friends in the assault.

Because of the heat and the fact that they were within sight of Jerusalem, more disputes broke out in the camps than at any time since Antioch. To see Jerusalem so close and to be forced to remain where they were was enough to make the men shed tears of rage. The women plaiting ropes let the work fall from their hands in sheer disillusionment. The sun seemed to stand still in the sky. It was as if an hour, two hours, had passed and there it was still in the same place. Jerusalem so near. Nearer than the walls of Antioch during the siege. These great square white towers with the vultures wheeling above them in a sky bluer than the sea.

It was then that Peter emerged from his tent and spoke to them.

The criers had proclaimed it everywhere before dawn. He went up to the top of the hill overlooking the city and his companions erected a canopy to protect him from the scorching sun. But he came out under the canopy and held up his arms. The crowd roared: first the poor at the front and then the soldiers.

"*Brothers, Jesus Christ has taken pity on you!* He will deliver Jerusalem up to us before the time of the vintage. To be worthy of this honor you must be washed clean of your sins and receive the baptism of union.

"He Himself had no need of the baptism of John and yet by His own will he was baptized by John in Jordan! You, miserable sinners though baptized with water and the Spirit, see, He calls you to him, to Jordan, so that the promises of your baptism may be renewed in the waters of the holy river.

"Prepare yourselves, take up your staffs, put your sick and your children on carts. The way is long and hard but soldiers will go with us. Let those who have work in the camp divide themselves into teams and relieve one another so that none may be deprived of the benefits of the holy baptism, except those who cannot go without putting the work of Jesus Christ in jeopardy.

"So that, purified and reborn, you may be the more worthy of the joys which Jesus Christ has in store for you."

He was so weak that two of his companions, like those of Moses, held up his arms and supported his frail body which was no heavier than a child's. His mighty voice was broken now. Seeing him thus, with his chalky skin, red-rimmed eyes, and ashen beard, all those who loved him had to struggle with themselves to keep their places and not run to him. All the sufferings of the poor had washed over him like the waters of the flood. He had kept to his tent, weeping and praying, burning himself out like an altar lamp before the Blessed Sacrament. Oh, the Lord preserve him for us: it is through him that we are still alive, for so many sins have been committed in these three years that Jesus Christ would surely never, never have borne with us but for the prayers of the saint.

He was poor and weak and lowly. For his poverty and his meekness God had chosen him. Even in the face of calumny and insult he had uttered no protest.

"Dearly beloved, know that Jesus Christ has shown me pure, clear waters, shining like diamonds. He has revealed to me the place where He Himself received the sacrament of baptism at the hands of Saint John. It is our part now to follow Him step by step through all the scenes of His earthly life. As you have seen Bethlehem where He was born and the well into which the star fell that guided the Three Kings, so now you shall go with Him to the sacred waters which He entered so that all should be fulfilled. You shall be baptized anew, for you must know, dearly beloved, that He has chosen you alone of all Christians to relive the Passion in your own flesh and to accomplish the great work of deliverance.

"Truly the whole Church is one body, but of this body you are today the heart. Do not weaken, my children, for on the day when the gates of Jerusalem shall open to you there will be such battle in heaven between the devils and the angels that you will need more than human courage to face that dreadful hour."

Some of the men among the pilgrims were so weary that they would have refused to walk even if they had been told they were to enter living into paradise. It is a journey of more than ten leagues over exposed roads. What is he asking of us? We shall die before we reach the Jordan.

"You must not think that Jordan is defended by high walls like Jerusalem. It flows between grassy banks bordered with willows and oak trees, and its sacred waters are sweeter than the water in the streams of your own lands."

They did not believe it. They marched along the burning roads, singing psalms, but it was hard to believe because it had been so long that even the most resilient were beginning to forget. They had never seen a more desolate land, unless perhaps during the crossing of the great desert, and that was not two years ago but thirty . . . At the end of the second day they saw woods of cork oak and villages set among orchards. Peter rode in front on a white mule, bearing a wooden cross in his hands and surrounded by priests on foot, carrying banners.

The waters of Jordan shone like rock crystal in the morning sun. The waters of Jordan flowed slowly between clumps of green trees, washing the gravel banks and sucking among the reeds. Above all, do not allow the children to run into them. Hold back the men crazed with thirst. This is not the Oise or the Eure or the Scheldt but of all rivers the most holy. To be worthy of it men fast and pray, for fear that God's punishment should fall on the sacrilegious.

Let there be no pushing and shouting. The leaders of each company are to draw up their men along the bank while the priests prepare to hear confessions. None must approach the holy river until they are free from their sins.

But for this good counsel which Peter had from God, half the camp of the poor would undoubtedly have become a graveyard, because what the water convoys brought back was barely enough for the horses, the soldiers, and the carpenters. There was not even enough for the animals, and the oxen perished by the dozen. Of the water that the civilian pilgrims brought into the camp by the sweat of their brows, the army quartermasters took three quarters, saying that those working for God's cause should be first served, and indeed this was only fair because in such heat the work of hauling timber and cutting and shaping the beams was so grueling that no man could have done it without drinking at least four times a day. The Greeks and Syrians were amazed at the speed with which the work progressed. Truly, they said, God and the saints are working with these people. The Count of Toulouse's wooden tower was a veritable castle. The first story was finished in a week and the whole camp could see the scaffolding and the thick tangle of ropes and pulleys. The teams of men were working together in such accord that it was like the order of a dance: not a single hammer stroke was wasted, not a single order repeated. And like the tower of Babel in reverse, the men understood the different tongues, so that Italians were able to tell Brabançons what to do without interpreters.

"This is what we shall do, brothers. When they have been purified and restored by the sacred waters in which Jesus Christ was baptized, the strongest of us will return to the camp so that their comrades working on the siege towers may be baptized in their turn. It is not fair that we should enjoy the delights of this pure and holy water and deprive our friends of the same happiness."

The sight of so much fresh water was enough to make you realize what paradise was like.

For half a league along the bank, camps had been set up hastily among the trees and bushes and shelters made of leaves and branches, like those of the Hebrews for the Feast of Tabernacles. All the banks echoed with singing.

Parties of naked men lay, half in the water, on the sandy banks, scraping their skins with pieces of bark and plunging their heads, rubbed with warm ashes, into the running water. So much dirt was carried away by the waters of Jordan that the river was covered right out to the center of its bed with a greyish scale mixed with yellow foam.

". . . And all they that live shall die so that all may be raised up together. And so the living will not be envious of the dead or the dead of the living but all shall be one in Christ."

"Brother Imbert, if that is so, why has God made the lepers and the blind and the little children and old women, and all those who cannot fight but are rather a burden upon the army, live so long? They all wish to see Jerusalem with their mortal eyes."

"And so they shall see it. But when the last infidel has gone and the city has been purified, then the miracles will begin. The sun will turn black and fire come down from heaven, and all shall die and rise again together: the sinners to be judged and the righteous to be saved. You must know that the longer men live, the more bitter shall be their martyrdom, and the greater their chance of absolution on the Judgment Day."

Brother Barnabé did not believe in these predictions. Peter had foretold nothing of the kind, or at least not for the immediate future. What he had said was that Jerusalem would be taken before the vintage, but would there still be talk of the vintage if the end of the world were so close? Besides, even if the miracles foretold in the Scriptures were to happen with the speed of lightning, surely the signs that preceded them would have been more clearly distinguished? *Ye know neither the day nor the hour. The day cometh as a thief in the night.*

It was strange to be alive, to be sitting there beside the river under a rotten willow tree whose leaves drooped like a tent over the little drifting eddies of blue-black water, to be there, so near the water that all you had to do was lean down and stretch out your hand to bring it up again dripping wet and press it to your forehead. Strange to hear so many voices singing hymns and, further upstream among the sandbanks, the shouts and laughter of children and the sound of splashing, and to see all the thin, naked bodies jumping and splashing in the blue river, sending up great sprays of living water all around them. Strange to think that in two weeks, if God wills, it will be all over and this land will no longer exist. These bodies, this willow, and this river, and this sky that is so blue and the bank over there with the reeds and the coppice of nut trees: the whole earth will be burned as if by lightning like a thousand suns. And naked, clad in their white, re-created flesh, the resurrected will crawl in their thousands and their hundreds of thousands to the valley of Jehoshaphat, below Jerusalem.

And Jerusalem will stand, purified, under a sunless sky, with all its gates and towers melted by the fire from heaven, their common stone changed to glittering gems. In two or three weeks: could any man believe that when he was told? Could any flesh not shrink with fear? It seems a little thing to die when you know that nothing will be changed and that the sun will still rise every day.

"Take heart of grace," Brother Imbert said. "You shall see our victory and touch the Holy Sepulcher with your own hands. On those who are in Jerusalem at that hour, the fire from heaven will descend first, and they shall hardly taste death before their bodies are made new."

"I don't believe it," said Brother Barnabé.

"You do not have to believe it. All that the Lord asks of us is to watch and keep faith."

The delights of carnal temptation, Brother Barnabé thought. There are souls for whom it is better to die of thirst than to become enslaved to water. Only one desire remains: for time to stand still and these days to go on forever! Lord, Lord, can Your holy river, where You were baptized, become a temptation of the flesh?

For the sake of all these children, all these anxious women, these scarred and verminous men, temptation catches me by the throat, for their bodies have become my own and I am so weary that every time a child laughs I am tempted. Do not take this joy from them too soon. We have too few waterskins and casks: how much can we take back to Jerusalem? For we must go back so that others may come and be purified in their turn. We must not forget the others. They must have time to make the journey and be baptized and return again before the great assault.

Just to listen to the water flowing past the willows. No Bedouin will attack us: the camp is well defended. We are used to guarding encampments. God knows, even the infidels, even the Turks would be ashamed to send an army to prevent poor people from taking their rest beside the water.

They washed, and the roughness of skins burned and tanned by layers of mingled sweat and dust and sand was slowly smoothed away and softened by the water, and the scabs and sores and vermin with it. Hair rubbed with ash and sand and washed, and washed again and rinsed, gradually became real hair once more, fine blond hair, light and soft, no longer plastered to the head. They rinsed it again for the pleasure of it, feeling the water streaming down their bodies.

The children were splashing about in gangs, like flocks of big pink birds, shrill voices shrieking and laughing, sending great fountains of water spraying noisily in all directions and a hail of pebbles skipping over the surface, making wide golden ripples on the blue water. Naked as the day they were baptized.

"Hey, Bertin, that's a pretty pair of tits you've got!"

"Go on, Mardoche! It's like two big fat boils." Bertin's left arm went up to protect the breasts that were like two round, rosy-pointed figs.

"You rude boys! You shouldn't look. I don't look at your dangling things."

"You're a girl, Bertin."

"I'm not. I've got short hair."

Bertin could use a bow as well as the boys. She whipped the water into their eyes with a willow branch. She had grown very pretty. Her pale-gold hair curled softly on her temples, and her eyes, beneath pink and softly swelling lids, blinked owlishly through yellow lashes.

"You're a girl, Bertin!"

"It's all the same."

"No, it isn't. Girls get raped."

"Well? So do boys. The Turks do it." Mardoche fell back gasping.

"They don't! What do they do?"

"Well," Bertin said, "this is what they do. They put the boys in a magic bath and turn them into girls. And then they do what they like with them."

"Show-off. It's not true." A fine boy, Bertin, with that skinny waist! "Anyway, you're not bad, really."

"Fornicator!" Bertin ran off and plunged into the deeper water where nothing could be seen but her disembodied head, perched on its thin neck, floating on the swirling water.

"Oh, those children of Belial! What a noise they make! In the holy river!" The women had taken the boards from the carts and were down on their knees pounding and thumping at the clothes, back suddenly in another world, a world where there was washing and washdays. Only these things were not easy to wash, so rotted with sweat and blood that they fell apart at a touch. Wool of ancient burnooses, sackcloth, a few shirts of finer stuff that were the spoils of battle: charitably they had gathered up all the clothes of the men who were baptized, while the men themselves paddled barefoot in the river with only a garland of leaves about their loins. Ah well, these breeches will be fine when they are dry. No one had any needles or thread.

They scolded, but they washed them all the same; rags or no, they might as well be clean. The dirt floated from the clothes in a greasy, stinking slime. Is it right to put so much filth into the holy river?

"Have no fears, friends. Jesus Christ forgives us our dirt, and Jordan will carry it away to the salt sea."

"Priestess. How are you, priestess? Still the same?"

The priestess was clutching her washing in both hands and slapping it down on the board. She was afraid to let it go. She felt as if she were plunging her hands into a bottomless and unbounded sea.

"Yes, since the baptism has done nothing for me. In Jerusalem, perhaps—"

"You mustn't mind what people say," Jean-Marc's wife told her.

"I don't care," said the priestess. "I don't care what anyone says, Mère Ludivine!"

"Our own people have never said a word," Marie said. "If it

were not for Brother Barnabé, there are some Picards who would get what's coming to them."

"I can't hear you," said Jean-Marc's wife. "I have wax in my ears."

"I'll say no more," said Marie. "You'll see what I have to say in Jerusalem."

"In Jerusalem, my girl, we'll have other things to talk about."

The priestess was crying. Oh, to have tears in your eyes and not one drop of light! What the Picards—and Jean-Marc's wife as much as any—were saying was ugly. They were saying that God had punished her for her sacrilege and that it was a sign that the clergy ought to keep celibate and not make themselves a scandal. Brother Barnabé had told Lambert, "Bear it patiently. We have not come all the way to Jerusalem to upset ourselves over petty gossip."

"Am I to let them call my mother a whore?"

"It is a sign, my son. Remember the infidels call the Virgin Mary by the same name."

The men went to work again in the cool of the day, feeling cheerful and refreshed. They dug trenches and erected palisades so that the comrades coming after them to be baptized should find the place all ready. In two days the banks of the river Jordan had begun to take on the aspect of a camp, with ditches and earthworks, heaps of chopped branches and wood chippings, freshly hewn tree trunks, and the black scars of dead fires, brushwood huts, and the ground all trampled and muddy. The men sang as they worked, wiping away the fresh, clean sweat that trickled down their faces with an entirely new enjoyment. They felt as if they had been brought to life again; freed from dirt, their skins were able to breathe again. They felt so bold that they decided to dig a real moat, joined to the river so that it would be permanently filled with water. "Yes, but suppose they come with horses and camels and jump over it?" "No, we'll drive stakes into the edge and strengthen the sides with boulders. If they try and jump, the horses will impale themselves on the stakes."

More trees were cut down in that place in those three days than in a thousand years before. The priests might say that it was a sin: it made no difference. When these men got to paradise they would start by building a fortified camp. They said there were known to be roving bands of Bedouin and other Arabs about, and they had wives and children.

It is so good here.

The nights were cool but mild. They heard the river flowing, slapping against the reeds and pebbles; they heard the fish jumping and saw the fires of heaven reflected in the Jordan and the moon slipping down softly into the water. Women and boys went fishing by torchlight on little rafts, and the low chant of hymns was punctuated by the cries of night birds.

They slept little, for even the night was alive. Married men came to their wives again as they had on their wedding night, although it was a sin and Peter had enjoined them to be chaste, while the unmarried, God forgive them, looked about for widows or young girls, French or Syrian, because there was one drawback large enough to make anyone act rashly, and that was that no one could tell whether such pleasures would still be permitted in Jerusalem, or how many would survive the final assault, or if their earthly bodies would still be as they were before.

The temptation was strong—because there was water to drink and the women with their newly washed hair had grown more beautiful—so strong that men and women alike were half intoxicated.

"Jacques, this time we shall have another child."

"And he will be born in Jerusalem."

"Will there still be children born?"

"Yes, and hardly any of them will die. We will have a beautiful house with a fountain in the court." Marie was not thinking of that. She was so full of the joy of love that she laughed and cried aloud.

"Jacques, you are the thunder and the lightning!"

"Oh, your hair!" said Jacques. "Your hair is better than fresh hay. If this is a sin, Marie, tomorrow we will wash ourselves again in Jordan."

Jordan washes away all the sins of the world.

Sinless, Lord, washed and baptized anew, I have shed no blood.

Today, le Grêlé was thinking, today, here is this great river flowing as darkly as if it were a river of blood.

I did not see her blood flow, in the dark. It gurgled as gently as this water among the reeds. It seemed to Élie that the great expanse of black water flowing away to the dark edge of sight was all coming from Euphemia's delicate throat. Speak to me in Greek, speak to me in Arabic, speak to your lover as you did on the day I stood beneath your window; laugh at me, laugh like a turtledove. I never wished you any harm, I loved you, Euphemia. Whenever I drink water, it is your blood that I drink.

The life of his soul was flowing away like this river through Euphemia's eyes.

He thought how strange to be sinless from now on: the blood that had been shed no longer a blemish but like wine, intoxicating the brain without weakening it. The sin is wiped away and I have been baptized anew in the river of her blood. The Jordan? To each his own. As the priest drinks the blood from the chalice. For it is truly blood, that is the Church's teaching. Jerusalem awaits us, our Bride by the baptism of blood.

We have seen toads as big as horses coming down from the towers. They had tails like snakes and their heads and their backs were all covered with bright eyes.

They came down, one by one, creeping all along the sides of the walls, and vanished into the ditch between the mounds of earth and the carrion. Many people saw them. Some even saw them climb back up into the city. How can God permit such monsters to defile Jerusalem? You do not understand, friends, these toads are the souls of the sons of Belial: when they take a siesta in the heat of the day, their souls come out of their bodies and crawl about the walls.

On the day of the procession to the Mount of Olives there was no one, clerk or baron, who did not go barefoot in his shift with a rope about his waist and a cross or a palm branch or a candle in his hand. The men walked ten abreast, keeping step so that ten thousand feet all struck the ground together at each stride and the rock trembled.

Everyone was singing and the air from the Mount of Olives all the way to Siloam vibrated as if with a mighty roaring: Behold the Lion of Judah come to seize His prey. *He that does not sing today shall not sing at the Last Judgment.* The sun sinking earthward transformed the city and the hills into a brazier of white light. The sky turned violet-blue, like the sea above sunken rocks. A vapor rose up from thousands of bleeding feet scalded on the heated rock. Rivers of sweat ran down each man's body until every shift was drenched and beards and faces wringing wet like Gideon's fleece.

Courage, Christians. You will not die of thirst while there is still so much water left in your bodies. God alone knows where it came from. Courage, and let no man spare his voice. God will restore your strength a hundredfold for the assault.

On this Mount where God sweated blood, may your sweat be as a dew, a dew of fire and suffering, a dew of tidings, for the day of the great assault is at hand.

O Jerusalem, we lay siege to you this day with our blood and sweat and tears. O Jerusalem of blood and tears, you are closed to us today but tomorrow you shall be full of blood to overflowing.

They may look down upon us from the ramparts today and laugh, but tomorrow they shall weep.

This was what the infidels had done: they had fetched the crucifixes from the churches and graveyards and stood upon the walls and on the Tower of David and held up the holy crosses, and then they had begun to dance about and smack one another on the buttocks with the crosses. They dashed the crosses on the battlements and flicked them with their fingers and spat upon them, and then they opened the front of their garments and made water on them. Infidel dogs, your God suffers himself to be insulted and says nothing! He is nothing but a bit of wood.

The procession had come to a halt, and some of the men were shouting and some women weeping aloud. Stop, stop, unbelievers, for the love of God. You know not what you do! There were no arrows and no mangonels in action that day: it was a day of truce and a holy day.

There was Arnoul, Arnoul who, God bless him, had a voice like the archangel's trumpet, standing with the bishops at the gate of the monastery at the summit of the Mount of Olives, and crying, "Pilgrims, let this be the final insult and the ultimate shame! We have beheld this with patience, but we shall not forgive!

"Leave lamentation to the women! You see how Jesus Christ needs you. You will not fail to avenge Him.

"You see that these are not men. Let them bombard us with the heads of our friends rather than commit this outrage against Him, the purest and the best of all, who is our only Friend.

"Woe unto you that laugh, for you shall weep! Not one of them shall be left alive, you shall spare neither women nor children, for they are a race of basilisks. Only serpents can be born of serpents.

"Today they are like the wicked rich man, keeping the priceless Treasure for themselves, and we are the poor Lazarus, starving and full of sores. They enjoy the riches of this world, fountains and granaries and fair gardens, but we, when we have sent them back to the Devil who is their father, shall enter into Abraham's bosom and living taste the joys of heaven.

"Woe unto you, heathens, that commit the sin against the Holy Ghost for which there is no forgiveness! Neither mercy nor the promise of ransom shall save you, for what use would ransom be to us? After your death we shall take all. Your lives are not worth a button. We want none of your gifts. Shame on any man that grants you quarter."

Men in the crowd were crying, "Well said, Arnoul! Jesus Christ shall not be betrayed!"

That day the Mount of Olives was drenched in Christian sweat and blood, and many scraped their hands and knees raw on the stones and grazed their lips with kissing the rocky ground. They remained there until the cool of the day, until the hour when the infidel priests in Jerusalem began calling men to prayer.

That night the good Count of Toulouse performed a noble act for which in other times he would have earned long praise (for in these days each day was like two weeks and so much happened that by the morning the events of the day before were quite forgotten). He purchased the casks of water brought by the Genoese the day before, at double their price, and his priests went all over the Mount of Olives and down in the valley where the pilgrim host was resting from the fatigues of the day, distributing water in great goblets, holding it to the lips of those who could not move, and splashing water in the faces of unconscious men. All who drank two sips of this water felt as much refreshed as if they had drained a cup, for on the Mount of Olives even water that had been brought from Jaffa became like the living waters spoken of in the Scriptures.

Courage, my friends, a short while hence in Jerusalem you shall drink from the real fountains, the very same from which Our Lord and the Holy Apostles drank. Water will no longer be measured out in payment for labor.

The people of Arras and Picardy were encamped at the far end of the great enceinte, near Duke Godfrey's camp. The night was cold and they shivered as they walked, and the stars shivered in the sky, their rays all trembling and clashing as if in fear of falling all together to the earth. High up on the walls were yellow torches aureoled with blue, and the Duke's tall wooden siege tower, illuminated from top to bottom and swarming with workmen, was like a reminder of the forges of hell. The teams of men worked in shifts all day and all night, and at night especially there could be no slacking and a strict watch was kept for spies and incendiaries.

Behind the piles of ladders at the foot of the tower, the oxen to be flayed the next day at dawn were already being rounded up. The earth in that place was saturated with ox blood and the beasts smelled it and stamped and pawed the ground, wounding one another in their terror, while the bellowing and the herdsmen's cries could be heard a long way off.

In the camp the men lay down beside the fires or rolled themselves in what was left of their blankets. The Count's water had been drunk, and already men were regretting it, as if it were possible to drink the water and at the same time keep it for the morrow. He is a fine speaker, Arnoul. He has shorn his sheep and spun the wool and woven the cloth before the lamb is even born! He thinks we shall enter Jerusalem just like that, overnight, and is already sharing out the spoils.

No, friends, such a man as Arnoul is no prophet, for if a priest calls for slaughter and pillage, what will the knights say? The victory is to the pure in heart. Has Jesus Christ ever commanded men to kill women and children?

Brother Imbert sat on a boulder with his hands clasped and stared into the dancing flames. "You think like children," he said. "In this place and on this day even Arnoul, like Balaam's ass, has prophesied. He is a priest and God is not sparing of His Spirit today. You do not know the justice of God. For what elsewhere is called slaughter and pillage bears here another name, for truly we know what shall be. Until now we have lived among shadows, but now we are at the gates of reality. If Jerusalem is taken in this assault, it will be by God and not by men."

There was another preacher among the Picards now, a man who had come with some half-dozen companions from the Norman camp. They were the sole survivors of their company, men from the Ile-de-France who had no wish to serve the soldiers. This Frenchman, whose name was Gilbert, had traveled formerly in many lands and heard more than a thousand sermons, and he said, "Arnoul is the barons' man. He is a friend to Duke Robert of Normandy and he flatters the soldiers to keep them from losing heart. But we are not soldiers and we have no need of his flattery. What we have already undergone is nothing. The real trials have not yet begun. How, with the few men we have here, can we take Jerusalem?

"Remember, we were nine months outside Antioch, and there we were five times as many and our enemies were men like ourselves. Our adversary here is the Prince of this world.

"He is sending a great army against us from Cairo in the south, and another great army from Damascus in the north. Then we shall retreat as far as the place called Armageddon and the enemy will surround us on all sides, and the earth in the place where we shall be will be rent asunder and flames come out and devour us, and those who try to flee will fall beneath a rain of arrows."

Jean-Marc pushed through the circle of men sitting around the Frenchman and went up to him. "You are a scholar," he said, "and they say you can even read books. The only Latin I know is my prayers, yet I will tell you something: we know neither the day nor the hour, and it may well be tomorrow. So why tell us these stories about armies coming from Cairo and armies from Damascus? Do you want to drive men into mortal sin? For if any should desert because of you and then we take Jerusalem, those men will not bless you, either in this world or the next."

"No one," Gilbert said, "will desert because of such words. We came here seeking baptism by fire and blood and those that remain fear nothing any more.

"It is known that before the great day of Armageddon, Jerusalem shall be in the hands of the unbelievers: sin shall grow there like unto a great tree and its pestilence shall spread over all the land. In this day we have been permitted to look on the face of the Devil, and even that is nothing yet! Do you think Duke Godfrey and Count Raymond and Duke Robert are mighty enough to overcome the Devil Lucifer? No. When they have come to the end of their pride, when the night shall be fire and the day darkness, then we shall see Jerusalem shining white and brilliant, washed by the rivers of blood. At every crossroads, springs of living water shall rise cool and bright as rock crystal, they will rise and flow down the steps of the streets and in the gutters and everywhere will be the murmur of running water . . ." He paused, his voice suspended by a sob, and more than one man felt his throat tighten, for ten times a day sermons and speeches ended in the same way. The talk turned to water and no one could go on.

Brother Barnabé lay at a little distance from the big fire; he was gasping for breath and his sides rose and fell like a blacksmith's bellows. He was very ill but he had followed the procession with the rest, bearing his cross on his shoulder, a heavy cross that he had made himself from two pieces of timber. He had not paused once during the march, walking at the same pace as the rest and singing. He had thought that he was better. Then while they were resting, blood vessels in his chest had burst so suddenly that he found both his hands full of clotted blood. Brother Imbert and Jean-Marc tried to reassure him, telling him it was bad blood and better out than in. "It may well be," Brother Barnabé said, "that all my blood is bad." He left his cross on the Mount of Olives and borrowed Jean-Marc's staff for the return journey.

In spite of the night chill, his shirt was drenched with sweat: how could so desiccated a body go on producing so much water? His shirt was wringing wet. It seemed to him that he was back at Antioch in the days when they had to sleep in the ice-cold mud. In the time of the great rains. Oh God, at Antioch at least there was never any shortage of water.

The raging fever that had made his teeth chatter and his eyes see double had passed. Brother Barnabé would have welcomed its return, for it was succeeded by a deathly cold that crept through the marrow of his bones until they all seemed to be melting away. He was in such pain that every particle of his body was sending out a separate cry of agony. His feet, his fingers, his whole body was crying out in such anguish that even the pain in his chest was as nothing to it.

They were beside him. Alix and Lambert, Jacques and Guillaume, even le Grêlé. Alix had begged a pint of water from Jean-Marc out of tomorrow's ration. They had built up a little bank with earth and dry grasses to raise the sick man's head and shoulders, and the herbs smelled strong in the darkness. There were aloes and some kind of lavender, and for some reason the sweet scents were painful to him. Even the warm water with which they moistened his lips, a few drops at a time, seemed to burn.

Even the gentleness of their warm, anxious love and their quiet sighs. They dared not talk. Brother Barnabé's breathing was quick and shallow, like a tired hound's. "It is the blood he has lost," said Jacques, and Lambert added, "We should have fetched the sorcerer from the Lorrainers."

This sorcerer was said to have the power to restore the blood to a wounded man with pieces of magnetized iron. But how could they pay him? "For Brother Barnabé, surely even a Turk would ask nothing."

Marie came, holding a pewter goblet between her hands as carefully as if it had been the Holy Sacrament. "I have got some wine," she said, "good wine. From Father Thibaut, God reward him. Take care, it's full to the brim." Alix raised the sick man's head and put the goblet to his lips. He drank a sip, controlling the quivering of his jaw for fear of losing a drop of the precious wine —as though that mattered now! The wine turned to vinegar in his mouth, while the others stood around watching with trusting pleasure, happy to have found this poor goblet of wine, happy to find anything from which to snatch a little comfort for themselves.

That night Jean-Marc's wife went mad. She was a good woman, a skillful weaver who had once boasted that she could make a piece of cloth fine enough to go through a ring, a woman who knew what to do to help in childbirth and how to sew up gaping wounds, a woman who would not have cut short her evening prayers even if her cart were on fire. During the procession she had been so shocked to see what the infidels were doing to the holy crosses that she had begun to dance up and down on the spot and scream, but she was not alone in that.

She had returned, tired and not herself, and when her two sons tried to make her sit down in a good place by the fire she had thrust them away roughly. Then she began to say that she had guessed it all, she knew the men on the wall well enough and they were Duke Godfrey and his brother Eustace and Count Robert. They had daubed their faces with soot deliberately and gone up on the wall to insult God. She had seen through their plot, she knew they had sold themselves to the infidels. Her sons and her Armenian daughters-in-law tried to calm her, but she did not know them. "You should be ashamed, my fine lords," she said. "I am not what you think. I am a decent woman! I know they have thought up this devilry to take the pilgrims' wives. I know because Duke Godfrey came to my tent yesterday to ravish me."

The daughters-in-law ran to find Jean-Marc, but when she saw him coming it was worse: she only shrieked with laughter, and pulling off her coif and after it her skirt and her shift, she ran toward the fire, leaping and dancing, all naked as she was. Her breasts and buttocks sagged like half-empty sacks, and she whirled around and around so fast that her braids flew out in the air and struck in the face any that tried to come near her. And all the while she was shrieking and laughing and calling out, "Who wants this pretty girl? Who'll take a fine girl? Who'll have my maidenhead?" until even the most hardened men stopped their ears and shut their eyes.

She paused for a moment and stared into the fire, her grey eyes fixed on the flames and shining so brightly that they seemed to squint. The marks of wisdom had vanished like snow from her grave, homely face. The careworn wrinkles on her brow, the lines at the corners of her mouth, had all gone and her lips were parted in a sly, happy smile as if she understood something at last and was congratulating herself on her cleverness. Those who were standing around the fire dared not move or speak, hoping she would come to her senses, and Jean-Marc, seeing her a little calmer, tried to throw a cloak around her shoulders. "No, King of the Turks," she said and laughed, "I want none of your ermine mantle. I am not for you but for any man who will take me! Come, my fine sirs, take me, all of you, my garden is open to you!" And she threw herself down on her back and writhed like a woman in the throes of love, but when the men tried to take hold of her to bind her, she slipped through their hands like an eel and began to run. She was a woman past forty and suffered from a stiffness in her joints, but it was as though age and infirmity had fallen away from her along with her wits, for she ran lightly as a young mountain goat, her arms in the air.

She ran off, a white figure like a big pale turnip, her dark hair swinging down her back. Some ran after her but none could catch her, and they saw her white shape flutter away and disappear behind the outworks of the Brabançon camp.

"Oh God, the shame of it," the men said. "Will the Brabançons respect her?" The shrill gaiety of her mad laughter still echoed in their ears. Jean-Marc's elder son had fallen on the ground and lay rigid and unconscious. They thought at first that he was dead, but soon brought him to himself by burning him. Then, in the midst of all the tumult, Lambert suddenly stepped up to the Picards' fire, and drawing himself up to his full height on his long legs, began declaiming in a high, singing voice like a cantor in church: "God shows us the punishment of pride! Praise the just God who confounds the hypocrites!" Jacques had enough presence of mind to go up behind him and fell him with a blow on the head, because if he had not there would certainly have been a fight with knives drawn, for which this was neither the time nor the place.

Brother Barnabé raised himself on his elbow and tried to sit up. "What is going on?"

"Jean-Marc's wife has gone mad."

"Lie still, Brother Barnabé," Alix said. "You will do more good by praying for her."

He let his head fall back. Mad—mad—mad—well, he thought, she will recover. People get over it. Just then it seemed to him unimportant compared with the deadly tiredness in his bones. Why were they all so frightened?

Jean-Marc was standing quite still, stiff and rigid as though struck by lightning. His sons were beside him and his daughters-in-law were wailing.

Madness of this kind was not uncommon. In two years many pilgrims had shed their reason in the same way, and their clothes along with it, but it was a dreadful thing to see a woman, and a woman in general well respected, in such a state. If she recovers her senses, Lord Jesus, she will hang herself for shame!

Brother Imbert climbed onto the big stone near the Picards' fire and made the sign of the cross. "Brothers, friends, do not distress yourselves. Think that our sister Ludivine, Jean-Marc's wife, has been given a great mark of grace. For you all know that she was almost a perfect woman, only lacking in a little humility, which was only natural considering the number of her virtues. By humbling her as He has done this night Our Lord means to show His great love for this soul. He has made her a martyr!

"And let none of you be shocked, for she has shown herself as we all are. Our nakedness is no fairer than hers and the hidden desires of our hearts may be more shameful. So shall we all be at the Day of Judgment, when all that was hidden is revealed. Brothers, God has granted her the grace of stripping her while she yet lives. She will have drunk her cup of shame and will enter into death as pure as a newborn babe. Let none condemn the chosen creature for this suffering!"

The men wept as they listened to him, and even the small boys who had laughed at Mère Ludivine's madness gaped. Jean-Marc neither moved nor spoke. He was a stubborn man. Even in paradise, sitting beside Saint Michael and Saint Gabriel, there could be no escape from such dishonor.

"Oh, that was a good speech. He is a saint," said Alix. Brother Barnabé had heard it, but his thoughts kept returning obstinately to himself and his own sufferings. He almost envied Jean-Marc's wife. What is it, he thought, that makes a man keep hold on his reason, retain his memory, keep on bearing on his shoulders the heavy head which even in his extreme agony still tries to collect his thoughts and call back to life the old man already falling apart? Why not start to laugh like a hyena, howl like a wolf? Why not simply let go the reins, like this woman who for three years has gone through hell with her head held high? At Dorylaeum, on the day of the battle, she moved among the enemy arrows with her two buckets of water, as straight and proud as if she were crossing some village square. No one judges you now, wife of Jean-Marc, for you yourself have ceased to judge.

Our Father. This is the day, this is the hour. Your servant is poorer than on the day of his baptism, all his talents wasted or buried, grant him a few more days, a little respite, time to find his way again!

The heart that has bled for so many friends grows slack and cold as a squashed toad, yet even now it tries to beat, pounding so furiously in your chest that it blots out all other sounds. Mighty is the terror of the flesh. Thirst. Alix was there, raising his head and holding the cup. Shame on you, letting yourself droop on a woman's breast, like a child! "I can still hold the cup for myself," he said.

The sky paled. They were all there, sitting around him, crouched on the stony ground. *Holy Land.* Cruel indeed, if even God suffered here. There they are, grey and haggard-eyed after a sleepless night, and not one of them thinks to fetch a priest. They were all waiting until he asked for one himself. They have loved me so much and already their love is a long way off, the warmth of their love no longer warms me. Le Grêlé bent forward; his long face with the white pockmarks was grave and his eyes were like a whipped dog's.

"Brother Barnabé."

"What is it?"

"It is I, Élie le Grêlé."

"Élie? I did not think it was the prophet." Élie grinned, the fixed, rigid grin that never failed to make him look stupid, glad to see that Brother Barnabé could still answer so well.

"Brother Barnabé."

"What is it?"

"Philotheus."

"What about him?"

"I did it." That hurt. Hurt badly. Brother Barnabé shut his eyes.

"It does not matter now. Leave me."

"Do you forgive me?"

"It is not for me to forgive you." Le Grêlé gave a sigh of resignation. He had known what Brother Barnabé would say.

If he has told me that, the sick man was thinking, it must be because he can see that I have not long left. Aloud he said, "Jacques." Jacques started out of a doze.

"What is it, Brother Barnabé?"

"Fetch a priest. Father Albert, if you can—if he can come."

"Better the healer, Brother Barnabé! You are not going to leave us, just before the assault?"

"Never mind. You will see Jerusalem without me."

"Oh God," said Jacques, "it will be sad to enter without you!"

In the dawn, the pilgrims climbed the hill in long lines for the first mass. Father Thibaut, a canon of Lille, celebrated it in the open air in full view of the holy city. The altar was set up facing the rising sun and to the right, beyond the long rows of tents, the white city lay, its walls bristling with scaffolding and mangonels.

In another week, if God wills, we shall be hearing mass in the churches of Jerusalem! Even those who said it dared not believe it and their hearts contracted with fear at a joy that seemed too near for safety.

They dragged themselves along, fevered, numbed, with dry throats and burning eyes, shivering with cold and staring with eyes of terror at the light breaking over the horizon: as though they were not used to it, as though they had hoped to see clouds there, as though fatigue had weakened their minds and borne them back in spirit to their own lands. Oh, sweet land where it rains in summer, where the grass is always green!

There had been little sleep that night.

Jean-Marc walked beside Brother Imbert, who carried his cross high in the air. What had become of Mère Ludivine, no one knew. The Brabançons had not set eyes on her. Jacques and Guillaume walked on either side of Lambert, holding his wrists because there was no denying that Lambert was a little out of his mind and had had words with Jean-Marc's sons. They had to keep reminding him: "Think of Jesus Christ. He suffered worse insults than you."

Such a quiet, decent lad, to lose his head like that only a few days before the great assault! "Brother Barnabé is dying," Jacques said, "and you can worry about what people say."

"I have forgotten it, Jacques. My mind is all confused. I snap at everything I see, like a mad dog that must bite something."

"Well, after the assault you shall bite the infidels."

Jacques and Guillaume laughed delightedly at this, but Lambert's eyes were troubled and there was a touch of foam about his lips as he said, "What are they waiting for? There has been time to die ten times over since they first promised the assault!" And whatever they said to him made him weep with anger.

During the mass several perfectly sane men in good health saw visions: crosses in the sky and white flames starting up on the churches of Jerusalem. They saw them quite clearly: great tongues of flame, white and smokeless, rushing heavenward from the towers and domes. Then the good Bishop of Le Puy was seen once again (for he had already appeared several times before). He passed through the ranks of kneeling men, walking without touching the ground, his hands joined palm to palm, his brow serene and grave. His garments were bright and clean, his beard shining, and it was clear that he was already enjoying the peace of Jesus Christ and that his enemies were wrong to believe him in purgatory. Many people saw him and were not afraid. On the eve of such great events it was natural for heaven and earth to come close together.

It is not death he foretells but life in Jesus Christ and victory at hand.

On the way back from mass, Marie saw an angel with blue wings walking toward the camp of the Picards, a very tall angel whose head rose higher than the mountaintop, swinging a censer which gave off a white smoke. "Do you see the angel, my Pierre? He is coming for Brother Barnabé."

The child, trotting sturdily at her side, answered, "Yes, I see him." But he was looking in a different direction. Marie picked him up in her arms and smothered his cheeks with kisses.

"Oh, you little fibber. You can't deceive me. I see you stargazing! The angel is over there. He is by Brother Barnabé now, and he will stay there until noon and then they will go away together."

Honorine from Picardy, walking beside Marie, said, "How can you talk of it so cheerfully?" Marie looked at her vaguely, like someone waking from a dream, then her lips began to tremble and she hugged the child against her and went on walking. The tears came welling up into her throat. Oh Pierre, oh Pierre, what will become of us without him? Oh Pierre, if he could only stay until the day of Jerusalem!

Oh, cruel angel! you were quite right not to look at him. He means to take our friend from us!

The priestess was there with Guillaume's wife leading her, and Rufine from Laon, and Jean-Marc's daughters-in-law and Marie of Calais. Only Alix had remained with Brother Barnabé. They walked quickly, urged on by thirst, but the fear of meeting the angel made them hunch their shoulders as though trying to make themselves smaller. If he so much as brushed you carelessly with his wing, the noonday sun would soon do the rest. Brother Barnabé could at least be sure of his place in paradise. "For him, Marie, it is a good day."

"Oh no, friends, surely not. He will pine for us. How unkind of God to try and part those that love one another."

"Stupid, how can God be bad?"

"Of course He can, He can do anything."

The two Armenians, who understood French, shook their heads: this was wrong, it was blasphemy, but this Frankish woman was protected; surely her guardian angel must love her dearly, for nearly all the infants in the company had died but hers was strong and handsome.

As soon as his mass was finished, Father Albert hurried to Brother Barnabé's side. When he saw him lying on the ground, grey-faced and gasping like a fish out of water, he crossed himself. God have mercy on him, he will not last the day. Then, when their eyes met, he forgot all about it: he knew those eyes so well, large, brown and shadowed, the eyes of a weary eagle. O death, where is thy sting? O grave, where is thy victory? He sat on the ground beside the sick man, hugging his knees.

"Courage, brother," he said. "Good news. A caravan of corn and wine is coming from Jaffa this very night. The good Patriarch is sending it to us from Cyprus. Once the victuals have been shared out, the barons will give the signal to begin the attack!"

"High time," said Brother Barnabé.

From a force of habit stronger than pain, Father Albert's voice took him back to a time when he had strength for argument. High time, he thought. Before Antioch there was no lack of water.

". . . and this time we shall win. They are holding a great council of war today. I have been talking to some Greek spies. Things are going badly in the city. People are burying their money and selling their houses for a tenth of what they are worth."

"Spies . . . always say that." Brother Barnabé's voice was a cracked whisper. His lips hardly moved, and in his heart another voice mocked silently: What is that to you now?

"Only yesterday they crucified three Greek monks!"

"As good news goes," Brother Barnabé croaked, "I've heard better."

"It's a good sign. They are losing their heads. A messenger arrived with promises from Cairo and the crowd in the market-place came near to stoning him. They do not expect reinforcements before the end of Ramadan. The rich are already fortifying their houses."

"It will be a hard fight," said Brother Barnabé.

"Brother, once our men are inside the city, the city's doomed. They can never defend themselves, not with all their women and children, the townspeople and the poor. The panic will be too great. It will be a real Last Judgment, you will see. One man of ours will kill ten of theirs."

"*A doomed city,*" Brother Barnabé said. "*Jerusalem.*"

Father Albert said that this was sure and certain, sure and certain. God Himself was putting fresh heart into the soldiers, and it was wonderful to see how joyfully all the men were waiting for the assault, how in all the camps they were going wild with joy, how even the sick felt suddenly better, so eager were they to enter into Jerusalem on their own feet and with their weapons in their hands.

Brother Barnabé listened. He wanted to speak but he could not, yet there were things he wished to say to this man. What? Father, *confiteor.* I have sinned. Many souls have been saved in this business, but many more have been lost. Why has God made His people suffer such ordeals? I have sinned against you, father, for but for me you would not be here.

"God alone can judge . . ." Jerusalem, great bleeding heart, Jerusalem the white-hot stone burning away our sins, the one place on earth where love is real—

the other man was still talking. The assault? Yes, the assault, *tomorrow*—

. . . they found the Sepulcher open

the stone rolled away. Why seek ye the living among the dead? We have longed with such great longing—I have longed with such great longing—to see and to touch—as a moth burns itself in the flame and is still drawn to it—a drunken soul forgets all and is drawn to the one true sun and sucked into a vortex of light THERE SHALL BE NO MORE SUN NOR MOON NOR NIGHT NOR DAY THERE FOR GOD SHALL BE THE ONLY LIGHT, FATHER FORGIVE THEM, FATHER WE ARE STRAWS

IN THE VALLEY OF THE SHADOW OF DEATH I WILL FEAR NO EVIL
thou shalt not be afraid for the terror by night
nor for the arrow that flieth by day
nor for the pestilence that walketh in darkness
nor for the destruction that wasteth at noonday
thou shalt tread upon the lion and adder

"Brother! Brother Barnabé!" He felt hands raising his head. Oh God, now he wants to confess me, and not before time! No strength to talk. "Wake up, brother, let me give you absolution at least."

"*Pater, peccavi.* Absolve me."

Brother Barnabé saw his forty years of life transformed under Father Albert's shaking hand into a clean white sheet. Nothing remained.

If I forget thee, O Jerusalem. Father Albert had shriven hundreds of dying men, but for once he was out of his depth. This man with his glazing eyes and shallow breathing made him feel as if a great stone had suddenly evaporated in his hands. He said, "He is still alive, give him some water and he will come around." The poor of Arras crept nearer, and Alix poured some water into the dying man's mouth and over his face. "It is the heat," Father Albert said. "He cannot breathe. He will be better soon."

"You would do better, Father Albert," said Alix, "to say the prayers for the dying."

And Brother Barnabé died.

A little before noon, at the time when the heat was so fierce that men who went bareheaded were struck down by it. They had stretched a cloth above him, and when he ceased to breathe they crossed his hands on his breast.

His face was the color of a smoky candle, and they were suddenly frightened to see how thin he was: the bones of his nose and forehead and cheeks stood out as though the flesh had all receded from his face, and his beard, still brown, lay in hanks. His mouth was shut fast in curiously stubborn lines. Already the vermin were deserting the body and running over his clothes and on the cloth placed beneath his head.

It was so hot that the women had no strength to wail, and they wept silently while the men lay under awnings of sacks or in the shade of the rocks and discussed the burial. They must have some strong cloth and some sound boards and not dig a proper grave, so that it would be easier to transport the body into Jerusalem. On the day we enter the city, he shall enter it with us, and his coffin shall touch the Holy Sepulcher.

This is not a day of mourning. Our friend has gone the better to aid us. He will go and plead our cause before Jesus Christ. He has gone on the eve of the great battle, he is with each one of us now, his great strength is released and he can share it among us as he will. He will become the real avenger of Jesus Christ.

Toward evening, the children went up the hill to watch for the arrival of the caravan from Jaffa. Praise God! There will be enough for us also, the good Duke has had it cried through all the camps. There will be corn for the poor and for every man of an age to fight, a double ration.

The knights shall go first, and then the soldiers, and after them the poor pilgrims, and then the Tafurs that do not fear death, all shall have their part in the task. God is not miserly; all, even the Greeks and Syrians if they will, for they too are able-bodied men, they have scythes and pitchforks and knives!

• • •

At night, after prayers and food, they buried the dead. In the Picard camp there were Brother Barnabé and a youth dead of sunstroke. It was not a proper wake night, everyone was too excited. Feverishly excited and glad with a strange gladness that made them utter incongruous cries and laugh as men laugh on the edge of the abyss. Deep in their hearts no one dared believe it: the barons would not agree or the siege towers would catch fire, or an Egyptian army would appear on the Jaffa road, but these things they said to propitiate fate. Do not believe, friends, do not think it is a little thing. To deserve such joy the ordeal must be hard and terrible, the day is not yet come . . .

Perhaps it may be at New Year's, at Easter, that this will come to pass, for it will be the year eleven hundred, the year of the new century, the first day of a new century. Those who said this were those who believed it least, yet even they were sure the miracle would happen. Tomorrow or the next day, with God's help and that of His army.

Tomorrow.

One more day and after that—instead of days a great light and a glory without end, for even those who did not believe in miracles and dreamed only of plunder could not imagine what it would be like when the city was taken.

It was a proud and noble city and if it was smaller than Antioch, it was ten times holier: it was all holy, a reliquary city, the whole city a relic. In other places a reliquary no bigger than a child's coffin would be carried in procession: here it was the whole city, with all its streets and houses and churches: the very steps of its stairways were holy and pilgrims carried away as relics the humblest stones picked up from the ground.

See the miracle of the Devil: as though swine were to feed on the Holy Sacrament and wallow in the consecrated wine, as though dung were carried on altar cloths, a vision incredible, a miracle of hell! God has permitted it, but the time has come. He will permit it no longer.

Already God has given us the victory. All is accomplished. Jerusalem is delivered. The cup is poured, and these hours that are so long for you are to God as the flash of a lifted sword. The sword is already raised, it shines, it falls on the enemy's neck!

You bear within you God's anger for this outrage. Forget all else and let this day of waiting be to you as brief as a lightning flash. Commend your souls to God, for tomorrow it is He who will direct the battle.

As the thunderbolt falls on the valley and turns it into a single sea of iron, so fired by the sacred anger of God, you will be one single soul with a thousand bodies, a torrent of flame with a thousand tongues!

From East to West, from Persia to Constantinople, from Cairo to the Black Sea, you will show them all tomorrow how mighty is your God.

That day Peter preached from the hilltop, bareheaded in the full sun, the silver cross between his raised hands flashing in the bright sun. Angels cooled him with the beating of their invisible wings, making his long hair blow about his shoulders.

"You have shed so many tears, but your sufferings shall not have been in vain! This day on which, for love of His poor, God gives the Christians victory shall be remembered for a thousand years.

"Let not your hearts fail amid the horrors of battle: *you have already conquered.* This night I have received the pledge of it. I see all the dead of this battle already living and transfigured, shining like suns in the heavenly Jerusalem."

"What of the living, Peter? What shall their glory be?"

"That, my children, I cannot tell you yet. God forbids me to reveal His designs to those souls that have not yet completed their pilgrimage. Pray, all of you, and refrain from sin, you who are bidden to the wedding feast."

It was a day of prayer and penitence. The proudest knights were to be seen kneeling humbly to their comrades, even to their sergeants, and asking forgiveness. Others went about the camps of the poor and right up to the lepers' palisade, giving away such wealth as they had left, coins and silver objects and even their crystal buttons. The ladies with the army, dressed that day in coarse wool with coifs of rough linen on their heads and riding humbly on donkeys, went around the camps, pausing especially in the poor pilgrims' quarters, and with their own hands poured out water for all who came to drink. In their zeal and devotion, they even visited the whores, who had been placed in the old sheepfolds, for there had been no sheep since the previous day, and these poor girls, who were for the most part baptized Syrians, received more gifts from the ladies than they ever got from the men. (Jean-Marc's wife had been found among them, but as she persisted in going about naked she had been bound and put in a cart.)

The camp seemed quiet, so quiet that the enemy garrison on the walls became uneasy, realizing that something important was about to happen. Count Raymond's wooden tower was nearly set ablaze by Greek fire because the oxhides dried quickly in the hot sun and as they caught fire they had to be detached with long poles and thrown into the moat. While this was being done a rain of arrows and abuse was maintained from the walls and the tops of the towers.

Mangy curs, stinking jackals, shame on your Mahomet! We spit in his face, gouge out his eyes, tear out his beard! We will drive you back to your Mecca, and make it a sty for pigs!

Dogs of Christians, worshippers of wood, not one of you shall enter this city alive, unless with your arms bound, for execution. You are good for nothing but to fatten kites!

There were interpreters on both sides, but they were beginning to understand a good deal even in Arabic. Death to you, dogs of Mahomet! We would not have your wives for our whores. They shall be skewered like pigs and your children roasted alive on the ends of our spears!

Idolatrous pagans, worshippers of three gods, when you are dead of thirst we shall make the wood of your crosses into pointed stakes and come and finish you off like dogs! You are not worth our arrows or our swords.

The army of our Vizier is already approaching, they are lions and you are jackals, they will fill ten ships with your heads and take them back to Cairo.

Oh, you dogs! God has already judged you and delivered you into our hands. Tomorrow you shall pay for all that we have suffered by your fault.

Is there really a day when desire becomes possession, when the promise becomes the reality, today and tomorrow joined in a single day and the pilgrim becomes the master of the house? *It can never be.*

The sky rippled with tiny flames and quivered like a taut hide stretched to breaking. Vipers crept out continually from holes in the walls, turned into yellow flames, and flew away into the air. Little flickers of lightning darted from man to man, driving like thorns into the flesh.

We are not mercenaries.

From every eye came a myriad circling sparks and the circles became spirals, turning and turning in an ever-widening gyre that eventually filled the whole horizon. Above the clamor of the camp, men heard a sound like a piercing cry, a howling and a singing that went on and on, the sound of a day that no man had yet seen.

No man, however wise or holy, has ever been able to make tomorrow into today, but out of the depths of God's thought the morrow was crying out and ringing in the ears of men until the very air vibrated with it. The sun poured down in torrents of invisible flames upon the stony hillsides, on the tent pegs, and on the walls and minarets of the city, with such intensity that it seemed as if at any moment everything would burst into flame.

There will be no tomorrow.

The men were working on the siege towers, and criers were sent out to recruit more laborers. The ropes and tackle of the flying bridges were greased. *Brothers, do not despise the work of men.* God is at work here. The wisdom of the barons, the strength of the knights, the carpenters' skill, and the soldiers' courage: all this is the work of God whose will it is that His whole creation shall share in the great work of salvation. Let all men obey the barons this day as they would angels out of heaven.

Two more priests had seen the Bishop of Le Puy. He was accompanied by a man of such great beauty that they could scarcely endure to look at him. All made of rock crystal and starlight, he seemed, and the good Bishop walked beside him dressed in white and bearing the martyr's palm, and rays like the noonday sun shone from his miter.

Do not be afraid if you should see your dead appear. Those who have fallen in this campaign for Jesus Christ are not like common dead. They do not come to summon you but to claim what God has promised them. God owes them a debt.

All men shall drink tonight, even the thieves and the forsworn, tonight all shall be pardoned and men in chains shall be released so that they too may win redemption tomorrow. As soon as the first heat of the day was past, the order was given to those farthest from the city to strike camp.

Let them see us coming. Let them know we still have men

enough, let them see us pouring like a torrent down the valleys!

They know us. We bring no useless mouths. Let even our lame beggars covered with sores strike fear into them, and those that have no staves arm themselves with tent pegs, shafts, and bags of stones.

Let all hold themselves in readiness behind the camps of the barons and the archers' lines. For God and Jesus Christ! All have sworn the oath that tomorrow there will be no retreat; if any men-at-arms give ground, then let the pilgrims drive them back to the wall or beat them down with staves.

When they pour down their rivers of fire on us from the walls, then cursed be any man that turns back.

Two men, fugitives from the city, had been found hiding under a heap of burnt hides near the moat. "Mercy," they said, "mercy, we wish to become Christians." But one of them carried a knife in his belt. They were killed and their bodies flayed and the skins hung up on the Duke's tower with the oxhides. The rumor went around that they had been sent by Iftikhar to kill Duke Godfrey, and the Duke's knights swore to have the skin of Iftikhar himself to punish him for such treachery.

For whatever people say, it is not to be believed that Iftikhar and his men are devils and wear horns concealed beneath their turbans, for God knows how many heads have been cut off before this, and none, however large their turbans, have ever been found with horns. The wickedness of these men is in their souls, and their bodies are made of ordinary flesh which is easily destroyed.

Those devils there are among them will escape whatever is done to them. When you cut them it is like cutting water, it leaves no mark. When a missile is aimed at them it stops in midflight and turns around. But if you call on Jesus Christ with a pure heart as you strike, then the devil makes a hissing sound and vanishes, leaving nothing behind but the clothes and the armor.

How can anyone believe such things? They are men and for all they may be proud and well fed, they are no more magicians than the Turks of Antioch.

The men of Arras had hidden Brother Barnabé's coffin in a crevice in the rocks that formed a kind of small cave. The children, tired out by the heat, took turns going in and lying on the coffin to find shade. No one stopped them. Brother Barnabé would never have grudged anyone a place in the shade. The candles for your vigil, brother, shall be the fires of battle: see the flaming arrows they are firing at Duke Godfrey's tower. We will all go to the ramparts, and the ditches before every gate will be choked with dead.

The men were preparing their weapons. Anything would serve, even stones and wooden mallets. Jacques and Élie had their axes, Guillaume his Turkish spear, and Bernard his long knife firmly attached to a staff. They sat on the rocks, silent, grave, and impatient as candlebearers awaiting the ringing of the bell which is their cue to join in the procession. Is all ready? We still have many prayers to say, but vespers is a long way off and the night will be long.

We must sleep, comrades, Peter has ordered it. In sleep God will send us strength and we shall awake while it is still night, at the hour of prime.

Jean-Marc came up to Élie and laid a hand on his shoulder. "I shall not dispute the leadership with you. As far as the battle goes, you are in command. My Picards will obey you. I did not come on pilgrimage to kill."

"That is not right, Jean-Marc," Jacques said. "This is God's work and you are as strong as any other man."

"I shall go to aid my friends. But le Grêlé will be more use to you in the battle."

"That is so," Élie said. "If you promise to obey me also, then I am willing."

The Picards were not pleased, but since Jean-Marc had voluntarily resigned his place there was nothing to be said. Not for nothing had God humbled Jean-Marc and glorified the people of Arras by calling Brother Barnabé to Himself.

The women were busy padding the men's caps with straw and dry grass, mending belts and straps. They had no energy to spare even for singing. That day seemed to have been the hottest ever and the flies buzzed around their heads more viciously than yesterday, enveloping them in a shifting black net. How was Mère Ludivine? No one dared to mention her. They were afraid of the malignant devil lurking in their own throats, making them want to scream like women in childbed and copy the poor creature's shrieks of insane laughter just to see, only to see, if it would ease their hearts.

"Sing, Marie, and we will join in the choruses."

"Oh my friends, there is a time for everything. We will sing tomorrow."

Tomorrow the carrion shall be consecrated bread.

Who, oh who would turn into a fly, a wasp, and fly, circling up into the air, above the siege towers and over the wall into the city—

It is not far, you could be there on foot in half an hour, but all around it is a wall of fire, and who would do the same as Peter Bartholomew? The Holy Lance did not save him but we, we have the Holy Cross in our hearts.

An invisible wall of fire, thought Marie, trembling and shimmering, its tongues licking the sky.

There will be more dead than living.

. . . and suppose it is true what they say, the Tafurs who go about naked, that this will be the end of the world and there will be no more living or dead?

All slain, heathen and Christian, down to the smallest child, even the lepers, and so long as there remains a single creature left alive in all Jerusalem the trumpets of hell shall sound the charge so that none may hear the voice of Jesus Christ! Happy the man who has the strength to pray.

It would be no victory if everyone were killed. Oh, you cursed flies, stop trying to devour our eyes. Go into the city, to the Devil your father, and eat the heathens, they are fatter than we are!

The boys were playing at killing infidels, but there were not really any infidels, not even dead ones. They had made puppets from sticks and waterskins with holes in them and were practicing shooting with the bows that they had made in the camp beside the Jordan. They still had some Turkish arrows left. They shot well, and when the puppets were stuck full of arrows they smashed them with stones and dragged them on the ground and danced around them. They were Iftikhar and the Vizier and Calixtus and Mahomet and Mahomet's wife.

> The blackbird sings and the meadow is gay
> Now sings the lark and blooms the may
> Arlette sings, for her wool is spun.

"If you will have me, I will be your man.
The skylark sings and winter is fled
I will give you the Vizier's head
And the heart of Iftikhar the dread."
"If you would have me, you must pay the price."
"I will give you the Vizier's head
And we two will live in paradise."
"For you alone I spun my thread
And you shall love me till you are dead!"
In Jerusalem the knot will be tied
Godfrey the Duke leads forth the bride.
Jerusalem has risen betimes
Decked with thyme and eglantine
Decked with arms and Turkish heads.
    O Jerusalem, washed in blood
    So long mourned, so well avenged
    On Mahomet and all his kind.

And one for me, and one for you! And one, two, three, there's nothing left alive! Gouge out their eyes, rip out their guts—

"Hey, you boys, that's enough of that shouting! The Devil will jump down your throats."

They whipped themselves up until they were half mad with excitement, whirling around and around until they could not stop, bawling their tuneless songs which in the end became no more than one shrill, endless scream. God knows where they found the energy. "Ah well," the men said, "let them tire themselves out and then they will sleep." They were a pathetic enough sight, thin, gangling, sunburnt creatures with eyes like drunkards and parched lips, so accustomed to being thirsty that they no longer asked for water except when it was given out.

They were happy because Élie had promised to take them with the men. They were to go into the city when the pilgrims' turn came, and each should kill his Turk, or more.

Alix took off her skirt and her long shift and put on the clothes of the boy who had died the previous day, and stuck a hatchet in her belt. With a woolen cap over her short-cropped hair, she looked like some strange kind of youth, already too old to be smooth-chinned. Her companions stared at her uneasily, thinking what a handsome boy she would have made. In better clothes she might have been taken for the holy archangel Michael! She was so slim and held herself so straight, and her fine, tanned features had recovered so much of their old grace under this deceptive masculine guise.

"Not that you look very fierce with that hatchet," Honorine said. "If it was a pike, now . . . or something a bit longer." The priestess, who was still blind, sighed when they told her and said it was a pity, that Alix had kept a good head on her until then but now she was madder than Mère Ludivine, and this was no time to play the mountebank. Alix laughed, softly and happily because she was fond of the priestess.

"You are right, sister, and I thank you for saying what you have. In these days there is no life or death, reason or madness, good or evil any more, everything is confused and we have all lost our way. I have more strength in my arms than a boy of thirteen, and God grant they may send my severed head back to you in camp. I ask for no better death."

Marie rose and put both arms around Alix's neck and kissed her hard on both cheeks. "May God protect you. Do not say such things! Tomorrow will bring life, not death. We shall see no more severed heads unless they belong to the infidels!" She buried her face in Alix's shoulder and wept, sobbing like a little child, and her grip was so tight that Alix was alarmed and feared she was falling into a fit. "Hush now," she said, "you will frighten your little Pierre."

Marie let go and huddled on the ground, her head in her arms, fighting to overcome her sobs. "Oh, enough, enough. We have all wept enough. As well to die! Oh Jacques, they shall not cut off your head! Or I will cut off theirs!"

"Oh God," said the priestess, "oh God, make us a day older or we shall all be stark raving mad."

The men had gone to the Brabançon camp in search of news. "Well, Saint-John, what about you? Aren't you armed? Surely now is the time to ascend living into heaven?"

"Do not mock, my friends. In this tumult wise men lose their heads and fools find theirs. It is said: A woman in travail is in pain, for her time is come upon her. Happy are those whose hearts shall not burst in pieces."

• • •

The knights have taken counsel and made wise decisions and prepared the attack in such a way that with God's help they are virtually certain of gaining a foothold on the walls and winning the gates. And if there are any fainthearts with the army, let them not rejoice. It is inside the city that the battle will be fought.

Do not think you will enter it as you did Antioch. There are few Christians here, and they have all fled to shelter behind convent walls and cannot come out. They will be no help to us, for they themselves stand in great peril of their lives.

There are fifty thousand Moslems in the city and more, and also many Jews. We are not half their number, indeed far short of it, and the barons have need of every man, for there will be fighting in the streets and in the houses.

But fear not, God has already delivered them into our hands. They have been weighed, judged, and condemned, like the impious Balthazar and the people of Jericho. For three whole days the barons will grant unlimited rights of pillage. Each house will be his that enters it first, each thing his that takes it, rich or poor, soldier or wandering beggar! No prisoners, better to feed the vultures than the heathen. Every infidel spared is a knife in your back.

Well said, friends, and may the barons' attack be successful. They can count on the men. A city once breached is lost.

Three days, friends! We must work fast. The Normans and the Brabançons will take everything first. "Oh, the fools!" Élie said. "Talking of plunder before the attack is even begun. A fine way to remember Jesus Christ."

"A fine way of serving God," said Jean-Marc, "using the Devil's tools: for what is a mortal sin in Lille or Maubeuge is more than ever in the holy city of Jerusalem. Murder and theft have never been acts of piety."

"Well, Gilbert, where is your Armageddon? We shall take the city in spite of all your prophecies."

"Wait, doubters," Gilbert said. "Even if we do take it, this will be only a respite, for this is not yet the true Jerusalem but only its earthly image, and well known to have been captured time and again. But the real, the one true day will come only after many signs and portents, and we may not live long enough to see them. For it is written that the great kings of the earth shall gather for this battle, and where are the kings? And even in our own lands we have no great kings, only dwarves for whom the crown of Charlemagne would make a belt."

"But look, Gilbert, down there in the crowd, by the Flemish tents. Do you not see the white columns of men moving to and fro and shining like the sun?"

"I see nothing of the kind."

"That proves that you have not the gift of sight. They are the souls of the blessed dead."

With the appearance of the first star, the noise ceased on the walls. The prayers began. Up there, the infidels too were praying to their God. They were breaking their fast of Ramadan and drinking cold water.

Christians, drink tonight, but let each company keep back some water for tomorrow, and let jars of water be put in the trenches. It is right that the knights and their men should have double rations, for theirs will be the hardest task.

The trumpets rang out. Share the water and the wine, Christians, and give thanks to Jesus Christ for His goodness! You have not died of hunger or of thirst, and if God wills you shall drink again tomorrow night.

The trumpets rang out. Remember, brothers, we were hungrier than this at Antioch, before the finding of the Holy Lance. Inside the city they have fountains, cisterns, good fresh water. Tomorrow night, if God wills—

Heads and bodies shall be reunited

the living and the dead shall be reunited.

Our dead from Hungary and our dead from Syria, our dead from Anatolia and the great desert. All those who died of thirst in the desert.

Our dead from Antioch.

and the martyrs of Nicaea.

Our dead from Syria and our dead from Jerusalem. If we had to avenge them all, each man would have more than twenty pagans to kill

And the women?

Shame on the man who, even before God has made known His Judgment, thinks to make the city of Jesus Christ a city of fornication! And even if the order cannot be given, let all Christian men respect God and let there be no rape!

Their women are unclean, like hyenas, like fruits rotten within, and let those inside the city not think that we have come so far to take their women. Our own, thin and ragged as they are, are to theirs as lilac flowers compared with thistles.

That night a young Picard boy named Gerbaud fell into fits and began to prophesy: he saw the four horsemen of the Apocalypse come down the hill and ride toward the camp; he saw the gates of the city open wide; he saw the streets and squares, and the gigantic horsemen were crushing the houses beneath their horses' hoofs. And the face of him that carried the sword was red as the rising moon

and the face of him that carried the balance was like a cloud of smoke

and the face of him that carried a bow and arrows was of silver

and he that sat on the pale horse ran with blood from head to foot and his eyes were no more than gaping holes crawling with flies.

As if an angel had lifted him up into the air, he saw the city full of white houses and the horsemen went through it like a rushing wind and it was filled with blood and the blood became a flood, a river in spate, it rose as high as the rooftops and covered the roofs. The boy cried out, "I see! I see! I swear it!" He was tense and vibrating like a taut string and blood trickled from his nostrils. Father Imbert wrapped him in his cloak and prayed.

"Fear not, brothers, the judgment is on the infidel, not on the Christians."

Jacques stared into the fire, polishing the iron head of his ax with dry earth. May it shine like new tomorrow! What he saw in the fire was fine houses and gardens more beautiful than those of Antioch, with pink marble fountains where the water spouted from lions' heads. He was dreaming.

"Hey, Grêlé."

"What?"

"If the houses are to go to those who take them first, we'll try and find out the rich quarters before the knights take all. We'll have a really beautiful house for ourselves."

"As for me," Élie said, "my share of the plunder is six feet underground at Maarat an-Numan. I shall return to Arras poorer than I left it."

"You mean to go home, then?"

"If God wills. Who can tell? Tomorrow may be the day of Armageddon . . . and then there will be no lands anywhere but here."

10 ✠✠✠✠✠✠✠✠✠✠✠✠

O Lord.

Forever and ever. IN SAECULA SAECULORUM INSECULASECULORUM INSECULASECULOR REMEMBER THIS DAY O LORD REMEMBER HOLY MARY MOTHER OF GOD REMEMBER, SAINT PETER SAINT PAUL SAINT MICHAEL AND SAINT GABRIEL, SAINT GEORGE AND SAINT JAMES REMEMBER

FOR THIS DAY WE HAVE ENDURED THREE YEARS OF MARTYRDOM.

We have died and who shall resurrect us?

See: the legions of angels have come down to earth. One at the Gate of David, one at the Sion Gate, one at Herod's Gate, and one at the Jaffa Gate. Night after night the slingstones sped toward the wall and smashed against it furiously one after the next; before you could shut your eyes and mutter half an *Ave*, bang! another stone and then another until your head rocked on your shoulders with the din of crashing stones.

While overhead the wooden birds with iron beaks flew so fast that none could see them coming. They buried their beaks in shields and beams, in leather casques and men's arms. They dug deep into the flesh so that the blood welled out around them and the flesh swelled. Oh, if you could only know, you there behind the walls. Lord, we are weary of this agony! Men walked with their heads down, bent double so that the arrows would pass them by.

The noise was sevenfold: the sound of the stones hitting the walls; the arrows whistling; the wounded screaming; men cursing and marking time: "Heave ho! Heave ho!" The hammers striking the machines; the axles creaking, and worst of all, the missiles falling from the walls.

Before dawn, the sky above the walls began to whiten. Screams. Such a screaming that the morning star trembled on its pearly wall.

The screams above were loud enough to split the sky. The fire arrows flew toward the wooden tower like huge glow-worms in the pale dawn light that made the torches up above gleam yellow. *Veni, Creator Spiritus*—to morning prayers, Christians, for all those fighting up aloft, the singing fires the heart and fills the body, every heart is filled with singing. Bellowing the psalm at the top of their voices, with parched throats and bellies gnawed by the Great Beast, consumed by the Great Flame, Hunger and Thirst the two sisters of the poor, Hunger and Thirst roared out the morning hymn.

And all the while, high up on Herod's wall the Christian shouts were rising above the voices of the infidels.

The fiery arrows fell on boards and shields and the little yellow tongues crackled. Smother them with buckets of earth. Oh, my children, if they were only buckets of water! The sky up there beyond the wall is growing red, up there where the men-at-arms are working the catapults. The chanted prayers are louder. Anyone that cannot sing, let him cry, cry, *cry to God.* He is here—listen, listen, the hiss of arrows is slackening, the wall is yielding, before noon a bridge will be thrown across between the wooden tower and the wall, before noon our men will have a foothold—

will have a foothold. Their feet, their mortal feet on the walls of Jerusalem, their mortal feet, their boots of leather shod with iron will run along the wall and down the steps.

O God, bless Duke Godfrey and Count Eustace his brother. O God, may they eat and drink their fill to the end of their days. O God, may they wash in fresh water every day: those mighty Christians, mighty warriors, beloved men, strong as angry bulls! From end to end of the camp the news was running by word of mouth, the whole camp was roaring, all other sounds were drowned in it, everyone was shouting, everyone was deaf from shouting, while up above the sun rose beyond the wall in a sky of bright blue. The carpenters were working on the wooden tower and no more missiles came to smash their bodies.

Men were clustered up there on the wall, their swords rising and falling, flashing bright in the sun. God help us! Our men have hooked fagots soaked in pitch to the ramparts. The wind is blowing toward the city, and the smoke on the walls is so thick and black that for the Turks it is day turned into night and the fires of hell! The flying bridge has been thrown across and they are fighting on the bridge and on the walls.

Ten scaling ladders were raised, their grapnels fast to the battlements, and a cry went up: "To the gates! To the gates!"

A great silence fell on the camp, as if all hearts had been made suddenly aware in that instant that God was there. They could see, from a long way off they could see that up there on the walls men were standing, men in Christian armor with Christian swords, and they were not fighting, they were pausing for breath.

On the wooden bridge and on the ladders of the siege tower a tide of men was rushing upward so fast the eye could hardly follow them, casques gleaming in the sun: almost at once they were on the walls, lightning flashing from their swords, and then what a cry went up, a cry so terrible that it seemed as if the whole plain before the walls were all one open mouth, shouting for joy. For joy. PRAISE GOD. PRAISE GOD. JESUS CHRIST. THE HEAT AND THIRST WERE CRYING OUT. DRINK JERUSALEM. DRINK TO JERUSALEM. THE BRIGHT SWORDS FLAMED ON THE WALL LIKE SHERDS OF A BROKEN SUN.

The gates. Who can hold back a river in spate? Shattered by the pounding rams, the gates were opening slowly, amid a rending and splintering of iron bars. Gate of paradise, tall, soot-blackened, misshapen from the boulders flung against it, it yielded and there was light beyond, there was sunshine beyond.

The soldiers poured in, forced their way through, jostling and scrambling over bodies and fallen timbers. The battle chargers in their heavy harness moved forward in long lines, snorting and trembling with thirst, and the crowd parted before them. The knights, lances at rest, faces streaming with sweat, rigid as blocks of stone in the saddle, waited their turn in the rush for the open gate.

Our men are already fighting in the city. We need a strong charge now to give the enemy no time to recover.

Their names were known by the devices on their shields, and never had they had such a welcome. Oh friends! Oh fellow Christians, avengers of Jesus Christ, God give you long joy of this world. God shield you, gallant warriors in your mail shirts, kill them all and let not one be left alive!

The horses were stamping and gathering speed. The gate was not wide, they could enter only two abreast, but the cavalry was soon within. No more enemies were left on this side: Duke Godfrey's banner waved on the tower above the gate, its gilded pole shining in the full glory of the morning sun.

Then the angels began coming down from heaven.

Inside the city, they ceased to know if it were day or night.

For they were inside. Make no mistake, all of them, through two wide-open gates, over wooden bridges twelve feet broad. Open, the double gates, the iron bars drawn, the locks burst asunder and the wooden beams as bloody as a butcher's stall. They went in blindly, like a crowd fleeing from a fire: across the moat filled with smoking debris and half-burned corpses and in at the open gate through which the cavalry had already passed.

Over the bodies of the dead, by now so thoroughly trampled that they lay like a deep red litter in the gateway, heads and ribs smashed, bones protruding through the flesh, a tangle of blue entrails mixed with scraps of clothing.

Over all this they walked barefoot, without slipping, because the horses had been over it before and so they trod upon a mash of horse manure with broken bones and teeth, and the men's feet, God be thanked, were hard as horseshoes.

And God be thanked, their ears were so full of the din and shouting that even the most hideous screams came to them muffled, as if through some enormous drumhead. They were screaming themselves, but they did not know it. Ever since dawn the screams had not abated, a screaming that rose above the pounding of the rams, the grinding of wood and stone and metal, the hissing and spitting, rending and groaning, and the dull boom of stone on stone, and the drums beating.

All drowned in the screams of men, men screaming with no human voice but bellowing with rage. There were no voices. The throats of a thousand men transformed into monstrous trumpets braying and thundering and howling for death.

Flayed oxen, wounded bears, a mighty cry of death so powerful that it was a weapon in itself. They fought upon the walls and at the gates, in the towers and on the roofs of the houses near the walls, dying men fought on with the flesh of their faces hanging in ribbons and their bowels half out, heathen and Christian clung to one another like leeches, and often one was dead and still the survivor went on hacking and screaming with rage.

But when they saw through the smoke that the wall was taken

the mangonels overthrown, the banners of the cross raised on the towers, and men with crosses on their tunics swarming along the wall

and the wall free, all defense at an end—

Then, as a sudden squall whips up a storm of sand, within seconds the camp was emptied of soldiers, they passed the wall and were absorbed into the city. It was strange and terrible to see those walls, once so feared and hated, become quite suddenly small and pitiful: it only wanted a few ladders and they could be climbed like an apple tree.

Then the shout went up, then the whole camp was shouting like a woman delivered of a child. Hearts flayed alive, seared by the vitriol of joy.

Lord God, we have won, we are inside, the day is ours!

This great day.

Clouds of smoke and dust were rising from beyond the wall, and the cries of battle, and then other cries. THAT OTHER CRY.

There was not a man, woman, or child in the whole army who did not know that cry deep in their bowels, know it even if they had never heard it: the death cry of a fallen city.

Swift as fire, the soldiers passed in and went to work with ax and club.

Already the news had spread that Iftikhar's men were in retreat, falling back toward the Temple of Solomon, holding up the Christian advance as best they could with improvised barriers of corpses and stone steps prized from their beds, while others kept up a running fire from the rooftops.

The gates were open, and after the confusion in the gateway the pilgrims found themselves inside, standing beneath ramparts devastated as if by an earthquake, while everywhere, on the mounds of slingstones and the piles of fagots, lay the bodies of Christians and infidels, sprawling disjointedly like stuffed dolls, like heaps of bloody rags thrown down at random.

The fighting had been fierce, and now they lay like discarded empty husks, of less account than wood or stone. Not one left to kill or finish off, and the wide street with its uprooted paving stones as full of people as on a market day.

Here it was hard to tell if the time were day or night; the light was red but not the red of the sunset, more like that of a great fire, only there was no fire. The sky was red with screaming. Everyone was screaming, the host pouring into the streets was screaming, and one continuous piercing scream rose from the courtyards of the houses. Red was the cry. The street led straight to the great Temple, where fighting was going on, and now and then out of the tumult came recognizably the war cry of the knights of Brabant.

A covered street opened like a cavern. A blinding red-gold light shone at the far end, and the body of a mighty Sudanese lay full-length on the steps, arms wide and head flung back, while the whites of the eyes and the bared teeth gleamed in the black face as though lit from within.

The cavalry had been sent in in the belief that they would most easily crush the resistance in the streets, but over the rooftops and through narrow alleys the garrison had fallen back on the Temple, barricaded all the doors, and were shooting at horses and riders from the windows. The principal streets were so choked with crowds of civilians fleeing to the citadel that the horses could make no headway.

But all began when the banners of Toulouse were seen floating from the Tower of David.

For the Provençals had borne the brunt of the fighting all that day and they poured into the city in their hundreds through a breach in the wall, crying, "Jesus Christ and Toulouse! The Cross and Saint-Gilles!" Swordsmen and spearmen hurling themselves on all they met with such fury that the crowds running screaming to the citadel recoiled and fled back the way they had come. It was like the shock of two great waves breaking against each other, and God alone knows how many died in the collision, trampled underfoot or suffocated. Then the hunt through the streets began. The city had gone mad.

The sky that was the color of red-hot iron paled suddenly and turned green as a corpse. But because of the screaming and the frantic rush of so many thousands of bodies, sweating with fear or fury, the heat in the narrow streets did not abate but became more terrible than ever, and men were seen brandishing lighted torches either in attack or in defense, and the cry "Fire!" was raised and fagots of flaming brushwood were flung down from the rooftops.

There were hundreds and thousands of them. People from all walks of life: big men dressed in embroidered robes, old men with colored cloths around their heads, poor people in tunics of coarse grey stuff, laborers in loincloths, naked to the waist, women swathed in veils and other women with a simple scarf over their heads, small boys and girls and infants in arms borne high above the crowd. They were not running any more but milling helplessly around and around in the same spot. There was nowhere left to run to. They flung themselves against the doors of the houses, banging hard enough to break the knockers, and voices could be heard calling and shouting above the crowd, so many names shouted at the tops of men's lungs, so many arms clinging, shoving with fists and elbows.

The pilgrims of Arras, with a group of Normans hard on their heels, thrust their way into the thick of the crowd sweeping slowly down the street, slowly because those in front were not advancing of their own will and others were pushing them from behind. People clung to the house walls, striving to thrust the others back; arms waved, eyes glared, hair was torn out, many lost their footing, and there were some who tried to clamber upon other men's shoulders.

Then the pilgrims came to meet them, brandishing all the weapons they could muster—axes, clubs, and pointed staves. They came on, howling and shrieking, because they too were propelled forward from behind, and all at once they saw the mass of humanity blocking the street waver and bend like a field of corn before the wind. One great cry of terror broke from hundreds of throats. In front were faces, eyes, eyes drunk with terror, a herd of living souls all mad with fear.

Drunk themselves, half stupefied, and yelling too with all the power of their lungs, the men struck out blindly with all their strength, using both arms, hewing like woodmen into the mass, and the bodies doubled up and fell; they were hacking furiously at anything that moved. Already the surging crowd had thinned, the people either taken into the houses or fleeing down another street, and the pilgrims waded on, hacking and hewing, forcing their way through, struggling to overtake each other so as to be among the leaders and have more play for their weapons.

There was no resistance. It was easier than slaughtering sheep. Skulls burst like pumpkins, arms and legs snapped like twigs, trickling, cracking, groaning, dying.

It was nearly dark now and no longer possible to see what was there, a heap of warm, pulsating larvae with here and there an arm stretched out and now and then, piercing the deep, baying clamor, a woman's high scream. No one fought back. They could not have done so even had they been armed. It was all over. The city now contained only wolves and lambs. The weakest Christian could have slain a fighting man with ease.

At the intersection they met some Flemish bowmen carrying torches who laid their hands on their quivers. "Stop, they are friends!"

"Greetings, brothers. What news?"

"The Temple of Solomon has fallen. Everything is cleaned up there."

"Then where is the fighting?" le Grêlé asked.

"Praise be to God and to Count Robert, the battle is over. The Provençals have got Iftikhar bottled up in the citadel. We are flushing out the men who have taken refuge in the houses."

Bodies lay on the ground. They kicked them aside and le Grêlé said, "The treacherous dogs have fled or hidden themselves. Where shall we search?" He began to run up a narrow stepped street from which screams were coming and a light that might have been that of a fire. All the men, Picards, Artesians, and Normans, followed him, none wishing to be lost. The intersection was swarming with soldiers by this time: Flemings with severed heads slung by the hair from their belts.

A fire had been lighted in front of a mosque at the end of the street and they were burning two men who, with hair and beards alight and garments smoldering, were trying to escape, but the soldiers thrust them back into the fire with the points of their spears. "It is their priests."

The door of the mosque stood open and men with flaming brands were running inside. All must be purified with fire. It was hot in the little square, the red light danced on the walls and flickered over the heads and shoulders of the soldiers. Long, wailing cries came from the houses behind the mosque. Come on, there are heathens there. Alix darted into the mosque and came back carrying a lighted brass lamp. "Here, Saint-John," she said. "You have no weapon. You carry it."

Saint-John was staring through the flames at the two Moslem priests, who now lay quite still on their pyre. The flames were leaping and spitting on their backs and on their necks, giving off a thick, black smoke. "Come away," Jacques said to him. "It is not good to watch." But Saint-John continued to stare, his eyes wide and his mouth trembling. "Jacques, I am afraid," he said. "My heart is bursting with terror."

"Now is a fine time! Come!"

They came to a kind of caravanserai, rather like a large courtyard, full of people. It was from here that the wailing had been coming. Two fires made for cooking were still burning, and shivering women were holding their children's cold hands to the warmth. The men were wringing their hands or lifting their arms to heaven and uttering long wailing cries like laments. When the pilgrims burst into the court, bloody and brandishing their weapons, there was no screaming but only a sudden deathlike hush.

The two groups looked at one another in a kind of daze. Then the children started to cry. There must have been a good many children and they were all crying at once. The men came forward with their hands up, striking their foreheads and bowing. Some went down on their knees. "Right," said le Grêlé. "Let's do what must be done."

The good work, and no easy task because the people began to run in all directions, some into the inner rooms, some up to the roof, but they were many, over a hundred at least, and they impeded one another. Some of the men grabbed staves and pokers, others drew their knives, but each was on his own like a hunted beast and could not stand against a company.

Let not one be left alive. No man, woman, or child. Let them feel God's vengeance.

Jacques alone felled six, striking at their heads with his ax. It was night, and yet by some miracle of God they could see as clearly as by day. They could see because they knew what to look for and how to go about it.

It was here that they lost Saint-John.

The boys had gone up onto the roof because the women had dashed up there, taking the children with them, and Mardoche said, "We'll deal with the children. The house is tall: we'll take them by the feet and sling them off into the street. Bravely, boys, a knife to the throat of any woman that fights back and then over the edge with the children." When he heard this, Saint-John lost his head and cried out, "Oh no! My children, my friends, do not do this thing!"

He wept and cried and clung to the boys' arms. "Oh no! Don't do it! No! Oh no, for the love of God!" As the little group of heathen children clung to one another cheeping like birds, he placed himself in front of them at the edge of the roof, his legs apart and his arms spread wide to keep the boys from pushing them over.

"Get away, Saint-John, don't be a fool," Guillemin told him, and Bertin said, "Go on, give him a push, boys." But he went on crying, *"Oh, my little ones, do not do it!"*

Mardoche stood back with narrowed eyes and slowly bent his bow. His lips curved in a smile. The arrow hissed and stuck fast in Saint-John's throat, and the poor fellow's arms waved wildly for a second before he fell backward over the edge. They caught a glimpse of his thin legs kicking for an instant in space before they disappeared. A perfect somersault. The boys shouted with laughter and Bertin clapped her hands. "Well done, Mardoche. Shoot him again!" She leaned over to look. Thirty feet below, bodies lay on the stones of the little square, caught in the glimmer of the distant bonfire: small black dots like birds beaten down by a storm.

"Can you see him?" Guillemin said.

"I'll say! Dead as dead, with his head all on one side." They laughed. What a liar, to say he couldn't die!

"Shoot him again, Mardoche. Take a big one and aim carefully."

The little ones screamed as Bertin and Onésime grabbed them by the hair and hurled them down. Smash and smash, and there's another!

There was quite a big boy, a lad of thirteen or so, nearly as tall and thin as Mardoche, who stood up and laughed back at them silently with a glint of fine white teeth. He had been crouching, hugging two little girls and a small baby, but now he rose and stood before Mardoche and looked him straight in the eyes. Then, still holding the baby in his arms and with the little girls clinging to his shirt, he put one leg over the parapet and so they jumped, all four, with a cry that held more joy than terror. Several others followed suit, the fools, like a lot of sheep. Mardoche bent his bow.

"That woman there, screaming blue murder! Aim for her neck!"

Torches were passing by down below and soldiers marching, brandishing heads and arms on the ends of their pikes.

"Hey, are you mad up there? That's dangerous. You could kill someone!" Onésime and Guillemin had just thrown a big girl down and she had fallen right at the feet of one of the soldiers, barely missing him.

There were still men in the courtyard hoping to escape by climbing up to the roof. They found a way of dealing with these. Guillaume the Picard stood at the top of the steps and as soon as the fugitives reached the top Guillaume hit them on the head with his club and knocked them down, and tipped them over the edge. But in their terror the poor wretches did not even realize what was happening, and they went on crawling up, lurching and bleeding, their fingers clutching at the walls, without a thought for what awaited them above. They did not see what was happening in the courtyard. For in the courtyard all those who had taken refuge inside the building were being dragged out under the arcade, and there the pilgrims were waiting for them with axes and mallets and the men worked like harvesters on a threshing floor, not even pausing to divide the living from the dead, and so many bodies were hacked to pieces on the spot that it was impossible to say which arm or head belonged to which.

"Shall we take the heads, Grêlé?"

"No, what's the use? We'd need a cart. There's work elsewhere. Hey there, Guillaume! Anyone left on the roof?"

Up on the roof the boys were charging about, leaping over the dead bodies and sliding on the pools of blood as though on ice in winter, so excited that they came near to precipitating themselves down into the street.

Oh, the blackbird sings and the meadow is gay
Now sings the lark and blooms the may
  I will give you the Temple of Solomon
  I will give you the Tower of David!

"Hey fellows, the mosque is burning, the devils have come out of it!"

Flames were dancing on the roof of the mosque, reflected in the low, blue-painted dome.

"Come down," Guillaume the Picard yelled. "Come down, you little devils, this is no time for dancing!"

Soldiers with torches came into the courtyard; by what they said they were men from the Ardennes: tunics, leggings, and arms black with blood, blood on their beards, they were leading two mules laden with sacks and baskets.

"Where are you from, friends?"

"We are the poor of Artois and Picardy. What news?"

"News? We've lost ourselves in all these streets. We are looking for the Temple."

"Well," Jacques said, "you've not been wasting your time. I'll wager it's not pagan heads you've got inside those baskets!"

"Mind your own business. We've earned our booty."

"Not tonight," said Élie, wiping his ax on a woolen cloak. "Not tonight.

"We didn't come here to take this house. There is work elsewhere." He looked up at the children running about on the roof: slim grey shadows against the rose-colored smoke.

"Well, come on then," Jean-Marc said, "give us a torch, you fellows."

The leading soldier obeyed without a murmur: tonight there were no more poor. Jean-Marc was a big man and held himself tall and erect as a bishop, his right arm resting on a club that was black with blood.

The windows of the mosque shone like so many suns. Inside, all was hissing and crackling and singing flames. It was as hot as an oven and the walls of the houses glowed red. Away beyond the close-packed houses was more smoke and screams, screams everywhere. The streets were full of dead bodies. The boys ran and shouted.

"Shut them up, Grêlé, can't you?" Alix said. But Élie did not care, he had only one thought in his head: to kill. A great joy was rising within him, as if a vast hole were opening in his chest, a hole deeper than a well and wider than a cistern, and it was filling up with warm red blood. The more he filled it the deeper it grew. He had drunk nothing since the day before and yet he was not thirsty. None of them had drunk since the day before.

They set fire to the Holy Sepulcher, they murdered the monks in their monasteries!

We will use the beards of their priests to wipe away our excrement, we will gouge out their eyes with red-hot irons. They killed all the Christians to the last man and flung their bodies onto dungheaps!

The sky was growing lighter, and in the great square before the Temple a crowd of men on horseback and on foot was milling about in a glorious fairground confusion. "It is not true, then, that they have burned the Holy Sepulcher?" "No, but the way is barred. Each in his turn, not all can go there at once."

"What are all those men on the Temple roof? They do not look like Christians!" In the pallid light they could be seen squatting or leaning against the turrets, their white cloaks hugged around them. The pilgrims and the men from the Ardennes rushed up the outside staircase to the roof. The Temple was a vast edifice with a gilded dome, and from its roof, paved with glazed tiles, it was possible to see over half the city and look down on the streets thronged in the half-light with a seething, boiling mob of people, and on the myriad flat white rooftops and the hundred rose-pink spires of the minarets.

Norman soldiers were guarding the roof and their banner was planted on one of the turrets.

"Well, brothers, what are you waiting for? There are infidels on this roof!"

"Go back where you came from. These are Tancred's prisoners."

But there were at least twenty of them on the roof by this time, and the Normans were but two. They were thrust aside and their battle-axes snatched from them. "By Jesus Christ and the Holy Virgin," Jacques said, "by Holy Sepulcher, Tancred shall get no ransom for these men!"

The men from the Ardennes ran forward with their pikes and the poor with their motley assortment of weapons. There were a few dozen soldiers of the Egyptian garrison with a number of women, sitting or lying, pale and too exhausted to do more than raise their heads. When they realized what was happening they did not even cry out, although a number of them ran and threw themselves down from the roof onto the crowd of bystanders who were there to see the Temple.

Lord Jesus, it was a sight worth seeing!

A Last Judgment indeed.

The Temple was almost as vast as the great cathedral in Constantinople. The arches that ran the length and breadth of it were supported on massive pillars and all around the great dome and the marble galleries hung shields inlaid with letters of gold. Walls and pillars were covered with brilliant mosaics, depicting circles and stars in white and blue and black. Lamps hung between the pillars, but these were not lighted. They swung gently to and fro, reflecting the light of the resin torches which appeared to be moving about by their own agency in the gloom below. A pale light came through the windows around the dome and fell on the balustrades of the galleries.

The torches were moving about slowly, pausing and wavering, because there were men still living within, indeed they were everywhere but they seemed lost in the vast emptiness between the hundred pillars of the nave. Hoarse voices called and there were groans and cries. The torchlight shone on broad expanses of red liquid from which protruded shapeless objects that were fallen bodies, lying alone or in groups of five or six together.

It was real, yet no one who had not seen it could believe. For the floor of the Temple was paved with marble and surrounded by raised steps, so that the blood could not run out. It stayed there, washing up to the first step. If a man had fallen full length it would have closed over his head, drowning him in blood. So much blood had flowed, Christian and infidel alike, because in the fighting men aimed for the throat and decapitated the wounded. The torchlight gleamed on the blood, congealing now into a turgid stickiness, bathing the whole Temple in a dull red glow.

There were so many dead that they had been pushed back against the walls and heaped about the pillars until the Temple seemed filled with worshippers gathered to celebrate a festival. A great host. The Last Judgment. In the center, under the dome, was a clear space, and soldiers and monks could be seen kneeling in the blood and turning over the bodies.

Many were so mutilated that it was impossible to tell Christian from infidel.

Count Robert of Flanders rode up with his knights and squires, their cloaks flung over their shoulders and their horses clean and shining, and all passed in through the great gate of the Temple and moved slowly forward toward the lofty throne, piled high with the dead. Even the destriers, though not afraid of blood, had never seen so much and pricked their ears, their nostrils quivering. The Count had lost some good knights here, but he had not come to mourn for them. It was a great day and a great victory.

See, Christians, see what happened. They fought here to the last man. It was God pronounced the doom. Some Christians came out of this hell alive, but not one infidel.

The knights of Provence appeared, cantering through the city as gaily as if they had come from a feast. Greetings, brothers. Toulouse and Saint-Gilles! Saint Michael and Saint George and Saint Saturnin! Praise God who has delivered the Holy Sepulcher.

Let all the cavalry ride through the temple. But this is not the day to turn it into stables, this is the feast of blood, *there is blood up to the steps.* It cannot run off, for the drains are choked with corpses.

Soldiers and pilgrims, wild-eyed, their faces streaked with dirt, went in to see, stepping on the dead to avoid having to wade through the viscous mass. Oh, what a salutary spectacle, worthy of the wisdom of Solomon, an image of human vanity! The splendid temple, shining with gold and marble and colored stones, becomes a slaughterhouse! Do not weep for your martyrs who fell here, they have deserved their joy. If your gorge rises, do not grieve, it is the weakness of the flesh.

O Jerusalem washed in blood
O Jerusalem washed in tears
O Jerusalem conquered and avenged!

Lines of Syrian Christians with long gaffs were dragging the bodies of those who had fallen in the street back to the ditches by the walls. A procession was coming, with candles and censers, a long procession of Greek priests on foot in their best gold-embroidered vestments. As they went they sprinkled holy water around them with sprigs of boxwood to purify the houses and the pavements. They were followed by a choir of monks singing hymns of deliverance. Their powerful voices rose above the tumult in the streets and courtyards, like a great ship forcing its way through a tangle of wreckage. The light of the candles was pale and wan in the sunrise, and wan were the solemn faces fringed with curling beards. None had slept that night, unless it were the last sleep of all.

Tancred shall take no ransom
Nor Godfrey nor any baron.

Who would have joy and pardon
Must serve God without treason!
Who spares the accursed traitors' lives
Spits in the face of Jesus Christ
He that betrays God for ransom
Let no songs be sung for him
Let him be scorned!
O so long mourned
So long desired
Vengeance is nigh.

Oh friends, they have not told us the truth, the Holy Sepulcher is burning! See the flames and the great smoke, the sky is already black with it!

They could not deliver it in time, the traitors have set fire to it, they mean to conceal it from us.

Can it be? The Devil has deceived the eyes of Duke Godfrey and his brother and Count Robert, and made a false church rise up before them, like a mirage in the desert, while all the time the Egyptians were setting fire to the real one! We did not come in time to prevent it.

The men ran forward, trembling, their hearts so full that they cried aloud with anguish. Some three or four dozen archers had joined the crowd of pilgrims and monks, and all were weeping and brandishing their crosses as if they would use them to strike down the infidels. They could not tell where the thick mass of smoke was coming from, but they could hear such an uproar, such a shrieking and howling and screaming, that they began to bay like wolves in turn. "What is it? Who is being murdered over there?"

"The Tafurs have entered the city through the Sion Gate."

No, good people, what is burning is the great synagogue, but do not go there, you will see nothing, there are too many people.

Praise God, the Jews have got their deserts. They are all in there, singing their last psalm. God have mercy on their souls, their sufferings are terrible.

Besides the dead, there were only Christians left in the streets now; everyone else had barricaded themselves inside their houses. There were thousands of houses, rich and poor, still full of the accursed brood. The soldiers broke down the doors with axes and burst into the courts, and the people ran to hide themselves in the cellars or in the corners of the rooms.

The Tafurs had invaded the rich quarter south of the Temple, and with their axes and their big knives and their Turkish scimitars were slicing off heads as woodcutters lop the branches of a tree. No one attempted to resist them: they were more terrible to see than knights in full armor. The pagans honestly believed that devils had come for their souls, for the bodies of these naked men were so thin and blackened, so covered with dried blood; and so inhuman were their weathered faces with beards like matted flock and toothless gums and vacant eyes that brave, strong men ran screaming at the sight.

Fear hung about them and went before them, for there is nothing more terrible than men who are beyond all fear.

They did their work, lips parted in a joyless grin, God's executioners, eaters of human flesh, going about their headsman's task unhurriedly. In one small white, marble-columned court they lined up all the women of the harem, panting like stricken deer, beside the pool and one by one decapitated them until the red waters of the pool were filled with pale heads and long black tresses floating like a random design of interwoven snakes. The Tafurs used their axes to smash coffers and glass and silver vessels, dishes, lamps, and boxes; they ripped up silken cushions, filling the devastated rooms with snowstorms of white down that stuck to their naked bodies, clothing them in a leprous whiteness which made them yet more hideous.

Duke Godfrey had sent a company of men under two knights to try and stop the destruction. The knights came to the courtyard of what had once been a rich man's house, paved with pink-and-white mosaic now awash with blood. The Tafurs were leading the horses out of the stables one at a time, and while one man held the horse by the bridle and forced back its head, another cut its throat with one stroke of his knife. The blood spurted out in a mighty fountain, the animal shuddered once and toppled over on its side. Seeing this, one of the knights stood up in his stirrups, lance in hand, and called on them to stop, saying it was madness to waste good horses in this way and the beasts could be useful to the army. The Tafurs only laughed their hoarse, mirthless laughter, and showed their rotten gums. Their leader spoke: "Tomorrow neither Jesus Christ nor the army nor any other man will need horses any more."

The barons will be punished like Saul and Ahab for their greed.

Meanwhile another horse was led out and the man with the knife prepared to strike. The second knight cried out, "Enough! Are we to let them slaughter these good beasts?" He rode forward to bring his lance up against the man's breast, though without meaning to hurt him. In one swift movement the Tafur sidestepped and with an upward glance darted forward again. The knight's horse shied and rose up on its haunches. In another second the knife flashed and vanished. A harsh, tearing sound was followed by a gush of blood. The knight had barely time to leap from the saddle as his horse leaped in the air, then crashed to the ground with flailing hoofs. Without a word the knight sprang up behind his comrade, and they galloped off with their men after them.

Saul has slain his thousands, and David his ten thousands.

Servants of Saul, your reign is at an end, God has judged you!

Tomorrow there shall be no rich or poor any more, but all you that covet wealth shall be food for jackals! Set on the left hand, and the sheep divided from the goats.

God is waiting for you beyond the wall of David in the valley of Jehoshaphat. You have made Jerusalem the holy into a den of thieves.

In each house where they passed they left behind them no living thing, man, woman, or child, horse, ass, dog, or fowl, and they left no object of any worth intact, not so much as a single earthenware pot, ripping open the sacks of corn, smashing the olive jars, and spilling all in pools of blood.

Drink. The sun is hot and the stones have not cooled all night because of the torches everywhere and the scattered fires and the fevered sweat of tens of thousands of bodies. Even those that had been dead for hours were still warm. There was a crossroads with a fountain where the water dripped into a stone basin. The water was red and the rim discolored with dark stains of blood, but they plunged their faces into it all the same and dipped their hands and drank from their cupped palms. The water tasted salt, like tears. Men looked in vain for their friends. The streets were full of people, but no way of telling a familiar face from a stranger's: all were alike, red and perspiring, red where they had wiped their brows with reddened hands.

Oh damned, accursed dogs, not even men. They had no faces, only eyes staring, eyes everywhere and gaping mouths. They were mad with fear, running like rats caught in a trap or coming forward with arms crossed above their heads.

Who cared if they were old? A white lamb's-wool beard and chattering teeth, lips blue with fear, long hands covered with a network of blue veins, and bleating like a sheep. Sing, old man, life is over for you, you are afraid, but we do not fear death! You have a nice bald pate, not so hard as olive wood, see it crack like an enormous nut, so much blood, see, he is covered with it, clothed in bright blood, such a fine red, a beautiful clear, deep color, the fairest color of all. Yet to see so much of it is wearisome. It dulls quickly. There must be more, always more.

I, Alix Malebouche, the fairest woman of Arras: see what God has made of the whore of Babylon. An unlikely woodcutter! The great tree of a hundred thousand living branches which has grown in the Sanctuary, the weeds that have invaded the sacred stones on which God walked: all cut down, the tree scattered, the serpent of a thousand heads, cut it down root and branch and bud! *You laughed when they fired our heads from the cannon's mouth.* To each his turn.

Our patience is ended. Finished forever. O God, Lord Jesus Christ, have mercy on poor lost sinners in Your kingdom! Alix ran down a covered alley, her chopper clutched in her right hand, her long legs bare and blackened, white, still youthful flesh showing through her torn shirt where the small ebony cross bounced between her bobbing breasts.

She ran on, holding her head up like a dancer, her mouth trembling in a grim smile and her cheeks smudged with tears. Red beads of sweat trickled from the strands of hair clinging to her temples under the bloodstained cap.

As she ran she struck out at the air left and right, but blindly: they were lying on the ground, crawling along the walls. The Normans had caught up with her and were hard at work with pikes and battle-axes, and the screams changed to dying groans. ACCURSED ACCURSED ACCURSED GOD WILLS IT!

All the same, the same black, staring eyes, the same brown faces blank with terror. Bodies that let go their hold on life at the approach of death, loosening their bowels, vomiting their bile, lacking even the strength to stand upright. In a low, smoke-blackened doorway a tiny plump woman with a birdlike face was clinging to a young Picard lad armed with a pitchfork. She was speaking, speaking in a Christian voice, and it was not hard to tell what she was saying, even without knowing her language: Mercy, lords, I have done you no harm, it is not right, think of your own mothers, for God's sake! The Picard shook her off almost shamefacedly and moved on. Some Normans came and split her head open with an ax and went into the house. There was a sound of children screaming and squeals of terror.

A big, rawboned fellow, with a look of more than swinish brutality on his lined and freckled face, was brandishing a spear on which was impaled the body of a little girl, the point sticking out between the small ribs like some monstrous thorn. The face, hanging upside down, was pretty, with the delicacy of all very young children's faces, and the eyes were wide open in an expression of dreadful surprise. Alix saw the face a handspan from her own with the small dimpled shoulders and the small arms dangling bonelessly. Dead, thank God, but still warm, with a sweet scent of curds. The soft, childish lips had scarcely lost their color. And the man carried this thing proudly, like a banner, his mouth half open in an idiot grin. Alix started back as if someone had struck her full in the chest. She felt suddenly dizzy. *Where am I, what is happening?* Father! Mother! Help me, take me away from here! She threw away her ax and began to run blindly, bumping into men whose jerkins were warm and wet and sticky to the touch. Maddened like rutting beasts.

Holding the flapping edges of her torn shirt across her breasts, she struggled to reach a wall to lean on, knowing that if she fell where she was the men would trample her.

God help us, what have we come to! Drink and be merry for tomorrow we die. To the uttermost depths of sin, Lord, have mercy on Your poor for truly You have led them into too great temptation. Up, coward, find your weapon, pick it up, go down into the depths of sin, lay bare your soul, it is uglier than that open belly there with the entrails like knotted snakes.

If you paused for a moment the weariness was so great that you would have given your life for one hour's sleep, yet all the time, running through your whole body from your toes to the roots of your hair, was a strange, tingling sensation like an invisible garment of fire: the exhalation of a host of men all blind with rage.

A priest was leaning down from the roof of a house, shouting with all the power of his lungs: "Good pilgrims, temper your zeal. Your enemies have been punished enough. Stop this killing. The barons have promised they will drive them from the city!" The men dragging the heathens from the houses heard his words and began to hoot and shout back, chanting in chorus: "Traitor, traitor, traitor! Death to the traitor! Death to the traitor!" Alix shouted with the rest. The priest was a broad, stocky man with a flaxen beard and he did not lack courage. He rolled a huge earthenware jar to the edge of the roof, as if he meant to tip it over into the street. There was a moment's silence. No one was anxious to get that on his head.

"Stop this madness, do not destroy your own souls as well as those of the people here. Take their goods but spare their lives. Jesus Christ never called for the death of sinners, and these are poor defenseless folk!"

"Silence, traitorous son of Ahab! Iftikhar has paid you a thousand gold bezants!"

The priest stayed where he was, unwilling to give the jar its final push because his own position was undoubtedly a perilous one. He was alone against a maddened crowd and the roof was not high or difficult of access. The rumor was spreading through the city that Iftikhar was still alive, shut up in the citadel with many of his emirs and his guard. The Count of Toulouse had spared him. He had betrayed Jesus Christ.

Why waste our energies on vermin, friends? Make for the citadel! If the Count refuses to take it and deliver the infidels into our hands, then let him turn his mangonels upon God's poor. Shame on us, to kill women and children and let Iftikhar escape.

Even now, none could tell if it were night or day, although the heat was like molten lead. The sun itself was lost in the blood and the screams, clouded by the ruddy smoke from the burning synagogue: a hotter fire among the many in that stricken city. The streets leading to the Holy Sepulcher were cordoned off and guarded by armored riders. Brothers, on this great and holy day it is not fitting to disturb the bishops at their prayers and the divine offices.

The Tafurs were climbing the street up to the citadel, and so great was the fear they inspired that none dared enter the street, but all stood back to watch them pass. They chanted hymns of their own as they went, which no one understood because they were not in Latin or French or German but something of all three, only more like the mouthings of the deaf than any words. They moved with a strange, loping gait like wild animals, shouldering their pikes and axes and staring heavenward with dull and burning eyes. Everyone thought they must be making for the citadel, but it was not so. They went out through the Gate of David, speaking to no one, ignoring the guards, still chanting as if they had been alone in the city. Their king marched at their head, a copper circlet on his brow, his clasped hands holding aloft a wooden cross. Still chanting, they went down the hill into the valley, their thin arms rising and falling.

They came and went like ghosts. Their prophets had seen visions. The angel of death was calling them to prepare for the resurrection in the valley of Jehoshaphat.

Some forty or fifty people followed them, mostly pilgrims but a number of soldiers even, tearing off their clothes as they went, and when their friends tried to restrain them they did not answer but only thrust them off with hoarse cries. They seemed to be in a kind of trance, and their eyes were glassy and unseeing.

Around the citadel there was a great deal of noise and excitement, but no fighting because the men were breathless from bawling out demands for the head of Iftikhar. There was a drumming in their ears and the shouting alone produced a strange exhilaration, the rhythmic chant drove every other thought from their minds.

Heaps of red maggots swarming around a huge block of stone. From the top of the tower there was a view of gilded domes and long vistas of stepped roofs with the dark patches of gardens and the minarets like tall candles, all wrapped in a haze of heat made thicker by the ruddy smoke. On the towers and dome of the citadel the flags with red crosses and the standards of Toulouse, of Provence, of Cerdagne, hung like painted banners against a flat, bright-blue sky. The crenellated ramparts were adorned with Saracen shields and severed heads, and an altar covered with cloth of gold had been set up on the roof of the tower. Priests were chanting solemn thanksgivings. Their hands shook and their voices were choked with tears, as if they could not yet believe in this great joy.

There is no city in the world like Jerusalem. Truly, there is no other city in the world!

Down below the whole city was buzzing and gasping as if in the grip of some mighty death throe. The clamor rose and fell and all else was lost in one vast, discordant growl of horror, while now and then such groaning rent the air that it seemed the very stones of the houses wept. The city wept and groaned, the city trembled under the shock of blows, the city bled like a thousand butchers' stalls in some vast slaughterhouse, the city reeked in the noonday heat, even the shadows in the dark streets exuded a fetid warmth.

The soldiers had occupied the houses in the more prosperous districts and were cleaning up, throwing the bodies out into the streets. They had destroyed all the dogs, also, because there were far too many.

Élie le Grêlé had lost half his company in the confusion. Jean-Marc had left the city to go back to the camp and take the news to the women and the sick, who could not be allowed inside the city until it had been cleaned up or while the soldiers were still masters of the streets. Because, Jean-Marc said, so far as could be seen there had been virtually no raping as yet, and the way things were going there would soon be no one left to rape.

"It is just as well," Élie said. "What would we have done with so many women and children? Sent them out to die of starvation in the valley?"

"We are powerless," Jean-Marc said, "before what is written in the Book of God." He was not unhappy, but felt rather as if he had been hit on the head with a hammer, not conscious of either joy or sorrow. His elder son had lost his right eye and he had barely glanced at him. He had merely shrugged. What was an eye, after all?

They had stopped at a two-storied house with a tiny court where a straggling fig tree grew. There was no one there. The people had fled. All they found, in the inmost room, was two women and five young children lying on some woolen cushions. Their throats had been cut. The man had killed them himself before he went out to meet his own death in the streets. There were many in that part of the city who had done the same, and none could blame them.

"Anyone sick or wounded," le Grêlé said, "stay in the house.

And say that there will be more than fifty of us. If we find a better house we will come back and fetch you."

The men who were unhurt ate a few dried dates and scooped some water from the big jar by the door, and then went out again. In spite of the heat they were hardly aware of hunger or thirst: they were possessed, driven on by an overpowering urge to destroy. They could not help themselves; the mere sight of a house with a tree in the courtyard made them physically sick.

"There's wine to be had in the Jewish quarter, lads. The Brabançons are in control there, and the Genoese, and already they are selling it at three deniers a pint." Jacques let out a great shout of laughter.

"Why not thirty? Suppose we start selling figs and dried onions, eh? The Italians would sell sunshine if they could."

The stone streets were black with blood and the bodies piled on both sides of the street left only a narrow passage between. Thank God the city is all paved, or what a mire we should have to walk in! Many people had been dragged from their beds and the bodies were half naked. The skin was grey, like stone. Many of the bodies were fat: great fleshy arms, powerful thighs, and livid, hairy bellies. Oh, those devils ate well, they had plenty of fat to spare! They wore shoes and their feet were smooth and clean! The flies hovered around them in ever-increasing numbers. All the better, they'll leave us alone.

On the other side of the Christian quarter, the shouts and screams were rising again as loud as ever. The people in that part of the city had hoped at first to escape because they were on good terms with the superiors of the Greek and Armenian religious houses and had asked them to intercede to obtain an armed guard for them. Fools! They had trusted to their wealth and to local Christians who, degenerate and schismatic abbots, had conspired with them for love of money more than Christian charity. Here were the streets of the silk merchants, the goldsmiths, and the dealers in carpets and furs. Besides the pilgrims, the Syrian peasants had made their way there and also the Christian workers from the potteries and the weaving shops, who were now being given their opportunity for revenge. They brought their hoes and sickles and heavy cudgels, and their knives as well.

"Brothers, enter the houses freely, let each man take what he wants! And if you have to fight for it, the greater your deserts." Rich men had stout servants who would know how to defend themselves.

Élie le Grêlé found himself standing before a door faced with panels of chased copper. Elsewhere in the room men were running, carrying lamps and enameled dishes. Élie, with Lambert and two Picards, was confronting a gigantic Negro, naked to the waist and wielding a curved sword. Lambert had a long lance, and he was looking at the black man with as much hatred as if this had been the very same who had cut off Baudry's head. The lance was long and the scimitar short, but the black was much quicker than Lambert. He dodged the lance, and the sword hissed. Lambert had time to throw up his left arm to guard his head, then he was staggering under the force of the blow, hearing the bone of his forearm snap as he fell.

Blood was flooding over his legs and the floor around him: his arm was almost severed near his elbow. In quick succession le Grêlé brought his ax down once on the Negro's sword and then again on his head. The two blows were struck so neatly that it seemed as if the ax had taken on a life of its own. The black man swayed slowly, his skull cloven as far as the nose, and the bright red blood spurted in little bubbling fountains down his face. He bowed forward, and Élie thrust his ax against the massive chest to fend him off because he was a giant of a man, broader than an ox.

Élie had seen many of his kind before, both dead and living, yet even so he stared, fascinated, at the smooth, black flesh and the ripple of strong, flexible muscle in the arms. It was not the same, that other had been younger, it was not the same but would to God, would to God that other could come alive again a thousand times over! While one of the Picards used his belt to make a tourniquet around Lambert's arm, Élie stepped over the corpse and shattered the ornate, copper-clad door with a few blows of his ax. "Stay here, lads," he said. "I'll go alone."

It seemed to him that if he could really go in alone it all might begin again and he would find himself back in the bright room with its marble-lined pool and see her sitting there, white and naked, with her black jewels of eyes and the soft, shimmering blackness of her hair. She would look at him, half dead with fright, not daring even to blink, the poor victim whose eyes were her only defense, and it would all begin again, down to the last night at Maarat an-Numan. But already he was no longer alone; soldiers, their leather jerkins black with blood, were running beside him and the usual clamor was rising within the house. The people were not fighting any more, it was too late for that. They ran to hide behind the hangings and the chests and were dragged out, holding out their arms in supplication, and the women fainted. And then there were long silken cushions, blue and pink, and two women, both very young, with skins that were white and soft as flower petals. Élie laid aside his ax and drew his knife.

They were not like her, no: beautiful but like sheep, their blood was sheep's blood, and no more real blood than water was wine. The real blood had been shed, once and for all, the white throat cut forever. There they were, two of them, and then a third, half dead, such a young thing with the eyes of a young kid; her neck fluttered like a captive bird under the knife and the blood flowed out gaily, like a long-pent-up spring, and ran in two bright rivulets over her white muslin shift. Sheep. The Devil had shaped them to look like women but his devices were too clumsy . . . Yet if it were only possible to feel again that little shudder she gave, the soft gurgle in her throat at the moment when the blood began to well out around the knife, a man could kill a thousand sheep in the same way, from dawn to dusk and all night long—

He said farewell at close of day
To fair Euphemia, his dear.
He said, I shall not see thee more
In sun or moonlight clear
Never shall I see thee more
Through all the turning years.

It was done; in that house there was no more to do. The others, and there were many of them now, were plundering. There were many fair things to take but no fighting over the spoils: there was enough for all. They were not even stripping the bodies. Élie stood watching them, his ax on his shoulder, his knife in his belt. They too were ghosts or animals. Flemish foot soldiers, men who were strangers to him. Élie could have made himself rich that day. There were silver vases and dishes and cups and women's jewels and embroideries. All these treasures turned to dust before his jaded eyes: lives, he had taken the lives of fair women and it had not made him richer. He had squandered all his treasure and it had not slaked his desire.

He left the house. Where Lambert and the two Picards and the rest had gone he did not know. He found them in the next court. Jacques and Guillaume and Thomas, Jean-Marc's younger son, were loading bundles onto the back of a mule. "The house is cleaned out," Jacques told him. "They killed their womenfolk themselves." There had been some trouble and a Basque archer had been split in two, in one stroke, from chin to chine. Jacques grinned, his wide smile seeming somehow fixed. He seemed at the same time very busy and very excited. Lambert lay beside him on a stone bench, deathly pale, his right hand nursing his nearly severed left arm. The boys had got hold of a dapple-grey horse and were crowding around trying to climb on its back. One, Guillemin, had died, not in the fighting but simply of sunstroke. His comrades said, "We'll put him on the horse and take him to the Holy Sepulcher and he will come to life again."

"What have you got there?" le Grêlé asked.

"A little of everything," said Jean-Marc's son, "except money. The Basques helped themselves first. But there are things that will fetch a good price."

"So you hope," Guillaume scoffed. "If they left anything for us it was because no one else wanted it. You'll be lucky to get a crust for it." Le Grêlé said they could always keep the things and use them for barter later on. He felt as if they were all talking in a dream. It did not seem possible that they could be in the city of Jerusalem, so drunk with the smell of blood that they could hardly breathe and talking about barter and subsistence.

By now the Christians of Jerusalem were emerging from their hiding places and from the shelter of the cloisters and going about the blood-soaked streets, praising God. They were led by priests and monks bearing the holy images, and as they walked they crossed themselves in horror at the magnitude of God's judgment. None but the very old, and they only from tales handed down to them from their fathers, could recall a similar carnage, but on that occasion the dead had been Christians. God is just and pursues His vengeance even unto the fourth generation. Praise be to the valiant brother Christians from across the seas, the blood of the murdered Patriarch had been repaid a hundredfold.

Do not be surprised, you Orthodox Christians, to see men so strangely accoutered, so savage in their aspect, so bloody and murderous. They are still drunk with holy anger and they are rude and ignorant, but their hearts are pure. Feel neither pity nor terror, but acknowledge the hand of God who avenges the righteous on the sons of their murderers.

You need not scorn your brothers from oversea, for their lands, though distant, are not barren: God has brought forth rich harvests there in former days, marvelous flowerings of martyrs and confessors, revered by our Church among the greatest: the blessed bishops Martin and Denis, the great martyr Sebastian, the virgin Blandina and the wise Genevieve, and a thousand more whose names are mentioned in our offices. They are not Monophysites or Arians, they are our brothers.

The Christians of the Greek faith rejoiced in the Christian victory; but when they saw the soldiers laughing as they ripped up dead bodies and carrying sacks of corn and precious things slung on their backs, they found it hard to believe that these wild men could be inspired by feelings of piety. There was enough plunder to be had in the Moslem quarters, God be thanked, but who could rely on the limits of a soldier's greed? They inquired after Peter, the holy man of the Franks, the prophet who had preached the deliverance of Jerusalem, and were told that Peter was still outside the walls in the fortified camp, together with the monks, the women, and the sick, waiting until the city was washed clean of all its impurity, and that they would be able to go and venerate him as soon as order was restored.

There were men that night who boasted of having killed more than fifty people with their own hands. It was not difficult: all you needed was a good weapon. There were even men who had not killed at all, not from unwillingness but from lack of opportunity, and yet others who had had no wish to kill, who had come to fight and not for butchery. But God had hardened men's hearts strangely. Chaplains had been seen, surrounded by the men of their companies, waving crosses in the air and crying aloud, "Courage, Israel, fulfill the vengeance of thy God! Slay the Philistine and the Amalechite!" while disheveled women fell on their knees and held out their little children in their arms, thinking that this would melt the soldiers' hearts.

But there is a time for cruelty as well as a time for love, and indeed, the more beautiful the child the greater may be the joy in killing, and some were bludgeoned to death in this way that looked as pure as the infant Jesus with their smooth cheeks and their big solemn, wondering eyes.

For if, in the midst of all this tumult and confusion and the sweat of mortal fear, any man was touched by pity it was only for an instant: who could afford to feel pity in the face of so much blood? Whoever yielded to pity would himself become one with these crawling maggots. By evening, when the air in the streets was red and filled with swarms of big black flies, slow and heavy from their feast of blood, even the most hardened were beginning to turn away from the bodies in disgust, for some of them had been lying there since the previous night and the day had been a hot one.

Many gaping wounds had become a seething mass of black and white: half flies, half worms.

May the same fate befall all the enemies of Christendom! Victory! Two separate races: one walking upright, gazing with living eyes at the fiery red sky; the other sprawled about the streets, a festering carrion in which the only thing still living was the worms. Their shame is laid bare and their false gods exposed for what they are!

Their Mahomet could not save them. Let the whole world curse his name.

Tomorrow is the Lord's day, brothers, and you will be able to hear mass in Jerusalem, in those churches which have been purified in time, but since these are not all, and very far from all, the men must wait their turn and five masses will be said in every church. Fast and prepare yourselves for the joy to come, and as for the cleansing of the city, from now on let that be left to the professional soldiers, acting under orders from their captains.

Brothers, they mean to rob us of our rights and keep the best houses for themselves. They are glad enough of our help when there is work or fighting to be done, but not in the division of the spoils. It is not Sunday yet and we shall not cease before midnight.

The sun was sinking toward the city walls like molten gold, the enameled domes burned with gold and rose-pink fires of unbearable beauty. Men were going up and down the narrow streets, stepping over the corpses and the swarms of flies, looking for a place away from the stench. A file of Provençal men-at-arms. "Hey, you cutthroat rascals, where do you think you're going? Get back where you came from."

"Hired mercenaries, this is our day! We are in no man's pay! In Jerusalem there are no rich or poor." And the men of Provence let them pass.

There was no fighting over the plunder; each man went into the occupied houses and took what he liked. Help yourselves, brothers, it is all there for the taking. This one was a weavers' shop but the weavers had fled, leaving the warp still on the loom and the cloth half finished. "Oh, what fine looms! See how close the weave. It would make a shirt fit for a king!" Le Grêlé shrugged. "Do you want to take them with you? You'd need a cart." Jacques scratched his head, thinking it a pity to leave such fine looms.

"The men," Mardoche said. "The men are hiding in the alley. Come on, lads!" Somehow he was acquiring an air of command. His voice was still thin, reedy, and unbroken, but he seemed within an inch of calling le Grêlé himself "my lad." He and his gang still had their bows, which were not very powerful, but they had fun with them all the same. Le Grêlé had no desire to go and kill weavers, but when he saw them crammed, wild-eyed and cringing, into the narrow alley, his rage descended on him again and he rushed out, brandishing his ax: let not one be left alive, they are not men—vermin, that's all they are, they will not even fight.

Screams. The squealing of stuck pigs, something flayed alive, howls, screeches, bubbling groans, piercing shrieks and doglike howls; the splash of blood, bones snapping, and soft, muffled thuds, and your own voice too breathless to rise above the incessant noise, gasping, take that, you dogs, and that, and that, on and on, were you a hundred thousand dogs, toads, soulless flesh, corruption, ordure of Mahomet, you with your full bellies, your fat buttocks, you that had so much water you didn't know what to do with it, whole cisterns full! We'll drown you in your own water, we don't want it. No, brothers, water, the water of Jerusalem, the living water, do not pollute it!

Except when they were killing, the men were so tired that they lost all sense of decency. When one of their number dropped dead from fatigue, they had forgotten all about him five minutes after they closed his eyes. They left him there in the street: they simply had not the strength to carry him away. The sun had killed many Christians that day, and the others thought: It is the Judgment. God has called him.

O Mahomet, what a great liar and a false prophet you are! The people are bitterly sorry now that they placed their trust in you, but it is too late. The Devil has ground them in his maw.

How they are ground, mangled, dismembered, disemboweled, trampled, burned, shattered, crushed, and torn limb from limb!

Destruction so appalling: the Devil's own belly burst open and his entrails hanging out, spilled through the streets in pools of blood and urine and vomit, the Devil's entrails poured, huge and noisome, over a whole city, a whole city! Oh God, the pity of it! A great city full of people who ate and drank.

And believe it or not, whenever they rounded a corner and came upon a head that was unmutilated and still beautiful, it was almost comforting, they would look at it without hatred or sorrow, after all, it is over, we do not hate you, we will not disfigure you.

The worms will do that.

Sounds of singing and loud voices came from the houses, but there was no more screaming. The din now was almost peaceful, although anyone hearing it from a distance would have taken it for a chorus of demons or goblins or some other unnatural beings. It was a noise like joyful weeping or grief-stricken laughter, like psalms bawled in loud, raucous voices and soldiers' catches piously intoned, like quavering war cries and blessings uttered like threats. Sounds of hammering, the crackle of cooking fires, and now and then a piercing madman's shriek. Those mad howls carried a long way, but they were accustomed to them now; no one so much as crossed himself any more.

Lambert had lost his left arm, all right. They cut away the part that was still hanging, along with the broken bone, with a sharp knife. Half fainting with the pain, Lambert stared at the bloodless arm as it lay on the ground in front of him, caked with dried blood, with the hand, the brown, sunburnt hand, all dirty and calloused and scarred, the thin fingers slightly curled. Dead. Does one ever think of loving one's own hand? He loved his at that moment, he loved it, it was a little like looking down again at Isabelle lying on the bier. It almost made him forget the agonizing pain. "Oh Jacques, it is a sign. It is a sign."

"What sort of a sign?"

"Those people we—back there—those people were our flesh."

"Rottenness," Jacques said. "Your mind is wandering. Here, drink this. Onésime has found some wine."

"Drink it yourself. I can't."

"Pull yourself together, damn you, you priest's son! It's the left arm and that's better than the right."

"Jacques, I won't need either right or left much longer." Jacques frowned but he said nothing. Such things were not to be spoken of.

Lambert might refuse the wine, but he had been made to swallow a good pint already. This was necessary to replace the blood he had lost, but he had lost far more than could be made up by drinking. He was breathing hard, gasping for air, and black birds were beating their wings before his eyes. His thoughts went to his mother. Jacques's heart turned over and he prayed without moving his lips: Holy Virgin Mary, make him recover, Saint James and Saint Gratian, make him recover, and I swear I will give all my share of the booty to the church of the Holy Sepulcher, I vow to sell it all to buy candles.

No, it shall not be said that Jacques of the Ax deserts his friends.

In two days or three we shall all go up in a great procession to the Holy Sepulcher. They will let us worship Jesus Christ in peace. He Who was poor in His life on earth has little pleasure in the baron's prayers; it is His wish that we should be allowed to come to Him.

"When? They haven't said. The Duke's criers have proclaimed that each company shall go in turn, but in a neat and orderly fashion."

"Oh, it is easy for them to talk! They have servants and baths. Was Jesus Christ scourged and crucified in a neat and orderly fashion?"

"No, Alix," le Grêlé said. "You would not have us go to worship at the holy place as we are now? We would frighten devils as well as angels."

They had lighted a fire in one corner of the courtyard, burning the stored-up pine cones in little iron braziers. They all stayed in the courtyard in spite of the cold. It was not easy to sleep, not only on account of the flies and the occasional smells that drifted on the wind from the street, but because the spirits of the former owners of the house were still there. They could not see them, but they bumped into them all the time: they were not hostile, they came and went through the low doorways or warmed their hands near their braziers, or tried to draw water in the big jars; they had died so quickly that they could not have understood yet what had happened. And so, in order to drive them back to where their bodies lay out in the street, they sang, not psalms, but everyday songs of home. Psalms might make them hostile, but when they heard the songs of Artois sung in French, they would think they were no longer at home.

They could not see them, but now and again they heard voices, children crying and the wailing of frightened women. Up on the balcony. They talked and sang, but all the time that sound was in their ears. The boys hovered around their new horse as it slept upright, tethered to the fig tree. How the boys could stand on their own feet was more than anyone could understand; they chattered like magpies, feverishly excited but still wide awake. They had done no more than eat a few dried figs and drink a sip of water. There was Guillemin, of course. "Guillemin—he is in paradise, Guillemin is. He will rise again on the third day." "On the third day?" "Yes, in three days we shall go up to the Holy Sepulcher."

Jacques said, "What about Saint-John? He must be lost in the city. No one has seen him all day."

"No, he is dead," Bertin said. "Mardoche killed him. With an arrow, bang, right in the throat. You should have seen him tumble down!" Élie rounded on the children wearily.

"What did you want to do a thing like that for, you little fools? You mad whelps! God forbids us to kill madmen."

Mardoche sneered. "He was a traitor."

"You hear that, Alix," Jacques said. "They have killed Saint-John."

Alix was lying on the ground with her head on a bundle of fagots, and her arms behind her head. She did not start, only frowned a little. "I don't mind," she said slowly. "He was not my brother, or my stepbrother."

The children were singing, clapping their hands in time:

> Tancred shall take no ransom
> Nor Godfrey nor any baron.
> Who spares the accused traitors' lives
> Spits in the face of Jesus Christ.
> The blackbird sings and winter is fled
> Marcelle weeps, for her lover is dead
> Ten times and more she has broken her thread . . .

Bertin was jigging up and down on a roll of carpets, waving her arms, her sharp voice rising to a pitch of earsplitting shrillness as she chanted:

> He was punished for his lies
> Never go to paradise!

The tune ended in a yell and a piercing squeal of laughter: "Bang! Bang! Go to hell! And the bogeyman as well! Here comes the chopper to chop off your head, chop, chop, chop. Rotten boys! Here come the Danes! Yeeeouw!"

> Have mercy, Lord
> The Danes are wild
> Put men to the sword
> And get maidens with child!

"For God's sake, Mardoche, shut her up," le Grêlé said. But there was no need. With unexpected suddenness the child crumpled at the knees and lay still. "Bertin. Hey, Bertin, are you dead?" No, she was not dead; she was sleeping the sleep of the blessed.

It was like that. People dropped into sleep as into a well, arms outflung, in the middle of a word—they simply rolled over on one side and began to snore.

Jacques sat by Lambert, holding his right hand in a crushing grip to distract him from the pain of his wound. "You won't get gangrene, you know, we cauterized it properly. We'll see the Holy Sepulcher."

"When?"

"We've waited three years, man. Now we are in the city, three days isn't the end of the world."

"Jacques, I keep seeing things. I see Brother Barnabé."

"Nonsense, you're dreaming. Listen, three days is not long to wait. The women will come and we will all go in procession. It will be truly the resurrection of the body. Your mother's eyes will be cured."

"I can see Brother Barnabé and he is weeping tears of blood."

"It is not real, it is the fever. Brother Barnabé is in heaven."

"Jacques, it feels good to kill. I have never been so happy."

Jacques's head was nodding. He jerked it up suddenly as if he were afraid it would fall off. Fall. Fall asleep. In through the great gates, ever open to those who have reached the end of their strength, the beautiful gardens of Jerusalem, the fountains of bright water and the fair houses built of rose-colored marble, a great white horse, Marie wearing a red dress, and the candles of the Holy Sepulcher like a thousand suns, the shouting and screaming, the screams of death, death, shame to Mahomet, shame . . .

Still half asleep, he raised his head and shouted aloud, "Shame to Mahomet!" Then he fell back and began to snore.

The street door was not locked. Not a door in the city was locked: most had been broken in. The door was not locked and the soldiers stepped through the low archway and burst into the courtyard with weapons raised. One of them carried a lantern. They looked around at the braziers filled with glowing embers, the huddle of snoring men, and the horse tethered to the fig tree. Le Grêlé, who slept with one eye open, got up.

"Lost someone?"

"Fool, why don't you mark your house? We almost took you for Turks."

But they had, they had painted the arms of Arras in blood and heaven knew how many crosses.

"How do you think we can see your blood in the dark? We heard there were infidels still in hiding somewhere around here."

The soldiers were Normans, tall blond men with long mustaches, wearing padded jerkins nearly down to the knee.

"So what?" said le Grêlé. "Have you no respect for the Sabbath? It is long past midnight."

"You with the face like a colander, what are you? A priest or something? God's work knows no day of rest."

They went away, cursing so foully that Élie crossed himself and spat on the ground. Beelzebub and all his nephews tickle their backsides for them, the murdering scum! They want their pay and double rations, and Jesus Christ into the bargain. He stepped over the sleeping bodies of his companions and crossed over to the door, only to recoil sharply as he encountered the stench of corpses that hung over the street like a noisome fog, while down below, oozing, bubbling, stirring quietly, the miasma of putrefaction was rising, warm and heavy with moisture. So soon, Élie thought. We must go carefully tomorrow.

The Normans had not been mistaken. In a few minutes the screams of the dying and the furious shouts of their murderers were heard once more.

• • •

It was clear beyond a doubt that the streets could not be left as they were. Many of the bodies had been lying there since Friday noon, and today was Sunday.

Outside the walls the barons had a hundred infidel prisoners, whose faith did not forbid them to work on Sundays.

The barons issued orders that any able-bodied men still to be found within the city, even women if they were young and strong, were not to be harmed but taken and put to work to clear the streets. The work they would have to do would be punishment enough.

You all say: Jerusalem. Jerusalem. Do you expect the filth of centuries to be washed away in a few hours? Do you expect the city to be delivered by blood and not to smell of blood, and the dead bodies of the enemy to give forth sweetness?

Look well at these gaping bellies and these shattered skulls, these severed limbs and this unspeakable mass of worms.

But for God's mercy, *even so would you have been this day!* Learn at least from this spectacle of horror to know God's goodness.

The city was very noisy all that day, with trumpets and clarions and drums, on the walls and towers and rooftops and in the principal squares. The soldiers were celebrating, and their instruments might be profane but their intention was not. It was a terrible music, solemn, harsh, joyful yet ominous, still throbbing with the screams of the dying and the clash of swords. Glutted with killing as they were, they could not change in a moment, or turn their rejoicing to pious orisons. Who but the soldier had won that stern and sacred battle, losing friends and brothers by Greek fire and shot and sword and battle-ax upon the wall and in the streets and in the Temple? The laborer is worthy of his hire, and common engineers and bowmen now had fine houses and gold pieces.

A kind of brotherhood had grown out of the sack, and on the house walls Flemish shields were to be seen displayed alongside those of Provence.

Tomorrow the gates would be thrown open, but today was a holiday. The barons had foregathered in what had been Iftikhar's palace for a great feast to which the abbots and arch priests of Jerusalem, Greeks and Syrians, were invited. The palace had been duly purified and sprinkled with holy water, all the Arabic inscriptions whitewashed over, and the walls hung with Christian banners. Trestle tables were set up, covered with gold and pur-

In the morning all the men who were able began to converg on the churches which had been purified. This was an ordeal i itself: the streets stank and in the narrow alleys the decomposin bodies had to be pushed aside with sticks to clear a passage.

Churches without bells, with bare, unpainted walls because the infidels had deprived the Christians of almost everything, and the churches that had not been desecrated were said to be so full of Greeks and Armenians and others of the local population that there was no getting inside them. Churches without bells, without images, without even candles: oh, what a pitiful mass for the first Sunday in Jerusalem! Be patient, brothers, such a glorious restoration cannot be accomplished in one day. You are asking too many miracles of God. Not two days ago you were still in the thick of the stones and arrows, without even water to drink.

God, was it less than two days? They had lost all count of time. Each day and night had been like a week—no, as if time had ceased to be the same, like the passage between sleep and waking, or between waking and dreaming.

O Lord God of glory, God of hosts, may this day never be forgotten.

MAY THIS FIFTEENTH OF JULY BE A DAY REMEMBERED BY ALL CHRISTIANS, A GREAT FEAST, THE FEAST OF JERUSALEM THE HOLY.

And of all the martyrs who fell there.

Knights and squires, sergeants, archers, men-at-arms, and miners and engineers and blasters, and poor pilgrims who were not trained for soldiers.

They labored so hard that their souls departed from their bodies and they know nothing of the battle they have won, unless it be from the songs of the angels.

You that have seen this day with the eyes of the flesh are richer than kings and princes. The Emperor of the Greeks and the Emperor of the Germans envy the meanest of you! Well may they come now and weep, for this happiness they can no longer buy, no, not for all the gold and silver in their palaces.

Let them keep their gold and silver, their armies and their engines of war. With a few soldiers and little money, men of France have purchased the Pearl of great price, with few men and little money, but a fortune in prayers and tears and blood.

And the strength of Jesus Christ.

As the sun is to the stars, so is Jerusalem to other cities.

• • •

ple silk, the water for the guests to wash their hands was offered in silver bowls, and pageboys brushed away the flies with peacock-feather fans.

Not a trace of blood remained on the floor of fine black and white tiles, and only some faint brownish stains on the long pale-pink Persian carpet.

Father Albert, washed, shaved, and dressed in a black woolen cloak, sat at the lower end of the table to act as an interpreter. There were few Latin priests with the army able to speak Greek, and because of this Father Albert knew that for as long as the Christians succeeded in maintaining themselves in Jerusalem his fortune was made. But as for whether they would succeed or not, *Domine, fiat voluntas tua,* not even the Duke or the counts or the bishops knew that.

. . . For if we are defeated now, not a child, not a monk or a leper will be spared. And all these proud, handsome heads that now wear a count's coronet upon their long fair hair will be embalmed like relics to adorn the treasure house of the Caliph's palace in Cairo.

The Greek prelates were equally aware of this and questioned Father Albert about whether the barons were expecting reinforcements, whether they had any news of the Emperor, and if the armies which had remained in the north, at Antioch, intended to come down into Judaea. In their cloistered lives they had not known, had not believed that the Christian army was so small and weak: well disciplined, certainly, but much exhausted by the siege. Father Albert spoke of God's goodness and the miraculous victories already won by the Christians. We have not been beaten yet. This victory was ordained by Jesus Christ.

It is His will, He cannot betray us now.

The Greek abbots, grave, dignified men with long pepper-and-salt beards and silver crosses gleaming on their black robes, expressed their gladness by sighing and raising their eyes to heaven and not by laughter: the day before they had appeared triumphant, chanting thank offerings at the top of their voices, burning with a vengeful fury. Oh glorious day! Blessed be the right hand of God that has wrought justice for us. The day before—

That was so long ago it was almost forgotten.

They were different now. The barons, the soldiers, all of them. And tomorrow we will no longer recall what we are today.

"To tell the truth—to tell the truth, father and worthy brother in Christ, these princes, although as pious as they are fearless, true champions of Christ, may perhaps have allowed their fighting men a little too much license."

"Reverend abbot, never believe it. These noble lords have hearts of mercy, their soldiers are no worse than other men, the poor pilgrims are honest Christians, but God has inflamed their hearts this day with a holy rage and they are no more to be blamed than the lightning that strikes from heaven.

"For God commanded the Israelites when they captured Jericho to spare no one, man, woman, or child, or any living thing, neither ox nor sheep nor fowl."

God be thanked, for otherwise in two days there would be famine.

They were served roast lamb stuffed with spices, chickens and ducks basted with palm wine, and good wine in silver cups; the laborer is worthy of his hire and those who had labored most in this campaign were still the knights. That morning they had all taken Communion at the Holy Sepulcher, as pure and shining in body as in soul, God bless them, but Father Albert was thinking of his poor, and of Brother Barnabé waiting in his coffin outside the walls. Surely it was a punishment from God to die almost on the eve of such a victory? Or was it a sign of grace?

All those left in the camp, the greater number of the monks and priests, the women and children, the sick and the few sound men who had volunteered to remain on guard to defend them, all these had gradually assembled on the side of the hill opposite the Gate of Herod, because this was where Peter had his tent. In this way they were not scattered and the camp was more easily guarded. All the carts had been brought together and lined up along the palisade, and all day Saturday, except when the sun was at its height, women and monks busied themselves searching the ditch for planks and timbers that were no longer needed, to strengthen the new barricades against possible Bedouin attacks.

When they saw the great mass of men pouring in through the open gate, like the waters of a lake through a breach in a shattered dike, when they saw that there was no more movement on the ladders and that the camp near the ramparts was emptying visibly, and that there was no more smoke upon the walls, only a headlong rush with Christian banners waving everywhere and the heathen banners hurled down into the moats, and that the greatest clamor had moved on from the walls to become dissipated through the city, then those who were unable to fight sent up such alleluias and hosannas and such a shout of joy and impatience as might have come from an army of madmen. For they were forced to remain where they were while their spirits longed to leap up and rush into the city, and so they waved their arms and danced or sprang forward down the hill and fell upon their knees. Brave, brave lads, God go with you. Blessed, brave, and holy friends. Oh God protect them. So good, the best of all, the very best, never were there such men since the Holy Apostles! Lord Jesus, they have given You back Your house.

THE CITY IS TAKEN
IT IS OURS

We are citizens of Jerusalem! Come, drink from the fountains of living water! The city is ours. We have taken it.

They were all slapping one another on the back and kissing one another's cheeks over and over again, kissing people they did not know from Adam or Eve, even monks kissing prostitutes. Everyone was crying out, "Lord!" Women fell into trances, some soiled their skirts, and others were taken with a bloody flux and lost that which they bore within them, while the youngest flung up their arms and danced: "Ours! Ours! Jesus Christ is ours!"

Exhausted, gasping between laughter and tears, they let the great wave flow over them, and when all was done there were those who had fallen in fits to be calmed and aid to be given to those who were taken ill, and the sick to be picked up off the ground where they had fallen from their stretchers. The strongest seized buckets and ran to the soldiers' reserves of water. There was still some left, a small ration for the evening. Ah, those brave lads have drunk nearly all. They have done well, what if they had drunk it all, oh for such good and faithful men we would have gone without a drink until the morning!

The buckets were emptied, the children quieted, and the sick revived. From the city, only a little way away, a dreadful clamor was rising. Sentinels stood by the banners, making sweeping gestures. Praise God, friends! The day is ours. Yet before very long joy turned to anxiety, for after all the fighting was still going on, great clouds of smoke could be seen hanging over the citadel, and the crash of missiles had not ceased. How can we tell if our lads have not rushed into a trap? Oh God, make them come out again, who knows, it may be a trick; who knows, the city is large and full of infidels. Quite suddenly the blessed gate, once gained, became the gate of hell. Who could tell what might be within the city? Would Iftikhar's emirs and the tall Sudanese and the Arabs of Arabia capitulate just like that because a few men had captured one wall and a gate? And surrender Jerusalem as they surrendered Nicaea? They have scaffolding behind the wall and great cauldrons full of boiling pitch standing ready up there.

Anxiety grew as the gusts of wind blowing back into the valley brought sounds of murderous screaming and fell cries. There was no way of telling who was screaming. The women went down in groups to the moat below the walls to question the sentinels. The sentinels gesticulated back: it's hot in there but our fellows are all right; it's all right, they are driving them back, they are running away. Suppose it is a trick? Suppose they have armed all the men?

But do our men realize? It is not like Antioch, their men outnumber ours by two or three to one. There are so few Christians. They are going into the lion's mouth.

"Hey, brothers, what news?"

"It's hot work but our men have reached the Temple!" All night long they listened to the screams and the roar of battle; there were lights on the walls and smoke rising from the city, but the news was good. That night there was feverish activity in the wreckage of the abandoned camps below the walls. People were running about with burning brands or even lighting fires near the edges of the moat, trying to drag out the dead and those who were not dead. A crowd collected outside the gate. The excitement was so great that none could sleep, however deadly weary they might be. Even the sick found strength to walk, leaning on staffs. The Count of Toulouse was inside the city, had gained the citadel! No, he had not taken it yet, but the Turks were besieged inside and the men of Provence were going through the streets dealing out great slaughter.

There was fighting around the Temple, fighting inside the Temple. There was fighting in all the streets. Oh Lord, do not let them be martyrs, make them come back to us alive!

"Oh no, my friends, this is no time to go running over the bridge; they will not let us in; our men are fighting bitterly, we will not add to their troubles by rushing madly into the city.

"Oh my friends, Alix was right to do as she did. How wise she was! I would not be so frightened now if I were inside fighting alongside my Jacques. I should get between him and the Africans' swords."

"Do not be afraid, Marie. Listen to what they are saying. God has broken their spirit and they are allowing themselves to be slaughtered like sheep."

There was no way of knowing what souls they were that fled with those great cries. Women were screaming, certainly, many women. Surely the city has fallen. This is not a battle, it is a massacre.

Marie no longer saw the high wall with its crown of torches against the dark sky. Instead, she seemed to see inside the city: the white streets were filled with light, and lined up in front of the houses were the Sudanese with their black faces and their lifted swords glinting like fire. The fiery swords swept off the Christians' heads and they went on, headless, while great fountains of blood spurted from their decapitated bodies. But still they went on running, running along without their heads, and everywhere the fountains leaped up, splashing the walls and turning the white pavements into running streams, and the Sudanese swords flashed again and again. "Alas, my friends, I see so much blood the streets are filled with it, the gutters are running over. It is pouring out of the doors and windows, it is dripping from the roofs!"

"It must be heathen blood that you see, Marie. Listen to the voices. It is not our men that are being killed."

"Oh my friends, the city is red like a flayed animal!" Marie was rigid, her hands pressed flat against her temples, sobbing with terror, harsh, dry sobs that left her sightless eyes parched and burning.

"Be quiet, you wicked girl," Honorine told her, "and take care what you are saying. You will bring bad luck on us."

A Norman priest standing nearby spoke to them: "Take courage, women, and do not mourn. There is no doubt the city is ours."

"Oh my friends, my head is all confused. I cannot see straight. Saint Michael and Saint George watch over our men. May we see them again, coming out through that gate, the same as they went in!"

"Tell me," the priestess was asking, "tell me, do you see any harm coming to Lambert?"

"I can't see anything," Marie said wildly. "I see nothing for anyone. The screaming, that terrible screaming. It is the wrath of God."

A storm of wrath. The night was cold and the city, with the torches moving about on the walls and the smoke and the din and the shouting, seemed to stand amid the cold dark hills like a monstrous heap of embers. Or a ghost city riven from another world, doomed every night for a thousand years to relive the day of wrath, a city without night or day, where horror and violence stalked the streets and flooded the open spaces like a river of sultry heat. Victory! Victory! God has delivered our enemies into our hands!

The first morning, the dawn of the first morning whitened, cold and pure, and the sweet morning star shone with its golden fire above the great furnace of the city of Judgment, the royal city ringed with the rocky hills like immense couching lions. Tremble and give thanks: down there men are meting out such a judgment as this world has not seen since the Resurrection of Jesus Christ.

The sky above the shoulder of the mountains beyond Jerusalem glowed palest primrose, the color of warm ashes. The mist in the valleys was white as snow and in an instant it was gone. Bless God in all His works; the new day dawning is the first day of Jerusalem delivered. The topmost towers and minarets blazed like beacons in the sunrise.

The trumpets on the walls were blowing fanfares of joy, and rising louder and louder above the din came the chorus of hundreds of voices singing hymns: all those without the walls sang with them. They sang, but in the city the screaming did not cease and the smoke of many fires rose and lay over the city, touched to gold in the sunlight.

Then the guards allowed the men to pass and they crossed over the bridge and separated, some to the right and some to the left, searching for the billets of their friends. Not many came out of the city: a company of the Duke's soldiers detailed to relieve the guard on the ladies' camp, and a handful of pilgrims. Those who saw them coming out felt a moment's fear that these were the only survivors, but the newcomers were making great gestures of joy, waving their arms above their heads and flourishing their weapons, so that it was clear they were proclaiming a victory.

Jean-Marc found his people and told them the names of the dead: Garin of Amiens and a young Norman lad who had been adopted by them. As for the wounded, they were lying in a good house where there was water and food.

Who had been hurt, and how? "Nothing serious, a few scratches. My son Mathieu has lost his right eye." Mathieu's wife began to scream and wail in Armenian, but Jean-Marc told her, "Take your howling elsewhere. This is no time to cry," and she was quiet. He was covered with blood: it had dried on his clothes and on his hair and on his beard and was like a thick crust on his feet. "Oh, Jean-Marc, what a fight it was! Say, are they fighting still?"

"There may be some fighting, but it's not a battle, more like a butchery. They were in no state to defend themselves."

"Oh, the fools, they thought we could never take the city!"

"Jean, have our men taken many heads?"

"Heads? The city is full of heads, no one bothers with them. All the good ones have been taken by the knights and their men."

"But they are all good ones, Jean, and we should have liked to see them! They are all good that are not our own."

"Jean-Marc, is it true they had filled the Church of the Holy Sepulcher with filth and ordure?"

"I have not heard so. The barons have been there, and their knights."

Brother Imbert came up. His long beard was quivering and his narrow shoulders were bowed, but his eyes were shining. He was very weak and shivering with fever and looked more than ever like an old bald vulture. "Beautiful indeed are the feet of the bearer of good tidings! Brother Jean-Marc, you are here as one returned alive out of the hell of battle, in anguish and in joy we have prayed for you this night. Do you know when we will be permitted to go and worship God at the Holy Sepulcher?"

Jean-Marc did not know, no one knew precisely: "In three days, yes, probably in three days when order has been reestablished. You cannot imagine what it's like, the very stones cry out, truly it is God's judgment."

"Do not let your heart be troubled, brother. Whom the Lord

loveth He chasteneth, and in truth few men have been more loved than the poor pilgrims on this great pilgrimage!"

When Brother Imbert spoke, everything seemed to fall miraculously into place. Courage, Israel, you have seen the fall of Babylon and triumphed over Pharaoh. God has granted to the poor and humble the miracle He has long denied to kings! Only let your hearts be great enough to contain the joy of God.

Dead tired and shivering with fever, the women climbed back to their camp. They placed the sick on litters and hitched themselves to the carts. The word went around to gather by Peter's tent. Those who had taken no part in the fighting felt lost in the empty camp, which now seemed suddenly too big, and the mounting excitement with which they waited for news was almost devoid of joy, so great was their fatigue. Happiness smoldered within them, slumbering secretly until the moment came for it to wake and burst out in earnest. Lord, who will have the strength to bear it?

The prostitutes were striking camp also, with tears and cries, for that day all were penitents, ready to swear perpetual chastity for the honor of being admitted to worship at the Holy Sepulcher. Saint Mary Magdalene, Saint Mary the Egyptian, Saint Theodosia, fair as queens, glorious saints standing with the virgins and the matrons in heaven, how many poor souls will run to shelter underneath their cloaks of celestial brocade! Jerusalem the holy has converted us: we will go to the Bishop and the Patriarch and ask for their protection. They too brought their carts, and gave away their necklaces, bracelets, and amulets to the wives of the poor: "Sisters, do not scorn these gifts. We are all Christian women, our necklaces are not dirty, we have all repented from head to foot!"

On one of their carts they brought Mère Ludivine, trussed up like a parcel, and the "Queen" of the harlots (so-called because she had charge of their supplies and all their business arrangements) came in search of Brother Imbert and told him that the madwoman, who was apparently a Picard, was herself again and should be restored to her friends. Accordingly, they released Ludivine from her bonds and gave her a dress to put on.

She let them dress her without a struggle. The poor woman's limbs were so numbed that she could not walk but fell down on her knees, and it was in this position that her countrywomen found her, sitting on the ground with her hair all disheveled and her eyes glinting like bright steel buttons in her curiously emaciated face. Yet, as if the bodies of the insane were not made of human flesh, within a few minutes Ludivine was as lively as a girl of twenty again. Leaping to her feet with such suddenness that the other women sprang back hastily, she ripped her gown down to the waist and dropped it at her feet.

She stood stark naked once more, her body still showing the marks of the ropes, her ribs and hipbones standing out and her breasts as flat as a pair of sandal soles. Jean-Marc went toward her, with Brother Imbert and an elderly weaver from Lille who was uncle to Ludivine's brother-in-law. The women tried to prevent them, but the madwoman rushed up to the three men and began flinging her arms and legs about, showing all that should not decently be shown. She lifted up the points of her breasts, saying, "See my little apples, see my pretty buds!" Brother Imbert and the old man turned away for shame and crossed themselves, but Jean-Marc stepped forward and gripped the woman by the shoulders: "Woman, it is I, Jean. For God's sake, pull yourself together!"

She threw her arms around his neck and spoke to him wheedlingly: "Oh my knight, how handsome you are, I kiss your blond hair."

At this, Jean-Marc drew his knife from his belt and brandished it before the madwoman's eyes. "*Divine. You see this, Divine?*" He meant to do no more than frighten her, since fear can sometimes cure madness. He held the knife to the woman's breast with a dreadful look, and his own eyes were so wild that he seemed on the point of falling into a fit. Ludivine twisted free, snatching the knife out of his hands, and what followed then was so swift that no one realized what was happening. The two of them were rolling on the ground, and such was the madwoman's strength that Jean-Marc was barely able to grasp her wrist and turn away the knife. The next moment the knife was in his hand and they saw him strike furiously several times, wrenching out the blade to plunge it back between the projecting ribs that fluttered like the gills of a fish.

For a moment Ludivine seemed to be herself again. She gazed around her with a look of surprise and murmured, "A priest, a priest." But by the time a priest could be found she was unconscious and breathing her last. Jean-Marc sat by her, his arms folded on his knees and his head down on his arms. Then one of the barons' provosts was seen approaching from the ladies' camp accompanied by two soldiers, having heard there was a man flown with drink who had stabbed a whore. Rumor traveled fast and the barons' law would not tolerate license, especially on such a day.

All the witnesses exonerated Jean-Marc and said that he had done nothing but defend himself; the woman had been mad, and furthermore he was her husband.

"Truly," Jean-Marc said. "A drunken man and a whore. The witnesses speak truth, lords. I did not mean to kill her. I am in no state to say anything." The sergeant looked with disgust at the dead woman lying on the ground and at the exhausted man with the blood dried black upon him, and said that it was a shameful thing that this great day should be marred by such sordid affairs.

"Cruel men, may your own wives be stricken with the same trouble." "You fool, these men have no wives, or if they have they are well fed and live with the knights' ladies." *Ludivine wore her heart threadbare.*

Oh Ludivine, this great day is your festival. Today your Christian soul tears itself free of the body with a fierce gladness, for so many heathen souls are damned in Jerusalem that the devils have no eyes for Christians; they ignore them and will not trouble your journey.

Like a great translucent sheet stretched over the city, trembling, rustling, crackling, riven with small lightning flashes, the thousands of souls parted from their bodies are contended for by the devils and the angels, and the noise of their battling wings drowns the roar of madness from the city.

My God, already the knights have attained their joy and see the Holy Sepulcher with their own eyes, but for us the judgment is not yet fulfilled; we are lost among the crying souls. Marie sat in the shadow of a cart, hugging Pierre to her breast, and gazed at the towers of the city and at the banners and the smoke, feeling the air vibrate as if with a long peal of thunder. Her own head felt full of thunder and lightning: Oh my Pierre, how shall we hold out for three more days? She wanted to pray for the men inside the city but the noise in her head prevented her. "Rufine, give me a drink, for God's sake. I think I have caught the sun." She drank. It was good water, scarcely warm. The soldiers had brought a wagon loaded with casks from Jerusalem. It hardly seemed possible that they had water in the city, so many cisterns full that it was like being in Antioch.

Stories went around. About the Jews, and how the Flemings had taken the glassmakers' quarter. The Jews there had their vats full of molten glass, heated white-hot, and welcomed the Flemings with a shower of molten glass, burning them to death. Apart from the soldiers of the garrison, the Jews had been the only ones to put up anything like a fight. In the end they had been overcome by a trick: they were told that their lives would be spared if they shut themselves up in their synagogue.

"That was not right, it was a lie."

"And have they never lied? They betrayed Jesus Christ. We had no time to spare to flush them out house by house, had we? Their lives would have been spared if they had chosen to be converted. They were offered that chance, which the Moslems were not . . . Besides, you can be sure that if they had not been made to go into the synagogue, not one house in their quarter would have been left habitable."

"Is it beautiful, Jerusalem?" "So beautiful, Christians, that one can never tire of looking at it. Churches and houses and open spaces as fair as in Constantinople, so much fine carved and decorated stonework, mosaics of gold and precious stones, and arches and colonnades all faced with marble!"

"And fountains?"

"Not so many as in Antioch, but finer, as big as chapels with domed roofs and golden grilles. Once it is cleaned up, the city will be paradise."

Because you must know that for the moment there is so much blood in the streets and courtyards, so much blood—so much blood that in the Temple of Solomon, their great mosque, men waded in blood up to the knee.

Oh, what a sight that must have been, how beautiful and terrible! Nothing like it was ever seen before, even after the fiercest battles.

"I saw so much of it," the men were saying, "that it seemed strange to see people that were in one piece, with heads on their shoulders and their bellies not gaping open. You see, the rumor had spread that the men and even the women were swallowing their gold coins and their precious pearls, and you should have seen those Provençal ruffians, and soldiers even, fishing about in the entrails with their knives and their bare hands: they were all but sniffing at them like dogs." The women listened, thoughtful and bewildered. Well, it was a strange way to get rich, all the same. "Was it any better when we used to hunt in the gutters for dead rats in Antioch, eh?"

"But to soil your hands with searching for gold in the holiest place in all the world!"

"Well, good women, soldiers are made like that. They are paid to get themselves killed, so they are bound to love gold."

It will not be long now, everything in its season. While there is still fighting in the streets and the division of the spoils is still going on and not even the knights know where to look for their men, the gates must be strictly guarded.

You must know that at this moment there are more dead than living in the city.

That was small comfort. They might say the news was good, but as the hours passed and the roaring and yelling and howling continued over there within the walls, when the hours passed and all that was needed was the time for a single scream to turn a living man into a dead one, how many men said to be alive that morning were so still?

If a count is killed, or a knight of great renown, the news is known at once, but our friends—even if all of them were dead, they would still tell us that the news was good. Who knows their names? Only God counts the poor.

Angels of death, tear out only the weeds: may our men shine like ears of corn in the sun of the great Judgment and let the corrupt put on corruption.

Shame to Mahomet who failed to protect his own. If God wills, we shall go all the way to Mecca, revealing his falsehood in the eyes of all men and putting an end to vain superstition. For now all the kings of Christendom will send us armies and our victory is like the grain of mustard seed, like the handful of leaven which soon makes all the dough rise. Ships have already sailed from Jaffa, bearing the good news to the Pope and to all our kings. And there is no need of messengers to carry the news to the kings of Damascus and Baghdad and Cairo: by tomorrow the screams of Jerusalem will be heard and the news will carry from mouth to mouth like a great echo. Already the Caliph of Baghdad and the Caliph of Cairo have put on mourning and curse Mahomet for his neglectfulness.

We must act quickly; there is no time to be lost. If the defenses of the city are not put in order within ten or fifteen days, men will talk of our martyrdom and not of our victory.

The harvest is abundant, but the harvesters are few. The harvest of damned souls and broken bodies. This was God's will, Christians, do not panic but remember that this harvest must be gathered swiftly and garnered in the barns that God has prepared on the sides of the valley of Cedron and in the valley of Jehoshaphat.

The work is hard but by no means shameful; all the poor with the army who register for employment under the authorities, either at the citadel where the Count of Toulouse has his headquarters, or at the palace of the Duke of Lower Lorraine near the Temple, or at the guardrooms of the Jaffa or Herod's towers will receive three dirhams or two Byzantine deniers for a day's work. All gangs to be ready by Monday morning, and for God's sake, Christians, do not be idle, for time is short.

The leaders responsible for groups of pilgrims or confraternities, of whatever nation or trade, should assemble every man able to wield a pick or shovel and register with the authorities: wages will be guaranteed under oath and paid at each day's end at the rate of so much per man. Women and children over ten years of age may also be employed at half rates, either inside the city or outside, digging pits, for the army's own miners would never be enough.

Gangs are to be ready to begin work at daybreak digging and removing the soil; trenches to be at least five feet deep and six feet wide. All those owning picks, shovels, axes, hoes, or other tools will receive an additional dirham for every two days' work; the rest will be supplied with implements which must be returned to the authorities.

From midnight on, those inside the city are to begin constructing as many hurdles and stretchers as they are able. Wagons will be provided by the authorities in the Temple Square, the Corn Market, and the Cattle Market, together with oxen to draw them. There will be some smaller hand-drawn carts also. But no cart is to leave the city until it has been filled, not to the brim, but up to two feet above the brim, and the load tied down with ropes.

Owing to the urgency of the task, workers are forbidden to delay in order to plunder or mutilate corpses as they are being taken up. If they see any objects of value on the bodies that may be easily removed, they are free to take them, provided there are no disputes: objects belong rightfully to the man who sees and points to them first.

Le Grêlé said, "This is not such bad news, lads. There are ten of us men here able to work, and six children."

"And one woman," Alix said. The sound of her voice, which was hard and dry, made them all look around: they thought she must be ill. She was sitting in a corner of the courtyard with her arms folded, as still as a statue.

"Good, and one woman," Élie continued. "That will earn us twenty-seven Byzantine sous a day, which in two days makes fifty-four. We have never earned so much money in our lives. Besides, the work must be done."

"But why?" said Guillaume of Avesnes. "Why should we do prisoners' work?"

"Because there are not enough prisoners," Jacques said. "You have seen our prisoners, they are out there in the street. It would be a clever man who could make them work."

"And Iftikhar and his emirs still in the citadel? They should be put to work first!"

"No, friends," le Grêlé said, "the barons are not going to wait for our advice about that. And the dead will not wait either."

"But why us?" Jacques said. "They should divide up the work by districts. We did not make the most. Is it for us to clean up the soldiers' refuse?"

Mardoche and Onésime and the others clapped their hands and called out, "Well said, Jacques!" Élie looked at them, but he was too tired to feel much resentment.

"I'm in command here. And you, Jacques, are talking nonsense. The soldiers would never do prisoners' work. It is different for us. Remember Antioch. If the city should be besieged, the price of corn will be tripled overnight and up ten times the day after. We have not taken as much plunder as all that. With our wives and our Syrians in the camp outside the city who can work in the trenches, we will have earned as much as eighty sous, if not more."

"You are daydreaming, Élie," said Mathieu of Lille. "They will never pay so much for digging trenches. For collecting the bodies, yes, but not for digging."

Jacques sat up so suddenly that his shirt, already rotten, split right across his chest. "Look, friends, is this Jerusalem or not?

Here we are in Jerusalem and everything is just the same as before. Already we are thinking about the price of corn."

"Only the dead do not eat," said Élie.

"Then you should have thought of it before," Jacques said roughly, "when you forced the doors of a sheik's harem without bringing away so much as a pin. The boys told me what you did there. You had your chance, and it was not worth Lambert's arm just to cut a few throats while the Lorrainers helped themselves to the goods. They say you walked right past the jewel box without even seeing it."

"Well worth it indeed," Élie said scornfully, "just to be in Jerusalem. I did not take the cross in order to steal jewels."

Jacques was in the mood to reach for his ax, and but for Guillaume of Avesnes, who was a powerful man of middle age, they would have come to blows.

"You must not blame him, Grêlé. He has a great grief on him."

"Which of us has not?" le Grêlé said.

Lambert was feverish but no worse. His wound was still healthy, and he lay dozing on a heap of blankets in the corner of the courtyard near the cistern, his body shuddering convulsively from time to time. There were grey shadows around his eyes, and his hair and his short curly beard were drenched and black with sweat. His whole body seemed bloated and disjointed, and looking at him Jacques was reminded horribly of the corpses, the masses of dead meat and fat rotting in the streets. They had been well fed, the dogs; no bones showed through their bellies and buttocks and legs. They had nothing to complain of, they had lived well, had never gone short of water, cisterns of fresh water even in summer, they washed and had no scabs, and yet people pitied them, while we are the ones who must clear up their rotting carcasses. Lambert, old fellow, don't give up. They shall not have you. Never think so. God damn their souls, they are all about us now, but they can do no harm to a Christian soul.

This deadly weariness. It hardly seemed possible to imagine that in three days' time they would see the place of the true light.

And what if the sun fell to earth this very day, and the moon, and a rain of stars, and a rain of angels? Suppose it were true what they say and this day's pains were the last? We have come to the brink of hell.

Oh, how we need our priests and our wives, so that we may go all together to the Holy Sepulcher by the Way which Jesus trod bearing His Cross—

When we have got rid of the stench.

You had to be strong for this work. In the houses and courtyards you did not notice it so much, for although the smell was strong you got used to it; you could get by even in the streets if you held your nose. It was almost incredible—almost incredible—yes, who could ever imagine the things men could get used to? During those days time stood still, and already they seemed to have lived all their lives in a city full of corpses, in this city, on this Sunday when the city was almost peaceful now that the killing had stopped and the streets were still too choked to allow processions.

Compared to the work all that was nothing, nothing at all, a pleasure, even.

Now is a fine time, you fools. That was what they were saying: Now is a fine time to turn your heads away and vomit up blood and bile, when two days ago you were laying about you with the best, spilling out guts and brains. You were not backward in that work, you were like ravening wolves, more ferocious than the soldiers whose only thought was plunder.

What they, the soldiers, are saying is that you did a lot of unnecessary damage, not only on the day of the assault, when every man was honestly beside himself, but all the next day and Saturday night as well, in a senseless fury, simply taking advantage of the confusion and of the fact that the barons and leaders were resting piously. The soldiers spoke contemptuously, and how could anyone retort that they had been seen at work all day Saturday and all night until Sunday morning, and that many of the dead in the parts of the city where they were quartered were still fresh? There were girls lying outside their billets, still white and clean but ravished for all they were worth, with more blood between their legs than ever came out of their throats. Hadn't they all seen them at it? And God knows the poor had weapons of a sort but no lances and spiked maces, no swords or crossbows, and there were some quarters where none of the poor had so much as set foot.

And if this was God's judgment, then no one is to blame.

Say, friends, suppose that God had sent a pestilence to destroy His enemies, as he did when the Assyrians were besieging Jerusalem, and all these people had died of the plague: we should have had the same work to do, and with the added risk of catching the disease in our turn. God has been merciful to us.

Take heart, already four big ox wagons have left the city. "Four wagons? Oh God, it will take hundreds."

If you have open wounds, bandage them well, there is no shortage of cloth now; bandage them, for if you do not you are certain to get gangrene. The juice that runs from the bodies is like serpent's venom.

Oh God.

In three years men thought they had grown used to corpses, but it was not so; they had seen nothing yet. Old soldiers turned green as moldy bread and turned aside to vomit. Most of all, it was the smell. Strong even when nothing was moved, as soon as the bodies were stirred with a pitchfork it rose in dense waves. The flies rose in clouds, so thick that the air in the streets was black and buzzing to the height of a man. The men moved through it as if through a storm of black hail coming, not from above, but from below.

All shiny black and green, heavy as ripe olives, swollen to bursting point with rottenness. They circled slowly, as if they were drunk, and settled anywhere, on the living and the dead. The men carting the bodies were covered with them and could not shake them off because they had lost all impulse to move; they would rouse for an instant at a shake of the head, then settle back again. The sun was climbing higher in the sky, scorching the roofs and beginning to penetrate into the streets.

The men brought flat hurdles which they dragged along the ground, and lifted the bodies carefully so as to disturb the putrefying flesh as little as possible, but it made no difference; the slightest movement was enough to release a burst of evil vapor that struck like a blow in the face.

The bodies burst open, releasing jets of black fluid, bodies covered with a black snow in which green lights shimmered, a devil's snow that lifted in slow spirals and got in the men's hair until it was crawling with them, got under the cloths they had tied across their mouths, they could not see for them—God be thanked, for even that was better than seeing what lay upon the ground.

Half blinded, with shovels and spades and pitchforks they scooped up what had to be collected. On hurdles and stretchers, piled as full as they would hold, and then they carried them to the nearest crossroads and tipped the loads onto the carts: heavier than bales of hay but not so heavy as stones, the weight of men's bodies, flesh weighed down by death as clay by water.

The carts were to be filled, not to the brim, but to a height of two feet above the brim; but some of the bodies were difficult to stack because they were as stiff as dead trees, arms and legs spread-eagled, twisted, leaving gaps to be filled in with severed heads and the bodies of little children. Oh God, children like that, whoever they were, stained black and eaten up with flies, their heads smashed to a pulp.

And oh the women, swollen faces, oozing with rottenness, a glimpse of fair white teeth still set in a fixed smile through the moist, seeping flesh, huge eyes black with flies in faces streaked with brown juice, and yellow claw-hands poking up over the edges of the carts in gestures clutching or menacing.

Well, they had stopped screaming now, and yet it seemed as if the sound of their screaming had continued for so long that it would fill men's ears for days to come, and although the screaming had stopped, the stench was so powerful that they seemed to feel it like a great scream all through their bodies. Lying there on the stretchers and the carts, stacked at the crossroads, the bodies were alive with a warm, dreadful life, sucking and bubbling, seething, whispering, like the subdued simmering of innumerable streams of fermenting barley.

Hour after hour, hour after hour, the dead pursued this life of their own, giving themselves to rottenness as to a feast. The carts were filled to bursting and the sound of decomposition was like heavy breathing, and all the time as the men worked they felt as if the bodies were beginning to move, were turning into the walking dead, in a little they might rise up and walk about the city, just as they were, all dripping with black juices, stuffed with worms—oh God, how grim and pitiful, too pitiful even for fear.

Yet some men were afraid and in their fear, when they saw an unmutilated body, before they laid it on the hurdle they would cut off the head, or if that was too difficult, the genitals, or even slide their knives quickly in between the ribs and cut out the heart, for God knows if these dead ever came to life they would make men mad—

A little girl, all bloated and greenish-grey in color with a head like a giant toad, sat propped against a wall, her legs drawn up and black hair lying in smooth, lusterless waves on her shoulders, her staring eyes so thick with flies that they seemed to flicker and a slow trickle of black blood oozing from the corners of her mouth. And that other, a white-haired woman, black and wizened as a prune, her hands crossed on her breast and her mouth gaping open: when the hooks pulled her over on her side a vomit of black bile came from her mouth and her stiffened hands clutched at the side of the stretcher. It was a fight to get to grips with them, they were more tenacious than the living, and there were so many that they had been left to stiffen in the posture in which death had taken them, legs and arms outflung, knees bent, so twisted and contorted that it would take an ax to make them move at all, rigid statues of putrefaction.

Beside them the flesh of the living seemed a poor thing, puny and insubstantial, flinching at the slightest contact, a flesh whose fleeting odors a little water would dispel. But these, this race of bodies without souls, their odor was more powerful than the sun's rays. Stunning, suffocating, invincible, *for but for that they would very soon have grown accustomed to the horror before their eyes, and even to the flies.*

The wagons rolled slowly to the gates. In the congestion at street corners, the men harnessed to the carts waited their turn patiently. They passed over the bridge in a continuous stream and drew their loads to the very edge of the trenches, then they emptied the carts, paused to rest for a moment, and went back into the city. Well, asked the men working in the streets, how is it going with the trenches? Not very fast, the ground is too hard, they will never dig fast enough. Those working on the trenches had the best of it. The air was clean there and a breeze was blowing, but except for the army quarriers they were not good workers: women and aged monks and children who could not lift even half a sack of earth.

At the very far end of the camp even the lepers had been taken on. There were some stout fellows among them, well able to work. As for the local Christians, they knew the ground and had good tools, but little heart: many had fled at the sight of so many bodies in such a state of decomposition.

The oxcarts returned and waited in the open spaces and the caravanserais while the piled litters were emptied into them. The smell upset the oxen, making them shy and refuse to go on. They went down on their knees, and even the best drivers had a job to get them moving. The sight of the bodies maddened them, and they tugged so awkwardly at their loads that they had to have their eyes bandaged and be pricked on with pikes, bellowing and rattling their yokes.

But worst of all were the men who had been trampled to death in the assault on Friday. They had been crushed almost to a pulp that same day, first by the rush of men and later by the horses, and then, because the street was a main thoroughfare, they had been heaped up in the side streets, and after that the Devil alone could have sorted them out; besides, they had stiffened and were so intertwined and stuck together that neither hooks nor shovels could force them apart, and they had to be put on the hurdles in lumps, five or six at a time. It was a real charnel house of arms and legs and heads, all jumbled together at random, hot and stinking and humming, a real witches' brew, while as for the worms, they dropped out in such masses that the ground was crawling with them, a white blanket before the eyes, white and black, worms and flies, flies and worms, not a particle of flesh but seemed alive. The stench was so great that men fainted from it. Those who were taken ill had to be carried into the houses and heaved up onto the roofs, and have water thrown over them.

Make way for the dead carts! Two knights on horseback, dressed in tunics of pale-green silk, with their squires riding behind driving laden mules, for the Marketplace had been cleared since Sunday and the soldiers were selling everything, cloth, vessels, jewels, perfumes, and spices.

But now, noble knights, kindly stand aside and wait, for today, today the dead still take precedence in this street and all the way to Herod's Gate the way is blocked, it is not fit for your mounts. They sat there, white coifs on their well-washed heads, their eyes light in their tanned faces, blinking in the sunlight, staring in horror and disgust, and when one of the men working asked them to move aside they all but crossed themselves at the sight of him.

For in very truth the men who were working there, their ragged clothes stained with the ooze from the bodies, rags wrapped around their heads and concealing their faces, as thick with flies as the dead themselves, looked like dead men burying their dead; their appearance was so ghastly that it must have come as a surprise to the knights to hear them speak in good French. With their pitchforks and their hooks.

Do not look so dismayed, brothers, or glare so angrily, for God knows in all this you had your part, and a fine part it was. All Friday's dead are yours. All the way from the wall and from Herod's Gate as far as the Temple and the Marketplace, Friday's dead belong to the knights. They cut their way through, to do them justice, they forced their way through like a spearhead, drawing the soldiers after them.

But when they did their work, these bodies were living men, good to look on and to kill, with red blood, crimson and ruby-red, great fountains of blood spurting everywhere from the headless trunks of Christian and infidel alike.

Then why do you not come and share in God's work? Why do you not take up your pitchforks for Saint Charity and wade through this corruption? You had your part in it and we, praise God, had ours, and you have by far the greatest share of the booty, but for the dead, doubt not that the poorest pilgrim did as much as any knight. There were enough for all, and in the joy of killing no one was denied.

A big white horse had run amuck and was charging about the packed streets, forcing its way past the carts and trampling the dead. The men had barely time to leave their work and leap back against the walls. Kicking, rearing and stamping, uttering shrill, almost human screams, it made short rushes here and there, then passed on out of sight. This happened just at the time of day when the sky was turning to molten gold and the towers and domes lit up with orange lights, while the heat had not yet abated but hung over the city, heavy with the smell of death, and the mad horse galloped about, screaming and showing its fearsome teeth, its legs and muzzle stained brown with blood. It seemed to be everywhere, in all four corners of the city at once, and none knew whence it came and no one dared to kill it. Long after it had passed by, men seemed to hear its heavy gallop and its anguished squeals. It was seen by men in different places at the same time, but only as a vision. Darkness fell and in the churches vespers were being sung, and still the horse loomed out of the blue shadows that lay between the houses, like a great white shape that blotted out the sky. Vespers were being sung and the laborers could rest in their houses until next day, but there was no rest.

Nearly all the men returned to their billets dazed and stupefied, their eyes filled with visions, for the dead that had lain quietly until they were disturbed seemed now to multiply: men saw them on the walls and against the sky; like the spots that dance before the eyes after looking at the sun, their bloated, inhuman faces would rise up everywhere, *even on the shoulders of a comrade.*

And although many streets had been cleared, the smell had not diminished. It followed you like a beast on the scent, it was in the water and the bread. Tomorrow the work will be done and we will go out of the city and fetch the women. Tomorrow. That night there were those among the men of Arras who said, No, mercy, we will not do it again tomorrow. We are sick. "Sleep," le Grêlé said. "Tonight we shall sleep. We have pledged ourselves to this work. There are seventeen of us, counting the children. We shall be seventeen tomorrow."

Alix drew water in a jar and gave it to the men to drink. They could not help admiring her; she held herself well in hand, as straight as a candle, tight-lipped, with never a sigh or an oath. Nor had she spared herself during the day, doing things the men could not bring themselves to do, scooping up armfuls of guts with her bare hands. Yet she was not like the children, who were tougher than the adults, not conscious of the same disgust and hardly even of fatigue. They could all see that there were times when she had to fight to keep herself from fainting.

The sick were beginning to revive and look more hopeful. Indeed, they had not been so well fed and lodged for a long time. There were stores of corn and dried fruit in the house, and it felt strange to eat and drink without a thought for the next day's rations. Inside the courtyards the smell was not too oppressive and they were almost able to forget it. Their wounds were healing well. Jean-Marc's son Mathieu was even talking of going to work the next day in his brother's place, for the wound in his eye was not deep; the eye had been gouged out but the weapon had not penetrated right through, and so Mathieu was not in pain and insisted that he could see as well as ever. His brother Thomas was reeling from exhaustion; he was convinced that worms were crawling all over him, but it was only fleas and lice. Although the night was cold he took off all his clothes and inspected his arms and legs and belly and insisted that he could see them everywhere, that they were burrowing in through the pores of his skin to devour him. Altogether, he made such a to-do that in the end

Élie grew tired of it. "You're not the only one. We are all seeing things. Say your prayers and then lie down and go to sleep."

"They will never dig enough trenches," Jacques said. "They say all the ones that have been dug are full to overflowing already, and the ones they are working on on this side and over toward Jehoshaphat will not be half enough. It is all rocks and stone, and they will hardly start uprooting the olive trees."

"In a little while," Guillaume said, "it will all be good soil. Wait and see how the vines will grow there. Let's hope it settles down before the rains."

"They will never dig enough trenches," Jacques said. He was thinking of the women. The heaps of bodies were not far from the camp and all the women who were able were working on the trenches. Some of them were pregnant: what would they give birth to after such a sight? Marie. Marie was strong, but she was young—oh God, she will not like to see this!

Lambert was still in great pain. His wound was not gangrenous but it was suppurating, and at times the ghost of his left hand came back. He could feel it, could feel the pain in his fingers. "Jacques, it is calling me."

"Don't be a fool. A hand does not have a soul."

"Jacques, when my mother comes, you must not tell her. Let her think it is just a little wound.

"Jacques, I want to last out until the Holy Sepulcher. I've earned that at least, haven't I?"

"Of course you have. Then you will be cured. And your mother too. Everyone will be cured, we shall all be born again."

Jean-Marc's sons were wondering if their mother would be cured also, for they did not yet know what had happened in the camp on Saturday. They thought that if they bound her and wrapped her in blankets they would be able to get her to the Holy Sepulcher. They wondered if Anselme of Béthune would lose his ulcers, and deaf Bernard hear again . . . *Miracles,* the knights and the clerks and the priests who have been there, to the Holy Sepulcher, and even their men-at-arms, they are all big, strong men and need only small miracles, but for so many poor would God Himself have power enough? First come first served, but who could tell you who should be first?

Not the Provençals, they have betrayed God.

"They let Iftikhar and his emirs go free with their guards and their families. They sent them out of the Sion Gate under an armed escort, with weapons and baggage!" "It's not true, the Count is too good a Christian! It's all rumors."

"Maybe, but that is what they are saying in the city. Even the Provençals don't look too pleased with themselves."

"Well, even so," Alix said, "the poor of Provence had nothing to do with it."

"They are all the same race," said Guillaume the Picard. "Certainly there are many more thieves among them than we have. Godfrey would never have let Iftikhar go. He has sworn to have his head."

"Were you there when he swore it?" Alix asked. "The Tafurs had the right idea, killing the horses on Saturday and the sheep and the fowls, and breaking the silver dishes and scattering the corn—there's no sense in being mad halfway, lads."

"That's all very well, Alix," Mathieu said, "but what then? Are we to eat Turk's flesh?"

"We are eating it already," Alix said with an odd, brittle laugh. "What else have we been doing since Friday?"

Élie said, "You are imagining things. None of us have done that."

"All right," said Alix, "I am imagining things. All day and all night."

There were rumors of maddened men who on Friday night had eaten hearts and brains, really eaten them, and these were not Tafurs but poor soldiers, driven insane by the heat of battle. They had gnawed like ravening wolves, and it was said that some had actually turned into wolves and run on all fours and howled.

There was a tale of a certain Norman woman with a dead son to avenge: she was half mad and went about the streets with a little knife and a pair of pincers, trying to flay the wounded alive, but she did not know how to go about it and only succeeded in tearing off great gobbets of flesh, which she folded up and put in her bag, saying she meant to make herself a cloak from them. "Was her son flayed alive?" "Apparently. It happened in Antioch on Easter Sunday."

"The dogs, to do such a thing on Easter Sunday!"

"Oh Lord!" Thomas was groaning. "Mathieu, see, they are coming back. Don't you see them, crawling all over my legs? If this goes on I'll scream." Mathieu wiped his legs with a wet cloth to calm him. Another Picard, called Stammering Jean, blinked at the children who had fallen asleep in a heap, one on top of the other, and said, "We must clear that lot away. They are even in here. Who put them in our yard?" They told him, "Those are our children, Onésime, Mardoche, Bertin, and Gerard, you see their fair hair."

"What, are they dead too? Better clear them away while they are fresh."

"God save you, they're asleep!"

"They're dead, I tell you, they're not moving."

They were not moving; they were so fast asleep that red-hot irons would not have wakened them. It was a miracle they were alive. God forgive them, as forgive them He must since He had saved their lives outside Antioch, for it was a fact that as many Christian children had died before Antioch as heathen children on Friday and Saturday in Jerusalem, and that was saying a good deal.

All the same, so many children had perished in this battle, even babes that could not say yes or no, *all the same—*

They lasted better than the others because they had fewer sins on them. There were some that were quite pale, hardly even grey, like faded flowers, *O daughter of Babylon,*

Happy shall he be that taketh and dasheth thy little ones against the stones.

Takes them by the feet and dashes their heads against the stones. And yet those of them who had killed their own children had the right of it. We found them in here, in this little room, lying neatly side by side beneath a coverlet, their throats cleanly severed, and the mother and grandmother by them. That man, Jacques thought, if that man had been baptized he would surely not be damned. It was not murder, that, but charity.

For four or five days yet he will haunt the house, he and his neighbors, the ones with a potter's shop. The street has been cleared and their bodies are far away, but they come back out of habit. We must think well of them, they do not know us, it was not we who dispossessed them, it was the Count of Cerdagne's Basque troops. We have done you no harm, infidels. We found the house empty.

Ours was the big house near the mosque, the house where Saint-John was killed; ours were the fine streets behind the Greek monasteries, on Saturday. How many? Jacques asked himself. How many? But he no longer knew. The Temple roof. How beautiful it was. The shining dome, like a second sun, and the wall below the dome all set with colored stones and the roofs of the city, glittering white and pink and blue and grey in the sunrise, and the motley crowd in the huge square with the Christian banners waving everywhere. So beautiful a man could die of it. The ax. God bless it.

You are no weaver, Jacques, son of Bernier, but a good foot soldier.

Be it known among you, all you knights and soldiers at home who have never gone farther than Rouen or Paris, that the meanest of us is more noble than you, and a better soldier.

We have entered alive into Jerusalem, with our mortal eyes we have seen it

> conquered, taken and fallen
> Jerusalem so long desired
> so deeply mourned, so well avenged
> now washed in blood.

And God grant that by tomorrow night no trace may be left of all this rottenness. With brooms of horsehair and of iron we shall clean away the dried blood and spread straw and brushwood on the stones.

Shame on Mahomet, the god of flies and carrion, shame on the coward who has so dealt with his own.

No, God did not will it or permit it. It is a great lie they have told us, how God loved the rich and powerful and meant to use them. The Devil only uses them. For see, my friends, look and ponder, it was not Jesus Christ who did all this.

They were in the valley below the walls. Near the trenches. The women should not have been put to work on the death pits, but hands were lacking and poor women are hardened to work. All living things have mercy on their own kind, excepting man. The women did not like to see the bodies of women and children. After all they had seen in three years, they were hardened to it, but even so the sight was too grievous. The loads were tipped into the trenches in heaps, packed down with spades, and when the trenches were three-parts full, the quarrymen began to shovel back the soil that was piled in long banks the whole length of the trench. The work was well ordered and progressed swiftly. It was good to see the stony weight of red earth slowly burying the hideous mess of mutilated limbs, to see the crust of black flies break into little ripples and then fall back: they were full and lazy, and they rose and buzzed a little as the earth and stones pattered down, then suffered themselves to be buried also.

All supplies of quicklime, saltpeter, and ashes were used up long since, for the dead from the ramparts and the Temple and the synagogue: that task had been carried out on Sunday by prisoners. There were not many prisoners, not above a few dozen men still fit for work, and they did not like the work. They were always fainting. As a result the workers on Monday had no ashes or sand or anything left, and this was why the quarrymen were so nervous, for although they had performed the office of gravediggers from time to time at need, they were not prepared for such a stench or for such vast numbers of bodies.

All day long without a pause they kept on coming; the living in the trenches were perhaps a few hundred and the dead tens of thousands. They were placed in a level heap along the edges of the trenches ready to be pushed in when the digging was finished, and it cannot be said that the laborers had any inclination to dawdle over their work but went at it as fast as if they were paid by the yard and not by the day. The women worked in pairs, filling the baskets with earth and tipping them out onto the bank. The sweat poured off their bodies, their clothes were wringing wet, and they were a dreadful sight, covered from head to foot with mud and flies. Old women went up and down beside the trenches with little donkeys carrying jars of water and dipped in long-handled ladles to give to the workers, and but for that no one could have endured for more than two hours at a stretch. *Thank God there was water, thank God there was no shortage of water in the city.*

No, it was not God's will. No. Jesus Christ never willed this or permitted it. "Get on with your work, Marie, and don't waste your breath." "Work, Marie. Don't stop. You are slowing us down." "For God's sake, you women, don't stop. You've just had a drink, there's no cause to faint."

Oh no, no. Jesus Christ has not willed it.

There are children here without heads. There is a whole load of children thrown down here, and some with heads no bigger than my fist. "She chatters like a magpie. Stop, for God's sake, we've all got eyes."

"Who did this, was it our men did this? Jean-Marc, did our men do this?"

Jean-Marc was laboring over his pick, his lips shut tight, himself as grey and filthy as a corpse. Marie let fall the bushel with which she was scraping up the earth and gripped the man's shoulders, in imminent danger of getting the pick full on her head. "Tell us, Jean-Marc, did our men do this too?" He thrust her away roughly and she fell.

"Mind your own business, she-devil, and fill your basket!"

"Jean-Marc, did you cut off children's heads?" He jerked upright and cast her such a look of hatred that Rufine, who was working at the same basket with Marie, took her by the arm and drew her away. Marie picked up the bushel again and went on working, but her eyes turned constantly to the heap of bodies above them, the dead that were ready to topple down into the trench on top of the men bending to their picks and hacking away at the ground.

So much discolored flesh, heavy and slack, foul, mottled and striped with black dried blood with here and there a face, looking pitifully lost with its useless semblance of life. It was not pity but a nausea that spread through your whole body and persisted even after you had vomited up your guts, invading your heart and soul, while a leaden chill rose from your bowels: flesh, flesh, so much cold flesh, so much human flesh turned into slime, everyone smelled of dead flesh.

"What if there are some there still alive?" There were sighs and creaks, and a gasping, oozing sound, the sound of decomposition proceeding. In this heat it happened quickly, the hum of decay and the hum of the flies so dreadful to hear that it drowned the sound of the picks. It is true what they say: there are so many we shall never get them all underground. More carts are coming out through the gates of the city all the time. They do not stop and will not stop until the Last Judgment, there are fifty thousand, a hundred thousand, two hundred—oh, they are a race accursed, they multiply before your eyes like worms in dead meat, they multiply and one corpse breeds ten more, the carts will never stop coming out of the gate. And why were there so many children in this city? They had enough to eat and drink, that is why, these people had many children living, in Jerusalem there are fountains. These children were never short of water.

They are up there on the surface and we are burying ourselves. Here we are, five feet below them already, the trench is ready and they will bury us in it. For a length of fifty feet your trench is ready, with God's help, comrades! Now climb out, everyone, the men to the bodies and the women to the earth. For Jesus Christ's love, let there be no delay.

Surely no army would ever have enough men for this job. It was not a battle but a Judgment of God. And so the men, many of them monks, had to dig first and then bury the bodies, shoveling them in with sows mounted on poles.

It was very hot. The sun was midway between the zenith and the sea, and the great mass of the walls, still blackened with the traces of the recent fighting, rose against a blue, blue sky, opaque as a painted vault. White flags with red crosses were etched upon it, and bright-colored flags, and rows of severed heads.

One day we shall go in, we shall enter the gate. If anyone had told us that we should wait for three days, we would not have believed them. Already the assault seems so remote that we have almost forgotten what went before it. A new trench is to be dug behind the Duke's tower. Christians, for the love of God do not spare yourselves, you shall have time to rest afterward but corruption will not wait.

The laborers marked out the site and the men got to work with their picks, each in his appointed place. And surely God was helping, for the work progressed quickly with hardly a pause for breath. The carts were still coming out of the gates, rumbling forward unsteadily, and by now the men did not know where to dump their loads.

"Why were there so many women and children? Could they not have sent them to Baghdad or to Cairo?"

"They believed the city would never be taken. They had water."

"No, truly, God neither willed nor permitted it. For if it was a judgment of God, God does not judge little children."

"Marie, have a drink of water, the sun is affecting your head. What is the use of talking? There is a time for everything."

"There is never a time for killing little children. There never was such a time, nor will there ever be.

"Our soldiers have killed these innocents here as Herod slew the Holy Innocents."

Marie's companions were resting under some olive trees with a dozen Norman women while they waited to begin shoveling the earth. Marie's lovely voice made some of them weep as they listened to her. She was standing on a heap of lumber in the full sunshine, holding up her arms as if in supplication.

Her voice was high and terrible, like a cry torn from the depths of her bowels. "Oh Herods, race of Herod, Jesus Christ never sanctioned this! In this place where God suffered Himself to be slain like a lamb, you have slain His lambs! Worse than Caiaphas and Pilate, you have come to this holy place to slay the Holy Innocents!"

She wept so bitterly that soon a crowd of women and sick people gathered around her and all, moved by her grief, began to weep and wail. Oh misery, for our sins God will take Jerusalem from us! Until at last a Norman monk approached the group and climbed onto the planks beside Marie.

"Be silent, woman. You have no authority to speak."

"Son of Satan, what have you got against me? Let me cry out or I shall die!"

"Be silent, if you would not be bound for a madwoman. It is not right to make trouble in the camp, and there is work to be done."

"Oh, servant of the Devil, lackey of the rich! It is the rich and the knights who have done this, Herods and sons of Herod are they all, curses on them!" She flung the words into his face, and spat at him. Her eyes were burning and rivulets of sweat ran down her quivering face. She was more terrible than beautiful, and yet she was beautiful too, like a tree blasted by lightning, sparkling and crackling.

The monk seized her by the shoulders and pushed her off her platform of lumber so that she fell on the stones at her companions' feet. "Do not listen to the woman," he cried. "Excess of pride has turned her brain! She blasphemes and will bring down God's anger on us."

Dazedly, Marie picked herself up. There was blood on her elbows and her knees were bleeding. Many of the women laughed at her, and all the more heartily because her lovely voice had moved them to tears, so that now they roared with laughter for no reason, finding comfort in it.

"You may laugh now," Marie said, "but you shall weep."

The Norman pilgrims were saying that the work would not wait and that if women were to begin prophesying and drawing crowds to hear them, their trench would never be dug before vespers. Brother Imbert of Cambrai ought to intervene, they said, and stop this crazy girl from making trouble and keeping folk from their work.

Brother Imbert, to do him justice, was digging gallantly but there was little strength in his arms. Martine, one of the Picard women, who was as big and strong as a man, hurried to take his place. "Marie is making trouble, you must calm her."

"You talk too much, Marie. We have always told you so. No one asked for mourners at this funeral."

"Back to work, you women, pick up your baskets and start heaping the earth." Brother Imbert hobbled forward, bent double from his labors with the pick so that he could not stand upright. "Woman, why do you trouble hearts already deep in grief? Do you think you can bring the dead back to life again? Wash your face and have a drink of water and then get back to your basket and your scoop. You volunteered for this work, and it is no worse for you than for the rest."

Marie picked up her basket in both hands and hurled it from her. "Oh, Brother Barnabé was right to die! At funerals no one weeps for the gravediggers! Are we to be pitied?"

"Girl, God has given your sex a tender heart, but the Devil has made your judgment weak and hasty. It is a sin for you to presume to know God's designs."

Marie's whole body was trembling and she stared at the monk with eyes like a frightened horse, without comprehending what he said to her. He took her hand and led her over to the foot of the nearest olive tree and made her sit down in the shade of the great twisted, hollow trunk, and himself sat beside her, stroking her head and shoulders with his calloused hands. She sat rigid and motionless, staring straight ahead.

"My daughter, if we could understand these things, we should be as God. The flesh in us cries out in revulsion at sights so full of horror. But Our Lord said, Father, forgive them, for they know not what they do. Violent men are like the burning sun and the waves of the sea.

"God said, Thou shalt not kill. And he commanded the Israelites to destroy their enemies, yes, even the women and children. Can it be, then, that God spoke falsely? We cannot believe that, or even think it. And if whosoever shall say to his brother, Thou fool, shall be in danger of hellfire, then surely there are no great sins or small but God has already forgiven all, for if not, no man shall be saved.

"You are shocked to see so many dead. Say to yourself that this is not the work of human hands. Earthquakes and pestilence kill as many innocents and God permits it. For on the great Judgment Day all shall rise from their graves and those that have never known God shall see Him in His glory. God remembers every living man unto all eternity, and not one soul shall ever be judged wrongly."

Marie listened to him, her arms hugging her chest, and tried to understand what he was saying, but the blood was pounding too fiercely in her head.

"My head aches," she said, "my whole body aches. My throat feels tight, as if I had swallowed a stone. My heart is breaking. Let me cry!"

"My poor child, Jesus Christ was spat upon and beaten and abused, and so it must be until the end of time. Men have never been good and yet He loved them enough to die for them."

"Why do you talk to me?" Marie said. "I am not a child to be comforted. I am older than you. I am tired of living. Oh, what a pilgrimage. The city is full of ghosts, as a corpse is full of worms!" Suddenly she screamed and sprang up like a frightened animal, pushing Brother Imbert away. Then she was on her feet and running, her long neck stretched taut and thin as a bowstring, her arms outstretched. She ran, leaping over mounds of earth and boards with the light, spasmodic movements of a frightened goat, and calling, calling at the top of her voice, *"Pierre! Pierre! Pierre, come away from here!"*

She ran up the slope toward the wagons where the children were and all who saw her stepped aside and said, There is Marie of Arras run mad, what a shame, a woman with her gifts. It was many days since the sight of madness had had power to surprise anyone.

She was stopped near the wagons. Two old women got a rope around her legs and she fell flat on her face. The priestess groped her way to her, and held her head because she was struggling and there was foam on her lips. "Do you want your Pierre to see you in this state? You would frighten him. Be quiet, now. Tomorrow our menfolk will come for us."

"Priestess, put out my eyes, and let me be like you."

"It is nothing, the heat and the thirst. Drink." Marie drank eagerly, a whole cupful in great gulps, and asked for more.

• • •

The laborers came up the hill again to hear vespers in the open air. Spears were stuck in the ground around the altars, surmounted by little triangular pennons with red crosses on them. Men and women sat rather than knelt on the ground, singing the responses in voices cracked with exhaustion, and it seemed to them that even the incense smelled of corruption. All seemed half drunk. When the service was over, the priests raised their arms to heaven and prophesied. There is no joy on earth without sorrow and no beauty without ugliness. You have seen God's judgment on His enemies. Gauge from it His love for those that love Him.

He has made for you a living parable of His enemies; see the wretchedness of the flesh revealed in all its horror.

Truly, it is your own sinful flesh that you bury here, at the gates of the Holy City. Leave your carnal illusions here. Shake the dust from your feet. You shall enter into Jerusalem bearing palms and olive branches, you shall have no thought but the joy of God.

The peace of God passes all understanding; do not seek to understand it. It lies on you like the cool of evening that descends upon you from heaven at the time of the first star. Your weary hearts cannot contain it but are lost in it like grains of sand in the sea.

Everyone was weeping. Not women only, but strong men fainted from the force of their sobs. The city showed white against the leaden background of the hills, and borne in slow waves on the breeze came the sound of psalms and trumpets calling.

Outside Herod's Gate men with torches were working among the heaps of unburied dead while dozens of vultures, startled by the light, flapped their wings and screamed above the charnel heaps. Men were coming out of the open gates, driving carts filled with bodies and others piled high with bales of straw. Thank God, there will be no more digging. They are going to try and burn the rest.

Burn them? There are too many, they will never burn. No, the engineers know what they are doing. They could burn sodden hay in the pouring rain.

Whatever else, the men that gathered up the bodies had earned their pay, and should have been paid more. Several of them had died on the spot, suffocated by the stench in the narrow alleys.

Surely God has been with us indeed, for these people never

went hungry: such stores of grain and fruit and oil and fowls were never seen. You can buy a sack of corn for three deniers! Truly Jerusalem is the queen of cities, and the land of abundance. In the market you can get jars of honey and olives and salted meats and fish for almost nothing!

"Have you been to the market?"

"Not me, no, but we were working not far off and you could see the soldiers bringing their donkeys back from the Marketplace."

"That is the way of it," the priestess said. "The soldiers take everything while our men work like galley slaves. Is it right?"

"To each his own reward," Jean-Marc answered. "The knights have honor, the soldiers wealth, and the poor have Jesus Christ."

"Must you do penance, Jean-Marc?" the women asked. "Were you not promised absolution in advance for this bloodshed?"

"It would seem so," Jean-Marc said somberly, "for I would not stay there to shed more blood, and God has punished me by making me kill my own wife. Surely that Saturday was a day of blood and no man could escape it."

God's goodness knows no bounds.

Even to the most sorely tried and tempted of men, those who are most sick and broken, whose bodies have suffered most from sores and vermin and sunburn, yes, to all, on hard stones, in the stench and cold, sleep comes freely. When the body is exhausted. After three nights of fever, three nights, or four or five. The devil must be clever indeed that would kill sleep. Men can sleep on the edge of a precipice, can sleep on nails, even in the midst of torture they can sleep.

Without the haven of sleep could any man live? It makes him strong and whole and himself again. For a few hours the most miserable sinner is made innocent once more. The pale light grows and the sentries beat their drums. Eyes open slowly and look about them without understanding.

What is it? The assault? What, are we striking camp? What ration of water this morning? No ration, a full pint. Jerusalem is ours! Our banners are on the towers. Long live Godfrey! Hail to the Christian soldiers, no more missiles will fall on our camp from those walls.

We are striking camp, Christians, striking camp for good!

Everyone into the city, except for the engineers, into the city and find your billets and your friends.

All, the poor and the soldiers, Latins and Syrians, Tafurs and lepers, for once the gates have been closed and the walls manned no one will be allowed to roam the open country.

We have still to keep what we have taken.

11

Believe it or not, there were many people who were sorry to see the end of work on the trenches, on account of the money. "What's this?" they said. "They promised us two days' work. We could still dig on the other side of the olive grove and in the old Brabançon camp. Let them give us the carts and we will move as many bodies as need be, and save the trouble of burning them." So, such is the greed for money among the poor, after cursing the work, they fell to regretting it. "The work is not so hard or so disgusting after all. You only have to get used to it, we have learned the way of it."

No, brothers, this surely is madness. Now at last you are permitted to enter Jerusalem, and for the sake of a little money you are regretting a task that the devils in hell would not make you do.

It is Tuesday now; our men have been in the city since Friday, and still you linger here, in your camps. When not a week ago you were saying, *God grant that we may but pass through the gates, and pray that our hearts do not burst for joy!* But truly, our hearts entered in on the day of the assault, and broke for joy and anguish. Oh God, why do the angels not lift us up on their wings and carry us to the doors of the Church of the Holy Sepulcher? Why must we go on foot as always, dragging carts and bundles, and all in the midst of such a stench and filth as never was seen, with the vultures to bear us company?

They all passed by the hill where Peter had his tent, and the holy man wept and blessed them. "Brothers," he said, "see, you are come at last to the end of the journey. God grant that you may forget your sufferings. Your dead walk beside you and go with you into Jerusalem! Sing, and think no more!"

They went on toward the gates in small groups, led by the priests and monks. Meanwhile the engineers were dragging beams and boards and buckets of pitch over to the dead and lashing the heaps of bodies together with huge rope nets to make a gigantic pyre on which the wood and the dead bodies were cunningly arranged. There were more than twenty thousand dead, and if these men succeeded in burning them all in one day and night, they would have done one of the best jobs of their lives.

O Jerusalem, bought at such a cost! We bring you more dead than living. From Hungary and Bosnia, from Nicaea and Anatolia, from Antioch and Syria and Judaea. So many Christians who never saw you with their mortal eyes are looking through our eyes. God unseal our eyelids at last, that we may see you in your true glory, cleansed of the mud and blood.

Surely until now we have seen you in a dream, as if through a red curtain of violence and death? After the days of Judgment come the days of peace.

Our feet shall stand within thy gates:
O Jerusalem.
Jerusalem is builded as a city that is
compact together:
Whither the tribes go up, the tribes of the
Lord, unto the testimony of Israel, to give thanks
unto the name of the Lord.

Pray for the peace of Jerusalem: they shall
prosper that love thee.
Peace be within thy walls, and prosperity
within thy palaces.

As the eyes of servants look unto the hand of
their masters: so our eyes wait upon the Lord our God.

Have mercy upon us, O Lord, have mercy upon us: for we are exceedingly filled with contempt.

Our soul is exceedingly filled with the contempt of the proud.

. . . Lord, we do not dispute with the proud for their inheritance; let them also rejoice in their palaces.

Receive us all into Your city, Lord, we who for three years have had no other wealth in this world but Jerusalem.

They shall say among the nations: the Lord hath done great things for them.

O so long desired. We will not wait another day.

Those who entered into the city on the day of the assault were strong and brave, and they were several thousand men, and one in three barefoot and almost unarmed, and in less than two days they had turned the city into a charnel house. God had fired their hearts to such purpose that even little boys of ten and twelve had killed their three or four or more, and many men already dead were hacked and hewn again, their bodies cut to pieces, so great was the lust to kill. Had there been three times as many people in the city, these latter-day Israelites would have got the better of them.

So great was their ardor that sick and fever-ridden Provençals were seen driving their small spears into the bellies of six-foot Sudanese, yes, even the Sudanese lost their heads and fled . . . So great was their ardor that no man thought of rape and hundreds of fair girls with flesh as soft as butter died unravished, and knights clad from head to foot in steel mail were seen spitting small babies on their swords. Yes and God be thanked that there were not three times as many people in the city, for they would have killed them all just the same and what would we have done with so many bodies?

The filth and stench in the streets was still horrible.

For although there was no shortage of water, no one was going to empty the cisterns in the middle of July only to wash the streets. All the ashes from the cooking fires were scattered outside, straw was burned and old rush mats and dried dung: after the blood the ashes, and the pilgrims coming into the city walked and knelt in ashes; the house walls on both sides were splattered and stained black with blood.

They had seen the bodies, but they had not pictured a city so laved in blood. The walls were stained, splattered, and smeared to the height of a man or more, to say nothing of drawings and recognition signs painted in blood, and the broad dark streaks that had dripped from the rooftops.

The men who had entered the city on the day of the assault were all active and sturdy, but now the whole camp was on the move, streaming in long columns toward the gates, and even the sentries and the knights on the walls were surprised, and even alarmed. They had not counted heads, not they, they were content to do their work, but now for every able-bodied man there was another sick, or a woman or an old man. Were there so many of them? Among the regular soldiers alone there were hundreds of sick and wounded, limping on crutches or carried on litters, and those scrawny monks, those bowed old men and bent, hobbling old crones, and those gaunt women carrying their possessions in bundles on their backs and holding small children by the hand. There were not many children but some here and there, skinny, naked, suntanned, their heads swathed in grubby rags.

All the sick who had been huddled away in tents or underneath the carts were now marching with the rest, carried, supported, dragged, or lying on the carts, thrusting up the covers at the sides with their eager heads. Outside Jerusalem the sick did not die: hope kept them alive. Legs monstrously swollen, pendulous goiters, ulcerated faces, mutilated limbs, verminous sores, bloodless features with the skin stretched taut across the bones, gums toothless and bleeding, suppurating eyelids over pale, cataracted eyes, sticks and crutches, splinted arms and legs, bandages with evil brown and yellow stains, unbelievably filthy, slavering lips and mouths crusted with blackened scabs: so many sick whom God had permitted to live to see this day.

The shouts of the engineers were drowned in the music of the psalms.

The Normans came first and after them the Northerners—Picards, Flemings, Lorrainers—and then the French, the Bretons, and the Burgundians. The little companies were piteous enough, for all the able-bodied men had been inside the city since Friday. God is great who has permitted these poor folk to live to see this day! There were living skeletons, coughing up their hearts' blood, bellies swollen to bursting point, infected limbs heaving with worms like those of the dead themselves, and all living and marching and singing.

There were the simple-minded, with fetters on their legs, twitching and giggling; there were others violent in their madness, lying gagged and strapped down to boards on the carts.

There were the recent dead, and a scattering of coffins belonging to those who were better off than most, or much beloved.

The lepers' camp was the last to move, and taken as a whole, not the most horrible to see because the majority of the lepers in the camp were comparatively well, those in the worst stages of the disease having been left behind at Antioch. There were several knights among them and two learned clerks, and there was order in the camp and the sane cared for the mad. It was a pitiful sight, for many were young and handsome, and because they did little work they showed few signs of exhaustion and since they could not fight they had few wounds; their garments were fairly clean and their faces terribly sad. There was a fine leper hospital in Jerusalem and the old lepers had all been killed, shut up and smoked to death and then sprinkled with quicklime; a fine leper hospital, indeed, but as for going to the Holy Sepulcher, it was by no means certain that the leaders and the bishops would permit it; they would have to be there in spirit, through prayer and faith. Nearly all the lepers were soldiers, and they said that if they had been allowed to bathe in the blood shed in the Temple they would surely have been cured. They had been sacrificed, they said, through lack of faith; for whom would Jesus Christ work miracles if not for the lepers?

One by one, singing the psalms of the way to Jerusalem, the slow processions crossed the bridge and passed in through Herod's Gate. The sentinels there were kept busy enough because the people, instead of moving forward quickly, no sooner reached the threshold than they stopped and fell on their knees and kissed the ground while those that came behind waited: to each his turn. But the soldiers said, Good pilgrims, you will all have plenty of time for your devotions inside the city: this gate is not holy. If you are as slow as this we will never get all the companies inside the gate by nightfall!

There were no more rich or poor, Jerusalem belonged to all, and above all to the poor. They were coming to take possession of their inheritance.

The barons had planned the attack and the soldiers and the knights had fought, and the prelates and canons had prayed to God by the celebration of the mass, but it was for love of His poor that God had worked the miracle. Never in any army in the world were there so many poor, dead and alive.

See: God did not deceive you.

They all told us it was madness, to seek Jerusalem was like looking for the sun at midnight. And the sun has risen at midnight and shines in the sky.

Cast off all thoughts of mourning, of grief and horror. Think, Christians, only four days, four days, this is barely the fifth.

When a thousand years to God are but a single day, your patience has endured for three years, and the patience of Jerusalem has endured for four hundred and fifty years! It is delivered from corruption, and has become a house of prayer.

You shall not thirst any more, you shall have a shelter for the night. Man is a pilgrim upon earth, but in Jerusalem the poorest is a citizen.

Marie. Marie of Arras. Look. This archway decked with banners above your head is Herod's Gate. You are entering Jerusalem.

She lay in the cart and watched the banners of the cross swinging idly in a breath of wind, and the bright blue sky away beyond the soaring, machicolated tower. Oh Lord, is it going to begin again? I am calm, you see, calm. They had tied her to the board of the cart and she lay quite still and watchful, holding her breath, as though gathering her strength, until the delirium returned and she fought with all her might like a deer caught in a trap and tied, and the women walking beside the cart laid wet cloths on her forehead. An old woman, half paralyzed, who was sitting in the cart started muttering: "It's not right, a strong, healthy woman, pretending to be ill just to get herself talked about!" By now Marie was in a high fever and there was such strength in her body that she made the ropes crack and the whole cart shake. She did not speak but uttered screams and angry sighs and brief rattles in her throat. "Oh God," the priestess said, "this is a dreadful sign, for so devout a woman to enter into Jerusalem in such a state. How has she sinned to be so punished?"

Marie heard the psalms, and she knew she ought to be singing but her throat was dry—our feet shall stand within thy gates, O Jerusalem.

Jerusalem is builded as a city . . . Pierre, where is Pierre?

where is Pierre? where is Pierre? Jacques, take care of him. Alas, the Sudanese have slain all the children of this city, and all the women, and we let them do it! Rachel weeping for her children and will not be comforted. Lord, Your great waters have overwhelmed me and gone over me, and lo, the third angel poured out his vial upon the rivers and fountains of waters; and they became blood. Lord, my mouth is filled with the blood of innocents, how shall I enter into Jerusalem? The voices singing the hymns were broken with weeping, men and women wept as they kissed the paving stones; pass on, good people, pass on, you will have all the time you want to pray now.

The small cart covered with branches on which Brother Barnabé's coffin lay moved slowly forward, drawn by four monks. A large wooden cross rested on the coffin, and the men walking alongside told the sentries, "He was a saint. This morning a white dove flew up from the lid of his coffin. He must be buried in the Holy Sepulcher." The Holy Sepulcher would have had to be as big as the Marketplace to accommodate all those who would be buried there.

They had not expected to find the city so gay. Each tiny square had become a festive hall. From inside the houses came cheerful shouts and sounds of men singing at the tops of their voices, and somehow, God knows how, the streets had been made gay with decorations: there never was such a riot of colored fabrics. The soldiers had hung out all the curtains and cloths they could find in the houses for bunting and vied with one another to decorate their billets. There were carpets in all the courts and squares, and people were sitting on silken cushions at their doors. Everyone was outside; these were not men who liked to be shut within doors. They had exchanged their torn leather jerkins for garments that were heathenish but clean: burnooses, surcoats, embroidered gowns, and slippers of painted leather, even turbans —a real carnival. And there was no denying that they stood in great need of a change of clothes, and unlike the barons, had no tailors to call upon.

The pilgrims of Arras and Picardy settled into their house, which in the event was rather more crowded than they had hoped. But it was a good solid, stone-built house and the rooms were cool. Le Grêlé assumed command, giving orders even to

Jean-Marc. "We must prepare ourselves fittingly, friends," he said. "We must fast all day tomorrow as Brother Imbert has told us and forgive one another all our wrongs. Let there be no argument over rooms. Those who are most sick shall have the best. And the women are not to leave the house today, for there is enough to do washing and mending and getting rid of the lice."

Still drowsy with the heat, the women unloaded the carts and sighed as they looked at their men. A fine state they were in, to be sure, reeking with filth, not to mention their wounds, which though not deep were ugly, and their hair, all matted and greasy with sweat and blood.

Jacques almost fainted when he saw his wife tied like a madwoman and his son in the charge of Artemisia, the wife of Jean-Marc's Mathieu. "Oh, children of the Devil, what have you done to her? What have you done to my Marie?"

"It's nothing, Jacques. Probably she caught a touch of the sun in the trenches yesterday." Jacques unfastened Marie and took her in his arms like a child, for her legs were numbed. She felt as hot as roast mutton.

"Oh God, my darling, my little flower, speak to me." Her face was red and raw and her blue eyes shining as if by firelight.

"Oh Jacques, Jacques, it is you. How I have longed for you! We will go into the desert and find the true Jerusalem."

"Silly girl, we are there already, in the truest of all. Rest now, you will not have to dig any more trenches." He carried her inside and laid her down on some rugs, but she was up again in an instant, bright-eyed and wary, and making for the door. He had a struggle to master her. She was possessed by a spirit of flight, and when that spirit was on her she became as strong as a man.

She fought him desperately. "Where is Pierre? I will not frighten him, I shall be very gentle. We are going to the river Jordan, Jacques, to be baptized anew. Jacques, I will try and be quiet for your sake, but it is hard! Fiery serpents are running all through my body."

"It is the fever, Marie. I am going to bring you a wet covering. Just think, Marie, we have a fine covered cistern three-parts full."

"Their water burns me, Jacques, everything burns me. We have killed the innocents to steal their water."

"Oh, you weak woman, to refuse God's gifts. It was them or us, and God chose us before them."

"Jacques, it is anger that has made me mad. Jacques, we have killed poor people to steal their bread."

And God has not willed it, or sanctioned it.

She tore herself from Jacques's arms and ran out into the court. She rushed up to some of the women who were picking over chick peas before throwing them into the pot and started grabbing handfuls of the peas and scattering them on the ground: "Here, heathen Moslems, here are your goods, your funeral offerings." They had to bind her again, and the women had little sympathy for her. They said, "She thinks she is a queen because she has a lovely voice, she, a poor weaver's daughter and not even a virgin, with her head full of nonsense.

"Because her child is alive," they said, "she mourns for the children of the heathen women." (In all the companies from Artois and Picardy there were now only two young children, Pierre and five-year-old Martine, the daughter of Guillaume the wheelwright, and Martine had been motherless since Antioch.) "She has nothing to avenge, it is easy for her to talk."

It is harder to die of hunger and thirst than by the ax.

"Yet it is true," Jacques said, "there are times when it sickens you to see a big Norman, as strong as an ox, spitting some poor little creature howling with terror on his pike. We did not do that, we left all that side of it to the children."

Brother Imbert was praying, resting his hands on Brother Barnabé's coffin. When he was lost in prayer like this he was oblivious of all else and his face looked younger, so fine-drawn and radiant that he scarcely seemed the same man. Clearly he was seeing heavenly visions. "See," the women said, "he is communing piously with Brother Barnabé, their souls are meeting before the throne of Jesus Christ.

"Surely he is asking for many miracles for us. For if we had to rely on ourselves, how poor our prayers would be."

Lambert watched the saintly man from his corner of the courtyard, a gleam of hope in his sad eyes. O Jesus Christ, grant him that, let him not forget me, even though I am not of his own country. His mother was there, her groping hands feeling for his hair and his cheeks, and he dared not shake her off although the touch of her roughened skin was painful to him. "Lambert," she was saying, "I would not ask anything for myself. I do very well as I am. Only for you—"

"I am not as sick as that, mother."

"Your arm must get better so that you can work for both of us. You must not pray for my eyes, only for yourself."

"Mother, if God wills, He is strong enough to cure us both."

There were two other dead laid out beside Brother Barnabé's coffin, Ludivine and an old man with dropsy who had died of joy on Friday night. No one hoped that they would be resurrected. What, on the fifth day? Saturday, Sunday, Monday, Tuesday—and now it is Tuesday night! Tomorrow is Wednesday, and not until Thursday will we come truly face to face with Jesus Christ. Oh God, the thought of it is enough to make you tremble so that in the end you wish the sun would stand still.

They had been preparing for this day for months, for years even, and yet they were hardly more ready for it now than on the first day! They were even burdened with fresh sins. From whom did they think to hide them? More sins on them than sores and vermin.

Today the soldiers of Provence had gone, all together, and the Basques also, and there had been cures. One man had seen all his scabs fall away from him at once; all his scabs had dropped off and there underneath was skin as pink and healthy as a baby's. And his were recent wounds, and infected besides.

"But it is not easy to come there, friends, there is such a crowd in the square all around it that not even an eel could slip through and the church is not a tenth as big as the Temple, and from what they say there are so many priests and rich men who stay there night and day that there is little enough room for other folk to worship. The people are almost treading on one another. They cannot even prostrate themselves."

"Well, the soldiers have more need of forgiveness than other men, we must let them have their fill of prayer. It is no small thanks to them that we are in the city at all. How they fought and how many of them died on Friday, Saint George and Saint Michael know! Do you know that a Basque is the equal of a Sudanese for size and courage . . . ?"

There was no jealousy or rancor that day, only high praise for the barons and the bishops, for the soldiers and even the commissaries. People were almost wishing the Sudanese could have been converted. What good soldiers they would have made if God had only wanted them!

• • •

So many candles burned before the altar, in the tall candlesticks and on hearses and in branches suspended from above, and in the hands of the pilgrims, as well as on iron brackets fixed to the pillars and on the screens that ran the length of the nave: so many candles, some as thick as your arm, some slender and set so close together that they stuck to one another: the inside of the vast church was brighter than daylight, so glorious was the blaze. Everywhere was the soft sputtering of wicks burning in the molten wax that dripped in hot white tears. The vault of blue and gold mosaic glittered all over like a starry sky in which the stars had all run together, and the heat was so great that men melted like wax.

The priests, their faces streaming and their hands shaking with exhaustion, in their heavy vestments shot with a myriad sparkling lights, seemed to have barely strength to officiate; their very weakness seemed to bear witness to their extreme piety, and indeed their piety was very great, so that between that and fatigue they were half fainting and visions of unspeakable splendor opened before their eyes.

Every priest with the army was entitled to take his turn at celebrating mass in the Church of the Holy Sepulcher. All, good and bad alike, were overcome with the great joy of this holy place so that whoever entered it straightway forgot all else in the world.

Come. Come all and see. The Sepulcher is empty. Here on this very spot death was laid low forever.

Brighter than a thousand lightnings, brighter than a thousand suns. The one true grave, empty for all eternity. There is no more death, death has been changed into life. You are here. With your mortal bodies, with your ulcers, your sweat, and your lice, with your acrid smells and your salt tears.

All may touch the sacred stone and draw new life from it.

As the poor prisoner touches the hand of a friend, as he recognizes a friend's voice in a strange land.

The great stone rolled away of itself and the tomb was empty, there was nothing within but a bright light and the linen clothes lying; the two angels shone so that the morning stars grew pale, O Mary Salome, Mary the mother of James, and Mary Magdalene, break your jars of spices! Death is dead, there shall be no more death than darkness in broad day.

And the city had no need of the sun, neither of the moon, to shine in it: for the glory of God did lighten it, and the Lamb is the light thereof.

A hundred thousand years are but a day in the sight of the Lord, this day we live now is true to all eternity, our affliction is a lie. How many tears were shed each day, from morning to night, in the great light of those thousand candles, it was impossible to say. None wished to leave the place, but go they must for there were others waiting. The singing was like thunder and the weeping swelled like the tide, sobbing and crying: O blessed Jesus Christ, born of the Virgin, hosanna to the Son of David! Let us die here, for this is already paradise.

The sick forgot their pains and stood up and sang with the rest, and there were many who believed themselves cured that were not so, so great was the virtue of that holy place.

When Brother Barnabé's coffin was carried up to the Stone of the Sepulcher, those who bore it seemed to hear the dead man's heart beating loudly through the boards of the coffin. Is it possible that he is living still? Should we open the coffin? A chaplain standing by the altar said that this was not necessary, the monk had been dead for a week. "What you hear is not a sign of life but the first intimations of the resurrection. It would be wrong to trouble the rest of the body that is now at peace."

He whom we loved so dearly is now on this great day blind and speechless, divided from us by boards of olive wood, he whose eyes blazed and were consumed with holy longing, he who wept for our sins. If they could have seen themselves, in the light of the thousand candles shining on gold and crystal, the pilgrims would have thought—but the thought was blasphemy—that God must be mad indeed to love such wretched creatures, emaciated, burnt black by the sun, sweating and scarred, diseased and covered with sores. Oh, truly, these are My people.

For the last shall be first.

(The last? Do not overrate yourselves, for the last may well be the lepers, or the poor Tafurs . . .) They were there, weeping for joy and pity for the body of Jesus Christ that had lain in this place pierced by so many wounds. They forgot to ask for their own miracles, for the sufferings of their mortal, perishable flesh were a little thing when God was there and had lain on that very Stone, the Lamb sacrificed from the beginning of time, the one true wound and the one true cure.

Élie le Grêlé was weeping aloud with great choking sobs like a child, and it seemed to him that his tears entered his heart through his mouth and quenched his great thirst, and that his heart grew light and all grief was melted and flowed away. Oh, if she were only there to see this day, she who died unshriven! Do not forget Your servant, Lord, since I must see this day without her! He did not see the altar or the candle flames, he saw the body of Our Lord stretched on the stone, white as marble, with blood on the hands and feet and on the right side, and around the brow. He was quite dead, His beautiful face with the closed eyes was smooth, cold, and deathly sad, but the wounds were bleeding and the blood that seeped from them was red and living.

The blood flowed quietly in bright rivulets over the white flesh, over the cold, blue-white flesh, and the subdued murmur of sighing and singing and weeping faded into the silence of death. As if he had gone suddenly deaf, Élie could hear nothing in his heart but this cruel silence and the sound of blood seeping from the wounds, and he was choked with pity and love. O Lord, it is I, I alone, who have caused these bleeding wounds, I who have killed You! Oh, that no one else had ever laid hands on You, that I alone had driven in the nails, struck with the spear, and that You should forgive me.

He stood there sobbing, so lost in his visions that people pushed and shoved past him without moving him from where he stood, with his head up and his hands clenched fiercely in the wild desire to seize a knife and strike at that pure flesh.

Beside him the priestess was praying, on her knees in the dark, craning her neck and holding up her face to the warmth of the candles. In all the noise and heat she felt like a black stone fallen into the sun. Oh no, I do not want it, oh no, Lord, let my eyes be, in six weeks I have got used to it. Oh Holy Mary, You are a mother, You know what it means. Oh best and kindest, pearl, dove, our living Water, our Morning Star! He is such a good son, You see, even Your own son was not kinder to His mother. He has suffered so much already. Do not take him, he is only twenty, hardly more! Oh Holy Mary, You know what it means. You are a woman, You would not do that to me. Lambert was beside her, kneeling or rather sitting on the ground, his face pale and set, his eyes wide open in a fixed and burning stare. I am here at last, all my sins burned away, and if only this pain would leave me, even this pain is the burning of God's love. Oh my friends, oh Jacques, oh mother, all our people, I know that God is calling me where I do not want to go.

Marie of Arras. You are seeing a new heaven and a new earth. As these moths drawn into the candle flame, even so are we, from Duke Godfrey down to the meanest leper, we are the same. You walk on a sea of dazzling flame, the sun has filled all the sky, everything is burning and you are no more than a straw in the sun.

Behold the new heaven and the new earth: a field of souls, living and dead, a field of standing corn in which every ear is a star and the fields stretch as far as eye can see, through all Judaea to Bethlehem and to the Jordan, and that is why there is no more night. The sky is not blue, it is all shining gold, and on that gold a blinding white cross. All around it great rings of flame, blue and rose and green, stretch out and spread to the four horizons, making shimmering rainbow circles ever changing, with angels falling like great sparks on the field of souls and rising up again.

They are all there, the living and the dead, even infants in swaddling clothes, flakes of golden fire that fly up with the angels, this is the real truth and the world as it is, as the soul sees it when the curtain of flesh is ripped from its eyes. Oh, why must it be? Oh, why? . . . Leave me, sisters, I shall not stir from this place. Marie felt herself falling into a blaze of light. Her eyes burned. She had lost consciousness, and her neighbors were holding her up to keep her from being trampled on. It was not surprising. What with the heat and the joy, they were all choked with tears.

They could scarcely hear the cantors intoning the psalms, everyone was speaking at once, like Pentecost. Oh alleluia, God be praised, oh most beauteous God, oh King of mercy! Who could silence them? Even the children. The smallest were chattering like little birds and the big ones shouting their heads off and clapping their hands as if they were in the public square. Long live Lord Jesus Christ, Father, Son, and Holy Ghost, suffered under Pontius Pilate, was crucified dead and buried—

Joseph of Arimathea laid him in a splendid grave
Wrapped in clean white linen, in a dark and gloomy cave,
Sing, Christians all, sing and be gay,
The pains of hell are done away!

They made up their own hymns as best they could, too excited to repeat the Latin psalms. Washed and combed as well as possible, they were not even bad-looking any more: lean as young colts, with bright red faces and clear eyes empty and sparkling; Bertin was dressed for once as a girl with a white kerchief and a grey dress. "Mardoche! I can see a departing soul." "Where?" "There, next to me! A naked, quivering soul." "Liar! I don't see anything."

Lambert was really going. He had forgotten where he was and the pain seemed to be leaving his body. He felt as if he were fainting, and yet he knew it was more than that. *Miserere mei Domine.* Father, mother, forgive me.

Oh cursed black face! I will torment you in hell. I did not want to die!

His mind was wandering. He saw himself as a child, his hands red with the juice of strawberries stolen from his aunt's basket. He saw his father, young and laughing, picking him up and tossing him in the air for a game. It was a little frightening but fun, his father was so strong and tall, with his white teeth and his bristly beard. Why was everything swimming? Why was it so dark? I too, he thought, I too am going blind. Mother, do not pray for me any more, it is not worth it, this is the end.

The priestess felt him crumple softly against her knees and her hands fumbled for his head. "What is it, what is the matter? Are you ill?" Feeling no breath on her hands, she panicked: "Oh God, all of you, Rufine, Honorine, Alix! Someone!" Alix turned at the sharp cry, took one look, and crossed herself. You learned by experience to know the faces from which the soul had gone for good: the sharpened nose, the lips drawn back. What to do? It was almost impossible to move. More pilgrims were coming in and they had to go. People were pushing, the men joining hands to protect the sick, coffins being used as battering rams. Jacques and Élie picked up Lambert bodily and carried him shoulder-high above the crowd. His breathing had stopped and his head rolled loosely.

The poor priestess clung to the other women, turning her face from side to side like a terrified linnet, too frightened even to cry out, Where is he? what is the matter? "Come," they said to her, "maybe when we get out of the crowd he will be better." It took a long time. Jacques could see his friend's head lolling on his shoulder. They were cheek to cheek and he had a glimpse of blue lips, slightly parted, and of the whites of the eyes. It filled him with dread but he dared not speak, he could only think: *No, not that, no, not that, no my God, not that not that . . .* He was clenching his teeth hard. The crowd surged about them and the clamor of voices rose until it was like a series of blows to the head, while all around the candles blazed in a great quiet conflagration.

Outside in the square the crush was worse than ever. People belonging to the same groups had to cling together like swarms of wasps to avoid being torn apart and lost in the crowd. Stretchers, coffins, small children, and unconscious women were borne above the mass on the heads and arms of the strongest men, looking as if they were sailing up and down the open space on a sea of heads. There were as many angry voices as there were joyful ones. By the time the pilgrims of Arras finally reached a quiet turning, Lambert's face was cold and his hand chilled. They could not doubt that he was dead. He had died in the church and was already dead when Jacques and Élie had taken him up. There was nothing left to do but lay him on the ground and close his eyes.

People passing the little group paused and said, "Poor souls, you are very simple. Why do you weep? There could not be a better way to die." "No," they answered, "you do not understand. This lad had his mother with him." The priestess had guessed long ago, but she refused to accept it and held his cold head fiercely to her breast: "Oh, give me back my eyes, give me back my eyes! Oh, let me see him, let me see you, my baby!" She was lost in the dark with the body lying against her, heavy as lead, and it seemed to her that if she could only see the dead boy's face she would be happy. "Oh my baby, oh my chick, my treasure! My darling boy, my sun . . ." She broke off her lament to scream like a woman in travail, then began again: "Lambert, Lambert, do not leave me! Oh curé, curé. See what God has done to us! Oh cruel lady, heartless and unkind. Oh Holy Mary, if You are good, what must the wicked be?"

The men tore their cheeks and pulled their beards, largely in sympathy with the mother, for it seemed to them a good death. The women wailed: "Ah, priestess, this is a cruel reward! Your son's bliss is your grief. The sword has pierced your heart. Oh Lambert, what have you done? Could you not wait? God called you and you went without a word."

The children, who were incapable of standing still, were

amusing themselves by twisting one another's arms. "There, you see," Bertin was saying, "I was right. I saw Lambert's soul going away." "Show-off," said Mardoche. He was looking at her strangely, breathing hard and fidgeting like a young colt newly caught. "You look like a scarecrow in those petticoats." "It is God's will," said Bertin.

He sniggered: "You'll get yourself raped."

"Stupid. There is no rape in Jerusalem." So she said, but for all that a sight of the tall girl with her fair hair and tiptilted nose skipping along was enough to make even middle-aged men check suddenly and catch their breath.

The question was where to take the coffins. Where shall we bury the dead here? The city graveyards were not large and they were already full. All the Moslem and Jewish bodies had been dug up and thrown out on the very day after the battle and the graveyards filled up that same day with Christians slain in the fighting. There could be no question of taking up the paving inside the churches: far too many people aspired to that privilege. The Christian priories were willing to accommodate monks and priests and the Latin Hospital of St. John took chiefly the poor, but here too there was no more room: bodies were waiting outside the monastery gates sewn up in canvas, while the monks dug graves in the gardens and cloisters and even in the refectory, but the truth was that there were too many dead, and more were dying every day.

In the valley, on the site of what had been the Flemish camp, the pyre was still burning, a vast hellfire, a hill of flame, of black smoke and red ashes, subsiding little by little. A light wind blowing from the sea drove gusts of smoke into the city and scattered the ashes until the ramparts and the moat, the walls and roofs on that side, were thick with the grey snow.

See, our enemies are turned into ashes, and borne on the wind. Fire has conquered corruption, and what there was on that pyre, only God or the Devil knows. Yes, on the pyre alone, so it was said, were more than twenty thousand bodies.

"Don't cry, priestess. Don't weep so loud." It was le Grêlé who spoke. "A good death is better than a bad life, and it is no life for a young, handsome fellow to have only one arm." The priestess leaped as if she had been seared by a red-hot iron. "What is that? One arm! Oh God, my poor boy! And he never told me. One arm, and what worse? That is fine comfort, Grêlé. He could have been one-armed and blind and leprous and a legless cripple, but not as he is now! . . . Oh Lord Jesus Christ, what a life we should have had, the two of us, begging at the gate of the Holy Sepulcher and singing psalms!" She began to cry again at the thought, and this time her tears were almost consoling as she pictured it in her mind's eye. "A good life. Oh, even a leper, Lambert, even a leper without hands or feet, you know I would never have left you." She racked her brains to think of the cruelest fates, rather than remember the truth which was worse than all.

They had laid Lambert under the fig tree in the courtyard, wrapped in blankets, leaving only his face uncovered, and the priestess sat on the ground and laid her son's head in her lap and set herself to keep away the flies that hovered around his dead lips. It seemed to her that all was not yet over, not while he was still there. Oh, if he could only stay like that forever, at least. As for Jacques, he was not thinking that it was a good death, he was crying too bitterly to think at all, possessed by such a rage that he struck the ground with his fists and bruised them till they bled. What was the good of all their prayers when on the very day of greatest joy God could hit you on the head and strike you down? Why could Lambert not have died on Saturday? That day it would not have been so bad, it was a day of blood.

God knows I gave you all my share of the plunder, I kept nothing back. Who was it lied and cheated? You are a bad comrade, Lambert, going away to God like that on account of the singing and the thousand lighted candles. Oh curé's son, I'll teach you to desert your friends! Oh Lord Jesus Christ, if this is Your reward! Jacques was drunk that night for the first time in his life.

The children sat in a huddle in the corner by the cistern listening to Bertin, who perched on a stone step, her thin arms hugging her knees, her shoulders swaying slightly as she talked. "Well, boys," she was saying, "the heathens let them all disembark. The eleven thousand and the eleven thousand and first. And I'll tell you what they did. One thousand they beheaded. And a thousand were hanged.

"And a thousand were burned to death and another thousand flayed alive.

"And another thousand were torn to pieces between four

horses, and another thousand spitted on pikes and roasted like sheep.

"And a thousand were thrown down from the walls, and a thousand drowned. And a thousand choked to death with smoke, and a thousand thrown into quicklime.

"And a thousand devoured by wolves, and a thousand chopped to bits. And a thousand were made to swallow fire, and another thousand disemboweled."

"That makes more than eleven thousand," Onésime said.

"There were more than eleven thousand, lots more," Bertin retorted airily, "maybe three times eleven—and a thousand had their eyes gouged out and their tongues torn out, and another thousand had all their sinews torn out with pincers . . ."

"Yes, but what about Ursula?" put in little Martine.

"Wait, you little pest, I'm coming to that. Ursula saw all this and she wept for pity and she swooned.

"And then the son of the heathen king said to her, 'You are so pretty I will give you a thousand gold bezants if you will let me rape you.' And Ursula said to him, 'The devils piss on your mother, I want to be a virgin martyr!' 'You wait, my girl, and see what's coming to you.' Then he told his archers, 'Fire away, boys!'

"And then they all started shooting and wham! an arrow in her arm, and one in her shoulder and one in her chest, and in her eye and in her other eye, and in her nose and in her mouth and in her neck, and one in her belly and one between her legs, and one in her side, oh what a martyrdom that was! So many arrows that not an inch of flesh was left, eleven thousand arrows!

"And she just stood there with her hands together, praying to the Holy Virgin. And lo and behold, all the arrows dropped off her and there she was as clean and white as a new-laid egg! Oh, you should have seen the heathens' rage. They were mad with fury. They broke their bows, and then they brought bigger ones.

"Then they began again. Wham, wham, wham! Whizz, bang, thump! And they broke all the bones in her face and her back, and stuck right in her heart, and smashed all her teeth to smithereens, and her brains spilled out all down her face and everywhere! Ooh the poor thing! Great big arrows, like crossbow bolts. Eleven thousand arrows and there she was still alive!

"So in the end the heathens cut off her head and stuck it on a spear, and her soul flew out, so white and beautiful that everyone thought the sun had risen in the middle of the night! And she went to paradise, to the gardens of the Lord Jesus Christ."

"And what happened then?" asked Jean le Brun, who, though a big lad of fourteen, was no brighter than a little boy because hunger had affected his brain.

"Then?" said Bertin. "Then they gave her a great big palm branch and a white robe and put a crown of stars on her head. And she forgot all about it. Everything! And she was as happy as a lark."

"Do you know any more stories about martyrs?" Jean asked. "Tell us the story of Saint George."

"Oh, Saint George is a good one," Onésime said. "The things that happened to him! And when he cut off the dragon's heads and the heads grew again and Greek fire came out of their mouths!"

"Bang!" said Jean. "One head and another head and another head and another head and another head and another head—"

"Will you shut up! Saint George was the best knight in all Antioch, boys, and he had a white horse! And its harness was all covered with plates of gold and hung with silver bells, and it was so beautiful that when he went out hunting all the people would go up on the roofs just to see his horse. A pure-bred Arab stallion, white without a single grey hair, and a mane like silk—"

"Oh God," said the priestess, "oh God, if it were only possible. If it were only possible."

"Drink a little wine, mother, it will make you sleepy."

"That's all I need! To get drunk, with my child lying there who will never drink again! Lord God, such a good boy he was, and never drank wine, except a little on feast days, and God knows he would have done better to have been a drunkard and a womanizer! God knows, instead of going about with idle good-for-nothings, listening to preachers, wasting his time with Garin and Bernier's Jacques and One-eyed Jacques and wanting to be a weaver . . . We always let him do what he wanted.

"Oh God, didn't I say this crusading was all nonsense and a scandal for good Christian folk, putting ideas into lads' heads that would swallow any foolishness so long as they had something to shout about? But there were married men and monks all saying it was a good thing, and the curé had to preach sermons and take up collections. I told him, Lambert, I said, marry the girl if you want to, but stay at home. Does God need you to deliver Jerusalem? Yes, I daresay! He's only waiting for you! But it was no good. I've had a vision, he said, God is calling us—oh, those murdering rascals that preached this pilgrimage, Peter and Brother Barnabé and the rest! God punish them for the harm they've done. Oh, the murderers, to come here and die of hunger and thirst and wounds, and kill people—when did God ever tell us to slaughter folk like fowls?"

"Woman, you blaspheme," said Brother Imbert. "It was God's will. Not a sparrow falls but by God's will."

"Then my blasphemy is His will also. He has a mother, He knows what it means. Oh Holy Virgin, why did he have to fight a Sudanese? He was no soldier.

"Oh curé, curé, what a pilgrimage! See where it has brought us all."

"Her mind is wandering," Brother Imbert said gently. "It is a mother's nature. A voice was heard in Ramah, lamentation and bitter weeping. Weep with her, you women. Share her grief with her." The other women were tired and almost asleep, and Jacques was dead drunk and snoring like a bellows, slumped down near the fig tree a few yards from his friend's body. The night was bright and clear and the white moonlight, sharply bisecting the court, shone cruelly on Lambert's grey face and made the three candles burning at the dead man's head pale and faint.

"Marie, you are not asleep, come and weep with her."

Marie was sitting by Pierre, who was wrapped in a blanket, near the red embers of a fire. She was not weeping but sitting stiff and straight, like a woman seeing visions. "Oh no, my friends, I shall not weep tonight. Our joy is too great. Let me go back to the Holy Sepulcher."

"Do you want to be tied again?" Rufine said. "Holy Sepulcher indeed! The streets are full of drunken soldiers." Marie did not answer. She pretended to be asleep, and then rose quietly and slipped through the shadows by the wall toward the gate.

Outside, she began to run through the dark streets. Torches were blazing on the rooftops, and through the open gateways were glimpses of candlelit rooms and courtyards with red fires burning and roasting sheep. Men were singing and laughing, and there were sounds of women's laughter also: it was a night of rejoicing. The torchlight showed pale yellow against the white moonlit sky and there were shields and banners. It was light enough to make out their colors, red lions and green crosses and fleurs-de-lis on a blue ground and gold crowns and red crosses. Drums were beating like a merry patter of hailstones, getting louder and louder, with answering trumpets. The soldiers were celebrating. Fires had been lighted in the square in front of the Church of St. Onyphrion and the front of the church was decked with red and gold cloths. Huge thornbushes crackled on the fires, and the firelight danced on the silken cloths and lit the soldiers' faces like torches.

The men were Flemings; they were singing in their own tongue, gay marching songs with a fine swinging beat, and at the chorus they all jumped up and roared out their battle cry. Camp-followers were dancing around the fire, shaking their long black hair and necklaces of brightly colored beads—native girls, all of them, who could not have understood a word of Flemish, but they laughed recklessly and rattled their tambourines.

Inside the church a high, ringing voice was chanting:

Libera me, Domine, de morte aeterna

O libera me. Through the half-open door could be seen a gleam of candles burning around three coffins covered with embroidered cloths: rich men, there are no more rich or poor, dead or living, sinners or righteous, O Jerusalem!

In a covered alleyway still clammy with the stale smell of putrefaction, a pair of lovers clung together laughing. The way was so narrow that Marie had to push past them, her senses momentarily roused by the scent of animals in heat. She came to a street strewn with palm branches and small twigs of aloes, their perfume mingling strangely with the acrid smell of urine. The street was filled with people, as if it had been broad daylight. Men emerged, half naked, from the houses, calling out to passers-by to come and drink. People were carrying lighted torches, others held tall candles. See, Christians, see, this is Jerusalem, not one stone but is holy, and your rejoicing is holy too. You have earned it!

"Hey, goldilocks! Come and dance with us!" They were men from the North, their blue eyes deep-set in tanned and furrowed faces, their leather coats gay with colored belts and scarves. They tried to draw Marie into a courtyard from which came a deafening rattle of tambourines. "Oh no," said Marie, "oh no, my friends, I am looking for the Holy Sepulcher, my heart is on fire, your joys are not for me."

"Come on, we'll give you embroidered silks, and if you're on fire we'll soon cool you down!" Half a dozen of them had gathered around her, and she shrank back against the wall and began to scream uncontrollably like an animal, so that the men stepped back in alarm. "Let her alone, she is possessed."

She fled from them and ran on, keeping close to the walls, running so lightly in her short skirt that from a distance she could have been taken for an overgrown lad.

The nearer to the Holy Sepulcher, the more filthy and crowded were the streets, ankle-deep in a slush of straw and excrement. Stretchers lay on the ground: the only way to get by was to jump over them. Here were the poor, either waiting their turn or simply staying where they were, so as to be nearer to Jesus Christ. They were camping in the streets, sitting on the broad stone steps, huddled in their cloaks. Many were sick, and the air was fetid although the night was cool. They sat there, searching one another for lice, and in the dim light of the thickly smoking torches the narrow street seemed filled with yellow fog. Some were fast asleep, stretched out across the streets; others were singing.

More sounds of singing came from the roofs. The moon shone down between the beflagged walls of the houses, white, with a terrible pure whiteness, so bright that after looking at it one saw only small green moons before the eyes. And the square before the Holy Sepulcher was cordoned off with chains and the chains guarded by soldiers.

What do you expect, good people, what do you expect? The poor and the sick will be trampled, you must be patient. Monks and priests were walking in procession across the square, hemmed in by long lines of people, many of them Greeks, but there were also some French knights and squires and other respectably dressed people. It is right and proper for Christians to rejoice at all hours of the day and night at the great favor which God has granted them. In the distance was the open door of the church. Never were so many voices heard singing the matin psalms together.

In the square the moon blanched the smoke from the torches and etched great black triangles on the white walls. A motley crowd was moving with a slow, rippling motion, and the singing was like distant thunder from the hundreds of cracked voices echoing the responses. The poor on the other side of the chains repeated the *Amen* and *Ora pro nobis* as near as they could, and the sound spread on down the streets to mingle with the groans and the varied singing.

Marie stood close by the chain, craning her neck to try and catch a glimpse of the church door and the candles that burned inside, but with all the people moving about the square with their long robes and torches and their arms raised—O Lord Jesus, O Lord Jesus, let me be a bird, let me be a fly and fly to You.

Let me stay with You forever
Wear me as a seal upon Your heart.
I love You as much as my Jacques and my Pierre.

Soldiers, you are here like the guard of Pontius Pilate, keeping us from the Sepulcher, do you think we will steal the body of Our Lord? The great stone rolled away of itself, and He came living from the tomb.

The candles were singing and the voices burning all together in one great flame, one Burning Bush. We are all the leaves and branches of the Burning Bush. Marie saw the square flooded with light as if the walls of the church had become transparent, and the men walking about the square were drowned in flame.

She saw a vision. The sky above the basilica was a jewel-studded arch of deep-blue mosaic and the face of the Virgin shone in the moon with a dazzling white light surrounded by three rings of fire, rose, blue, and green, and the rings were made of the wings of angels flying upward in a spiral.

They whirled around, faster and faster, until the whole sky was filled with a shimmering, swirling light that merged into the lights of the square. The thunder of voices singing the matin psalms was a great fire in which the angels danced. While up above, in the moon, the Virgin wept, Her face wet with tears, shining with a pearly glow, so compounded of light that the face itself was scarcely visible. Her love is so great that even in the midst of joy She weeps, weeps for Her children and will not be comforted. The three haloes are made of tears. They flow down silently in shimmering spirals, filling all the sky and sweeping the earth.

Marie saw herself in the church close to the Holy Stone, one with the flame of the candles, fused and burned away, plunged in the fire, her body transmuted into fire, wavering and trembling with the candlelight in time to the singing. She was singing with all her might and the square around her burned, the chain and the walls of the houses and the soldiers with their halberds. You there, you are the soldiers that nailed Jesus to the Cross!

All of us nailed Jesus Christ to the Cross, and He has come to life again. The city is burning. For He is risen and His wounds shall bleed to the world's ending! The streets are filled with blood up to the cornices and paved with severed heads, He has conquered death, there are no dead or living any more, all have been burned together in the great furnace of the sun.

O Lord, two hundred of us set out from Arras, now we are twenty-five. Truly, Lord, You are the God of the living, not the dead, they are all living, the city is all light in the midst of darkness, lit by the souls of the dead.

Oh Jacques, Jacques, do not weep, do not weep any more, your friend is not dead but living, a veil of light hides him from your eyes, but he is living.

He is more alive than we. The stones crack, all the stones are cracking, the walls of the church are falling. He is risen! Why seek ye the living among the dead? For He descended into hell and brought them all back with Him. Oh, dazzling light! Friends, I am parched, I am dying.

I am a woman of Arras, I see visions, I burn with fever, a mouthful of water for the love of God. I thank you for your great charity, it is the living water of the fountains of Jerusalem.

The moon has gone down into the great pyre, down there beyond the ramparts, she has gone to comfort the spirits of them that died an evil death and cool their burning flesh. See, the valley of Jehoshaphat is filled with the living and the dead, there is no more night, it is the Judgment Day.

Since Friday, there is no more day or night for us, but only one Judgment Day till we die!

At daybreak carts drawn by mules brought fresh supplies of candles to the Holy Sepulcher. In the square before the church rich and poor bought candles according to their means. Pale, exhausted, with burning eyes, the priests came out of the church reeling like drunk men, and other priests came, surrounded by men bearing candles, to take their place. In the morning light they too were pale, but glad, newly washed, and straight as lances.

The barons, dressed in their long silk robes, came in a great procession to pray. Ever since the storming of the city there had been no end to the celebrations and processions around the holy place. The common people dragged away the chains, pushed past the soldiers, and surged across the square, and they received more alms than they wished for, for their one thought was to get inside the church. For that night many that were wounded or covered with sores had seen their scabs fall away from them with their bandages, and there were many more who hoped for the same miracle.

A boy about ten years old was running about the square quite naked, dancing and whirling like a top and singing:

Holy Mary, Holy Mary
My sores have all gone! My sores have all gone!
Let them go to the heathen
The Turks and Egyptians
The Greeks and the Syrians . . .

And it was a fact that his body was smooth and clean. The rest of his people—he was from Lorraine—were calling and shouting to him: "Come here, you bad boy, or your sores will come back. God has given you a miracle and you can't even say thank you." The boy was a bit simple and did not really understand that what had happened to him was a miracle, but many good and devout people prayed in vain and obtained no relief.

Because of this there began to be some murmuring about the church, and people said it was not right or decent for the shrine to be surrounded by so much dirt and stench, for the sick and dying were never a pleasant sight and could not always control their bodily functions or keep covered their maggot-infested sores. No, it was not decent, and the holy men and the nobles who came to pray there were put out by it. Was the holiest spot on earth to be made a dungheap and so justify the sacrilegious name the Moslems had bestowed on it? Those who complained most were the Greeks, who were known to be a proud, hardhearted people. Had they no sick of their own?

There was a time and place for everything, they said. The Lord cured the centurion's servant with a word, without going near his house, and the Latin bishops and clerics would be well advised to explain this to the poor. The Greeks were sad because their Patriarch, the venerable Simeon, had just died. Like Moses at the entry into the Promised Land and like the other Simeon who sang the *Nunc Dimittis,* the good old man had rendered up his soul to God on the very day after his people's deliverance. Not, as the Latin priests observed, that he had behaved like the Patriarch of Antioch, who had remained in his city and narrowly escaped martyrdom at the hands of the Turks. The Patriarch of Jerusalem had fled to Cyprus where he was in no danger of martyrdom, and it was for this reason that God had not permitted him to see with his own eyes Jerusalem delivered.

Jerusalem belonged, not to the Greeks, but to all Christians, and it was clear that God no longer wished a Greek to be patriarch of His city.

The Greek priests walked in procession through the streets, looking thoughtful and tight-lipped. In the Via Dolorosa they had their servants put aside the pilgrims who lay on the ground, crawling toward the Holy Sepulcher and kissing the stones with raw, bleeding lips. In all fairness, these priests had to get by also without walking on the prostrate bodies, but there was little humility in the way they went about it.

The dead were carried to the churches, each to the church of his own quarter because there was no room in the Holy Sepulcher. They were carried on stretchers, wrapped in sackcloth with wooden crosses resting on the sacks. Christians, pray for those who saw Jerusalem with the eyes of the flesh but did not see it long. No, there is no more room in the city's graveyards, and the poor are to be buried without, in the shadow of the sacred walls. Do not let it grieve you, they will still be close to God—less than a quarter of a league.

The people of Arras filed through the narrow streets in the wake of the two men bearing Lambert's body on a stretcher. Brother Imbert walked in front and Élie and Jean-Marc followed him, using their shoulders to force a passage for the dead. *Pray for him, Christians, he was a lad of twenty summers and his mother was with him.* Jacques and Guillaume of Béthune carried the stretcher and the priestess hobbled after, supported by Marie and Alix. She had stopped crying and her face, with its reddened eyes and nose and purple lips, was like that of a woman in a drunken stupor, vacant and dry-eyed. Passers-by bowed and crossed themselves as they brushed past her, even the wealthy Christians of those parts crossed themselves: A mother, clearly, may God comfort her.

The stretchers were lining up at Herod's Gate and soldiers were letting the little processions through: Go then, good people, but do not stay too long praying at the grave, be back before curfew. The black smoke was still rising from beyond the walls, drifting lazily into the blue sky. The drawbridges and portcullises and the road beneath the arched gateway were grey with ash. All this from human bodies, and enough ash down there around the pyre to cover all the streets. All the olive trees at the bottom of the hill were grey, and men breathed ashes and swallowed them each time they opened their mouths. Human ash is no more bitter to the taste than any other.

Ah, Lambert, you too, you too, as though enough dead had not been carried out through this gate, enough trenches dug. "Move on, Picards, no dawdling there, there are others to come after you."

"We are not Picards," Élie said. "We are from Arras. Only this man and this and this woman here are Picards."

"What is it to me?" the soldier said. "Pass along, there." They passed on, with decent lamentations.

"Now then, you brats," le Grêlé said, "no squabbling. This is no time for it."

"It never is, Grêlé," Mardoche retorted. "People are dying all the time."

"You won't, that's for sure. Neither God nor the Devil would have you."

"Hey you," the soldier said suddenly, "you with the pocky face. Are you Élie le Grêlé, the weaver of Arras?"

"Aye, what if I am? You're not from Arras. I'd pick you for a Walloon." The soldier, a youngster with a brick-red countenance, was staring at him with an air of disbelief. "So you're Élie le Grêlé, the lover of the fair Euphemia?"

"Seems so. What's that to you?"

"Just that if I'd known you had such a boar's head on your shoulders, that song would not have made me cry so much."

"And who asked you to cry?"

A shade of sadness crossed the soldier's face. "You see," he said, "I had a girl in Antioch. Her name was Zenobia. Not Euphemia, Zenobia."

Élie shrugged and hurried after his friends. There were no songs made about any Zenobias. God knows there might have been many in Antioch, but only one was fair. There would never be another so fair again.

Fool that I was, Élie thought, not to have stayed one more day, at least to bury her decently. I could have made it out to be some drunken soldier's crime—such things happen. I could have looked at her for one more day. And now they were taking the dead out from Jerusalem to the old burial ground, the one that had been made for the Christian dead during the siege. Not six weeks ago, and already it was an old burial ground, away beyond the great pits where, beneath its thin covering of fresh earth, the vast seeping mass of corruption exhaled its heavy odor in the sun.

Down in the valley, deep in the grey snow, the remains of the pyre were still smoking. In the center around the dark-red, glowing heart, the black scaffolding of bones subsided from time to time and flames shot up and died away. The engineers and their volunteer assistants were scattering the cooled ashes over the ground, and many were down on their knees still grubbing among the charred bones, still searching, remembering the rumors of those who had swallowed gold coins, or of rings overlooked on dead hands.

It was not very different from striking camp at any other time. The teams of carpenters sent their criers into the city: Who would take service dismantling the siege towers? There was plenty of work because these towers were like real castles, and it was worthwhile saving some of the timbers because, as everyone knew, there were few trees in these parts. Once the dead were buried, all the men who were able made their way down the hill and settled among the debris of what had been the Walloons' camp to wait for the work to begin. It was by no means as well paid as the work of clearing up the dead, but better than the same work at Antioch or Arqa. The trouble was that the poor were always in need of money. You thought you had got plenty of plunder, and what with candles and the vows that you had made it was all gone in a few days.

To the ladders, men! The large timbers from the top were lowered from the wooden bridge straight onto the ramparts and piled up at the foot of the wall inside. For this job, men were needed who were used to working with ropes and tackle.

Moreover it had to be done quickly, or there would be nothing for it but to set fire to the wooden tower, and that would interfere with the work of the masons who were repairing the walls and filling in the holes made by the missiles, for the wall on this side was a grim sight.

"What then? Are they coming to invest the city?"

"So they say. They are even saying that the great army out of Egypt is already on its way, that they are putting five hundred vessels under arms."

"Mercy! What of our dead? They will desecrate all the graves."

"That is how it is, my lad. To each his turn. Leave God to take care of the dead."

The carpenters burned through the big wooden bolts with red-hot irons, and once freed, the huge cedar trunks swung out slowly, stayed by the ropes which teams of men paid out a little at a time. If it had not been for the heat and the strong smell of scorched meat (for the great pyre was still burning) the work would have been pleasant enough, for from the top of the tower there was a view over the roofs and domes of the city, with its gardens and belts of crenellated walls, to the beautiful blue mountains beyond. Oh, it was a beautiful city, who would ever believe that so much blood had been shed within those walls? But what is that, that beating of drums and roar of voices coming from the Temple?

"Haven't you heard? This is a great day for the Walloons and for all those from the Ardennes and for all the French army. Duke Godfrey has been made King of Jerusalem."

Jacques wiped his brow with the back of his hand and took a fresh hold on his rope. "That's no bad news. The Duke has deserved it."

"The barons granted him that honor because he was the first to enter Jerusalem. For you must know, friends, that his purity is such that every night God permits him to see visions, for he spends his nights in prayer in his chapel."

"God grant," Jean-Marc said, "that his visions may be good ones and foretell victory for us."

"What's this, my man? Are you a heretic?" asked the master carpenter. "God did not deliver Jerusalem into our hands for a mockery, only to take it back again in a fortnight. The victory is ours already."

"Woe unto you, Christians, for you have been deceived! See, the army of Gog and Magog is come upon you, and because God has not judged us worthy He will deliver us into the power of the infidel, as He delivered up the Hebrews to Nebuchadnezzar.

"Woe unto you! For three transgressions of Israel and for four I will not turn away the punishment thereof. For you have ripped up women with child and trampled infants beneath your horses' hoofs! See, the armies of Pharaoh shall come down upon you like lightning and God will no longer defend you.

"See the sign which God sends us and how He has judged us: your bad shepherds have appointed as Patriarch of Jerusalem a man unworthy of the name of priest and of the name of Christian!"

This speech came from a Poitevin monk standing on the roof of a house not far from the ruins of the old mosque; he had a powerful voice and the look of a holy man, being very thin, with a shaggy beard and a habit worn so threadbare it was transparent. Because of this, people listened to him in horror. What he said seemed to make sense, and it made no difference that he belonged to the Provençal camp; even the Normans and Flemish were shocked to see such a man as Arnoul, a bad priest and a man known for his scandalous living, elected patriarch of the holiest of cities.

That he was wise and clever and brave and a fine speaker and had the ear of the barons, no one denied, and when he rode through the streets on his fine grey horse the soldiers cheered him gladly and he responded laughing to their cheers. But from that to making him patriarch, just like that, without the approval of the Pope or the Patriarch of Antioch, was another matter. One did not have to be a very learned man to understand that trying to turn lead into pure gold by the workings of the Holy Ghost was no work of the Holy Ghost but trickery, and some laughed and others shook their heads, but all agreed that Arnoul must be a wizard. He must have given the barons and the bishops with the army some kind of magic potion to drink.

But tell us, holy man, is it just that we should all be rejected by God for the sake of a single sinner? Let Arnoul be struck with leprosy if he got himself elected by a cheat, but it is no fault of ours.

"Oh, the foolishness of men! They cannot see the signs. The whole body is rotten within and you take fright at a single boil. And do not say it is no fault of yours, for surely the rich and the mighty shall pay most dearly but you have all of you your share.

Pray and repent, for it may well be that the Lord will spare Sodom for the sake of ten righteous!"

There were some Norman soldiers in the crowd who, because they liked Arnoul and disliked the Count of Toulouse, began to mutter that this was no time for sermons of this kind and that Jerusalem was a Christian city and would remain so in spite of traitors. "And your Count," the pilgrims added, "got more than ten thousand bezants to let Iftikhar and his emirs go free. Whatever anyone may say, Arnoul was never a traitor." The Poitevin made an attempt to go on speaking, but his voice was drowned by angry shouts and no one listened to him.

A mounted company in long robes embroidered with gold rode through the square, among them ladies with veiled faces and hands covered with white gloves. Mercy, Lords, mercy for a poor soldier who had his eyes burned in the first assault, pity for an archer who lost his right foot, a little bread for the love of God for a poor old man who has lost his tongue! The knights flung some small coins at random, and they needed to have a good many about them when they rode through the city thus.

For Jerusalem was becoming a city like any other. So soon had people grown accustomed to its stepped streets, its covered alleys like dark, vaulted passageways, its narrow lanes debouching into spacious arcaded courts, and to the open squares before the churches, the great gateways with their Roman arches, the walls adorned with mosaics of colored marble, the gilded cupolas and domed and pillared fountains, to the rich palaces surrounded by their gardens and the ramparts that were always there behind the terraces of white roofs, to the huge citadel itself with its square keep dominating an area of rich houses with domes and gardens planted with orange trees, and to the big Marketplace lined with arcades where little shops were already beginning to open.

They had grown so used to it that they would never have confused it with Antioch or Maarat or anywhere else. Men talked of the Market and the Temple, of the Tower of David and the Holy Sepulcher, as they might have done about St. Vaast's Square or the castle in Arras.

And if there was still black blood set hard between the stones in the streets and walls, no one noticed it. It seemed as if the city had always been like that and would remain so: bloodstained, soiled, and scarred, with here and there the marks of burning. The sites of the synagogue and of a number of mosques were heaps of broken beams and blackened stones: these would be cleared up later, later, the good stones kept and a new building erected. It was a city of empty houses and shattered doors, a spoiled city with too much room in it for the people that occupied it, so that ten days after the sack there were still quite good houses left for anyone to move in and hang up his shield or his knife above the door.

It was a city where they were still camping, waiting for the next battle. Nothing was real there, except the Holy Sepulcher, its finest houses no more than a poor reflection of what was to come, all glorious and resplendent in marble and gold

descending out of heaven, like unto a stone most precious.

Twelve gates: twelve angels, twelve tribes of Israel, twelve apostles.

And the first foundation shall be jasper, the second sapphire, the third, a chalcedony, the fourth an emerald, the fifth sardonyx, the sixth sardius, the seventh chrysolyte, the eighth beryl, the ninth a topaz, the tenth a chrysoprasus, the eleventh a jacinth, the twelfth an amethyst.

And the twelve gates shall be twelve pearls.

The Lamb shall be the light thereof and He shall shine on the altar of the Holy Sepulcher. And through its walls, translucent and bright as crystal, the light shall shine on all things and there shall be nothing hid. Yes, all the stones, down to the smallest piece of pavement, shall be made of crystal and pure gold.

It is because of this that today they must remain blackened with smoke and stained with blood, awaiting the day when the seven vials shall be emptied. We are pilgrims on earth and pilgrims in the city: the earthly pilgrimage is done and the pilgrimage of the heart is about to begin.

My poor friends, you thought to be delivered from sin, and God has brought you here to reveal to you the magnitude of your sins! Humble yourselves and pray, for what has been hidden before is now revealed. The horror you have witnessed in these days is the horror of your sins. God has shown it to you so that victory may not make you proud!

"This is all very well, Brother Imbert, but what is going to become of us now? If sins are not forgiven in a place as holy as this, then where will they be? Already, since Thursday, the price of corn has almost doubled, because of the rumors of a siege. Indeed, it seems that everywhere, even in paradise, there will be rich and poor."

"My friends, if God's angels cannot tell the good seed from the bad, how then should we? The sword of God has passed over you, your hearts are laid bare, do not let the devils enter, do not let your thoughts swerve from the Holy Sepulcher.

"See, the army of Egypt is approaching, but fear not, God will not permit them to take Jerusalem from us. If He has permitted Arnoul to be made patriarch, then honor Arnoul, but know that the more he is honored, the greater the punishment God has in store for him. If God has permitted Godfrey to be named lord of Jerusalem, then honor Godfrey, but know that his sins will be judged the more severely. If you are citizens of Jerusalem, all Christians should honor you for that, but your debt will no longer be counted in deniers but in gold bezants."

The people of Arras listened, and the Picards and the French from the neighboring houses with them. Brother Imbert spoke well, and since he had been in Jerusalem his face seemed to have grown lighter and brighter and his pale eyes no longer blinked but remained wide open and piercing, like an eagle's. His high voice was shaken with sobs, so that he seemed to be singing rather than speaking. People were glad to listen to him, though they found his words hard to understand: it was a fine thing to come so far and suffer so long, only to be burdened with more sins than you would have committed staying at home. "You all know," Brother Imbert said, "that so great is the virtue of the Holy Sepulcher, so great is that virtue that all sins are consumed in it as straws are in the fire."

Then on Saturday night, something happened which gave the people of Arras and Picardy something to talk about. On the way back from vespers, Bertin was jostled somehow by the crowd and became separated from her own people. Two hours later she came home, bleeding, with her clothes all torn, and howling fit to wake the whole street. She had been raped, she said. Some Norman soldiers had raped her in a courtyard, a whole bunch of soldiers, a whole company. By some miracle she had made her escape over the rooftops, but they had treated her so roughly that she had fainted twice. She went on crying and sniveling, flinging her arms around Alix's neck—of all the women of the house it was Alix for whom she had the greatest fondness—and saying that she wished she could put the evil eye on all the Normans, even on their Duke Robert, and that she wanted to die and become a virgin martyr and then the filthy beasts would be damned, damned, damned.

"Fear not, my child, they will be. Just tell yourself it was better to lose that than your head."

The men looked at the girl and scratched their beards: such things ought not to happen in Jerusalem, the captains ought to keep a closer watch on their men, who was to be blamed now?

"Thank God," Brother Imbert said, "it was the soldiers that did it and not some poor pilgrims from another quarter. At least you are not tempted to attack your brothers with picks and axes."

"To think that in Jerusalem," Élie said, "we should have no protection against the soldiers and that a girl gets raped because she obeys God's law and puts on women's clothes! We must go and find out the captain of the Normans."

"By tomorrow," Jacques said, "they will be raping married women and old crones, and shall we have nothing to say about it?"

The women said they must take the child with them to the Normans' quarters and get her to point out the guilty ones and denounce them to their officers. The poor should have better protection in Jerusalem than anywhere else.

"You fools," Alix said. "How do you expect this poor creature to point out the soldiers to you? She will point to every Norman she sees, and they will all say they never set eyes on her."

"It was all the Normans," said Bertin, "every one of them! There were a hundred of them. They all raped me."

"She's making it up," Mardoche said. "A hundred! Why not a thousand?"

"There were a thousand! Cross of Jesus Christ, I'm telling the truth. A thousand!" She dabbed at her bruised face with a wet cloth and turned her small head from side to side, like a snarling wolf cub.

"There's nothing to make such a fuss about," Jean-Marc said. "It could have been worse."

"You have a hard heart for a Picard," Jacques said. "After all, the girl is from your own country."

"We've none of us any country now but Jerusalem. Normans, Provençals, Bretons, and Picards, we have all been through the same baptism, my lad, and we must learn to harden our hearts. What do you expect us to do, sit here weeping all night?"

It was three days now since Lambert's death and it was true that Jacques no longer wept, but twenty times a day he found himself wanting to say, Well, Lambert, or See this, Lambert? and he would turn around, as if his friend were standing there, invisible. He had only to turn a corner, go up onto a roof, and there, like bumping into a friend, so he was always bumping into the absence of Lambert, and everywhere that Lambert was not made him feel a small ache in his heart.

It was a good feeling, Jacques. I never felt happier in my life.

Yes, my lad, and you know I gave everything to the Church, down to the last sou. I did not even keep one pin for Marie. What more could I have done? Perhaps I should have cut off one of my own fingers at least, yes, probably I should have—don't worry about your mother, I'll see she does not want for anything.

"Jacques, stop prowling about. Stay with me."

"No, Marie, you are feverish, you make me too hot."

"Don't you love me any more, Jacques?"

"It's you that don't love me." Marie was lying on some mats close to the brick oven where the next day's bread was baking, warming her sleeping Pierre with the burning heat of her own body. Her eyelids were so swollen with fever that she could not close her eyes. She saw the courtyard filled with strange men, women, and children. They were the dead infidels, dark-skinned men with short black beards dressed in faded blue tunics, and women swathed in striped veils. They must be the people who lived here, Marie thought, they do not understand why we have taken their houses. They died too suddenly. You see, good people, we are Christians, and it was God's will to give us this city. Do not grudge it to us, we are all in God's hands, and the man is not yet born who shall understand why God has judged us all so.

Oh Pierre, let us go away from here. She sat up so suddenly that the child awoke and began to cry out, "To arms! To arms!" "What arms, my poor baby?" His little hands went around her neck and he was asleep again almost at once. *Oh Pierre, Pierre, let us go away from here.* She braced herself to keep her shivering body from troubling the child.

WALK THROUGH THE STREETS OF JERUSALEM AND STRIKE. STRIKE EVERY LIVING THING. LAY INTO THE CROWD WITH YOUR AX, HEADS,

BACKS, EVERYWHERE TRICKLING, SPURTING, CRACKING, GROANING, SCREAMING. GO TO IT, JACQUES. IT IS SPURTING IN GREAT FOUNTAINS, YOUR FACE ALL OVER BLOOD, YOUR BEARD IS RED GO TO IT JACQUES OH JACQUES JACQUES JACQUES GO ON—if only I had been with you.

They were fighting now, over there in the middle of the courtyard, underneath the fig tree, and they were all shouting at once, it was hard to tell the dead from the living, and women were crying. What did you do that for, you dog, you swine? Why did you do it, and you a married man? There were some hard knocks and the one the others were hitting was groaning. The children were yelping like jackals. "What is going on, Rufine? Have the spirits of the dead come back to torment us?"

"No, silly. Jean-Marc's youngest has raped Bertin."

Oh Lord God, soon Jacques will have raped Bertin too. All the men, even Brother Imbert, will do it, even Duke Godfrey himself. Bertin, doubled up with pain, her hands clutching her belly, was shrieking to them to kill him, kill him, kill him! Grêlé, cut his throat like you did Guillaume the fuller's!

"You, a married man, to do that!" The boy fended off the blows. "The Devil fly away with Lydia! I'd give twenty like her for one fair one. And Bertin had nothing left to lose, had she?" The two Armenian women were clinging together, sobbing loudly and wailing in their own language.

Marie saw Brother Barnabé move through the crowd of dead and living and come to a halt three paces away from her. His clothes were in rags and his whole body oozed black corruption; his beard and hair were coming away from his skin, and the bones of his cheeks and forehead showed through the pallid, riven flesh. His eyes were wide open, two deep holes from which flowed tears of blood, and his expression was like that of a man under torture. "Oh, Brother Barnabé, is it you or a spirit of the Devil that has taken your face?" "It is I, Marie of Arras, do not be afraid of me. Where I am, I am plunged into a vat of rotting corpses and the stench is so great that for pity they let me come out and breathe from midnight until cockcrow." "Oh God, how many days will you endure this ordeal?" "Many days, for the grief that I have for the sins of my poor."

"And we were glad, thinking of you in paradise!" "I shall be there surely, Marie, but not until I have accounted to God for all your sins. I see many souls in danger of damnation." "Oh, do not tell me which, Brother Barnabé, I am afraid." "Marie, if you would serve me, go and find Father Albert for me. Tell him that he is on an evil course and threatened by great peril. Let him do penance and return to live among you as he did at Antioch." Before Marie had time to answer, Brother Barnabé was gone, taking with him in a luminous red mist all the dead that were walking in the court.

Jean-Marc's Thomas, lashed to the fig tree, naked to the waist, his face covered with blood, braced himself and sniffed up the tears that blubbered his cheeks.

"What?" said le Grêlé. "Shall we punish him when we can do nothing to the Normans?"

"I care nothing for the Normans," Jean-Marc said. "But we are not dogs."

"What are they going to do to him?" the women asked. "They will not kill him unshriven?"

"Let his forehead and his cheeks be branded with a red-hot iron and drive him out into the street. And may he never come back here again."

They lied when they told us that in Jerusalem there would be no more rich or poor. Then better be like the Tafurs and live naked among the rocks, feeding on jackal's meat. Anyone can be poor, but in Jerusalem are many who think only of growing rich, and that is not given to everyone.

There were rumors of a Flemish potter who had taken possession of a house and found treasure there, and now he was lord and master and ordered his friends about like servants and had two armed men to guard his gold, and wore a silken robe and a belt studded with gold, and was employing masons to repair his house. Not everyone has the gift of avarice, and the poor less than the rest. The poor, my friends, are civil folk, and even when they have not charity they have some shame and share that which they have rather than be thought bad comrades, and give to the Church rather than be called bad Christians. When they have money they cannot keep it long.

So that in two weeks there were many soldiers and many poor knights also that became rich, and also many clerks, which was no good thing because they took the goods of the Greek Christians and robbed convents and churches. And the great lords and barons took a great deal, but they did not grow rich because all their money was spent on the purchase of arms and supplies for the army. But the poor that became rich were very few.

They had to look for work, and though there was no shortage of work they had little heart for it, because of the great heat and because they were dead tired. Get to work, idlers. You that did the great cleansing, will you refuse to rebuild and repaint the houses and strengthen the defenses, when you are promised a good wage and have as much water as you want? Will you ask a knight's fee for mason's work? In heathen lands it is clear for all to see that the knight's work is the most useful of any, his money is well earned!

Here is the Pharaoh that is called the Caliph of Egypt sending unnumbered armies against us; the Vizier himself commands the leading vessel, and the sea from Gaza to Ascalon is white with their sails and on each sail the crescent of Mahomet gleams. Unless we defend Jerusalem better than Iftikhar did, there will be no more rich or poor in very truth, for do not think that a single Christian will escape, whether pilgrim, Greek, or Syrian.

Know, brothers, it was a good deed that you did to slay all the citizens of Jerusalem: for now the enemy approaches and every man spared, every woman or child old enough to think, would have been so many knives planted in our backs. Remember all the cartloads of carrion that you dragged outside the walls and threw into the pits. You saw for yourselves: there were so many that we could not have spared all or even half of them. It was a miracle of God that with your small numbers you were able to overcome them all! Carrion, food for worms, and ashes scattered to the winds, that is all they are, that and no more. Do not fear their ghosts. For God surrounds His city with an invisible wall and their spirits cannot get through it.

If you should see their ghosts, if you should hear their screams, know that they are no more than the images of delirium, false and empty; they cannot harm you.

Jerusalem so dearly loved
So long desired, so well avenged
Washed in blood
Saved by the Cross.
Jerusalem so dearly loved
So closely guarded
So purified

Painted and gilded
Restored in God!
And may we all burn in hellfire
If we let the heathen come near you again!

There will be no siege, brothers. We shall go out all together to meet the great army. We will not let them disperse among the valleys, but go out and meet them where they disembark from their ships and hurl them back into the sea. This the barons have decreed, and they are more skillful in battle than Alexander.

All men of an age to fight are to form companies of foot, each according to his country, for the harvesters are few and the harvest will be great. Wages will be paid in advance and the reward will be either spoils or martyrdom.

For it is known that the Vizier brings more wealth with him than was found in the tents of Kerbogha and the Sultan of Nicaea.

They are bringing their Sudanese and Armenian guards against us, and you know the Sudanese are mightier than the Turks and the Armenians so fierce in battle that they never draw back. If we let them get away from the coast and move inland, then we are lost and ours will be not the glory of martyrdom but the shame of having betrayed Jerusalem. Let even those women who are able go with the army to help the fighting men in case of need and succor the wounded. Let not one mule or a single cart be left in Jerusalem, let no one think to save his own house and goods, *it is a case of one for all.*

Men began to see Saint George galloping on his white horse, the horse's hoofs scarcely touching the ramparts. He circled the walls at a swift gallop, bearing in his hand the banner of the cross, his scarlet cloak billowing like a sail in the wind. His lance, dripping blood, pointed toward the sea and the road to Jaffa.

Then the citizens of Jerusalem made ready to set out, and it took all their courage. In two weeks they had almost forgotten what camp life was like, the thirst, the marching, and the enemy arrows. They might have believed that life was done with forever.

The overriding weariness which they were just beginning to forget returned so fast that by the time they were organized into companies again, the men already had their heads full of noise and shouting and their throats parched with thirst. They were past caring even for the armies of Egypt. Let them lead us where they will.

Battle lay out there before them on the Jaffa road, the great red clamor shot through with arrows and glittering swords, the clamor of raucous voices and the clash of steel, the clouds of yellow dust, the black smoke and the bloody reek. What they felt was not fear, only a wild longing for the battle to come soon, as soon as might be, to hurl themselves into it, deaf to all sounds beyond the thunderous shouting, while the white horse of Saint George swooped above the fray amid the flashing swords and the helmets gleaming in the noonday sun.

And see the tent of Alafdal, vast as a palace hall, all hung with silken carpets and decked with round shields overlaid with letters of gold, and filled with open chests with gold up to the brim; see Alafdal lying in the middle of his tent, with gold coming out of his mouth, his gaping belly stuffed with gold pieces, and the golden coins, glittering like stars, flowing from his severed neck in place of blood. For gold he sold himself, he denied Jesus Christ, he is not a man but a sack of gold pieces.

He leads his army against the Christians but his gold shall not avail him; his tent shall be pillaged and his head adorn Godfrey's lance, while his limbs are scattered on the field. Oh, Vizier, you have traded the true God for the false, and though you offer the city of Cairo in exchange for your life, you shall not escape the justice of Jesus Christ.

Ah, you boast that with your great army, covering all the plain from Gaza to Ascalon like a forest on the move, you will easily overcome a small force of men. The men about to fall upon you now are so terrible that ten of yours will flee before a single one. See what these men have done to Jerusalem: they will do as much to Cairo and Alexandria.

No men so cruel and terrible were ever seen in any land. This is the vengeance of God, the men He sends against you fear nothing any more.

The army moves fast, with the cavalry at its head, and once past the mountain valleys, once in sight of their camp, brothers, we have got them; they will never stand against us on the plain, they will be like a flock of sheep, they will not have time to empty their quivers.

The infantry advanced rapidly in the full glare of noon, spread out over the slopes on both sides of the road which was choked with mules and carts. The men marched quickly, leaping over boulders as if they were fleeing before an enemy. Flies swarmed about them as they went and their bodies steamed from the sweat that poured off them, while out in front the ground rumbled and shook and a great cloud of dust rose up where the horsemen were heading on down to the plain. White shadows dodged in and out behind the ridges and arrows hissed. From time to time a man staggered and fell, and those not killed outright were dragged back to the carts. The Bedouin were everywhere, but like the vultures they would not attack an army, and there was no time to deal with them.

At dawn, after a brief prayer, they went on again under a cool, pale sky, the stones underfoot wet with an ice-cold dew. The cavalry had already begun their gallop toward the plain and their close-packed ranks were visible through a distant haze of whitish dust as they broke into the charge, racing for the long lines of tents and campfires and the droves of horses grazing among the olive trees.

Hurry, men, for God and Saint Michael! There will be work for us when they have ridden down the tents! Everyone was running, with only one thought in mind: not to arrive too late. Fall on them before they have time to rally and form into battle order. By this time the foot soldiers were swarming down the final slope, the tight columns fanning out over a widening front. This is it, men! The battle has begun. Listen to the shouting!

The thunder of the charge had given way to a sustained roar as all the knights shouted with one voice, a cry that seemed to shiver the rocks themselves and split the trees asunder, and followed almost at once by a great wail of terror from the camp strung out along the shore below the walls of Ascalon.

The archers advanced on both flanks while in the center the bulk of the men on foot rushed forward in the wake of the knights. And what work there was then, God knows, with men and horses overthrown, trampled and maimed, some fleeing, others standing to fight, falling back a foot at a time, but the men bearing down on them with maces and battle-axes might have been so many massive boulders hurled with gigantic force, too breathless to shout but laying about them for all they were worth.

It was not a battle but a rout. Good. And a massacre. No, hardly even that, hardly a massacre at all, simply a speedy end to the wounded, and there were many of them because the knights' charge had wreaked such havoc that men and horses were lying in heaps ten feet high and all they had to do was walk along hitting anything that moved. In some places the soil could not soak up the blood and the ground was like a quagmire. There was no time to spare the horses, and few in any case were worth saving.

No, no time to strip the corpses, there would be plenty for everyone. The knights' horses were curveting on the shore, jibbing at the long lines of blood-reddened foam. Those infidels who tried to escape by swimming were mostly drowned trying to reach the ships, because of their numbers and because they clung to one another struggling in the water. So many had been driven into the sea that the mere sight of the host contending with the waves was enough to rouse a belated shudder of fear: but for God's help they would have annihilated us. Oh Lord, the sight of those ships alone is like the harbor of Constantinople, all those galleys with square white sails heeling over under the combined weight of the human beings clinging to them. A city on the water, a city in the grip of panic, the water all along the shore solid with human heads and arms and the vessels shuddering like frightened horses.

Hundreds of vessels, the whole surface of the sea was covered with them.

Alafdal has got away, men. See, his galley is leaving harbor.

The barons may have been vexed, or the knights, but not the men. It was hot. The sea itself seemed to boil, a foul red stew of bodies of the dead and living. For a league around Ascalon there was not a clear space to sit down: bodies entangled in the wrecked tents, dried blood, hot dung, trails of fire in the dry grass, and several thousand men roaming here and there like ants from a turned-up anthill, looking for spoils.

Sticky with sweat and blood, reeking, wild-eyed, half laughing, and calling in cracked voices, so drunk with fatigue that they almost forgot to rejoice, yet dazed with joy nonetheless: the whole of the Vizier's army, the greatest they had yet seen, broken, not one in five escaped alive. Ah Mahomet, come and see, come and see what has become of your people now, deceiver who failed them in their need!

Duke Godfrey and the Duke of Normandy with their knights were outside the walls of Ascalon so early in the morning that only a few emirs and their horsemen had time to get inside the city. Then the gates were shut and men could be seen lining the walls, crowding along the ramparts and on the towers, throwing up their arms and wailing in despair. Be it known that we have much to gain by taking Ascalon; we must strike while the iron is hot. Camps are to be set up to encircle the city by land. There is such panic in the harbor and such a screaming inside the city that given the scaling ladders, we could have taken it by storm this very day.

The criers rode about the battlefield and the men laden with their spoils heard them proclaiming the order to form up and converge on the fortress, ready to make camp. Tomorrow they will bring us ladders from Jaffa and Jerusalem and we will launch a general attack. In three days the city will be ours!

Oh, but say, friends, what a handsome fortress, so regular it might have been drawn with a plumb line, with its fine square towers so identical and so crenellated and serrated it is a pleasure to see. What a triumph it would be to take it without spoiling it! We should have thought of it sooner and brought ladders.

For after the miracle God wrought for us, the inhabitants would certainly have offered no resistance. So they said, leading their captured horses laden with sacks and baskets, for the camp was a rich one and if the Vizier's own tent fell to the knights' share, there were others, veritable storehouses of corn and oil and jars of olives and figs and even preserved oranges, as well as copper vessels and cushions. Egypt must be wealthy indeed if their soldiers take cushions and chests of clothes to war with them: any humble knight of theirs is better equipped than a baron of ours.

Gasping for breath. A fiery mist before the eyes through which ships, crenellated towers, and banners passed in endless succession. Ears pounding with an interminable clamor of bells, all the tocsins and the knells that were ever heard filling the heavens with a muffled, rhythmic booming. The dead sprawled on the ground, half naked, so much mangled grey-and-red flesh, were objects as commonplace as the stones along the road. A man is nothing, a man is nothing, thank God we can safely leave them to rot out here in the open fields, no fields of ours. They are so much clay, nothing more, to be trodden underfoot, bellies and faces trodden underfoot without a thought, like so many clods of earth.

It did not even occur to anyone to take the heads, they were not worth a moldy orange. After so many heads, severed or not, even a Christian head made no more impression than a pile of horse manure. We'll divide the spoils, friends, in Jerusalem, if ever we get back there.

Get back? Of course we will. The people of Ascalon will put up no defense so long as we get the ladders in time. Do you hear them screaming inside the city? They will surrender maybe before they are attacked.

The men of Arras were digging their section of the trench. The heat of the day was not yet over and their picks and mattocks were heavy in their hands, but all the same the trench must be dug before nightfall, and God be thanked the ground was lighter here, much better than around Jerusalem. They would camp here —how long? Three days or more? Élie le Grêlé was banging in tent pegs collected from the enemy camp, which would do well enough for a palisade. Not far away the Lorrainers were setting up camp and roasting a sheep for their evening meal. They were serving now in a company of Picard foot, and the captain left them free at night to associate with their own friends.

Our carts have not come up yet. They must have gone astray back there beyond the sycamore woods. Thank God the soldiers will not be in a mood to violate Christian women tonight.

It is getting dark. How can we look for them?

Sounds of soldiers singing rang along the shore. Men still black with blood were bringing stray horses and camels into camp: rich prizes these, fine camels with one hump, rolling on their long legs like ships at sea. A joyful shout, long drawn out, swept through the army like a wave. God save them! Down tools, everyone! It is the good Duke's banners!

He rode on toward his tents, his knights around him, still fully armed, with brown bloodstains on his white surcoat and his tarnished helm stripped of its plumes, but his head held high and his gauntleted hands resting on his horse's neck. He wore his vizor up and the clear eyes gleamed in his stern face, grey with weariness, with the calm, steady brilliance of an eagle's. Men straightened as he passed and put down their picks and spades and raised their arms in salute: God save him! The King, the Advocate of the Holy Sepulcher, lord of Jerusalem! The horse moved on with a slow, heavy tread, and in the fading daylight the banners of the Walloons and Lorraine fluttered like pale birds from the lances.

The new Patriarch, Arnoul, rode surrounded by the clergy, in helmet and coat of mail, bearing a gold cross in his hands. There were shouts of "Long live Arnoul! May God forgive his sins! Everlasting salvation to Godfrey. He has not shamed Jesus Christ!"

The men dropped into heavy sleep as into a vault of stone; souls left their bodies and went wandering over barren mountains where the jackals cried. The sentinels strove to prevent themselves from falling asleep by laying their arms on the glowing embers and woke again with a start, all dazed and thinking themselves at Jerusalem or below the walls of Jerusalem.

Jean-Marc was to keep watch for the rest of the company until moonset, when le Grêlé would relieve him. The camp was very quiet; sleeping, the living looked like dead. Beyond the camp, over by the still-burning sycamore woods, pale shadows came and went, like ghosts mounted upon invisible steeds.

Yet these were no ghosts, but Bedouin. They crept close up to the camp and then withdrew again with a faint clatter of hoofs, and now and again a javelin buried itself in the ground near one of the sleepers or a stone fell, a dark circular object that landed with a soft thud.

A man was making his way toward Jean-Marc, a tanner from the Lorraine camp, half asleep, shivering, and stumbling over the sleeping forms. "Hola, you Picards. Bad news. My chief sent me to tell you."

"What for, curse you! If the news is bad we would have heard it soon enough." The man crouched down beside the embers of the fire. He held a human head in his hands. The head had a long grey beard, now stained with blood. The mouth and eyes were wide open in a look of horror and the skin was the color of dirty stone. By the long hooked nose, Jean-Marc recognized Brother Imbert.

He crossed himself, hardly believing what he saw, and indeed the face was barely recognizable. Yet the hair was the same, and the beard, yes, and the nose. Jean-Marc stared down at the agonized face and then looked at the Lorrainer. Both men bowed their heads. What was there to say? The Bedouin had fallen on the wagons and there were too few soldiers with the rear guard. The Lorrainers too had women and cattle there.

"We don't know yet," the tanner said. "We can't tell yet who has escaped."

"Tomorrow," said Jean-Marc. "We'll know tomorrow."

All the same, he woke Élie. Élie said, "What? The moon has not gone down." It hung still, like a big red copper axhead, only a little way above the horizon.

"I think we'll keep watch together," Jean-Marc said. "I don't feel much like sleep now. Come and see."

Élie did not speak. He sat for a long time, very still, with his chin on his fists. At last he said, "At least you and I have no women now."

"I have my sons' two wives," said Jean-Marc.

"Yes, but Armenians."

"Maybe that makes it worse." Ever since the young women's parents had died outside Jerusalem he had been wishing he had not encouraged these two innocents to leave Antioch.

Not all the convoys bringing water and supplies had taken the same route. The object had been to avoid congestion and speed up arrival, for no one could have foreseen that the battle would be over so swiftly, that there would be no need to entrench, and that they would find more than enough provisions on the spot. The barons had planned things all too carefully. Jean-Marc laid Brother Imbert's head down on a saddlecloth and drew the fringed ends over the dead face. Élie was putting some cypress branches on the fire, building them up into a cone to make the blaze last longer, and the ruddy light flickered over the sleeping forms. God, what an awakening for them! Would that the night were longer. The Bedouin were notoriously wild and savage men who violated women before they sold them. Oh God, Élie said to himself, it may be after all that what I did was for the best.

Even though she had been dead for six months and more, the mere thought of her in the hands of the Bedouin, the mere thought of her terror, was enough to fill him with such pity that he could almost have wept. As though she were still alive and screaming with terror in the arms of the men of the desert, and God be thanked, it was not true. Never again, never again.

Weep for Élie of Arras, him they called Grêlé
Who once was a good weaver, but a better crusader
Who left everything for Jerusalem's sake
Wife and little ones and house and loom.
If he had not taken the cross, he would never have loved.

Not but what the songs were a comfort in sorrow. But who would make the songs if they had taken Marie of Arras? Lord, she was a good comrade, was Marie of Arras. Already he was thinking of her as of one dead, almost without grief.

But the living were another matter. It was to be expected that they would howl and beat their heads against the rocks. Especially those who still had womenfolk brought with them from home.

By dawn the news was coming into the camp. Heads were picked up, thrown in by the Bedouin, about twenty in all, monks and soldiers of the rear guard. Only a small section of the convoy had been taken by surprise; the rest had been in camp since the previous day. Two young Normans had escaped by dodging among the rocks. How many Bedouin were there? God knows. Fifty or a hundred. On small black horses. They hurled javelins and ropes with running nooses, uttering earsplitting yells, and how the women screamed also!

Those who had lost their wives in the affray could still be thankful they had not found their heads lying on the confines of the camp. Thankful? That remained to be seen. There were many evil tales told of the Bedouin, it was even said they raped women to death. No, surely not, lads, the Bedouin are fond of money. They will not spoil their merchandise. They say that prizes taken by the Bedouin are numbered in their thousands in the slave markets of Damascus.

The men seemed stunned, too dazed for grief. Well, friends, this is a business. Where can we look for them by this time? How can we catch up with them when we do not even know which way they went?

They must be a long way off by now. They know this country like the palms of their hands.

They never camp two nights in one place.

Barons' orders to reinforce the camp's defenses. Set up all the captured tents and erect poles over a space of half a league. Make them think our numbers greater than they are. Drums are to be beaten loudly and fanfares of trumpets sounded, and all men are to shout and sing at the top of their voices. Give them no chance to get over their fright.

Shout, ah yes, they felt like shouting! Oh, the perfidious dogs, if we take the city not one shall be spared! Be calm, Jacques. What is the good of breaking the oil jars? The booty belongs to all of us.

"What good is oil? What good is booty? Now we are rich indeed!" He flung himself face downward on the ground and wept, striking his forehead with his fists and sobbing more like a bull roaring than a man.

There were Jean-Marc's elder son Mathieu and Guillaume, Rufine's husband, and Pierre who was married to Honorine and six more besides, all rending their cheeks and tearing out their beards, and swearing that the barons had betrayed them, had failed to put a sufficient guard on the convoys. Some Walloon soldiers of the Duke's army stood by in great distress, comforting the poor men as best they could. In such a great victory there were bound to be losses; it was a sin to grieve when God had performed such a great miracle for His people, for if the army of Egypt had not been destroyed, then we would all be dead and tomorrow Alafdal would have been in Jerusalem and slaughtered all the Christians, young and old.

Be sure of one thing, lads, whatever may have happened to your wives, they will have little to suffer in purgatory.

It was a consolation they had heard often enough before, but it was hard to know nothing, harder even than to have watched them die of fever, because they could not help picturing the worst.

The men flung themselves furiously into their work, seeing that it did more good to hammer the stakes of the palisade than their own heads. Oh, those Bedouin! As soon as we strike camp we'll be after them. We'll brand their faces with red-hot irons before we cut off their heads. Oh Marie, MARIE, MARIE.

"You have not lost everything," Jean-Marc told him. "You still have the little boy, in Jerusalem. And you have the priestess as well. You promised to take care of her."

"Yes," Jacques said, "I will take care of her. And I'll go for a soldier in any company that will hunt the Bedouin."

There being no more talk of taking Ascalon by storm, the poor that were on foot returned to Jerusalem: from there, friends, you can go down to Jaffa. The good Count of Flanders and the noble Duke of Normandy will pay the passage for all who wish to sail home again.

12 ✠✠✠✠✠✠✠✠✠✠✠✠

As long as everyone knew there was no means of getting away, no one had thought of going home. People had forgotten they had ever known another country.

But as soon as there was any mention of ships and sailing, even the most hardened became suddenly homesick and started to weep with nostalgia. Oh, just to see the faubourg and our old church, just to see the mist and the rain and the green grass of midsummer. They seemed to feel already the breath of the cool breeze on the Somme, or the Scarpe or the Seine. They went on foot, leading the captured horses by the bridle, the horses' saddles piled high with sacks and jars and rolls of cloth. Fools, horses are for riding, will you be poor forever? Forever, or so it seems. If we mean to sell the horses in the market they may as well be fresh: our legs cost nothing.

Amid joyful shouts and a beating of drums they marched into a gaily decked Jerusalem.

> Jerusalem, so dearly loved
> So closely guarded, so well avenged
>   So highly honored
>   So faithfully kept
> Our Bride richly adorned.

The walls were newly washed with lime and ochre, and every man down to the meanest groom was dressed in brand-new clothes. The Via Dolorosa was decked from end to end with green palm branches and altars with lighted candles.

The pilgrims of Arras returned to their own house with bowed heads and bitter feelings, for through no fault of their own they had suffered a grievous loss: seven women, all young and strong, gallant women who had gone as volunteers to help the fighting men. Was this the reward that Jesus Christ reserved for them?

Was this their reward?

Jesus Christ had better harden men's hearts, turn their hearts to bolts of stone. Those who had remained behind, the sick and the children, did not even mourn. They were more inclined to rejoice, because all kinds of rumors had been rife in the city and they had feared that all their folk were dead in the battle, so that to see the men back alive was something.

Alix was recovering from a bad bout of fever and was still too weak to walk properly. "You had a narrow escape, Alix. Why did God not send the other women a fever?"

"Oh no, friends, it is too much, indeed it is too much, the share of paradise that all of us are winning." She gave an odd little cracked laugh, gulping back her tears. *"Oh my sisters, my sisters, how shall I live without you!"*

One by one they knelt before the chest studded with copper nails in which they had put Brother Imbert's head. Now we have neither priest nor monk. He was a holy man, he wore iron chains under his habit. He was as meek as a lamb and he spoke like an angel out of heaven: shriven or unshriven he will surely win salvation!

Marie and Rufine and Honorine

and Artemisia and Lydia and Guillemine and Lucienne

may God forgive you your sins. Courage, friends, it may be that we shall find them again alive, anything is possible—

They say it is even possible to find a needle in a haystack, if God wills—

Oh, the poor little needles, the stack is so large: from Cairo to Damascus and from Mosul to Baghdad, but however large it be, it is not in the next world.

"It might as well be, my friends."

The priestess was nursing little Pierre on her lap, stroking his hair with her blind, groping hands. "No, no, my son, do not listen to them. She will come back, your Marie will come back, all beautiful in a new dress."

"Why do you lie to him, priestess?" Jean-Marc asked. "Better he should pray for her."

"Such a baby, Jean-Marc. He's not yet two years old!"

"Better he should learn to know life while he is young."

Pierre was a pretty child, clean and well nourished. He had blossomed since the capture of Jerusalem and was like a little apple, with ruddy golden skin and flaxen hair and big round blue eyes, deep-set between white, puckered lids. He had Marie's mouth, red and soft-lipped. Everyone loved him because already he could talk well and understand all that was said to him. He was listening now, looking up at Jean-Marc solemnly. He said, "I want to go to the Bedouin with Marie."

"Oh, poor darling, God forbid!" the priestess exclaimed. "You will grow up and go and get her back from the Bedouin." Jacques could not bring himself to look at his son, merely to think of him made him want to scream.

Make up your minds, good people, and for God's sake do not delay too long, because the two barons are sending their armies home and they are willing to take on board their vessels all those who long to see their homes again, but they must know how many they can take. Moreover, unless you set out at the same time as their convoys you too will be in danger of being captured by the Bedouin, or even by fugitives from the Egyptian army who are living in the mountains.

Why, when the time came to end the pilgrimage and say farewell to Jerusalem, should they be hustled and forced to pack up their belongings in a hurry and stand in queues outside the guardhouses? They were barely given time to run and take one last look at the Holy Sepulcher, while as for getting inside, not even a fly could get in, it was so full of Norman and Flemish soldiers saying their farewells to Jesus Christ.

The desert wind had risen suddenly, wreathing the city in an incandescent haze. It was hard to tell if it was vapor or dust, but no one could remain on the rooftops and men fainted in the public squares, suffocated by the waves of parched air laden with hot sand, sand so fine you breathed it in with every breath and it seared your eyes and throat even at night. The sky was yellow and the sun melting in a red-hot oven.

People began to see the angel with the trumpet above the Temple of Solomon, and lived in daily expectation of the rain of fire. For it was in Jerusalem that all was to be revealed first, and this was where all the prodigies were to begin, the time that was foretold had come after all! The angel towered above the dome like a red whirlwind and the gigantic trumpet in his hands glowed with a dull fire, like burnished copper.

However, the learned men said this was by no means the first angel with the trumpet but merely a vision, to be put down to the sacred nature of the place. Those who would depart should be not troubled; the signs of the last days were yet far off, and there would be no more peril in voyaging by sea this year than in any previous year.

Those noble men the Duke of Normandy and the Count of Flanders are not abandoning the Holy Land but are returning to their own homes because they have toiled enough for Jesus Christ, and they will send new armies from their provinces so that other Christians may also win salvation. And you, God's poor, shall go back to your towns and villages to bear witness to the miracles of Jesus Christ, and tell your brethren that God's land has need of men of good will: you can see for yourselves that three quarters of the houses in Jerusalem will be left without a master.

God, in a wind like this a man must be a good Christian indeed to wish to remain in this land! Once it has begun it lasts for a whole week. It is a gust from the furnaces of hell. Mahomet is avenging his own, and indeed it is the least that he can do. The wind nearly blew the sentries on the towers off their feet and carried away lances and banners like so many straws. In the streets and courtyards there was shelter from the wind, but the heat was worse than in calm weather and all was roaring and banging overhead. Dead leaves whirled like mischievous spirits about the rooftops and broken tiles were smashed to pieces on the pavements.

The gaunt fig tree in the courtyard was coated with yellow dust and had lost its topmost branches. The men crouching or lying in the shade of the wall could barely summon up the energy to sing. But if they did not sing it was worse, because they felt sick. The two little ones, Pierre and Martine, wriggled and cried as if they were being stung by invisible bees. "For God's sake, priestess, can't you keep them quiet!"

"How can I? They won't even drink."

Alix crossed the courtyard with a pitcher in her hand and took it to each of the men in turn to drink. Then she went into the back room and dipped her hands in the jug and pressed them to her face. Jacques had followed her. He took the jug from her and emptied it over his head, then he slid his arm around Alix's waist. She did not understand at first, then she tried to push him off, but he was stronger than she; he was caressing her, kissing her face and throat, trembling so violently with desire that she could hear his teeth chattering.

She pinched his arm sharply, making him wince, and managed to free herself. "You poor boy. Think what you are doing."

"Alix," he said as if he were drunk, "you are so beautiful. I will make you a lady, you'll see." He was between her and the door.

"You'll have the Countess of Toulouse sooner than me," she told him. "Do you think I would do that to Marie?"

Jacques flushed darkly. "Don't talk to me of Marie. No one is to talk to me about Marie! Alix, I am going mad, be kind to me."

He had sunk to his knees, burying his head in the woman's skirts and crying like a child. Alix picked up the jug and broke it over his head, then she pushed past him and ran out into the court, the tears streaming down her own face. But there Jean-Marc's Thomas and Guillaume of Béthune got slowly to their feet, red-faced and trembling, and began moving around her like hounds about a cornered boar.

"Sons of Satan, what do you want with me? Élie, Jean-Marc, look at them, they have gone mad!" Then Jacques the Picard and Bernard got up also and went toward Alix, holding out their arms. She started to scream.

Jean-Marc moved to stand beside her, and drew the knife from his belt.

"Shame on you," he said. "Have we sunk to assaulting our own women?"

"She's a whore," Guillaume said. "We had her for nothing from Belgrade to Constantinople. Let her do her work."

"Fear God," Jean-Marc said. "She is our sister."

Alix ran for shelter behind the priestess and old Marguerite of Picardy. "Oh, this wind," she said, "this Devil's wind. Holy Mary shield us! Look well to Bertin, my friends."

"Bertin?" said Marguerite. "The boys have been playing rape with her for a long time now."

"The boys! God forgive them. Pray the men don't take a hand."

The old woman sniffed. "Anyone would think you had your maidenhead again," she said.

That same night Alix took Bertin by the hand and left the house.

Jacques picked himself up. There was blood all over his face and a deep gash on his forehead just below the hairline, but his head was tough and he was not even in much pain from the blow. Élie spoke sharply to him: to have assaulted Alix was not right or decent, and since Marie was surely still alive, it was even adulterous.

"As for you, Grêlé, the sooner you go back home the better. You think you're Brother Barnabé already!"

Of the people of Arras (as they were still called, though not all were from Arras; some came from the region of Cambrai or Béthune), weavers, fullers, and peasants, only twelve were left of the two hundred that had set out three years before. Not all were dead; thirty or so had been left behind at Antioch. Of these they had no news for although Christian vessels plied quite freely between St. Simeon and Jaffa, those vessels were not there to serve humble folk.

It took courage to go home and be the bearer of so much ill news. Fathers, mothers, wives, and little children, give thanks to God: your loved ones have become glorious martyrs! Or: Don't worry, they are happy there, it is a beautiful land with sunshine all the year round and vines and olive trees and corn and flocks of sleep, they have fine houses with wells and gardens and orchards, and have married local girls, beauties whose like is not to be found here . . . Or perhaps you could say: Mère Gilberte, your son killed six Sudanese with his own hand. They are singing songs about him over there. Mère Perrine, your daughter was cured of her hump by a miracle. She has grown straight as a candle and is a lady now. Since her Lambert took a chest full of gold bezants as his share of the spoils.

Whatever you told them, surely those poor souls who had stayed at home would believe it readily? That Jerusalem is paved with pink marble and the grilles around the gardens all gilt and the apple trees in blossom all year round, and any man that enters the churches is instantly cured, that there is so much bread they throw it away by the basketful, and in the houses everyone has oil lamps and carpets. And let me tell you, at every battle our people hardly even had to fight: crosses made of lightning fell from heaven onto the heathens and burned them up on the spot, and an angel with a shining sword was to be seen marching beside every knight.

And the devils that were in the heathens came out with frightful yells and vanished in black smoke. And nothing was left of all the heathens that were in Jerusalem but ash; the city was cleansed of them as if by a miracle.

Jean-Marc was going with both his sons (he had forgiven Thomas), and taking old Marguerite and four more Picards with him. All of them were weeping tears of joy at the mere thought of seeing their own land again. Jean-Marc did not weep, but neither did he feel any great joy. He had sewn his hard-won booty into a little bag which hung around his neck: a little chip of stone from the Holy Sepulcher and five gold bezants, old ones of good weight. He had succeeded in selling the things that he and his sons had taken for a good price (the Genoese must not think that a weaver of Picardy was a fool).

No one back there at home would know, except the lads who were returning with him and they would soon forget, for what was the naked body of one poor madwoman to a man who had waded through heaps of naked corpses? For two whole days they had shoveled them up by the spadeful and tipped them into the pits, bubbling and oozing, guts and white maggots. And please God those two poor girls far away in the mountains would not cry too much, or live too long, raped to their deaths, it might be. While once they were home again, since they were set on going, the boys would take new wives, for the Bedouin were a surer means of breaking marriages than the Pope.

"Me?" Jacques said. "Am I going? Spit in my face if ever I think of it." "But what of your parents?" "Why, they may be dead by now. What, go home and be laid off work because I've lost my touch? You tell them, Guillaume, if they are still living, tell them I am well. That I shall have my own house. That I have become a soldier of Christ for good now."

"What shall I say to them about Marie? And to Marie's people, if they ask me?"

"Tell them nothing. They will understand."

"It is better to be a martyr, Jacques, than rich. Heaven is full of martyrs."

"Do women understand that? Look at the priestess."

With him, Jacques kept Mardoche and Onésime and Pierre from Béthune and Guillaume who had been married to Rufine. They all went to the Church of St. Onyphrion and swore a solemn vow to become soldiers of Christ and never to leave the Holy Land. Then Jacques set out to find the knight of Vireleu, because he had no intention of remaining under the orders of a mercenary captain.

The knight, freshly bathed, was resting in his house. He was back in Jerusalem briefly to pack up his belongings preparatory to rejoining the Duke's army outside Ascalon. Nowadays such men put on no haughty airs when they met a man who had lived through three years' campaigning. "Saving your honor, I have always respected the knights. If you will take me into service as your man just so that I can get in a few blows at the Turks, then I will thank you. I fought with your men in Cilicia." The knight laughed gaily, and Jacques laughed with him.

"Well, my lad, you've still got all your teeth, I see, and bear yourself as straight as a professional soldier."

"I have a horse that I got from the battlefield. Only I have pledged it in the Marketplace so as to send a little money to my parents. In Arras."

"Good. How much does he want, this Genoese of yours?"

"Fifty dirhams."

"Very well, take them and come back with the horse, and men if you have them. You will lodge with my men."

"Also," said Jacques, "I have an old woman and my son."

"Good, the old woman can do the washing. A woman of your own country, is she? Not a Syrian?"

"Of course not. She is from home, the widow of the curé of our parish!" Jacques went back to the house and began to pack up his things. He redeemed the horse for forty dirhams, and with the remainder paid for a candle at the Church of St. Onyphrion, for Marie. He wondered if he should pray for her as one dead or alive. *Alive.* Surely she is alive.

He placed the lighted candle in a prominent position before the image of Saint George. Look at it well, Saint George. It is for Marie of Arras, the wife of Jacques of the Ax, and I will buy you a candle as big as this one every Sunday. Do not forget Marie of Arras.

O Lord Jesus Christ, I have come very near to cursing You.

• • •

The wind was still blowing. It was said that in the desert, pillars of sand got up like a whirlwind and towered right up in the sky and chased you so fast that even a horse could not outrun them, and rains of sand would fall from the sky, burying the caravans. Away there in the desert lived men with blue faces who never slept by night or day and fed on sand. But in Damascus there were orchards and fountains at every street corner, and the people were rich; even the slaves ate figs and barley cakes. Damascus was a white city, with so many minarets that it was like an army of knights with their lances erect. Oh Marie, Marie.

Let me forget that you ever lived.

Let me die if I cease to remember you.

The house was emptying. Those who were leaving camped in the square outside the barracks, waiting for the Norman and Flemish armies to be ready. The wind was so unbearable that some of the women and the sick began to scream aloud.

Le Grêlé went about the city, visiting the churches and repeating the pilgrimage along the Via Dolorosa three times a day, with his ax on his shoulder and his slender prize money sewn into his belt. His knees were raw from climbing the steps of the holy street and his beard black from kissing the paving stones. Many of those who made this pilgrimage fell unconscious from exhaustion, overcome by the stifling hot wind. When they came to the square before the Holy Sepulcher they would lie down on the ground, croaking rather than singing the psalms.

Élie had made up his mind to go home because he had a wife and children in the faubourg of Arras. At his age a man does not forget his trade. But it was hard to leave Jerusalem, for no one could ever have enough of that holy place; a man could spend years on end hoarding up the joy of the Holy Sepulcher within himself. Yet as soon as you passed out through the city gates the holiness left you: outside Ascalon it had not been at all the same. Prayer had become like a shriveled nut, whereas in Jerusalem it was strong and full, even the wind had a smell of incense.

The walls of the houses in the main streets of Jerusalem were decorated and the priests walked in procession through them, and the soldiers made merry at the street corners, for whenever they were not fighting and had wine to drink they were always merry. In the evening when the wind had dropped at last, le Grêlé paused outside a white stone house with gilded latticework at the windows. The house was brightly lit with torches. Torches set in brass rings blazed before the entrance, while from inside came the sound of music and laughter, and voices singing. Élie had paused because the song they were singing was one from his own land.

Two pretty Syrian girls, bare-shouldered with black painted eyes, stood in the doorway, their smiles revealing small white teeth. Next to them was a man with a halberd. Élie frowned and drew himself up in surprise because the man was a Picard from their own house, Pierre the Tinker by name. "Son of a heathen, what are you doing here? This is a fine trade!"

The other, who was a young man of no great wit, laughed awkwardly. "Well, but I'm with Alix. She's given me a job."

"And since when has Alix employed men for such work? So she lives in this house, does she?"

"It will be a week now. She has joined up with Giscarde, but she is what you might call the boss, seeing that Giscarde's getting on."

"That's as may be," said Élie, "but she must be brought to her senses." He stepped inside and found himself in a pretty arcaded court, brightly lit with candles burning everywhere. People were sitting on cushions drinking, and in the middle of the court were two boys, one singing and one playing a vielle, while from underneath the arcade came the sound of women's laughter. Élie had never been in such a house before and he stood looking about him in bewilderment. The drinkers had noticed him, and there was some loud laughter. "He has got the wrong inn," they said. "He thinks there is soup here for the poor." Élie stood blinking and listening to the musicians. It was a song of his own country that he knew well but had not heard for a long time.

Then he saw Alix emerge from under the arcade in between two great hearses covered with candles. He knew her by her height and by her walk, but then he thought he must have been mistaken. He had never seen her like this. She had drawn black lines around her eyes, her cheeks were colored pink, she wore innumerable glittering bangles around her neck and wrists, and her hair, which had miraculously grown again, was the color of saffron with shining golden lights. He would never have believed that she could still be so beautiful. She walked straight up to him, and he said, "Get thee behind me, Satan. Do you want to damn your soul?"

"How did you find me out, Élie? You know I would have come to say goodbye to you in any case. I know you do not leave for three days yet."

"You know more than I do, then."

One of the men called out, "Hey, Alix!" He looked more like a clerk than a knight, his hands and face were so smooth and soft. "Hey, Alix, are you taking on that bumpkin as a bodyguard?"

"No," she answered. "He is a man of my own country. Come into my room, Élie, there is too much noise out here."

"I have never been in a whore's chamber," he said. She was slightly drunk and tears and laughter mingled in her eyes.

"You are a bad man, Élie, but I am fond of you. We have been through too much grief together. I am fond of you, Grêlé, and I shall be sad to see you go. Just to see you warms my heart."

"Well, so it does not mine. Is Bertin here?"

"Yes, of course she is. If she's going to get herself raped, she need not do it for nothing. She'll earn herself a handsome dowry, you'll see, and marry an Italian." Élie spat on the floor.

"Tell them at home, Grêlé—if anyone asks you. If there are any that remember me. Tell them Alix has the finest brothel in all Jerusalem, that noble knights and clerks to the Archbishop come here and it would be no surprise to see the Patriarch! I shall have money to have masses sung at the Holy Sepulcher."

Élie looked at her as though at some strange exotic bird, as if he could not believe that this was really Alix. A heavy scent, warm and oversweet, was invading his senses, making him feel slightly sick.

"Here," he said, "is it you, reeking like that?"

"It is essence of jasmine, my lad, and I paid a high price for it. The most noble ladies anoint their bodies with it."

"Then they are as much whores as you. You would do better to bring Bertin and Pierre the Tinker and come home with us."

Two richly dressed men entered the court. They wore long mantles of striped silk and their beards were scented with perfume. Alix went forward to greet them with a broad smile: But yes, certainly, the noble lords could see for themselves, such sweet young things, rosebuds no less, all milk and honey. Assuredly they would not be robbed, they should pass an hour in paradise.

The men, who were knights, said little, but they looked askance at Élie, possibly in some apprehension of being obliged to share their pleasures with this boorish oaf. "Oh, Grêlé, wait," Alix said. "At least let me call Bertin. If you could see how pretty she's grown, she has even put on weight, and her tan has washed away with the dirt. Do not worry about us, we have a good life."

"And Baudry?" said Élie, "and Brother Barnabé? and Brother Imbert? and all our people?"

"No, wait, Élie, you must tell them—tell them if you get home—tell them that Alix Malebouche has settled down. She has finished her pilgrimage, and each to his own trade. Tell them I have a fine life, I burn wax candles, I have baths and music, and sweetmeats and cinnamon wine, and I do not rob my clients! My old crone—my bawd, I mean—she would be glad for me if she knew . . ."

"Farewell, Alix. It is a pity, all the same."

He turned away and resumed his roaming of the by now almost empty streets, wondering if it had been a dream. Surely it was a sin to illumine such a house with wax candles, like a church? The money that rich men spent here—as if they had Alafdal's tents to pillage every day. The sky above the roofs was clear again at last, encrusted with cold stars that blazed with a hard white fire.

The eyes of the dead. What was it like, up there in the sky? How was it now, up there, with all the friends they had seen die? Did they dwell in groups, each with those of his own land, glad to be together again—or were all the best together and the poor martyrs placed unwillingly at the foot of the first circle of light? Surely they must still be quite close to earth, right at the bottom of the sky, and still able to remember many things.

Up there where there was no night, on the far side of the great vault of heaven, close to the angels that hold up the stars—they say there are even some that fall out of the sky remembering. That is why there are so many shooting stars in these lands.

The starlight clashed like sword blades. There was battle up there, the sky was all blue and white swords, growing longer and then vanishing again, like slow lightning flashes. The chivalry of heaven was in full panoply of war.

How many unworthy souls were turned back, to fall down, down like dead flies through the black sky. And why are they so heavy when, leaving the body, they weigh hardly more than a moth? They are falling, black against the black sky.

But such must be the weights and measures of God, Élie

thought, that under certain souls the bridges would collapse. Holy Mary, have mercy on souls gorged with blood.

For heathen blood is like water to a drunkard, Christian blood like wine—it is the blood of Christ.

Pity Élie of Arras, him that men called Grêlé
if he had not taken the cross, he would never have loved.

. . . If he had not taken the cross he would never have killed
. . . If he had not taken the cross he would never have wept
—oh coldest of women, even in life she was as cold as a corpse.

A guttering torch was still smoking faintly outside a house from which hung a Brabançon archer's shield. A soldier sat on the doorstep, fast asleep with his lance in his hand. His head had fallen back against the wall and he was snoring. His snores were so peaceful and regular that he might have been a country lad fallen asleep after a day's haymaking. Élie stopped, his eyes on the white throat above the open collar lined with grey wool and the faint bulge of the Adam's apple. Why did the torchlight fall just on the throat? Like a thief in the night. Ye know neither the day nor the hour. Death comes like a thief in the night. There would not be so much as a cry, the throat neatly slit with one stroke of the knife and the hot blood spurting out like Moses' water from the rock. Élie felt his knees buckle with desire and his heart thudding. And yet, this lad has done me no harm.

It may be that he is a phantom, sent to tempt me. The knife slipped from the wooden sheath of its own accord. Élie had no idea how it came to be in his hand. O Lord Jesus Christ, protect him, indeed he has done me no harm. He bit his lip and walked on along the empty street, and each step cost him an effort as if he were dragging hundred-pound balls, so terrible was the temptation. When he reached the little square where scaffolding had been erected over the burnt-out ruins of the mosque, he paused for breath and suddenly began to howl in a voice he did not know for his own, like an animal. The people in the nearby houses thought it was a stray dog run mad after the days of hot wind.

Coming to the place where, from what Mardoche had said, Saint-John had fallen from the roof, he leaned against the wall, remembering the children's bodies thrown down there, and for a moment he saw again the scene in the courtyard of the big house, the uproar, the groans and screams of agony, the yells of fury, and the dreadful heat of that great settlement of accounts. It was over so soon, it should have begun again each night.

He knew then that he was not going home.

The next day he asked Jacques to put in a word for him with the knight of Vireleu.

"Hey, what about Mardoche and Onésime? If you are here they will want to go with you."

"I'll leave you Onésime and take Mardoche. You don't need four men. And it's better to serve men of your own country." Jacques shrugged. At heart he was not sorry. The sight of so many people leaving made his head spin.

Fresh companies of soldiers and pilgrims were arriving from Jaffa, people who had never seen the Holy Land, and there were crusaders from Antioch who had come down the coast in ships, and even those from Antioch were like strangers, men speaking a different language.

"Did you know Alix had become a rich man's whore again?" Jacques roared with laughter.

"If I get rich I'll go to her. We'll all go."

"Not me," said Élie.

The side streets were deserted, but in the main streets and the squares the crowd jostled as though on a fair day. Columns of new arrivals passed those who were leaving, both mingling with processions of Greeks and Syrians, and there was a great clamor of voices speaking every known language: it was like Pentecost and the tower of Babel all at once. Pedestrians took refuge in the courts and side streets to make way for the Provençal horsemen assembling before the Tower of David ready to set out. A huge brazen bell, sent to the Holy Sepulcher by the Greeks of Cyprus, was brought in at Herod's Gate on a painted and carved chariot with enormous wheels. Priests walked at the head of the procession, blessing the crowd, and those that saw the bell pass by, shining like gold beneath a canopy of blue cloth, shouted for joy.

The fact was that a great many wealthy pilgrims of all nations—Greeks, English, Spaniards, Venetians, and Danes—who had come by sea had been forced by the siege of Jerusalem to make a landfall in Crete or Cyprus for two months, and were now beginning to arrive, escorted by armed sailors. And these people marveled greatly at the crusader pilgrims who had not, as they had, spent the hottest months of the year in Crete at the Emperor's expense, but had fought for the glory of Jesus Christ. Moreover, it seemed to them a good thing that there were no mosques or synagogues in the city any more and that the Christian pilgrims no longer had to pay taxes to the heathen in order to visit the shrines, for it was contrary to all the laws of heaven that Christian piety should serve to enrich the Moslems.

They came, these people, well fed, dressed in clean clothes, and tanned but not burned by the sun, complaining a little of the heat and exclaiming in wonderment at every step, for God knows there were fine things to be seen in the city, so many churches and palaces, arcaded squares, and wealthy priories. The repairs to the outer walls were almost finished, the damaged houses replastered and freshly painted, and the new citizens of Jerusalem were adorning the outsides of their houses with shields and banners and carpets which had cost little enough. Cartloads of sweet-smelling herbs and branches of cypress were brought in daily to strew the Via Dolorosa and the square before the Holy Sepulcher.

The crowd in the church itself was still so thick that altars and stations were set up in the square, with monks standing before them with bowls in which the pilgrims placed their offerings. And if the sellers of holy relics made their fortunes in those days, this was no cause for offense: the Patriarch had commanded it so. Certain accredited merchants had to stand outside the church and prevent the pilgrims from getting at the walls or lingering too long, for otherwise the whole wall up to the height of a man, and the pilasters around the door, would have resembled some dreadful leprous growth in stone. Already, in the days immediately following the victory when there was no control, the crusaders had helped themselves as far as they could and even some whole stones had been removed. Hawkers had got to work on some of these stones with hammer and chisel and chipped them into heaps of tiny fragments, some the size of a nut, others like grains of wheat: Be fair, good pilgrims, and remember it is not the size of the stone that matters, the virtue is the same, complete in every sliver of stone, as God is complete in the Host.

When Alix went to the church, preceded by two bodyguards and accompanied by old Giscarde and two young maidservants, even monks and pious citizens said, Truly, here is a woman to be proud of, there are none fairer than the women of the North. You had to look very close to see on her washed and painted face the ineradicable traces of dust around the long blue-grey eyes and at the corners of her mouth, and that her neck under the many rows of necklaces was thin and scrawny.

Giscarde, a tall, gaunt Flemish bawd with a hawk-face and red eyes, wore as many jewels as her age and status admitted and cast shrewd looks at all the men, summing up their worth in terms of money. She was a woman who would have sold Jesus Christ and the Virgin and the Twelve Apostles into the bargain. She had already done penance several times, herself driving the prostitutes from the camp with a whip, only to corrupt fresh ones the next day. She needed Alix because she had been suffering for some time from the evil eye and her clients had died within the week. People made the first approach to her, as the elder, but it was Alix who answered.

Pilgrims came to their house and found what they sought, and Alix led the revels, though she did little reveling herself, for it was true that she no longer had the body of a girl of eighteen and she feared to be rebuffed or that unkind persons might call her a whited sepulcher.

In church she prayed devoutly, beating her breast like the publican in the parable, so that people said, Truly, this woman of evil life may be placed in heaven above many honest women.

. . . Pray for poor Alix, Christians, Alix of the Thirty Pieces, Alix of the Thirty Pieces of Silver!

She who betrayed the Lord through pride and sought to put on a crown that did not belong to her, and who renounced the pitiful sins of a harlot only to come in the end to running about this city knife in hand in the company of murderers.

Pray, Christians, for those who know not what they do, and even more for those who know full well. It is not enough to suffer for three years, to endure hunger and thirst and fear, and to watch the deaths of your dearest friends; it is not enough to pass through the hell of sin and the joy of forgiveness. Christians, pray for Alix, who would live to be old and rich and respected, and win this world since she cannot win heaven. For it is a great honor for you, Alix Malebouche of the faubourg of Arras, a great honor to keep the finest brothel in the holy city of Jerusalem.

Jacques presented himself at the house of the knight of Vireleu, bringing with him his horse, a neat little dark-brown animal. On the horse he had placed the priestess with the child and their bundles. His three men followed him. Élie and Mardoche were already waiting for them at the great gateway into the big courtyard.

"Don't worry, Grêlé, even the Duke would take a man as stout as you!"

Mardoche, somewhat nervous but making an effort to be calm, was intent on checking the string of a bow almost as tall as himself. Over his shoulder was slung a bag filled with the arrows he had collected here and there and mended: Turkish heads and fresh wood. "Let them give me a mark to shoot at, and I'll show them. An arrow in the eye at fifty paces!"

In the courtyard, among the soldiers and grooms and the horses being led out to drink, the men of Arras stood close together as though afraid of losing one another. Little Pierre, in the priestess's arms, was shouting war cries. "That's a fine child," the soldiers said. "A real count's son!"

"That's a fine child," said the knight of Vireleu. "He should have been born a knight's son."

"God willing," Jacques said, "he will be a knight. It is a good trade."

The other laughed: "Ho, ho! And I thought it worse than a cobbler's! So you think it good enough for your son, do you?"

Jacques flushed, conscious of having said something foolish, then blushed more than ever because he had blushed. "Sure he'll be a knight," he said, "and he'll marry Ondine."

"And who may Ondine be?"

Jacques had thought the whole camp must know the story of Ondine, so aptly named, who now dwelt with the ladies of Boulogne. But knights do not tell tales about the poor. Jacques shrugged awkwardly and was silent.

Marie gazed up at the stars turned by her tears into great balls of fire. Her whole body ached so that her mind was a blank, for they had beaten her and dragged her over the stones with ropes. O Jerusalem.

The night was cold, and the women lay on the ground and huddled close together for warmth. Too bruised to complain. Lost amid the black mountains that had become suddenly so wild and strange. As though in the old fireside tales, a magician had taken the poor women and transported them in a single night to a desolate land a thousand leagues from Jerusalem; a thousand leagues or a thousand years. How will they set us free? A dark shadow loomed over them, moaning softly. Oh God, is it a departed soul? No, sisters, it is Artemisia, the wife of Jean-Marc's Mathieu. "They did not want me, God be thanked, because I am with child."

The Armenian sat down on the ground and began praying quietly in her own language. They dared not ask, "And Lydia?"

The men had set up their light tents not far from where the camels were lying, and from them came sounds of women screaming and a growling as of wild beasts. They were raping the Christians. The Bedouin had taken the Armenian and Syrian women for themselves, leaving the others because they thought them too dirty. For it was well said in the camps: Make yourself beautiful for the Turkomans, but for the Bedouin, make yourself ugly. They were slave-traders, they did not kill women.

They were bruised and shivering with fever, for to be seized and carried off so suddenly is a shock to the whole system. Oh, the poor men that were beheaded! It all happened so quickly. Their swords were sharp as razors, and what a shame about Brother Imbert, such a holy man and he did not even have time to pray to God. How can you be sure? Oh no, he just cried out like a man in terror. Oh, the poor man, ever since the crusader pilgrims came to this land these Bedouin have hated anything that wears a beard.

"And what of us, my sisters?"

"What they do," Honorine said, "is take the women to the city and put them in the marketplace, in a pen."

"Oh, we knew that without your telling us. But what then? Our men will never find us. They have other things to do. They are fighting the great battle."

They have the whole army of Egypt marching against them.

O Lord, let me remain a captive forever, only let Jacques come out of the battle alive! If you live, Jacques, and if you are not hurt, I don't care if they sell me in the market.

Jacques.

You are so handsome, Jacques, you are as good as the sun. They have not violated me and perhaps they will not. Do not fear for me, Jacques—Jacques, I know you will be safe, the Sudanese cannot harm you. Holy Mary Mother of God, pray for us poor sinners, watch over our men in the battle. My friends, someone must pay, and it may be that when God sees our sufferings He will be merciful to our men.

"Do you think God reckons everyone's sufferings, you silly girl?" Rufine said. "What would it have cost Him to protect us too, and Brother Imbert who prayed to Him day and night?" They were thinking: I am hungry, thirsty, in pain, but they did not say it, they were used to it, so tired they were no longer even frightened. At daybreak the Bedouin fell to prostrating themselves, touching the ground with their foreheads and both hands, and chanting their prayers aloud.

One by one the women got to their feet, their heads so thick with sleep that they hardly knew where they were. There were thirty of them all together, lying in bunches of five or six on the sand of the dry river bed, among clumps of bleached willows. The sky was dazzling white and they saw each other's faces grey and drained of color, more faded than the sparse leaves of the willow trees. Their throats were almost too parched to speak and their voices were hoarse croaks. *Ave Maria gratia plena Dominus tecum ora pro nobis peccatoribus*. The thought even occurred to them as they watched the Bedouin prostrating themselves: We should prostrate ourselves also so they will not take us for unbelievers. "Oh my friends, let us pray softly. What if in their hatred of Jesus Christ they should kill us?" They knelt and made the sign of the cross, too wretched to pray.

The sun rose as on any other day and the mountains looked like the mountains around Jerusalem, yet nothing was the same any more. The black-bearded men in burnooses and the camels lying near the tents and the dry river bed all seemed flat and inconsequential, like the images seen in a dream; only the thirst and the pain in their limbs was real. If they shut their eyes the women could think themselves back outside the walls of Jerusalem, or somewhere on the way between Bethlehem and Jerusalem: if they could only hear the familiar sounds of the camp, songs and oaths, and men's voices speaking a Christian tongue. These Bedouin were not unkind; they gave them water to drink, such good rations that it almost broke the women's hearts to have to drink it all at once, for lack of gourds or waterskins, and not be able to keep any for midday. And they gave them mutton bones to gnaw with whole mouthfuls of meat left on them.

"Yes, my friends, they mean to fatten us up to rape us." The Syrian women had come back, or most of them, weeping and moaning and hiding their faces in their hands. The others tried to comfort them: "It is no shame, it is a martyrdom endured for

Jesus Christ." "And what a martyrdom! Sisters, there is less pain in childbed, these men are wild beasts!" "We will carry you," the Frankish women said. "We will make slings of our cloaks, and those that can walk can lean on the shoulders of two of us."

Well, believe it or not, they did not have to walk. They were lifted onto camels and tied there with strips of cloth. The creatures swayed so that it was like being on a boat; it made you giddy, with the sun beating down on your head and your legs and arms growing numb and swelling, while the grey hills rose and fell on all sides like gigantic waves under the hard blue sky.

In the evening, between a red sky and orange-colored hills, they saw another company of Bedouin leading a file of men roped together behind their camels. They had only to look at them to know that these were no Christian crusaders: they were dark-skinned men of small stature, half naked, with white cloths wrapped around their heads and neat pointed beards.

It was then the captives learned the great news. Dumped on the ground behind the camels, they begged the Syrians to try and hear what the men were saying and where they came from, for they looked like soldiers. Some of the Syrian women were from Antioch and spoke quite good French, and they all grew very excited. "Oh sisters, sisters, they are fugitives from the great battle. I think they are saying that not many escaped. They say our men are more terrible than demons and they made such a slaughter as was never seen and drove the Vizier's army into the sea! And already they have carried the city of Ascalon by storm!" They hardly dared to believe it.

"Do not cry out too joyfully, sisters, or they will come and punish us." But it was hard not to cry out. O Lord God, who are truly the God of battles, You have not abandoned Israel, and soon our people will come as far as Damascus and Bassorah and free all the Christians. Oh, our good knights, oh, brave and holy men, may God bless them!

Lord, may our men have come unscathed through the battle.

It may be, my children, that we shall never know until we get to paradise.

When we are dead and they also.

"Be quiet, you crazy girl! If God wills they will reach Baghdad. Not one Christian will be left a prisoner." They drank warm, brackish water that smelled of camel's urine and marveled again at the kindness of these Bedouin: truly, during the siege our knights had less to drink. Courage, friends, it may be this is a good sign, that tomorrow we shall make camp by a real well where there is good water. Or even by the river Jordan.

Fifty yards away the prisoners of the other company sat in rows because they were all fastened to the same rope, passing the waterskin from hand to hand and making such a noise as they drank that the women could hear them. They must be thirsty, over there! These Moslems must be what you'd call bad Christians, taking captive people of their own faith, soldiers that have suffered enough misfortune already. The Bedouin make money out of everything, that is why they give us water to drink, so that we will be more beautiful and more salable.

They said their evening prayers, not forgetting to thank God for the victory, for surely it was true? Surely? Oh, but we know what it is like with fugitives, perhaps they know no more than we. No, no, I heard them. The Bedouin know also. The whole army was drowned or killed on the spot. They are saying that the Roumis came so suddenly it seemed like a bolt of lightning. O Lord Jesus Christ, who in Your great goodness have succored Your people Israel, and scattered the armies of Pharaoh! Glory and honor throughout all ages, thanks be to You, Lord, who did not let our friends be covered with shame.

"Surely," Honorine said, "if my Pierre were dead I should have known it. The fillet I wear around my neck would have broken."

"That is a sin," Lucienne said. "I would rather not know than bind myself by sorcery."

"You would not say that if you loved your Guillaume."

"Well?" said Lucienne. "What of it? I loved my first and Guillaume is my third!"

"Pierre is my third also," said Honorine.

"Your fillet, Honorine," Marie said, "how many years does it last?"

"As long as love lasts. It is woven from both our hair twined together and dipped in the blood of a male and female pigeon killed at the same time, and salted with both our tears, mingled at midnight under a new moon. As long as love lasts the fillet lives, and if one dies it will break of itself and writhe like a snake. And if love is dead it will lose its color and become rough as hemp."

"I should be too frightened," said Marie. "Oh no! I would rather pray for a living man."

"Did you know that jackals are murdered children that died without baptism? . . . That is why they cry at night."

"Then there will be many jackals here this year. And what happens when the jackal dies?"

"They pass into the bodies of other jackals. It is like the owls at home, that are widows who died of grief, cursing God."

"Superstitions! How can a Christian soul be in the body of an animal or a bird? Why not a fly?"

"No: in anything warm-blooded. And there are so many sinful souls wandering like that in the bodies of animals that some people say if you eat beef you might be eating a person."

"Heretics say that, people who do not believe in Holy Communion."

"It may be true, even so," Marie said. "Listen to the jackals. It is pitiful to hear."

"I'm sure it's true. What about werewolves? My godmother had a cousin that was one, and just after he died they saw an old wolf prowling around the village sheepfold and trying to get into the houses. No one dared lay hands on it."

"What happened?"

"The curé sprinkled it with holy water and it screamed with a human voice and ran away and never came back. True, he was not a bad man."

"If we turned into swallows, we could go back to our own country," Rufine said.

"Some say that is the purgatory for souls who have committed mortal sins unwittingly."

"Well, as for me," said Rufine, "let me tell you, my children, I never stole anyone's water ration, but during the siege I went among the soldiers of Brabant and lay with them behind the engines, and I shared the water they gave me with Guillaume."

"Is there anything one would not do for water? There are plenty more would have done the same if they had only thought of it."

"Exactly, my dears. I thought of it."

"Listen, at Antioch we would never have held out if there had not been water. When we were shut inside the city, after Isabelle died, for two whole days we lived on nothing but water. You can live for as much as forty days with water. If you know how to drink."

"Jean le Roux, Mardoche's father, died from drinking too fast.

Do you remember, Marie? . . . how he used to imitate all the bird calls, and how we laughed."

They talked softly, huddled in their cloaks. If only they would let us have a fire. And they talked as they had never talked before, God knows why, with a tenderness that made the silliest things sound like sweet music. They were neither sad nor happy; they had the feeling of being in another world, as if this night would never end and they would not even notice, like the man who listened to a bird singing in the forest and went back to his village to find that a hundred years had passed and his children had died of old age long ago . . .

These sleeping Bedouin, these camels lying like heaps of sacks, had turned to dust and dry bones long years since, a thousand new stars had appeared in the sky . . . if only they could sleep.

They had slept on colder nights than this. "Is it fear, my friends?"

"We have known worse. Listen. In the morning, let us rub our cheeks with earth and spittle and show them we are ugly."

"Do you know, the women that are sold for the harem, they wash them for three days, wash them and scrub them and polish them like copper vessels, and take away all their lice and rub them with oil, and cram them with food till the filthiest slut becomes pretty!"

"Oh, did you ever, what vicious men! They say one girl tipped a pan of burning incense over her face. They flogged her to death for it."

"Then she went to paradise. Artemisia, would you have the courage?"

"No, but the Mother of God preserve me. It is wrong to destroy your own face. If I did God would not recognize me at the Day of Judgment."

At dawn they had to walk in double file behind the camels, and they sang as they walked to keep their spirits up. The familiar marching songs almost made them forget that this was not a journey like any other, that they were missing the men's voices and the creak of axles and all the warm, confused sounds of the host on the march. The Bedouin were dismal fellow travelers, silent as death except when going into battle, and the Egyptian soldiers had no heart for singing.

Where are they taking us? From the direction of the sun it must be Damascus. But surely this is not one of the great caravan routes. A dry wadi, full of stones and dusty scrub, with a few vultures planing in a sky that was growing bluer all the time: beware the hour when all around us is one great white-hot oven and the stones begin to crack from the heat!

Jerusalem so dearly loved
So long desired, so deeply mourned
Now lost to us and far away
We cannot tell what year or day
Will bring us to your golden gate
Your Sepulcher where our life began.
By Holy Mary, crownèd queen
Virgin Mother, maiden bright
And by all saints that in heaven are seen
Who then would envy our sad fate?

Their voices were roughened by the heat and their parched throats seemed to be filled with hot sand. Courage, it was worse in Anatolia. You Syrians don't know what it was like.

The caravans halted in a pleasant place of cypress and palms and olive trees where an abandoned village straggled up a hillside. There was a well, and one of the men with the caravan made signs to the captive women that they were to draw water for the animals. Oh, the joy of drawing water! They did not need telling twice but took the skins and gourds and leather buckets, whatever they were given, and ran to the well, praying that before they fled the peasants had not filled it with carrion. But no, these Bedouin knew the country. Come, we'll form a chain. All set in line except for two to turn the wheel and two to relieve them. Hook on the buckets. The wheel is heavy! The camels first, then the horses, and the men when they have finished their evening prayer.

The sun was already going down toward the sea, taking the heat with it, but the air was heavy. The tops of the trees bowed ominously northward and the sky was redder than usual. If the wind begins to blow from the south it will go on for a week. (And where shall we be in a week?) They drew water, fighting against the lethargy that turned their arms and legs to lead. Before passing the bucket to her neighbor, each one dipped her hand in the water and drank from her cupped palm quickly, not daring to do more for fear of these Bedouin who did not even deign to speak to them. How could they tell what these people might do to slaves who paused to drink in the middle of their work?

What they did know was that these men regarded them as animals, better than sheep but not as valuable as camels. They were all used to drawing water, and the Bedouin, squatting in the shade of the cypress trees, glanced at them now and then, idly but with considerable shrewdness. They were thinking, in fact, that the Franks trained their slaves well: each of these women was worth nearly as much as a Negress from the Sudan. But they must be monsters indeed to treat their servants worse than animals, for the women were clearly inured to hunger and thirst and blows and used to living in the most shameful poverty. The merchants of Damascus would have to soak them in water for hours on end to make them look presentable, and yet they were good merchandise, God confound their faith!

The women stayed by the well, taking it in turns to lean over and breathe in the coolness and the smell of moss and mold that rose from it like a fragrant memory of the wells of their childhood. For a change, the evening air brought no chill and on the far side of the hill little eddies of fine golden sand could be seen, like small clouds against the pale sky. To drink was such a joy that no mother could have felt a greater gladness at seeing her children again. Oh, the fresh water sent the joys of heaven flowing through your whole body. Oh, if every halt could be like this!

None of them knew how it started. Someone laughed, at nothing, at some silly joke that was after all not so silly, because by the time it had been repeated two or three times, several more and then a dozen and then all of them were laughing helplessly, without really knowing why, and the more they tried to stop themselves—thinking it a sin in their present plight and that the Bedouin would punish them—the more they wanted to laugh. So that after five minutes all the women, even the ones who had been raped, were shrieking in paroxysms of laughter, and the sound of their own gurgles and hiccups of mirth only made them laugh more than ever until they were all writhing and choking and holding their stomachs.

They paused for breath, biting their lips and wiping their streaming eyes, then someone caught her neighbor's eye and giggled and the laughter began again. "Oh no, sisters, oh no, stop, think of God . . . think of something sad!" Then one of the Syrians, gasping for breath, cried, "The evening star, the hour when they say their prayers!" And then, knowing that now they must stop laughing at all costs, the women were quiet in an instant, but the Devil prompted them to look at one another again, all exhausted and shaking, and they burst out again with such a shout of laughter that the camels looked up and began to roar. And now it really was the time of prayer.

One of the Bedouin, a heavily built old man armed with a whip, advanced on the women, and even then he did not speak to them, although these people talked to their animals and knew that many of the women understood Arabic. Such was their contempt for the Christian women that he did not speak, but his long whip cracked and the captives bowed their heads and flattened themselves as hard as they could. The whip flickered over several backs and took off one or two coifs. The women were not laughing now; most of them were writhing and sobbing convulsively. All the time the men were praying, they did not stir but remained curled up on the ground with their eyes shut, pressing their lips together until they could hardly breathe in the effort to keep their bodies still.

Too much laughter easily ends in tears, and some were crying now while others prayed. Oh my friends, who would have believed it? That we should have to force ourselves to think sad thoughts! Who can tell when we shall feel like laughing again? They dared not look at the men, who were now eating and drinking, exchanging brief remarks in their own tongue. Oh, if we look at them we shall want to laugh again, and it is not right, or prudent. What if they think that because we can be gay we cannot be chaste, and when they have eaten they seek to violate us? We should rather weep, for who knows when—who knows if—if ever —if ever—if we shall ever see—oh God, perhaps this is the last time we shall ever laugh. Oh, heartless women, when our men may be dead in the battle! Heartless women, what of our freedom and Jerusalem? THIS IS NOT TRUE. THIS CANNOT BE TRUE!

Oh Jacques!

Marie began to scream first. Just that one cry, OH JACQUES. But it was the cry of one who feels a red-hot iron in her bowels, the cry that is wrenched from the body before the mind is even conscious of pain. She lay on her back and dashed her head against the stones and screamed, and in a moment the others had begun screaming and sobbing too. Oh, why don't they come and kill us! Why don't they trample us to death with their camels! Anything would be better than this. Oh God, it is not true, it is not true that they are taking us away forever, that we shall never see our own people again!

Jacques! Jacques! Come and find me, find me if you love me, do not leave me, do not desert me, I want to see you again, I want to live! Jacques, Pierre, this cannot happen, it is not Christian, God will not allow it. Jacques! Pierre! Pierre!

Let us escape, or throw ourselves into the well! Let us run away, let them kill us, let them rape us. Honorine, Rufine, Artemisia, oh my sisters, we are innocent, we have not killed anyone, then why? Why?

The Bedouin, hardened though they were to the screaming and sobbing of their captives, listened in surprise to this sudden outburst from the women, who had seemed quite calm until that moment. Two of them got to their feet, reluctantly, not liking what they did, because it was a nuisance to be obliged to mark slaves they had in mind to sell at the next day's halt. The whip was a good cure. Some of the women who had been hit squealed for a little while in pain; the rest were silent, biting their arms to stifle their sobs. One by one they fell into a drugged sleep, so deep they could have been raped ten times over without waking. In fact, there was no thought of raping them, for that day even the Bedouin, although hundreds and hundreds of slaves had passed through their hands, felt something like pity.

All the women were young, between eighteen and twenty-five years old, tough as stray dogs, wild and ignorant: in their Godforsaken lands where the light of true religion had never penetrated, women were treated with such contempt that they were not even taught the simplest laws of decency. But then, the people of those lands were known to be like children, credulous, easily frightened, quickly moved to tears and cries, and incapable of understanding. By dawn the envoys sent by the merchants of Damascus were at the appointed place to discuss the price of the haul. Once they were cleaned up, these women would be worth three or even four times the price asked. They were young, hardy, and quick workers, and could be usefully employed instead of eunuchs for the heavier work of the harem.

They were beaten awake. The men of Damascus, less proud than the Bedouin, were not above shaking the creatures if they were too long in getting to their feet. Yes, they were tall and slim with strong legs and broad shoulders—too thin, of course, but no doubt about their youth, so young that some of them still had quite good breasts, though all except the Syrians from Jerusalem had clearly suffered from starvation. (Most of the Frankish women had bad teeth, and two of them had hardly any teeth to speak of.) But they had suffered no permanent damage: they were thin but healthy and the marks on their skin, apart from the scars, could be cleaned up in a few weeks. Out of curiosity, the interpreter—a eunuch and an old soldier who had been a prisoner of the Normans—asked how they came by these great scars. His speech was so unintelligible that the women frowned and shook their heads, but when they finally understood they shrugged: from arrows, naturally. What else?

More frightened than ashamed, the Frankish women tried to push away the hands of the eunuchs who examined them. They stood in a sulky silence, holding their elbows tight against their sides. The Syrians hid their faces in their hands and wept. The interpreter asked the youngest whether they were virgins.

"No. Married, all married. Neither maids nor widows."

The six Norman women were able to understand what the interpreter was saying better than the rest, and one of them was brave enough to clutch at the man's arm, telling him they were no ordinary women but women of great piety, held in high esteem by the men of the army, and that there would surely be a good ransom for them in Jerusalem. She said their husbands were gallant soldiers and could pay, but the interpreter, a man in a blue turban with a face that was at once dry and flabby, only shrugged her off and eyed the other women appraisingly. He had not in fact understood a word of what the Norman woman said because she spoke too quickly, but he guessed that she was talking of ransom and he was well accustomed to the boasting of poor prisoners. If these creatures were indeed married, then their husbands must be the very dregs of mankind to let their wives travel the roads in the wake of the army, barefoot, with their faces uncovered.

The Bedouin were bargaining. Guessing what was going forward, the women found themselves beginning to look back on the Bedouin almost with regret. A dull, speechless fear was creeping over them, as if the act of changing hands would make them somehow more truly prisoners than before, as if each new step into the unknown carried them more deeply into misfortune.

Oh God, when the Bedouin found us we were free, walking along the road. They fought the men of the rear guard and cut off their heads. The Bedouin are something we understand.

They are selling us—to whom, for what, to go where? Damascus, ten days' journey from Jerusalem, had now become the end of the world, the place from which no traveler returned, the enchanted castle to which no road led, the city not inhabited by men, not men, only ghosts and shadows, and when you opened your mouth no words came out, no sounds came to your ears, a place where anything could happen and where nothing that happened mattered any more . . . Whether you were chosen as the favorite wife of a prince or were flayed alive in the marketplace no longer mattered to anyone, no one would ever hear of it. Oh sisters, sisters, do not let them part us, let them send us to work in the salt mines so long as we are all together, let them shut us up in a brothel for soldiers so long as we are all together. There is no shame or wretchedness in shared misfortunes. If they do not separate us we will pray for them.

They clung together as hard as they could to combat the chill that was creeping over their hearts, making each other wild vows of friendship, saying all the fond things there had never been time to say to those who were close to them. Oh, can't we tell them it is the custom of our country, that we must always be together, that like the ox without his fellow, if they take us from one another we shall die!

They traveled like this all the way to Damascus, clinging together in groups of five and six, saying little and trying not to look at the men leading them, as if by ignoring them they could make them disappear. The Egyptian soldiers who had been sold at the same time marched in front of them, legs shackled and heads bowed, and they too walked in tight groups as if they feared separation.

"Can you see any visions, Marie?" "Oh no, we are too far from the churches of God! I see nothing but a great white light, as if the moon had grown as big as the whole sky, and there is nothing there, neither angels nor beasts nor men, only a white, empty sorrow, as big as the sky."

My heart burns so that I wish I could forget even my Pierre's face and become a brute beast . . . "Perhaps if we try to escape they will kill us and our souls will go back to Jerusalem, to our own people?"

"Don't you believe it. They won't kill us just for that. Do we kill the sheep when they try and get out of the pen?" They walked on in a daze, lacking even the energy to sing, surprised to find they were not more unhappy, almost glad now because the worst had not yet happened, because they might go on like this for days yet. The worst? What was the worst? Damascus? The slave market? Masters? A harem? The mines, or work in the fields or in a workshop somewhere? Or in a brothel? What if some Moslem were to buy us and torture us in revenge for the women of Jerusalem? Suppose they try to make us spit on the cross? Force us to couple with asses or with dogs? Suppose they force us to eat Christian flesh? And oh, my friends, what if their sorcerers give us a philter to drink to make us forget everything and become madly enamored of some heathen, suppose they put us in baths of perfume? Or what if God should happen to touch the heart of some rich man and make him buy us out of pity and send us back to Jerusalem?

What if God inflames the hearts of our barons and kings with zeal so that they come with armies and take Damascus and deliver us? Oh, what tales we can tell! Oh God, we'll see Duke Godfrey and the Count of Toulouse and the Duke of Normandy with their armies marching into Damascus and scouring the streets, sword in hand, and severed heads and arms flying in all directions . . . *Friends, friends, we are the Christian slaves, our prayers have gained you this victory!*

The Moslems are cruel to women, they shut them up in houses and courtyards, and only the men go about the streets. They are so cruel, friends, that the more rich and respected a woman is, the less freedom she has, and whenever they do leave their houses they are carried in cages, shut in all around. If they sell us separately we shall not even be able to meet in the marketplace.

While as for escaping, how could we, even if we knew Arabic? The people here are all dark and the women are small . . . If our men take Damascus they will have to search, house by house.

And when they come, my friends, on that day, when they have got a foothold inside the city, then every one to her poker or her cauldron or her pitchfork! We will find cleavers in the kitchens and cut off their heads . . .

Who spares the accursed traitors' lives
Spits in the face of Jesus Christ.
Who would have joy and pardon
Must keep him from all treason.
No Frenchman shall take ransom!

Oh say, there is a man here who understands our language. What are you singing? It is a man's song. Let him silence us if he likes. Jerusalem!

Jerusalem, so dearly loved, so well avenged,
Jerusalem recovered from the heathen
Restored to Christendom
Given to Christendom
For more than one year
For a thousand years
To the men of France
To the people of Provence
Of Brabant and of Flanders
And of Picardy.

Ah, do you think that man cares what we are singing? The man did not care, he was not listening to the words; he was thinking that these slaves were indeed worth a good price, all they needed was training. They had plenty of spirit!

Marie was the first to be sold.

They were sitting quite still, all on the dusty ground not far from the arcades of the great caravanserai, in an enclosure surrounded by chains and guarded by dogs. Their legs were shackled. They heard the cackling of fowls, the bleating of penned sheep, and the barking voices of the men crowding the square. Loudest of all was the voice of the slave merchant, haggling continually with passers-by, waving his arms and lifting them up to heaven, bowing, smiling, nodding, a real mountebank.

The men who passed would stop, eyeing the group of women with heavy, thoughtful looks: yes, foreign women, it was not often you saw so many all at once, or so tanned: as a general rule they had been captured by pirates and were well fed and in good condition. These, thin, brown, and toothless, seemed to have nothing that belonged to their sex but their smooth chins, for in those lands of the Christians in the West, even the men often wore long tresses and the women uncovered their faces shamelessly.

They did not talk. It was the first day and they were nervous, vaguely humiliated to find themselves offered to view like cattle. It had been explained to them, however, that they would not be ill-treated, that true believers took good care of their slaves and they would not be forced to renounce their faith. They were told there were many Christian churches in Damascus and that it was even possible they might be bought by Christian masters. *They are saying that to keep us quiet.*

Marie looked beyond the barrier of chains into the square. A little way away some small children were playing with a big black dog. They were pretty children, laughing excitedly, the youngest hardly more than two years old, with a little lilting voice, just like Pierre's—oh, if his hair were only white and not brown! Oh God, he has a lovely laugh, like a goldfinch's! Some bereaved mothers turn against other children, while others are filled with love for everything that reminds them of the one their eyes can no longer see, and the joy of the eye momentarily replaces the joy of the heart. So Marie looked at the little boy with his fine chubby cheeks trying to climb onto the black dog's back, and thought how brave and eager he was with his lovely red mouth . . . It was like a draught of water, fresh and at the same time bitter. Then a man came up to the enclosure and his black-and-grey striped robe hid the little group of children. Marie sighed, and her eyes encountered the man's glance.

She gazed back vaguely, surprised to find him looking at her so intently; then her heart began to thud as she recognized the same look she had seen in the eyes of the Norman knight who had pursued her so hard in Antioch. She was suddenly frightened. She was not in a Christian country now, how could she defend herself? She turned away quickly, pretending to retch, and Rufine, sitting beside her, gripped her arm: "Oh look, that man wants you!"

"Be quiet. I know. What is he like? I daren't look!"

"He has shoes of red leather and a fine belt, and a red silk cord around his head veil."

"Is he still looking at us?"

"Yes, Holy Mary defend us, what a look! Like a man bewitched." Marie crossed herself and began muttering prayers under her breath. Now the man could see only her back and he would go away; people looked and then passed on.

I am ugly, my God, I am hideously ugly! Holy Mary Mother of God, make my face come out in spots.

"There," said Rufine, "he has gone." Marie scraped up some dirt from the ground and spat on it and rubbed her cheeks with it. As God is good, make my spittle poison, make it burn me like hot embers, make it sting like a hornet! Then the eunuch who spoke Norman came to fetch her.

It was a small, vaulted chamber with cushions disposed around the walls and a low table on which were cups and jugs of copper. Three men reclined on the cushions, talking among themselves. One, the fattest, was smoking a long pipe. One of the three was the man in the black-and-grey striped robe and red leather shoes. Marie tried her hardest to screw up her nose and twist her mouth out of shape without looking too much as if she were deliberately making faces.

The merchant was explaining to his client, in between puffs of opium, that if it was a matter of choosing a concubine he would never bring himself to sell a slave who had been put on public view; he had far better slaves inside the house, Persians and Georgians, young virgins plump and white, the blessed in paradise could wish for none fairer. The man in the red shoes said nothing. The eunuch saw Marie screwing up her mouth and jabbed her in the back with the knob of his staff. She rounded on him, too startled to be angry, but at least he understood French! "By your Mahomet," she said, "have pity! I am sick." The eunuch told her the man wished to buy her for his pleasure and that she would have an easy life if she was sensible.

"Tell him I am already married."

Two of the men conferred with the eunuch. The third, the man in the red shoes, said nothing. Marie looked up and saw that he was still looking at her, and could not even bring herself to make a face. Does one make faces at the lion about to eat one? He was quite young, with a short black beard, high cheekbones, and narrow black eyes. A Turk. Still without a word, he laid a purse of green silk on the table.

Marie felt her arms and legs growing heavy as bags of sand, soft as cushions. The men's voices sank to a long, muffled whispering, their heads were floating in a dark mist, and she thought: Jacques, I am dying, oh I feel so ill. Then she fell and knew no more.

When she came to her senses, Honorine was bending over her,

crying, "They are taking you away tonight. They are coming to fetch you." So it was true, she had not been dreaming.

"I shall kill myself," she said. "I shall kill myself."

"Don't be a fool," Lucienne said to her. "You may do very well. If the man wants you he will try to please you, and you will find some clever trick to escape."

"I am not clever. I am Jacques's wife. I will never be a concubine! Least of all to a Turk! I shall get a knife and kill him.

"Oh my sisters, my sisters, weep for me. To leave you is like dying. Don't be afraid, I shall not hang myself, but pray for me, and God grant that you may all be sold together, or at least in pairs.

"Oh, pray for me, who mourned so well for others. I helped the Christians to mourn. Whom shall I sing for now, alone among the Turks? Do you think a living soul can exist alone among the Turks? Pray for me, my soul will die of loneliness. I am not afraid to be raped but I do not want to be alone. Pray for me! If I forget thee, O Jerusalem.

"O Jerusalem, if I forget thee, our sun, our joy, our great ordeal! If I forget you, Jacques, if I forget all our friends, Sir Evrard and Brother Imbert, Alix and Brother Barnabé and Saint-John and Élie le Grêlé! Do not forget them, my friends, let us not forget one another.

"I know it will be long and our men will not come to deliver us, not in ten years or in twenty years. *We shall be like beasts if we forget.*" They were all crying. Even the Moslem slaves who did not belong to them were weeping. The Syrian women in the crusaders' party explained to them, exaggerating a little as was natural for slaves, that this Frankish woman had been a famous beauty in the Christian camp, a woman endowed with great virtues, the wife of a man who was young and brave, and the mother of a boy as fair as the morning star. Oh indeed, she had good cause to weep!

Marie, Marie, do not destroy yourself. Submit, it is no sin. Do not destroy yourself, become a favorite. The man is rich, perhaps you will be able to find us and make him buy us.

"Oh my friends, I could not even if I would. Do not forget our battle songs or the songs of our own land, or the songs of Jerusalem."

The eunuch who acted as interpreter came with two old

women and took Marie into the house, and washed her all over once again, and wrapped her in flowing veils of mauve and pink and put embroidered silken slippers on her feet, and unbraided her hair and rubbed it with scented oils. The old women tried to make her eat and drink something, but she clenched her teeth for fear there might be a love philter in the drink. Then they bore her away like a parcel in a kind of small closed litter through the heavily latticed sides of which she caught a faint glimpse of daylight. The light was red, it was evening, and through her tears she saw the grille spangled with rosy stars. She who had always used her tongue to such good purpose was silent now; no one would understand her any more, she would be like an animal.

A single Turk intent on raping you was certainly less perilous than ten Bedouin with the same thought, but what if he tied her to a bed with her legs apart and her mouth gagged? The Normans had done that, and to very honest women. The house in which she found herself, though not so rich as the grand houses of Antioch, was hung with carpets. All around her were women who stared at her in amazement, shaking their heads over her hands and feet. Vaguely hoping that she might after all be employed merely as a servant, Marie looked around for one who might be the lady of the house, but none seemed to want to give her orders, and so she made her way to the darkest corner of the room and set about plaiting her flowing hair. Did they expect her to look like a young girl? She had forgotten that she still had lovely hair: these devils had the art of cleaning it to restore its golden sheen. Probably, she thought, the man was tired of dark women and was looking for a fair one: they were a vicious race, always seeking after perverted pleasures.

What could she do? She knew enough about the ways of men, and had known for a long time now. The Turk wanted her that night, she could sense it as a bird senses a coming storm. The thought so terrified her that she could think of nothing else. He would have her beaten to death, like the girl with the pan of incense. There are dreams in which you try to run and your legs are tied: this was such a dream, for she still had her legs and the room had doors, but she knew there was nowhere to run to.

She was taken into a small windowless room with a fretted door giving onto a gallery, but the door had no lock. A burnished copper lamp stood on a small stool and there was a jar of water by the door and red woolen cushions on the floor. A young, dark-skinned servant girl was waiting for her. The girl was saying something, but there was no understanding what it was. Marie stood in the middle of the room, rigid and motionless, as if turned into stone.

All Turks are soldiers. Perhaps he will come with his saber at his belt and cut off my head. Oh God, my fair head! She thought of her face as she had seen it reflected in the basin, a young face, not unattractive, with big round grey eyes. Oh, my poor head, he will put it on that stool beside the lamp! There are men who like to violate headless women.

She did not see the servant leave, but she saw the man come. There was no mistaking it, he was blowing like a rutting bull. She took one look at the red silk headdress and long robes and his face burning as if from some inward fire; then she started to scream.

She backed away to the far wall with the cushions, but only to spring up again and go for him, her arms outstretched, her hands spread out before her like claws. Stamping, foaming at the mouth, herself unconscious of the source of those dreadful, braying shrieks, those sounds of bellowing and trumpeting, she only knew that she was pawing the ground and reaching out with her hands for something she had to grasp and rend with her nails, but what it was she no longer knew. Her eyes were blind. A bloody redness. She was drunk with the cry that tore itself from her whole body, like the terrible howling of some human animal. In that moment she felt such strength within herself that the very walls trembled.

She knew that she must not stop screaming, not if the veins of her throat should burst. She knew with what conscious thought remained to her that it was this screaming alone which kept her alive, and she roared with all the power of her lungs, the full-throated roar of a soldier charging furiously on the enemy. The man had gone now. There were three women around her, pouring water on her head and into her mouth. She thrust out wildly with her elbows, spitting out the water and plunging like a wild horse caught in a noose. I will kill him. I will drink his blood. I will kill them all. She got up and sprang for the door. The women tried to stop her, but she spat at them and slashed them wildly with her nails, and she was taller than they, and stronger: she had not known she was so strong. They were saying something and their foreign speech grated on her, making her respond with more piercing shrieks. She had not spoken one word since they brought her from the slave merchant's house.

The next day she was beaten and branded on both cheeks with a red-hot iron and taken out of the city on a donkey to some kind of fortified house set among olive trees. They made her understand that she was to clean out the stables. Her back was bleeding and the wounds on her swollen face were thick with flies. She had barely enough strength to walk, but all the same she took up the shovel and the fork. I have known worse. They won't frighten me with farm work. Two Armenian women and an old man worked on the farm, and there were shepherds also. But for her injuries the work would have been easy. She thought of nothing, she did not even remember the man who had tried to rape her; it was as if they had simply beaten her and sold her onto a farm.

Nothing remained of her great fury and terror but a faint feeling of surprise, at night when her back was breaking with weariness: Well, God came to my rescue. He stopped that man from wanting me. Strange to say that the easy life, the carpets and cushions and gilded lamps and baths and dishes of sweetmeats, even apart from the shame that life seemed to her much more frightening than life on the farm. In two weeks she had learned to talk to the Armenians a little; she had known a few words of their tongue since Antioch. But all day and all night she thought and dreamed: O Lord, let them send us one of the women from our group, oh, even one of the Normans, or any woman who speaks a Christian tongue. Oh Rufine, Honorine! To think that I could ever have quarreled with them. Oh, send any one of our women and I will work for her, do anything for her! As she scraped at the muck in the stables she listened for the sound of voices, the sound of footsteps, with such a hunger to hear people speaking her own language that there were times when, in a kind of delirium, it seemed to her that she could really hear them, and she would drop her shovel and run outside . . . When her face was healed she began to sing again.

Reckoning the years on her fingers, she thought she must be more than eighteen years old. Nineteen. Escape with the chain on her leg and her branded face was impossible. She talked about it with the Armenians and they shook their heads. No. Even disguised as men it was not possible. Jerusalem was too far away, they would die of thirst in the desert. It would be suicide. God would not permit it.

. . . It took them three years to capture Antioch and Jerusalem; perhaps in another three years they will take Damascus? Three years! "I have a child in Jerusalem," she said. "I cannot wait three years to see him. I have my husband."

The Armenians too had husbands and children, lost in some market, God knows where. Five years since.

. . . When our armies come to invest Damascus they are bound to set up camp in the olive groves, and I and my Armenians will hide and then at night we will make our way straight to the trenches. Who goes there? Christian captives. God bless you, dear brothers, Saint Michael and Saint George have brought you here! Where is the camp of Picardy and Artois? . . .

Sing to us again, Marie, sing the songs of your own country. How can you ask me? Oh, how can you ask? O Babylon! By the rivers of Babylon. If I forget thee, O Jerusalem. Oh, do not fear, for how could I forget? The soul dies of thirst. Better to die of thirst in the desert. One night she slipped off her chain and escaped and was found three days later by a caravan, half dead and suffering from sunstroke. She was taken back to her farm and flogged, beaten so hard that her nose was broken . . . Jacques, if you find me, perhaps you will not want me any more? No, love me still, Jacques, do not marry again or I will put a spell on you. How long can one live like this, suffocating, going slowly mad, how long? O cruel Jerusalem, lost Jerusalem

let them not call me mad.

To the Holy Sepulcher, blazing with the light of a thousand candles. Like moths to the flame. Destroyed, incinerated, burnt out.

Too dearly loved, too long desired
So well avenged, so well deserved
Washed in blood, in blood reborn
Regained but lost again too soon!

Sing, Marie of Arras. Do not forget, Marie of Arras.

In this marvelous evocation of the Middle Ages, Zoé Oldenbourg returns to the novel once again to tell the dramatic tale of what it was like to be part of the great mass of the poor who joined the long and arduous trek to Jerusalem on the First Crusade. Her main characters are a group of weavers, in particular a young teen-age couple, Jacques and Marie, who, following the inspiration of Peter the Hermit, leave the comparative safety and comfort of their homes in northern France to embark upon months of misery, war, death, even slavery, to liberate the Holy Land. It is an epic tale, spread upon a vast canvas and copiously illustrated by a thousand and one descriptions of the everyday sufferings of this enormous horde. With her fantastic knowledge of and passion for the times, Mme. Oldenbourg overlooks no detail in presenting her own exciting vision of the Crusade, imbuing her poor people with an incredibly human reality and ordering their lives among a multitude of events. Beyond history itself, this is fiction of the highest order, an unforgettable book by one of the great masters of the form.